INFERNO

KAREN HARPER

INFERNO

MIRA®

MIRA®

ISBN-13: 978-0-7394-7910-0

INFERNO

Printed in U.S.A.

To all our fellow travelers on the Ohio State Alumni Rocky Mountain trip, especially Marilyn and Jack, Debbie and Nadine.

And as ever, to my fellow traveler through life, Don, for all the help and support.

Prologue

August 29, 2005

The sound of sirens always soothed his soul. In the pitch-black night, the throbbing lights of the fire engines and cop cars did not make his pulse pound, but rather made it slow and steady itself. As ever, he was completely in control.

Curtain up! Showtime! Evan Durand lay flat against the porch roof across the street, four houses down from the conflagration. He had a front-row seat in the balcony to watch the actors in the grand pageant. For he was both director and producer of the chaos he had created with such care and cleverness.

They would never catch him, never pin the multistate string of arsons on him. *In Like A Ghost, Out Like A Ghost*—that was the name of this epic drama, Evan thought as he twisted his mother's onyx ring around his little finger with his thumb.

Both the wildfire in the woodlot 6.4 miles away and this blaze in a house a stone's throw from a suburban fire station were in his script. He was the genius in the Durand family, not his father. Let the hotshot FBI Serial Arson Team think they could identify him by his M.O. That's what they were desperate to do. He was so proud his work was getting national reviews now, not just local ones! Finally, the morons had figured out that his successes were linked, were from the same brilliant brain.

The cops shouted at the growing crowd of onlookers to get back. An EMS vehicle and two more fire engines screeched up, much too late. They'd been pulled away by his smaller decoy fire. Firefighters piled from the ladder truck. It reminded him of a circus act where the clowns spilled out, and he shook with laughter. Some carried axes; some dragged hoses. They were fighting a smoke-belching fire less than a third of a mile from their station house, yet they'd been suckered in again. Evan Durand—rave reviews and standing room only; America's firefighters—a one-night stand. And the FBI team—beneath contempt.

On his belly, Evan inched away from the edge of the porch roof, closer to the house. He'd been hiding in the bushes when a young couple ran out to watch, and he'd used the woodpile they had stacked close to their house to get up on the porch roof. Man, if he'd chosen them instead of Jane Stinchcomb, he wouldn't have had to do much more than throw a low-grade liquid accelerant here, then toss a match. The pile, the porch and the entire wooden frame would be ablaze in minutes.

But Evan always chose the house of a woman living alone. That had made the firefighters and local arson investigators in Helena, Mission Viejo, Boulder, Seattle, Salt Lake, Reno, Lake Tahoe and Boise blame themselves even more when they failed. And now that the FBI had been called in, this would make them feel like the fools they were, he thought, and gave his ring another hard twist. A little woodlot fire made them late for their big entrance.

For the first time, Evan heard the woman's screams from the burning house. Rising action! At least the protagonist had great voice projection.

He'd jimmied her front window and heaved the jar of liquid white phosphorus where it would ignite the bottom of the staircase and trap her upstairs. WP or Willy Pete, his source had called the volatile stuff when he'd sold it to him. And all the research Evan had done on it was absolutely on target. He could smell its garlic-like stench; its flames were as yellow as the glare of a spotlight. Its dense white smoke was a curtain ready to go up.

Had the doomed heroine of the tragedy been sleeping through all the noise and flames and smoke before this moment? Had she missed the sound of shattering glass? She was probably so used to hearing sirens that she didn't react at first, not even when they came close. People living near fire stations, much like firefighters themselves—especially those cocky crews battling wildfires—were way too certain they were safe. He'd proved that.

Evan watched four firefighters charge inside while one climbed a ladder. Incandescent, canary-colored flames waved merrily from the blown-out lower windows, even as the hoses poured in water. Sand smothered WP better than water, but this would work eventually. Meanwhile, the cops kept the growing cluster of neighbors and fire junkies back from the belching heat.

And then he saw something that made his pulse pound. An unmarked black car pulled up and three men and a woman jumped out. They showed the cops something in their hands—no doubt their badges—and charged right through the yellow-tape perimeter.

One of the men was broad shouldered and blond, while another was gray-haired. The third, a heavyset man, limped badly. He could tell that the woman was fairly young and had long, brown hair. It had to be the vaunted FBI arson team.

Now they would realize that their so-called Boy Next Door Arsonist had brought his operation to their own backyard. This fire was just nine miles from their FBI office in downtown Denver, where they tried to track him with all their forensic evidence and wild profiling theories. Evan had a good notion to drive right over to their office and start a fire there.

The thought made him laugh so hard he felt the shingles vibrate under him. He tried to make out the faces of the new arrivals, but they didn't turn his way. Besides, it was difficult to see through the smoke screen created by the WP.

A crick in his neck suddenly pained him, so he rotated his head to ease it. And then he saw the old woman. Her face lit by dancing flames, she was staring out a second-story window of this house. How long had she been there? And had she glimpsed his face? Evan longed to savor this Dante's *Inferno*—no, *Durand's* Inferno—but knew he had to get the hell out of Denver. Yet not before he left some sort of insulting message for the government crew. The sobriquet Boy Next Door Arsonist was all wrong. He was not a boy, but thirty years old. Besides, he wanted to be called something worthy, like the Fire Phantom or Smoke Ghost. Speaking of which, he had to disappear now, and fast.

Evan pulled his baseball cap down over his forehead and belly-crawled away from the woman's window to the edge of the roof. What if she phoned the cops? He had a mind to bust in her window and shut her up for good, but that was not the way he operated. Peons worked with brute strength, not with the finesse and intellect that were his calling cards.

Evan scooted to the side of the porch, scraping his stomach right through his black T-shirt, and then dangled his legs until his feet found the top of the woodpile. When he let go, he snagged his ring, yanking his knuckle. At least the ring didn't pull off.

Fortunately none of the cops at the scene so much as looked his direction as he walked calmly away between two houses. After about a hundred yards, he began to run. He hoped that old lady wasn't a glitch in his master plan. Maybe, with this pièce de résistance tonight, it was time for a break, another change of scenery. Back to the wilds for a while, like that little California working vacation two years ago. Only this time he'd go somewhere he knew, somewhere farther out so he could get lost—really lost.

And he knew just the place.

1

September 5, 2005

Lauren Taylor left the Lost Lake area and flew her white Cessna 206 combination wheeled-pontoon plane over the crest of Salish Range and down into the Flathead Valley. The county seat of Kalispell lay beneath her as she followed the Flathead River and Route 93 south. Though she'd made many instrument approaches to the city airport south of town during rain or snow storms, it was great to be able to just fly by the landmarks today. That always made her feel more in command of her life, which had spun badly out of control.

The firs, pines and spruces lining the lake and Bigfork Bay looked green from this height, but it hadn't rained in weeks and all of northwest Montana was bone dry. At least this weather made for an easy trip, thought Lauren, though she had no fear of flying, even in the mountains. In fact, she loved it. Up there, surrounded by massive granite peaks, or soaring over vast snowfields and glaciers, she found an escape from her great loss.

The monumental tragedy of her thirty years was losing her husband Ross when he fought a wildfire two summers ago. He'd left her with a log house on the edge of a small town, this plane and their son, Nicky, now six years old.

Thank heavens Ross had taught her to fly this trusty old warhorse. They had nicknamed the plane *Silver,* after the Lone Ranger's pure white steed in the old cowboy stories. *Silver* was her and Nicky's livelihood and her lifeline to the outside. Their mountain-sheltered town of Vermillion was miles from any populated areas and could be reached on the ground only by twisting roads, which rockslides or winter avalanches sometimes cut off completely. Still, as far as Lauren was concerned, after once seeing the jade green, glacial-melt Lost Lake, its alpine meadows and protective ring of mountains, nothing else compared.

Silver and six other pontoon or ice-runner aircraft flew everything—from mail and food, to hikers and skiers—between Vermillion and Kalispell. Her plane could seat up to six, but Lauren usually took out the back four seats for cargo. Today she was picking up newspapers, mail and cartons of dairy products for the general store, plus one passenger, a hiker named Rocky Marston who had contacted her via her Web site.

From Kalispell it was an hour's flight to Vermillion and Lost Lake. At three hundred dollars an hour per passenger, she figured this Marston guy must really like solo hiking. There were fewer passengers in the summer than in the winter when the ski lodge was open. If Marston had bargained with her, she might have come down in price, but he'd e-mailed her only once from Phoenix. She was grateful for the money. Nicky's birthday was coming up, and she wanted to buy him a beginner's mountain bike.

"Cessna Niner One Zulu," came the crackling voice on her radio, answering her earlier call for permission to land. "Cleared for approach into Kalispell. Welcome back to the big city, Lauren."

"Good morning, Jim. Cessna Niner One Zulu out of Vermillion, following clearance into the airport."

Jim Kline, the chief air traffic controller, wasn't kidding. Kalispell, with a population around fourteen thousand, was the big city to a girl from Vermillion, which boasted six hundred and eighteen year-round residents. And to Nicky, who came along with her sometimes to hit a restaurant, movie or the stores, this place was about as exciting as seeing New York or London.

This summer she'd brought him, her friend Dee Cobern and Dee's grandson, Larson, to Woodland Park, where they used the water slides and floated on inner tubes in the lazy river. Another time, the four of them had gone swimming in Foy's Lake, which warmed up in the summer, unlike Lost Lake. And another great memory—Ross had proposed to her in Lawrence Park's picnic area in the gazebo.

Over the intersection of Routes 2 and 93, Lauren started her descent. As usual, *Silver*'s landing gear came down with a clunk. Lauren backed off the power and drifted down, lowering the flaps to coast in. She landed the plane gently; Ross would have been proud. She taxied down the single northwest to southeast runway toward the only refrigerated storage shed. After locking the parking brake, she shut down the engine at the tie-down on the east side of the tarmac.

She waved to Stan Jensen, the guy who helped load cargoes. He was all smiles, no doubt because he was headed for a month's vacation camping in Canada. Then she noted a dark-haired man in new-looking, brown-green camouflage heading across the tarmac toward the plane. He carried a big backpack and some other gear. Sunglasses and unruly, blowing hair obscured his face, but he reminded her of one of the First Nation men in the area who had Blackfeet or Crow blood. He was probably her charter.

As she opened the door to get out, she whispered to herself, "Calm down, mister, 'cause you're going to have to wait 'til Vermillion's milk and mail gets loaded."

She jumped down, surprised to feel the warmth on the tarmac this early in the morning, but the temperatures had been above average all summer. Striding to meet the man, she held out her hand to shake his. She noted he had pristine-looking gear and new hiking boots.

"Rocky Marston?"

"Yes, ma'am. Figured it was you by the timing and the picture of your plane on the Web site."

"You must be a real veteran hiker to head up into the hills around Lost Lake alone."

"I'm a veteran, at least. Done my time in Iraq and want some peace and quiet for a while."

So, she thought, the fatigues were not just for effect or camouflage in the forest; he was used to them. His big, expensive backpack did make him look like a guy who could take care of himself. It had the kind with aluminum supports, which often indicated a pup tent.

"Where did you come in from?" she asked.

"Flew into the Glacier Park airport from Arizona. Love the mountains."

"Ever been to the Lost Lake area before?"

"Nope. Look, I don't mean to take up your time talking."

She took the hint. Besides, she wanted to be back soon after Nicky got out of school. "We'll be airborne as soon as I load up and refuel," she told him, glancing toward Stan, who was already pushing a dolly of cartons toward the plane. "Would you like to ride upfront? Or I can set up a seat for you behind the cockpit."

"Definitely in front," he said, twisting a surprisingly dainty onyx ring on his small finger with the thumb of the same hand. "Flying's not my thing, so that way, I'll feel more in control."

"I can't believe we must have been near the bastard, but we're no closer to stopping him," Brad Hale told his boss, Mike Edwards. The other three members of the FBI Serial Arson Team nodded.

"Despite this insulting letter, I think we're at a dead end 'til our 'Boy Next Door' torches something—or someone—else," Mike admitted. "Even the report from our Behavior Analysis Unit says we don't have the typical torch here." Swearing under his breath, he dropped the FBI profiling report on the table along with the letter they'd received from the arsonist.

Brad, age thirty-four, the newest member of the team with only two years under his belt, had been staring at the gruesome photos of the latest arson scene; now he glared at the letter, too. The national FBI database had sent it and its envelope back, claiming they were clean—no prints, not even saliva on the flap to test for DNA. The paper was standard, its handler must have used gloves; and the printer was a commonly used laser type. So what if they'd deduced the arsonist was right-handed from the burn marks left by flammable liquid splashed at several of the arson scenes? The majority of people were right handed. They had next to nothing.

And VICAP, the FBI's Violent Criminal Apprehension Program, was no help. The arsonist had used different accelerants in every fire and left behind nothing but sanitized crime scenes. And now, to add insult to injury, the bastard was trying to call the shots in this letter.

But what really infuriated Brad was that his research into the accelerant used this time—white phosphorus—had turned up next to nothing. The minute his eyes had begun to burn and he'd smelled the sulfur stench at the fire scene, he'd guessed what the BND, as they called the Boy Next Door arsonist, had used. Then, sifting through the charred ruins the next day, his guess had been verified.

But even knowing BND had used liquid white phosphorus had not helped the team trace him.

The military had employed that highly volatile compound since World War II, and as recently as last year's Battle for Fallujah, but military supplies of WP were closely guarded. And though WP was also a common product in the manufacturing of soft drinks and tooth-paste, Brad's calls to businesses that used white phos-phorus had turned up no reports of any missing. Besides, the stuff was extremely volatile to transport. It was like the guy had spirited it in. No wonder BND thought he deserved to be called phantom or ghost.

Though he was listening to Mike, Brad stared so hard at the photos of this latest BND arson scene that his eyeballs ached. The woman's house was a blackened shell, her body badly burned. Though the firefighters had gotten her out without losing any of their own this time, Jane Stinchcomb had died of second- and third-degree burns in the hospital the next day. That brought the deaths caused by the string of ten arsons in seven western states to four—three women living alone and a firefighter.

"Now I get why they called in the FBI," Clay Smith, another old hand at this, said. "And I don't mean because anyone thinks we can solve this mess. If this is allowed to turn into a cold case, we take the heat—'scuse the scrambled metaphors."

Usually arsons were handled by local investigators, but this case had been given to the FBI team not only because it concerned interstate crime, but because it fell under the new antiterrorism laws. Though he was only thirty-four, Brad had worked for years to get on this team. He'd been trained as both a firefighter and an FBI agent, then gone to the National Fire Academy at Emmetsburg, Maryland. It was pure chance he was currently working in his hometown of Denver. The FBI team was sent all over, but the field office here was fairly central to the scattered arsons.

It wasn't only that Brad was on a mission to stop such heinous crimes or that he wanted to make good on his old home turf. He was driven to atone for a family tragedy. This case was the worst he'd seen, and he'd do anything to solve it.

"Not only is the press on our backs, but now the torch himself!" Jen Connors, the only woman on the team, said in her usual sardonic tone. She kept playing with her empty coffee cup; they'd all drunk enough java lately, they could have taken a bath in it. She suddenly slammed both fists on the table, which was cluttered with maps, photos and more than one psychological profile of typical torches.

"Give me a break!" she went on, gesturing at the letter. "The perp doesn't want to be called the Boy Next Door because it's 'too cute and common.' He demands we call him the Fire Phantom or at least the Smoke Ghost? Maybe he should just do our press releases for us!"

"Hell," Mike muttered, "maybe he *is* a ghost."

"I think he's a gamer," Brad said. "He's having the time of his life with all this. But how does he support himself with all the moving around he does?"

"And," Jen put in, raking her fingers through her long brown hair, "why does he hate firefighters so much?"

"Listen up," Mike said. "I've haven't earned these gray

hairs for nothing. Let's go another round with theories on that, however far out or old hat. Go! Brad?"

"Okay," he said, tearing his gaze away from the photos. "Someone BND loved was killed in a fire, and he blames the fire department for not getting there in time."

Jen said, "Or how about he wanted more than anything to be a firefighter, but was turned down for the job. Then his girl left or betrayed him, and he's out to get both single women and firefighters."

"But he's a smart guy," Brad insisted. "He could surely pass the tests to get to join a fire department. If he can pull our strings, he could play the system to get in."

"Unless he bombed out on the psych part of it during interviews," Mike said. "Still, some screeners don't pick up on wackos who are fascinated by fires for the wrong reasons. Hell, too many torches turn out to be volunteer or even pro firefighters."

"But don't you have the feeling BND's been passing as a normal guy?" Clay asked, leaning back in his chair and clasping his hands behind his head. "I know he moves around a lot, but we've had media articles out on him, and *America's Most Wanted* usually turns up some kind of lead. We don't have a face to go with the crimes, but he's evidently passing for Joe Schmo—Mr. Nice."

"Not exactly a Joe Schmo, because he's bright and proud of it," Jen added. "It's a typical arsonist profile in that respect—above-average intelligence but still some sort of a failure."

Brad noted that Clay's hands were shaking. Clay had been trying to quit smoking, but the pressure was about ready to suck him into the habit again. He got up to pace, despite the fact he was out of shape and limped badly. They seemed to be going in circles—and they were starting to get on each other's nerves.

"Other theories?" Mike prompted, rapping his knuckles on the table. "Even if we've hashed them over a hundred times before, let's hear it."

Brad said, "Though a lot of arsonists are adrenaline junkies, he's an attention junkie. He loves looking at the fire and saying, 'I made that,' but he wants others to be impressed, too. 'I am smarter than the cops, than the fire guys, than the FBI.' He wants media coverage and wants to manage it by naming himself. He wants to control others' lives—and deaths. He's having a real good time playing God."

Though he had more to say, his voice drifted off. The three of them were staring bleary-eyed at him. It was only midmorning, but since they'd gotten the taunting note from BND, they'd hardly slept. Yet Brad knew that wasn't why their attention was riveted on him right now.

They thought he was speaking about his own father, who'd been an eco-arsonist here in Denver and was now serving eighteen years in the federal prison system for torching luxury homes built on the fringes of a nature preserve. The shock and shame had killed his mother—the doctors had called it sudden cardiac infarction—and disillusioned and humiliated Brad. But somehow, when he was trying to stop other arsonists, his own anger and pain receded—at least, for a little while.

Mike cleared his throat in the tense silence. "Now listen up. I'm going to the Stinchcomb funeral this afternoon to see if I can spot any smoke ghosts or fire phantoms. Maybe the perp's so pleased with himself he'll drop by or hang around the burial site. Not that likely, but frankly, I'm grasping at straws. Brad, man the office 'til I get back. You other two get some shut-eye so you can pull the all-nighter. Until we get a break, we'll work this in shifts round the clock, 'cause we're all so damn tired we can't see straight."

Lauren hoped Rocky Marston didn't mind that she kept talking, because a wave of exhaustion had washed over her just after they took off. Ever since losing Ross, she hardly ever slept straight for more than a couple of hours at night. But she could hardly tell a guy whose life was in her hands as they soared toward jagged mountain peaks that she was sleepy. She knew, if she'd just get through a couple more minutes, that her exhaustion would pass. Yet Rocky Marston had hardly said a word, even as she'd pointed out interesting sites in Flathead Valley.

"So what did you do in Iraq?" she asked.

"Tried to stay alive."

"I mean security, engineering, supplies? My husband was armored division in Desert Storm—tanks."

"Actually, I guarded the big brass. Black-ops stuff I can't talk about."

"Oh." She started to feel impressed, but she wasn't sure if she believed him. He might just be trying to shut her up.

"You should be aware of bears and mountain lions, especially if you hike alone," she said, trying another subject. "Black bears will stay out of your way, but the brown bears and grizzlies can be aggressive. The mountain lions are sneaky and dangerous but are seldom seen. They're called the ghosts of the Rockies."

"Yeah? I like that name."

He got quiet again. Maybe the guy just wanted to enjoy the stunning scenery. An occasional glacier field glittered in the sun. Snow still clung to the highest peaks while snowmelt streams slammed down cliff faces in silver torrents, however dry the weather had been.

After a while, as if he'd read her mind, he said, "You're in a drought around here, right?" He was twisting his ring again.

"A long one, so please watch your campfires."

"Oh, I sure will."

Brad could have danced around the table when he took the call from one of Jane Stinchcomb's neighbors. The FBI's hotline number—which he had wanted to call something else but was overruled—had been printed in the local papers.

"You probably think it's strange that we're not at the funeral," Peter Lockwood went on as Brad pressed the phone to his ear, "but we didn't know Ms. Stinchcomb that well. My mother's been living with us until we can get her into a good assisted-living program. She doesn't have Alzheimer's, but her memory comes and goes."

"And she saw something the night of the fire that

might help?" Brad prompted when the man hesitated. "I promise you, we protect our sources."

"Yeah, she saw something all right. Susan and I went out to watch close up, but my mother stayed in her room because she could see the fire from there. It's been a week since the fire, but today she told us that she had seen a strange man dressed in black, lying flat on our porch roof right under her bedroom window, also watching the fire. When he saw her, he took off. We both talked to her, Agent Hale, and we think she's telling the truth. I mean, unless the guy was trying to hide, why not just join the crowd watching the blaze?"

Brad's heartbeat kicked up. "And could your mother describe this man? We could have her work with an FBI sketch artist."

"Like I said, sometimes we're not sure stuff she says is legit, but she insists she can describe him, what he was wearing and especially his profile."

Brad gripped the phone hard and threw his head back in relief. It was something. It was a start.

"Quite a view," Rocky Marston said as Lauren banked the plane. Finally the guy had offered something. His silence and brusque nature had made her nervous.

"That it is. People who see it from above or below never forget it."

"That's the ski lodge there?" he asked, pointing.

"Yep," she said. "The Lost Lake Ski Resort, a tiny town unto itself, at least in the winter months. There's always big competition for sports tourists in the Rockies, but the Vermillion City Council is also trying to build up tourism during the off-season."

"Hey, you never know," he said, becoming animated for once. "Something really big could put this little place on the map someday."

"Advertising costs big bucks and people here are torn about needing tourists yet not wanting this area over-run with them. We don't even have cell-phone service yet, though we have plans to build a couple of towers—one down at the far end of the lake."

She could tell he was looking at her now, not staring out the window for once. "You born and bred here?" he asked.

Lauren shook her head. "Grew up in the little town of Fostoria, Ohio. I spent one year of college at Ohio State in Columbus, not sure what I wanted to do. I came here to work one winter at the lodge, met my husband and never left. He used to be a fire warden for the district. Would you believe his first office was in that old wooden smoke-spotting tower, there on the hillside at four o'clock?"

"That thing isn't still staffed, is it? I heard Montana's got choppers, air tankers to drop water or retardants, spotting planes and all that. You or your husband ever fly this plane for smoke spotting?"

"My husband used to, but I stick to commercial flying. Ross got separated from his hotshot crew and was trapped with a friend in a wildfire in California in 2003. A government investigation ruled it a freak accident."

"Oh, sorry." He looked quickly away, as if to hide tears.

"Yeah, me, too. He was very smart about fires, so it's

hard to understand how he and another guy got caught by flames—and on an upslope, too—when he knew better. It wasn't even a fire Mother Nature set— lightning, I mean. Not arson, either. The so-called experts were thinning and sculpting the forests around a populated area for safety. The blaze got out of control in a place called Coyote Canyon."

"Morons! It just shows you can't trust anyone."

She sniffed hard. Marston cleared his throat as if he couldn't find other words, but then neither could she. The worst of her waking nightmares pressed hard on her heart. Again she saw in her mind's eye what had only been described to her, scenes she had read about in official reports and newspapers.

Her husband's death haunted her as if she'd been there with him. Ross and his friend Kyle separated from their crew and squad boss. Ross in the blast of super-heated air and flame. Ross without his lifesaving, body-hugging fiberglass shelter that could have saved his life. Ross trapped and burned beyond recognition, beyond all sanity.

She jerked out of the horror but still hit the water a bit too hard. The pontoons bounced, skipped, hit again. Beside her, Marston braced himself against the control panel and swore.

"That's why my son and I call this plane *Silver*," she told him, trying to sound normal, even light. "You know, like 'Hi, Ho, Silver—away?'"

She figured he'd make a comment about women drivers, but he said, "Yeah, like 'Who was that masked man, because I wanted to thank him.' My dad used to watch that show on TV years ago. I heard it all the time from him, just like all the other trivial crap he knew and thought everyone else should, too. He was a real hog for attention and glory."

As Lauren steered the plane toward the dock at the west end of the town, she was relieved Marston didn't seem angry with her but with his father. After all, he'd only agreed to pay her half the three hundred dollars until she got him safely here.

2

By the time Lauren had stashed the rest of her passenger's fee in her purse—all cash again, three fifties—and had overseen the unloading of her cargo, Rocky Marston had simply disappeared.

Unlike most of her charters, he hadn't asked her where to buy supplies or anything about the town. But maybe for a guy who'd just finished a grueling tour in Iraq, wilderness hiking was nothing that needed concern or preparation. Besides, the general store was labeled just that, so anybody could find it.

Lauren made certain *Silver* was locked and tethered to its small space of dock, one big, winged bird among the small flock huddled there. The dock also sat on pontoons and was hauled out of the water in early November, when the lake began to ice over and they put sled-type runners on their planes.

Thinking about supplies for hiking reminded her that she had to pick up a few things and drop off the mail; the grocery store served as the post office, too. Then she'd pick up Nicky at her friend Dee's. Anytime Lauren couldn't meet her son after school, which was at the other end of town, Dee walked her grandson, Larson, and Nicky to her own house until Lauren could pick him up.

Lauren got into her old SUV and headed into town. Her house was located in what locals jokingly called the "burbs" of the tiny town. As she paid for her groceries, she asked Fran, the checkout worker, postmistress and cousin of the store's owner, "Did a hiker dressed in fatigues stop here for some supplies? I just brought in a new guy who's determined to hike solo, so I'm sure he needed to stock up."

"Haven't seen anyone but the same old same olds," Fran said and popped her gum. The smell of banana-strawberry emanated from her as she went back to sorting mail for the array of post office boxes lining the back wall of the store. Vermillion had no postal carriers, and like many residents, Fran held a variety of jobs to make ends meet.

"Well, he did have a large backpack," Lauren went on. "He probably came prepared."

"You tell him to watch out for bears?"

"Sure did, but after fighting terrorists, that probably sounded pretty tame to him."

"He comes in here, I'll give him ten percent off," Fran said as she cracked her gum again. "It's Clyde's policy for somebody who puts his life on the line to protect our freedoms, and all that. Here, you want to take your mail and Dee's?" she asked and handed over two packets as well as Dee's day-old *USA Today*. After losing Ross, Lauren had canceled her newspapers and magazines—and not just to save money. She did much better if she just shut out the world's woes.

Lauren arrived at Dee's as the boys were eating cookies and milk and playing a game of war with an old deck of cards. Despite their whooping and hollering, Nicky gave her a big hug around the waist as she stooped to ruffle his auburn hair and kiss the top of his head. The boy was a blend of her and Ross—her red hair and green eyes, his broad forehead and quick movements.

"And how was first grade today, gentlemen?" Lauren asked.

"Mom, we learned all about how you should call Indian tribes First Nations or Native Americans!" Nicky cried, his freckled face turned up to hers with his milk-mustache smile. "And never call them red men or redskins or nothing like that. And we're going to learn all about the Blackfeet who lived right around here. Did they really have black feet?"

"I'm not sure how they got that name, hon," she admitted, "but I just bet Mrs. Gates will teach you all about it."

Lauren reveled in the fact that her son was so open and affectionate today instead of distracted and moody. Maybe this new interest in local Indians would replace his obsession with superheroes like Batman and Spiderman. Since last Christmas he'd gone around the house with a towel pinned to his shirt for a cape and insisted on wearing his Batman pajamas all day when they didn't have to go out. He'd had more than one imaginary friend since Ross died, usually some powerful hero from a book or video. At least the Blackfeet really existed, and he'd be learning local history and respect for other people.

"And," Larson piped up from his place at the table, his mouth so full of cookie he spewed crumbs, "a Blackfeet chief named White Calf had to make a treat."

"Make a treaty," Nicky corrected, heading back to their card game as Dee gave Lauren a little smile and wave from the kitchen door. "A treaty means the tribe had to give up their land in change for peace. That's what Mrs. Gates said, 'member?"

"Land that is now Glacier National Park and all around Lost Lake, too," Larson said, his eyes huge through his glasses. The two of them were like a tag team now, picking up on each other's news. The fact that the classes were sometimes grouped put the younger students in with some older kids, and Lauren had noticed that this accelerated Nicky's vocabulary and learning speed.

"And when they lost their land to the U.S.," Nicky plunged on, "Chief White Calf said even if he died, he'd live in the mountains forever, like—um, 'The mountains are my last refrig,' so it must have been warm weather then, just like now."

Lauren bit her lip to keep from laughing. Behind the boys, Dee shook her head, threw up her hands and said, "I hope their fridges were big enough to keep a lot of buffalo meat cold all summer if they had weather like this."

"I've read what Chief White Calf said," Lauren told the boys, "and I think he said 'my last *refuge*,' meaning his last place to go, his safe shelter."

"I'll ask Mrs. Gates," Nicky said, as if his teacher was the be-all and end-all of wisdom. Lauren was so glad he was excited about school this year. For the last two years, he had suffered from separation anxiety anytime she so much as went into another room.

"Hey, come in here a sec while I work on this casserole and let them finish their game," Dee said. Lauren joined Dee in her cozy, pine-paneled kitchen. Dee handed her a large sugar cookie, then went back to chopping onions.

Like most of the houses in town, the Cobern place sat slightly above Vermillion's single paved street on a rise of ground that slanted up toward the alpine meadow at the skirts of Mount Jefferson. Just beneath this chalet-style house lay Dee's small fashion and ski shop, Just Fur You, which, like the other shops and stores, faced the lake. Dee's place, like several specialty stores, was open limited hours in the off-skiing season. During the warm-weather months, she helped care for her only grandchild so her daughter, Suze, a local wildlife artist, could paint in peace, while her son-in-law worked at the lumber camp on the other side of Mount Jefferson.

As warm and wonderful as Dee had managed to make this home, it felt strange now, hollow, compared to when Dee's husband, Chuck, had lived here too. Despite the Coberns being almost twenty years their seniors, Chuck and Dee had been the Taylors' best friends, and they'd helped her survive these terrible last two years. But having lost Ross so tragically and permanently, Lauren couldn't fathom why Dee hadn't either forgiven or divorced her husband by now.

After Dee had learned that Chuck cheated on her with his old high-school sweetheart in Kalispell, he'd been living in a rented room at the ski lodge—for five months. Chuck was not only the town sheriff, but he headed the volunteer fire department, so he'd be sorely missed if he left the area—at least, by everyone but Dee.

It was Lauren who had flown Chuck into Kalispell and gone with him to the Regional Medical Center last week to get his shoulder set. And it was Lauren whom Dee had interrogated about whether Chuck had made any phone calls to unknowns or been out of Lauren's sight while he was there. Dee did care, so why didn't she show it to him?

"He's not ready to be forgiven yet," she'd said more than once, shaking her blond head while her blue eyes snapped. "Right now, it's out of my control."

Their breakup was the talk of the town. If little Vermillion had had a tabloid publication, their story would have been continual banner headlines to rival paparazzi coverage of a couple of feuding movie stars.

Now poor Chuck had broken his shoulder in a hiking accident. He couldn't drive, couldn't fish, couldn't do much but pop painkillers and try to rekindle his relationship with his wife over the phone. Still, Dee wouldn't take him back.

"I've heard all about the kids' day, but how are you doing?" Dee asked. "I saw you come into the dock."

"Did you see my passenger get off and walk uptown?" Lauren asked as she finished her cookie and started to chop a red pepper for the casserole. More often than not,

Dee insisted she take half of a meal home for her and Nicky since Lauren had refused to let Dee pay her for their flights into Kalispell this summer.

"Nope. Didn't see hide nor hair of him, and it's a long dock. He probably stopped for a bite at the Bear's Den or hit the general store."

Lauren stopped chopping. "He didn't. I checked—the store, I mean."

"No big deal," Dee said, suddenly turning away to sort one-handed through her mail. She flopped her newspaper she jokingly called *USA Yesterday* open on the counter between them as she started sautéing onions. "You think he dropped off the dock and drowned or something?" she teased. "Maybe he stopped at one of the B&Bs this end of town to get a room before he went into the wilds. So, was he weird or something?"

"Not exactly."

"Then I'll bet he was. Tell Dee."

"Not weird—just quiet."

"Man, he ought to blend right in around here. Except, that is, for the loudmouthed town sheriff who tried to talk me into letting him come back here in the after-noons—just when Larson's here, he said. Must be high on his pain meds. I told him he has plenty of places he can see his grandson—if you count his ski lodge digs, his office and the firehouse."

But Lauren had stopped listening. She stared at the secondary headline, which read, FBI Most Wanted: Boy Next Door Serial Arsonist/Murderer Finally Has a Face.

And beneath it was a profile sketch that looked frighteningly familiar to her.

Her insides cartwheeled. It can't be, she thought as she leaned closer, then picked up the paper. It just can't be!

"What?" Dee's voice pierced her panic. "You look like you've seen a ghost."

"Don't say that. It says here this guy told the FBI he wants to be called the Fire Phantom or Smoke Ghost. And he's killed people—with fire."

"What?" Dee demanded, crowding close, putting her hands on Lauren's shoulder. "Lauren, you're just having one of your moments about losing Ross…"

"No, that's not it. He—this looks like my charter."

"Get a grip, girl! The guy just creeped you out. What are the chances that someone on the FBI's Most Wanted List would be here in Vermillion? When pigs fly."

"Or when arsonists do. Dee, I've got to call this national hotline number. And I should call Chuck, too."

"What's he going to do?" she said. "You're the one who told me he's not supposed to move around with that shoulder, and he's obviously completely out of it on narcotics, even if they are legal."

"I have to do something, just so I can sleep at night."

"As if you're doing that now. All right, go use my bedroom phone. But speaking as someone who used to love the local sheriff, let me warn you not to get everyone around here panicked."

"I know, I know," she conceded, heading for Dee's bedroom. "It can't be him. Like you said, not here in Vermillion. Don't worry, I'm keeping calm."

"It's not even a very detailed sketch," Dee called after her. "And did you read here, the information came from an elderly woman who saw him in the dead of night? Not exactly a solid source. Might be the FBI's grasping at straws and you probably are, too."

But that didn't help. Nothing did. Some of the things Rocky Marston had said… She wasn't actually keeping calm at all, because her heart was trying to pound right out of her chest.

"I wish we had an Indian story, but David and Goliath is a pretty good one," Nicky said, his voice slowing as he stretched and yawned in his bed. "Mostly 'cause the bad guy gets kilt with just a little stone."

"I think the idea behind the story is that even little people—like you and me—can fight back against something bad."

Sitting on the edge of her son's bed, Lauren thought again of the call she'd made to the FBI today in Denver. Was she crazy? Or could Rocky Marston be the serial arsonist and murderer they sought? It suddenly seemed so impossible and unreal, especially since no one else had seen him. He'd more or less disappeared into thin air.

"Indians could have stones like David threw," Nicky went on, his one-track mind riding the rails of his latest obsession. "There's stones everywhere round here, more than feathers birds have lost. Mom, Chief White Calf could fight back with stones to keep his land. He was a good guy, wasn't he? Some kids at school said the Indians were bad."

"I think White Calf had every right to want to keep his land here, just the way you and I want to keep Vermillion and Lost Lake beautiful—and safe."

"Could our house be on the land that was his?"

"I don't think the Indian tribes believed in owning land the way we do today, but it's possible he could have camped around here. The settlers back then wanted to live here too. They said the tribes should go to stay on reservations—places of their own, like we still have here in Montana. Remember when we went to see their pow-wow with the dancing?"

"I 'member only the pictures, when I was standing between you and Dad. Maybe I was too little then. I try to 'member lots of stuff we did when Dad was with us, but sometimes I can't."

"Then I'll take you to see a powwow again next summer. Listen, hon, let's talk about all this tomorrow, okay? You need to go to sleep so you can be wide awake for school."

"Yeah, 'cause Mrs. Gates is going to tell us more about how the Blackfeet lived. Mom, I have black feet, too, when I run around without shoes, so maybe that's where they got their name—if they didn't wear moc'sins…"

His voice faded and his eyelids drooped. After he said his prayers—always asking God to say hi to his dad—Lauren brushed his bangs back from his face and kissed his forehead. His little arms came tight around her neck, and she hugged him hard. She longed to rock him and cling to him, but she didn't want him to know how shaken she was. They let go; he sighed and snuggled into his Batman sheets.

"Be safe, Mom," he whispered their parting mantra. That was the farewell often spoken by those who fought wildfires in the West, a saying Ross had taught them both. They were the last words Lauren and her husband had ever said to each other.

"I love you. Be safe, my Nicky."

As she snapped off his bedside lamp, she thought how small he looked in his bed in this peaked-roof loft that used to be her and Ross's master bedroom. The top part of the A-frame second story of the house, it had sliding doors to a balcony with a great view of the mountains, but she almost never went out there anymore.

In the half darkness—Nicky insisted on a night-light in the adjoining bathroom—Lauren gazed out at purple shadows crouching in the trees and shrouding the mountains. Realizing she still held the book she'd read from, she leaned over to replace it on the shelf. Nicky often wanted her to read from this *Children's Book of Bible Stories* that had once been his father's. Before Ross died, the boy's favorite had been the creation story, with its drawings of all the animals in the garden, but now it was any sort of tale with "bad guys."

Though Lauren never closed the curtains, she suddenly yanked them shut. The familiar view seemed not protective but oppressive. She hurried downstairs to close the other curtains and recheck her window latches and door locks. Dear God in heaven, what if she'd brought a snake into this Eden?

* * *

The FBI team kept at it, renewed by calls pouring in about the BND arsonist. Mike and Brad were working the day shifts, Jen and Clay at night. They'd borrowed two secretaries from the field office here and were trying to follow up on any tips or intel that seemed credible.

Just as Brad got ready to go home at 9:00 p.m., Mike called him into his office and told him about a possible sighting in rural Montana, which didn't fit the perp's M.O. at all.

"Yet it makes a crazy kind of sense," Brad insisted when Mike relayed the phone call received from a female pilot living in a tiny town in northwest Montana. "He knows he could possibly be I.D.'d now. We've splashed his picture everywhere in the last couple of days. So he takes off for a while to podunk. I say we check this woman out, at least interview her so we can get an idea what her passenger was like—and even what she's like. We sure could use another eyewitness besides an old lady who doesn't know what year it is and saw him in the dark by firelight."

"'In the dark by firelight.' Sounds almost romantic," Mike murmured, rubbing his eyes with his thumb and index finger. "Yeah, my sentiments exactly about our lady pilot, Ms. Taylor, so you're catching a plane first thing in the morning for Kalispell, Montana."

"Can't I fly clear into— What's the name of her town you mentioned? Vermillion?"

"I'm having her meet you at the Kalispell airport, though you'll be flying into big Glacier International. I have no idea if taxis exist to get you between airports, but you'll handle it. And do some background work on her before you leave here tonight. If you think she's squirrelly or not worth more time after you meet her, thank her and get the hell back here. If she seems credible, use your own judgment about flying to Vermillion with her to look around a bit—without stirring everyone up there so the guy disappears again. It may be a wild-goose chase, but it's probably almost goose-hunting season in Montana."

Just above Lauren Taylor's small spread of land, Evan Durand hunkered down in the line of shivering aspens. It was after dark but the three-quarter moon shed wan light. He'd never had a more picturesque place to live and work for a while. What a great vacation spot! It was more beautiful than he remembered, but then again, the other time was in the dead of winter.

He'd been watching her place for several hours, but he already had the area almost memorized. Above the aspens stretched an alpine meadow in late-summer bloom. Even in the darkness, the ring of mountains seemed to occupy the sky. He could still hear the crooked snowmelt stream in the small ravine that passed the house not far from her lot line. A row of blue spruce six feet tall marked her property boundary. He would not have been able to pick it out otherwise, since she had no neighbors in sight. She'd been home since about four-thirty with the boy, and no one had stopped or even driven by on the narrow gravel road.

Evan studied the silvered silhouette of the cozy log house, one and a half stories with steep roofs to shed snow. In daylight, the logs looked shellacked on the outside, like the ski-lodge cabins, which probably protected the wood from insect borers, snow and water damage. He had planned a respite from his work here, but this was pretty tempting. There was no fire hydrant in sight, though a hose could suck water out of the lake about twenty yards beyond her lot line. All these things he filed away in his infinite memory.

Since he couldn't ask anyone and didn't want to be seen—ghosts and phantoms were only seen by their chosen ones—it had taken him almost until dark to find out where she lived. When she'd left the dock, she'd driven off uptown. That had misled him at first, but then he'd seen her SUV go by with her and the boy in it. He could have asked her where she lived, but that might have made her nervous. He wanted to know everything about her, but from his own observation, his own homework, not what others, including her dead husband, had told him.

Yeah, the master actor, not the Phantom of the Opera but the Phantom of the Fires. Evan Durand was taking his act on the road. Like summer-stock theater, he told himself. New drama, act one! Light the lights!

So, first things first. Since he'd arrived, he'd been eyeing the large vegetable garden she had surrounded with a six-foot-high wire fence. Protection from marauding animals, but not the human kind. From here it looked as if she only grew root vegetables, but he believed in a healthy diet. Though he'd packed plenty of tuna and peanut butter, he fully intended to also live off the land, and that included people's gardens and castoffs. It was shameful what individuals, grocery stores and restaurants threw out these days.

A batting cage and a small soccer net were set up in the backyard, and her son had draped the soccer net with an old blue-and-gray-striped blanket. Earlier tonight, the kid had been playing Indian with a ribbon around his head and a feather stuck in it. When his mother had seen him out the window, she'd hustled him back inside. That meant to Evan, who had to admit he was a great student of character, that the boy was obedient but still had a mind of his own. And that his mother was too damn controlling.

He was a cute kid, though too short to be spotted easily through the cabin windows unless Evan went to higher ground. But then, he was too distant to see what was going on. The moment it got dark, Lauren Taylor had surprised him by closing her curtains.

That made him uneasy. There was nothing but wildlife—including himself, he thought, with a chuckle. And since she had seemed so at home here, he didn't take her for one who would be fearful. Her husband hadn't been a bit scared, only too nosy, too dangerous.

Evan had figured out who Lauren was the second he'd seen her Web site. Imagine stumbling on Ross Taylor's widow. Taylor had talked about her and the boy, but when Evan had chosen Vermillion for his little vacation, he'd never thought she'd be sticking it out on the edge of the frontier, living—almost—alone. On the other hand, her friend, whose mailbox read Cobern, evidently really did live alone.

Evan sighed. He'd surveil them both, get to know them better than they knew themselves, then decide. Or maybe he'd outdo himself in a blaze of glory—he smiled at another of his brilliant double entendres—with two women going up in flames instead of just one.

3

Lauren's stomach was more knotted than the macramé purse she had beside her in the restaurant booth. Under the table, she kept bouncing her foot; she was biting the inside of her lower lip. As high-strung as she got sometimes, she'd never felt this jittery.

She glanced at her watch again. Five 'til. At 2:00 p.m., just one day after she had phoned the FBI hotline listed in Dee's newspaper, she was to meet Special Agent Bradley Hale from Denver in the Western Wings Coffee Shop at the Kalispell City Airport. She was early and kept an eye on the front door, chatting with people when she had to and trying not to get too jazzed on caffeine.

When her insomnia started to get worse, she'd cut caffeine out completely for two weeks, but had quickly learned that wasn't to blame. Her grief, regrets and the nagging feeling she'd tried so hard to bury with Ross were the culprits. Official government report or not, something had been very wrong about the way he'd died.

And now she wanted help from the government, from one of their own, on a completely different matter, even though she'd told herself not to trust them. She sucked in a quick breath. That was surely him coming across the street. At least he hadn't shown up in a suit and tie. But his khakis looked pressed and he wore a jean jacket over a light blue shirt with a button-down collar, no less. Slung over one shoulder was a black duffel bag. Wearing opaque aviator sunglasses, he kept looking around as he crossed the street. Agent Hale reminded her of those no-nonsense Secret Service guys who protected the president. His boss, Agent Mike Edwards, had told her to keep this man's presence a secret for now. Except for telling Dee, she had.

As he came closer, Agent Hale both assured her—he looked so in charge—and distressed her, because he was a real hunk. She shifted on the hard wooden seat as he opened the door and stepped in, swiveling his head right and left as if he expected to be attacked. His face was angular, with a strong jaw, prominent brow and aquiline nose. His Nordic coloring made him look like a Viking. On the other hand, as he came in through a door in the middle of the mural with life-size painted figures of Lewis and Clark heading west through this area, he looked as if he belonged with those rough-hewn heroes. She might feel uneasy with this man, but Nicky would love him.

It was no miracle that he spotted her immediately, because she was the only woman in the place. Suddenly, Lauren wished she'd dressed less like a bush pilot and more like a businesswoman. She shoved her wayward red tresses behind both ears. Darn! She could feel her cheeks heat; she hardly ever blushed anymore.

"Lauren Taylor?"

Low voice, slightly raspy. He took off his shades to reveal clear blue, narrowed eyes, which seemed to take in every atom of her being. He extended his hand and she offered hers. His shake was warm and very firm. He was tall. She guessed he was about six feet, at least five inches taller than her, but maybe his broad shoulders made him seem even bigger.

"Agent Hale," she whispered, "thanks for coming. I'm sorry, though, I don't know where he is. I mean, he just disappeared after I flew him into the Lost Lake area."

"If it's him, he's good at disappearing. Can we talk here for a minute?" he asked, sliding into the other side of the booth across the narrow wooden table.

He was only going to stay a little while? He had come all this way for a few minutes?

"Oh, sure. Montanans are good at minding their own business—except for me, I guess. But I'm so worried." She clenched her hands in her lap where he couldn't see them. "I'd just die if my plane was the Trojan Horse that brought someone dangerous—deadly—into our town. And it's been tinder dry around here."

Lauren knew she sounded shaky. She hadn't meant to blurt out so much at once, but she was so glad to see him, to get some help on this. Dee had been right about Chuck. His injury made him pretty useless as a sheriff right now. And since his painkillers had him so doped up that he was delusional at times, she hadn't even tried to tell him about this.

"Ordinarily I sit with my eyes on the door, but you're

the one who knows what this guy looks like," Brad Hale
said, turning around once to glance at the entry. She
could tell he noticed the Lewis and Clark mural, but he
didn't remark on it.

"Coffee there? Menu or piece of pie?" the café manager, Jerry, asked Agent Hale from behind the counter.

"Coffee, hold the rest," he told Jerry, then got up to
get it himself from the counter before she could. He sat
back down and slid what she thought was a wallet toward her. "You'd better start with that," he said, keeping
his voice low. "Arsonists don't announce themselves, but
special agents have to. These are my creds."

"Oh, right." She studied a gold badge pinned to a
leather oval. It flaunted an eagle with arrows atop a
shield that read: Federal Bureau of Investigation. U.S.
Department of Justice. And under that was his photo;
he looked so stern in it. Though she knew he was who
he said, she skimmed the words with his photo: *Bradley
Hale is a regularly appointed Special Agent of the Federal
Bureau of Investigation and as such is charged with the
duty of investigating violations of the laws of the United
States in cases in which The United States is a party of
interest.*

A party of interest, she thought. That was a strange
way of saying it.

His knee bumped hers under the table. She sat back
a bit, then turned the badge and slid it toward him. He
was watching her like that golden eagle, his gaze as steel
tipped as those arrows.

"Where should we start?" she asked.

His taut mouth tensed as he took a sip of steaming coffee. She was so close she could see his thick blond lashes and the slightest shadow of his beard. She was surprised she was so physically aware of him. Since Ross, she couldn't have cared less about another man.

"Did anyone else see this guy?"

Did he think she was making it up? She suddenly realized how Nicky must feel when she tried to talk him out of his bad-guys-hiding-in-the woods fixation.

"Stan Jensen. He works as a sort of porter here at the airport," she said. "But he left yesterday for a month's camping somewhere in Canada." At least that didn't seem to faze him; he only nodded.

"Besides the sketch of his profile you thought you recognized from the newspaper," he said, "give me the top three things this Rocky Marston said or did that made you suspicious."

"Fine," she said, wrapping her hands tight around her lukewarm coffee mug. "Besides the fact that he just disappeared into the woods without even buying supplies, he asked me if we were in a drought."

"Though that's pretty obvious," he countered, "and could pass for normal chitchat. People always start with weather-type talk."

"He knew that Montana used choppers, air tankers and spotting planes to fight forest fires. Does this guy's résumé include forest fires?"

"Small ones, usually woodlots, but we think those are just to draw firefighters away so he can hit his real targets."

"Which are homes near fire stations?"

"Affirmative. Let me ask you this, Ms. Taylor—"

"Lauren is fine."

He nodded again. "Then I'm Brad. Please don't take this wrong, but I'm just wondering, considering your husband's occupation and his tragic loss, if you said anything leading to make Marston discuss firefighting?"

Her eyes widened and her lower lip dropped before she could hide her surprise. "Well, I guess I would expect you to do your homework on a potential witness. Yes, I did point out Lost Lake's old fire tower and mentioned that my husband was once a fire warden and that he'd died fighting a wildfire. You—do you know all that?"

Damn, damn, she thought. Maybe he believed she was just obsessed with fires since Ross died that way. Brad Hale wasn't going to help her.

"Sorry to bring that up," he added when she hesitated. "Yes, I know all that."

"Agent Hale—Brad—I just feel that that man had a hidden agenda. There was something strange and—and wrong about him. I know that sounds like women's intuition, but I think he was seething with anger. I landed the plane a little rough on the lake and told him I'd named the plane *Silver,* as in the Lone Ranger, to calm him down, chitchat as you say."

Lauren sat forward now, leaning over the narrow table with her hands palm down on it. Her pulse pounded again; she knew her face was flushed but she didn't care. This man had to believe her. Ever since she'd brought Rocky Marston to Vermillion, she'd felt she was being watched, that Marston or whoever he really was had his eyes on her. Obsession, maybe. Paranoia, probably.

"Go on," he urged. "Angry about what? Could you tell?"

"Anger at or hatred for his father just spilled out of him. His tone got almost threatening when he told me his father flaunted a lot of 'trivia crap' that everyone had to know. And one more thing," she added, talking faster and faster. "He paid me all in cash when ninety-nine percent of my charters either pay the three-hundred-dollar fee by credit card or check."

She was actually winded. Realizing she was almost touching his hands, she sat back, folding her arms across her chest.

"The anger at his father may be significant," he admitted, nodding slightly. "It often fits an arsonist's profile—absent or superior father figure, weak or doting mother, who is also resented. Do you still have those bills he gave you?"

"I spent one, but I have the others at home."

"He didn't wear gloves?"

"No—and he grabbed his side of the control panel when I made that rough landing. I haven't cleaned that area."

"Since you've flown at least once since then, any prints may be gone from dust or even cold air. Still, now that I'm this far, Lauren, it's worth a try. I think the BND arsonist may have panicked when someone saw him at his last fire, so he took off for the hills—literally. Sad to say, we have him pegged as a very careful, bright guy, so it may be difficult to snag him. But I'd like you to write down everything physical about him you can remember, especially any distinguishing feature or unusual trait."

"I just remembered, he kept twisting a dainty onyx ring he wore on his right little finger. Things like that?"

"Anything. Anything that will help to nail this bastard," Brad gritted out through clenched teeth as he hit his fist on the table. Lauren sat up straighter; she wasn't the only one who was desperate here. This man was on a mission.

"Another thing," she added. "Marston said he just got back from duty in Iraq. When I asked him what he did there, he first said, 'Try to stay alive.' Then he told me he'd guarded the big brass, but that it was black-ops stuff he couldn't talk about. That could have been true, of course, but it struck me as phony."

"I'll check that out. If Marston's lying about a service record, even if it's so-called black-ops stuff, we should be able to discover that quickly."

"But you do believe it could be him?"

"Let's just say it's a big possibility. And since I have a fingerprint kit with me, I'd appreciate it if you'd show me your plane."

She felt relieved and much more at ease with him. That is, until he got up to pay the bill and she glimpsed a shoulder holster with a handgun under his jacket. But then, the arsonist was a killer, one who needed to be stopped with anything it took.

When her back doorbell rang, Dee threw down her dish towel and went to answer it. Most folks in Vermillion didn't even lock their houses, but she had ever since she'd thrown Chuck out. If some of Dee's friends were here for a chat, they'd have to cut it short or else walk to the school with her to pick up Larson and Nicky, because the kids were out in fifteen minutes.

Chuck stood at the door, looking so like a specter of himself that she gave an involuntary moan deep in her throat. She hadn't seen him since his accident; now she looked at him without the red haze of her anger for the first time in five months.

He'd lost weight. His usually neatly clipped, silvering hair was scraggly—she'd always cut it for him—and his bronze complexion had faded. He wore a shoulder sling, with his arm resting on a pillow that was attached by Velcro to a wide band around his waist.

Her heart went out to him, but that's no doubt exactly what he wanted. In these tough times, why didn't he just go move in with Jidge McMahon, since he'd gone to her for the good times?

But Dee opened the door.

"I hope you didn't walk clear down here from the ski lodge," she told him, "but then I guess you can't drive."

He tried to force a jaunty grin that was more like a grimace. "Hello, sweetheart. Can't drive for maybe two months or so, the doc says. But I wanted to see Larson."

"You know he's not here yet. I have to go pick him and Nicky up. You—you look faint."

"Naw, just haven't done any exercise since this happened. Dee, truth is, I had to see *you*."

She blinked back tears that prickled behind her eyelids. "You better come in before you fall down. You can stay to see Larson, then I'll drive you back to the lodge."

He didn't argue, didn't get riled as he had during their other few confrontations since a friend in Kalispell had told her she'd seen him and the newly divorced Jidge, his old high-school flame, going into the Best Western Hotel. At least he hadn't tried to deny what he'd done. But in a way, that made it worse.

"I don't want the boy—or you—to see me like this," he said, his usually robust voice sounding so shallow. "But I can't help it. Suze said to come stay with them, but I need to get back to work." Their daughter was trying to stay neutral in this family mess.

"To work?" Dee cried. "You can't work now—shouldn't even be out walking the streets!"

He half sat, half slumped onto a chair at the dining-room table, pulling it out first so he wouldn't bump his pillow support. He'd ripped the right sleeve of his shirt so he could drape it over the cast. She wondered how he managed to get dressed at all without help.

"I'm going off the meds," he announced. "They mess up my head."

"Lauren said the doctor told you that you'd need to take them for weeks. That even when you begin physical therapy, the pain will be severe, and—"

"Dee, damn it! My body pain's nothing next to how I feel about hurting you, about screwing—sorry, bad choice of words—messing up what we had."

"You didn't throw your meds away, did you?" she demanded, bending down to get right in his face. His eyes were bloodshot and unfocused; she was afraid he'd pass out. The stubble on his usually clean-shaven chin and cheeks made him look like one of those grungy rock stars. Thirty years of marriage and he was still a handsome man, damn him.

"Left my meds at the lodge," he muttered.

"Good, because when I take you back—drive you to the lodge, I mean—you're going to start on them again. Why don't you lie down here. I'll prepare Larson for what he's going to see and I'll tell the boys they can't be as noisy as usual. And after we all have something to eat, you're going back to bed at the lodge."

Grabbing her jacket off the peg by the back door, she left him where he was. Lauren had said he was strung out on the meds, but he was obviously in agony without them.

Dee went out and closed the door, then leaned against it, all strength gone from her legs for a moment.

Chuck had been the center of her life for more than thirty years. He was a man who became sheriff here— and fire chief—almost by default, for his real loves were leading camping-and-hunting trips, like his buddy Red Russert. But that was so iffy and seasonal around here. Chuck had taken the law enforcement job to support her and Suze because they loved life here, and she had thought he had loved her. It just showed you couldn't trust men, not even the ones you were willing to die for.

Brad Hale seemed to fill the interior of Lauren's plane in a way not even Ross had. Brad was polite and businesslike, but he seemed a raw, huge presence in any size space.

"Under ordinary circumstances, do you touch this side of the control panel much?" he asked as he brushed graphite powder on the surfaces, then bent close to look at the results.

"No, and I keep it pretty spic and span in here. But he did grab it when I landed, right there below the oil-temp gauge."

"I see a few latent ones, and maybe this is a handprint," he said. "This *C.S.I.* stuff usually isn't my thing. And I'm going to have to print you so I can eliminate any of yours."

"Oh, sure. Besides, you could use them to check me out more than you already have."

"Standard procedure," he said, glancing up at her tart tone. "I'm sorry we had to background you. And I'm really sorry about the loss of your husband. I'm sure it's really impacted your boy, too."

She pressed her lips together and sighed hard through flared nostrils. "He's doing a little better, but he still has his own escape mechanisms, I guess you'd say. He has a terrific fantasy life."

"So do some grown men," he said, then added quickly, "but in some of them it's out of control. I'm theorizing that our arsonist thinks he's justified somehow, that he deserves to be king of the world."

"Rocky Marston seemed nervous, but he did say he liked to be in control."

Brad's head jerked up. "That really fits the profile. A lot of arsonists light fires because they feel inadequate and that helps them get their pain or failure out. It's like, 'Look at me, I am important, I am in control.'"

He got out another kit within that kit, then inked and rolled her fingers and thumbs.

"This seems old-fashioned," she said.

"It is, but we're not exactly in civilized territ—sorry, didn't mean it that way. I'm going to go express mail these to my team in Denver from that UPS drop box I saw back by the restaurant. Then I'd like you to fly me to Vermillion to look around, spend a night. Surely there's a motel."

"There's a ski lodge with rooms and cabins and several B&Bs."

"Sounds good. Are you game?"

"Anything to get that guy—if it's him."

Brad, who knew the beautiful mountains and towns around Denver well, was awed by the rugged beauty of the Salish Mountain Range and by the stunning woman who flew him over and through it. Lauren Taylor didn't wear a bit of makeup, but her shoulder-length, wild, strawberry-colored hair framed an animated, heart-shaped face highlighted by amazing green eyes. Her big, droopy sweater over snug jeans and scuffed western boots hid what must be a lithe, shapely body, but she got to him in a way no woman in a bikini ever would. Lauren seemed as natural and alluring as this territory over which they soared, cut off momentarily from the rest of the world.

"There's something I forgot to tell you but should have," she said, interrupting his thoughts.

"Shoot."

"Cell phones don't work well around Lost Lake, if at all."

"Yeah, you should have told me."

"I do carry a cell, but it only works when I'm not at Lost Lake. You can use my home phone anytime you want."

"I think we'll have to use our heads to locate this guy—and maybe some footwork, too. If he said he went hiking, maybe he did. Are you familiar with the backcountry there? He's sure not intending to stay out a long time or pull some sort of escape over these mountains."

"Yes, I know the immediate area. But if we find him, won't he think something's fishy when he sees me?"

"If I can get someone else who knows the area, I will, but I don't want the word out right away about who I am or what we're doing. I don't want to induce panic among the locals or our suspect. And I'll be armed and ready. As for something fishy, everyone in town will think that of me if I don't get a cover story at least as good as the one Rocky Marston came up with. I'm thinking we'll put out the word—through you, too, if you'll willing—that I'm a nature writer doing a story on the area for a travel magazine."

"You mean, tell no one the truth? My friend Dee Cobern already knows."

"We'll clue her in. She's the sheriff's wife, right, and your initial phone call to us was from her house?"

"Yes, but they're estranged right now, so he's living in a room at the ski lodge."

"Is there anything else I should know?" he asked and turned in his seat to put his hand on the back of her pilot's chair. Her hair, brushing against his inner wrist and palm, was as soft as it looked.

"Is there anything else *I* should know?" she countered.

In this bright light up here, even with his sunglasses, he could tell her slanted cheeks were coloring up. She'd blushed when he'd first sat down at her table at the airport too.

"You're still uneasy I backgrounded you?" he asked.

"Was it my entire bio? Including a Columbus, Ohio, speeding ticket when I was a freshman in college?"

"Okay, let's even the playing field. We're going to be partners in our hunt for Rocky Marston, after all, though I'll bet that name is bogus."

"So that evens the playing field—that you're telling me you suspect he used an alias?"

"No. I want you to know that I understand how hard it is to have something like your husband's loss hanging over you, always a part of you."

"You lost someone in a fire, too?"

"In a way. One of the reasons I'm so dedicated to my work is because my father was an arsonist."

Her eyes widened; she gripped the wheel hard, lifting and stiffening her arms.

"Everyone who works with me knows it," he went on, "so I have that always on my back, the invisible monkey clinging, making things I say and do be seen in that light. Yet it's a part of me that doesn't hold me back. It makes me better, more determined to stop others who use fire illegally and immorally for their own ends. And frankly, if that's the way you feel, too, so much the better to get this guy."

"Did your father's fires kill anyone?"

"No, thank God. He was what they call an eco-arsonist. He torched half-built luxury homes on a wild-life preserve outside Denver near our horse farm. I was in high school then. And despite being ashamed of him—and angry that we lost our business and our home and that it killed my mother—I missed him like hell. Still do. He's in prison and will be for years."

"I appreciate that you told me," she said as they descended into a cuplike valley with an amazing green glacier lake at its heart. He saw the little town along the western shoreline, looking like a toy village under a Christmas tree. Only this town was rimmed by meadows, deep, blue-green forests, and then the slate-gray mountains. It was so lovely that, for a moment, he forgot to breathe and even blinked back tears. What a sin—a sacrilege—if someone destroyed all this beauty with nature's precious, perilous gift of fire.

4

From above Lost Lake, where they landed at 6:00 p.m. that evening, Brad noticed the single block of false-facade, shoulder-to-shoulder commercial buildings and scattered houses that made Vermillion look like a Wild West movie set—minus the horses.

A sharp memory stabbed him. He'd loved horse packing in the backcountry around Denver with his parents. After his father was imprisoned and fined, they'd had to sell the stable of registered quarter horses they'd raised. Brad had been devastated to lose his big, sorrel gelding, Sam. He'd never forgotten the look in Sam's soft, doe eyes when his new owner led him away. All that had broken his mother's health and his heart.

"Anybody around here do backcountry horse packing?" he asked Lauren as she smoothly headed the plane toward the only dock on the lake. "You know, wilderness outfitters for camping trips?"

"If you're thinking of trying to track Marston on horses, it's probably not a good idea. A lot of the hiking trails are too narrow."

"No, I wasn't thinking of that."

"There are no local public stables. A few folks have a couple of horses they ride around the lake trail. I've borrowed two from the Fencer twins—teenage girls—before, just to get Nicky on a horse. We had a great time riding together."

"Give me a quick layout of the town," he said, anxious to change the subject. He'd told her enough about himself and only because he wanted her to trust him. No reason to get all emotional about his own losses. She didn't need to know that he hadn't been on horseback since he lost Sam, or that he could still bawl like a baby at the mere thought of the day everything he loved went up for auction—went up in smoke because of his father's fires. Brad made himself focus on Lauren's recital of places.

"Starting at this end of town, that's the only gas station," she said, pointing. "That first house belongs to one of the other pilots, Jim Hatfield, and his family. The other six regular pilots are all men. Anyone who wants to fly in or out checks in with Jim's wife, Carol, who keeps track of which plane is going into Kalispell and when. They use their living room as a sort of lobby."

That made Brad realize he needed to start thinking in terms of small-town America, at least from the last century if not before.

"And that large building anchoring the main street, the only paved street, is the general store," she went on.

"I was going to say Vermillion reminds me of a Wild West town, but that's exactly what it is—with a sheriff and, no doubt, a schoolmarm. And you and I are about to become the posse."

"Oh, yeah, it's wild all right. Nothing ever happens." She gave him the first smile he'd seen. It surprised him, lifting the tips of her green eyes and transforming her tired, worried look for a golden moment. Despite the cloud of anxiety that hung over her, he felt as if sunshine bathed him in warmth. He tore his gaze away.

"It's not a one-room schoolhouse," she was saying, "but it's all in one building, about a hundred and twenty-five kids, K through 8. The grades are grouped, and we have a total of five teachers, four women and one man, who is also the principal. Most families who have high-schoolers send them to boarding schools in Kalispell or Missoula, but a few homeschool. My son's a first-grader and loves his teacher—she's a real veteran. She actually taught my husband, too. But back to what you asked. Between the gas station and the school are shops for the ski season and the two restaurants. It's not a big choice in town, but during fall and winter the excellent ski-lodge restaurant is open, too. The two churches at the far end of town are Community Protestant, where Nicky and I attend—the one with the white steeple— and Saint Mark's Catholic, beyond that. A few homes you can't see are hidden by foliage or the uplands."

"And your home?"

"There," she said, pointing toward the shoreline quite a ways from the town as the plane cozied up to the dock. "You can just make out the peak of our A-frame roof. I can walk to town in about twelve minutes, but I usually drive."

"I checked on the roads in and out—or I should say, road."

"And that's sometimes blocked by rock slides or even avalanches in the winter. So my plane—"

"Heigh-ho, Silver!"

She nodded and smiled again. Though Brad was always hell-bent on chase and capture, he savored the light moment between them.

"*Silver* and these other pontoon planes," she went on, "are the stagecoaches that bring passengers and goods in and out in one hour instead of four on a scenic but tedious and sometimes dangerous, road. We are pretty isolated here, but that's part of the charm and beauty of the Lost Lake area. That is, unless a demented arsonist gets loose here."

Her smile tightened to pouted lips that trembled. Brad fought to keep his emotions in check, to stay rational, even as she gripped the wheel and blinked back tears. She was blushing again, with anger this time, he could tell. He was tempted to touch her, to reassure her, but he sat solemn and silent until she blurted, "You know the truth about what neither of us is saying! One smoking cigarette butt or spark from a campfire could mean an inferno with this drought. I want to help you find out if it's him and then find him!"

"We will," he said, annoyed his voice sounded rough with emotion. Unless they caught a break, it was going to be hardheaded, cold and calculating detail work that would capture Rocky Marston, or whoever he really was. "I'll do everything I can," he told her, "and the Bureau and I are grateful for your help."

After they stepped onto the floating dock, she tethered the plane, then led him ashore toward a gravel parking lot to an old black SUV that looked as if it had seen better days. They were heading first to pick up her son, where he planned to ask Dee Cobern to keep his identity a secret, except from her own husband.

"So Rocky Marston walked down this dock and just disappeared," he said, looking around and thinking the man must have hidden in the nearby trees or headed for the gas station restroom. "And no one else seems to have seen him. I'll have to ask around about him, say he's a friend of mine."

She bit her lower lip and narrowed those amazing green eyes, almost the color of the glacial-melt lake. He put his duffel bag in the back seat next to a Frisbee and soccer ball.

"You do believe me?" she asked as they closed their doors. "I mean, I realize people don't just vanish."

He turned to face her, close across the console. "Lauren, I believe you or I wouldn't be here." She looked exhausted, yet passion—even power—emanated from her. "Let's go, partner," he urged. "Like they say in the old western reruns, 'Time's a'wastin.'"

Dee Cobern used Lauren's oven to bake the chocolate-chip cookie dough she'd mixed at home. When she'd seen how happy Larson was to see his grandfather, she'd decided to bring Nicky home and let Chuck and Larson have some time together at her place—not that she was getting soft on Chuck's betrayal.

To keep the cookies large, round and uniform in size, she spooned up dough with a small ice-cream scoop. Most of them were for a bake sale at the school. Dee prided herself on neatness and perfection, at least in cooking, housekeeping and the layout of her shop. Her marriage, on the other hand... Heck, she'd once thought that was under control, too.

Peeking out the living-room window, Dee could see that Lauren's plane was at the dock, so it surely wouldn't take her long to learn that Nicky was already at home. When Lauren arrived, Dee would head back to her house, where her daughter might have already shown up, and send Chuck back to the ski lodge with Suze. Or even talk Chuck into going home with their daughter to be sure he got back on and stayed on those meds. She hoped Lauren hurried because she couldn't wait to hear what the FBI guy had said. More than likely, she thought, the whole thing was going to be a dead end.

Dee could see Nicky from the kitchen window that overlooked the backyard; he was playing Indian in a tent made from a blanket draped over his soccer net. He was in and out of it, looking for feathers, he'd said, but evidently collecting small stones that he piled just outside his doorway. Maybe he was making an imaginary campfire.

Evan Durand had just washed his hands in the snow-melt stream that rattled down the ravine next to Lauren Taylor's house when he looked up—and realized too late that he was facing her son about six feet away. The kid must have quietly and quickly come down the side of the ravine from his makeshift tent above. Evan had been watching him for a quarter hour as the boy scoured his backyard for small rocks.

What to do? Gag him and take him so he wouldn't tell his mother? But that would trigger a manhunt. That friend of hers who'd been watching the boy from the kitchen window could be down here in a flash.

But before he could either flee or grab the kid, the boy blurted, "Are you real or are you an Indian ghost?"

"Me Indian ghost," he said in a low, singsong voice. He'd played Squanto in a Thanksgiving play once, the last performance his mother had allowed. He knew darn well that Indians didn't really talk like that, but maybe the kid had seen some of those old flicks that stereotyped them.

"Are you the ghost of Chief White Calf?" the boy asked, his eyes big as dinner plates.

Evan nodded. Was this kid serious?

"You're not dressed like pictures of the Blackfeet I seen," the boy accused, studying his green-and-brown camo outfit. "But I guess you have to be careful no one sees you."

Evan almost hooted a laugh at that. This was too good to be true. If he played his cards right here, this opened up all sorts of possibilities.

"That true," Evan said, frowning. He crossed his arms stiffly over his chest. "Chief White Calf of the Blackfeet not let enemy see him. Only chosen one can see him— that you, my friend."

"My name's Nicky Taylor, and we're learning all about what happened to your land in school. And that you said you'd live in the mountains forever. Did you fly in here from your sacred burial grounds in the Vermillion Valley?"

Evan nodded solemnly. "That all true. But you not tell anyone you have seen me. You alone can see me, my friend."

Evan squinted quickly up at the house. Even when he was standing, no one could spot him, unless they were on the balcony or roof.

"I want to be your friend," the boy vowed, crossing his heart. "I won't tell anyone, even my mom."

"And not any friends. Not the teacher tell you about my people. If you tell, White Calf disappear for good."

"I can keep a secret! Honestly, I can."

Evan hoped the woman in the house thought the boy was in his tent. He had to set this up quick and get the kid out of here, back in sight.

"You help feed White Calf?" Evan asked. What the hell? He'd been raiding the Dumpster behind the Bear's Den Restaurant and had taken carrots and radishes from the fenced-in Taylor garden, but he could smell something good baking out here. He'd love to supplement his canned tuna and peanut butter.

"Sure, but where will you be waiting?"

"You put food for White Calf in your Indian tent. He get it at night."

"Well, okay, but be sure to get it early so it doesn't draw bears or 'coons. But you know all about that, right?"

"White Calf know all about mountain animals. We meet in this ravine again sometime, but you go out back of tent to come down here, so you not seen. No white man or woman but you, my friend, must see White Calf."

"I won't tell. I'll get you some stuff. Will you be watching for me?"

Evan nodded slowly and deliberately, trying to keep from smirking at how this had worked out. He actually believed the kid would keep the secret. And if he told someone, so what? They'd obviously take it with a huge grain of salt. Evan knew this type of child—sensitive, bright, imaginative. Maybe even brilliant.

"Remember," he told Nicky, "White Calf watching."

"Hi, Lauren." Suze, Dee and Chuck's twenty-five-year-old daughter, greeted Lauren and Brad at the door. "Come on in."

"This is Brad, a charter I just flew in," Lauren introduced them as briefly as she could. He had his black bag strapped over his shoulder. She wondered what was in it besides the fingerprint kit, since he seemed unwilling to let it out of his sight.

Suze and Brad shook hands. Suze wasn't pretty but she was striking with her huge mascared eyes and gypsy costumes. Not only did she draw stylized versions of local wildlife, but she seemed to be her own artistic production with flowing gestures and garments. Today she wore a full black skirt and magenta sweater over her boots, an orange silk scarf tied around her long tresses to hold them back from her vibrant face.

"Dad's here with Larson and me," Suze said to Lauren. "Mother took Nicky back to your place over an hour ago."

"Oh, okay. I'm glad Chuck's got a foot in the door anyway. Too bad she vacated."

Suze rolled her eyes. "She's not listening to anyone. I know Dad made a big mistake, but he's been eating crow for five months and needs his family right now."

She seemed to take Brad in for the first time, to really study him as if he was a subject for a drawing. He calmly studied her back.

"Brad's a nature writer," Lauren said. "He's here to do an article on this area."

"Man, I hope it helps attract off-ski-season buyers for local art," Suze said, pointing a thumb at herself that jangled her big bracelets. "Listen, I need to get going with Larson because I have to pick Steve up today. I'm going to leave Dad here so Mother has to deal with him—get him up to the lodge at least and back on his meds."

"Go ahead," Lauren urged. "I'll just see how he is, then I'll head home so I can free up your mom."

"Great. Thanks," Suze said, hugging Lauren lightly. "Larson, we've got to get going!" she called as she darted into the other room.

"Way to go," Brad told Lauren. "When she's gone, you can sound out Sheriff Cobern to see if I can parlay with him on this or not."

Suze came back through with Larson in tow. "Will you be staying long in Vermillion, Brad?"

"As long as it takes for me to get my work done."

"Have Lauren bring you to my studio—though in this weather, I usually draw outside."

"Suze, keep an eye out for wild animals and be careful," Lauren blurted.

Brad thought Chuck Cobern seemed to come to attention when he showed him his creds and introduced himself. But the guy looked like heck, and one glance made it obvious he'd be no good to him in searching for or arresting a possibly violent criminal.

"Most wanted?" Chuck repeated, sounding dazed. "Arson and murder?"

"We're still not certain that Rocky Marston is the Boy Next Door Arsonist," Brad admitted, "but I believe it's a valid lead. And right now, this is undercover work, except for what your wife knows from Lauren and what I'm telling you."

The sheriff winced each time he moved, even when he drew a deep breath. "Understood, Agent Hale, but if you get any proof this perp is here, we've got to spread the word to keep people safe." There was a long minute where Brad thought he might say something else, but he just stared off into space. "Will you keep me informed?" he added.

"Affirmative. And Lauren has agreed to give me some necessary information so I have an idea where to search."

"It's like you're after a wild animal—and in a way, you are." The sheriff had broken out into a sweat and was obviously having to concentrate on his thoughts. "I'm up at the ski lodge for now, if you need me. Or I can walk down to my office in town, even show you around the fire station. It's not much—one engine and one EMR vehicle, all volunteer help including me, the fire chief."

"Much appreciated," Brad said, realizing that last designation would make this man an automatic target of the BND arsonist, too—at least for humiliation. "I plan to look around the lodge ASAP. From the air, I thought some of the cabins looked pretty far-flung. If they stand empty this time of year, it might be a place the suspect could hide."

"He did show a lot of interest in the ski lodge," Lauren put in.

"I can check the cabins, save you time and effort," Chuck said and grimaced as he tried to gesture with his good arm.

"I'll handle that," Brad said. "I'm afraid you'd be at a disadvantage if you ran into him. First time I spot him, I'll call in help from the Bureau if I need to."

"Did Lauren tell you we have to call out by conventional phones? No cells, 'cept way up on the mountains or the fire tower."

"She told me," he said, though she hadn't mentioned a cell might work from the fire tower. It didn't look that far away. "I'd like to check that fire tower, too. It should provide a great view of the entire area."

"It does," Lauren said. "I've been up there, but not for—for over two years."

Her gaze met Brad's intense stare. He nodded, then glanced back at the sheriff. The guy looked as if he was about to keel over in his chair.

"I hope you'll be better soon, Sheriff Cobern," Brad told him. "Anything productive I learn, I'll keep you posted. I'm going to surveil the area and check around to see if anyone's seen Marston. I'll claim he's a friend who said he'd meet me here. If nothing turns up, we'll have to decide whether to warn and maybe protect some of your citizens. Or set some kind of trap."

"My wife gave me a photocopy of the newspaper article. Lauren can give you the list you'll be needing. But if it comes to that, I'll move in here and take care of Dee."

"Dee?" Lauren cried. "Why would Dee be in danger?"

"Because," Sheriff Cobern said, his voice shaky, "when you give Agent Hale a list of women living alone near Vermillion's fire station, she'll be on it, 'less she comes to her senses and lets me back in here. She told me once it would take Armageddon to make her take me back, but maybe this is it."

Evan thought the sunset over Mount Jefferson that evening was breathtaking, all smeared in red and orange, as if the sky itself was aflame. He lay on his back on his sleeping bag beneath the stand of aspens above Lauren Taylor's house, savoring the view and congratulating himself on how he'd handled her kid.

But it still annoyed the hell out of him that the Cobern woman had kept peeking out the window and had finally called the boy back inside, just the way his mother had henpecked her little chick. Just like his own mother...

He closed his eyes and let the red rage pour through him, though he stayed calm, completely in control. His hands clasped behind his head, he felt the pressure of the ring that he always wore, not because it bound him to his mother but because it freed him from her.

Evan, sweetie, you come on in right now! He heard her shrill voice from the depths of his soul. Years and years of that voice, even when he was no longer a child. *Time for your piano lesson! Be a good boy and come on now.*

The neighborhood kids had laughed at that for years. Some had even mimicked her voice, mocked how Evan had to get right home. They were playing touch football and poor little Evan had to go in to practice his musical scales, damn her.

And then when he'd tried out for the play at school, Agatha Christie's *Ten Little Indians,* no less, she'd said that was too arty, just a waste of time. He'd found his life's calling, but she said it would take too much time from his real studies and his piano practice—which he hated—and take too much time away from helping her at home while Dad was on the road so much. He hated them, too—*HATED THEM BOTH!* Couldn't they see how talented he was? Couldn't they let him run his own life? His senior year he didn't even try out but was asked to be in Shakespeare's *As You Like It*—and she didn't like that, either. No, he should major in science like his brilliant father.

Totally composed, he whispered,

> *"'All the world's a stage,*
> *And all the men and women merely players.*
> *They have their entrances and exits*
> *And one man in his time plays many parts.'"*

Including, he thought, the part of the ghost of Chief White Calf of the Blackfeet. Including acting like a dutiful son while he played his greatest part and planned his mother's exit. And the colors of the fire that had consumed her and left him with just this ring were the very colors of the sunset now fading through the trees, fading to the cold ashes of death....

Evan Durand sighed as he got up and rolled his sleeping bag so it would be easier to carry back to the ski-lodge lift-control shed where he'd been staying. He knew the small building inside out; he'd memorized the mechanics of the lift the summer he'd worked at the lodge, the summer he was finally free from his mother and his dad was off telling everyone in the universe how to fight wildfires.

5

The last vestiges of a beautiful sunset lit the sky as Lauren waved goodbye to Dee and watched her drive away. "Mum's the word on everything I know about the Boy Next Door Arsonist," Dee had promised Brad. Lauren could tell she was shocked that an FBI agent had actually come to Vermillion—and that Rocky Marston could mean big trouble. "Since I'm not actually speaking to Chuck," Dee had added, "I have no one to discuss it with anyway."

Brad didn't comment as he carted his black bag into the house. Lauren intended to fix him and Nicky dinner, then call a friend's B&B to see if they could take him in on such short notice. Dee had said Nicky was in his room and that he'd fallen asleep, but she wanted to look in on him. He never took naps anymore, so she hoped he hadn't caught some bug at school.

"Make yourself at home while I check on Nicky," Lauren told Brad, "then I'll fix us some food before I make you a diagram of who lives where, especially near the firehouse. You know, I was thinking—" She knew she was babbling as she led him into the living room and went over to draw the drapes "Since Chuck is out of commission for this, Red Russert, our local hunting guide, might be a big help to you. He's a real veteran of the area, knows every nook and cranny for miles."

"Lauren," Brad said, turning her to face him before he let go of her arms, as if touching her had burned him, "you do not have to go one step with me outside this house. But I really do need your advice on where to look, who to ask if they've seen him."

"I want to help, even beyond these walls."

"Don't do it because you feel guilty for flying him in. If not your plane, it could have been one of the others. If he wants to hide out around here, it is not your fault. He would have come anyway."

Though she still had her jacket on and the day was warm, she suddenly felt chilled. She hugged herself. "I said I want to help and I mean it. Excuse me a sec. I'll just run upstairs to check on Nicky and tell him we have a guest. There's a bathroom right through there if you want to wash up," she added, turning toward the stairs that led to the loft. "I hope cheeseburgers are okay with you."

"Sounds great."

With a smile and a nod, she started upstairs. But she heard a noise from the kitchen below and went there first. Nicky was stuffing crackers, two big chocolate-chip cookies and an apple into a plastic sack.

"Dee said you were taking a nap, hon," she said. "Are you hungry? Packing your own lunch for school tomorrow?"

"Just getting some stuff for at night," he said, coming

over to hug her. "Sometimes I wake up like you do and I feel hungry."

"Didn't you hear a man's voice? The charter I flew in today, Brad Hale, is going to eat with us before we drive him to Lacey's B&B."

"Does he have a reservation there? And is that why they call the place the Indians stay a reservation, like you can sleep there all night and get breakfast, too?" He looked guiltily down at the stuffed sack in his hands, then back up at her.

"I think it's because that was the land reserved for them," she said, opening the fridge to be sure she actually had defrosted the ground beef. "Brad's a writer, and I'm going to show him some places around here he can write about. And I'll just bet you can tell him some things about the Blackfeet."

"Oh, sure, even while you're fixing dinner."

"Come on and meet him then," she said and started for the living room. Brad was staring at the far wall, at a picture of Ross in full wildfire fighting gear, just above the pine bookshelf next to her desk.

On the shelf she still displayed several of his things: his Pulaski fire ax, his first set of Whites fire boots and his bright yellow, dog-eared copy of the federal handbook of firefighting, open to a page titled "How to Properly Refuse Risk." Why had she clung to those things? she wondered. Was she actually still angry with Ross that, at the last minute, he hadn't refused to risk his life?

Brad turned to her and said, "Big shoes to fill," before he surprised her by squatting to get to Nicky's height.

"I can see why your mother's so proud of you," Brad said when Lauren formally introduced the two of them. He offered the boy his hand and they shook, sizing each other up.

"If you're a writer," Nicky said, "you might want to do a story on the Blackfeet Indians. They used to be all around here. But don't go out looking for any, 'cause there's bears and mountain lions, and it might be too dangerous."

"You know," Brad said, straightening to his full height, his eyes meeting hers over Nicky's head, "sometimes the only way to win is by doing something dangerous." He glanced at the yellow book, then back at her.

"Despite the odds," Lauren said, "wildfire fighters, like Nicky's father, always have a can-do spirit, and I like to live by that, too."

But it wasn't Ross now in her home, standing here strong and sure, asking Nicky about local Indians while she bolted back to the kitchen to fix supper. Soon she was going to put away that shrine she'd made to her husband. She had to get on with her life, and to do that, she had to help catch an arsonist.

If Brad turned his eyes, he could see Nicky, with a sparsely feathered headband on, watching a video while Lauren made a quick sketch of the town. The boy was engrossed in Disney's *Pocohontas,* though Lauren said he'd long outgrown the movie and hadn't asked to see it for a long time. He seemed as wrapped up in it as the striped blanket he'd tugged around his shoulders.

Nicky had easily accepted his mother's explanation that she was drawing the town for their guest so that he would be able to say who lived where when he wrote about it. Lauren Taylor was as good at well-worded half truths as anyone on the arson team, Brad thought.

He had used her phone to call the Denver office and talked to Jen, who was on the night shift with Clay. He filled her in and told them to watch for the express package with the fingerprints. He explained about the phone situation and gave them Lauren's number and the number of the B&B where he thought he'd be staying. He told them he was also planning to try to raise prints from three fifty-dollar bills Rocky Marston had given to Lauren, but wasn't sure when or how he'd get them out to them.

"Sounds like you're on Mars," Jen said, her voice sardonic. "So what's she like? Rough and ready?"

"Let's just say credible."

"Old, young, pretty, not?"

"I'm not saying this line's secure," he'd told her, frowning. "Read the dossier I e-mailed to Mike if you're so curious."

"Touchy. I thought this might give you a chance to get out of this rat trap and relax."

"This isn't some side trip to Disney, Jen."

"Not even Frontierland? Good luck, then. We'll process the prints the second they arrive and let you know pronto what turns up. And seriously, you know we can call in the cavalry if you need them—if this turns out to be anything."

"I'll check in tomorrow after I look around."

"Copy that. And I'm serious. Watch your back."

"Okay," Lauren announced when he hung up, "this is Vermillion, Montana and vicinity." She rotated the drawing toward him. She'd printed the names of who lived where and who owned what shops. She'd put a big X on the fire station, which also housed the tiny attached sheriff's office. "And," she went on as he bent over it, "the two women who best fit the possible target for Boy Next Door would be Dee—since she's been living alone lately—and Marilyn Gates."

"My teacher?" Nicky asked and hit the pause button. "What about Mrs. Gates?"

"I didn't know little pitchers had ears that big," Lauren murmured and twisted in her chair to look at her son. "Go back to your show, hon. I'm just telling Brad who lives where in town."

But he came closer, dragging his blanket. "She moved from her house outside town 'cause it was too big for her after her husband died," Nicky said. He glanced at his mother's sketch. "She lives in a 'partment above the gift shop. Larson and I got to help her carry some things home from school once."

"I'll bet she's a good teacher," Brad said.

"The best. And she wears earplugs at night so if the sirens go off for a fire, she won't hear it as loud, but it doesn't happen much she told us."

"I'd like to meet her if your mom would set it up for me. I believe she's lived here a long time, so she might be able to help me with my writing."

"Oh, yeah, she can write really good. You should see

the words she prints on the board, with no mistakes at all."

"With no mistakes at all," Lauren said as she straightened one of the new feathers in the boy's headdress and reached for her phone. "Now, wouldn't that be great?"

"She's the obvious choice for best teacher—and best possibility," Brad said. "So maybe you can ask if I could meet her tonight, when you take me into town."

"Sure, it's barely eight o'clock," Lauren said. "Unless she goes to bed early. She's no spring chicken."

"She's not chicken at all!" Nicky started to protest, but Brad rose from the table and gestured for the boy to follow him back to the sofa, away from the table where Lauren would make the call. He was pleased that Lauren got through to the woman at once, and he tried to keep her son occupied for a moment.

"If we stop to see Mrs. Gates tonight," Brad told the boy, "will you give me a little private time to talk to her about my project?"

"Sure."

"I can tell you really like to help your mother. You're getting to be a big boy. Would it be all right if I call you Nick?"

He looked surprised. "My dad used to call me that, but no one else does now."

"What do you think?"

"Yeah, it would be all right, just between us."

"It's all set," Lauren announced. "Turn off the TV, hon."

"She calls me hon, too," the boy whispered and clicked it off, then went back into the kitchen to look out the back window through the blinds as he'd done several times earlier. He was, Brad had guessed, keeping an eye on that makeshift Indian camp he'd made out back.

"You can vouch for this woman?" Brad asked Lauren as Nicky darted ahead of them to knock on his teacher's door. They had to walk up an enclosed staircase to get to her apartment, but Lauren had told Brad the view of the shoreline and lake from the second-story side porch was spectacular. And that there was a side entrance onto the porch.

"Vouch for her? You mean that she won't announce in class that there may be a deranged arsonist loose?" she whispered back. "I don't know how she'll take your news, but you might want to get her promise of secrecy first."

Suddenly looking grim, he nodded. Lauren was amazed—not only that Brad kept his black bag with him again, but that she was starting to read his mind. And she was surprised at how smoothly he orchestrated everything once they were inside. After a few minutes of conversation, he maneuvered Nicky into another room to look at a book with pictures of Blackfeet Indians, and the three of them huddled in the kitchenette where Marilyn Gates had just vowed she'd do anything to help the FBI.

But then, Lauren recalled, the woman had not one but two American flags in her classroom, and the kids always said the Pledge of Allegiance. She even had a blown-up photo of the Statue of Liberty over her fireplace, where one of those artificial logs burned easily and cleanly. The entire apartment looked absolutely spotless.

Marilyn Gates was in her mid-sixties but looked much younger, with her taut-skinned face, spry body and vivacious demeanor. She always joked that her white hair was from teaching two generations of Vermillion children, but she loved her work. A bit of a taskmaster, she was still filled with life and fun—which had not escaped the hawk eye of Russert, to whom, talk said, she'd given the cold shoulder. But as Marilyn Gates listened to Brad's calm, clipped explanation, Lauren noted that she looked neither lively nor amused.

"But that's dreadful," she said, wringing her hands when he explained the situation. "Most Wanted List for arson and murder? It's been bone dry around here all summer. If he burned this building, this entire block of the town could go up in flames."

"Yes, ma'am, I realize that."

"So you are warning me to keep a sharp eye out. Teachers have eyes in the back of their heads, you know."

"Yes, that's part of it. But because this arsonist has always set a perimeter blaze to draw firefighters away before he ignites a single woman's house near the station, I'm asking you to vacate this place immediately anytime you see or smell anything suspicious. Lauren says you have a second exit out the side. Is there anyplace nearby you could get to quickly to be safe?"

"Not many people live in this block, with all the shops," she said.

Lauren, realizing she might be treading on shaky ground, put in, "Red Russert lives over the Bear's Den

Restaurant just two doors down on the other side of the firehouse."

"Unacceptable," she clipped out. "I can't be running to him for help, possibly in the middle of the night."

"But he's out on the trail so much in the summer," Lauren countered. Didn't this bright woman realize they were talking life and death here? "When he's away, he could at least leave you a key."

"I'll arrange something," Mrs. Gates said, her warm voice starting to ice over. Lauren could see now how this veteran teacher managed to keep kids in line with just a look or a word.

"And what does this firebug use to set his fires?" she asked Brad.

"Unlike most serial arsonists who are quite consistent, he amuses himself and tries to confuse authorities by using a variety of methods and accelerants."

"Such as?" Mrs. Gates quizzed the big, stern man in a way that surprised Lauren.

"He's used everything from an old-fashioned Molotov cocktail made of a gasoline-filled bottle with a cloth wick, to a new version of it with sugar, gasoline and potassium chlorate. He's employed 151 percent rum in one case, where the victim lived near a bar. In a house where the woman was a chain smoker, he used a smoldering cigarette with matches, cotton and a rope wick attached to a container of charcoal lighter fluid. We believe he even used potato chips because of their natural oil, but we're not certain because a fire started that way consumes all the evidence. Most recently, he used volatile white phosphorus at great risk to himself, but he may have chosen that because the woman who died in the fire once worked at a factory which used that chemical."

He stopped his recital; his intense gaze locked with Lauren's. Her stomach cartwheeled, partly from the intensity of his stare and partly because the devious intelligence of the man they were up against finally hit her with stunning impact.

"In short," Lauren said, exhaling hard, "he likes to research the place and victim he's chosen and use appropriate accelerants."

"Bingo," Brad said. "We can profile his basic method of operation, but he has no exact signature, such as one source of fuel we can use to trace him or lay a trap for him."

"But," Mrs. Gates put in, "speaking of profiles, didn't he come to Vermillion to keep a low profile? To hide out from your Most Wanted publicity Lauren saw in the newspaper? Which reminds me, Lauren," she said, turning to her. "Are you reading newspapers lately or watching the news? Because you've cut yourself off from the world that way, Nicky is woefully unaware of current events."

Lauren felt as if she'd been caught cheating during a test. "I just happened to see Dee's newspaper," she admitted. "I realize now that Nicky's older I need to change. It's just, after all that publicity over Ross's death, I needed to shut myself off some…"

"I know. I do know, my dear. Well, I certainly will heed your private, privileged warning, Agent Hale, and I thank you for it. Where can I reach you, should I notice something—or someone—awry?"

"You can call either Lacey's B&B or Lauren, and I'll check in with you on a regular basis," he told her. "Also, I'd like to have your phone numbers here and at the school."

He scribbled down what she recited in a small, black notebook he'd pulled from the inside of his jacket.

"Oh, you have a gun," Mrs. Gates said, clasping her hands together and pressing them to her pursed lips.

"Yes, ma'am. This man needs to be stopped, hopefully to stand trial, but stopped."

"My, all this seems so unreal," she marveled. "But I promise you I will keep my eyes peeled and my doors and windows locked. Nicky," she called, suddenly heading for the living room, "have you found any pictures of black feet on the Blackfeet Indians in that book?"

"Lauren," Brad said, touching her arm to hold her back as she started to follow, "I'm going to ask around first thing tomorrow if anyone's seen Marston. I'll describe him, not use the drawing. But I'm wondering if you'd have time to drive me to the fire tower at the other end of the lake about ten. Since you said Marston showed some interest in it, I'd like to take a close-up look and see if my cell phone works from there."

"We can't drive there. We'd have to walk, which would take a while, or use a boat or ride horses."

He frowned, looking suddenly very upset. He was just going to have to accept that this area was wilderness, she thought, and not what he was used to.

"Even if we took a boat, we'd have a hike after we got there, right?" he asked, shifting his weight from one foot to the other.

"Right. Horses are the best option. I could borrow two from the Fencer twins."

"Fine. I'll meet you at the dock at ten if you can get the horses. But what about your flying schedule?"

"I'll ask someone else to bring my cargo back tomorrow."

"Won't that put a dent in your pocketbook?"

"I told you I wanted to help and I meant it."

"There's a large reward for this guy, if your information leads to his arrest…"

"I don't care about any of that, nothing but getting that madman out of here before he hurts someone!"

"Mom, Mom!" Nicky cried as she and Brad joined him and his teacher. "I didn't learn if their feet were really black from this book, but see the red dirt in this picture? It's just like where our little stream goes into the lake. The Blackfeet visited places like that for sure!"

"That red soil is what the Blackfeet used to make ocher or bright red paint," Mrs. Gates explained. "That color is also called vermillion, and it's how our town was named. The tribe daubed vermillion paint on themselves for war, the color of a flaming sunset that signified death."

She stopped talking, then mouthed, "Sorry!" to Brad and Lauren. Brad just shrugged, but Lauren thought he looked more determined than ever. As for her, for the first time in two years, when she began to flashback to Ross's dreadful death, she stopped that violent vision before it could devour her. But that didn't stop the horror of her mounting terror that her little town could go up in an inferno of vermillion flames.

6

Lauren ran from the towering wall of orange flames, but her feet were like lead. The inferno reached for her. She was running scared, so scared. Was Ross with her? Surely this was her haunting nightmare where they ran together. She had to wake up—*wake up!* But, no, Brad Hale ran by her side, pulling her, helping her escape the devouring heat only to pull her into his arms where flames still licked at her...

Perspiring, Lauren sat up, wide awake, her covers churned to waves and wrapped around her. She groaned when she saw the bedside clock read 3:00 a.m.

She tried to snuggle down again, but when her mind began to replay the nightmare, then what had happened yesterday, she knew she was doomed. Better to get up and do something quiet, then try to sleep again.

She stuffed her feet into her terry-cloth slippers and padded to the window overlooking the backyard. Her bedroom was now on the first floor since she'd given Nicky the loft for his bedroom and playroom. Leaning her shoulder on the wall, she peered out through the curtains.

The three-quarter moon washed the area in wan light. She had always loved to sleep with the curtains, even the windows, open, to wake up and see the black silk sky, the moon and stars, to hear the breeze and night sounds through the trees and dream of dawn's new day. But on this warm late-summer night, she'd closed all the windows. No use being careless until Brad found what Rocky Marston was up to. Dear God, she prayed, don't let him be up to arson.

She went into the living room. In the dimness lit only by a night-light out in the kitchen, she took Ross's boots, his Pulaski firefighting ax and rule book off the shelf, then put them on the floor of the hall closet. Yes, she could admit now that she'd been angry with him for dying, for leaving her and Nicky alone. Ross had experience, and he knew the rules of fighting wildfires. How had he ever been trapped in that flaming canyon?

For a while after she'd buried him, she'd found herself imagining he was still alive, that someone else had been burned to death. Not Ross! Ross would come walking out of the forest behind the house someday to explain he'd had amnesia from a knock on the head or a fall, that the dental records she'd given the coroner had been someone else's.

She closed the closet door and sank to the floor, sitting cross-legged, and put her head in her hands. But she didn't cry. Nor, for once, did her brain replay scenes of her days with Ross. She pictured not her dead husband emerging from the moonlit darkness outside, but the arsonist, the Boy Next Door. And he looked just like dark-haired Rocky Marston.

She jumped up and made a circuit of the house, peeking out each window through the curtains. She went upstairs to listen to Nicky's deep, regular breathing, wondering where he'd put that sack of snacks he'd said he wanted at night. Again, she checked the lock to the balcony and peered out.

And gasped when she saw a bear move in the darkness. No, surely it was just shifting shadows in the breeze. Not only was this summer dry but it was windy. Besides, she made certain that her garbage can was always secure and nothing was left out to attract a bear. Thank God the grizzlies usually stayed higher in the mountains, but the smaller brown bears could be dangerous and the black bears were notorious marauders. There was no food outside but that in her garden. Though a bear could easily knock down her garden fence, it seemed to deter them. Still, she thought a raccoon might have gotten a few carrots or radishes the last two nights.

With her knees pulled up and her arms circling her shins, she sat in the beanbag chair in Nicky's room, thinking of places she could suggest Brad look for Marston around town, places she could take him besides the fire tower.

What if nothing—no one—ever turned up? What if no one else saw anything? That would be best, of course. But would Brad then wonder if, as she did with her son and his fantasy world, she'd imagined and embellished the whole thing? She suddenly wished this entire experience was just one long nightmare from which she would soon wake.

As good as her word, Lauren met Brad at the gas station with two saddled, old bay horses at 10:00 a.m. At least they weren't quarter horses, he thought, fighting to keep his mind on locating and trapping a possible criminal. He gave her a boost up, then easily mounted.

"That's right," she said, watching the way he took the reins and turned the horse, "you used to live on a horse farm. I think that would have been great fun. I can't recall who said, 'There is something about the outside of the horse that is good for the inside of the man.' What? What did I say?"

"Nothing," he told her as they headed north along the shore toward the water tower. Lost Lake's narrow beaches were not soft sand but packed hard with small stones, so the horses' footing was good. "My memories of my horse-riding days are bittersweet, that's all."

She sobered instantly. "Because so much was lost when your father was convicted? I didn't mean to bring it up. But to even the playing field, as you put it yesterday, I feel the same way about the fire tower. When I first knew my husband, the winter I waited tables at the lodge, he was the fire warden there."

"We're a pair," he said, then wished he hadn't put it like that. No fraternizing with witnesses or suspects. But then again, he needed her help.

"Changing the subject," she said, riding beside him as they moved their mounts to a faster gait, "what kind of background does one need to be on the arson team, besides FBI training?"

"In my case, college major, criminology, University of Colorado at Boulder. Then Butte College Fire Academy in Chico, California. I worked in a fire department in Virginia, while applying repeatedly to the FBI Academy in Quantico. I think it took them a while to decide on me because of my father's incarceration. I never wavered about what I wanted to do, never looked back." He paused, then said, "But let's stay on track, in more ways than one. I checked at the gas station. The guys there did not see the man I described use their bathroom the day you flew him in—and their john has an inside entrance. Ditto for the stores and restaurant where I asked around and at the three B&Bs Mrs. Lacey called for me."

"It sounds as if Marston wants to earn those nicknames Fire Phantom or Smoke Ghost, except, thank God, he hasn't evidently lit so much as a candle here."

"Unless he's hiked out of town and lit campfires."

"You know, when I told him to watch his campfires in this drought, he said, 'I sure will.' Now, that sounds ominous."

"Have you remembered anything else he said?"

"Unfortunately one more thing. When I mentioned our area's competition for sports tourists, he said, 'Something really big could put this little place on the map someday.' Brad, I know he seems invisible, but I think he's the one. I just do. A huge fire could not only put Vermillion on the map, but erase it from the map, too!"

"Keep calm," he said. "The worse the situation, the

better it is to keep calm." But they both urged their horses faster toward the old fire tower.

Evan heard a door slam nearby. It jolted him wide awake. He'd been out half the night foraging for food and for something better than his old drip torch to start a fire. He was burning the candle at both ends and felt as if he had a hangover.

He crawled out of his sleeping bag and peeked over the windowsill of the small building from which the ski lift was operated. It was less than a mile from the lodge itself, in the direction of the outlying cabins. Since this ten-by-ten shed hadn't been occupied for months, the windows were filthy, but he dared not wipe a spot clean. He looked, instead, through a glass darkly.

And saw a big man with a huge sling on his right arm lurching past toward the cabins. Evan had thought about sacking out in one of those but didn't want to break in—too obvious. Here he'd known where the extra key was hidden, just as it had been years ago. It almost made him wonder if Red Russert didn't still run the ski lift in season.

But what sobered him even more, that guy going by could be the sheriff. Last night Evan had overheard the cooks from the Bear's Den Restaurant when he'd had to hide behind their Dumpster. While they'd had their smokes out back, they'd talked about Sheriff Chuck Cobern and mentioned a huge sling with pillow support. When the cooks had said he'd been kicked out of his house by his wife, Evan had surmised that she was the one who had watched Nicky Taylor like a hawk. But if that was the sheriff, why was he here, and what—or who—was he looking for? Or was it standard practice in this backwoods place to check the lodge buildings off season?

And what if he looked in here?

Evan grabbed his sleeping bag and backpack and shoved them into the only corner from which they wouldn't be spotted if someone looked in the two windows. He hid behind the large wheel-and-cog mechanism that ran the lift as the man walked past on the path, his slow feet crunching gravel.

Still in control, Evan exhaled, then chuckled—chuckled at Chuck, if that's who it was. He'd really give the guy a shock if he started the lift from here; the loading platform with the cable of dangling double chairs was just a few yards away. Red Russert used to let him run the tramway from time to time, especially when he wanted a snort of whiskey from that little flask he always carried. Evan had loved running the massive machine, mostly because he imagined that the people riding it were on a spit to be roasted. If only he could have ignited those pine trees over which they were hauled up the mountain.

The returning sound of footsteps drew Evan from his reverie. Was the man heading back this way already?

A shadow dimmed the small shack as Sheriff Cobern peered in, lifting one hand to shade his eyes, then rubbing a circle of soil from the window. He moved away and rattled the door handle. What if he knew where the extra key was kept?

'Fraid so, Evan thought when he heard the key in the lock. Before the door could open, he darted behind it and grabbed a wrench from the pegboard on the wall, holding it over his head, poised in case the man came in instead of just looking.

A crystal-clear snapshot of hitting Ross Taylor over the head, then placing a rock near his prone body to make it look like he'd fallen and hit his head, flashed at him. How he detested *mano a mano* violence. Evan shook his head to clear it.

The door creaked. Looking really unsteady, lumbering like a big bear, the man stepped in.

When they reached the far end of the lake, Lauren and Brad followed a twisting forest path upward for ten minutes on horseback, then had to tether their mounts and hike the rest of the way. When they reached the concrete base of the fire tower, they climbed twenty sets of ten metal, very steep steps to the wooden-framed, tin-roofed structure. The view was both stunning and sobering, Lauren thought as she fumbled with the key that opened it, one she'd had to look for through all her old keys this morning.

Such a beautiful area, she thought, but so much to catch fire in this drought and wind.

"Quite a view," Brad said, gazing out over the panorama as they stepped inside, out of the breeze. She recalled that those were the very words Rocky Marston had used when she'd flown him into the area. Would she always be haunted by that hour with him? What else had she not recalled that he had said? At least she didn't feel Ross's presence here. She had thought she would, but Brad seemed to dominate the small area, despite its cinematic vistas.

"I don't see any signs that someone's been up here," he said, tearing his eyes away from the windows to look around on the floor. At first the place had the scent of dust, but with the door open, it quickly smelled fresh and new. Brad had her binoculars around his neck, but had only used them when they'd ridden past the ski lodge.

"I agree," she said. "Nothing but spiders and their webs."

"Tell me what I'm looking at out there and where a lone camper might have headed," he said as he gazed excitedly out the windows in one direction, then another, like a kid on Christmas morning who didn't know which package to open first.

"That's Mount Nizitopi at three o'clock," she said, pointing. He spun around to look out toward the west, lifting the binocs to his eyes. "Called, as I'm sure Nicky would tell you, for the Blackfeet name for themselves, meaning 'The Real People.'"

They were silent for a moment. Was he thinking Rocky Marston didn't seem real?

"The elevation is 3,363 meters or 11,033 feet," she went on. "Pilots have to know all that. It's the largest mountain, as you can see. Behind the town is Mount Jefferson—"

"Named for the president who sent Lewis and Clark west?" he asked, dipping the binocs to study her. When she nodded, he said, "I'm not as one-track-minded as I seem. Skip the stats, but tell me where the hiking trails go."

"They spread out all over from the lake, in almost every direction except due south," she said, pointing again. "The valley between Mount Nizitopi—there—and Mount Jefferson has trails. It's been called Vermillion Valley for years, but the Blackfeet used to call it the Piskun Valley, one of their sacred burial grounds. It's strange, isn't it, that the white settlers not only took native lands but renamed them? Wrong, too. But then again, I heard the word *piskun* means deep blood kettle, which sounds pretty scary, though I'm not sure what it is."

He nodded. "I'm sure your boy could fill me in on that."

"Here's hoping Mrs. Gates isn't teaching those kids *everything* about the Blackfeet, because they were fierce warriors. Anyway, that valley's very narrow and rocky, with a braided river and tiny lake, but there's no town in it or past it that Marston could have hiked to."

"Maybe he doesn't know that. It's pretty obvious he's not going high since there's still snow and even glaciers. And he's not heading around the mountain, because those waterfalls full of snowmelt would cut him off. If he's hiking out or is just camping in the area, he wouldn't go much higher than the tree line because of the cold. I don't know. I'm just thinking out loud. Are there any houses distant from town that we should check, just to be sure he isn't holed up there?" he asked, skimming the vista with the binocs again.

"Maybe even taken hostages, you mean?"

"That's not his M.O. I'll bet he's a guy who doesn't like hands-on violence, but you never know about someone when they're threatened or cornered. At least he's not going to feel trapped here with all this space. It may be partly why he picked the area. And even if he sees me, he can't possibly know who I am. Nor, probably, does he know who the sheriff is since Chuck is more or less out of commission. No, I'll bet—I hope—our Boy Next Door still feels things are completely under his control."

"I can call the families that live outside town and ask how things are in general. But let's just hope he doesn't know what single women live near the firehouse in town."

"That, unfortunately, I do not put past him."

"What about the big lumber camp on the other side of Mount Jefferson? Dee's son-in-law is a manager there. It has one of the oldest wooden flumes still in service. You know," she said, gesturing, "those huge wooden chutes on stilts that they fill with water to get the logs down from the slopes to the river and to trucks waiting farther down toward Kalispell. A lot of lumber operations use choppers for lifting logs now, but it's not cost effective here, with the distance and the price of fuel."

"I supposed if there are piles of wood there, an arsonist might be interested in a lumber camp. But it's just not him. Those are the ski slopes?" he asked, suddenly pointing. His hand accidentally bumped hers.

"Right, the bunny trails are the lowest below the first stop of the ski lift, then the serious slopes start up higher there and on the other side of the mountain. The Lost Lake Ski Lodge has twenty groomed runs, which are mostly alpine meadows right now, and almost three hundred inches of snow fall annually. I can take you up in the plane if you'd like a better view of the runs. The ski lift itself isn't in operation this time of year."

"It may come to that later. Let me see if my cell phone's going to connect from up here, as the sheriff mentioned."

He went outside and turned away to make the call, but she could see how animated he was and hear his deep voice lift when the call went through.

"Yeah, Mike, I found a place my cell would work besides an airplane around here, but it takes almost an hour by horse and foot to get to this spot, so I'll still be using Lauren Taylor's phone…. Not hide nor hair of him yet…. I know how busy it is there for you, but I still think I should stay at least another day."

Her hopes fell, not only that his boss might make him leave, but that they'd found no proof of the arsonist's presence yet. If Brad left, not only would she feel less secure, but wouldn't it mean that he—that the FBI— didn't believe her?

"No," Brad went on. "We're hardly ready to initiate a search and sweep here yet. You know how slippery he is. I don't want him bolting somewhere else, though there aren't many ways in or out of here. I'm trying to come up with a plan…."

A plan, Lauren thought. She wondered if he'd share it with her, but she wouldn't ask, at least not directly, or he'd know she'd overheard. She turned away but listened intently.

"Copy that. So he was lying about any kind of service record, special ops or not, at least with the name he gave? Of course, he might be telling the truth about Iraq, but be using a false name. Still, none of that would prove he's our arsonist. Maybe he was just trying to impress a beautiful woman."

Lauren gasped. Brad thought she was a beautiful woman? That touched her. But if anything at that point, Marston had been trying to shut her up, not impress her.

"Since the prints from the airplane cockpit aren't back yet, I'll call you later today…. Hoping for a match from the Criminal Master File or the civilian ones stashed in the paper files… I took more prints from some money he touched…. Right, right, I've got that covered…."

As he came back in, she was looking out over the lake. "It's awesome up here," he said, "but we've got to keep moving. I want to check the outer cabins of the lodge today, then get back into town. You okay so far, Lauren?"

She turned to him; their gazes met and held. "Okay up here, you mean, or trying to track down Marston?"

"Both. Up here, I guess."

"This danger to the area—and my bringing it in— has made me start to let some things go. The idea of a murderous arsonist loose is so potentially devastating that my troubles seem small by comparison. It helps me that you are letting me help."

"I'm sorry about your husband—and that he died fighting what he wanted to conquer."

Words burst from her like a broken dam. "The thing is, besides being skilled in fighting wildfires, he had lived through one catastrophe already, one they called a major rager. He knew how to avoid blowups, how to avoid back-fires. He'd saved himself once already by what they call 'Keeping one foot in the black'—you know, standing or lying down on charred ground to let the flames race by. The government report said there was supposedly a black area he and his friend Kyle could have run to. As a matter of fact, it was what they call a big black, a decent-size area already burned. His salvation was just twenty yards away, and he knew it was better to run through the flames to that charred area than to run uphill!"

Brad put a big, heavy hand on her shoulder, gripping it hard. "I've read a lot about wildfires, but it's a whole different bag from the structural blazes I'm usually assigned. I really admire what wildfire fighters do, literally in the heat of things. My team usually goes in afterward to figure out the what, how and why—and the who."

"Yeah, the who. Let's get going," she said, pulling away before she clung to his arm. "We can check on how the sheriff's doing today, too, if he's at the lodge."

"Some news," he told her. "Marston was lying to you about serving in Iraq, let alone in black ops, but there's no fingerprint match yet."

"I hope you can come up with a plan to trap him."

"I need to look around more, learn more first."

When she locked the door and started down behind Brad, staring at the trees blowing below, at the closest waterfall crashing eternally down a cliff, Lauren had a strange moment of vertigo. For a pilot, that was disaster; she'd never felt like this before.

She gasped, grabbed the metal railing and clung to it.

Why did these steps have to be so steep? It was almost like descending a ladder.

"Lauren? What is it?"

"Just dizzy for a sec. I'll be all right."

He scrambled back up behind her, his body pressing against her back to hold her safe against the metal steps. His knees strengthened her shaking legs, almost as if she was going to sit in his lap up here. His black bag, ever on his shoulder, blocked a bit of the kaleidoscope view that had made her feel tipsy.

His mouth was so close to the nape of her neck that she felt his warm breath even in the stiff breeze. "Tell me when it passes."

When it passes, she thought. When my old life with Ross passes is right now. I have to let him go, except for honoring his memory as Nicky's father. I have to go on, find the arsonist, safeguard this area, my home, my people. I have to get past my fear that there was foul play involved in Ross's death, and maybe even a government cover-up.

"Lauren, should we go back up where you can lie down for a few minutes?"

"No. It's passed."

"You didn't eat much at dinner last night. Did you sleep?"

"I'm an insomniac, but I got four hours straight, which is great for me."

"We're going down step by step, pretty much like this, with me just one step behind and under you."

"That will take forever. I'm all right. It was probably just low blood sugar. I've got a candy bar in my saddle pack."

"I'm sending you home."

"No, you're not. You need me at the lodge."

"An insomniac who gets dizzy flies planes?"

Meaning she wasn't to be trusted in the air—or on the ground? Damn, she was going to show this man he needed her, that she could help him find Rocky Marston. She'd get some more sleep tonight, she'd eat better. She'd been part of the problem and she would be part of the solution. There are no problems, her can-do husband used to say, only solutions, but he had been wrong.

They started down slowly, step by step almost in tandem.

"I'm just fine," she insisted.

"In general, I'd agree with that."

"Then let's go faster."

"Faster can be good sometimes. We've got a lot to do, but I'll keep it in mind."

7

At first Evan thought he'd just leave the sheriff on the floor with his head bleeding right next to the ski lift mechanism, as if he'd fallen there and knocked himself out. Totally believable, the state he was in. If the national park investigators had accepted that Ross Taylor tripped and hit his head, these rubes around here ought to assume this.

Evan patted the man down but found no gun on the guy. He probably couldn't draw one with his arm busted up like that anyway. Evan didn't like guns any more than he liked hitting someone over the head—much too violent—but he would have taken a revolver and buried it if he'd found one.

Evan did feel comfortable that no one would come looking for the sheriff right away. The lodge seemed almost deserted this time of year, except for an Asian guy who was maybe the janitor or groundskeeper. Other people from town evidently came and went now and then to clean the place or tend the area, but Evan had spent most of his daylight hours near Lauren's house or watching the village, so he wasn't sure.

But then, looking toward the lodge, he saw Lauren Taylor ride in on horseback, as if his mere thoughts had conjured her up. She was with a tall man Evan hadn't seen before. They dismounted and went up the steps and into the lodge.

Evan took the sheriff's ring of keys and left him unconscious on the floor. Then he went out and hightailed it to the lodge and darted around to look in various windows. He finally located them inside, standing before the huge fireplace in the rustic, pinewood lounge, speaking to the Asian guy, but he couldn't tell what they were saying.

He tried to read their body language. Was this man Lauren's friend, brother, boyfriend, lover? He was big and blond. Too clean-cut for Evan's tastes. Rough-hewn enough to fit in around here but not ragged or rangy-looking like most men in the area. But wait—Evan was pretty sure he'd seen that man go into the Cobern house with Lauren and her kid his second night in town. He now knew it was the sheriff's house, but since the two women were friends, it probably wasn't official business.

Maybe it was time to show everyone—the sheriff, Lauren, Mr. Clean-Cut here and this whole town that anything he wanted to do, he could. He would just think of this as a little warning, a subplot in the epic drama. He made the rules, he was in control.

As for the main plot, it was starting to look as if a fire at Lauren's house would be a good diversion for a bunch of local-yokel volunteer firefighters, though he was considering keeping Nicky safe. And then either the sheriff's very own home and wife or that of the older, single lady who lived next to the firehouse would provide the grand denouement of this drama—and provide his curtain call in Montana.

But he was also writing the script for a grand exit. To be or not to be a kidnapper? Should he force Lauren to fly him out by threatening her kid or let her go up in flames and coerce someone else to get him back to civilization after this little respite? Meanwhile, to illustrate who was in charge here, he wasn't just going to leave the sheriff on the floor. No, he was going to take him—all of them—for a real ride.

Like all Lost Lake locals, Lauren was proud of the lodge and not just because it poured money and vitality into the little, isolated community. It was a handsome, sprawling building, rustic but state-of-the-art. The central pine-and-cedar building was a combination of hotel, restaurant and lounge. The eight outer cabins, each with its own fireplace, were for larger groups than the rented rooms in the lodge. During the season, a ski school and ski rental were available outside. And the two-person-per-chair ski lift skimmed over a skating rink and took skiers up the mountain for ski runs, cross-country trails, snowshoeing and extreme snow sports. The place came alive in the winter but seemed a ghost town now.

After she had introduced the lodge chef, Peter Lee, to Brad, she once again admired how her very own special agent questioned someone, this time assuming the role of a curious visitor and writer. Peter was an ebony-haired man of Asian descent, who had the disconcerting habit of rocking slightly back and forth on his heels.

"Nothing much goes on in the summer," Peter assured Brad with his long-fingered hands clasped before his chest. "Still, we hoping to have music camp here next year, more hiking in the future. You come back, write about it and my cuisine in the winter, busy then, very busy, not only Asian food but fusion with good American winter food, venison, buffalo steaks, other wild game."

"I'll have to do that. Do you know if the sheriff is around right now? We might as well see him since we're here," Brad added. He'd evidently convinced himself Peter hadn't seen anyone unusual around.

"That's a good idea," Lauren chimed in, realizing she wasn't half as good at this kind of smooth duplicity.

"Saw him outside," Peter told them, rocking slightly forward. "Was going cabin to cabin, checking to be sure all is well. I tell him herbs and acupuncture instead of that strong medicine he take be good for his pain. He should take it easy, but will not. I fixing him food though. You stay for lunch, too?"

"If you'll let us be paying restaurant guests," Brad said, and Peter nodded his acquiescence. "Lauren, let's go enjoy the view outside and see if we can find the sheriff, then bring him back in here for some of Peter's fine cuisine—summer style."

"Still good," Peter promised. "Things always fresh and very good."

Outside, they didn't see "hide nor hair" of Chuck, as

Lauren had overheard Brad tell his boss about Rocky Marston. Brad even yelled for him twice.

"He probably went back to his room in the lodge," she said. "I'm glad Peter's keeping an eye on him and feeding him."

"I want to get some food into you, too. That candy bar wasn't much after that incident on the tower steps. What's that cabin over there by the ski lift? It has a small circle of glass rubbed clean in all the dirt—like a little spy hole."

"I think that's the place that runs the ski lift—you know what I mean," she said and jogged after him as he headed toward it.

But something else snagged her attention. Just beyond the small building, the ski lift was running, the double chairs moving down and around through the empty loading ramp before being hoisted high into the blue, windy sky to climb the mountain. Of course, she realized someone could be here to work on it. Red Russert had run the lift for years, and a younger man, Greg Pierce, did it now.

Peering into the locked building, they could see it was empty. Brad kept looking inside, and Lauren, gazing out at the lift, saw no one.

No one, that is, except Chuck Cobern, fifty yards away, slumped in one of the chairs, being lifted farther out and up into the open air.

Evan had liked to run the ski lift, not to ride it, but he had no choice now. In addition to amusing himself by sending the sheriff out into the wild blue yonder, he needed a fast stage exit from this area and some sort of diversion. With his left arm, he held his sleeping bag and backpack on another ski-lift chair so they would not roll off. As soon as he made it to the top of the beginner slope, the safety bar would automatically disengage. Then he could jump off, hopefully control the lift from up there and make his escape through the trees just above the town.

He kept twisting around to look back. He'd dragged the unconscious sheriff and barely managed to heft him onto a two-person seat four chairs behind the one he had used to stash his gear. Then he sprinted to make it in time to his chair as they swung around the platform ramp.

Still unconscious, maybe dead, Cobern rode behind him. The only gamble Evan was taking here was that someone who knew how to stop the lift might get to the controls before he got to the first disembarkation point. Then he'd be dangling for anyone to see—or catch. But he was still just Rocky Marston. He'd say the sheriff was out of his head when he turned on the lift and got on, while Rocky had just been sitting in a lift chair, admiring the fabulous view.

"Brad!" Lauren screamed, seizing his arm and pointing. "Chuck Cobern's on the lift! Out there, look!"

"Slumped over, maybe unconscious. The binocs are in my saddle pack."

"There's a safety bar over him, but what if it doesn't

work, especially when the chair swings around at the first stop?"

Brad ran back and rattled the door of the ski-lift control shed. "Locked," he muttered before he tried to use his shoulder like a battering ram. The door didn't budge. "Do you think Peter has a key or can work the lift?"

"I doubt it. Let's just break a window."

"If I can just get in there and reverse the thing, we can bring him right back to us."

He picked up a large rock and yelled at her, "Get away!"

She moved to the edge of the loading ramp and heard the window shatter. She looked back and saw Brad get another rock to knock off the jagged pieces of glass that still framed the window. He couldn't reach the door by putting his arm through.

She could see the lift chairs going by. If Chuck fell off at the bunny ramp, he'd need help. Had he gone onto his meds and out of his head again? For his sake—and Dee's—she had to help him.

Yes, Lauren thought, for Dee, who loved and needed Chuck, though she was stubbornly, stupidly acting like she didn't.

Since Brad was almost inside, she could just wait here. But even from this distance, maybe twelve cars back, she could see Chuck leaning lower, lower... Safety bar or not, he could slip out and fall several hundred feet.

Before she knew she would move, Lauren jumped in front of the next moving double chair and let it take her. The safety bar came down over her lap and she held tight to it. With no one beside her, she listed slightly, just as Chuck's chair had.

She felt her chair give its usual little shudder as it lifted away from the platform, the same movement she recalled it would make when it went under each of the cross-arm pillars that kept the cables suspended high above the valley.

She heard Brad's voice behind her, loud and angry. "Lauren, what the hell?"

She twisted around, cupped her hands and shouted, "He'll need help if he falls off at the first ramp—just above the town! Don't stop it until I get that far!"

But she didn't see Brad. He must have gone into the building through the jagged window. She looked ahead again, praying Chuck wouldn't fall off way up here.

The changing view seemed to rotate under her, around her. Too late, she realized it was worse than on the fire tower steps, but she fought to keep control of herself. A collage of colors from late wildflowers carpeted the slant of meadow, the area that would be the bunny slope and powder bowl when the first snows fell. Seemingly marching downward beneath her, the tops of parched blue-green spruce and tall lodgepole pine gave way to other alpine conifers reaching up above their canopy of dried, brown needles on the ground. The jagged mountain peaks came closer, shutting out the sky.

She held tightly to the safety railing, hoping she wouldn't have another dizzy spell. Lost Lake looked so small from here…. She felt lost in the whirling vortex of space, one little leaf blown about in the vastness. But she kept hold of herself. She'd come to help Chuck and wanted desperately to help Brad. She had to stay strong.

Then, as she squinted far ahead at the chairs strung out like toys on a wire, she saw something else and gasped. Several cars ahead of Chuck's, someone else was in a chair, someone with a big blue backpack on the seat beside him, someone who had almost reached the first disembarkation platform to which Chuck and Lauren were now headed.

Panicked and furious, Brad made a quick study of the levers and moving parts of the ski-lift mechanism, then tried to move the largest lever backward.

It didn't budge.

Forward.

Nothing.

But why not? Was there a lock on this thing?

He tried to move two other, smaller levers. Nothing shifted, so there must be a lock release somewhere. Had Chuck set this thing in motion? But why?

The noise he and Lauren had made—or the maddening, steady hum of the lift motor—evidently drew Peter out of the lodge. He stuck his head in the door, gaped at the broken glass on the floor, then frowned at Brad.

"Why the lift going?" he demanded. "You break window? You not to touch that machine!"

"Somehow the sheriff started the lift, got on and blacked out. Lauren's jumped on to help him. Do you know how to work this thing? The levers won't budge."

"I only king of the kitchen. That not been on all

summer. But maybe it got overriding from one of the terminals."

"What?" Brad demanded, glaring at the man while still trying to unjam the controls.

"It not have to be worked from here but can be worked from the first platform—or way at top," he said, pointing at the ceiling of the small shed. "Up at the bunny slope or the one where the best skiers go. You know, override."

"You mean these controls can be overridden by controls above?"

"That it," Peter said, nodding, "if you know how to do it. I can go to the lodge and phone Red Russert. He used to work on it. Can't call Greg Pierce since he gone to Helena to see his mother. Or maybe I can call Mrs. Cobern, tell her sheriff coming home a new way."

"Yeah, you call Mrs. Cobern and tell her to get up here right now, in case I can get him back," Brad muttered and turned to the mazelike machine again. "And call Red Russert if you can get him!"

Lauren knew Brad would like to kill her. She was no doubt done as his partner. But in that split instant where she had seen Chuck needed help, she had just reacted. She only hoped that someone else didn't try to kill her before Brad got to her.

Because as the chairs ahead of her climbed toward the top of the intermediate and advanced ski runs, she saw that the third person must have gotten off. Would he be waiting there for Chuck's and her arrivals, or was he fleeing? And after all this looking high and low, could that big blue backpack mean it was Rocky Marston?

She breathed a sigh of relief as the chairs came to a swinging stop. Brad must have figured out the controls. Perhaps he could get the chairs to stop at a place where Chuck could get out on the platform, if he was able. But unless Brad had her binoculars or superhuman vision, how could he see this far to stop Chuck's chair at the upper platform? Maybe he was going to reverse their direction and return them to the lodge.

Lauren tried looking back down the slope, but the chairs behind blocked her view of the lodge terminal. She squinted upward into the bright midday sun. Both the first rider and Chuck had disappeared over the rim of the platform above her while she dangled here, the chairs and her booted feet swaying slightly in the increasing breeze, high above the ground.

Then the lift shuddered. It jerked. Reversed the direction of the chairs, then slammed forward into motion again.

Lauren screamed, let go of the safety bar across her lap and grabbed for the side handholds to stay in her rocking chair. Ahead of her, the empty chairs shook violently. Brad didn't know what he was doing. Or the mechanism was malfunctioning. She almost dry heaved from fear.

The chairs started forward again, stopped, then advanced.

She recalled that the lift could be controlled by someone at any of the terminals, despite the fact that it was usually run by an operator down at the lodge.

As the ski lift began taking her up toward the platform she could not yet see, she wished Brad were here, or at least his gun. Despite living in the wilds, she and Ross had never owned a gun like most of the towns-people did. Some would have called Ross a tree hugger, some a greeny, because of his stand on the environment. Had Brad's father been like that, she thought, and fought back with fire?

A jumble of emotions and jagged thoughts consumed her. Frenzy, frustration, regret and fear raced through her as her chair jerked and rocked again. Nicky. She should have put her own safety ahead of Chuck's because of Nicky. She had no immediate family left. If something happened to her, would Dee or Suze take him in? She needed to make out a will. She should have stopped mourning Ross long enough to take better care of herself and Nicky, too.

In awe and terror, she forced herself to watch the double chairs ahead of her as they climbed higher toward the top platform. Would she see Chuck or that other man? Or had they both disembarked on the bunny slope platform?

As she cleared the tops of the last of the spruces, she crouched in her seat, holding on tightly, bracing herself against some sort of attack.

She could see the platform now. Only Chuck was in sight. But he was sprawled on the ground—and he looked dead.

Dee was in Just Fur You, checking inventory for the coming season, when the phone rang. Grabbing the receiver, she heard Peter on the other end. Instantly she knew something was wrong with Chuck. Her heartbeat accelerated and she repeatedly punched a stack of down-filled parkas as she listened to him.

"He what?" she asked. "Slow down. He went for a ride on what?"

She squeezed her eyes shut to concentrate on what Peter was saying. The sheriff had gone on a ride on the ski lift, and Mrs. Taylor went after him. The travel writer had said to call Dee and tell her to come to the lodge. All Dee could think was that Chuck was back on his meds and had overdosed on them.

"Never mind about the override!" she interrupted Peter as he rattled on. "You tell Brad Hale I'll be there as fast as I can."

She left the parkas and sweaters where they'd dropped and was halfway out the door when she remembered that she'd told Lauren she'd pick up the boys again today so she could take Brad around. No doubt that's why they were at the lodge. Why hadn't they kept a better eye on Chuck? Lauren had gone after him. On horseback, or on the lift?

She dialed the Fencer twins, who babysat for a lot of kids in town. Eighteen this year, Ginny and Gerri weren't sure what they wanted to do with their lives, but Dee had promised them winter jobs at the shop. She prayed they'd be home.

"Hi, Dee! We can tell it's you because we just got caller ID," a young voice said.

Dee didn't even take the time to think how pointless

that was here in Vermillion, nor did she ask which girl she was talking to. Trying to keep her voice steady, she asked them to pick up Larson and Nicky at school, but to go into the office first to get permission. She asked one of them to take Larson to her house—the door would be open—and the other to take Nicky home. He knew where the extra key was.

Dee slammed the shop door on her way out, not bothering to lock it. Within two minutes she was in Chuck's truck and on her way out of town toward the lodge.

She should have kept Chuck at home, she scolded herself as she sped up after passing the school. Maybe not forgiven him, but taken him in while he was hurt. Why in heaven's name had he taken the ski lift up the mountain? At this time of year, there were rocky precipices up there with no snow to pad a fall.

"Oh, please, Chuck, don't do anything desperate."

The moment Lauren's safety bar lifted from her lap, she jumped from her chair and stumbled away from the next ones as they rotated past on the platform. Her legs shook; her pulse pounded.

Just off the pavement, Chuck lay, his bloodied face up. His broken arm was still in its sling, but at a strange angle. His other arm was splayed straight out, palm down, as if he were bracing himself. He did not move. He might not even be breathing.

Lauren looked around and saw no one else. Could Marston be hiding in the trees and bushes about ten yards away?

"Chuck? Chuck!" she cried, gripping his good shoulder and shaking him slightly. Trembling, she knelt beside him and felt for his pulse. She couldn't tell if it was fast or slow, but it was there, so he was alive. Chuck Cobern had always been one tough cookie with everyone, except his own wife.

The wound on his head looked as if it had stopped bleeding. Had he hit it against the chair? No, the wound was starting to scab, so it wasn't completely fresh. Maybe he'd fallen and hit his head, then had no clue what he was doing. Or maybe Rocky Marston had knocked him out.

Lauren knew she'd never be able to heft him onto one of the moving chairs and make it in herself to steady him while they rode down the slope. Since the lift kept going smoothly now, maybe Brad would ride up here to help her. She'd just try to keep Chuck comfortable until help came.

Scowling again at the bushes, she prayed Marston had fled. Yet she wished she'd catch a glimpse of him, so she could be sure of what she'd seen—that he was real. Of course he was real, she scolded herself. If only Brad had seen him!

Lauren sat down with her back against one of the pillars supporting the cables and chairs. The metal was warm from the sun, and she could feel the hum of the cables running through it. Help would surely be here soon.

She patted down Chuck's lightweight jacket and came up with nothing. No gun, no holster. Nothing. He'd probably disarmed himself when he got so woozy from the meds.

She heard a rustle in the leaves and a snort. Turning, she expected to see Rocky Marston emerge from the foliage. Instead, a huge brown bear cocked its head and stared at her, as if to size her up.

8

"Mrs. Cobern, this way, this way!" Dee heard a shout and saw Peter windmilling his arm over by the ski lift.

Dee ran toward him, wondering where Brad was.

"He is there!" Peter said, as if he'd read her mind. He pointed out over the valley. "He say you stay here. He bring them back, and I keep the lift going."

"What happened?" she cried, shading her eyes and staring at the back of Brad's ski-lift chair. He hadn't gone far, maybe not out of earshot. It would be nearly ten minutes more before he'd reach the top of the bunny-hill runs.

"Sheriff must have started the lift," Peter said, darting back and forth between her and the ski-lift shed.

"Brad!" she screamed, waving both arms. "Brad, I'm here! Find him, help him!"

He evidently heard her because he turned in his double seat. He waved an arm but didn't shout back. Her instinct was to jump into the next chair, but what if Chuck rode back down here while Lauren and Brad were after him up there? Then, too, she had the feeling that the FBI was to be obeyed. But had Lauren done that?

She bit her lower lip and blinked back tears at Chuck's predicament—and at hers, treating him so coldly these last months when she loved him so much, despite his stupidity and his sins.

"That travel writer," Peter called to her from the door of the shed, "he gonna have a lot to write so far."

Dee nodded and kept her face turned away so he wouldn't see her tears.

Lauren moved slowly, deliberately. She rolled Chuck over, facedown, despite what that might do to his hurt arm and shoulder. Then she stood. Bears always tried to roll a prone person onto his back to get at the stomach, the softest spot they could attack. It was good to play dead, and Chuck was doing a fine job of that. Hopefully, he wouldn't regain consciousness right now.

At least this bear wasn't a grizzly, she thought. Still, she averted her eyes and watched the animal sideways. Brown bears considered a direct stare a challenge. She'd seen many around here over the years, but never this close. And never one that looked interested in her. They usually preferred avoidance to attack, but this one must have smelled something.

Unfortunately, her standing stock-still in a non-threatening posture didn't deflect its curiosity. In addition to not wanting to abandon Chuck, she knew it was not a sane option to turn and flee. Everyone in these parts knew never to run from a bear, since they could go up to forty miles per hour. And to them, flight signaled prey. It was best to talk low or sing in a soft monotone while you backed slowly away. But if she did that, she was leaving Chuck to the bear.

The five-hundred-pound animal reared on its hind legs to its six-foot height and wriggled its nose, trying to identify her and Chuck by smell. Food? A threat? Everyone said bears were very complex, unpredictable animals, but always vicious if cornered.

An errant thought raced through her brain. The arsonist must be like that, complex, unpredictable, and if cornered…

Though her voice snagged in her throat, she began to recite a singsong rhyme that came to her, half remembered, half created on the spot: "Bear, bear, go away, come again another day and not where people like to stay. Bear, bear, go away…"

But it didn't. It snorted again. "…where people like to stay…" It could have cubs around, too, though she didn't see any "…another day…"

She thought of Nicky, how desperate she'd been to protect him after his father's death. Yet she'd endangered herself now. Ross should not have risked his life, but here she was facing down a bear on a mountain.

Brad, where are you? The ski lift was still running. Brad, where are you? "…come again another day…"

Lauren knew that if the bear came close, she should try to intimidate it, though that had always sounded pointless and stupid. One should shout, hit it with a branch or rock, she'd heard.

She felt slowly through her jeans pockets. She found only a candy-bar wrapper and the key to the fire tower.

Most weapons other than a high-caliber rifle would be powerless against this raw power.

Don't panic, she told herself, chanting the silly song aloud again. Keep calm. Brad had told her that very thing just today. The worse the situation, he'd said, the better it is to keep calm.

But she couldn't fight the frenzy filling her.

The bear dropped to all fours and charged. Lauren dropped to her knees beside Chuck and shredded the air with a piercing scream.

When Brad heard Lauren scream, he was still four chairs below the break in the trees where the platform must be. He drew his gun, glad he had it. But would he be in time? And what would he find? Had she come upon Chuck injured or even dead?

It took an eternity for his chair to lift the last, short distance. He was closer now to the other chairs heading down, coming at him empty.

Lauren had come to mean a lot to him in a very short time. And so had Nick, with his wild imagination, his passion for Indians. He'd sensed instantly how much the boy missed his father and felt protective of the little guy. Though Brad had been older when he'd lost his dad, his whole world had shattered. But Nick had a father to be proud of, not one to be ashamed of, not one whose deeds now drove Brad to right wrongs.

Brad heard no other sounds after the scream. In his line of work, he'd never had to rescue anyone directly, hadn't since his stint in the Alexandria, Virginia, Fire Department. He'd saved a woman from the flames there once, but like the BND's victims, she'd died later of burns and smoke inhalation.

Despite the safety bar across his lap, Brad shoved himself up in the chair as it crested the treetops over the platform he would see now. If only this damn safety bar would free him...

He didn't see her or Chuck at first. And then he did.

They both lay, facedown, on the grass just beyond the concrete loading ramp, not moving as a huge bear faced them, just a few feet away.

Wishing he had a rifle, Brad lifted his Glock .45. Despite the bar lifting before his face and the chair swinging as he jumped off, he took a shot at the bear.

Still out of breath from his run down the mountain, Evan heard the boy's high voice from here in the ravine beside the Taylor house. Since the kid's mother must still be somewhere up on the mountain, Evan hadn't expected to find anyone home. Maybe Dee Cobern was keeping an eye on Nicky again.

"Can I go out and play in my Indian tent just in the backyard?" Evan heard him ask. Evan instinctively ducked, though he knew no one could see him except from the balcony or roof.

A young woman's voice he hadn't heard before answered, "Oh, yeah, nice tepee. Sure, but come back in for this PBJ sandwich you asked for, okay? I'm going to turn on a TV show here while I straighten up this kitchen a little for your mom, but I'm right here if you need me."

"Thanks, Gerri," Nicky called to her. Evan heard the back door bang.

Almost immediately, Nicky stuck his head out from under his makeshift tent, just the way Evan had told him to. Yeah, he liked this boy. He followed orders well.

"I was hoping you'd be there, Chief," the kid called to him in a stage whisper. "I'll be right down."

He half slid, half scrambled down the slope and managed to put on the skids before he fell into the stream.

"I got a banana and graham crackers for you," he said, digging things out of the back of his shirt where he tucked its tails in. "But I'll have a peanut butter and jelly sandwich for you soon!" His eyes were huge as he extended the food and studied Evan.

"White Calf not know what those are, but any food good."

"Oh, yeah, I forgot, those are modern things, but I don't have buffalo and bittersweet root and all that we've been reading about. I saw that in the books about your people at my teacher's place last night."

"Where your teacher live on White Calf's land?" Evan asked, taking the food from the boy. He was careful not to touch his hands, but he could probably explain that ghosts had to have real bodies sometimes, especially when they ate.

"She lives in a 'partment over the Montana Range Gift Shop in town, by the firehouse. Ever since her husband died, she lives alone there 'cause she needed a smaller place."

"Good. That good for her."

"I went with my mom and her new friend, the writer, to visit her there."

"Big, blond man?"

"That's him. He calls me Nick, not Nicky, just like my dad did."

"He write for newspaper?"

"I think he writes travel books. But at Mrs. Gates's, I figured out another reason you appear to me here by this stream."

"What that?"

"Because it runs into the lake at the place where your people used to dig out the clay with the vermillion to make war paint."

"You very wise, boy. I give you name Running Deer, but you tell no one."

"Oh, I won't. Running Deer? That's way cool. I guess I better go up and get your sandwich—that's two pieces of bread with some really good stuff between them. My mom's not here right now 'cause she's taking the writer around town and to the fire tower."

"The fire tower?"

"That's why I'm here with a babysitter. I'm not a baby—it's just the way white people talk. I let her in with this," he said and showed Evan a single key dangling from a coiled neon-orange elastic bracelet around his thin wrist.

"That beautiful with bright color of the sun," Evan said. "You make peace and friendship gift of that to White Calf?"

"Uh, well, I guess so. I can just take the key off."

"But that shiny silver. I not know what key for, but if it that metal charm, I like that, too."

"Oh, okay. We have other keys, even ones just like this, so I guess so," he said, slowly pulling the whole thing off and extending it to Evan.

His dramatic triumph over his kiddie audience made Evan want to break into laughter. He managed to stay in character until the boy scrambled up the ravine and crawled into the back of his tent to emerge out the other side and run into the house.

Ah, what recompense for his performances today! The Smoke Ghost, stage name White Calf, long-dead chief of the Blackfeet, was now the proud owner of the key to the sheriff's house and the key to Lauren Taylor's place. It was just too perfect—kismet!

Evan laughed out loud. He might have lost his familiar *pied-à-terre* in the ski-lift cabin, but he now had a choice of attics in which to make a nest. That is, until he decided to light a mighty big campfire in one place or the other. He was on such a roll, surely he could find a way into Teacher Gates's apartment, too. Then the entire town could search for him high and low outside, but he'd be all cozy and closer to them than they'd ever know. Why, when his vacation was all done here, they'd have to dub him not the Boy Next Door but the Man in the House!

Cursing and shouting at the bear, Brad squeezed the trigger again and again, but the recoil and his rush to get out of the moving chair made him miss. He thought he might have hit him the animal the first time, but maybe the noise scared him more than anything. Thank God the bear turned and lumbered away.

Brad kneeled by Lauren and Chuck. Chuck had blood on his head, but it looked dry. And Lauren…

He bent down to her, afraid to move her if she'd been mauled—or worse. He wanted to cover her body with his own, pull her into his arms and race to safety with her. Tears blurred his vision. He was afraid to roll her faceup. Check for blood and injuries first, he told himself.

"Lauren? Lauren, it's Brad. Are you hurt?"

She had her eyes squeezed shut, but they blinked open. She'd been crying; her face was streaked with tears.

"Just terrified. Is it gone?" she whispered. "It charged at us, but it stopped after we didn't run. Still, I was so faint, I thought I'd better play dead. You—did you shoot it?"

"Yeah, but it wasn't like firing at a shooting-range target. It may be back. How's Chuck?" he asked, feeling for the man's carotid artery with his left hand. As he did, Brad realized he, too, was shaking all over.

"He's out cold," she said, getting to her knees, then sitting unsteadily back on her heels. She glanced around and brushed herself off. Damp with sweat, she trembled as if she had a fever. "Let's get him down the slope. I can help you get him in a chair. I'll be all right," she insisted, but her knees buckled when she tried to stand, and she broke into tears. Both kneeling next to Chuck, they hugged hard. She spoke with her mouth against the side of his warm neck.

"I thought it would kill me. That I'd never see Nicky

again, that I wouldn't be able to help you find that man so he doesn't hurt others. Brad," she cried, pushing herself back from his hard embrace but gripping both his arms, "I swear to you that Rocky Marston was on the lift just a few chairs ahead of Chuck. I swear he was! You have to believe me."

Frowning, helping her up as he stood, Brad scanned the area again. "Was Marston in sight when you got off the lift?"

"No! No, and neither was the bear. I got off because I saw Chuck lying here. He looked dead. I saw Rocky on the lift but not when he got off. He just disappeared. Brad, I saw him!"

"You can tell me all about it when I get you two back down to the lodge. We're not doing any sweep for Marston here, with bears loose and the sheriff hurt. Let's try to get him into a chair. He's heavy, so I'm gonna need your help. I'll ride down with him so he doesn't roll out. Can you get in the next chair on your own?"

She nodded and swiped at her tears, smearing dirt on her cheeks. "Did you make the chairs stop and shake?" she asked.

"No, but I saw that. I think someone up here was overriding the controls—and it sure as hell wasn't that bear. Of course I believe you about Marston. It opens up all sorts of new possibilities."

It scared him how limp and unsteady she looked. But he and his entire trained-to-the-teeth team would probably be blithering idiots after what she'd just been through. FBI teams didn't do bears.

"You did the right thing, Lauren," he assured her, his voice catching in his throat. "I'm just glad you're not hurt. Now let's get the sheriff back to Dee. Peter called her. She's at the lodge."

Together, they got Chuck on a chair next to Brad, and he held the big man upright until the safety bar came down. Brad craned his neck to look back at Lauren as she made it into the chair right behind. Though the ride was smooth, she held on with both hands as if her life depended on it.

"You've been a great help, pard'ner," Brad called to her. "But I think it's time for you to retire from the posse and just hole up with your boy at the old homestead."

"No way! I'm going to help the FBI get the Fire Phantom before he pulls any other deadly stunts! And I'm not doing it for the reward money but to get him off the streets and off the slopes!"

Brad grinned despite himself as he turned forward and held hard to Chuck Cobern. She was a hell of a woman, and one he absolutely refused to let get hurt again. Somehow he had to get her off the case before anything else exploded in her face.

Dee was so happy to see Chuck, however terrible he looked, that she burst into tears. Peter ran to phone for the town's only EMR vehicle and to alert the health clinic. As Dee knelt to cradle Chuck in her arms and kissed his dirty cheek, he opened his eyes.

"Wha're you all doin' here?" he managed to say as Dee, Brad and Lauren bent over him.

"I guess you have the magic touch, Dee," Lauren said. "Sleeping Beauty awakened by a kiss. He was out cold the whole time we were with him."

"Am I in heaven?" Chuck said, sounding as if he'd been on an all-night bender.

"His pupils are dilated," Brad said. "He's probably in shock, or he may have a concussion. Sheriff, we think our arson suspect put you on the ski lift." Dee gasped, but Brad went on, "Can you remember anything about how you got knocked out?"

"Did I?" he said, frowning, even as he nestled his head tighter in Dee's lap. "Can't recall."

"Loss of short-term memory's not unusual with a head injury," Brad said. "Just relax, Sheriff. That's okay."

"Las' I 'member," Chuck went on, "I was checking cabins. Yeah, that's it—for him. So maybe I flushed him, huh?"

"Brad," Dee said, "can't this wait until later?"

Brad nodded and went over to the ski-lift shed. Lauren squeezed Dee's shoulder and started to rise, but Dee mouthed, "I can't thank you enough—both of you."

Lauren nodded too and got up to follow Brad into the shed. Through its open door and broken window, their words floated clearly to Dee as she held tight to Chuck.

"What are you looking for?" Dee heard Lauren ask Brad.

"Wish I knew. But if Chuck didn't start the ski lift, maybe Marston did."

"Because Chuck had him almost cornered?"

"Or we did."

"But he can't know who you are. So what if I'd see him? He can't realize I know who he is."

"Lauren, we can't underestimate this man or even predict what he'll do next. I tell myself I can—I want to, but I don't know. It was tough for me to figure out how to operate this thing. And Marston must have gotten to the top and used the override up there. Now, who would know how to do that?"

"Someone who knew machinery? Someone who'd operated a lift somewhere?"

"Or maybe operated it here?"

"What? No way! I'd never seen him before."

"I'm guessing that no one has run this lift for years, except for the current guy who's not around, and Red Russert. And we know this building was locked. Whoever started the lift got in here without breaking and entering like I did. Dee—" Brad popped his head out and called to her "—did Chuck carry keys to this place?"

"Never have," Chuck answered for her. "There's one under that big rock over there, left of the door," he mumbled and Dee repeated what he'd said to Brad.

"It must be the rock I grabbed to break in," Brad muttered, and she heard him swear under his breath. "Yeah, the key's still here. It doesn't make sense," he said as he tried it in the door to be sure it worked. It did.

"Sweetheart, check to see if I still got my badge," Chuck whispered to Dee. "You got my permission to frisk me."

"You're sounding better," she told him, secretly thrilled he was feeling well enough to tease her. "Yes, he has his sheriff's badge," she called to Brad and Lauren.

"Marston might have seen that and wanted to get rid of Chuck or make a fool of him," she heard Brad say, speaking again to Lauren.

"More proof it could be him," she insisted. Dee held Chuck tighter. He'd either blacked out again or gone to sleep. But if he had a concussion, she needed to try to keep him awake.

"So did Marston accidentally find the key?" Brad asked Lauren. "This whole case has been one big, locked room. I need to find Red Russert, and now."

"I think he's out camping," Lauren told him, "but he comes back now and then. We can check his house, leave him a note."

"I want you to go home and stay with Nick! If we can't find Russert on the ground, could you spot him from the air? Do you know where he might be?"

"Marilyn Gates might."

"I got the distinct idea she detested the guy."

"I can tell you've never read a romance novel. Opposites attract, and bickering is foreplay. Brad, what's this sticky stuff on the floor here? See?"

Dee could finally hear the distant wail of a siren. Like the fire department in town, the EMR paramedics were volunteers who received a call, then reported to the station house. It comforted her to hear the siren and to have Chuck safe—though evidently unconscious again—in her arms.

He could have been killed more than once today. And it hardly calmed her when she heard Brad tell Lauren, "Looks like blood. Maybe Chuck's."

After a long silence, Dee heard Brad say, "I think Chuck cornered Marston, who then used this wrench here on the wall to knock him out. See the hair and blood on the metal? It hasn't quite been wiped clean, so our mastermind's made a mistake for once. There have to be prints on here. We can at least charge him with assault and battery, if we can get him to materialize again."

Dee shuddered and held Chuck even closer as Peter pointed the EMR vehicle their way.

9

Though Brad had insisted she go home and stay there, Lauren could tell he was torn. He had to find Rocky Marston fast, before he could do more harm, especially the kind of harm he specialized in. So, he needed her to find Red Russert. Up on the mountain today, they'd both realized how dry the grass was, how wilted even the big conifers looked from lack of rain. And the wind whipped up through the valleys and howled around the cliffs incessantly.

They had just left their horses at the Fencer place, although the twins were babysitting Nicky and Larson in their homes. In Lauren's SUV, they drove directly into town.

"I hope we don't shock her," Brad muttered as they hurried up the stairs to Marilyn Gates's apartment. "We look like something the cat dragged in."

"Or something the bear did."

Halfway up the enclosed staircase, he put his hand to her elbow and turned her to him. He started to speak, then seemed to choke up. Picking a piece of leaf out of her wild hair, he brushed her tresses back from her face.

"Don't tell me again that I need to go home," she said. "I will tuck Nicky in tonight and be with him as best I can. But I can't really be at home until this is all over, when my son and I and our friends are safe and can sleep at night. I'm running on adrenaline, though I'm so exhausted that I think even I could get a full night's sleep."

"Then I can't ask you to take me up in the plane to look for Red Russert, whether or not Mrs. Gates knows where he is."

"I'm the best sleep-deprived pilot around," she insisted, tapping her finger in the middle of his chest. "Actually, I'm the *only* one in town since Wednesdays are big flight days and the other five planes are probably in Kalispell or in the air right now. Come on, Agent Hale. Let's hope that Mrs. Gates knows as much about Red Russert as I think she does."

Almost the moment they knocked, Marilyn Gates flung the door open, her face alight with expectation. She was prettily dressed in a soft aqua jogging outfit.

"Oh, hello!" she said, sounding startled and looking crestfallen before she composed her expression. "I thought it was someone else. Come in, come in and—whatever happened?"

Lauren shot Brad an I-told-you-so look as they followed her in, but he said only, "We've been searching for the suspect up by the ski lodge and had to help Sheriff Cobern, who was almost attacked by a bear. That's the short version of it, but we need your help again. The suspect is obviously hiding—maybe camping—in the area, and I could really use Red Russert's tracking skills."

When Mrs. Gates only nodded, Lauren put in, "He's such a loner, but I know he sometimes tells you where he's going."

"Yes, he does, and I sometimes tell him where he should go, too," she said, her voice angry but strangely wistful. She led them into the kitchenette and pulled out two bar stools at the high counter. They saw she had been fixing herself a sandwich and had a pitcher of iced tea. Both of them started to sit down.

"No, wash your hands first at this sink, both of you. Your face, too, Lauren. I won't ask you for details and you won't ask me for any, either, but while I feed you, I'll tell you what you need to know."

They obeyed without a word as if they were first-graders in her class, then sat at the bar, while she bustled about her little work area. She cut the chicken sandwich she'd evidently made for herself in two and gave each of them half, then poured some potato chips out of a bag onto their plates. Dill pickles followed. "Eat, I said. I'm making other sandwiches for myself and more for you."

Despite themselves, ravenous and parched, they leaped at the food. They'd had nothing but water and her candy bar since they'd set out for the fire tower. They'd left the ski lodge without the lunch Peter had promised them.

"Yes," Mrs. Gates said as she bent over the counter with her back to them, "Red Russert usually tells me where he's going—just in case something befalls him. This time, he's at the high camp, as he calls it, waiting for me this weekend."

Lauren almost choked on a big bite, then managed to chew and swallow. "For you?" she said, but Brad kneed her leg and she shut up.

"Red and I go way back, but I married someone else. That should have been end of story, but it wasn't—isn't." She heaved a sigh but kept busy. "The thing is, after Glen died, Red tried to, well, to retie our ties, but I said no. First of all, we're as different as night and day. Secondly, he had a knock-down, drag-out fistfight with my husband once at the general store that shamed them both.

"You know," she went on, just staring at her cupboards now, her hands momentarily still, "when I was a girl, I always loved those stories where the armored knights jousted for the affections of their lady love. Well, I digress, and you are in a hurry."

She cut the two sandwiches she'd made in half. "You see, Glen was a conservative, mild-mannered man, and Red is just the opposite. You can imagine who got the best of the other in that fight. I feel I'm honoring Glen's memory by keeping clear of Red Russert, tracker and trapper that he is...

"I'm sorry," she said, whirling to face them. "You didn't need to hear all that. I'm not going to meet him at the high camp, but I can tell you where it is. It will take you about two hours by foot—it's the only way up to it."

"Red's a tracker?" Brad asked.

"Oh, yes, the best around," she said, her voice swelling with pride. "If you took him to the spot where you said Sheriff Cobern had a problem with a bear, he could track that bear for you."

"Has he ever tracked humans?" Brad asked, the last piece of his sandwich suspended in his big hand halfway to his mouth.

"I'm afraid they leave different calling cards, but I'm certain he could help you there, too," Mrs. Gates said with a decisive nod. "I should have thought of that before. Do you have any sort of trail for him to start with?"

"The top of the bunny slopes," Lauren said to Brad. "I'm not sure which way he ran, but it was probably down—maybe back toward town. Can you tell us where the high camp is?" she asked Mrs. Gates. "Since time is of the essence though, maybe you could draw us some sort of map we could use from the air. We can fly over the camp and either buzz Red or drop a note to meet us at the first stop on the ski lift. That way we'll avoid hiking two hours, only to find that he might not be there."

"That would be great," Brad added. "Whether we spot him or not, we can drop a message out of the plane to his camp."

"I have just the thing," Mrs. Gates said and left them for a moment only to return with a bright red beanbag pillow. "You can attach the note to this. It should be heavy enough not to snag in a conifer. And it will drop all the way to the ground but not hurt anything. I'll stitch a small American flag to it while you write your note, Agent Hale, and I'll tell Lauren exactly where Red is up Mount Jefferson. And if you do find him, just tell him I wasn't coming to the camp anyway, and we'll talk about it all later."

"Yes, ma'am," Brad said, sounding excited when he usually stayed icy calm. "And may I say, Mrs. Gates, *you* get an A for the day."

"Nonsense, though I have decided that one chapter of the memoirs I intend to write someday will be titled, 'Marilyn Gates, Special Counsel to the FBI.'"

Evan used the key in the back door of Lauren's house and stepped inside. Nicky had told Chief White Calf that his mother wasn't coming back for a while and that he was leaving with his babysitter, Gerri. He would spend the evening at her parents' house with his best friend and his babysitter.

"And they have some horses there, and I might get to ride them!" the kid had said. "I might ask if I can ride mine without a saddle, the way your people did."

"You be careful. That not easy," Evan had told him.

But getting into Lauren Taylor's house was a piece of cake.

As soon as he relocked the door, he went straight to the refrigerator, hoping for some sort of gastronomic indulgence he'd been missing lately. He'd noted from his observation of Vermillion that no one had security systems. Many people didn't even lock their doors. But he wasn't taking this risk just to forage for extra food. That wasn't why he was here at all. He was doing research on what accelerants would be best to torch his three candidates' houses.

Evan drank milk directly from the half-gallon plastic bottle and, without using a knife, piled together a slapdash sandwich of bologna and cheese with a squirt of mustard. The food the kid had brought him helped, but he was hungry and sick of canned tuna. He ate cookies and crackers that he found, and took an apple off the counter that he crunched into. Lauren probably wouldn't even realize she had three instead of four there now, not with a kid and babysitter in the house.

He searched through the cupboards, and turned up a cache of miniature Mr. Goodbar candies, individually wrapped like those given out at Halloween. They were stashed high, not like the jar of M&Ms the kid could reach on the counter. He took handfuls of both kinds of candy and jammed them in his pockets.

Were the Mr. Goodbars Lauren's secret chocolate sin? He remembered a movie called *Looking for Mr. Goodbar,* about a woman who picked up a guy in a bar who killed her. He would have liked to play that part onstage. You could hardly do a realistic drama about an arsonist without the props catching the whole theater on fire. His shoulders shook with silent laughter.

He'd observed that the kid slept upstairs and Lauren down, so he went next to reconnoiter her bedroom. It was a small room with white pine paneling and a single twin bed covered by a yellow and blue quilt. There were four framed drawings of local wildlife on the opposite wall, all signed by an artist named Suze M. The animals were a bison, a bighorn sheep, a moose and a wolf. He liked the wolf best.

Evan bet the boy's bedroom upstairs had once been hers—hers and Ross Taylor's. Too bad the guy had been so nosy about how the wildfire they were fighting had spread so quickly and into virgin areas. He'd asked too many questions and had challenged Evan's answers. It was his own fault he'd had to die. And how fitting, by the very fire he was fighting. Ross's demise had been Evan's inspiration to have each later arson ignited by an accelerant that fit the victim. In a way, he owed Ross Taylor a big debt of gratitude for that.

Unafraid now of leaving fingerprints that he so assiduously avoided leaving at the scenes of his masterpieces, he opened Lauren's closet door.

There weren't many dresses and skirts, but lots of jeans, some nice slacks and matching jackets, blouses and T-shirts. He saw boots and running shoes—and even one pair of red heels. A few extra purses were stacked on the single closet shelf. And there were lots of bulky sweaters there, each in its own plastic zipper bag. It smelled good in here, Evan thought, a sort of fresh-wind scent. No expensive perfumes for Widow Taylor. Did she miss having a man? From the way she'd talked about her husband when she'd flown Evan in, she might still be mourning the guy. Get over it, he'd tell her if he had the chance. Life is short and you just never know when your time is up, so enjoy.

He closed the closet door and suddenly wondered if she kept a gun. Gingerly, he felt beneath her pillow. Nothing there. He wondered if she was sleeping with the blond man —not Mr. Goodbar, but maybe Mr. Good-blond. He'd really like to know more about the travel writer.

Evan knelt and looked under her bed, where he found dust and a couple of scrapbooks. Flipping through the books, he found articles about Ross's career, and one from the Kalispell paper about them being a husband-and-wife pilot team. He hoped he had time to look through them later, as it was best to be very well informed about the chosen ones. He was still undecided if he'd need Lauren to fly him out of here after the inferno or whether she was expendable. At one time, he might have spared her because of her boy, but he'd learned that some young men were much better off without their mothers—or either parent, for that matter.

He went to the white, eight-drawer bureau and pulled open the top left drawer. It was full of lingerie, rather fancy stuff for a woman who went around looking like she was camping out. He fingered the items, letting the silky material slide through his fingers and over the sensitive skin of his inner wrist. Deep aquamarine, fuschia, salmon. Pretty lace, sexy stuff. Maybe this was her other little indulgence, besides the Mr. Goodbars.

Ha! If he had to choose an accelerant for Lauren's house, wouldn't these hot little items be the perfect fire starter, especially if doused with gasoline from her plane?

Lauren took off into the western wind and circled the lake once, gaining altitude. Brad sat in the copilot seat with the beanbag pillow on one knee. Mrs. Gates had sewn his message to Red inside with the words CUT OPEN TO SEE NOTE on the outside.

The note within read,

To Red Russert. Lauren Taylor and her friend Brad Hale need your help to track a stranger who endangered Sheriff Chuck Cobern's life earlier today. Please meet us at the top of the beginner slope near the ski-lift ramp ASAP. Marilyn Gates suggested you would be excellent to assist us with this task.

Lauren Taylor and Brad Hale.

Poor Red, Lauren thought. He'd probably get his hopes up, thinking he was getting a gift or love note, but at least the mention of Mrs. Gates might encourage him. She had even attached a small American flag to the package. It seemed the woman had flags and patriotic memorabilia stashed everywhere inside her little place.

As they flew back across the lake toward Mount Jefferson, Brad said, "The mountains here are awesome, from both the ground and the air."

"They never change and yet they are never the same, especially with the shifting sun and clouds. The Blackfeet called the Rockies 'the backbone of the world.' This area was sacred to them. The early white settlers said this is 'the land of shimmering mountains.' To me these mean just plain home."

"From this height, what amazes me are all the yellow and gold colors mixed in with the green and brown.

I know it's early September, but is the gold all dry terrain, too?"

He was looking out at the far reaches of the Vermillion Valley, which Lauren intended to fly through to approach Red's high camp from the opposite direction. That way they'd be able to spot it, maybe even see him, before they soared beyond the surrounding trees.

Lauren had quickly memorized Mrs. Gates's map. She'd hiked up into the area once with Ross years ago. The stark contrasts in the area were stunning. The Vermillion Valley and the canyon beyond both had an eerie aura about them, one Ross had laughed off as "just the old Indian ghosts of fierce warriors hanging around." Again, she hoped Mrs. Gates hadn't shared with Nicky's class the fact that the Blackfeet left their dead to rot on platforms until nothing was left but bones, which they buried on-site.

"No," she answered Brad, "those colors aren't a sign of autumn or, thank heavens, dry grass or foliage. You can't tell from here, but that's late-summer yellow yarrow and, higher up, glacier lilies along the snow line. The rest is alpine larches, which look like evergreens, but their needles turn yellow-gold by winter. Still, the area is tinder dry."

"Don't I know it. Look, an eagle. We're soaring with eagles!"

He sounded like Nicky, as if his troubles and tension had dropped away for a moment. She wondered if he was picturing that fierce-looking eagle on his FBI badge, but thought not. Despite all they had to worry about, she'd learned long ago that flying lifted you in more ways than one.

She flew *Silver* down the valley. It was not a glacial, U-shaped one like the Lost Lake area. This one looked sculpted from stone. Lost Lake was really a tarn, a small, deep lake that occupied a basin scooped out by the glaciers. But this steeper area was waterfall-cut cliffs with jagged peaks above and timber below. The braided river flashed beneath them and then the small, skinny lake it fed. As they flew farther north from the town, the Vermillion Valley continued to narrow until it became a forested area that ended near the lumber camp.

"We're going pretty far," Brad observed. "Surely this wouldn't be a two-hour hike. How old is Red Russert, anyway?"

"About Marilyn Gates's age is all I know. No, I'm going to swing around and head back, but I can't do a big turn until we're over the lumber camp. Look down at ten o'clock."

He craned his neck as she made a large loop. "That's a big operation," he said.

"Dee and I took the boys there earlier this summer, and Larson's dad, Steve, gave us a great tour of the place. Of course, the kids loved all the massive machinery— tree-harvesting monsters with names like the slasher, the skidder, the feller and the dozer—not to mention the log flume itself, which reminded them of a theme-park ride."

"I can imagine. Yeah, I see that log flume now. At least this area is probably too far for Marston to go. I have a feeling that if Red can help us, we just might be able to find where he's holed up around Vermillion. Look, there's someone down there on the edge of that rock!"

Lauren tipped her right wing slightly to look. "It's Suze Milliman, painting. That's called Cedar Ridge. As you can see, it overlooks both the canyon and the lumber camp—a panoramic view. At least Suze isn't near town where Marston could find her, though she's always carried a gun."

"I don't think she'd be in any danger from him anyway. He's never assaulted or raped a woman. He obviously likes to kill them from afar."

"In short, the bastard fries them to death. Hang on. I'm going to dip both wings, though Suze will know it's me by the plane."

She waggled the wings. Suze looked up and waved, crisscrossing her arms over her head before she was out of sight again.

"Get ready," Lauren warned. "High camp will come up soon. Your toss will have to be fairly accurate, especially in case Red's not there and has to stumble onto the pillow later. Get ready, just past this waterfall called Weeping Wall. There! In that clearing? You can even see his tent. Do you see him?"

"No!"

"I'm cutting back the speed a bit so we can coast down, but I'll have to climb before that line of trees. There he is—see?"

"Yeah, and I see where he gets his name Red."

"He used to kid me that we were related," she said as she saw the big man walk out into the clearing and look up, shading his eyes. His coppery hair gleamed in the sun. "Brad, open the window. Ready, set…"

She watched as he waved an arm out at Red, then heaved the pillow. With its little, flapping flag, it made a bull's-eye drop on the small clearing near Red Russert's tent.

The Taylors' attic was no more than a crawl space accessed from the second-floor ceiling. It was jumbled, hot and airless up there, so Evan decided he'd still camp outside and just visit when they were away. He left his backpack hidden in some bushes about a half mile behind their house. Wrapping his precious, good-luck drip torch—the one he used to set back blazes while fighting wildfires—in his sleeping bag, he set out with only those two items on the campers' trail toward town. He had all of the sheriff's keys, and hoped their attic would be bigger or cooler, their larder fuller. Those chocolate-chip cookies Dee Cobern had given Nicky yesterday were great.

He trudged along on a narrow hiking trail, just slightly up the rise from the only road into town, making certain he was behind a tree or bush when a car or truck went by. Rush hour in Vermillion, he thought, snickering. Maybe twenty vehicles went by in twenty minutes.

He wedged his bedroll in the crotch of a tree and surveyed the Cobern house and the nearby shop where Dee went from time to time. The sign outside it clearly said, Dee Cobern, Owner, and listed the brief summer hours. She didn't sell ski equipment, the display windows indicated, but ski-weather clothing.

He half expected to find the front door of their house draped with black crepe for the sheriff's sad demise, but cops were just plain mean and that often pulled them through. Just plain mean, like his father the world adored. Lecturer, author, consultant, expert on fighting wildfires—expert on absolutely everything. Hell, if the man couldn't even take care of his own family, he was a complete and utter failure as far as Evan was concerned. Talk about King Lear or Hamlet's uncle being a loser. David Durand was a walking tragedy and didn't even know it. But he would learn that someday, when he too became trapped in a fire, the last inferno in his son's long and illustrious career. Evan vowed to be certain that his father knew who had set it and why.

He had planned to just stroll across the street and try one of the sheriff's keys on the Coberns' back door. But then he saw the lady of the house drive up in a truck, jump out and go in. In five minutes, she came back out, carrying a small suitcase. Then she drove off.

Was she staying somewhere else for the night? Maybe the sheriff was all right and she was taking extra clothes to him at the lodge. He wondered if she'd even locked the door.

Then, looking out across the lake between the Cobern house and the shop, he saw Lauren's plane land and taxi toward the dock. Surely she was flying it. So she'd gotten down from the slopes, he realized. Maybe she'd brought the sheriff down, too—with help from her big, blond friend, no doubt.

Evan swore under his breath. He simply hadn't made

enough of an impact around here yet. He didn't like the way life went on after he presented the ski-lift drama for them. Something great and grand was needed soon, something big that would bring in all the tourists and publicity they could possibly want. But the thing was, once everyone came to gawk, there'd be nothing left.

10

Brad knew he should listen to Lauren, but he was anxious to get going. She kept assuring him that they had time to clean up and pack food before they set out. It would take Russert way over two hours to get to the ski-lift terminal.

He took a fast shower at her place while she called the Fencers and talked to Nick. Brad came out and sat at the kitchen table, stuffing the extra backpack she gave him. He'd wear one gun and carry the other with the extra ammo. He could hear her still on the phone, and it was just as well she didn't see all this.

"No," she was saying, "I do not want you to ride bareback. I don't care if that's what the Blackfeet did or not. You need that saddle horn to hold on to because you haven't ridden that much and you're still small on a big horse. Hon, Brad and I rode those horses to the fire tower today, so don't you get them too tired, okay? I will come to pick you up as soon as I can this evening. Now let me talk to Gerri for a minute. Yes, give her the phone. Be safe, my Nicky."

After she hung up, she told Brad, "It won't take me a minute to shower."

"My kind of woman."

"Are you set to go?" she asked. "I've got two walking sticks for us." When he rolled his eyes, she said, "Honestly, they will help steady us going up and coming down. They can even be a bit of protection."

"Not from bears."

"A walking stick saved Dee's daughter, Suze, from a rabid raccoon once."

"I'm carrying protection. I have a real feeling we're going to find out where Marston's been besides the lodge. We may even find Marston himself."

While Lauren showered and changed, Brad called the Denver office for an update. The fingerprint search had turned up nothing, which didn't only depress him but made him mad as hell. When were they going to catch a break on this Fire Phantom–Smoke Ghost case? If they didn't find more evidence than Lauren's distant sighting of him, Brad feared Mike would order him back to Denver, where they were still fielding leads from a panicked population. Mike had even joked about him being on a sabbatical while the rest of them covered for him.

They locked up her place and waded knee deep through confetti-colored alpine flowers in the throes of their final blooms, then cut around about half a mile of the foot of Mount Jefferson on a slight slant upward.

"We'd be nuts to go straight up without climbing gear," she said. "And we'd be cut off by the Trident waterfall, which becomes a couple of small streams, including the one that cuts through my backyard."

"Trident? Not named after the chewing gum, I'll bet."

"It's three-pronged," she said, not relaxing her swift pace. "We'll walk upstream by the Otter River, which eventually feeds into the lake. Then we'll cut up to the ski-lift terminal. It's almost three o'clock. We're lucky it still stays light until late."

He was content to follow her, buoyed by her grace and determination, the swing of her shapely hips under her bouncing backpack. He quickly learned she was right about the walking stick helping. He thought he was in good shape, but keeping up with her was a challenge. They both kept looking off to the sides and behind, especially when they got into the woods. But there was no way Rocky Marston would be camping way up here in these deep forests. They finally hiked out of the trees to the edge of one of the beginner ski slopes and followed it steeply upward, the now unmoving ski lift in sight.

To Brad's amazement, Red Russert was waiting for them, sitting on the ground with his back against the ski-lift pillar near where he'd seen the bear closing in on Lauren and Chuck. That seemed ages ago. It was hard to believe it had happened earlier today. In fact, so much had happened, he could hardly believe he'd been in the Lost Lake area for only twenty-four hours. Yet he had the overwhelming sense that time was running out.

The big, red-haired man had already turned his head their way and stood in one smooth movement as they emerged from the trees that edged the ski slope. He looked the way Brad had always thought the legendary lumberman Paul Bunyan must, black-bearded, tall, broad-shouldered with a red-and-black-checkered flannel shirt rolled up over brawny forearms and big, brown leather–laced hiking boots. All the guy needed was a huge ax and a blue ox named Babe.

"Hey, Lauren my girl!" Red cried and leaned down to peck a kiss on her cheek. "And Brad Hale," he added, shaking Brad's hand. Very few people made Brad feel small, but this guy did. "Got your air mail message," Red said and grinned, flaunting strong, white teeth that contrasted with his sun-browned skin. Mrs. Gates wasn't that big a woman; the picture in Brad's mind of them together was almost funny. Which reminded him, he'd better clear the air about that.

"Mrs. Gates said to tell you she won't be coming to high camp, but she'd like to talk."

"Oh, she's good at that, all right," Red muttered with a shake of his big head. "So our prey assaulted Chuck Cobern?" he quickly changed the subject as he bent to pick up his backpack. "On top of that broken shoulder, how's he doing?"

"Concussion, we think," Lauren said. "Dee's with him at the clinic."

"Well, that's a start back for them, lucky bums. So we've been deputized to track this guy or what?"

They had decided they would tell him that Chuck's assault was the reason they were after Marston, but since Marilyn Gates knew the whole story and Brad instinctively trusted this man, he said, "That's part of it. I am a friend of Lauren's but I'm also here because I'm law enforcement in pursuit of a serial arsonist we believe is hiding in this area—one and the same with the sheriff's attacker. It's highly possible that our man headed down toward town after he got off the ski lift on this platform. We're hoping you can pick up his trail from this end, maybe find his camp. He prides himself on not being seen or found."

"Yeah, and I pride myself on finding anything that moves. I'll give it my darndest."

"He's going by the name Rocky Marston," Brad added. "Dark, chin-length hair, olive skin, stands about five foot ten, military green-brown camo outfit, bright blue backroll and backpack."

"Got it. Good thing Marston didn't head thataway," Red said, pointing up the slope. "'Cause I see signs a big brown bear went in that direction, recently, too."

"I told you the man was good," Lauren said, folding her arms across her breasts. "And I mean Red, not Marston."

"One more thing," Brad said as Red donned his backpack and picked up his walking stick. "Marston evidently knew how to run the ski lift or figured it out."

"I ran the thing for years, half-asleep or half-soused," Red admitted with a shrug. "It doesn't take a genius to figure it out."

Brad winced at that, but he surely would have handled the mechanism if it hadn't been jammed or on override.

"But the interesting thing is," he told Red, "Marston was able to override it at another terminal."

"Well, that does show some know-how."

"Other than you and the current operator, can you think of anyone else who's ever worked the ski lift?"

Red gave another shrug, this time with a shake of his head. "Who knows, especially recently. Well, there was this kid who worked at the lodge one summer, and I taught to use it. I was into the sauce pretty good back then, after a fight I had with a guy. But I can't recall the kid's name. He was a funny kid, a loner, liked to do different voices. Wanted to be an actor, I think."

"Dark-haired?" Lauren asked.

"Bet way more'n half the world's dark-haired," Red said. "Truth is, I can barely recall what he looked like and sure can't call up a name."

"Any idea about when that would have been?" Brad asked.

"Had to be the winter of '91."

"And the kid was how old then?"

"Just outta high school, I think. He had some sorta sad story about him. I think he'd lost his mother and his dad was on the road a lot, so he got him a summer job to pull his life together. The dad may have been some sort of big shot in protecting the environment," he went on, frowning and scratching his head. "Maybe he wrote books and gave talks or some such, a real Smokey the Bear. I don't recall exactly. Hell, I've probably got bears on the brain, now that I spotted that brown-bear track right over there."

"Maybe we could find lodge records on who was hired to work the ski lift in 1989," Lauren said.

"Naw," Red insisted. "Besides, he wasn't hired *for* that. But I can't recall what else he was doing, bussing tables, maybe. You know how that goes, Lauren." Red walked to the edge of the clearing and lifted his hand to hold them back while he bent to scan the ground. "By the way, I gotta tell you, it's too dry all over this immediate area for good prints in the earth."

Brad exhaled hard. This case was a maze, with a series of wrong turns and dead ends. He needed backup but he had nothing concrete to justify it. He'd be a laughingstock if he got the team here and nothing happened, nothing was found.

"Okay, got something," Red said, jolting Brad from his agonizing. "Dry grass here will help. I see some scuffed up right by the roots in the shape of maybe a boot tip, heading in a hurry this way—down. And since it's the boot tip without the heel marks, this person might have been hustling. Let's get going," he ordered and headed for the trees.

The Lost Lake Health Clinic had four small private rooms where patients could be tended to or simply held until they could be flown to the Kalispell Regional Medical Center. Dee sat in a chair pushed tight to Chuck's bed while the nurse-practitioner, darting in and out of the room, kept an eye on him.

The doctor said his concussion was mild, but being tossed around had reinjured his shoulder, so he was back on his pain meds. Which meant, Dee realized as she listened to him mumble and rave, that he was out of his head again.

They'd even strapped him down in the bed with buckled ties across his ankles, hips, torso and good arm to keep him from flinging off his covers or pulling out the IV drip. He'd settled down at last, with Dee holding his hand. She talked calmly, quietly, to him. And though it seemed to help, she could tell he still plunged from one disturbing dream to another.

"I'm going to go back to the house. I want to be there when Suze comes for Larson," she told him, though she thought nothing was registering right now. "Larson's at the Fencers' with Nicky. Maybe Suze can stop to see you on her way home. She's been out painting near the lumber camp all day, even planned for Steve to have lunch with her up on Cedar Ridge. Remember how we used to have picnics out there years ago?" she asked, blinking back tears.

Suze would be relieved that this was the beginning of her parents' reconciliation, Dee thought. These last five months had been an eternity. Dee couldn't picture her life without this man. She had to get him back to being healthy, vital, in control—and happy. Dear God, she prayed, let us both be back together and happy again. And please protect this town we both love.

As they walked through the forest, Lauren kept up with the two men, but couldn't quite tap into some wavelength they seemed to be on. Nods, grunts, pointing—Brad and Red had some sort of macho telepathy going.

"Scuffed pine needles," Red muttered. "Still running, but not as wide strides as before."

"He feels safer at this point," Brad said.

"Or he's not really in good physical shape," Red added.

"What about these tracks?" Lauren asked, seeing other footprints in the carpet of dry needles. "They're far apart, too."

Red glanced over. "Ten-inch-long bear tracks, almost human, but look closer. Bear's big toe is on the outside of the paw."

"Oh, I didn't see the toe marks, just the heel."

"Brad, look. He hunkered down here," Red said as they left the thick trees and came to the bank of the Otter River, with its braided streams and stony islands amidst divided waters. "Maybe he needed a rest or a drink."

Lauren and Brad had skirted this area earlier. Now, despite their rush, she admired the brilliantly hued harlequin ducks that had returned to this ancestral stream just the way the cutthroat trout in it had.

"Ducks the colors of the American flag," Brad remarked as they followed Red along the path. "Very patriotic."

"Very stupid," Red said. "The Otter River's full of their namesake, and those little devils are trouble. Cute as can be, swimming on their backs and all that, but real vicious. Besides diving for fish or grubbing for frogs, otters get ducks underwater and rip them apart."

"The animal version of a criminal undercover," Brad said.

"You're not kidding. Otters even tear beaver dams apart along here—" Red pointed toward a pile of logs and debris a bit upstream "—and when the water level goes down behind their destruction, they snatch up the stranded, flopping fish. Nature giveth and taketh away."

They moved on, slowly, stopping and starting. "You're probably right about Marston heading for town," Red said, bending down. "I hope we can find him this way since he's made himself scarce there."

"To everyone but me, he's been invisible," Lauren put in.

"I've been thinking," Red said to her. "You knew to bring Brad up from town the way you did, but I doubt an outsider would know how to get down to town this way. I've had tenderfoot campers and hunters up here argue with me about going straight down the mountain 'stead of roundabout. Your man could have taken the longer trail blazed clearly on the trees, but he took this shorter, easier way. Maybe this Marston isn't a newbie 'round here after all."

"But I've lived here for years," Lauren protested. "I know everyone and I'd never seen him before two days ago."

"Then maybe," Brad said, "he was just here skiing or hiking once and noted how the ski lift was run."

"He told me he hadn't been here before," Lauren blurted.

"Listen to yourself," Brad said, rounding on her. "Are we believing what he says now?"

"Then why did you want me to tell you everything he said?" she countered, hands on her hips.

"Whoa, you two," Red put in. "Sounds like you been spending lotsa time together, but kinda like a shotgun marriage."

Lauren only gasped and cried, "Look!" She pointed but was stunned when Brad whipped out a gun from under his jacket. She'd finally realized it was his weapons and ammunition he guarded so closely in his duffel bag.

"Where?" he said, pivoting with it lifted in both hands.

"Not Marston," she said. "An elk drinking up there. See?"

Brad swore under his breath, and for the first time since they started down, Red chuckled. He stretched as he and Brad exchanged a look she couldn't read. Brad holstered his gun.

Red said, "Yeah, look at the rack on him. It's a big bull getting ready for the autumn rut. It's usually in August, but this drought's thrown off more'n the vegetation. The moose'll probably mate later than the first frosts this year, and the bighorn rams may miss November, too. Everything's off-kilter. But they'll get to their rough love-making, you bet they will."

Brad's laser-blue gaze snagged with Lauren's. She felt a fire arc between them that made her knees weak and her stomach go into freefall as if she'd just jumped off a cliff.

"Cedar Ridge used to be our favorite place to go, Chuck. Do you remember?" Dee went on. "We even made love there one time with the sky so blue and the sun so sweet."

She kept one eye on her wristwatch. She'd better get going if she wanted to catch Suze, but she couldn't bear to leave Chuck. Still, if she and Larson weren't there, Suze might panic—or drive to Lauren's, where no one would be, either.

Chuck began to mumble. Was he waking up? Those darn meds.

"Ridge…" he was saying. She held on to his hand but stood and bent over so she could get closer to his face.

"Yes, Cedar Ridge," she prompted, thrilled to think he might remember. "Do you recall what a wonderful time we had there, sweetheart? You proposed on the ridge, and we always…"

"—idge…"

"Yes, Cedar Ridge."

"Jidge."

Dee gasped and dropped his hand. She straightened. He hadn't said *ridge,* but had clearly said *Jidge.* Here she was pouring out her heart to him, forgiving him, worrying about him, and he said that woman's name. He was dreaming about that woman!

With a sob, Dee grabbed her purse from the table by the bed and ran for the door.

"You seem to know all about the mating seasons," Brad told Red, elbowing the big man as they picked up their pace. Marston had evidently walked closer to the river here. His booted footprints were clearer now since the shore was silt as well as stones.

"All 'cept my own," Red muttered. "Like my pa used to say, I hope I haven't missed the bus I'm interested in catching. Now, Lauren, don't you dare repeat that to Mari Gates."

Mari Gates, she thought. She'd hardly heard anyone call Mrs. Gates Marilyn, let alone Mari.

But she held her tongue as they started across the alpine meadow just above the town. The roofs of the shops and houses were in sight below. Suddenly, Red stopped in midstride.

"Don't know if others been out walking through this tall-grass meadow," he said.

"Lauren and I—" Brad began.

"No, your paths are over there where the flowers and grass are freshly bent in the direction you walked. But see that other faint pathway over there? It's not heading toward town but southeast, a bit away."

Red and Brad both turned to look at Lauren. "And that," she whispered, "could take him toward my place."

"Let's cut across to that path and see," Red said.

Evan tried the sheriff's set of keys until one fit in the back door of the Cobern house. He let himself in and looked around. The walls held photos and lots of artwork, all signed by Suze M. There was a signed photo of her painting, standing next to her mother. She must be the sheriff's daughter. If she lived nearby, he had another possible chosen one. After all, she worked with oil paints, and those artists always had turpentine around to clean their brushes. With some paint rags and a canvas or two—*whoosh!*

He turned on the desktop computer in the corner of the living room, hoping he didn't need a password. Why would anyone have a PC in this rinky-dink town? He got online easily but waited impatiently for everything to come up on the screen.

He was tempted to read the *Denver Post*'s report about the BND arsonist's fire and the obit of the woman who had died in it, but he'd already done that at the library in Phoenix and time was of the essence here. Instead, he Googled *Blackfeet Indians* and *northwest Montana sacred burial grounds* just in case Nicky Taylor had any more questions about where Chief White Calf had "flown" in from.

The kid must have been referring to the Vermillion Valley, which the tribe used to call Pis'kun, and which early settlers had claimed was haunted. Heck, he thought as he turned the PC off, people could probably call any site haunted if they knew the entire history of the place.

As he passed an upstairs window of the bedroom, he noted how close the fire station was, just two doors away, on the other side of the Montana Range Gift Shop. How could he pass this up? The sheriff's own wife was living near the ladder truck that would rush to put out a distant fire while her own house went up in flames. And it would have to be gasoline for this blaze, gasoline he'd siphoned directly from the fire engine itself! What could be more perfect?

And then he saw the omen on the wall, the sign that meant he was making the right choice. In the bedroom office hung a large, framed photograph of Chuck Cobern, sheriff of Vermillion, Montana, in full firefighting gear, one booted foot on the bumper of the bright red ladder truck as if he owned it. Evan squinted closer at the photo. Cobern was not only the sheriff but the fire chief here! That meant Evan had already made the fire chief look like a fool. But it wasn't enough, not nearly enough.

He rifled through the desk drawers until he found what he was looking for—a pistol. He had figured the sheriff would have one around that he could borrow, especially since he hadn't been carrying one up at the ski lodge. Evan hated firearms, but things were getting so dicey here that it was a necessary evil. And it was the kind where you rammed a clip up into the handle. He'd figure it out and just hope that fire did his talking for him so he wouldn't have to resort to this. He was lowering himself by taking it, by needing it. Crazy, trigger-happy Americans with their gun fixations, from the minutemen to cowboys to mobsters to today's mafia and street gangs. Degrading and disgusting!

He opened the door to the attic and hurried up to look around. With one glance, more plans fell into place. There were two big, old trunks he could stretch out behind with his sleeping bag, and two dormer windows through which he could watch everyone who came and went. Best of all, there was a small, railed balcony facing the lake. He could use it to get out onto the rooftop so that he wouldn't be trapped.

Hoping he'd have time to get his sleeping bag and precious drip torch up here before anyone came home, he headed downstairs.

But he heard a car door slam nearby and froze. He hadn't heard a car, but the drone of another plane landing on the lake could have muffled the sound.

The front door slammed. "Mom? Larson?"

Perhaps the painter. Since she didn't live here, it was doubtful she'd come upstairs, but he knew he'd better hide just to be sure he wasn't forced to act prematurely. This young woman had become an artist, so maybe he shouldn't think so poorly of Dee Cobern. If his own mother had let him follow the path less taken, let him follow his heart, she wouldn't now be an incinerated corpse buried in Saint Louis's Bellefontaine Cemetery.

Another car door slammed outside; someone else came in the house.

"Mom! Mom, what is it? What's the matter?"

Maybe the sheriff had died. How frustrating! Evan wanted him alive so that he could suffer. Muffled words, more crying.

"But is he going to be okay?"

"You'll have to find out for yourself! I was going to take him back—I tried."

"What did he do?"

More muffled words, more crying. Stomping around. Slamming cupboards. Evan wanted to risk going to the top of the stairs, but he'd better not. It would be just like a distraught woman to run upstairs to cry on her bed. He'd seen more than one female trapped in a fire who fled up to the supposed safety of her bedroom, not down toward a better chance at escape.

"But you said yourself that the meds screw up his thoughts," the daughter protested. "And maybe he said *ridge*. I'll go back, but you've got to go with me. He's just hallucinating."

"Which is the same thing as dreaming about her.

No!" Dee's voice exploded clearly at last. "You've always been Daddy's girl. You sided with him in this, just like he's always sided with you! 'Let her get married early,' he said. 'Let her go off in the wilds all day, even when her son's so small.' Your father spoiled his only child, and now you're all for him! Did you know about that woman before I did?"

"Mother, of course not!"

"Your father may not have left Vermillion lately, but he would if he could. He still loves her, I swear he does."

The two women went on arguing, but all Evan could think was that, once again, he was going to have to change his mind about Dee Cobern. She wasn't the one who had let her child pursue her dreams. Dee had put herself right back near the top of the list, with Lauren still in first place for the diversion blaze. Dee was a lot like his own mother and needed to be taught a final, fatal lesson.

"Are you sure we're still on his trail?" Lauren asked Red as he tracked Marston closer to the line of aspens above her house.

"'Fraid so," Red told them. "See the same distinctive design on this boot print—two wedges and the waffled sole? You might have problems getting his fingerprints like you said, Brad, but I'll bet we've got his footprints here."

"Sometimes that doesn't prove a thing," Lauren argued despite the glare Brad shot at her. "They had clear footprints in blood at the scene of Nicole Simpson's murder, which matched a pair of O. J. Simpson's distinctive shoes. Yet he still got off."

"Lauren—" Brad started but she interrupted him.

"But why would he be watching my place? I don't live near a firehouse—or alone. Still, there's a clear view of my property from here." She stated the obvious. Her voice got very small. She felt scared, then angry.

Brad put his arm around her, and she leaned gratefully into his strength.

"There is a trail that parallels the road along here to town," Red said. "He could have gone that way, but it's so well walked, I may not be able to be sure. He may not have been coming here at all, Lauren, but just passing through."

"But to where?" she asked. "Where?"

Though she was perspiring, she felt chilled. She longed to hold on to Brad, with both arms tight around him, and bury her face against him. But she stood stiffly at his side.

"Let's go down and have Red look around your backyard," he said.

They walked down with Red still leading.

"Your boy's footsteps are all over here," Red said, "so I can't be certain about where Marston went now. Let's look in the ravine. Maybe he just drank from that stream en route to the hiking path into town. He may not even know this is your place."

"Though we'll have to take precautions," Brad added.

While the two men went into the ravine, Lauren looked at Nicky's piled stones, then peeked into his little blanket-over-soccer-net tent. She got on her knees and peered inside. It didn't look as if he'd even used it, though he had left his headband with feathers here. And one of the feathers was from the bright harlequin duck's back on the path where they'd just tracked Rocky Marston.

11

After thanking Red—though Lauren was hardly grateful to know that Marston had been anywhere near her house—she and Brad watched him walk toward town on the hiking path, his head still down, looking for signs and clues.

"Whew!" Lauren said. "That makes me want to get Nicky home and turn this place into a fortress until Marston's caught."

"My sentiments exactly, but I need to look around here some more first. You go on in and call about us picking up Nick."

That sounded strange, yet so right to her, as if they were both the boy's parents. Brad made a point of not calling him Nicky like everyone else. Everyone, that is, except Ross, who had always thought it sounded too cutesy, even when he was a darling baby.

"I'll stay out here with you," she insisted. "Four eyes are better than two, even when two of them are trained FBI."

"Red Russert ought to teach a class at Quantico," he muttered and went back down into the ravine.

Lauren poked her head into the tent again and picked up the Indian headdress. Nicky's other drab, common feathers were taped on, but this bright one had been poked through the ribbon headband itself. She carefully put the headdress in her backpack, before placing it by the back door, and went down into the ravine. She almost couldn't stop running and had one foot in the cold stream before Brad grabbed her with an arm around her waist.

"Don't walk around too much down here," he said, pulling her past him, then loosing her. "Nick's been down here, too. Is he allowed?"

"He's never come down before. When he was younger that was a rule. We even had a little chicken-wire fence up there once, but lately—I guess I haven't made a point of it."

"Well, young Blackfeet Indians certainly wouldn't like a fence. Lauren, over here…"

"What?"

"Here, by the stream. It's the same boot print we've been tracking from the ski lift."

She edged closer to him. Holding on to his arm, she peeked past him, careful not to disturb anything.

"At that angle," she said, "it looks like he drank from the stream. Hopefully that's all he did around here. Brad, Nicky knows not to talk to strangers when we're in Kalispell. But here in Vermillion, at least off-season, there just aren't any strangers."

"There are now. Come on, let's go call the Fencers and pick him up."

"Why? So that you can question him about being down in the ravine?" she asked. Her voice sounded a bit too sharp, but she couldn't help herself. She stood with her hips canted, her fists on her waist, blocking his way.

"Hardly. But he needs to know more about me—and about the dangers."

Biting her lower lip, she nodded. She was starting to act irrationally, arguing with this man who was here to help her. As she walked toward the back of the ravine, she noted scuff marks under Nicky's tent. After spending so many hours listening to Red Russert, was everything starting to get to her? She was trying to keep calm and be civil, but panic and paranoia kept crashing through her like an avalanche.

"Brad, does it look to you like Nicky's been coming down into the ravine by sliding out the back of this tent? See?" she asked, pointing.

"Looks that way. Typical boy. Fastest, funnest way."

"But he does overdo the imagination stuff."

"Lauren, I used to alternate between being Luke Skywalker and Darth Vader while staging entire intergalactic battles with just two friends. When I was alone, I became both Luke and Darth at once, making light sabers from tinfoil-wrapped yardsticks and having duels with myself. I fell down the basement steps once because I wouldn't take off my Stormtrooper's mask and couldn't see where the heck I was going."

"But that must have been before you lost your father. Nicky's only been that way since his father died."

"We can both talk to him tonight. Let's go in."

But he started to walk around the house, looking at the ground under her windows. After she unlocked the back door, she hesitated, wanting to rush in to phone Nicky but curious and even more unnerved by Brad's actions.

He disappeared around the corner and she hurried after him. "Do you think Marston was trying to lift a window to get in?" she asked.

"See this other waffle-soled print where you've evidently watered these flowers? He was either trying to get in or was looking in. Lauren," he said, frowning as he turned to her and grabbed both of her upper arms, "regardless of what he's been doing here, I want to stay."

Her stomach cartwheeled at his putting it that way, but she knew what he meant. "You mean move in. All night?"

"I'll bunk on your sofa just in case. You—and Nick—could use a bodyguard."

The phone rang before Lauren could call the Fencers. It was Suze, sounding really upset.

"I wanted to be sure you were there before I brought Nicky home," she said. "I'm at the Fencers' getting Larson, so I can pick up both of them if you want."

"Thanks. And Suze, be careful. Are you— You sound out of breath."

"Not out of breath. Temporarily out of tears. Dad evidently blurted out that other woman's name in his drug-induced delirium, and Mother's on an absolute tear. I'll tell you when I get there," she added and punched off.

"Brad," Lauren called to him, "Suze is bringing Nicky home, but she says that Chuck and Dee are feuding again. Suze is pretty upset. I think we have to tell her more about what's happening and who you are."

"Affirmative, partner. I still don't want to cause mass hysteria, but I'm starting to think we may need all the help we can get."

To give Lauren some time alone with Suze, Brad took Nicky and Larson out in the backyard to play catch. The two women sat at the kitchen table where they could see Brad with the kids. Suze's eyes were red. Her mascara had run and been swiped at so many times it looked as if she'd been finger-painting under her eyes. "It was horrible," she told Lauren, blowing her nose. "Mother turned on me, as well as on him. I think she's getting ready to snap."

"Aren't we all?"

"Lauren, what's really going on with Brad? You know my motto is that Picasso quote, 'Everything you can imagine is real.' I'm imagining too many things. What is he to you? He seems so—in charge."

"He wanted secrecy at first, but I can tell you now. He's with the FBI, a serial arson team member."

"Go on!" she cried, her voice mocking as she smacked her palm down on the table.

"Just listen. I saw an arsonist's Most Wanted picture in your mother's newspaper and called the FBI hotline on Monday."

"Wow. You called the hotline and got a hottie. But who's the arsonist?"

"I flew him in—obviously, before I knew. He goes by the name Rocky Marston. He's been practically invisible, but we think he's the one who hit your dad over the head. Your parents are both in on this."

"So this Marston guy might start a fire out in the forest?" she demanded, getting up and starting to pace. She kept dabbing at her eyes with a tissue. "Can I warn Steve and the guys cutting timber? You know they have buildings full of logs, and the trees up there are dry."

"Marston might have been staying on lodge property. But in general, it looks as if he's sticking close to town. You'll have to ask Brad about telling others. We don't want to start a panic."

"Oh, great, just great! Are you sure this guy you flew in is the arsonist?"

"Almost sure. He's clever, Suze. At first, when no one else had seen him, I was blaming myself so much."

"Who else has seen him now? My dad?"

"We're not sure. We still have to talk to him to see if he can remember more about the assault. We do have the wrench he was hit with, so that will be checked for prints. And we have some other prints that were checked."

"These other prints... Did they turn up who the arsonist was?"

"Not exactly. I'll let Brad tell you what he thinks is best."

"In other words, I'm supposed to trust someone who probably thinks our government can do no wrong?" she cried. "Since that National Parks Service investigation over Ross's death, I had the distinct impression you didn't trust anything any government agency decreed or did."

Suze was right. Lauren had vowed not to trust the government after that, yet now she had a G-man ready to move into her house.

"So what's this guy's M.O.?" Suze was back to her interrogation. She leaned stiff-armed on the kitchen table, as if she were a cop grilling a hostile witness.

Despite how exhausted she felt, Lauren popped up from the table. "I'll feed the boys in the kitchen and let Brad talk to you. Brace yourself, because this arsonist is one really sick, dangerous man. You can't imagine—"

"Oh, yes, I can," she said, seizing Lauren's wrist in a tight grip. "Remember, everything you can imagine, in a way, is real. For an artist that's good. For an arsonist, it's really bad."

When Lauren got Nicky out of the bathtub, she let him go back down to the kitchen for cookies and milk. Brad had called Mrs. Gates and was just getting off the phone.

"Did you convince her to rely on Red for protection?" she asked.

"I didn't, but Red did. She wouldn't let him stay at her place, but she did finally agree to switch places with him for the night. He said she was complaining all the way that his apartment needed cleaning and that she couldn't abide the stuffed animal heads staring at her from his walls."

"Better that than to be staring at Rocky Marston peeking through her window. First thing in the morning, maybe we should check around her place for the telltale prints. And Dee's place, too."

"You know, Lauren, you're starting to read my mind and that scares me. Is it okay if I talk to Nick before you tuck him in?" he asked, nodding his head toward the kitchen.

"Fine. It's probably best if some of the explanation comes from you. I just don't want him so scared that I can't leave him at school or with Dee. It's only recently that he's let me out of his sight without tears. Mind if I eavesdrop so I know what you told him, or I could come with you—"

"Listen if you want, but I think it should be just us guys for a couple of minutes."

She nodded. For too long, Nicky had not had a man in his life.

"Hey, Nick," she heard Brad say as he went out into the kitchen.

Suddenly feeling sad, Lauren sat down on the staircase.

"Hey, Brad."

"Why'd you smash that cookie all up on your plate, pal?"

"So it would look more like Indian pemmican."

"Oh, yeah. Listen, I just wanted to tell you why I'm staying here tonight. I'm really a police officer, and I'm trying to find a man I need to question. I think he might have come to Lost Lake, so—"

"Which plane flew him in?"

Brad hesitated for a beat. "Your mom's did."

"So she knows what he looks like and is trying to help you find him?"

"Right. We've been looking at the fire tower, the

lodge, even around here. We want you to know why you can't go outside for a few days, just in case. He's not a nice person."

"I can't even go to my Indian tent?"

"That would be okay if I go out with you, but we're going to be pretty busy tomorrow and you'll be in school. Nick, I don't want you to tell your buddies there, though Mrs. Gates knows."

"She does? Why?"

"Her friend Red Russert was helping us look for the bad man, so we told her. Can you keep a secret for us?"

"Sure. Brad, if you promise someone you'll keep a secret, that's really what you should do, right? Even if someone asks or you kind of change your mind?"

"Absolutely. That's what I'm asking you to do."

"Okay, then."

Lauren took that as her cue to join them, but Brad passed her in the hall. "You thought that would be easy, didn't you?" she whispered and went in to see Nicky making a mess, trying to eat a smashed cookie with his hands.

"Time to head upstairs to bed, my Nicky."

"Can I ask you a favor, Mom?"

"Of course, if I can do it."

"Could you start calling me Nick like Dad and Brad?"

"Sure, if you want. It might be kind of hard for me to switch over, though."

She walked him upstairs to brush his teeth and then pointed him toward his bed. There, on his pillow, she'd laid out his ribbon Indian headdress with its drab feathers surrounding the one bright one.

"Wow," he exploded when he saw it. "Look at that neat feather! But why is it here in my bed?"

He glanced around the room, then at the windows as if it had floated inside of its own accord.

"I brought it in from your tent since you can't play out there for a while—at least until Brad catches that bad guy he's after. But where did you find that harlequin duck feather? Nicky—Nick—I know you can't have been up by the Otter River where all those bright ducks are."

"I guess they just flew over here and dropped it, that's all," he told her, putting the headdress quickly aside as if it meant nothing to him now. "So where's Brad going to sleep?" he asked.

"On the sofa. And you're not to disturb any of his things—not in the pack he carries around or anything else."

"Sure, I know that. Be safe, Mom," he said and held out his arms for a hug. The moment she kissed him, he turned away from her and covered up his head.

"Be safe, my—Nick," she said. She was on her way downstairs before it hit her how cleverly her little boy had changed the subject from his actions to hers. For the first time since she could recall, she had not read him a bedtime story. He didn't want to be her Nicky anymore.

It really scared her how much he was changing. And how much she was changing, too.

As soon as it got reasonably dark, Evan tiptoed down from Dee Cobern's attic. Taking his flashlight and ever-present, precious drip torch, he first headed for her kitchen. It had been over an hour since she'd stopped pacing in her bedroom, though the house creaked in the breeze. Actually, he liked both sounds. And he liked that the breeze didn't let up after dark around here, either. When he chose to release the flames, the wind would feed them.

By the light of the open refrigerator door, he drank some orange juice from a carton, though he preferred the pulp-free kind. Using his flashlight, he searched her drawers until he found a butcher knife to borrow, an eight-inch one with a serrated blade. He already had the sheriff's gun, but that wouldn't do for what he had in mind right now.

He quietly let himself out the back door and relocked it. The night air smelled fresh and brisk, but he could almost imagine it laced with smoke.

As he had last night, he tiptoed up the steps to Mrs. Gates's large side porch. But this time he did not take one of her tidily stacked E-Z Lite logs, for he'd already taken three from her stash and had them hidden nearby. But he did need something from this neatly kept elevated area with its lovely views.

He took out the butcher knife and cut off a six-foot length of the garden hose the teacher evidently used to water the plants she had lined up in plastic containers. Unfortunately, she would notice this, but perhaps she'd ascribe it to teenage vandalism. He knew how women thought.

He had started down the steps when he realized he could also use the three-gallon plastic container she evidently mixed liquid fertilizer in. Holding it upside down over the railing, he dumped out the small amount that was in there, but cursed the gurgling sound it made.

Then he froze.

The back kitchen curtains were drawn shut, but someone swept one aside. Evan pressed his back to the house near the balcony railing. If someone looked out or came out, he'd have a long jump from here. Or could the person just be looking out at the aurora borealis? It was aglow in the sky again tonight, as if watching over him.

He recalled the night in Denver when the old woman had been watching him from her window, the night he'd decided to lie low in Vermillion for a while. But how could he ignore the abundance of fire fuels, local accelerants and the perfect conditions here, as well as the signs he must act and soon: Ross Taylor's widow, her son playing a part, the vast stage this area offered for a grand spectacle!

To Evan's amazement, the shadow thrown onto the floorboards of the porch was not that of petite Mrs. Gates. It was a big form, with broad shoulders.

The widowed schoolteacher had a male visitor?

Evan held his breath. Had the man heard him? Whoever he was, he went from kitchen window to window, opening the curtains so more light spilled out.

Then the kitchen went black.

Was the man trying to see out better? Hopefully, he was just trying to watch the northern lights.

Swearing under his breath, Evan heaved the plastic container off the porch and onto the side of the building that had no windows. It almost hit the nearby firehouse, but made very little sound. He hooked his drip torch over the back waist of his jeans, then quickly looped the piece of garden hose around one of the boards that supported the railing. Holding on to both ends of the hose, he scooted over the edge of the porch.

Suspended by the hose, he let more and more of it slide through his hands until he was close enough to drop to the ground. Letting go of the hose with one hand, he pulled it down to him and, keeping low, ran toward the firehouse. He snatched up the plastic container he'd thrown and darted around the back of the building.

From there, peering around the corner, he watched a large, bearded man come out onto the porch and look over all the sides, then go down the stairs with a flashlight to look under the porch. The big brute was looking for more than lights in the sky.

Mrs. Gates had a protector? Why? She'd looked like an old-maid type to Evan when he'd peeked through windows or watched her from the Cobern attic. Was she loaning her place to this man? He had seen her go into the front door of the Bear's Den Restaurant this evening and not come out. But so what?

When the big man went back in and closed the door, Evan darted to the back door of the combination firehouse and sheriff's office. Getting excited now—but not out of control, never out of control—his hand shook as he tried different keys on the sheriff's ring until one fit. He entered slowly, listening, peering into the darkness, then realized a dim light was on somewhere within. Surely no one was here at this hour.

His hand still on the back door in case he had to run, he called out, "Anyone here?"

No sounds. He was home free. His luck held.

Ahead of him loomed the dark silhouettes of the single ladder truck and the boxy, white EMR vehicle. He snapped on his flashlight and stroked the sleek, cold, crimson metal of the truck. Vermillion Fire Department—THE EQUALIZER, it read so pompously that he had to laugh out loud.

"You're no match for the Fire Phantom," he whispered. "In like a ghost, out like a ghost. You'll see."

He set about siphoning gas from the truck, using the garden hose. He sucked on the end of it to get the flow started, then fed it into the plastic container. Ah, the clean, sharp smell of gasoline!

When he had enough accelerant, he decided to take a ladder, too. They would miss it, but probably too late. This ladder truck was small. It probably had only one automatic extension ladder, which would emerge from the back of the truck by pulling a lever. But it had a full array of horizontally stacked, aluminum extension ladders on its side, which could be freed by the turn of a handle. He assumed these were standard-length extension ladders of fourteen-, sixteen-, twenty-four and thirty-five feet. He freed and lifted off the shortest one. That would surely be enough to look in or get in second-story windows at night, including Nicky Taylor's, alias Running Deer's, bedroom.

12

Her nightmare was different this time. A huge bear had her down, pressing into her, mauling her. It had thick brown fur—no, its hair was black and she was bleeding black blood. The bear turned her face up…it was Rocky Marston, and Suze was crying trying to draw his face, but his features were burned beyond recognition…

Lauren sat bolt upright in bed. Reality came crashing back. Had she heard something in the house? Was Nicky all right upstairs? Brad was here. Perhaps she'd heard him.

She glanced at her bedside clock—4:00 a.m. She'd slept almost six hours straight—a miracle! But she still felt tired to the bone.

It was finally pitch-black outside. This time of year nights stayed semilight so long, just the opposite of the lengthy winter ones. If Marston lit a fire, would he want it to be in the blackest time of night?

She thought she heard another sound, maybe just a floorboard creaking. Even in her utter exhaustion, it had been hard to go to sleep with Brad just down the short hall. He had been too tall for the couch, but when she'd given him a pillow and blanket, he said he'd be fine.

Lauren shoved her feet in her slippers, wrapped her robe around her nightgown and peered out into the living room. Pitch-dark. Maybe he was asleep and she was imagining things.

She shuffled down the hall toward the stairs. She'd just look in on Nicky—Nick—then go back to bed if Brad was asleep.

"Are you okay?" His voice came from the dark. As her eyes adjusted, she could make out his form sitting on the couch. He was in his dark jeans but his white T-shirt showed. "I just peeked in on Nick. He's fine."

That's what she'd heard. Brad on the stairs.

"Thanks. Yeah, I'm all right," she whispered, and sank into the chair facing the couch, curling one leg under her. "In one respect, at least. I just slept six hours straight. I'm going to have to hire you for security after this is all over. Did you sleep?"

"Sure, I'm fine."

"I thought I heard you pacing earlier."

"Just looking around now and then."

"Looking outside, just in case?"

"It's been quiet. I've been trying to lay plans for where to look next around town," he said, rubbing both eyes with one hand. She heard him stifle a yawn. "And to decide whether to call in the troops or not."

"The rest of your team?"

"Yeah. I'm trying to talk myself into risking that."

She sat forward in her chair. "Risking?"

"If we're wrong that Marston's the guy, or if he suspects something and bolts, or makes his move with a fire…"

"Then you'd look really bad. And that's one thing he loves to do, make those who could catch him look really bad."

He nodded. "You are a very astute woman, Lauren."

"I don't think so. I've tried to wall myself off these last two years, and that was a mistake. You heard Mrs. Gates—it's not helping my son. It's probably not helping me, either. Brad, I've got to tell you something," she said, jumping up and starting to pace. He turned his head each time she passed; she could feel his gaze riveted on her.

"Since Ross died," she said, "I've been really angry with the government for the shoddy job they did investigating his death. He knew better than to be trapped by that fire. I tried to tell the investigators that, but they said he just panicked and made some very bad choices at the end. But I still can't accept that his death was accidental, because he wasn't stupid. He knew fire rules, he knew fires."

"But he died with a friend, too, so doesn't that make foul play look less probable, if that's what you're implying?"

"Yes, but the thing is, I want you to know you've changed how I feel about the feds."

He rose and took her arm to stop her pacing and make her face him. "You're telling me that a while ago you might have liked the feds to look bad—just like our arsonist?"

"I had never thought of it like that, but yes. I was

hurt and furious. But as angry as I've been, I'm trying to help."

"You are helping. A lot."

As he reached for her shoulders, she took his wrists in her hands and held tight to them. It was as if they propped each other up.

"Brad, I realize you have so much on your plate now, but sometime, when all this is over, I'd like to show you the articles and transcripts of the government investigation about the Coyote Canyon Wildfire in northern California two summers ago."

"The Coyote Canyon Wildfire. I've heard of that. By government investigation do you mean the Department of the Interior, the National Park Service or what?"

"Both. I have scrapbooks under my bed that cover the whole thing—court proceedings, witnesses who testified, photos, even some tabloid magazines that did pieces. They brought in some really big guns to prove themselves right and Ross wrong. I kept everything. Though I haven't been able to look at any of it, I'm sure I can now."

He pulled her close and gave her a hard hug before he set her back. "Lauren, something Red said today about that kid who helped him run the ski lift years ago has been bothering me."

She felt deflated, but she couldn't blame him for having a one-track mind. For a moment, she'd been certain he was going to tell her to show him the scrapbooks, or at least vow he'd help her once this nightmare was over. Had he even been listening? Blinking back tears, she turned away.

"What?" she asked. "Red said a lot, none of which he was sure of."

"He said more than he knows, more than I picked up on at first, given how anxious I was to get him tracking. Red thought the boy had lost his mother and had a 'big-shot dad' on the road a lot, who evidently tried to solve the kid's problems by sending him off to an isolated place on his own. All that might fit the profile of an arsonist's parents. But Red also said he thought the dad wrote about the environment, and that *he was a real Smokey the Bear.* What does that last comment mean to you?"

Intrigued, she turned back to him. "That the dad wrote about fire prevention, maybe wildfire prevention?"

"What if that's correct?" he cried, putting both hands atop his head as if his brain was going to explode. "And what if we can track the kid—who would be around thirty now—through his father? You said some big guns testified at the Coyote Canyon hearings. They were probably wildfire-prevention experts, maybe authors. Lauren, go get those scrapbooks and put some coffee on."

They huddled shoulder to shoulder at the kitchen table with the two dusty scrapbooks spread before them. Brad felt jived and not just from their first pot of coffee. He was thrilled he actually had his hands on something concrete that might lead somewhere. He was sick of the specters of Smoke Phantoms and Fire Ghosts. He needed a lead, any lead.

But he stopped flipping pages when he came upon a

newspaper photo of two knee-high white crosses in the burned grass and trees in Coyote Canyon.

"Lauren, is this where they fell?"

"Yes, but they're not buried there. It's a memorial the Park Service put up, either because that's tradition or because they felt guilty for the way they handled things. I don't know. The flames raced up that slope and caught them. Kyle's buried in Seattle and Ross in the cemetery of the Community Church on the other end of town. I used to visit a lot, even took Nicky daily for a while, but it wasn't helping either of us. He became more fearful and I stayed mad as hell."

He gazed into her impassioned face. She looked wildly beautiful, with her red hair mussed and free, like some goddess of nature.

"You couldn't help him or his legacy," he told her, his voice breaking, "but you're making up for it now."

"Thanks for understanding."

"How could I not with my own past? I don't need a shrink to tell me that my drive to stop arsonists is caused by what my dad did."

He reached out and cupped her cheek with one hand. They stayed like that for one breathless moment as the wind howled outside and another pot of coffee gurgled on the counter. He wanted more than anything in the world to haul her into his lap and hold her, but with a brief press of her hand to his, she jumped up to get the coffee.

"The information on the trial is in both scrapbooks," she said, "but the newspaper articles will probably be best to list and identify the so-called expert government witnesses."

He forced himself to flip pages, skimming headlines like Fatal Fire Trial Continues and Panic and Distortion Cause Double Death. As she sat back down with two mugs of steaming coffee and—to his surprise—a pile of tiny Mr. Goodbar candies, she pointed to one big article entitled Fire Swept Up Slope, Trapping Fleeing Men. She told him, "More than one witness implied Ross and Kyle not only dropped their protective personal body tents in their headlong flight, but that they would have been smarter racing through the flames or keeping one foot in the black."

"Meaning it was their fault they didn't get to an area already burned out and hunker down there so the flames would go around them?"

"Right. That's a known tactic and has been proven to work. Firefighters should stay near some black, or if there isn't any, make their own. Twelve smoke jumpers died in a fire near Helena years ago, but their crew boss survived because he lit dry grass beneath himself and lay in the burned area while the inferno blazed around him. In that fire, they say the grass had dried to a consistency of hay and the firs were as dry as kindling. It was a lightning-set fire with whirling winds."

"Drought conditions, like here?"

"Yes. It was in rough Montana backcountry, too."

He took a swallow of coffee and bent over the articles, scanning them for witness's names. "Do you have a paper and pen around?"

"Go ahead and dictate," she said, relieved to have

something to do as she scrambled for the items. "I'll write everything down. Jenkins and Sterling were two of the witnesses, but I can't recall their first names."

"Right, Marlin Jenkins, longtime environmentalist and wildfire expert. Two others were Andrew Sterling and David Durand."

"And Durand was an author, I think."

"I'm looking. Yeah, he had some input in the *Forest Service Manual,* plus he's the author of *Fighting Fire Without Fear* and a list of other titles. He was also a fire consultant to many western states, a lecturer, etc. Here he's called the 'guru' of wildfire investigation, though Marlin Jenkins and—here's another—Jackson Smith sound like big boys too. Do you recall if there were any photos of these men?"

"One of the Sterling guy, I think, but I can't recall where."

"You didn't attend all this, did you?"

"I couldn't stand to. Besides, Nicky had chicken pox about that time, but even if I had been in court, I would have been arrested for standing up and screaming that they were pompous asses and didn't know Ross at all, that he would never have made the mistakes they implied. *Fighting Fire Without Fear,* my foot!"

"Lauren, I promise you I'll study all this later, but right now I'm going to call these names into Denver to see if any of them had a wife who died shortly before 1991 and would now have a son in his early thirties. As soon as I get off the phone, let's use your good old dial-up computer server and see what we can find online."

"I'll check in on Nicky and be right back."

* * *

Evan saw that Lauren was burning the midnight oil in her kitchen. He'd intended to put the ladder up to the kid's bedroom window and knock on it to try to wake him up—just to see if that would work for later, when he really needed him. But from the rise under the line of aspens, Evan could see that she was with Mr. Macho Blond again.

Considering that it was about 5:00 a.m., it was pretty obvious the guy was staying with her. Evan could only glimpse them through the windowpanes of the back door because they had the kitchen curtains closed, but if he moved just right, he could catch glimpses of them at the kitchen table. It was chilly out here tonight, despite how warm it could be during the day. He half wished he'd decided to conserve his strength in Dee Cobern's warm attic, but he had an important agenda.

With his sleeping bag protecting the drip torch strapped to his back, he hid the fire ladder in the bushes where he had left his bulky backpack.

He noticed the pale kaleidoscope of lights in the northern sky, pink, blush, bluish green. The aurora borealis, he thought, arrayed just for him, as if the heavens themselves burned with faint fire. It was a good sign, an omen, lights scooting across the sky for the ghost of Chief White Calf.

He stretched and smiled, forcing his brain back to work. His props were scattered all over, each piece now in place. Gasoline and the quick-start E-Z Lite logs were hidden where he could access them for igniting either the

Cobern place or Mrs. Gates's—perhaps both. He had gasoline he'd just siphoned from Lauren's pontoon plane hidden in a metal can he'd borrowed from the gas station. And he had a ladder to get to his pal Running Deer, if he needed the boy as leverage for a ticket out of here.

It was almost time for curtain up on his pièce de résistance. He'd use little Vermillion for his prologue and, hopefully, the dry hills behind it for the rest of the extravaganza, all of which he would watch from Lauren's plane before making an exit from this vast stage. Unlike his impromptu work with his only other large-scale wildfire in Coyote Canyon, this was perfectly scripted, all but for who the tragic heroine would be, and that he would decide by tomorrow night.

Something he couldn't quite name made him feel he'd almost overstayed his welcome here. Flat on his back now, hands behind his head, he peered again at the glow of soft spotlights in the sky. Yes, the stage was set for another opening—tomorrow night.

When Lauren tiptoed in to check on Nick, she saw that he'd pulled his Indian headdress next to his pillow. Had they woken him up with their talking? She tucked him in again; he always kicked the covers off. As she headed back downstairs, she had another idea.

"Brad, before we get online, let's call Red at Mrs. Gates's to see if any of those men's last names remind him of the boy's name. Something might jog his memory."

He was just hanging up the phone. "That didn't take long. They're on it, but you're right. We could do that, too."

She read him the phone number and he called Red. "Sorry to wake you up," she heard him say. "She's called you four times? Well, sorry but it's Brad. Listen, I have some names for you…"

Lauren handed him the list of names she'd written. He explained their relevance, then read them off. "Are you sure? That one rings a bell?"

Brad started to nod as if to encourage Red; he began to bounce on his bare feet as if he heard some silent musical beat. "You think his name might have been Ethan Durand? E-t-h-a-n?" he spelled out. "Look, if we get a photo of the guy, we'll be down to see you. But we'll call first so we don't get our heads taken off, or get swept in the door in a big bear hug. Yeah, I hear you. Later."

"What?" Lauren asked. "He recalled the kid's name who could work the ski lift?"

"And who was such a loner and fit the profile of a possible budding arsonist. He thinks it might have been Ethan Durand."

"We're starting to get somewhere!"

"It's a start. By the way, Mari's called Red more than once to tell him he needs to get rid of the mounted bighorn sheep and moose heads on his walls. And to tell him she'd cleaned his kitchen but wasn't lifting one more finger to help him. I'd put a year's salary on their ending up together."

Lauren smiled grimly, but she was already heading to boot up her desktop computer. Brad was right behind her. She waited for her screen to fill.

"I see you put away the pickax, boots and books,"

Brad observed, looking at the empty shelf where a shrine of Ross's firefighting things had once been.

"They're in the closet—for Nick someday. I guess if Mrs. Gates were here, she'd make me dust the shelf, too. Okay, here we go," she added and signed on her server.

As soon as she got online, she Googled Ethan Durand. Nothing hit but family-type Web sites and blogs that didn't appear to be about the man they wanted. Then she Googled David Durand and found a lot of sites, including all of the commercial ones that sold his books.

"See if you can find his bio," Brad said, hovering over her shoulder as she perched on the edge of her chair.

"Here's his own Web site. He's also been an investigator for the Federal Occupational Safety and Health Administration and a consultant to the Bureau of Land Management. You'd better sit down and take notes on this. Yes. Yes!"

"Yes, what?" he demanded, trying to see the screen from the side.

"Wait, I'm still reading."

"Lauren, what?"

"Shh! You'll wake up Nick."

Muttering something under his breath, Brad swung his leg over the back of her chair and sat down tight behind her, pushing her closer to the keyboard and screen. His splayed legs pressed against her hips, almost as if she sat in his lap. His cheek pressed tight to her temple so he could read the screen too, and his hands wrapped around her waist to make her as breathless as what she was reading. She didn't protest, but read aloud, in a tremulous voice,

"In 1965, David Durand married a woman whose maiden name was Jeanette Marston. Marston! Ethan Durand, alias Rocky Marston, is using his mother's maiden name! No, it says here their only son's name is Evan, not Ethan."

"Red almost had it. This has to be him!"

"Jeanette Marston Durand died in a single-car accident when Evan was eighteen. She's buried in Saint Louis where Durand still lives—and where Evan was reared, I guess. There's nothing else about the son, only about David's career, his publications, where he's lectured—and cases where he's testified as an expert witness, including at the Coyote Canyon fatal wildfire investigation. It sounds like the guy's traveled all over, especially in the West."

"And so has his son, I'll bet. Incognito, lighting fires to defy his father in some sort of warped hatred, some kind of power play."

She scrolled farther down David Durand's bio and gasped. In a color photo of AUTHOR, LECTURER, one with his hand contemplatively lifted to his chin, "Rocky" Marston's father stared at her. Perfectly groomed, black hair going silver at the temples, olive skin and that intense look that reminded her of his son's even though he had sometimes seemed distracted.

"Do you believe it?" Brad said, his mouth so close to her ear that her hair rustled. He'd never seen Rocky Marston, so he obviously wasn't referring to the photo but was reading something else on the screen. "David Durand has been a special agent for the U.S. Forest Service and—get this!—for the International Association of Arson Investigators. That's it—arson investigators! And his kid's been running amok for years fighting battles with a father who has no clue. No clue!"

"Brad, this photo isn't a profile view like the newspaper photo, but Rocky Marston—Evan Durand—looks a lot like his father. It's him! We've found him!"

He hugged her tight, lifting them both out of the chair and spinning her once around so hard her feet left the ground. Then he put her down. His expression changed to a grim, determined look, as if his features were sculpted in stone. "But now that we've found him, we've got to *really* find him," he said. "Before it's all too late."

13

Brad and Lauren knew they had to get off the computer to clear the line. The moment they were off, Lauren started upstairs to check on Nick again. Almost immediately the phone rang, and she heard Brad answer it.

She couldn't hear what he said at first, but it was obviously his boss calling back. Then Brad's voice rose. "No, Mike, it's not a one-horse town." He sounded suddenly annoyed. "I can testify that they've got at least two horses, so what did you find out?"

She paused on the stairs.

"You told him what? Why didn't you detour him to Denver and relay whatever he told you in interviews? No kidding? Evan worked at the ski lodge here? Bingo! But I still don't want David Durand or anyone else coming here to panic BND. No, she's staying here. Get someone else to fly you in if you're set on coming."

Lauren didn't care if Brad knew she'd been listening. She raced back downstairs and into the kitchen where he was pacing from window to window, looking out as he talked.

"What?" she mouthed when he saw her, but he held up his hand.

"Mike, if we get too many people coming in, I'm telling you, it will spook our ghost. I need a little more time. I know, but I've got a gut feeling on this. Okay, yeah, I know who's head of the team. Then bring fishing or hiking gear with you so you don't look obvious. At least give me that."

Muttering to himself, he punched off and skidded the phone down the counter, where it stuck between her flour and sugar canisters. Stiff-armed, head down, he leaned over the sink.

"Your team is coming here?" she asked.

"As fast as they can, on an FBI jet into Kalispell and then to Vermillion on a pontoon plane."

"I don't think it will be on one of ours, unless they manage to commandeer one that's already in Kalispell."

"Which I don't put past him."

"But if Rocky, a.k.a. Evan, sees a lot of action going on here, new people and—"

"I know, but I don't think he'd strike in the light. That gives us several hours. I was overruled, damn it. But that's not the worst of it."

She pressed her clasped hands against her chest and waited. He turned to her, looking angrier by the minute.

"David Durand threw his weight around when the team phoned him to inquire about his son," Brad said, raking his fingers through his hair, making it stand up on end. "And from questioning, he figured out where sonny boy is, though he claims they're estranged."

"That could be true."

"Durand says he hasn't seen Evan in three years. Expert that he is, Daddy Durand insists the serial arsonist Boy Next Door couldn't be his son, but he's coming to help out anyway. He could even be here soon, since they traced him to a speaking engagement in Seattle, not Saint Louis where he lives. Hell, we get a break, then everything gets broken."

"And out of your control."

"It never was in my control, but that doesn't mean I—we—are going to sit around here waiting for others to take over. As soon as we get Nick safely to school, we'll visit the sheriff to see if he's recalled anything about his assailant. And I need to ask him who to call in for a briefing meeting at the firehouse. It's past time to tell the Vermillion firefighters, even if they are volunteers, what we may be up against." He turned away from her to glare out the window again.

"Brad," she said, laying a hand on his shoulder. "You have done and are still doing everything possible. And you've warned the arson team to give you more time, so if they crash in here and things get out of hand…"

She bit her lower lip and sniffed hard.

"Yeah, out of hand…" His voice trailed off as he turned toward her and stared into her eyes. He seized her wrist. She was certain he would kiss her. She *wanted* him to kiss her so hard that all this would go away, stay away, and it could just be the three of them here, safe together…

"Mom, is it time for breakfast yet?" came a voice from the bottom of the stairs. "I'm hungry and if Brad's eating early, I can eat with him before school."

"Sure," she called to her son, her wide gaze still held by Brad's intense stare. "I think we're all starved."

Brad let her go when she tugged back, but not before he quickly kissed the soft inner skin of her wrist.

Brad and Lauren checked in at the school office and applied for visitors' passes to take Nick clear to his classroom.

"But why?" the boy asked as they signed in.

"Because we want to talk to Mrs. Gates," Lauren said.

She wanted to hug Nick goodbye again as she had at the house, but she had to be content just to see him run happily into his classroom. She was grateful for the way he'd changed from clinging to her when she so much as made a move to leave him alone. Mrs. Gates saw them and told her students, "Now, do not let the noise level go up, up, up in here," then joined them in the doorway to her classroom.

"You see I survived the night," she told them, but she looked sparkly eyed and as sprightly as ever.

"Mrs. Gates," Brad said, "we're going to have to ask you to stay at Red's for at least one more night. We believe we've had a break in the case, but we don't have an arrest yet. Others on the team are coming in, so it's likely that they will want to position themselves in or near your house and Dee Cobern's to keep an eye on things tonight."

"And if they take over my house, that means Red Russert would be where?" she inquired, her voice icing over.

"I'm not certain," Brad admitted, "but I'm hoping, whatever it comes to, that you will still be as cooperative as you have been so far. And if Red does need a place to stay tonight, his own home is obviously the best place."

"I see. Well, for God, country and the FBI, I suppose I could abide him underfoot for one night. And it's fine with me if some of your arson team joins us for dinner, or all night for that matter. No one would recognize Red's kitchen right now—it's immaculate. But one more night in that museum of dead animals and I may turn arsonist to get rid of them!"

"Let's just say," Brad told her, "you're adding more to that chapter in your memoirs."

With a little shake of her head, Mrs. Gates said, "We mustn't make light of all this. And you needn't ask about my keeping a special eye on Nicky until you pick him up this afternoon, Lauren."

"You've been great through all this, Mrs. Gates," Lauren said. "And, I must tell you, Nicky has asked to be called Nick now."

"A good sign, I think," she said with a pert nod. "Now, if we can just keep him from turning into a Blackfeet brave when this Indian unit is over, that will be another step in the right direction!"

They left her and drove to the health clinic to see Chuck. The nurse didn't want to let them in at all, let alone this early, so Brad flashed his badge at her.

"FBI working with the sheriff on an old case," he told the astounded woman. Then as he and Lauren headed down the short hall toward the door she'd pointed out, he whispered, "What the heck. If the arson team and the arsonist's father are crashing this party, I'm not going around undercover anymore. Too many people know, and the volunteer firefighters will soon know. I just hope Evan's staying undercover so he doesn't overhear what is probably about to become great Vermillion gossip."

Lauren was trying to act calm, but his words made her stomach knot even tighter. To their surprise, they found Suze sitting by Chuck's bed. At least he was awake. And alert enough to lift his good hand in a shaky, two-fingered salute to Brad, who stood at the foot of the bed.

"I see some of your short-term memory's back, Sheriff," Brad told him after they inquired how he was doing. "Any recall on the guy who assaulted you?"

"Not a damn thing. But I do remember going into the ski-lift shed to check it before I finished the cabins. And I guess, from what Suze said, that almost finished me. A ride up the ski lift and a bear attack?"

"He didn't attack," Lauren put in, "but he was thinking about it, planning it."

"Like this loony we got loose in our paradise?" Chuck asked with a half-suppressed groan. "You close to an arrest yet, Agent Hale?"

"We think we've got his identity nailed down," Brad said, "but as for the man himself, we're still working on it. The arson team's coming in to—I hope—help."

"Federal Bureaucracy of Investigation?"

"Something like that. Sheriff, is there anything else you can think of that might help us find him before he leaves one of his calling cards around here?"

"First let me just say, since my wife's not speaking to

me again," he went on, as Suze patted his hand, "Dee needs to be coerced—forced, whatever—to go stay with Suze and Steve."

"I agree," Brad said.

"She's so stubborn," Suze said with a sniff. "She's mad at me, too, and won't come to stay with us. She'll have to be carted out of there."

"I'll arrest her and lock her in with Lauren, under my guard tonight, if I have to," Brad promised.

"Much obliged," Chuck said, his voice getting weaker. "And what you just said reminds me of something I did think of. Unless Dee has them, and Suze says not, I lost my ring of keys somewhere. I had them on me when I was making the rounds of the lodge cabins. I had Suze call up there and the groundskeeper found only the cabin keys, not my ring of them."

"Which had your house keys?" Brad asked.

"House, office, firehouse and fire engine, our truck, you name it. I should've told you sooner, but I didn't even think of it." He threw off his covers and tried to roll onto his good elbow, but Suze and Brad pushed him back.

"Dad, you're not getting out of bed."

"Dee would let the arsonist in 'fore she'd let me in, but I've got to warn her. Let go now, Suze…"

"Lauren," Brad said, helping to hold Chuck down, "please send the nurse in here. Then go call a locksmith and get the locks at Dee's house and the firehouse changed immediately, FBI orders. I'll be right out. And then call Dee and tell her we're stopping by to talk to her."

Lauren nodded, patted Suze's shoulder and ran for the nurses' station.

Because Dee didn't answer her phone, Lauren and Brad headed directly to her house from the health clinic. But as they passed the Montana Range Gift Shop, they saw Red. The big man was hard to miss, although he was just emerging from between the fire station and the gift shop.

Lauren braked, and Brad yelled out the window, "Red! What's happening?"

Red lumbered over to the SUV and rested one forearm on Brad's lowered window. "Thought I heard someone on Mari's elevated side porch last night, and today I see I did. Someone's hacked through her garden hose. Could have been some crazy kid, I guess, but we don't get much of that stuff here and considering what's been happening, figure I got a right to be paranoid."

"Any footprints around?"

"That's what I've been looking for, but don't see any."

"A garden hose. Someone just cut it, or maybe took a piece of it?"

"Didn't think to match up the loose ends, but guess that's the kind of stuff Uncle Sam pays you for. I'll check it and let you know."

"We're going to be at Dee Cobern's for a few minutes."

"Be right down."

The Cobern truck was in the driveway, which worried Lauren. "First we find Chuck unconscious..." she began.

"Don't worry about something that hasn't happened," he said, then shook his head. "As if that's not what we've been doing for the entire time I've been here."

They pounded on Dee's front door. Nothing.

"I'll bet she's in the shop," Lauren said hopefully, then added, "but the house phone rings there, too. Since the truck's here, she must have gone for a walk or on an errand."

Frowning, Brad tried the knob on the front door. At least it was locked. Before Lauren could answer, they heard the latch, then the door swept open.

"What?" Dee cried, standing there in a bathrobe with a towel wrapped around her hair. "I was taking a shower. Is Chuck all right?"

"He's fine but—" Brad got out before Lauren elbowed him and interrupted.

"He's not fine. He's guilt-ridden and sick to death of hurting you, of loving you. The man was out of his mind on those meds when he said whatever he said, Dee, and you know it. And Suze hasn't stopped crying over all this. We're here to tell you that we think the arsonist may strike soon, and you live too near the fire station to be safe. Since you won't let Chuck back home—not that he's in any shape to protect you as he wants so desperately to—you had better spend tonight with Nick and me. Brad may be there, too, but some of his other arson team members are coming in today."

Dee listened to the tirade with wide eyes and an open mouth.

"A couple of other things," Brad put in when the two women just stared at each other. "Because the arsonist may have taken the sheriff's keys after he assaulted him, a man—what's his name, Lauren?—from the general store is coming to change your locks."

"Ken Cecil," Lauren said.

"And if you aren't at Lauren's place by nightfall," Brad went on, pointing a finger at Dee, "I'm going to arrest you and take you there myself. Let's go, Lauren."

Before they could turn away from the dumbstruck Dee, Red came loping around the side of the house.

"Your hunch was right, Brad," he said, then nodded at Dee before rushing on. "Mari's hose wasn't just cut but had a piece cut out—maybe several feet of it. And I'm pretty sure that at least three of the E-Z Lite fake logs she burns in her fireplace are gone, too, 'cause I bought her a dozen of them last week and she told me she didn't intend to burn any 'til I learned to sweep out my own fireplace. Brad?"

"I heard you. I'll bet our invisible tourist is planning to use those artificial logs to start a fire, but I can't figure out the hose."

"Surely those packaged logs couldn't start a big blaze," Lauren challenged, hands on hips. "They burn slow and clean. He'd need some kind of accelerant."

"Which could be funneled through a hose?" Red asked.

"Those logs only burn slowly and steadily," Brad explained, "when they're not cut into or broken open. Then they burn with a hot, fast flame, about 100,000 BTUs of it. They're oil-treated sawdust with some copper-based coloring and can go up big-time, especially with a liquid accelerant. He might have been using the hose to siphon gas out of cars or trucks parked outside around here. Dee," he said, swinging back around to look at her, "we're not playing games here. Will you be at Lauren's tonight?"

Looking stunned, she nodded. Brad turned back to Lauren. "I'm betting that our boy figures Mrs. Gates's tidy little logs would be perfectly appropriate to set her house on fire—or maybe even Dee's. Can you phone the volunteer firefighters and get them here to meet with me about noon for a quick briefing? The sheriff gave me a list of their names, but we can look up their num—"

"Come in here," Dee spoke at last. "I have all their numbers. You can use my phone."

Evan knew he was fated to succeed with his plans tonight when he saw that men kept showing up at the firehouse. From his vantage point in a clump of spruce trees on the hill above the town, he could see far down the one-sided main street. How he wished he could be a little mouse to eavesdrop inside, or at least get a peek in a firehouse window.

But what really caught his attention was that Macho Blond had gone inside, too. Who was he really? More than Lauren's lover, he'd bet. Or was he one of the volunteer firefighters? If so, Evan could only hope he'd be "lost," as polite people like to put it, fighting the fire tonight. Yes, *Lost at Lost Lake,* a great possible title for this masterpiece.

Watching the firehouse with the pair of binoculars he'd borrowed from the Cobern place, Evan counseled himself to be content waiting where he was. The men—six of them, not counting the blond—came out after about fifteen minutes, still talking to each other as they got back in their separate vehicles. Five of them drove away.

Besides the blond, one man lingered, then walked several doors to the Cobern house, knocked once and was let inside by Dee Cobern. A little later, the daughter showed up and hugged that man in the door of the house, then went inside arm in arm with him.

Evan recalled seeing the guy in the family photos. He was obviously the artist's husband. In one picture, he'd looked like a logger. And in another shot, he'd been dressed as a firefighter, just like his father-in-law.

Ah, the plot thickens, Evan thought.

Suddenly hungry, he wolfed down some barbecue sauce on sourdough bread, both of which he'd taken from the Bear's Den Dumpster last night. He'd started stashing food in case he needed it when he blew this place. He'd found plenty to eat. Restaurants should ask their customers whether they wanted bread, he mused, or how much they wanted, before they served it to them. Some Americans were still on that silly diet that made you swear off carbs. And the amount of food Americans wasted in one day could probably feed a Third World country for a year. What was wrong with people these days?

Evan decided he'd best stay put until nightfall, then ignite everything fast. But he'd have to be sure he had Nicky Taylor in hand and hidden first so that Lauren would cooperate. And so that she'd willingly ditch

Macho Blond. No way did Evan want to tangle with him at close range.

Evan had almost nodded off when he heard the drone of a small plane. It had pontoons, but he didn't recognize it as one of the town's fleet. It circled the area once, including the town. So as not to be spotted, he scooted farther under the blue spruce branches and cursed when the dry needles pricked his back through his shirt. The plane finally landed on the lake, though not on the usual trajectory the others did.

It headed for the dock: the pilot seemed to hesitate about where to put in to tie up. Finally, three passengers, two men and a woman, got out on the dock, loaded down with what looked like big, matching tackle boxes and other fishing gear. Then their plane taxied out and took off again, leaving them here.

As the three headed toward shore, something familiar about them struck Evan. A woman with long brown hair was completely common. Two gray-headed men, so what? But that guy with the distinctive limp—where had he seen that? Where had he seen this assortment of people together?

Then he remembered and gasped. Only they'd had a broad-shouldered, blond man with them then—a macho blond.

The FBI team from his last fire, in Denver!

Could it be? Could it really, really be?

Had they found him? No, he'd been too careful, too clever.

No one met them at the end of the dock. Darting

from tree to tree with his binocs, sometimes sprawling on the ground, Evan watched them walk to one of the B&Bs at the end of town.

At least they weren't headed for Lauren Taylor's place. Could she have ID'd him? Or had the Taylor boy told his mother or the blond man about Chief White Calf? Could someone in town have spotted his Most Wanted FBI picture that old hag in Denver had described to an FBI artist? He'd been proud of the publicity but horrified by it, too.

Despite the heat of the day, Evan broke out in goose bumps. The FBI team was here to stop him, but no way he would allow that—ever. To calm himself and stay in control, he began to sing, "The hills are alive with the sound of music," then changed the lyrics to "The hills are so dry they will be a huge fuse…"

He chuckled. He was so inventive. And he'd give Vermillion, the state of Montana and the entire country an extravaganza to remember, one definitely entitled *Lost at Lost Lake.*

14

At Lacey's B&B, where Brad had spent his first night in Vermillion, the FBI Serial Arson Team set up its on-site command post. When Brad brought Lauren in, he introduced her to the team, then everyone sat around the dining-room table while Annette Lacey, a friend of Lauren's, served them coffee and sandwiches. Annette was plump, middle-aged and always joked she liked her own cooking too much. Her family went way back in these parts, supposedly descended from French trappers, but Annette was the last of the Laceys around.

"Lauren, sit here by me," Brad said and pulled out a chair for her at the table. "You've been in on locating BND in Vermillion from the start, and we need your local knowledge and input."

Lauren saw the only woman on the team, Jennifer Connors, roll her eyes. Brad didn't seem to notice, but Lauren knew that Jen, as everyone called her, didn't want her around. Maybe she liked being the solo female in on all of this, or maybe she just thought civilians should stay out of the way. The two men, both considerably older than Brad, had thanked her for her initial tip about BND.

"Frankly," Brad told everyone, "I was hoping you could hold off on this a little longer. We've obviously been making progress here."

"Not enough, if you can't produce Evan Durand," Mike put in. "Though now that I see the rugged vastness of this area, I can see why not. I'm tempted to bring in choppers with night-vision capabilities."

"But you've also seen it's dangerous flying this terrain day or night," Brad said, before she could tell them that. "I think tracker dogs might be more useful."

"No way," Clay Smith said. "Once BND lights a fire and moves onto burnt ground, dogs would have one hell of a time following him. At the World Trade towers, the cadaver dogs burned the pads right off their feet days after."

Brad leaned forward and looked down the table at Mike. "We all know this guy has a volatile personality and delusions of grandeur. But I still say, if he finds out he has the vaunted FBI team to impress, which he's already lectured once before—boom!"

"I hear you," Mike said. "But we cannot—I repeat—cannot have this man running loose, not while I'm in charge."

Lauren thought the air shimmered with unspoken tension. Poor Brad. This was his boss, and the team he had to work with in his mission to catch arsonists. She was so grateful for being a self-employed pilot with her own plane. If she could only be soaring alone above the mountains right now, or maybe with her son. Brad, too...

"Okay, people," Mike said. "I'm going to take just a few minutes to bring Brad up to speed on what we all know about Evan Marston Durand."

"So," Brad said, narrowing his eyes and leaning his elbows on the table to prop up his chin, "that's his middle name as well as his mother's maiden name. The guy doesn't make many mistakes, but using the Marston alias with Lauren was a big one."

"Yeah, she helped us with that, all right," Jen put in, but she sounded almost sarcastic.

Evidently ignoring her, Mike went on, "Now here's the need-to-know intel we have on Evan Durand so far. Only child, thirty years old, born and reared in Clayton, Missouri, a suburb of Saint Louis. Mother, almost forty when he was born, was once a concert pianist, father you all know about."

"In other words," Clay said, "two high achievers who probably demanded that of their only child."

"Fits so far," Mike agreed. "Mother died the month Evan graduated from high school, when her car engine caught fire and she was evidently trapped in the vehicle—"

"Burned to death? No kidding!" Brad said, hitting both fists on the table. "You don't think—"

"I have no idea at this juncture," Mike interrupted, "because we don't know Evan's relationship with her. Field agents in Saint Louis are trying to interview old neighbors and the like. Car engines do catch fire."

"How has he supported himself?" Brad asked. "His father can't still be picking up his bills if he claims they're estranged."

"As far as we can tell so far, through acting," Mike said and shrugged.

"Acting? Like in what?"

"One report says miming on street corners."

"More or less panhandling?" Brad asked, looking doubtful. "What's that word for performing in public venues with a box of coins nearby?"

"I think it's called busking," Lauren put in. "Street musicians are called buskers."

"But busking can't be all," Brad insisted. "There has to be more to how BND's moved around, fed himself and kept a low profile —though acting skills could serve him well in changing his appearance and even getting in tight with people. I'm thinking of how he must have conned someone into letting him buy white phosphorus for the Denver arson. Anything else?"

"Only that he's pretty much dropped out of government records since he turned twenty," Mike said. "He's not even paying income tax."

"At least we can arrest him on that," Clay muttered.

"Ten years," Jen said. "For all we know, his serious arsons could have started about ten years ago, though we've only been onto the BND fires for about five. But I think Brad's right that this lunatic must have done more than mime on street corners to support himself. Maybe he's a thief, too, or cons people with his acting background. There have to be more pieces to put together."

"Which reminds me," Mike said, "Jen's going to debrief Lauren again. I know you've already done that, Brad, but it won't hurt for our reports to have it not by word of mouth, so to speak, but officially recorded."

Jen scooted her chair back and reached behind her to rip open the Velcro top on her black case. If that bag was supposed to pass for a fishing-tackle box, Lauren thought, these people were really city slickers. Suddenly she was terrified that Evan Durand would outsmart the lot of them.

She could tell Brad was seething, either with excitement or frustration. And he seemed barely able to keep from trying to take over from Mike, she was sure of it. Somehow, she had learned to read him in these few days, to tap into his feelings and needs. But she would lose him soon. And if these people couldn't somehow stop Evan Durand, she might lose much more than that.

"Sorry about all that—your being interrogated again," Brad said.

Lauren was driving him to her place to pick up some gear he'd left there and to bring back the scrapbook photo of David Durand, partly so the arson team could check his identity when he arrived, and partly, she thought, just to get her—or maybe both her and Brad—out of their strategy meeting. As he talked, he kept fussing with his two-way radio that linked him to the rest of the team. It looked a lot like the walkie-talkies wildfire fighters used.

"It's all right," she assured him. "I only told her what I've already told you."

"If Durand tries anything at your place, Jen's an excellent shot, though I'm sorry that I won't be spending the night with you, Dee and Nick. Mike thinks the men should be deployed at the fire station, Mrs. Gates's and Dee's."

"Maybe Dee's made up with Suze and will go to their house instead of mine."

"You're more likely to get them all there, since Suze's husband will be on call in case a blaze is set. It's weird how I feel as if I know your friends already. I haven't had that kind of thing—neighbors I knew—since we had to sell our place in Denver."

He sighed and hooked the radio to his belt. She noted how wistful he grew each time he mentioned anything to do with the "good old days," before his father's arsons brought everything in his childhood crashing down. She prayed that her own son's loss of his father would not take a toll like this. For the first time since she'd lost Ross, she wished desperately that she could give Nick a good man in his life, someone to be a father.

"Small-town living has a lot of rewards," she told him, "as does escaping the daily-pressure grind of a job like yours."

"I know," he said, turning to her. "Lauren, whatever happens tonight or hereafter, and as difficult as what we've been through together has been so far, I want you to know that I've enjoyed working with you, enjoyed getting to know you. If it hadn't been for you, we wouldn't be this close to finding Durand. And I will look into what happened at the Coyote Canyon fire when this is over, I promise."

She nodded, afraid she'd choke up. "You've been great for Nick," she whispered. "It's helped me to have you here." Her voice snagged. How ridiculous would it look if she cried or tried to cling to him, she scolded herself.

They got out of her car and started for the house. But on the stiff breeze they heard a thwack thwack sound that grew louder and louder.

"A chopper?" Brad shouted over the noise, shading his eyes and looking up. "If Mike's called in choppers, he's really nuts!"

A black helicopter buzzed the lakeshore, and they both ran to the water's edge to watch it. There were no official markings on the side of the big bird, but there were two men in it. It tilted into a turn, then headed for an open piece of ground between the town and Lauren's house. "This ever happen before?" Brad yelled as the descending bird kicked up a whirlwind of dry debris.

"Choppers? Not much," she shouted back. "Sometimes the owners of the lumber camp go in and out like that, but not on this side of the mountain. Every now and then someone wealthy comes to the lodge in the winter this way, but they usually land on the other side of town."

"I'll be back," Brad shouted and ran down the rocky shore of the lake toward the chopper, his shoes throwing the red mud the vermillion pigment made at the water's edge.

Despite what he'd just told her, Lauren ran after him.

Evan had been carefully shifting from tree to tree along the ridge above the town, working his way toward

Lauren's place, when he saw a helicopter fly low overhead. Grand Central Station, he thought. More of an audience arriving early for his standing-room-only performance tonight? Perhaps even the director of the FBI or a newspaper reporter? How he wished a television logo had been emblazoned on the sleek skin of the helicopter. CNN, FOX, ABC, NBC, CBS—he'd like to invite all of them to attend, then to write reviews of his greatest performance, which he had to get going right now.

He wanted to be in place before it got dark so that he could take out his hidden ladder and have Running Deer in the tender care of the ghost of Chief White Calf before he set the fires. With the rising wind, the entire area could be one giant lighted stage when Lauren flew him out of here.

He'd decided to leave the ransom note the old-fashioned way—her son's life for her compliance. In this podunk place where cell phones didn't work, who knew if he could even get to a phone. And even then, one of these FBI lackeys might have tapped it. He'd written the note wearing gloves so he'd leave no prints.

Hunkered down behind a cluster of thick conifers, Evan lifted his binocs to his eyes, pointing them toward the helicopter landing on the shore near Lauren's property. He adjusted the focus dial; the scene leaped large into view and etched itself on his mind. He saw that both Lauren and her blond friend were racing toward the big bird as its rotors slowed. And the man who emerged and jumped down to the rocky shoreline was—was...

Evan bucked so hard in shock, he threw himself back

and hit his head on a tree branch. He steadied himself and gripped the binocs. The two sides of them came together to pinch his fingers. Then, furious and frenzied, he fell flat on his back to the ground and rolled under the tree, suddenly terrified he'd be spotted, that he'd be stopped. Finally he forced himself to kneel and looked through the binocs again to be sure.

Yes, it was his father. His omnipotent, almighty, perfect father was here! But why?

Evan tried to control his racing pulse and ragged breathing. He was hyperventilating, and blood pounded in his ears. His father turned away, started walking in the opposite direction…

No! Oh, no… He was a little boy again, shuffled off, left behind, ignored. His father beat him and locked him in for starting the fire in the trash can, told him he'd end up a pyromaniac. Evan could still hear the way he'd said that horrid word, as if his voice echoed from the bottom of a barrel: py-ro-maaa-niii-aaac. Evan didn't know what it meant then, but that word had sounded so dreadful. Did his father mean he was crazy? That he was sick? The word sounded so dirty.

Evan threw himself down again. He pulled his hair and kicked the ground, beating his fists on the dry pine needles until he got control of himself again. After all, wasn't this what he'd always wanted? Although his first impulse was to get close enough to just shoot his father, they'd catch him then. Besides, his father deserved to be engulfed in a fire, just the way his mother had been. In more ways than one, he wanted his father to suffer.

Tonight the master arson investigator David Durand, and all of them, were going to be made into laughing-stocks, the butt of all bad firefighting jokes. As Shakespeare wrote in the last act of *Othello*, *"Here is my journey's end, here is my butt."* How his fellow thespians used to laugh at that line in high school, though Evan told them that *butt* meant the final target, the final ambition for one's life. Yes, this great tragedy was a comedy, too, and the second-greatest playwright since the Bard would have the last laugh in presenting his drama, *Lost at Lost Lake.*

So why was he curled up in a ball crying? Crying like he had not done since he'd so successfully rigged that fuse and fire in his mother's car?

"David Durand?" Brad called to the man who bent low and hurried away from the circle of wind the chopper blades made.

Brad saw it was definitely him, then noticed that Lauren stood just behind him, gaping at the new arrival. Durand frowned at them, then walked closer.

Lauren kept her arms folded across her chest, but Brad thrust out his hand. "Agent Brad Hale, FBI Serial Arson Team," he introduced himself. "Mike Edwards, the head of the team, told me you were coming in from Seattle. That was quite an entrance."

"I flew from there into Kalispell and at considerable cost to myself," the man said. He had, Brad thought, an upper-class East Coast accent. Boston maybe, shades of the Kennedys. "I had to cut short a speaking tour to set things straight. Obviously mistakes have been made. In my profession, I hardly need such a cock-and-bull story to get out about my son—or, by association, me."

"This is Lauren Taylor. She flew your son Evan into Lost Lake, before she knew who he was, of course. He was going by the name Rocky Marston then."

"Indeed?" Durand said, looking startled.

But rather than admit to recognizing the use of his wife's maiden name, the man plunged on, with a slight, stiff bow in Lauren's direction. "I'm afraid you—as well as that old woman who spotted the Denver BND arsonist in the middle of the night—are sadly mistaken and are causing me a great deal of trouble, my dear."

He was ingratiating and arrogant, Brad thought. And not to be trusted since he hadn't come clean on "Marston" being a major clue that BND was his son. But that fit. It all fit.

"As for trouble," Lauren shot back at Durand, "the arsonist is causing this town a great deal of that, not to mention the tragic deaths of the four women and the firefighter his blazes have caused so far."

"I hardly meant to cast aspersions on anyone, Lauren. My entire life has been spent in the cause of fighting fires and stopping those who start them. And where, Agent Hale," he said turning his back on Lauren, "am I to meet with your team?"

"Back in town," Brad told him. "We can either hike along the lakeshore, though you don't seem dressed for it," he said, pointedly looking at the man's polished wingtip shoes, "or Lauren can take us in her van."

"I'll take you," she said, looking at Brad. "But after that dramatic entrance, most people in town will realize someone who thinks he's important has arrived. Wait here, gentlemen. The chauffeur will bring the limo on the road right up there."

Brad watched her stalk off down the beach. He grinned behind Durand's back. He'd love to be there when Lauren took this guy on about his testimony against Ross during the Coyote Canyon hearings.

But there was one good thing about Durand's arrival. A pompous, self-important and preoccupied father like this was the classic kind to produce an arsonist, and if Durand was too blind to see that, he just might be enlightened soon. The trouble was, it might take flames to do that.

As Lauren drove David Durand and Brad toward town, she knew she should think of herself as Brad's assistant and keep her mouth shut. But she couldn't. She just couldn't. This so-called expert was one of the witnesses who had testified at the trial. And he had made it sound as if Ross's own carelessness had caused his death.

"I have to tell you, Mr. Durand," she began, fighting to keep her voice in check. She intentionally slowed the van, so she'd have time to say her piece. "I can't put much faith in your vehement claim that your son's not an arsonist. Not after the shambles you made of the Coyote Canyon hearings."

From the back seat, she heard Durand gasp. Beside her, Brad shifted in his seat but said nothing.

"And why would you be following those?" the man

demanded. "Or think you know enough to question my testimony?"

Brad turned partway toward the man, who sat behind Lauren. "In case you didn't catch our driver's last name, Durand, it's Taylor. Her husband, Ross, was one of the experienced, *expert* firefighters your testimony implied was acting like a novice and partly caused his own fatal entrapment in that fire."

"Uh," Durand choked out, sounding as if he'd been belly-punched. "Sorry, Mrs. Taylor, but the evidence clearly sh—"

"The evidence was flawed," Lauren interrupted. "Maybe even skewed. I've kept a record of every word you said, not just from newspaper articles but from word-by-word accounts taken during the investigation. Brad's seen some of it and is going to look the transcripts over more thoroughly later. There's something wrong with two veteran wildfire fighters being trapped without their protective body tents. There's something wrong with a man who hears that Rocky Marston is the suspect's name and doesn't instantly tell an FBI agent that Marston was his wife's maiden name."

As she approached Lacey's B&B, she hit the brakes hard for emphasis. Brad bounced against his seat belt and braced himself on the dash. As she suspected, Durand hadn't fastened his belt, so he banged into the back of her seat.

"Quite a jolt to realize that you can make serious mistakes, isn't it, Mr. Durand?" Lauren goaded. "Maybe you'll think over the slight possibility that you're human and can be wrong once in a while. And maybe you'll decide to be honest enough to admit it and then get on with helping the FBI find and stop your son."

She hit the gas and jerked the cursing man back into his seat as she pulled up in front of Lacey's and came to a smooth stop.

Sounding shaken now, Durand muttered, "I insist you turn the engine off before I try to get out. Agent Hale, I demand you talk to this woman."

"Good idea. Lauren," Brad said, turning to her again, "I agree with everything you said. And I sure as hell am going to look into the ramifications of this man's testimony about Coyote Canyon as soon as we get our hands on Evan. Of course, I can only hope he chooses to—as you so expertly suggested—cooperate with us now. Durand, let's go."

Brad winked at her and got out, then pulled Durand from the back seat and hustled him inside.

Evan Durand pulled on his old firefighting gloves and tamped them carefully between his spread fingers. He made certain the note to Lauren was in his pocket. He felt again to be sure he had the long strips of cloth he'd cut from his extra sweatshirt for ties and a gag, should the boy not be convinced to come quietly. This was more than he'd ever risked before, but the isolation of this place, the presence of the FBI—and the brazen arrival of his arson-expert father—all made this necessary. Though he felt completely in control, it would be all their fault if anything went wrong.

From his observations, Evan knew that Lauren's house was full of women, including the female FBI-team member, but that might work to his advantage. Dee Cobern and her artist daughter were there, too, so they must be speaking again. They might all keep each other occupied, talking and fretting. At least, as far as Evan could tell, Macho Blond wasn't there tonight to get in the way.

He squinted up at the sky. Racing clouds—scudding clouds, poets always said. It wasn't pitch-black yet, though dark enough for what he intended.

He could tell by when the lights went out in the boy's bedroom that he'd been put to bed about ten minutes ago. Too early for Lauren to check on her son already, Evan reasoned. The boy was upstairs and they were probably all downstairs, feeling safe out of town, safe in numbers, safe in knowing that someone would have to go through them to get to the boy. But since the BND arsonist had shown no interest in harming children, and since fools like the FBI relied on their adversary's previous M.O., he wasn't worried about this part of the plan at all. Besides, Nicky Taylor, with his wild imagination, had played right into his hands.

And since everyone was preoccupied with fires on a large scale, one little boy hardly played into their fears, just as another little boy had hardly been noticed by his parents in their busy, busy lives. At the last minute when the flames devoured her, had his mother known? At least his father would recognize the power and importance of his son on this night.

Evan made certain he leaned the fire-truck ladder against the sharply slanted roof shingles, where it couldn't be seen from a window. Someone would actually have to make an outside circuit of the house to see it. He loved the fact that the ladder was labeled Property VFD. All he had to do now was hope that his little Indian brave would open the upstairs window when he knocked on it.

He climbed quickly and tested the roof with one foot first. Sturdy, not slippery. But then again, why should it be in this drought? That surely was another sign that tonight was meant to happen. He knelt outside the boy's curtained window and rapped as lightly as he could, then a bit louder. Women's voices were discernible from here, not the actual words, but the murmur of them. Didn't they realize they might keep the boy awake? He wondered how much they'd told Nicky about what was going on.

To Evan's delight, the bedroom curtains parted slightly, then swept wider open. The boy's pale face pressed to the window, his eyes wide, his mouth in an O. Maybe he had gone to sleep that quickly, Evan thought, because he looked dazed, half out of it. But that might help, too.

Evan had his arms crossed, Indian style, but now he lifted one palm out in greeting, while he pressed the index finger of his other hand to his lips to signal silence. He gestured to Nicky to open the window. He did. There was a screen behind it.

"I'm not dreaming, right?" the kid asked.

"This no dream, but White Calf want you come out for special campfire. Then you come back before your mother worry."

"A campfire? With other Blackfeet ghosts, too?"

Evan nodded.

"I'm not dressed. Should I get dressed?"

"You have robe? Indians like robes. Or blanket."

"Are we going to fly down or just disappear or what?"

"You take screen from window. You know how? I come in, help you get ready."

The boy began to fumble with the screen. There must be something on the frame inside that held it in place. Evan gave it a shove. When it pushed inward, he grabbed at it so it wouldn't make any noise. He shoved the sill up farther and crouched to step into the bedroom, putting the screen aside.

"I have my feather headdress right here," Nicky said, backing away and picking something up from his bedside table.

The bedroom door was slightly ajar, and the women's voices were more distinct now. If only he had time to eavesdrop.

"Did you put the bright feather in it?" the boy asked as Evan grabbed the blanket off the bed, wrapped it around the kid like a robe, then dropped the note on the bed pillow.

"Bright feather special gift for you," Evan whispered, pushing him gently toward the open window. "More gifts when you come out with me. You come see northern lights in sky, like ghost lights."

"Yeah, I've heard them called that before. Chief, I didn't tell my mom that you gave me the bright feather, but I thought you were the one."

This was working so well that Evan again knew his plans were fated—kismet! He helped the boy step through the window onto the roof. Nicky wore long-legged pajamas and socks, so his footing ought to be good, though Evan realized he might have to carry him down the ladder.

When they were both out, Evan lifted the screen back into place as best he could, then closed the window from the outside.

When Nicky saw the ladder poking up above the roof, he asked, "Aren't we just going to fly away, like a ghost would? Or like in *Peter Pan* when they go out the window to Never-Never Land? Indians don't use white man's ladders, 'specially not ghosts."

"Other Indians waiting. We make you honorary member of tribe, have feast."

"I don't want to go down the ladder. Just make us appear on the ground like you do in the ravine."

"White Calf carry Running Deer down," Evan said and reached to pick him up.

"No!" the boy cried and darted back up the roof until his blanket tripped him and he sat down hard. "I'll see you in the ravine tomorrow. And why are you wearing gloves? Blackfeet don't have gloves like th—" he went on, his high-pitched boy's voice rising.

Evan shoved the gag in his mouth. As Nicky started to kick and flail, Evan wrapped the blanket even tighter around him, trapping his arms down at his sides. Using a fireman's carry, he slung the writhing boy over his shoulder and, with more difficulty than he'd imagined, went down the ladder.

Laboring, breathing hard, he ran with his bouncing bundle up into the clumps of aspen. He lay the sobbing boy next to his backpack and carefully tied his feet. Evan also loosely tied him to his big backpack, so that the boy would not roll down the hill where someone could spot him. Then he darted back down the hill for the ladder and stashed it in the foliage above the house.

Even if Lauren did not obey his orders in the note, it would take her quite a while to locate the boy. By then, the town would be on fire, and people she'd need to help her would be in disarray or even endangered, fighting the fire. If she did not meet him at her plane, he might be able to roust out that other pilot. He had a gun and a knife, after all. If worse came to worst, he could try to force his father's chopper pilot to get him out of here.

"You not cry," Evan told the boy, not certain why he kept up with the Indian lingo. "I get your mother here later and we go for airplane trip, see lots of pretty sights. Chief White Calf be back for you soon. You be brave, Indian brave."

Evan smiled grimly at the way he could come up with clever lines even in the busiest of times. He took a deep breath. Yes, he was in control. So far so good.

He removed his drip torch from his bedroll, being careful the butcher knife and gun were still there. He patted the kid on the head, then took off running for town where he had his kindling and accelerants stored.

15

Brad thought Mike's plan would probably work—or would if they were facing a more common criminal. He'd come to believe there was a fine line between genius and insanity. And Evan Durand, alias Rocky Marston, fell somewhere in between.

Although Jen, who hadn't been too happy about her assignment, was stationed out at Lauren's, Mike had deployed the three men to key sites to watch for any activity in town. He'd ordered Clay to spend the night at Dee Cobern's deserted house. Clay had set himself up in the attic with night-vision goggles because, as he'd just said on the radio, "There's a window up here with a perfect view of the Gates place, the edge of the firehouse and the main street."

"As if BND would be coming down the main street," Mike muttered into his two-way from his post in Mrs. Gates's front window. "Clay, just be sure you can get down fast to ground level if you spot anything. And don't be smoking up there. You gotta get off the weed again when this is all over. I'm not having a smoker on a team when cigs start blazes. Brad, you in place?"

"Affirmative, babysitting the fire engine. But I'm worried about David Durand's helicopter entrance. If BND spotted his father, he might try to face him down one way or another at Lacey's B&B. I think I could be better used there, since—"

"Granted, the father's a jerk," Mike interrupted. "We saw that in the meeting with him. But David Durand has enough smarts to keep an eye out at Lacey's. The guy's a survivor. Since he's finally acknowledged it 'could possibly' be his son behind all this, he wants to do everything to stop him. But do you know why? 'Cause it's the only way he can salvage his reputation. He's worried about himself, not his son. I know we're spread thin, Brad, but just sit tight. Jen, you there?"

"Affirmative. Lauren Taylor says I can take her vehicle to the B&B or drive into town if anything goes down."

"The sheriff's wife and daughter staying put there?" Brad asked.

"So far so good," Jen said. "That BND bastard just better pick another place to light his diversion fire, or I'll be all over him. Besides, with her son and the other two women here, Lauren's hardly a woman alone tonight. I've been making interior circuits of the house here and everything looks calm outside. I do think both mother and son are missing you though, Brad."

"Knock off the social commentary," Mike said. "Everybody, just keep your eyes peeled and these lines open. If we get this guy, I'm gonna see that part of the reward money goes to getting a cell-phone tower around here. Man, I feel like I'm back in the twentieth century— or even the nineteenth."

Brad was tempted to defend Vermillion and its people, but he kept his mouth shut. He'd defend them another way, by stopping the Fire Phantom if it was the last thing he ever did.

He'd tried to keep from missing Lauren and Nick, from wanting not only to protect them but just to be with them. It was hard to believe that four days ago he'd never so much as heard of Vermillion, never laid eyes on the Taylors.

And he couldn't keep from wondering how Red and his Mari were doing at Red's place above the Bear's Den Restaurant. He'd lay odds that Red would take good care of her—and that she really wanted him to. Brad had asked Mike to give Red the extra two-way he'd brought, but Mike had told Red to phone him at Mari's home number if he spotted anything. Or if he saw flames, to phone the number at the firehouse that set off the alarm. The volunteer firefighters were in earshot tonight. After dark, they had sneaked into Dee Cobern's shop and hunkered down in sleeping bags on the floor. By running about fifty yards, they'd be here in the firehouse, ready to roll in a matter of minutes.

Partway up the wooded hill behind the town, Evan uncovered his cache of E-Z Lite logs. He strapped his drip torch to his back, as if it were a small scuba lung.

Nineteen inches of beautiful, bright red stainless

steel, the drip torch was his favorite firefighting device, but it could also set amazing arson blazes. He hoped not to have to use it tonight, though it always thrilled him to smell its heady mixture of diesel oil and gasoline. He shivered at the thought of its gobs of accelerant drooling to the ground to produce darts of fire. Yet he wanted to keep that as his best, last weapon; he had plenty else to use before he had to rely on it.

Evan had spent hours trying to figure out exactly how the FBI Serial Arson Team had psyched him out. They'd expect him to act as he always did, which meant starting a diversion fire away from his primary target— a single woman's abode near the firehouse. And though he hated to disappoint them, he had a few special surprises in store tonight.

He knew the FBI team wasn't at Lacey's B&B anymore, but he wasn't quite certain where they were. How excellent it would be if he could trap one or more of them just as they yearned to trap him. He regretted having to get Nicky Taylor under his control tonight. Otherwise, he'd have had time to surveil the town continually and known exactly where all the actors in this drama were waiting in the wings.

Evan carried two of the three E-Z Lite logs down the hill toward the back of the Bear's Den Restaurant. Let them watch the Cobern and Gates places—surely that's what they had under guard. He did regret that the restaurant that had fed him so well would have to be sacrificed, but it was the only building he could get to completely undercover. Not only did its Dumpster provide protection for him to get close to the building, but the long, metal, open-air barbecues were perfect for crawling under between the Dumpster and the building itself.

No way he was going to lower himself to starting a mere Dumpster fire. Drunk college kids did that, gangs in the 'hood did that. No, the Dumpster and barbecue grills were merely his paths in and out, especially in case the FBI team had brought night-vision goggles.

He belly-crawled out of the foliage and around the Dumpster, then under the ten-foot-long, raised barbecue grill, squeezing himself and the two logs between its regularly spaced sets of metal legs. He carefully placed the logs where he wanted them, one at the back corner of the restaurant where the wind whipped through from the lake, the other on the second step of the back entrance to the restaurant and the apartment above. The second story evidently belonged to a single man.

Variety was the spice of life—and death. But it was dark upstairs, so he couldn't tell if anyone was up there or not. He assumed there was a front exit, probably through the restaurant itself. If he did this right, flames and smoke would quickly cover the entire upper floor.

The wooden stairs reached clear to the second story, and like the teacher's upstairs apartment two doors away, the stairs were covered, perhaps to keep the snow off or the cruel winter winds out. Once this log ignited, anyone trying to go up or down would have to run the gauntlet of fire.

Evan crawled all the way back and darted to the hollow tree where he'd wedged the plastic container full of gasoline siphoned from the fire engine last night. Pushing the container ahead of him, he made it back to the logs.

Pressed tight to the rear exterior wall of the restaurant, he used Dee Cobern's knife to hack into the logs to free their highly inflammable guts. How nice that so many of the western-style Vermillion buildings were made of rustic wood. This one even had a shake-shingle roof.

Evan laid a little trail with gasoline to both logs and backed away, dragging the almost empty container with him. He still had a second metal can of gasoline he'd siphoned from Lauren's plane at the other end of town. The extra log and some of that gasoline was destined for the B&B where his father was. The last of the accelerant would be used to set the dry grass field behind Lauren's house afire before he took the boy and headed for her plane.

A three-act play! This restaurant, the place sheltering his father and the field to provide the lighted backdrop to it all!

His hands shook as he lit a match from a half-used book he'd found in the Dumpster his first night here. *Nothing better than BEAR'S DEN chow,* it read.

"Except a Bear's Den fire," he whispered and struck the match.

Lauren hoped the women's chatter downstairs wasn't keeping Nick awake, but she doubted it. His eyelids had been heavy. He'd been excited to have Dee, Suze and Jen, "a friend of Brad's," here for dinner. To avoid upsetting him, Lauren had asked Jen not to talk arsonist business until she'd put him to bed.

"If BND strikes," Jen had told her in a whisper, "your son's going to know all about it anyway."

"But I'm trusting all of you to stop him," Lauren had countered. "Besides, Nick's father died in a fire. He's been doing so well lately that I don't want him upset."

"Oh. Sorry for your loss," Jen had said, though it sounded as if she was reciting a recorded response.

Lauren pushed open the door to Nick's room and tiptoed in. He'd opened one side of the curtains, probably to look out at his Indian tent again. Would he ever grow out of his wild flights of fancy?

He wasn't in his bed. She turned toward the attached master bathroom. She didn't want to startle him. He had downed a lot of orange soda at dinner, but she gave him credit for not wetting the bed anymore.

Lauren tiptoed over to the bathroom, but before she reached it, she sensed he was not here. "Nick? Nicky?"

She looked inside the bathroom, even pulled back the shower curtain and glanced behind the door. She darted back out into the upstairs hall, half expecting him to be leaning against the guardrails, asleep where he might have been eavesdropping on them downstairs.

But he wasn't there either.

She tried to stay calm. She wanted to scream for him, for help, but she didn't.

He had to be here. No one had come down the stairs. One of them would have seen him. She snapped on the bedroom light and ran to look under his bed.

And saw a folded note on his pillow.

He'd left her a note? What was he thinking? Was this some sort of Indian game? Was he going to tell her he was hiding and she had to find him?

As she opened it, her legs went weak and she collapsed on the empty bed. The handwriting—hardly Nicky's big printing—was small but ornate, with loops and embellishments. The message was laid out on the page like a poem or screenplay.

LOST AT LOST LAKE *STAGE DIRECTIONS.*
EPILOGUE

Dear leading lady, this drama's the place
Wherein to settle the FBI's hash—or case.
The Smoke Ghost has spirited your son away,
Gone for good, unless you costar in my play.
So come <u>alone</u>—no FBI, no friend in tow
To the airplane dock at 1:00 a.m., prepared to go.
For the finale, you bring Nicky home. Oh, happy days!
Or else, he'll be gone with the wind
In a big, beautiful blaze.

It was unsigned, but Lauren knew who the note was from. Her hands shook so hard as she skimmed it again that the words jumped and trembled. Wrapping her arms around herself, she rocked back and forth on her son's bed, fighting to keep quiet, to stop the moaning, keening sound inside herself.

She struggled to clear her head and control her fears. She had to act coldly, calmly.

How had Evan Durand gotten Nicky out of here? Without a sound, without a struggle? Had he sneaked in somehow?

Her heart thudded so hard she was certain those downstairs could hear. She almost screamed for Jen to get Brad on her two-way radio, but then he'd leave his post to rush here and everyone would know. Besides, it was obvious Evan must be watching.

She grabbed Nicky's pillow to her and hugged it hard, almost smothering herself in its depths—the smell of him, pictures and memories of her baby.

Then she got up slowly, dropped the pillow on the bed and walked to the window with the curtain shoved aside. The window was not locked, when she was certain she had checked it earlier. Had Nicky opened it from the inside? Surely he hadn't gone out via the roof.

The screen had not been slit, but the entire frame was loose. Like the window, it could only be freed from the inside. Had Nicky let that man in?

It didn't make sense. Nothing did. But she knew she must do whatever this madman said to get her son back. If Brad were here, she'd ask him what to do. She trusted him that much. But the entry to the dock was an open area, and the dock itself long and bare. There was nowhere Brad could hide to get close to them. And if Durand was holding Nicky with a gun or a knife…

She even thought about getting David Durand to help her, but that could set Evan off. When he'd so much as mentioned his father that day she'd flown him in, his anger had been explosive.

Lauren could only pray that the arsonist had seen the show of force here and was getting out before anything went up in flames. And then, as the note said, she and Nicky could come home.

Whoosh! went the flames behind Evan as he scrambled into the protection of the foliage behind the Bear's Den. He could see that both logs caught quickly, belching coppery-colored light. Then the dancing flames flared to the wooden exterior of the restaurant. The logs were strategically placed to engulf the back of the building, but in this wind, the flames would vault to the second story and devour the eaves and shake shingles above, catching the front of the building too.

It was soon a roaring good fire, at first hidden from the street until it had a strong start. Then it turned into a thing of beauty as it leaped around the sides and caught the roof.

Taking the path above the town, Evan headed in a dead run toward Lacey's B&B.

Brad noticed that a diffused golden glow seemed to settle on the street. He'd been ordered not to go outside unless he saw the arsonist or flames, or if he smelled smoke. But he didn't care what the hell Mike's orders were. He sensed fire. But it wasn't where they'd all been looking. So where was it? Where?

Brad was unlocking the front door as the call came in to the firehouse. It set off an alarm that sounded like screams in his skull. He nearly jumped through the roof. Then the overhead lights came on. No one had told him to expect that. Backlighted like this, he was a walking target if he went out the front, so he tore to the back door and fumbled with the lock and the knob. This alarm would bring the volunteer force, and they'd be here soon.

The moment he tore out the door, the stench of smoke and gasoline hit him. It was obviously nearby, but where?

As he rounded the corner between the firehouse and Mrs. Gates's place, he saw red-orange flames roaring out the back of the Bear's Den Restaurant on the other side of the fire station.

Mrs. Gates and Red were there! Had they called in the alarm? Why weren't they outside where he could see them?

Keeping back from the impact of the heat, Brad made a jogging circuit of the restaurant. The fire must have started in the back, but the wind had already fanned it to the front. Most of the building was already engulfed. Clear to the roof—shake shingles, damn it—was ablaze, and the wooden-covered entry to the back stairs was a tunnel of flames.

"Red!" he shouted. "Red!"

Out of breath, Clay appeared at Brad's side, his face and form lit crimson by cavorting flames.

"Those two still up there?" Clay bellowed.

"Not sure, but that staircase is an inferno! Red! Mrs.

Gates!" he yelled. "Clay, meet the firefighters out front and have them hack in the front door. See if that front escape will work. Go!"

For one split second, Brad feared Clay would balk at taking his orders, but he ran around to the front.

Even over the wild crackle of flames, Brad could hear the fire engine and the firefighters. They could walk to this blaze; BND had not lured them away first. Of his own dire necessity, he had changed his M.O. What else had he changed in his plans?

And then, looking up as he heard a first-floor window shatter from the heat, Brad saw a face appear in the window above—no, two faces half hidden by smoke and fire. Red was waving and shouting, but he knew not to try to open the window. They must be right above the back stairs, near that entrance, checking if they dared to open that door to get out. With this side of the building so engulfed already, the firefighters would never get ladders up to reach them. And there was no escape to the roof. The blaze had been cleverly set; it had spread like a wildfire.

And unless the firefighters could break in the front entrance, Mrs. Gates and Red were trapped in that inferno.

"I'm going to turn in," Lauren told the three other women when she went downstairs. She'd washed her face with cold water and was still drying it with a towel, just in case her tears started again. "I've been trying to keep awake by throwing cold water on my face, but I need some sleep." She faked a yawn. "Dee, you take my bed and Suze can take the couch. Jen said she's pulling an all-nighter. I'm going to put a sleeping bag on Nicky's floor. Let me just get a few things out of my bedroom first."

She got a ring of keys from her drawer and jammed a credit card in her jeans pocket. If *Silver* was out of gas when she let Durand off in Kalispell, she'd need the card for a fill-up or to get to the police there. She fully expected him to just disappear into the crowd and become the Fire Phantom again somewhere else. Maybe he'd leave her and Nicky tied up in the plane. It would mean that she and the FBI team had failed, but at least she would have her son back.

From her closet she took a down-filled, sleeveless vest because she knew it could be cold flying at night in the plane. She already had jeans, a shirt, jacket and shoes for Nicky laid out upstairs, ready to go. As far as she could tell, he'd been taken out the window in his pj's and socks. With Jen on guard down here, going out the upstairs window and chancing a drop to the ground might be her only escape route too.

Lauren thought immediately of the Lindbergh-baby kidnapping so long ago. Someone had taken the son of the famous flyer, Charles Lindbergh, by using a ladder at his nursery window. The baby had turned up dead. Oh, why did she have to think of such a dreadful thing now?

Nick had become Nicky to her again. Her boy. Her baby, who she would fight to defend with her life. And with Evan Durand, it might come to that.

She went out to the kitchen and pocketed a steak

knife. Her kitchen was immaculate; Mrs. Gates would be proud. Dee and Suze had cleaned up all the dishes for her while she'd played Slides & Ladders with Nicky. Lauren went back into her bedroom for a pair of knee-socks, the tight ones she used to keep her legs massaged when she was flying long hours. She'd wear the socks and put the knife in one, just in case. Then she went back into the kitchen and dumped all the candy from Nicky's jar into a small plastic bag. The rest of her Mr. Goodbar candies went in another, and then she wrapped every-thing in her terry-cloth robe so that no one could see what she had.

"'Night, best friend," Dee said to her as Lauren started back upstairs. "Thanks for throwing the truth in my face today. I'll go see Chuck tomorrow. And," she added with a rueful laugh, "if he doesn't blurt out that he's leav-ing me, we can start to rebuild again—I hope."

Dee hugged her as Suze smiled at them. Lauren hugged her back, trying to be responsive but not desper-ate. She didn't want to give her panic away, yet she wanted to cling to Dee and sob out all of her fears.

Lauren said good-night to Jen and waved to Suze, who had gone back to the table where she'd been sketch-ing a golden eagle. Lauren thought of Brad again. Only three days ago, he'd pushed his eagle badge—his creds, as he'd called them—toward her across the table at the airport coffee shop. So short a time, yet it felt like an eter-nity ago. Would she ever see him again? Would he understand what she had to do?

As she started up the stairs, Lauren heard the distinctive crackle on Jen's radio that usually meant someone was going to talk.

"Jen!" came Mike's voice clearly over it. "Borrow Ms. Taylor's vehicle and get in here. BND's hit, and we need all the help we can get looking for him. Like last time, I'm hoping he's staying around to watch."

"Did you hear that?" Jen cried, coming to the bottom of the stairs and looking up at Lauren. "That still okay with you?"

"Yeah, anything to help," Lauren told her, wrenching her SUV key off the ring. "I'll hold down the fort here."

Dee and Suze came out into the living room at the bottom of the stairs just as Lauren tossed her key to Jen, who caught it handily.

"What's on fire?" Dee asked. Lauren chimed in too, just so she didn't stand out, though she was amazed at how little it mattered to her now. Nothing was going to stop her from trying to get her boy back.

"What's on fire?" Jen cried into her radio as she raced for the front door. "The what? He said the Bear's Den," Jen called back over her shoulder, then slammed the door behind her. Soon Lauren heard the engine start and the SUV roar away. She prayed neither Red nor Mrs. Gates were in the apartment above the restaurant tonight.

"It could spread, Mom," Suze was saying. "And where's Red? He must be safe. Why didn't they say? Let's drive in. What if the fire spreads to the health center?"

"Steve and Brad both told us to stay here," Dee argued. "But I guess we could go—if we keep out of the way. Of course, Lauren has to stay here with Nicky. Lauren, we'll leave you one of the cars. Will you be all right here alone with Nicky? I hope we didn't wake him. He'll be scared to death when he hears there's a fire."

"Go ahead, but be careful in town," Lauren told them. If she got rid of them, she could meet Evan easier. She knew she sounded like a robot, speaking slowly, one word at a time, but Dee and Suze were so distraught they didn't notice.

"And don't worry," Lauren added as they rushed for the door. "I'll take good care of Nicky."

She put her hand in her pocket and fingered the note from Evan. Yes, she had to risk meeting him alone. She couldn't wait for Brad, but she had to let him know what had happened.

Lauren raced out to the kitchen, grabbed a pencil and scribbled a few words, then dropped the note on the counter. Brad would be desperate when he found it, but not as desperate as she now felt.

16

The crackle of flames became a roar in Brad's ears as he gestured and shouted up at Red. "Go around! Other side! Front!"

More windows exploded; the two faces disappeared. Two firefighters ran around to the back of the house with ladders, only to take one look and run back to the front.

Brad followed, his lungs pierced by thickening smoke. He hacked and his eyes ran. The wind made cinders shoot aloft and drift down in erratic showers. A crowd had gathered in the street, but Clay and Mike ordered them to stay back.

Brad saw Suze's husband, Steve, take down the heavy wooden restaurant door with an ax. Thank God he was a logger, Brad thought. But only smoke belched out; no people emerged.

Steve and Suze Milliman had a son Nick's age. In another change of plans, the Fencer twins were taking care of Larson tonight. Steve had a whole life of his own to live, but Brad watched him plunge into the roiling smoke to try to save Red and Mrs. Gates.

Brad's firefighting days came back to him in bright fragments. Hot, heavy gear. Feeling his way in the blackness inside a burning building, lit only by incandescent flames. Stay low. Pray for no falling beams, no collapsing floors. The heat, the stench, the fear in your throat and gut like—

Suddenly Jen was there, pulling on his arm, tugging him away. "You can't help with that, Brad! Get back!" she screamed over the cacophony of noise.

She had David Durand with her. He wore just loafers, slacks and an open shirt, his face, lit by shimmering flames, looked both awestruck and enraged. At least he had a front-row seat for what his son had been doing, Brad thought.

"BND's also lit the B&B!" Jen cried. "Annette Lacey is safe. Mr. Durand insisted on coming with me, but Annette wouldn't leave. The chopper pilot's with her. At least there aren't any buildings close by for the blaze to spread to. But with the fire guys here, there's no help for her place."

"Is everything all right at Lauren's?" Brad demanded. "It sounds like the arsonist could have been heading that way."

"For all I know, he could have lit the B&B first and be heading *this* way," Jen insisted. "But, yeah, everything's fine at Lauren's."

Lauren put her supplies into a backpack, checked that her kneesock was going to hold the knife secure and went out the back door. For the first time, she wished she and Ross had kept guns, or that she had one of Brad's. She knew she had to hurry. Even at a sprint, it would take her ten minutes to get to the dock, and she wanted to be early. Luckily she made a habit of filling *Silver* with fuel each time she returned, so she didn't have to do that now.

Rather than taking the road, she ran along the shore she and Brad had run together toward the helicopter only a few hours ago, the shore they had ridden together on the horses toward the fire tower on the other end of town. Her flying feet didn't make the usual crunching sound on the wet pebbles, but a hissing instead.

She could see the flames from the Bear's Den fire in the sky, but she'd steeled herself for that. She prayed again that Red and Mrs. Gates had escaped safely. Then she realized the fire seemed so close, too nearby.

She gasped and paused a moment to get her bearings in the dark. Could Annette Lacey's place be on fire, too? That made dreadful sense. That's where the FBI team had met earlier and David Durand was staying. Worried now for Annette and even for the arsonist's father, she began to run toward the dock.

The black helicopter in which David Durand had made his grand entrance sat near the edge of the lake. She'd never piloted a chopper, but if it could help her, then she'd try it.

Lauren ran on until the long dock and its tethered planes popped out in silhouette before the distant flames in town. Finally she slowed her stride. She did not want to be gasping for breath when Evan Durand appeared with Nicky. She had to be in command of her mind and body in case she had an opportunity to push him in the water or use her knife on him. She would do anything to save her son and herself.

Lauren walked out onto the dock. Widely spaced pole lights cast puddles of yellow on the wooden boards. The air here smelled of smoke and was peppered with flecks of floating ash. From the Bear's Den or from the B&B? It didn't matter. She knew what she had to do. If her beloved fellow townspeople blamed and banished her for bringing destruction in, she couldn't help it. With Brad, she'd tried to help stop all this. But now she was doing what mattered most.

She went to her plane and unlocked it, then threw Nicky's clothes onto the copilot seat. When no one appeared, she paced back toward shore. Five minutes passed; her stomach knotted even tighter. What if they weren't coming? What if that note had just been a ruse to get her out of her house so that Evan could burn it, too? What if he knew about her involvement and meant to punish her for bringing in the FBI? And what if he hurt Nicky to get his revenge?

A heavy man emerged from the trees beyond the dock. No, not a heavy man, but one carrying a big bedroll. No, it was Durand, carrying Nicky wrapped up in a blanket.

She had meant to stay in control, but she tore toward them.

"Stay back and do what I say!" Durand commanded. "I have a knife at his throat!"

"Is he all right?" she asked, skidding to a stop at the end of the dock. "Nicky, are you all right?" She saw the gag now dangling under his chin.

"He lied to me, Mom. The Blackfeet ghosts will get him for lying to me about White Calf."

She understood none of that. Had he drugged the boy? But Nicky was all right—alive and feisty.

"Evan," she said, gripping her hands together so hard her fingers went numb, "leave him here on the dock, and I'll fly you anywhere you want to go."

"You'll do what I say," he said, enunciating each word exactly.

Lauren could see part of the bright blue backpack he'd arrived with beneath the bedroll strapped to his back. The knife he held to Nicky's throat glinted in the light.

"Yes, yes, fine," she told him, taking a step back.

"Then let's go. And we'll take Nicky, on his best Blackfeet behavior, with us. Now move! Let's get Heigh Ho Silver in the air!"

Brad's eyes were streaming with tears as Steve staggered out, guiding Red, who had an unconscious Mari Gates in his arms. Both Steve and Red fell to their knees in the street, then were helped up to move farther away from the flames. Brad saw that Steve had been sharing his breathing mask with them, but Mrs. Gates looked limp.

Brad rushed to help Red, but the big man wouldn't let her out of his arms. His face was black, his nose and mouth drooled mucus. His beard and hair were singed.

As for Mrs. Gates, Brad couldn't tell if she was actually breathing or if Red's shaking was just jostling her.

"Didn't see it—'til it got started," Red gasped out to Brad. "We were busy…" His words dissolved in his choking.

Did he mean in bed together? Brad thought. Suddenly both Dee and Suze appeared, rushing the security lines toward Steve. Brad recognized the nurse from the health center with them. Red finally laid Mrs. Gates on the ground and the nurse began to give her CPR.

"Dee, Suze," Brad said, catching both of them in his arms and dragging them back. "Give Steve and the nurse room. He's a hero—he saved them. Where are Lauren and Nick?"

"They're back at the house, all locked in," Dee said. "Did you get the arsonist?"

"Not yet. Can I use your truck? I've got to go check on Lauren."

Mike was suddenly at his elbow, looking distressed and distracted. "You'll do nothing of the kind," he ordered. "You, Clay and Jen are going building to building with your guns drawn, then up into the hills at first light, to flush BND out. I swear, he'll be watching this and gloating. He may have a unique—a flexible—M.O., but he's never deviated from it so far."

"Mike, he's not going to get trapped here. This place is like an island. He'll try to disappear again," Brad argued, taking the keys Suze handed him. "He came with hiking gear for a reason, and he knows the area. We need someone to watch the valley toward the mining camp, maybe even look for a hitchhiker on the single road out."

"If we don't bag him tonight, I'll order just that. But right now I'm ordering you to help the team, Agent Hale," Mike insisted, his voice cutting, despite an occasional cough from the smoke. "Chain of command, remember? Now follow orders, or I'll have you off the team so fast it will make your head spin!"

Lauren felt nauseous and dizzy, but adrenaline raged through her as she turned the key to start the airplane's engine. Behind her, Durand had tied Nicky into a seat and took the other one directly in back of her for himself. She felt as if he was breathing down her neck.

"Keep that knife away from his throat," she ordered. "It might be a rough takeoff with this choppy water, and if my son gets hurt, you'll have lost the only bargaining chip you have with me."

"Is that right?" Durand asked, his voice mocking. "What makes you think we're not just going up so we can crash right into the action uptown? I want a smooth takeoff or else."

She was amazed at the command in his voice. He'd seemed so quiet and nervous when she'd flown him into Vermillion. Surely he wanted to escape, not treat her little town the way the 9/11 terrorists had attacked the World Trade Center buildings. A terrorist—that's what Evan Durand was. An arson terrorist.

She glanced at the glowing instrument panel and throttled up, forcing herself to pay attention to her task.

Nicky had stopped whimpering, but she'd heard him breathing hard before the propellers started. They bounced a bit on the waves. There would be no smooth, skimming takeoff this time.

"Nicky, hang on, okay?" she said. "You always like to fly."

"Sure, Mom. But aren't you gonna call me Nick like Brad does?"

"Brad," Durand muttered, sitting back away from her for once. She heard him click his seat belt in. "Wondered what Macho Blond FBI's name was. Maybe we can all wave goodbye to him as we fly over. Once you get this thing aloft, I want you to circle the town once. I'm mighty proud of my magnum opus, and I want a last look."

She didn't like the way he'd said *last* look. Still, as they picked up speed across the water, she forced herself to go through her preflight routine, all the things she usually did at the dock. She checked the RPMs monitor, the fuel flow and oil pressure gauges, wishing something would go wrong so they couldn't take off.

But the plane began to climb away from the fire, into the wind. She eased off the throttle. With its lights streaming out ahead into the darkness, *Silver* rose in a long curve and then banked, heading back toward Vermillion. The roar of the engine increased with the speed, then settled into its steady hum. Usually when that sound became a constant, she felt comforted as the world slipped away.

But not now.

As Lauren looked below, a primeval blackness seemed to hover around her little town, pierced by hellish flames. The Bear's Den and perhaps the gift shop, which meant both Red's and Mrs. Gates's places, were on fire. She could see the fire engine, even people. Many had come out of their homes. Vehicles parked haphazardly showed that some had driven in from the hills. And then she saw, for the first time, that the dry grass and flower meadow on the rise behind her house was aflame.

"You lit the meadow, too?" she cried.

"The restaurant, the B&B and the field," he said, sounding so proud. "My three-act drama."

She calculated quickly. At least the wind tonight was blowing east to west off the lake, so perhaps the meadow fire would not spread to her land, her house. Winds generally blew upslope in the day and downslope at night, but tonight was different. Although the meadow fire was already spreading in the grotesque shape of a hand with grasping fingers of flame, she tried to take the wind direction as an encouraging sign. Then, too, maybe the Otter River would stop the growing conflagration before it leaped into the Vermillion Valley and from there to the canyon, lumber camp and dry conifer forests that stretched for miles.

But if she lost Nicky—or Durand killed both of them—what would any of that matter?

She wanted to live, and she swore she would win the struggle this madman had challenged her to.

"You want to waggle the wings at them?" she asked. "Just to show them you've won?"

"I've only won if the fire at the B&B caught my father there, and if he realized I lit it because I hate him. Because he deserved to die that way," he said, his voice suddenly so loud, so passionate and furious.

"You want your dad to die in a fire?" Nicky piped up. "But—"

"Shut up!" Durand screamed.

"Nicky, be quiet," Lauren said and waggled the wings right over the main street. People looked up and pointed, then the plane was out over the blackness of Lost Lake again.

"I didn't give you permission to do that!" Durand shouted and flashed the knife at her, reaching up between the seats so it caught in her hair and nicked her right earlobe.

She almost went into a steep dive to see if she could shake him or get him to drop the knife, but it was too dangerous. If only Brad had seen *Silver* and guessed what had happened! Meanwhile, she had to stay calm—deadly calm.

"I'm setting a course to get you to Kalispell," she told Durand, ignoring how her earlobe burned. She was certain it was bleeding down the side of her neck.

"Hardly," he said, surprising her again. "You think I'm really going to risk your putting down there and having the cops or more FBI waiting to arrest me? Come around again and head up the Vermillion Valley toward the logging camp. And no more tricks!"

"But that's a narrow valley, bad enough to fly in during the day. The winds are weird tonight. The up-and-down drafts can almost rip wings off planes near the mountains, so—"

"Just do it—or else. You've got much more to lose than I do, Mrs. Ross Taylor, so just do it!"

"Did you see that?" Brad demanded, pulling Mike's arm and pointing up as the silver plane seemed to disappear into the cloudy darkness after a long loop out over the lake. "Damn it, that's Lauren, and two to one, Durand's forcing her to fly him out."

"We'll alert all the airports within the radius of her gas tank," Mike told him, still squinting up at the sky. "That can't be too many places."

"BND's proved he's no fool, but we are if we rely on that! The plane turned south between Mount Jefferson and Mount Nizitopi, not east toward Kalispell. I'm going after her. None of us would even have a lead on BND if it wasn't for her."

"Going after her how?" Mike demanded, swinging Brad around as, keys in hand, he started for Suze's truck. "In that?"

"I'll get someone who flies one of the other planes. We'll never find them if we wait until daylight."

"I'll help you," David Durand said, stepping up. "It's the least I can do. My chopper pilot said he had extra fuel, though I guess we'd have to pay him overtime. He's back with Mrs. Lacey, trying to comfort her."

Comfort her, Brad thought. There was no comfort in any of this. He didn't care what Mike said or did to him. He didn't care if his entire life's goal to make and help the FBI arson team went to hell.

"All right, Durand, let's go," he said, nodding. "The

chopper may be able to put down places another pontoon plane wouldn't."

Still, Brad didn't like or trust the man. Even though Evan Durand was ultimately responsible for his own actions, and other kids who'd been ignored by their fathers didn't turn to arson and murder, David Durand was partly to blame for the monster his son had become.

Mike muttered something, but Brad kept going. As he backed the truck away from the fire, he saw that someone had pulled the EMR vehicle out of the firehouse. Next to it, Red Russert was being cared for, laid out on the ground, breathing oxygen. But Brad didn't see Mrs. Gates's petite form anywhere. Hopefully she was in the EMR being tended to.

He skidded the truck in a half turn, the way he'd been taught to drive at FBI school in case other cars blocked in a vehicle for an abduction. Was that what Lauren was facing? With Nicky or without? He hit the brakes and backed up again, sticking his head out the window.

"Dee! Can you and Suze borrow a car and go to Lauren's house to see if Nicky's there?"

"That was her plane!" Dee shouted, running up to the truck. "You don't think he has her and Nicky?"

"I'm going to take Durand's chopper and find out. But Nicky may be at their house, may be hurt..."

"Yes, Suze and I will get a car and go together. We— oh, no!"

She gaped past the truck, toward the other end of town. Brad craned his neck. Sheriff Chuck Cobern walked unsteadily toward them, wearing pants under his flapping hospital gown.

"Take him with you, Dee. Get him away from here," Brad told her and gunned the truck toward the B&B. It would have been easy enough to find from the light in the sky, but the entire area above and beyond seemed to be aglow too. Could the B&B fire have leaped to some parched trees? No, the lights in the sky were too bright, like a thousand aurora borealis. And that couldn't be the reflection from the flames in town.

"Looks like your son's set the meadow on fire, too!" Brad said.

"Then we'll have to call in air tankers and hotshot teams," Durand said. "I can recommend several good crew bosses to assess the extent of it and what else will be needed."

Brad slowed to pass a car coming at him, no doubt other area people drawn to town by the flames and smoke. He tried to get a grip on himself. He could not believe this man. So calculating and calm. If his own son had done this… If *he* had a son…

Nick. Nick had to be safe.

"And if your son's lit all this," Brad challenged as he sped up again, "and is heading up the Vermillion Valley, what's next to be torched?"

"What's up that valley past the Otter River?" Durand demanded. "More than forests and subalpine meadows? Any problems beyond that?"

"Other than the fact that it's almost too narrow to fly during the daytime, let alone at night? After a narrow canyon, there's a lumber camp on the far side and access to dry virgin timber up to the snow line for miles of mountains."

"Is that the area Annette Lacey told me used to be sacred to the Blackfeet, with burial grounds and all that?"

"Yeah, maybe, but it's not the Blackfeet I'm worried about. We're going to have Mrs. Lacey get in this truck and go back to town to find Mike. He can call in help."

"But I'm the one who's the expert on wildfires, not your FBI boss. It seems to me he's made a mess of things."

Brad gripped the steering wheel so hard he could have wrenched it from its base. "Durand, you can put all this in your next book, or explain your expertise on how to raise a serial arsonist murderer on your next lecture circuit. But right now, you're taking orders from me."

"I'm the one who hired the helicopter, Agent Hale!"

"And I'm going to arrest you for withholding evidence, for not coming forward earlier with everything you knew about your son, so just—"

"I had no idea! I swear it!"

"You know what's sad? I believe you!" Brad yelled as he braked a distance from the still-seething shell of the B&B. Two figures emerged and walked toward them. "Now get out and explain things to the pilot while I tell Annette Lacey, as shaken and grieved as she must be, what she needs to do."

17

It was challenging enough to navigate the Vermillion Valley in the light, but this was a nightmare. Lauren tried to level off, to fly between the cliffs and crags from memory as much as by her headlights and instruments. Above the rock-walled valley in the ricocheting winds, she fought the rudder pedals, fought the wing flaps and the wheel. And fought her fears.

They had left behind the burning meadow and the Otter River. If she had to crash-land, she could only pray that, despite the drought, there would be enough water in the smaller braided river that fed the Otter or in the slender, shallow lake beyond to handle a pontoon-plane landing. But the pontoons could be pierced by rocks or ripped apart by logs; the plane could tip over. It would be dangerous to land, but she had to convince Evan to let her try. She'd tell him that she could show him where to follow the road down from the lumber camp. He could hitchhike or even take a vehicle by force there—anything to make him let her land and let Nicky go.

Her mind raced. She had a CB radio on board, but she couldn't turn it on without static that would give her away. She wished she'd bought that expensive Emergency Locator Transmitter, which would have gone off automatically in a crash or could be manually activated so rescue forces could locate the downed plane. The baggage compartment behind the wing contained survival gear such as flares, mess kits, water and blankets, but you first had to put down safely to get to—or need—any of that.

"If you insist on flying in this direction," she told Evan, trying to keep her voice steady though the plane trembled, "there's no way to land in heavy forests. And our gas won't go far enough to get us to any sort of runway in this direction."

"And I siphoned some of it off," he said with a little laugh. "Great accelerant for the B&B and the grass field."

She was beyond being shocked and only squinted at the gas gauge. About an eighth of a tank less than she had assumed.

"Yeah, we should land soon," he went on, "because I have much more planned."

"Mom, he's got a drip torch just like Dad's that he's unwrapping from his sleeping bag!" Nicky cried out. "He's going to start more fires!"

"Quiet! Evan, there's only one place I can turn near here to circle back and try to land in the small lake and stream that feeds the Otter River," she said. "The turn must come over the logging camp, then I'll have to go lower than I'd like until my headlights reflect off the water."

"Mom, you might hit some otters or beaver. And Brad said you saw an elk when you were walking back from the ski lift."

"Ah," Evan said, "out of the mouths of babes. Brad, Brad, Brad. I see I should have talked a great deal more to Nicky and not just about Blackfeet business."

"You lied to me!" Nicky yelled. "You—"

"Nicky," Lauren shouted, "do not argue or say one more word! I need to concentrate."

"In short," Evan said, "your mother doesn't know the first thing about the bond between Running Deer and Chief White Calf. Always use your imagination, boy, and don't listen to your mother. I learned not to listen to mine. I did better without my father around, too, the SOB."

"What does SOB spell?"

"Nicky, please!" Lauren cried as she began to bank over the lumber camp she could not see below. Her compass and her gut told her she was right, but if not, both Mount Jefferson and Mount Nizitopi could be much too close.

She brought the plane around just as she had the day she and Brad buzzed Red's high camp. How excited Brad had been to fly with eagles, to see the reach of the valley and the beauty of this place. Now the land she loved most had turned terrible and terrifying.

Dee and Chuck sat in the back seat of a borrowed car while Suze drove. "Once we check on Nicky," Suze said, "I'm going to the Fencers' to get Larson. I don't care what time of night it is."

"They live far enough around the mountain that they may not have seen the fires," Chuck said. Dee could tell he was in pain, but he was covering it up. His voice had even regained some of its strength. "He may be sound asleep and best left that way for now, honey," he told Suze.

"I just have to see him, be with him, Dad. You understand."

"Sure. Sure I do."

He scooted closer to Dee. She knew he longed to put his arms around her but couldn't manage with one shoulder broken and the other wrist sprained. With one arm, she reached around his back and hugged him hard.

He shifted his hand to her knee and squeezed it weakly. They hadn't said the words they needed to yet, but they were together. And Suze, too, all talking, all working in unison.

"Look!" Suze cried. "The lights are on at Lauren's. At least that pyro didn't torch this place, but that meadow fire's too close for comfort."

"We'll check the house for clues—for Nicky," Chuck said, "then hightail it back so I can help coordinate the wildfire teams we've got coming from Kalispell and Missoula."

They climbed out of the truck, Chuck with difficulty, though Dee sensed she should not help him. Suze ran up to the door and tried the knob. "It's locked."

"Here's the key!" Dee cried. She wanted to sob against Chuck's shoulder but she needed to be sure it wasn't just the emotion of this dreadful night affecting her. No, she was sure it wasn't. What had happened in town—and at the B&B they'd passed—had broken her heart, but not as much as how she and Chuck had hurt each other.

Suze took the key and opened the front door. "Nicky?" she shouted as she went in, followed by Dee and Chuck. "Nicky!"

"Mom," she said, turning back to Dee, "I'm scared to look upstairs."

"I'll case the place down here," Chuck said. "You two go upstairs and be careful. At least the arsonist isn't here, we know that much."

Dee and Suze tore through Nicky's room, bathroom. They even looked in the closets. "Nothing!" Dee called to Chuck as the two of them thudded down the stairs. "I'm not sure if that's good or bad, but— What is it?" she asked as she saw Chuck leaning against the kitchen counter, carefully holding something with a torn piece of paper towel to avoid touching it.

As she went closer, she stepped on several spilled M&M candies. They crunched under her feet on the pine-plank floor.

"On the counter," Chuck said, "I found this crazy note that says the arsonist took Nicky, and threatens his life if Lauren didn't help him. The damn thing rhymes like a poem."

"Oh, no. Oh, no!" Suze cried, craning her neck to read it. "Do you think she left it here for us or dropped it?"

"Left it, but not for us—see?" he said, and flipped the note over so they could read the back of it.

BRAD—HELP was scribbled in big but shaky printing.

"Nicky's writing?" Suze asked.

"I think it's Lauren's, written in haste," Dee told them and threw her arms around Chuck's neck.

"Never thought I'd say this," he whispered, his voice rough, "but later for that. We've got to get going."

"But Brad's already gone after her."

"It's too vast out there—and too damn dry if that pyro has so much as a few matches with him. Now, if I could hug both of you to me and never let you go, Dee, I would."

She sniffed hard and pulled herself away, swiping at her tears. "What's happening to Lauren and Nicky makes me realize that I never should have wasted so much time between us."

"Save that thought, sweetheart, 'cause we've got to save this area from an inferno. And Brad and whoever else we send in have got to save Lauren and Nicky."

Determinedly, with more speed than Dee thought he could muster, Chuck started for the front door. Yes, she admired the sheriff as much as she loved him, she realized, and hurried to catch up.

After her half circle over the lumber camp, Lauren headed the plane back into the Vermillion Valley, into the wind. It lifted *Silver* and she had to fight it to descend.

Both Nicky and Evan were silent now. Did he have the knife to her son's throat? If only she could risk grabbing the blade she had in her kneesock under her left pant leg, she might be able to lunge at Evan with it. But he could hurt Nicky before she even got her seat belt loose. And in a struggle, it wouldn't take much for the plane to veer, to crack a wing into the cliffs, to go down.

"The lake will come up before the river." She spoke aloud, mostly to herself. "I'll try to land on the lake, not the river, unless there's no other way. Nicky, put your head between your knees and hug your legs."

She gasped when she saw that she had come down too steep and too fast—too soon! She slammed the flaps down full and backed off the power. Treetops rushed at her before she saw the distant glint of water. Yes, the north end of the lake was almost under her. If she could just miss these trees…

One of the pontoons brushed, then clipped a treetop. Nicky screamed as the plane jerked and shuddered. Lauren struggled to control its path and descent. She was over water now, choppy in the wind funneling down the valley, the waves coming at her with small whitecaps. That was good, she told herself as she flew even lower. Movement on water could help her to judge distance and height. She glanced at her altimeter again. Next to nothing—nothing…

She was tempted to shout at Evan to loosen his seat belt, hoping in the trauma of the moment that he'd mindlessly obey and then get knocked around. But Nicky might unlock his, too. And even a small body could go right through the windshield if the plane landed wrong.

The minute they were down, even though the waves made them buck a bit, Evan had the knife to her throat.

"Nothing funny now," he told her.

"Get that away from me," she ordered. "How am I going to lean forward to shut down these engines and coast us in? Or do you want to get out in the middle of this rocky water—Rocky?"

"Very good," he said. "Touché—or 'touchy' as an actor friend of mine used to say. Touchy, touchy, Lauren—knife to throat," he taunted, bouncing the blade width-wise against her skin instead of cutting her with the edge.

"You leave her alone," Nicky said. Lauren could tell from his nasal voice that he'd been crying. If Evan didn't leave them with the plane—if he insisted they continue as his hostages—she was going to have to keep Nicky quiet. Evan's already volatile temper was dangerous, and he'd probably keep that knife on the boy. She prayed he'd leave them here. Rescue efforts might find the plane, but if they set off into the tree cover between here and the lumber camp, they'd never be spotted from the air.

"How much flying time do we have?" Brad asked Len Woodruff, the chopper pilot, as they lifted off and tilted toward the Vermillion Valley. They had to shout to be heard over the rumble of the rotors. Brad had comman-deered the copilot's seat and put David Durand in back.

"I'm not sure—hour and a half, maybe," Len told him.

Durand's hired pilot had been more than willing to help. Evidently he thought it was a grand adventure to be chasing one of the FBI's Most Wanted.

At least, Brad thought, a chopper didn't need to take long turns around the lake or large curves to gain alti-tude. As late a start as they were getting, maybe they could make up for lost time. This baby had a big sweep-light, too.

Brad had seldom been in choppers, and flying in this one made him nervous as hell, though he was grateful for its ability to turn on a dime or hover. From within the invisible bubble of the cockpit, he had a 180-degree view of the yellow-and-crimson meadow fire before they flew into drifting, blowing smoke and night again. Ahead loomed a vast, blind blackness. Nothing was visible except for what the front lights or sweeping beam beneath the belly of this beast illumined.

"Since you're not used to flying in these mountains, Woodruff," David Durand shouted from the back seat, "no heroics. We can't stop or rescue anyone if we go down. And what if we catch up to them and crack into them in the dark?"

"We're at a much lower altitude and with more control than a prop plane could handle, Mr. Durand. I feel like I'm playing a video game, but a real one with escarpments and narrow passages—as you can see."

Despite the man's bravado, Brad could see the pilot sometimes struggled to keep the controls steady and to work the directional pedals. The turbulence up here was buffeting them around, not only side to side, but up and down.

"I'm trying not to look," Durand shouted, "except straight ahead. But the smoke's starting to get pushed through here, too. We'll never see a red taillight, never see—"

Brad exploded, "If you don't have anything to contribute but grief and fear, Durand, don't say anything!"

He hadn't been this upset since his father had been

declared guilty and was taken out of the courtroom in handcuffs and leg hobbles. Lauren and Nick—they had to spot them, save them from this man's brilliantly crazy son and his lust for fire. He tried to calm himself, to speak more civilly.

"To the best of your knowledge," Brad said to Durand as they kept scanning the sky ahead of them, "could Evan have set wildfires before? He's done a couple of woodlots, so I think the urge is there."

"Absolutely not—just the opposite. I think he's temporarily insane, and I intend for that to be his legal defense. Like me, he's fought fires. He worked for the National Park Service each summer, usually in California. And I'll have you know, he got the jobs himself without my pulling strings. I didn't even know at first, but I was very pleased to learn it later."

"California? Did he work the Coyote Canyon wildfire there?"

"Not that I know of. Besides, that wasn't an arson fire."

"But once it got going, some of it spread as if it was," Brad argued. He hadn't mentioned it to Lauren yet, but he'd picked that much up just from skimming the articles in her scrapbooks. And now he couldn't help wondering if Evan had had something to do with the Coyote Canyon wildfire.

But Brad kept his mouth shut on that for now. All that mattered was finding Lauren and Nick before it was too late.

However, he had learned one other thing from Durand. He now understood where Evan had earned the money to live on the rest of the year, which allowed him to move around, study his victims and torch houses. Lauren had told him that even firefighters at the lowest levels, the grunts who worked with spades and root rippers to fight high-risk wildfires, could take home paychecks of up to thirty-five hundred dollars for two weeks of work, not counting overtime and hazard pay. And those guys went from blaze to blaze during the fire season. Whether or not Evan had been a busker or an actor, his personal arson schedule would have meshed perfectly with wildfire fighting.

"We're above some sort of divided river with islands between its strands," Len told them. "I'm going to have to go up a bit—trees too close ahead."

"There's a little lake beyond, then trees, a narrow canyon and then the logging camp," Brad told him, recalling how it had all looked from the air when he and Lauren had flown over. "After that, forests stretch forever. Lauren's plane has probably gone on, but see if you can slow down and sweep the river and little lake with that beam. I don't know if she could put down there, but we have to keep our options open."

"Will do, but slowing and hovering in these winds will take more fuel."

The minute Lauren opened *Silver*'s door to get out, she thought she could hear the *thwack thwack* of a helicopter's blades somewhere above and beyond them. Surely that's what it was, not just the strange echoes from Weeping Wall Falls. If she could get her lights back on for a signal, or just start talking and make some noise, so that Evan didn't hear the chopper until it was too late…

"Nicky, are you all right?" she asked loudly, clicking her seat belt off and turning in her seat. She hit the interior light on. Now to get the wing lights going…

But Evan reached forward and grabbed her shoulder. He slammed her back in her seat.

"They're coming," he said, "but they're not going to get me until I've completed my work. I've got the knife you know where, so kill that dome light and start up again—and no exterior lights. I just hope the illustrious firefighter and king of the world, David Durand, is in that helicopter. Lauren, start the plane up again and run it up onto the shore here. Get it under those trees now!"

She clicked off the dome light but tried to stall for more time. "We hit tree limbs before we landed," she said. "I think one of the pontoons is damaged. We may be taking on water, so I don't know if—"

"Do it!" he shrieked.

She blinked back tears. Turning the ignition key, she revved up the engines again. Unable to think of any way out of this but to obey him, she hit the throttle and let the plane coast toward the shore. As she did, she saw a sweeping beam of light zigzagging across the water behind her reflected in her front windshield. This maniac had been right. They were searching for her plane!

She heard Nicky whimper as the pontoons hit several rocks in shallow water. They bumped and crunched while the plane skidded sideways onto the stone-littered shore. The wings and fuselage made it under the aspens untouched, but swept into the lower branches of spruce and pine that swiped at the windshield like brushes in an automated car wash gone mad.

The nose bounced to a stop against a tree trunk, jerking them in their seat belts. Lauren could hear the propeller hacking into the branches as it slowed with a final shudder.

Overhead, the chopper sounded louder. For one second a searchlight blinded them like a strobe, then jumped away as the chopper noise faded.

Lauren sucked in a big breath. To be so close and yet so far from help was almost too much. Tears streamed silently down her cheeks, but she swiped them away with her palms. Nicky's safety—that's what she was living for now.

"I see nothing along the river or lake," Len Woodruff said. "Is there any kind of landing pad at the logging camp?"

Brad's neck ached from craning it to look down. The spotlight from the chopper helped, but its reflection off the water sometimes made him think he'd seen a light or distress signal where there evidently was none.

"Yeah, there must be a landing spot at the camp," he said. "Lauren mentioned that some of the logging company bigwigs fly in on choppers sometimes. Her plane couldn't put down in that small of a space, but maybe in an opening there at the camp."

"Such as a concrete driveway for logging trucks," Len said.

"I saw the camp once briefly from the air, but I can't recall," Brad admitted. He felt disappointed and exhausted—but not defeated. "I think they send most of the logs via an old flume down to trucks waiting below."

"I'm not only thinking of Lauren putting her plane down," Len admitted. "We're lower on gas than I thought, so unless you want to try to make it all the way back to Vermillion, bucking that big wind and the smoke blowing into the valley, I think we'd better land at the camp. First light's only a few hours off, and they'll be looking for her—and us—by then."

"If they can spare men from fighting that meadow fire," David Durand put in. "The thing is, with these tricky winds and the draft this valley makes, let alone the narrow canyon you mentioned, the meadow fire could possibly leap into it and sweep this way. Canyon fires are notorious for fast spreads."

"And if your son is anywhere around," Brad added, "he could just start another fire."

Maybe Len sensed another shouting match, because he asked again, "You want to try to make it back to Vermillion, Agent Hale? I see the logging camp up ahead, so tell me now. I think I even see a helipad with a big X."

"Let's go back," Durand said.

"Put me down here first," Brad ordered. "Evan didn't make Lauren head into this valley without a plan, and that probably didn't include flying into endless mountains and timber where he couldn't get back on firm ground to do his thing. And take Durand back with you. The arson team thought the mere sight of his father might be enough to set BND off, so maybe I shouldn't be gambling on letting him help me—and his son."

"I resent that!" Durand shouted as the chopper descended toward the helipad. "I had no idea how sick—temporarily insane—Evan is, but I'm probably the only one who could help him, who could talk him out of any more fires. I should be back advising everyone on controlling that meadow fire, but if Woodruff here is willing to refuel and come back for us tomorrow morning, then I'll stay."

Brad was torn. He actually was afraid that, if Evan spotted his father, he'd try to impress him with more fire. On the other hand, he probably wanted his father to suffer more than he did Lauren or Nicky. And getting Evan distracted long enough to jump him could be priceless.

"Then I'm staying too," Len said. He was a big man, a bit too old to be tramping through the brush looking for a plane, but Brad admired his fortitude. "Besides, this bird's right on the borderline of not having enough fuel to get back," he admitted.

"Len," Brad said, "if you can surveil the logging camp and try to contact help on your radio—either from the chopper or from any phones you can find on site—I'll head back up the valley with Durand. I swear, Lauren's plane has to be behind us."

Brad didn't know if David Durand could keep up, but he wasn't going to let him slow him down. He reached under his feet for his duffel bag with his guns and ammunition. Lauren and Nick's safety was what he was working for now.

18

"I think the helicopter's gone. Get out. Get out!" Evan shouted, shoving Lauren's shoulder. She opened the door, pushed some spruce branches back and jumped out onto the ground.

Evan took his time, keeping the knife against Nicky's throat, emerging from the plane while holding the boy tight to him.

"Get back and stay back!" he warned her. "We may be on the ground, but don't think you're safe. No way."

Her insides cartwheeled when she saw Nicky's face glazed with tears. He was biting his lower lip, trying to hold himself together. No way was Evan going to drag her son any farther with that knife to his throat.

"Evan," Lauren said, "just leave us here and go. I've done what you asked. I'll show you the path to get out of this area."

"And you'll go with me on it."

"But Nicky will slow you down. I might, too. You can follow one of the two hiking trails out to the logging camp and its access road."

Months ago she'd heard Red say that there were two trails here. One trail followed the valley and canyon floor, while the other wended its way along a slightly elevated ridge. Surely one or both headed north from this end of the lake, where the valley narrowed to the canyon.

When Evan didn't answer, she thought, so much for the bravado. Now for the begging, which might get her further with this self-centered, volatile man anyway. She gripped her hands so hard together that her fingers went numb.

"Evan," she said, forcing herself to look at him instead of Nicky, "I will be so grateful to you if you leave us here in the safety of the plane."

"You want to make a deal? How about this? I'll leave him, and you can lead me out of here."

"I can't leave him alone."

"Someone will find the plane. You're right, he would slow us down. I'd like to just vanish like a ghost, but—"

"Then get going. I'll point out the path to the logging camp and the access road. And you'll get the Boy Next Door back in business, having made fools of your father and the FBI."

"My, my, very well spoken and quite a fine attempt to manipulate me. I told them I wanted to be called the Fire Phantom or the Smoke Ghost, and after this I will be."

"You told me you were a ghost," Nicky choked out.

"See, it wasn't really a fib at all," Evan said. "And isn't this the area where the Blackfeet ghosts still roam?"

"Y-yes-s," Nicky managed to say, wide-eyed. For the first time, he glanced away from Lauren to skim the spruce branches bowing in the blowing darkness. Beyond, the quaking aspens shivered their leaves.

"Please stop scaring him more than you already have," Lauren said.

"Mom, don't leave me here."

"All right!" Evan shouted, and for one moment Lauren thought she'd won. But he shoved Nicky toward her, pocketed the knife, produced a gun from that same pocket and pointed it at her. When Nicky clung to her, she thrust him away so a bullet couldn't hit him, too.

"Don't use that, don't point it!" she cried. "I'll do what you want."

"You just bet you will," he shrieked, then seemed to quickly gain control again. "Now, you have been of help to me, so I'll give you five minutes to end this charming soap-opera scene by bidding him goodbye. Then he stays and you go with me."

She gaped at him before she closed her mouth. Survival for Nicky was the goal of this game now.

When Evan lowered the gun, she pulled Nicky to her and hugged him hard. What if she never saw him again, her Nicky who wanted to be a big boy?

"Nick," she said, holding him at arm's length in a crushing grip with both hands, "listen to me. You must not be afraid, because someone will be looking for the plane as soon as it gets light, and that's in just a little while. You are going to have to stay not only with the plane but *in* the plane."

"In case of bears or mountain lions?" he asked, his voice very small. "Or ghosts?"

"There are no ghosts here, that's just stories. But yes, stay in *Silver* to be safe. But if you hear a plane overhead after it gets light, look carefully around for wild animals…"

Dear God, she thought in a fragmented, frenzied prayer, a wild animal is here with us now. Please keep my son safe.

"…and if you don't see any, you could run out and wave your red jacket so they see you. But if they pass overhead, get back in the plane for protection."

"I don't have my red jacket."

"It's in the plane with a pair of shoes and some M&Ms for you. And I'm going to leave you my candy bars, though I know you don't like peanuts and—"

"You know, Nicky," Evan put in, "the Mr. Goodbars from the top shelf to the left of the sink in the kitchen."

Lauren's heart pounded harder. Evan Durand was a ghost; he'd been in her house, in the downstairs as well as in Nicky's room. But she went on, "And whatever happens, honey, I want you to know I love you and think you are the best son ever."

"Cut!" Evan roared, suddenly sounding angry again. He lifted his gun at them. "Great acting job, Mom. Now let's go. If you've got any gear to help us, get it."

Holding Nicky's hand and pulling him along with her, Lauren went over to open the hatch behind the wing. As Evan came closer to watch what she was doing, she took out two canteens she always had filled with water, showed them to him, thrust one at Nicky, then slung the strap of the other one over her shoulder. However pristine the streams and lakes around here looked, they could carry a microscopic germ that messed up your intestines worse than Montezuma's revenge. Black-feet revenge, Red Russert had called it when he'd warned her and Ross. Maybe Evan didn't know that and she could convince him to drink the crystal-clear water.

The knife pressing against her calf seemed to burn her. What if he discovered she had the weapon before she could use it? She picked up two flashlights and checked both, then held one out to Nicky.

"No," Evan said. "Charity only goes so far. Both of us will need one of those, at least until daylight. As you said, it will be light soon and a brave like Running Deer won't be afraid, will you?"

"I don't want my mom to leave me."

Lauren started to cry. How terrified he'd been after Ross died if she even went into the next room in broad daylight. He'd come so far since then.

"You'll be all right," she told him, fighting to keep her voice steady. "And if the meadow fire should come near here, wade out into the lake until it goes by and—"

"You know, Running Deer," Evan cut in, "for the Black-feet tribe, rivers and lakes have a special power. I was just reading online the other day that they're inhabited by the sacred underwater people called Suyitapis and—"

"I don't believe anything you say about them any-more!" Nicky insisted. "I won't believe that unless Mrs. Gates says it's true! Mom, I do smell smoke."

"Yes, but it's just blowing in on the wind. Get up in the plane now. Be safe, my Nicky—my Nick."

"Be safe, Mom," he cried. It broke her heart. She bent

to hug him again but, the gun in his hand, Evan dragged him a few steps away and boosted him up into the cockpit, then slammed the door on him.

Lauren almost seized her knife to lunge at him, but he still held the gun, and she didn't want Nicky to see what would happen. Their eyes had greatly adjusted to the darkness under these thick trees. What if Evan shot her and no help came, or Nicky got back out of the plane to help and got hurt…

No, she'd lead Evan a little ways off before she tried anything like that. And if she could stop him somehow, she'd run back to be with Nicky. But she had no chance to tell him that. She waved to him and tried to force a smile, but her face felt frozen.

"Let's go," Evan said. She tore her eyes from the pale circle that was her son's face in the plane's window. Evan swung his big backpack at her, keeping the smaller bedroll for himself to carry. "And no tricks like trying to lead me back toward town. You just get me to the lumber camp fast. Above all, don't get clever or cute. To paraphrase Shakespeare, 'Thus do all things conspire against you.'"

He wagged the gun at her and grinned as they started away. "You see," he rambled on, "as much as I hate guns, I had to borrow this from the sheriff's own desk."

"You've been inside their house, too?"

"Oh, yes. I didn't want to use this in the plane in case I hit some of the controls, but I have no problem using it on terra firma. Now, I may be the best of arsonists," he went on, his voice lighthearted as he clicked his flashlight on and shined it in her face, making her stumble, "but I can't claim to be the best of shots. Still, I assure you, we will be close enough that I would have no trouble hitting you."

She clicked on her flashlight and moved away from him, searching for a sign of the trailhead that must be near. Behind her, as if he didn't have a care in the world, Evan was humming the tune to "Follow the Yellow Brick Road" from *The Wizard of Oz.* To that same melody, he sang, "Follow the trail to the camp. Follow it right through the night. And find me, find me, find me, find me a forest to light."

"Why's this thing moving?" Red Russert asked, startling as if coming out of a trance.

Dee knew the EMR vehicle was bouncing him on his gurney as it pulled up to the dock. She hoped the movement wasn't hurting Mrs. Gates, who was already in a great deal of pain. Dee had volunteered to come along to watch Red while the more seriously hurt woman was tended to. The doctor had a wide-open saline drip going in her arm, and she was swathed in sterile, dry dressings on both legs and one arm. Her hair, like Red's, was singed, including the hair in her nostrils, which indicated—Dee had overheard—severe smoke inhalation. Dee wasn't sure what they had given Mrs. Gates for her pain, but the woman had been moaning.

Red turned his head and stared at Dee. "Are we at the health clinic?" he asked.

"At the dock. Jim Hatfield was going to fly Mrs. Gates into the Kalispell Regional Medical Center, but they're sending their air ambulance for her. We're meeting them on the shore here."

"I'm going with her," he insisted, trying to get off his gurney. Perched in the jump seat at the head of Red's gurney, Dee leaned closer to him, hoping he wouldn't guess how touch-and-go it had been for Mrs. Gates so far.

"The fires out now?" he asked.

"All but the one in the meadow. Because of the prevailing winds, that blaze is spreading upslope and into the Vermillion Valley. You're not as badly burned, so you're going to be admitted to the health clinic here."

"Like hell, if they're sending her to Kalispell."

"Red," Dee whispered and tried in vain to hold him down, "you need to rest. You've inhaled enough smoke to—"

"To be smoking mad!" he finished for her, then started coughing and fell back momentarily. But it didn't stop him from adding in a raspy voice, "That idiot arsonist must have targeted Mari and me, known where we were, maybe 'cause I tracked him back to town. But if they're transporting her, I'm going, too."

Dee was amazed at the man's strength as he firmly pushed off her attempts to hold him and swung his big, bare feet over the side of the gurney.

The doctor and nurse must have heard him, but they didn't budge from their positions bent over Mrs. Gates. For a moment, Dee was afraid Red would push them away, too. She could glimpse Mrs. Gates's profile, and her usually alert, animated face was almost completely covered by an oxygen mask that hissed softly.

The nurse started to protest, but Red wedged his broad shoulders between them and knelt in the narrow aisle between the gurneys.

"She conscious?" he asked, then didn't wait for an answer. "Mari? Mari, my love."

The nurse and doctor stepped apart and looked at each other but they didn't interfere. Dee sank onto the edge of the gurney that Red had vacated.

"Mari?" he repeated.

Dee leaned closer. She could see the woman open one eye, just above the top of the oxygen mask. Had she and Chuck gone through the years of their marriage like that—with barriers between them, wearing masks?

"Mari, I'm going with you," Red insisted. "And you're gonna be all right. We're gonna finish what we started— you hear?"

She seemed to answer with what little was left of her singed eyebrows, moving them up and down. Then she lifted her unbandaged hand, wagged her index finger at him and tried to speak.

Red lowered his head, right ear down, close to her mask. "What?" he asked. "Who? FBI—oh, Brad? He went after Lauren and Nicky in a chopper, 'cause it looks like the arsonist took them. Mari—Mari, don't you move now, sweetheart."

They heard the *chop chop* of the arriving air ambulance getting louder as it set down on the shore in the halo of its own lights. Mrs. Gates's protruding finger pointed at Red again, then out the door.

"You're not sending me away, Mari, 'cause I'm not going."

He started hacking. She repeated her motions even as the doctor said, "We're going to carry her out to the evac chopper now, Mr. Russert. You'll have to move aside."

"I told you, I'm going with her!" Red insisted as Mrs. Gates made her two jerky motions again: You—out.

"Red," Dee said, jumping up to take his arm and trying to pull him back. "For her own good—for her health—you've got to let them take her."

Red was crying. Whoever thought Red Russert—trapper, hunter and former lumberjack—would cry, and over a woman who hadn't given him the time of day for years? But what was really getting to her was more memories of her and Chuck. He'd been hurt, flown to Kalispell, and she'd intentionally stayed here. Unlike Red, she had said she didn't want to go with him.

When Dee tried again to tug Red back from Mrs. Gates's gurney, he felt like petrified stone. He didn't budge, and Dee feared he might gather the small woman up in his arms and race off with her into the night. She could tell the doctor didn't know what to do.

"You realize," Dee told Red as the thought came to her, "that she asked you first about Brad, and you told her that he, Lauren and Nicky were in trouble. I think she's telling you to go find them, help them, not to stay away from her."

Red sniffed hard as the doctor and a paramedic from the chopper rolled Mrs. Gates's gurney out, then carried it away. He stayed on his knees. "You think that's what she meant?" he asked with a sniff.

"She's the one who said you'd do a great job tracing the arsonist from the ski lift," Dee assured him. "Lauren told me that. I'm going to ride back to town with you, but I promise I will send someone in a plane tomorrow morning to stay with Mrs. Gates in Kalispell. She won't be alone, Red."

"No. If the two of us live through this, Mari Gates won't be alone anymore, I swear it."

"So get a good rest tonight at the clinic. And when the firefighting crews get here tomorrow, you'll be ready to—"

"I'm ready now," he told her. He turned and sat down hard on the narrow platform where Mrs. Gates's gurney had been. "I'll let 'em patch me up, borrow some boots and gear and head out. I know a back way into that valley where it meets the canyon. I'll leave that info with the FBI team and the sheriff. But I'm not waiting around for outside help. Brad Hale didn't, either, 'cause, just like me, he fell fast and hard for a woman, though he might not know it yet."

Since Brad already had a jacket, Len Woodruff gave Durand his. Then with the only flashlight Len had to loan them, shoving back foliage with three-foot tree limbs, they set out on a fairly discernible floor-level canyon path back toward the Vermillion Valley. If Lauren had given this canyon a name when they'd flown over, Brad didn't recall it.

He wondered if this was the path Suze had taken to get up to Cedar Ridge where he and Lauren had seen her painting less than forty-eight hours ago. But if so, she must have cut up on a higher trail somewhere. If he could find Lauren and Nicky and they could make it to that high rock, maybe the flames would pass them, even if they roared this deep into the canyon. If only these damn winds fanning it in his face would let up. He knew sometimes their direction shifted at dawn, but sometimes they kicked the flames up more, too.

Time seemed to have collapsed this week; now it dragged. Though he was exhausted, he forced a quick pace. He was risking everything on his hunch that Evan had ordered the plane put down somewhere so that he could light more fires to impress his father. And he was praying that Evan did not let Lauren fly on where they would have to crash-land into thick forests, mountain peaks or even high altitude glacier fields.

He tried to block out the terrifying images: the plane down and broken, people broken…Lauren, Nick…

It astounded and scared him how much the two of them had come to mean to him in such a short time. The people of Vermillion, too, and the town itself, set like a jewel in a raw wilderness that could become a fatal, flaming caution.

Brad kept a firm hold on his duffel bag. He had a single-action .45 automatic in his shoulder holster but carried his Hi-Power Browning 9mm with fourteen rounds and extra ammo for both guns. He wished he'd thought to bring Clay's night-vision goggles.

The terrain was rough and night sounds shook him. Did bears roam at night? What about mountain lions? Surely cats hunted at night, and they had built-in night-vision goggles.

"I ran out of that fire without any socks," Durand said from behind him. All he'd done so far was pant and wheeze, trying to keep up. "I'm going to be crippled from blisters if I don't jam some leaves or something between my heels and these loafers."

Brad was tempted to say, "Too damn bad," but he stopped. "Make it fast. I think we're at least a half hour from that water where she could have put down safely."

"We saw nothing there from the air," Durand said as Brad heard him ripping leaves from a tree. "I just hope none of this is poison oak."

"I've been meaning to ask, how did your wife die so young?" Brad asked, though he knew she'd died in a car wreck.

"Been profiling me as well as my son?" Durand asked, his voice accusing.

"Wise up. Arsonists are made not born. We always try to figure out what the parents were like."

"As if no one's responsible for his own acts anymore. That's partly what's wrong with this country. We have a victim mentality. Poor me," he went on, his voice mocking. "It was how I was raised. It was just an accident or a mistake but not really my fault. Or, Agent Hale," he continued in his own voice, "let's just crucify the parents for what a wayward child does."

"Be sure to tell Evan's defense lawyer to use all that when you try to pony up an insanity defense for your *wayward* child, especially since the charges will be multiple counts of arson and murder."

"I refuse to let you blame me and his long-dead mother, for heaven's sakes! If you must know," he said, madly stuffing leaves in the back of his shoes, "she died in her car when her engine caught fire. She couldn't get out in time. The St. Louis police investigated it thoroughly—a tragic accident, that's all."

"A fire. Ever have any strange fires around your house when Evan was growing up?"

"It's not uncommon for kids to play with matches."

"And he did. In spades, I'll bet."

"As you just sarcastically mentioned, I intend to get a lawyer for him, Agent Hale. And right now I'm going to invoke my rights—"

"Miranda rights?"

"First Amendment! No more questions except to my lawyer or I'll have you out of your elite FBI position so fast—"

"You know, Durand, you're the second person to tell me that tonight, so I'm used to the threat. You want to be on your own out here, fine. See you. And if you run into your son, be sure to tell him you're going to get him a lawyer to help prove he was temporarily insane while he cleverly lit separate fires with carefully chosen accelerants on widely separated dates all over the western

U.S., and outfoxed, for a while, not only the FBI but his own father. Sounds pretty insane to me."

"No, don't leave me out here!" he shouted as Brad walked away with the flashlight. "I just don't want to be blamed for something I didn't do, that's all. I do want to help you."

Brad shook his head and kept going. Durand thrashed through the foliage behind him and eventually caught up. He was panting, but he said, "I'm so shocked and horrified by what my son may have done that I can't accept it. I— As Mrs. Taylor pointed out, I may have made some mistakes, yet they weren't my fault. But I do want to help—to atone, as she put it. Don't you understand wanting to make amends for something like that—crimes committed by someone you thought you knew and trusted?"

"Yeah, I do, Durand. I really do."

19

Lauren was grateful to find a hiking path that led north from the end of the lake, climbing over the canyon floor. She thought there was a path that went lower, but she didn't want to act as if she was confused. With her flashlight, she spotted the I-shaped slash on a tree, the sign for a marked trail around here since the days of Lewis and Clark. But this was a seldom-traveled path with no wooden, carved placard at its head. In the dark, facing foliage and underbrush, she prayed it would lead them toward the lumber camp.

Her biggest fear was that, if that meadow fire kept coming this way, the entire area, including what they walked through now on this slightly elevated ridge, could ignite like a pile of dry kindling. True, the canyon didn't have as heavy a ground cover or as many trees as the valley, but it was narrower, which could concentrate smoke and flames. Ross had died in a canyon.

Worse, if the fire approached the plane, Nicky would be afraid to get out and wade into the lake. And what if he did get in the water? She should have told him not to go in too deep. He could swim, but with that heavy coat on, he could get waterlogged. He'd have to duck his head down if the air became superheated. The horror of that scenario kept gnawing at her.

"This trail traverses the entire canyon?" Evan's voice pierced her agonizing.

"Clear to the logging camp," she said, but she had no idea if that was true. Hopefully she could keep him distracted so he didn't light fires on the way with the drip torch as he had hinted he might. Had he actually been a wildfire fighter like Ross? Could he even have known Ross? If so, could she play on his emotions to let her go and to not start a blaze here?

"Should I call you Evan," she asked, "or do you still want to go by Rocky?"

"Evan's fine. My latest stage name is no longer useful."

"I was just wondering about the drip torch Nicky recognized."

"What about it? It's my favorite prop, just waiting for its cue."

"Your possession of it suggests that you know something about wildfire fighting as well as fire setting."

"Smart girl."

"Could you have known my husband? He used to fight wildfires. He served on a hotshot crew in the summers, not around here, thank God, but usually on the West Coast."

"Never met him."

"I guess I told you that the day he died he was fighting a fire. Did you always stick to burning buildings, or did you ever set one in the wild?"

"Planning to write a tell-all after this is all over? If so, I really should get part of the royalties. Since your FBI lad Brad has obviously done his homework, he must have learned that my illustrious father is an expert in fighting wildland fires, as they are properly called. So, of course, I would stick to house fires—except for the meadow—because I wouldn't want to make him look bad."

Though he sounded breathless from their hike, he laughed, a strange wheezing sound. Brad had been right, Lauren thought. Evan Durand wanted not only to make himself seem important and brilliant, but to outsmart his father—and everyone else.

"I heard," she went on, though she too was getting out of breath, "that the BND set fire to a woodlot or two, though I guess that wouldn't count as a real forest fire."

"You and Macho Blond spent your time together talking about woodlot fires, did you? I do love sparring with you to pass the time, but since you asked about my drip torch, would you like to see a demonstration of it?"

"No! Ross had one. I know how they work."

"Enough of this little scene, my dear leading lady. Just get us out of this narrow canyon. Should a fire start here, it could be deadly, with the winds funneling through. Can't outrun those once they get going, you know."

"As I told you before, Ross was entrapped in a flare-up in a canyon, the Coyote Canyon in California. Have you ever heard of th—"

"Enough!" he screamed. "Cut the scene, I said, or I'm going to use a prop besides my blowtorch and that's this gun, with real bullets. You'll just have to wait for the epilogue when we get near the lumber camp, my little guide. Now, keep quiet and keep moving!"

Sniffing back tears, Lauren held her flashlight steady, looking for the next blaze on a tree and praying those were the only kind of blazes she would see from now on.

Suze made an urn of coffee at Dee's place, then Dee carried a tray of steaming mugs to Chuck, Steve and the FBI team. They had set up a common command center in the fire station. The fire at the Bear's Den had gotten a fast start, but the VFD had put it out before the lower front level was completely destroyed. Sparks had ignited the gift-shop roof, but they'd put that out before it burned more than Mrs. Gates's side porch.

At least the town was safe—unless the winds shifted at dawn and blew the meadow fire this way instead of just north into the Vermillion Valley and canyon beyond it. That would mean the lumber camp and the forests could be threatened too. And then, God forbid, their little town could be engulfed by flames whipping around the far side of Mount Jefferson.

"No, I don't know how many acres are burned yet!" she heard Chuck yell into the phone as she entered the station house. Steve was holding the phone up to his ear. "I said, I need a burn boss, initial attack crew and air support in here pronto."

The FBI team was huddled at the other end of the long table. Brad's friends had spread out a map, and Red Russert was pointing things out to them.

Dee had thought of telling the nurse to give Red a sedative, but if he heard she'd said that, he'd come looking for her. He was Marilyn Gates's knight in shining armor, and it was better to let him go after the dragon and, hopefully, slay him. She desperately wanted Lauren and Nicky—Brad, too—to be safe.

"Fresh coffee here," she said as she put the tray in the middle of the table.

Jen nodded her thanks and reached for a mug. Mike hardly looked up, but Clay took one, too.

"Are you going in after them?" Dee asked.

"I am," Red said.

Under these bright lights, he looked so different with his beard and hair partly singed away. During his stop at the clinic, he'd had both wrists bandaged. He'd borrowed a shirt and jacket that were too small on him. Dee wondered where he'd gotten boots his size so fast, but then she'd noticed that the general store was open. She planned to go down there later and ask Fran if she could fly into Kalispell to stay with Marilyn Gates.

Barely lifting his gaze from the map, Clay said, "We hope to fly over the valley and canyon at dawn, unless the smoke or flames make a close-to-the-ground search impossible. The fact that neither Lauren's plane nor Brad's chopper have returned..." His voice trailed off.

"But that could mean a lot of things," Dee said, trying to argue against her own fears. Suddenly all the coffee she'd been putting away herself made her stomach feel sick—bitter.

She wanted to tell them that Lauren was a good pilot, and that in the few days Dee had known Brad, she'd been impressed with his take-charge attitude and dedication. But she knew her voice would crack, and she might burst into tears.

Nicky's life was at stake, too. How would she explain all this to Larson? Suze had let him stay the night at the Fencers' after all, but she phoned them every hour to be sure they neither saw nor smelled a fire. And she'd told them there would be no school today, let alone in Mrs. Gates's classroom.

Dee moved to the other end of the table near Chuck and his men. Her husband was using Steve as a secretary, writing things down, fielding calls from a phone he couldn't lift on his own.

"More fuel for you," she said, putting several mugs on their end of the table. Then she added, "I guess I shouldn't have put it that way. Is help coming?"

"Working on it," Chuck told her with a nod and a stiff smile. As distracted as he was, his eyes went briefly over her like a physical caress, and her legs went weaker than they already were.

"Chuck," she said, "I could do the support work for you to free Steve up for other things."

"Good," he said with a nod. "I need you, Dee. Don't think I could even lift a mug of that good coffee without help right now. Feed me like a baby, baby, but I'm gonna roar like a lion into these phones till I get all the help we need in here."

Thrilled she could help, could be close to Chuck, Dee lifted and tilted a mug to her husband's lips.

"I suppose with just one year of college, you've never read Dante's *Inferno,*" Evan was saying as they plunged through the leaf-lined path that made Lauren think of a dark tunnel into oblivion.

It surprised her that he'd remembered that tiny detail she'd mentioned about her college years. It showed how sharp he was. Yet, was he crazy? And how was she going to get his gun to turn the tables on him? Talk, keep him talking, she told herself. She'd never known anyone who'd been abducted, but establishing a relationship with the captor was supposedly the thing to do.

"No," she told him, "I haven't read *Inferno.* Is it about a fire?"

"It's about the author's idea of hell," he said, "though, of course, fire plays a part in that." His pleasant, professorial tone unnerved her more than cursing and screaming would have. "You see, according to Dante Alighieri," he went on, "there are nine circles of hell, and evildoers are punished in highly appropriate ways for their sins."

Where was he going with this? He was a man of many moods and bizarre thoughts.

"Well?" he said, "I assume, though you haven't read it, that you can draw some comparisons. What I really like in the *Inferno* is the idea of two souls wandering, seeing the hellish sights, so to speak, just like us. And at the gates of hell, as Virgil leads Dante in, there is a sign which proclaims, *Abandon all hope, ye who enter here.* I rather like the allegory, the symbolism of it all. There will be an inferno, Lauren, and I can't wait."

Despite stuffing his shoes with leaves, Durand kept slowing Brad down. The smell of smoke was getting stronger. What if Lauren had been forced to crash-land the plane and she and Nick were unconscious? What if the flames racing up the valley from the meadow reached them? What if?

"Durand, I'm going to pick up the pace. I've got to get at least as far as the small braided river and narrow lake before I turn back. Light should have filtered down into this canyon by then. If you look straight up, you can see hints of dawn."

"Or the aurora borealis. I can't go any faster, but don't leave me. We only have the one light."

"I'm going to look around, see if I can find where Lauren might have put the plane down. If I find nothing, I'll head back out on this same path, so I'll find you if you stay *on this* path. You could even sit down here and wait if you want to."

"I'm not an outdoorsman!"

"An expert on wildfires should learn to be. Just don't panic. I'll be back ASAP."

"But if you find them injured, you'll need help!"

"Which should be flying over at first light."

"But there could be wild animals, especially fleeing that fire up ahead," Durand cried as Brad took off at a jog.

As much as Brad detested David Durand, he hated to leave the guy. But the thought of Lauren and Nick out here alone—or with that damn arsonist was far worse.

After that spiel about a hellish inferno, Lauren knew she had to change her plans. She needed to get back to Nicky. She somehow had to get away from Evan without being shot or torched with that horrible fire starter he cradled as if it were a child. And she had to do it soon. Daylight was coming, and she'd never escape him then.

Lauren considered different possibilities. She could fall to the ground and fling herself back into him, like a tackle in football, then scramble for the gun. But if it came to a wrestling match, he was stronger.

Or perhaps she could turn on him. Even if he shot at her, she could just jump aside or duck, and hope he didn't shoot to kill. Then she could grab the gun. Or maybe she could find a break in the bushes or the trees and dart away before he could react. Though he might shoot in her direction, she could scramble down this slope they were traversing, hide behind a tree and pray he didn't take the time to look for her in the dark but keep going. She could try to elude him in this thick, dry brush. But what if he started a fire to flush her out? Besides escaping him, she had to keep him from starting a blaze for as long as possible.

Just beyond another slash mark on a thick tree trunk, she noticed an opening through the foliage. Old moose or elk trails, heading down toward the sparse glacier meltwater on the canyon floor, were frequent along here.

Nicky would probably say they were Blackfeet trails—
ghost paths. The next one she passed, she was going to
try it. It made sense that the other trail Red had mentioned would be just a ways below.

She'd have to sit down, skid on her rear and try to
keep branches from scratching her eyes. She could click
her flashlight off but would have to hold tight to it.
Though she had no idea what was in this big backpack
he'd forced her to carry, she would drop it behind her
or throw it at him to keep him from following her down.
Perhaps she could veer to the side as she descended and
escape the trajectory his bullets might take.

Yes, here came another opening, not only between
trees but one that looked slightly beaten down.

Now or never! she screamed silently to herself.

She swung around and heaved the heavy backpack at
him, at the gun. Bending low, she clicked off her light.
She leaped into the open space, sitting down to slide, but
her legs straddled a sapling partway down, banging her
thigh. She thrust herself up away from the snag, then
down again. This time she rolled, hitting herself from
tree to tree.

"Damn you!" came from Evan above her somewhere.
Then the crack of his gun—just one shot.

The sound—or was it the bullet itself?—echoed,
zinged off bark, through leaves. Still clutching her flashlight, she lay on her face in a pile of dry leaves.

She stayed still, trying to control her breath. Her head
hurt and she felt dizzy. Things were spinning. Had she
hit her head on the way down?

Where was Evan? Surely he'd head toward the logging camp, not back toward the plane where they'd left Nicky.

Then a voice, controlled and calm, rang out above her as she gripped the ground to stop the earth from tipping.

"Lauren, call out your position and turn on your light. Right now, or I swear I'll set a fire with this drip torch you will not outrun, an inferno just like in the deepest rings of hell."

She didn't speak. She had to call the bastard's bluff.

"Lau—ren—nn!"

He was furious; he was losing control. Please, dear God, don't let him light a fire.

She kept silent but tried to calculate how far they had come. At least any blaze set here wouldn't buck a breeze this strong to get back to Nicky. And Evan would have to run from the fire; he could be trapped too.

She strained to listen. Was Evan using the drip torch, or had he lied or left? Was he walking away or coming silently closer?

Surely she had blacked out from her tumble. Maybe she'd hit herself with the flashlight she'd been clutching. It would be dawn soon—if the smoke she could smell even from here didn't blot out the sun.

"Hallelujah!" Chuck cried. "If I could clap my hands, I would. We've got a big air-crane helicopter coming in from the National Park Service with on-the-ground support!"

Cheers and applause filled the firehouse. Even, Dee noted, from the solemn FBI team.

"And," Chuck went on, "it's an 88-footer that can dump water into areas with steep ridges and narrow canyons. Its 300-gallon-per-minute cannon launches water or foam up to 160 feet through the air, and it can draw its supply of water right out of the lake!"

Despite the smiles and relieved looks, Dee thought they still had enough problems to sink an 88-foot chopper.

"Also," Chuck informed them, "they're sending a crew boss to the end of the canyon through the lumber camp entrance. If he determines that the fire could well spread beyond the canyon, we'll also get the use of a foam-dumping air tanker, one of the big babies, so it won't be able to land around here. It'll be flying in from Missoula to Kalispell, then over the fire—estimated arrival time, mid to late morning. Some of you might want to take a break or get some quick shut-eye. We may have a long battle ahead of us. There are still sleeping bags on the floor at Dee's shop, and our daughter, Suze, is serving as chuck-wagon cook at our place—and that's no pun."

Chuck sank back into his chair beside Dee at the table. She was proud of how he'd handled things despite his obvious exhaustion and pain from going off his meds again. He closed his eyes and seemed to waver.

"Chuck," she whispered, putting her hand on his knee, "both of those planes are too big to put down in the valley or canyon, even if Lauren's plane or Brad's chopper was spotted. We'll need another smaller chopper, one that can set down or at least put a rescue basket down."

"That's already on its way. I took care of that before

you took over for Steve. Dee," he said, opening his eyes and turning slightly to her, "can you take Suze's truck and drive Jen to the dock to wait for that rescue chopper? It'll be here soon, and she's going up with it."

"Sure. Anything to help."

"I guess Red Russert's loose out there somewhere," Chuck said with a shake of his head. Dee almost told him that she was partly to blame for that. Red had done it for Mrs. Gates's sake, and with a happy heart that would have cracked had he thought his Mari was sending him away. Actually, Dee wasn't sure yet whether the woman had meant for Red to get away from her or to find Brad.

"I'm scared for Lauren and Nicky, Chuck. And for Brad."

"I know. Me, too. But daylight's coming—in more ways than one, I hope."

Lauren floated in and out of consciousness, then the horror rushed back, jolting her wide awake. The smell of smoke was so much stronger, more acrid. As she slitted her eyes open, she could see it now, drifting above her. In a burning house, she knew to stay low in the fresher air as long as possible. It was obviously the same way for the open air.

How long had she been out?

She was quite sure it was dawn, but the wan light had a strange, pearly cast to it. And it seemed to be snowing, she thought as she sat up and rubbed the knot on the back of her head. No, the snow was actually drifting ash from the fire.

And worse, through the foliage around her came a skittering sound and beyond her on the rocky canyon floor, other occasional echoing noises. To her amazement, she saw a sporadic animal exodus—mule deer, elk, moose—loping toward the lumber camp, away from the fire. And in the underbrush that she'd evidently fallen through, a few ground squirrels and pikas darted past her.

With her hand against an aspen, she tried to stand. A doe and a large fawn raced by along a trail on the canyon floor not ten feet from her. And by the looks of the panicked parade, even bears wouldn't stop to give her the time of day now.

Nicky—she had to get to Nicky.

Thank God, Evan seemed to be nowhere in sight. How long had she lain there?

She glanced at the wristwatch she'd obviously smashed against something. Despite the flight of frightened beasts, time stood still until she could get to Nicky. Was it her imagination or was the distant fire pumping heat out ahead of it? She shuffled and slid from tree to tree down the rest of the slope to the edge of the canyon floor. Carrying a dead limb and her flashlight for weapons and, avoiding the larger animals heading down the center of the canyon, she began to run in the opposite direction from where she and Evan had been heading.

She was almost to the area where the canyon opened up to the denser growth of the valley. Ahead, she saw a small body partly covered with dried foliage and leaves. Dear heavens, it was all bloody. Surely—no, it couldn't be! Nicky hadn't tried to come after her and…and what?

She gasped and shuffled closer. It was the half-eaten body of a small doe. She knew that bears buried the rest of the carcass they couldn't eat. It was mountain lions that covered their kill and came back later. But surely mountain lions would be heading out of here too. She had to get back to Nicky fast.

Just then she heard a hiss and turned to see a big, caramel-colored cat crouched in a tree about five yards away. As she screamed and lifted her stick, it bared its fangs and sprang.

20

Apocalypse now! Brad thought as he saw animals heading down the canyon, from south to north, and smoke roiling in the sky ahead of him. How much could the meadow fire have spread? Maybe he'd never make it back to the small lake and river where he'd hoped to find Lauren's plane or maybe Evan Durand too.

And then he heard a woman's scream.

Or was it? Did wildcats around here sound like that?

Sucking smoky air into his lungs, he broke into a dead run toward the sound. Another scream. Human? Close, very close.

He exploded around a pile of boulders and saw Lauren heave a flashlight at a big, snarling mountain lion. She lifted a limb before her to ward it off, then swung it, clipping the cat across the nose.

Brad dropped his duffel bag and drew his Glock from his shoulder holster. He lifted it and, stiff-armed, steadied it with both hands. Where was Nicky? What was that bloody body between her and the cat?

In the split second it took to fire, all his senses slowed.

Sounds stopped, the smell of wood ash settled in his stomach. His Quantico training came back to him: hold breath, sight, shoot!

The bullet hit the animal. He shot again. With a scream of its own, evidently wounded, the big cat backed away from Lauren and vaulted at least twenty feet before it sprinted off, limping and trailing blood.

Brad had barely lowered the gun before Lauren ran and threw herself against him so hard they almost both went down. Her arms tight around his neck, she trembled against him. He was amazed she wasn't sobbing; she looked in shock. They held tight, rocking each other back and forth.

"Where's Nick?"

"With the plane, hidden under trees by the lake. I ditched Evan, and I'm heading back there. Evan has a gun. He made me leave Nicky behind."

She pushed him away. Reluctantly, he let her go. Her face was streaked with dirt, tears and scratches. Her hair was wild, her green eyes wide.

"Thank God," he whispered. "That body over there…"

"The cat's kill, I guess. He must have been full but wanted to protect what was left."

"Where's Evan? He's got to be stopped."

"He's heading toward the lumber camp. He says he's going to light fires. How did you get here?"

"I came after you in David Durand's hired chopper. It's over at the lumber camp but with little fuel, not even enough to fly back to check on Nick."

"I have to go to him. With that fire coming this way… I never thought it could move so fast."

"It's been light for over an hour. Surely someone's found him, rescued him."

"But if the fire's there already…"

"I left David Durand behind me, told him I'd be back."

"You were heading this way from the logging camp but didn't see Evan?"

"No," he said, holstering his gun and retrieving his duffel bag.

"There's another higher trail I came down from. That's the one he's probably still on. I've got to try to get back to the plane!" she said again. "I told Nicky if he saw wild animals not to get out, but if the flames come, he'll have to get in the lake until it passes. There's still some gas in the plane. It could explode. I should have prepared him better. If he sees both animals and flames, I'm not sure what he'll do. I know you have to go after Evan."

She was right. Brad knew he was duty-bound to find and stop the arsonist. And she wasn't begging for his help. She cupped his cheek with her trembling hand, then turned away, running back toward the thickening smoke.

Brad knew he had to head in the opposite direction. The arsonist could burn the entire area. He'd taken an oath to protect the country's interests; that was all he'd worked for and once desired. Besides, one more defiant, maverick move and Mike would dismiss him from his longtime dreams and desires in disgrace.

But he wanted to fight for Nick's life, wanted to protect Lauren. He'd never forgive himself if something happened to them he could have prevented. He had new dreams and desires now, emerging bright and warm through the smoke of the past.

His weapons and ammo bouncing against his body, he broke into a run behind Lauren.

With Agent Jen Connors sitting beside her, Dee pulled up to the dock in Suze's truck. The rescue chopper landed on the same spot where the air ambulance had picked up Mrs. Gates earlier. Both rescue chopper pilots wore helmets that dangled oxygen masks; she could tell by their silhouettes in the pale light of dawn. One of them got out—he wore a bright blue jumpsuit—and jogged toward the truck as she and Jen got out.

"One of you an FBI agent?" he asked, lifting the opaque visor of his helmet. He was young and clean-cut.

"I am. Jen Connors, special agent to the FBI Serial Arson team," she yelled over the roar of the rotors. "This is the town sheriff's wife, Mrs. Cobern."

"Change of plans!" he told Jen after a stiff nod at Dee. "We need to take someone up ASAP who knows the area. We can't take two because we'll need the space in the back in case we find evacs. What's the intel for numbers trapped on the ground?"

Jen started to protest, so Dee interrupted, "In the fire area, there are a woman and a boy in a silver pontoon prop plane. Three other men went in a helicopter. We just got word that the chopper made it clear to the lumber camp beyond the fire, but two of the men have gone back into the endangered area. Then there's the firebug."

"Ma'am, I wouldn't call whoever set that raging fire we just saw from the air a firebug or even an arsonist. He's a maniac. The wildland fire's already crowned on the northern mountain slope and is heading way up the valley. Now, I'll take whoever knows the terrain or wait for someone who does—incident commander's orders."

"Listen," Jen said, looking angrier by the minute, "I have a map of the area, and I've gone over it with local experts. And if you find the arsonist, I'll make an arrest on the spot—or stop him if I have to."

"We'd like to borrow that map, Agent Connor," he clipped out, "but we have our orders. Now, if Mrs. Cobern here can't go, please find someone authorized who can, and fast."

"I'll go," Dee heard herself say. "I've hiked the area and seen it from the air. And I know what the plane looks like—and the people."

Jen was sputtering something as Dee pressed the truck keys into her hand and grabbed the map. Bending low, she followed the young man toward the maelstrom of the chopper wash before she turned back and shouted, "Tell Chuck I'll be all right—and that I love him!"

Several times as he ran toward the lumber camp, Evan was tempted to use the drip torch. But the winds were at his back so strong he might be caught in the blaze himself. He'd wait until he saw the open spaces of the camp and then light fires within it on all sides—that is, after he figured his escape route. He'd done that when he'd knocked out Ross Taylor and his friend Kyle, then laid their bodies on the hill where the flames would get them. He could only hope that Lauren would get her just desserts by being trapped, just as her husband had been.

Ha! What's good for the goose is good for the gander. Which was maybe one reason the animal kingdom seemed to be vacating en masse in the same direction he was. He laughed low at his continual cleverness and wit, even under duress and stress.

He jogged up over a small rise, then stopped dead in his tracks. Ahead of him, plodding toward the lumber camp, was his father. He recognized him instantly, though he was limping and the usual arrogant set of his shoulders sagged.

Again, kismet! Act four of his magnum opus!

Just in case the wonderful, the marvelous David Durand gave him a hard time, Evan drew his gun. Only one bullet had been shot from it, but he wasn't sure how many he had left. Enough, no doubt, if he needed them.

"Hail, David Durand, guru of wildfire fighters of the world!" Evan shouted. Holding the gun, he crossed his arms, spread his legs in a defiant stance and smiled. Arnold Schwarzenegger, governor of the tinderbox state of California and cinema star of *The Terminator,* could not have done better.

His father's gasp was audible from here. "Evan! What in the— Where did you come from?"

"From your loins and Mother's womb, unfortunately. That kind of makes all this your fault, doesn't it? I won't ask if the FBI and the mediocre American media have poisoned your mind against me, because it was poisoned from the beginning, wasn't it?"

"You're not making sense. And why the gun?"

"Because I wasn't sure I could catch you with a fire, so perhaps firing this will be my new M.O. And may I offer my belated congratulations on your miraculous, phoenix-like resurrection from the blaze I set at the Vermillion B&B."

Pointing the pistol at his father's chest, Evan walked closer.

"Put that down. Aren't you in enough trouble already?"

"You're not talking to a ten-year-old who used to worship at your feet—your absent feet. Why are you even here? Researching a book about moral deviants?" Evan taunted. "Preparing a talk about pyromaniacs, using your own son as exhibit A?"

"Evan, just calm down. I came because I didn't believe what the FBI said. I want to help you. I'll get a good lawyer. I'll—"

"I don't need a lawyer. I just need a little more time and for you to shut up for once. And of course, I need my trusty little drip torch. Just keep away—you've always been good at that," Evan ordered as his father kept coming closer.

"I see you still wear your mother's ring from Grandfather Marston. I've been wondering recently if the fire your mother died in kind of got you started."

"What do you mean?"

"When you lost her in that fire, you got so angry with the world. Maybe you decided that others should have to die the way she had."

"Close but no cigar," Evan told him and laughed.

"But I do suddenly have a fierce desire to explain it all to you."

"Good. I can help you, I said. I'll get you professional help. We can get out of this and—"

"*We?* If you had ever wanted to be in my life, this wouldn't have happened, so don't bother trying to climb in with me now. What I do, *I* do, including explaining everything."

"Fine. That's just fine. I want to know, to understand," his father said, holding up both hands as if to ward him off. "Maybe we should start with the past. Would you like to tell me about your mother's death?"

"Yes, let's start with the sacred past. There's a sacred spot right down in the center of this canyon that I want to show you. I read about it online just the other day. It's sacred to the local Blackfeet Indians, now sadly gone from this area but for their ghosts."

"You always were so bright, Evan. Are you still acting?"

"All the time. And don't try to change the subject or manipulate me. Head across the canyon just a little ways, to that flat rock over there," he said, pointing with the gun. "We can climb it to watch the animals vacate the valley while I explain."

"Let's head for the logging camp instead. I've got a helicopter there. It's almost out of fuel, but we can wait there for help—then I can get *you* help."

"After I show you the sacred spot. Go on."

The animal exodus had almost ended, Evan noticed. With his father walking ahead, they crossed the shallow, dry gully and headed for the rock. He would shoot his father if he balked, just enough to wound him, then do what he had to do. An ingenious idea had been forming in his brain ever since he'd read the Blackfeet beliefs about this area.

"That rock?" his father asked, pointing at it. "What about it? What's the story? Evan, that smoke from the valley fire's funneling down this way, and I don't doubt that the flames will, too. Tell me quickly and then let's get back to safety. What about this area and this rock?"

"Let's climb up for a better view, then I'll tell you."

They scrambled up strewn boulders to reach the fairly flat top of the ten-foot-wide rock, set like a small mesa in the middle of the canyon.

"All right, I'm listening, but make it quick," his father demanded, crossing his arms and frowning.

"Oh, sure, I'll make it quick. Wouldn't want to hold up your schedule. This area was sacred to the Blackfeet tribe," Evan said, drawing out the words and speaking in a sonorous voice. "It was, Daddy Dearest, where they laid out their dead. And you've been dead to me for years now."

Still holding the gun on him, Evan swung his backpack down and fumbled in it for the strips of torn sweatshirt he had left over from tying Nicky Taylor. He heaved them at his father. "Sit down and tie some of that around your ankles, then put your hands behind your back."

"How ridiculous! I will not!"

Evan fired the gun at his father's feet. Rock fragments splintered and flew. The report echoed. David Durand jumped back and sat down hard. Then he leaned forward, grabbed the strips of cloth and began tying his own ankles together.

Lauren knew she loved Brad Hale when she heard him running behind her. In four days together, they'd lived a lifetime of danger. Now if only they could find Nicky. If only they could save him and then all stay together.

She tried to ignore the stitch in her side as each deep, smoke-laced breath she took bit into her lungs. Where was that narrow lake and that shallow river? They had to be near because the canyon widened to the valley here. But she saw only gray clouds of smoke beyond, and above that, orange-gold, leaping flames that were much higher than those which had swept the meadow grass. Trees must be on fire. But surely not those surrounding the plane! she thought in desperation.

"It's close—too close!" she cried and started to run again.

"Lauren!" Brad shouted, grabbing her arm to swing her back toward him. "Wait! Quiet!"

"No! I have to go—have to find him!"

Brad grappled her backside to him and put a big hand over her mouth. "Listen!" he ordered. "A plane!"

She strained to hear. The terrible crackling of fire was all she heard at first. And the continual, low rumble of Weeping Wall Falls blurred with the other sounds. But then— Yes, he might be right.

A chopper? A rescue chopper. Going or coming? Could it have pulled Nicky out of that inferno and be taking him back to Vermillion—or to a hospital?

When she nodded, Brad loosened his grip. Her eyes streamed tears, not only from the smoke but from hope, even relief. She hugged Brad hard, and they clung together, both looking up, squinting through the pall of thickening smoke. To her dismay, the roar of the chopper didn't seem to stay in one place. It got louder, then sounded as if it passed right over them.

"Maybe they've got him," she cried. "I don't know if they hovered long, but maybe we only heard it when they were taking him away."

"Smoke's too thick here and flames are coming!" Brad gasped out. "We have to retrace our steps, try to beat the wall of it. The animals knew."

"And that wild animal, Evan Durand, knew exactly what he was doing. Let's try to get to him, stop him no matter what. You came with me to be sure Nicky's safe, now I'll go with you to find—"

A big blast jolted them, then echoed down the canyon walls. They threw themselves flat, but no other sound or repercussion followed. There was no falling rock, only a rain of brown pine needles and sifting, silver ash salting the ground and their skin. They shook their heads to get it out of their hair and flicked debris off themselves.

"That chopper didn't go down, did it?" she asked. "It came from the other direction…" She saw the stricken, frightened look on his face. "Not my plane's gas tank?" She started to sob. "Dear God, please don't let Nicky have been in it."

Brad threw one arm over her and pressed his face close to hers as they huddled on the ground. "If the chopper didn't pick him up, maybe he was in the lake water like you said. Lauren, we have to go or we're going to be roasted here. We're going to have to run like hell now."

"Evan promised me it would be hell," she said as they staggered to their feet. "And I'm going to help you get him for that. For everything."

"What was that blast?" Dee demanded of the two men who sat in the helicopter seats ahead of her. The impact from it buffeted the aircraft and made more ground smoke mushroom ahead of them.

"Sounded like a fuel explosion," Tony, the one who had asked her to come along, said. "But sometimes big trees get superheated and explode into flames."

Dee hoped and prayed it was the latter. She'd zipped herself into a fireproof, silver jumpsuit and had an oxygen mask she could pull over her face, though when she did, it got in the way of her looking out the window. She gripped the mask in her lap and squinted through the coiling smoke and stabbing flames to see where they were. She had thought she would be able to tell exactly where that little lake and river were, but she hadn't been sure—until now.

"I see a rock formation I recognize!" she shouted to the pilot. "It's called Cedar Ridge. We've gone just a little too far north. Can you turn back? And that blast. Could it have been an airplane's gas tank exploding?"

"Could be!" Tony told her. "But even if we see something below, smoke's too thick to put down. We're gonna have to head for the lumber camp."

"Please just go back for a minute!"

The pilot pivoted the chopper and tilted them back toward the worst of the blaze. "Yes, there!" Dee screamed. "See that little lake? That's where I was thinking she could have landed."

Both men looked down as they hovered.

"Something bright red on the water at four o'clock," Tony shouted.

"A flare or something burning out in the lake?" the pilot asked.

Dee pressed her forehead to the glass bubble of her window. "I think it's a red coat! Nicky has a coat like that. Do you see him? Maybe he got in the water. But where is he? And Lauren?"

"There's a coat, but there's no body with it, so no boy," the pilot said. "Ma'am, maybe the blast blew it there. But I repeat, we can't set down. If we'd spotted the boy I'd risk it, but there's no telling if he's even still in this area. We'll let the ground teams know though. They can check it out as soon as they can hike in. Sorry, ma'am, but we're gonna have to gain some altitude and sweep the canyon to see how far the fire's spread. We need to report in to Incident Command."

Dee wanted to scream at them to descend over the water. She'd go down in their rescue basket herself, though she knew she'd be baked if she tried. She kept picturing Larson, her own grandson, and how that could have been him down there.

She threw herself back into her seat and sobbed silently. "I'm so sorry, Lauren," she whispered, pressing her face to the window. "I'm so sorry."

* * *

Partway into the canyon, Lauren and Brad stopped and gasped for air. They'd heard a chopper fly over again, heading north, but it had sounded higher than the one before. Or maybe it was the same one doing reconnaissance. Brad had only pointed to the sky but not remarked on it this time. They were trying to save their breath and strength. Lauren prayed silently, repeatedly, that the chopper had rescued Nicky.

"We're not going to make it running," she told him, panting between words and holding her side. "That was part of the mistake Ross may have made. The flame wall's got a head start on us, and with this wind…"

"Yeah. But it's also burning any vegetation to climb the canyon walls, so we can't go up."

"There's one place that may be safe if we can get there in time," she gasped out.

"Under the waterfall?" he asked as if he'd read her mind. "It's a big one. We'd get battered to pieces and not get a breath there either."

"I think we can get under the cliff behind it, but it's…still a climb. And they say never go up. It's better…to run through it. I think we've got a little while…before it gets us…like it must have got to the plane."

"But it didn't get Nick!" he told her, his voice fierce. "He's all right, I feel it."

She nodded but started to cry again. At least he couldn't tell; her eyes were streaming with tears from the smoke. He hugged her, quick and hard.

"We've got to save ourselves before we can stop Evan. I swear to you we will stop him," he vowed.

She didn't want to let go of Brad. She was desperate for his strength.

"Let's go!" she said. "Next stop Weeping Wall Falls. Follow me."

21

"I really need to be going," Evan told his father as he stood over him. "That was the line I've heard from you over the years, so I've perfected it."

"Evan—son—you can't leave me here. The smoke is bad, and with the wind direction, the flames will follow."

"What a brilliant deduction from the wildland fire-fighting guru of the nation! But before I ring down the curtain here, let me fill you in on why I've chosen this exit for you. As I said, this land is sacred to the Blackfeet because it was their ancestral burial grounds. They put the corpses on elevated platforms until they had decayed and came back later to collect and bury the bones. I'm afraid, though, I won't be back for that part. Too busy! Onward to new challenges, greener pastures, so to speak."

"Evan, I'm begging you. I'm sorry for whatever I did to make you so angry. I've made mistakes, lots of them, but you cannot leave me here!"

"You left me here!" Evan roared, looking down into his father's panicked face with the pistol pointed at him for effect. "Not exactly here, but you sent me into exile to work at that ski lodge right after mother died. You couldn't even spare time for me then!"

"I had to support you. I had a full schedule I couldn't change without losing fees and honoraria. The alternative would have been to put you in the care of doctors—psychiatrists. And you refused, don't you remember? If you want to know the truth, I was terrified of what they might get out of you!"

"Oh, sure. I might make you look bad. And Mother."

"You—you didn't have anything to do with that engine fire in her car, did you? I wouldn't let myself believe it, and accidents of that type happen. The investigators said such a thing couldn't be rigged so skillfully, even by an expert, so—"

"Granted, it would have taken a brilliant mind to devise that fire with a timer and a fuse. A fire that burned up all the evidence. A mere eighteen-year-old who loved his mommy—no way! Surely it isn't that a mere lad had outsmarted professional investigators and my own genius father!" Evan cried. And then he smiled.

"You—you can't mean it. I— Your mother didn't deserve that, and I don't deserve this. Just let me go. You can take off again, and I won't—"

"Just shut up, David Durand, expert witness, expert human being! This is an honorable death. If you don't like the Blackfeet Indian comparison, let's say your denouement entails a funeral pyre like that of a Viking king going up in flames. Or think of all the great martyrs and saints of the world who shared this fate, like Joan of

Arc. Now I really must be going. But I will do you one last favor. I'll pile some brush closer to you so that things will go quicker once the flames get here—and I'd judge that will be in less than a quarter of an hour. Farewell, Father!" he cried with a sweeping gesture. "Farewell, for parting is such sweet sorrow."

He jumped down and started to gather dried branches and underbrush from nearby bushes. He dragged those up onto the flat stone, shoving them against the writhing man. His father continued to beg, jabbering, making promises Evan didn't even listen to, let alone believe. He was done with him now. His unjust, brutal past was over, and there was only a very, very bright future.

At the last moment, before Evan had to flee to get a good enough start on the encroaching flames, he got out his drip torch and waved it over his now-sobbing father in an elaborate flourish.

"We who are about to start more fires salute you!" Evan declared, hacking from the smoke. "I would ignite your pyre with this, Daddy Dearest, but I want to save it for fires today that are much more important."

He could think of nothing to top what he had already said, so he wrapped the drip torch in his sleeping bag, hurried down from the funeral pyre and ran north.

When Brad got close enough to see beyond the trees guarding the foot of the falls, he knew they were in trouble. The trail they'd have to climb to get up and behind the torrents of the wide waterfall was blocked with fallen rock.

"Oh, no!" Lauren cried. "I don't think it used to look like that."

The water pool they'd expected to find below the falls, which they could get into as Lauren had told Nick to do, was nonexistent. Brad knew the thundering water from above did not run into the canyon, where it could have acted as a firebreak. Now he saw that it ran off between the rocks and was swallowed by clefts in the cliff behind it, perhaps becoming an underground river. But even worse, the strands of crashing water had dumped a lot of debris, rocks that ranged in size from boulders to golf ball–size talus.

"An avalanche hit here last winter," Lauren went on, "but I didn't realize… When I fly this narrow canyon, I always have to look straight ahead."

"I can see where the cave shelter is higher up, but let's go closer and look for something on a lower level. Can you do it?"

"Yes—go ahead."

They scrambled up, around and over rocks, then started to climb a talus field of broken stones. But the area was wet from the spray of the falls, so it was like trying to climb a pile of slick ball bearings. More than once, Brad rolled down into her. They slammed together, sat down and slid in a rumble of small, round rocks.

Bruised, they got to their feet, still at the foot of the falls. "At least the smoke seems lighter here," Lauren said.

"Airflow from the falls is pushing it back, at least for now. But I can't see any place where the impact of the water is light enough for us to stand in it and survive when the fire wall gets closer. The water would pound us, suffocate or even drown us."

"Maybe we'll have to burn out an area in the canyon, then hunker down in it. You know, stay in the black, while the worst of it sweeps past us," Lauren suggested.

"We don't have anything to set a fire with. And there's no way to get ourselves a blackened area ahead of the flames."

"If we could just get up these rocks a ways, there would be nothing to burn under us and—"

"These trees around the falls could topple into us when they burn, or throw flaming branches or embers," he argued. "I've seen that happen even at house fires, where they end up igniting the next roof. Maybe we could make it to one of the bigger rocks out in the canyon, get on or behind it, be sure there's nothing that could burn near as it roars past. Are you sure there's no other trail around here that goes down the canyon toward the logging camp? Something high? We can't outrun the fire on the canyon floor, but if we could just get some protection…" He started hacking again.

"I don't know. I recall some things Red said about this area, but I've never hiked it. I told Evan I did, but I was lying in the hopes that I could get away from him and get back to Nicky."

Brad felt helpless as Lauren put her face in her hands and sobbed. He pulled her to him and watched their massive enemy approach, marching with orange and red strides down the canyon, leaping from tree to tree, devouring bushes. As the temperature rose, the fire seemed to suck air from the entire canyon.

Through the scrim of marauding smoke, Brad scanned the area, looking for a rock formation or a boulder that could shelter them. Even hunkered down in the relative shelter of one, they would have to hope that the superheated air or flames didn't make them casualties of Evan's grand-scale arson.

Then he saw what he prayed was the perfect rock: large, flat on top, one they could maybe hide behind or even under. But something moved near it. An animal—no, a man was running toward it.

"Lauren, look. There's a man running toward that flat boulder, closer to the other side of the canyon." He turned her and pointed while she swiped tears and drifting mist from her cheeks. "And there's a pile of something on the boulder."

"I can't tell what," she said, "but that looks like Red Russert running toward it. Is it? Where could he have come from?"

"He knows the area, so we have to get to him. I think something's moving amidst a pile of brush."

"Is it Evan?"

"Can't tell. I hate to leave this cool mist where the air is better, but Red may know a way out and what's happening back in Vermillion."

"Let's go!"

Holding hands like kids, they slid the rest of the way down the slippery slope and ran as fast as they could across the canyon.

* * *

"There's the commercial helo, just where Command said it would be!" Tony shouted, pointing as they hovered over the lumber camp.

"My son-in-law's a foreman there," Dee told them. "I know the area well. That chopper is sitting on the only landing pad."

"Doesn't matter," the pilot said, lifting one of his headphones to hear her better. "I see a lot of open area where we can set down. The pilot radioed that he was out of fuel, so we'll take him back with us, or his two passengers if they've turned up yet. So, Mrs. Cobern, where have they been logging?" he asked. "It looks like virgin timber stands for miles."

"That's what everyone's afraid the arsonist will burn, or the fire will spread to next. They try to keep this area looking pristine, partly because it can be seen from the ski runs, but also because they've logged just around the curve of both mountains to the east and west. They send the logs down to the service road at the bottom of Mount Jefferson on that wooden-log flume there," she said, leaning forward and pointing between their shoulders.

"An antique!" Tony said. "It looks like that Disney ride where you get splashed at the end. Could some of that water flow be diverted to fight the fire?"

"I don't know!" she cried. "Look, there's a man waving at us."

They put the rescue chopper down in an open area between massive piles of logs and the huge machines that hauled, delimbed and lifted them into the flume.

The man, who Dee didn't recognize despite her desperate prayers it might be Brad, ran up to them as Tony opened the door.

"My two passengers went into the canyon and haven't come back!" he yelled without introduction or preamble. "I don't have enough fuel to get back to town, but I hate to leave the bird!"

"I see heavy equipment here!" the pilot shouted to him as the man leaned into the cockpit, trying to hear over the wash of the rotors. "There has to be a gas pump around!"

"I don't want to be caught fooling with gas if the fire's coming this way."

"Unless this wind shifts, it's plowing its way right up the canyon," the pilot told him.

"Then I will head back with you."

"Did you spot a silver plane?" Dee demanded as the man scrambled into the back seat.

He gasped, evidently surprised to see her. "No. Agent Hale was determined to find it, and that's why he headed back, but he was dragging my charter with him, David Durand, so I don't know how much headway he made."

As the man buckled himself in and Tony slammed the door, Dee bit her lower lip hard to keep from crying. Worse than Durand out there, somewhere his maniac son was on the loose.

Drifting smoke obscured their view of Red and the rock, while the roar of the falls and cacophony of flames muted their desperate shouts to him. Between clouds of smoke, they saw Red half drag, half carry someone—David Durand, they thought—toward the lumber camp. Lauren knew they'd never catch him now, not exhausted and choking like this.

"He may get safely to the lumber camp, but I'm not sure about us," Brad told her and she nodded grimly. "But let's try to make it—at least as far as that rock."

They had both pulled their T-shirts up over their mouths and noses for smoke masks, though it didn't help much. Despite how parched Lauren felt, she knew they had done the right thing not to soak the shirts in water at the falls. Ross had said that could steam your lungs, which was deadlier than inhaling smoke. And since Brad had been a firefighter, he must have known to fight that instinct, too. She wanted to ask Brad so many things about his life, but now…

They pushed on, staying toward the middle of the canyon because it was the shortest distance toward the logging camp—and the smoke was thinner here than along the canyon walls.

The dry canyon floor, which offered the fire less fuel than a thick forest or field might have, brought new problems. Behind them the conflagration seemed to leap from bush to bush, tree to tree, vaulting faster and closer than it might have if it had more fuel to take its energy and time.

At the head of the fire, which they could see now boiling up behind them, flames surged and pulsed in fire fingers grasping at the canyon. Still holding hands, they stared aghast as the wind sucked burning pine needles, cones and branches into a twenty-foot updraft that leaned sideways to spew out embers like a thermal sling-shot. But all that became an erect pillar of flame again, roaring and breaking loose from the main body of the fire and roaming the edge of the canyon as if of its own accord.

"A fire whirl," Brad said, his voice raw and awed. "I've only heard of them. It looks like an evil giant. We're going to have to make a stand. Let's get as close to the downwind side of the big rock as we can and hunker down." They began to run again.

"But the brush around it and on top of the rock where we saw Durand… It'll catch on fire. We need to have it burned off—gone."

"We have nothing to light it with!"

They stumbled toward the rock with the inferno's hot breath on their backs. Lauren yanked her hair into a knot and tied it back with a dry vine she pulled from a bush. Better not to have the bulk of it loose, to be ignited by an ember or even the huge pieces of ash falling now.

"I'll try to clear the brush," Brad said. "We'll get on the leeward side and maybe the worst of the fire will go by fast."

"If it doesn't devour the oxygen here. But we're not get-ting caught like Ross was. Evan is not going to do us in!"

Another thought hit her hard. She'd almost said that Evan was not going to do us in, *either.* Could Evan have had something to do with Ross's death? Evan had claimed he'd never heard of him, but he was as skilled an actor as he was an arsonist.

"I'll be right back with a firebrand to ignite whatever you can't clear!" she shouted.

"What? No! Lauren, you can't—don't go…"

But she was off at a run toward the nearest burning bush.

Evan was exhausted but exhilarated as he reached the edge of the logging camp and gazed back into the tinderbox canyon with the smoke-filled Vermillion Valley behind it.

Magnificent in its power, the inferno lit the sky with its fury. Tall, blowing columns of gray-black smoke and tongues of golden flame filled his view and his vision for his future. His enemies were sacrifices to the power of the fire and to his own might: his father, Brad of the FBI, and maybe Lauren, too. Sad about Nicky, though. Evan would have considered taking on a boy with that fine an imagination. Yes, he could have taught him all he knew.

He tore his gaze away and forced himself to survey the central open area of the camp behind him. Tall piles of logs lay waiting to be moved and sold—or, in this case, burned. Huge machines that did the bidding of the men who timbered in these mountains were parked nearby. Yes, he'd burn this place, too, sending a blaze into the forested mountains. He would then get down to the service road Lauren had mentioned and hike out to a new life.

He laughed and looked back into the canyon, where he saw two figures struggle from the periphery of smoke, staggering toward the camp, almost on the same path he'd just used. At first he thought it could be Brad and his father, but—

He didn't know the burly man, but whoever he was, he had rescued Evan's father from the flames! Oh well, in many of the great tragic operas, the dying singer came back to life for a swan song before croaking for good. Now he'd simply have to find a way to write the epilogue to his masterpiece tragedy by eliminating—in an appropriate, clever way—anyone who emerged from that glorious conflagration.

Dee was shocked to see Chuck himself meet their chopper when it put down by the dock. And she was even more surprised when, despite his sling and bandages, he held her to him the moment she ran out from under the rotors.

"I couldn't believe it when Agent Connors said you had gone instead of her!" he cried.

She hugged him hard, pressing herself against him as she had not done in months. "I thought I could help find them, but we couldn't. All we saw was Nicky's coat floating in the lake. Chuck, I think her plane was down there. We heard the gas tank explode."

"That doesn't mean they were with the plane. Lauren's a smart woman."

"But who knows what the arsonist did to them. And if that was her plane, he could be on foot out there somewhere, doing his damndest to make things worse."

"Come on back to town," he urged and led her toward a car Steve was driving. "This fire's got a red alert now—

all kinds of help being flown in. They were going to set up their command at the lumber camp, but they figure it's in the path of the fire now, so they're hunkering down here for the duration. It's best, Dee, 'cause it'll protect the town if the flames spread around the mountain or come rushing this way. The weather report says the wind should shift soon. Then we'll see what we have on our hands. Meanwhile, you and I've got to make up time—just make up."

She let him put her in the back seat of the car. Slowly, still guarding his shoulder, he got in beside her.

"Suze was really shook when she heard you went in the rescue chopper, Mom," Steve told her. "She went to get Larson, and he keeps asking where his buddy Nicky is."

"And I keep wondering where Lauren is. Chuck, if they're lost out there, I'll just die!"

Stunned by the hot wind that slapped her, Lauren grabbed a two-foot limb that looked to be only half on fire. The unburned part was hot, though, and she had to steel herself to hang on to it. She turned and tore back toward the rock, surprised to see that Brad was coming after her.

But when he saw her returning, he did as she had ordered, and started yanking brush away from the rock, even climbing it to heave off bundles of sticks and grass that someone—Red, or David Durand?—had piled up there. With her flaming brand she quickly lit everything he threw down, then darted from bush to nearby bush, lighting them.

Is this how Evan Durand felt when he burned something? she wondered. It sickened her, but it must thrill him.

Huge silver ashes continued to rain down along with
embers. The smoke was thickening. She could see flames
that now flanked the canyon on both sides where vegetation, maybe seeking shade, had grown along the paths
they had been on earlier.

"Lauren—now!" she heard Brad scream as the
winds increased their turbulence and almost lifted her
off her feet.

Was this how it had been for Ross in the last minutes
of his life? She was grateful her brain no longer bom-
barded her with the horrible scenes of his death. Even
in this hellish inferno Evan had promised, she was not
swept back again into her living nightmare.

She ran toward Brad. She wanted to live, wanted to
help him stop the man who had done this. She wanted to
find her son and to tell Brad how much he meant to her.

She expected he would lead her up on top of the large
rock where they could lie flat as the fire passed over and
around them, but he grabbed her and pointed at a split
in the side of the stone away from the fire. He wedged
her in face-first, pushing her into a triangular-shaped
cleft, so that she was standing with her back to the opening. Then he shoved in tight behind her.

"This is good," she cried to encourage him. "We're in
the black. It's not like having an aluminum survival
tent, but—"

"Save air!" he ordered, nuzzling the top of her head
with his chin as he fitted close behind her. She could feel

his shoulder holster pressing against her back. Where had his precious duffel bag gone? He managed to get one hand between her and the stone at the level of her waist. He held her there firmly, his fingers on her bare flesh under the T-shirt she still had over her mouth and nose. He pressed his thighs against her bottom. It took her back to the day he had protected her as they'd climbed down from the fire tower and she'd felt faint.

She felt faint now. Her head was spinning.

Even in the shelter of the rock, they heard, as well as felt, the conflagration coming. The sound of it was like a freight train with its wheels ripping by right above their heads.

Lauren worked one hand free and took the hand that gripped her shoulder. As they interlocked their fingers tight, she felt so close to him. He had been so good for her in the short time they'd had together.

It was hard to breathe. If they died like this— suffocated or burned—would anyone ever find them? Or would they be wedged here, hidden, their bones like those of the Blackfeet, together in this sacred area for all eternity? Suddenly, strangely, the thought of such horror didn't scare her at all.

But Nicky needed her.

Sweat poured into her eyes, making them sting. She thought she could smell singed hair. Save air, he'd told her, maybe the last words he'd ever say.

Save air, she chanted to herself. Save air, save air, save us.

She tried to breathe slow and shallow. Smoke seeped in, worse, thicker as the temperature rose. Save air.

Lauren tried to picture swimming in Lost Lake, so cold, so good. To remember skiing down the slopes, breathing in the brisk cold, the frosty air in her face.

She felt someone shift behind her, come closer. Brad, taking care of her. From the first moment she'd seen him in the airport coffee shop, coming to help, he had taken her breath away...taken her air.

The fireplace was putting out too much smoke and heat as she and Nicky roasted hot dogs and then gooey marshmallows to make s'mores...if Brad would only stay with them... He knew a lot about fires, and he'd built one inside of her.

She wasn't sure, but she thought he said, "I love you, Lauren," before she stepped into the void of utter blackness.

22

Brad was kissing her and murmuring her name... Pressing close over her...

Lauren opened her eyes. Was it night? No, the sky was seething gray.

"Lauren, thank God," he gasped, pressing his cheek to hers.

She sucked in a breath of sooty air and started to cough. Was Brad crying? Maybe it was just the smoke, the fire—the fire that might have hurt Nicky.

Brad must not have been kissing her, but using mouth-to-mouth to make her breathe...

"Did I faint?"

"I was scared I'd lost you. The winds shifted. The flames went by us, then came back. The fire's turned on itself. It's not out but it's better now."

"Are you burned?" she cried, trying to get up. Her hands were black with charred soil, with soot. Her head spun. He helped her up and she leaned against him, dizzy. She felt so dizzy.

"My jacket roasted right off my back when the winds

changed," he said. His voice was a rough whisper. He coughed every few words. "The fire went past us, then came back," he repeated, as if he, too, was dazed. "Behind us it seemed temporarily stalled. I don't know if the shift is permanent, but we have to try to get to the lumber camp. If Red went that way, it's got to be the best way out. Do you think you can walk?"

"If I have to, I can run."

But her legs were wobbly, and they had to walk together at first. He held her hard to his side, as if they were in a three-legged race. Then, up ahead, on both sides of the canyon, she saw green trees and unburned brush edging the lumber camp.

"Out of hell into heaven," she gasped.

"This is where the wind turned it back. There are hot spots, pockets of fire still. Unless we get some planes dropping water or retardant in here, this area might ignite, too. But yeah, it's a paradise compared to what we've been through."

The air was better here, pumping in from the forested mountains beyond the camp. They tried to breathe deeply of it, but her throat felt so raw even that hurt. The stench of smoke and death sat in her stomach.

"We can't just go rushing in," he said as he steered them along the lower path of the canyon's eastern edge, "in case Evan's at the camp."

"If he's there, it's probably only to find the service road and escape. He must know people are after him. If he lights another fire, it will give away his position."

"No, I'd bet all this has only whetted his psychopathic appetite for more. He believes he's invincible. And, I swear, that's why we're gonna get him."

We, he'd said. He must mean his team, but they weren't here. Anger at Evan and strength to help Brad poured back into her. Reluctantly letting go of his hand on the narrow, shaded trail where they had to walk single file, Lauren steadied her legs—and her heart—and went on.

Evan figured he had time to break into the office in the center of the camp. Each building, he'd noted, was clearly identified with a carved, wooden sign. He'd literally held the key to Vermillion—those to Lauren's and the sheriff's houses, at least—and he wanted to see if he could find any here. These big, sleeping monsters, with their shovels and sharp blades entranced him. Before he lit other fires, he could picture himself riding one of these to mow his father down.

He headed for the log cabin–style edifice labeled Main Office. Beside the building, on a post, was a metal State of Montana Historical Landmarks sign, which read in part,

In this area, including the lower reaches of the Nizitopi and Jefferson Mountains, the Blackfeet tribe once buried the bones of their dead. The spirits of these great people, including their powerful Chief White Calf, are said to yet inhabit this sacred area.

"*Perfectamente*," Evan muttered. "Just like my stage character, White Calf. Once again, I'm in like a ghost, out like a ghost." He laughed, but the thought made him shiver, too. He was fated to burn his father's body near here, not down on that rock in the canyon.

Evan broke the window of the office with a piece of log and smiled as he listened to the crash of the glass. Not quite the same sound as when a roaring house fire shattered windows, but music to his ears anyway. He found the keys hanging on hooks in the office, all nicely labeled: delimber, skidder, dozer, feller, knuckle boom and crane. Now if only someone had been kind enough to identify the big beasts, too. But he was just going to have to guess which was which.

He took the keys labeled skidder and crane and rushed back outside. As he saw the two men staggering over the slight rise to the camp, he found the machine that took the key for the skidder. Boasting massive tires, the dusty, yellow vehicle looked like a huge tractor with a sharp shovel in front. It was something like the dozers he'd seen scrape vegetation from the path of a blaze to help hotshot crews make a firebreak. He climbed into the cab and crouched, peeking out to see what his father and his father's rescuer would do. Then, his hand shaking with excitement, he fumbled to fit the key in the ignition.

Imagine, another chance to kill his father! The man with him looked big and burly, though he was no spring chicken. Could he be someone from this camp? Too late, Evan realized he should have cut the phone lines, but he'd been so intent on the keys. At least he'd made so few mistakes that, hopefully, this one wouldn't matter.

The key slid smoothly into the ignition. Just to be sure he had all the protection he would need, Evan pulled his gun from the pocket of his camos.

The men were close under him, panting hard, their sentences punctuated by gasps. The lumberjack-looking guy was saying, "…call for help…tell them what your son did so…"

Then he heard his father's voice, one he thought he'd never hear again—never wanted to. "Thank God the wind shifted, or we might not have made it out. We'll tell the FBI, too…"

Evan studied the dashboard controls of the skidder: steering wheel, stick shift, pedals. He'd turn it on and roll it right over them. But what if they made it to the safety of the office? He'd hate to waste time trying to knock the building down to get to them. Besides, there could be a back way out.

Damn, he'd left the office door open and one window was shattered, so they'd smell a trick. What was the matter with him? It infuriated him that the winds had indeed shifted to stop the progress of the valley and canyon fires. He had to start new ones here, quickly, before those who would interfere came. Once his father summoned help, he'd have to leave his life's work unfinished here, and he could not allow that.

Instead of using the skidder to chase them, he realized he needed to move stealthily and quietly—especially to get control of that big man. Leaving the key in the ignition, Evan dropped from the cab to the ground and tiptoed after the men, drawing his gun.

If he could just tie them up, it would be much easier, so much quicker. And once their remains were shoveled by this big skidder to the edge of the camp, he'd start the first fire there, right on top of them. He so wanted his father to have his funeral pyre.

Just before Brad and Lauren started up the slight rise that would take them to the lumber camp, he stopped and turned to her. Breathing hard, they leaned together. They both looked like hell, but that hardly mattered. And he knew she was even more exhausted than he.

He'd been terrified she'd actually suffocated, jammed in the rock during the onslaught of the fire. But she'd only fainted and had come right back with mouth-to-mouth. Lauren Taylor was a fighter, but he could not bear for her—or Nick—to be hurt anymore. He needed not only to corner Evan Durand, but to get Lauren in touch with rescue operations so that he could prove to her that her son was safe. He had to be!

"Okay, partner, let's lay some recon plans," he told her. He almost didn't recognize his own raspy voice. "We know Red and David Durand headed here, but we have to assume, from what you said, that Evan might have, too. I'm just hoping Durand's pilot is all right. If he's still here, he'll have a radio that we can use. If not, are there phones here?"

"Yes, in the main office. And they use two-ways when the teams are out harvesting or in the vehicles. Steve gave the boys a tour this summer, so I know the layout of the place pretty well."

He expelled a rush of air through flared nostrils. Then he might do well to take her in with him, he realized, though he wanted to keep her here until he surveilled the area.

"Unfortunately," he told her, "Evan's M.O. has included cutting phone wires, so we can't risk just waltzing into camp and trying to find a phone. For all we know, he could have laid a trap, so—"

They both jumped and instinctively ducked at the sharp crack of a gun. Did it echo off the rocks or had someone shot twice?

"Where was that from?" she asked, gripping his arm.

"The camp. Does Red carry a gun?"

"A hunting rifle sometimes."

"That wasn't a rifle. So much for plans about how we'll recon the place. You stay here. I'll try to sneak up on Evan," he told her and drew his gun.

"Where are your other guns? I could help."

"My bag with them burned up. You stay here."

"Listen! What's that sound?"

"Maybe one of the big vehicles starting. Could he drive out of here in one of those?" Brad asked as he jogged up the slight rise in the path, Lauren right behind him.

"The single, narrow service road out of here twists and turns, so he couldn't go fast and he could plunge over the side. That's why they use the log flume."

He thrust his free arm out to his side to stop her. They peeked up over the rise to the camp.

"Stay back," Brad repeated. Keeping low, darting from tree to tree, then from massive machine to machine, he carefully worked his way closer to the heart of the camp. The chopper he'd arrived in was sitting on the landing pad, but it looked empty. He wondered if the pilot was anywhere around. Maybe he was hiding so he didn't get shot.

When Brad peered around a machine—one with huge blades with SLASHER written on its side—he *finally* got a good look at Evan Durand, alias BND and Rocky Marston. The trouble was, he held a gun on his father and evidently on Red, too, though Brad could only see the Durands. Brad didn't have a clear shot at Evan from this spot, nor could he shift his position without being seen.

But Brad could see that the arsonist was dark-haired with a good tan, just as Lauren had described him. His camo fatigues may have once been green and brown, but they were now smeared by soot and charcoal. He was a villain all in black.

Despite his bad position, Brad was actually tempted to just try to shoot the bastard. But he wanted him alive to stand trial, to be studied so that they could find out what made such a sicko tick. He had to stop Evan before he harmed anyone else or set another fire.

When Evan turned his head slightly away, Brad shuffled slowly to his left. Since Evan controlled Red and David Durand, this had become a hostage situation with new rules. Too bad he'd never taken sniper training at Quantico.

Slowly, Brad sidestepped farther. Holding a gun on

his two prisoners, Evan was evidently forcing his father to pull the big, inert body of Red Russert—shot or dead?—into the lowered, front shovel of a tractor-like machine that was already running. Its glassed-in cab was set high on huge tires, but the wide shovel had been lowered to ground level.

Struggling with his rage, fearful that Evan could have killed Red, Brad pressed himself behind the cab of the crane likely used to lift logs to the flume overhead. Even now, he could hear the rush of water within the elevated wooden trough. Just before he could dart closer, he heard something behind him and spun back.

Damn! Lauren had followed him into the camp and was hunkered down behind one of the tresses supporting the flume.

He gestured broadly and mouthed at her, *I said, stay back!*

Her mouth formed the words *I am!*

Brad glared at her before turning back to assess whether to rush Evan or wait to see what he was up to. If he'd already shot or knocked out Red—and Brad couldn't imagine the guy cooperating—he had to move fast.

But just as Durand bent over to lift and drag Red, Evan hit him on the head with the butt of the gun so that he crumpled into the shovel beside Red. Praying Lauren would stay where she was, holding his gun up with both arms stiff in front of him, Brad rushed Evan's position.

"FBI!" he shouted. "Drop the gun, Durand! Hands in the air!"

But Evan wheeled, ducked and shot as he darted to the other side of the big machine. The shot went wide, pinging off metal somewhere nearby; Brad kept charging.

He saw Evan's head appear in the tall cab of the bulldozer. The machine roared to life, lifting the shovel with the two unconscious men inside, and jerkily started off, away from Brad's position.

His first instinct was to shoot out the glass in the cab. But what if he hit or killed Evan? He wanted him alive. And what if that made the machine, with Red and Durand in the raised shovel, go over the edge of the camp or crush them to death?

The bulldozer wasn't fast, though he supposed Evan had it going full tilt. By jogging, Brad could keep close to it as it rolled on its huge tires toward the Mt. Nizitopi side of the camp. The dozer took out a bush or two and bumped the bottom of a fifteen-feet pile of logs that began to roll.

His gun still raised to keep Evan in his sights, Brad ran out and around the thudding, bouncing, cut and delimbed tree trunks. He looked back to see where Lauren was, but in the avalanche of logs, he didn't see her anywhere.

"The incident commander's here, Dad!" Steve shouted in the front door of the house. Dee scrambled off Chuck's lap where they'd been sitting half sprawled, half embracing on the sofa.

"Send him in!" Chuck yelled and gave Dee's bottom a quick pat.

"Please," she said as she straightened her shirt, "ask him to send whatever choppers he has in to look for Nicky and Lauren."

"You know I will. We out of coffee yet?"

"I'll get you some."

Their gazes held before she turned away, and he went to greet the man who would coordinate the wildfire-fighting operations. As they'd been praying for, the wind had shifted when the temperatures rose after dawn, sending the fire back upon itself to partly burn out.

As Dee fixed coffee and food in the kitchen, Suze and Larson came down from upstairs. "Are they going in after Lauren and Nicky?" Suze asked.

"The cavalry just rolled in," Dee said. "Actually, I was trying to overhear what they were saying to your father."

"I can go listen!" Larson volunteered. "I want to know if I can go with them to find Nicky."

"You're not going anywhere near that fire, buddy," Suze told him. "Let's just you and I sit here quietly at the table and make Mrs. Gates a get-well card so your grandma can eavesdrop."

"Does that mean drop on the floor and listen real easy to what people are saying? 'Cause Nicky and me, we've done that."

"I'll bet you have," Dee told him, feeling sick over Nicky and Lauren again. "But I don't plan to drop to the floor," she told him, trying to sound normal, in control. She was shaking so hard inside she might just drop to her knees in desperate prayer that not only Nicky and Lauren, but Brad, too, might be safe out there somewhere.

Lauren gasped as the cascade of piled logs rolled at her. She'd been trying to keep Brad in sight but not stay right behind him. Had Evan intentionally bumped the lower, supporting logs, or had he hit them because he wasn't used to driving that big skidder? They were tumbling like Nicky's Lincoln Logs, which he used to build forts and castles.

Lauren ran, but they kept coming at her. At least the rumbling pile slowed as it leveled out, but Evan just kept going. And Brad must have been far enough ahead to miss getting crushed.

She fell, but scrambled on all fours until she got to her feet again. She threw herself behind the slasher and let it take the hits of the logs that rolled this far. Against the big vehicle, they bumped and thudded until there was just dust and silence.

To her surprise, Brad came running around the corner. "You all right?" he asked.

"At least he won't be burning that pile of wood," she told him, trying to sound bold. "Let's go, FBI!"

He nodded and ran around the now-wide pool of logs with her right behind him. "Next time I say stay back," he said, "I mean it."

"Roger that."

But they gasped when they saw that Evan had dumped both Red and his father on another pile of logs, one about six feet tall, under a long wooden shed. Lauren shaded her eyes to see what Evan was going to do next and recognized the shape of what he was holding up in the glass cab of the truck.

"He's got his drip torch out!" she cried. "He's going to start a fire there! Can you shoot at him through that glass?"

She watched as Brad ran closer and pointed his gun at the glass window of the skidder cab. He shot. It shattered around Evan, but he still managed to launch flames into the pile of logs. Then he leaned out to shoot a line of flaming oil and fire at Brad, all the while laughing.

Brad jumped back, then shot at Evan again. Bending low, Evan hunched down in the cab and headed the skidder toward the trees at the foot of Mount Nizitopi. Brad scrambled up the end of the flaming pile of logs to drag first Red, then David Durand down. Lauren rushed to help, pulling Red away from the spreading flames while Brad hauled the screaming Durand to the ground. He looked woozy; he was bleeding from a blow to the head.

"Red's breathing!" she shouted to Brad over Durand's hysteria. "He has a pulse, but he's been shot. He's bleeding from his belly."

"Durand!" Brad yelled in the other man's face. "Durand!" He slapped the man hard to shut him up. "You're safe now and Lauren's going to stay with you. Lauren, see what you can do for Red. I'll be back with him soon. And I mean it this time—stay back."

23

Lauren ignored the trembling, cursing Durand and turned immediately to Red. He was conscious now, obviously racked by pain, but not making half as much noise as the other man.

"Not been shot for years," Red ground out through clenched teeth.

"What can I do to help?" she asked, leaning over him.

"Get me a hospital room with Mari."

She blinked back tears at his grit and devotion. "I think I should try to stop the bleeding, but I don't want to hurt you."

"It already hurts. Do it. Lauren? In more ways than one time counts."

"The only chopper here doesn't have fuel, or, I think, a pilot. But help should come soon. I'm sure it will come soon."

"If we—have to wait—don't know."

"I've got a horrible headache, but I'm hiking out of here down the service road," David Durand interrupted. "I'll send help. Where is that—the road?" He was hunkered down as if to use Lauren for a shield. "Evan's tried to kill me twice, and I've got to protect myself."

"Red can't wait that long for you to send help. Hiking down could take over an hour."

"I'm not staying here where I'm a target!"

"Then shut up," she ordered, "or Evan just might find you again. And don't mind Red here. He only saved your life in the canyon, didn't he? But there is a way to get to the highway fast—though you'll get soaked."

"Fine with me after nearly being roasted twice," he said, glowering at her and holding his head with both hands. "You—you mean down the flume?"

"Yes—with Red. You and I can get him up the service steps to the top. No logs are in it when the men aren't working. The flow of water is cut way back clear down to the holding ponds. Those are just off the highway that connects Vermillion to Kalispell. And firefighting or rescue vehicles should be on the road to give Red help."

"But he's bleeding bad," Durand whined. "You don't mean I should get him down that way by myself, do you? I couldn't hold him all the way down in a flume. Now, if you go with me, Lauren, I—"

"She can't leave Brad, Durand!" Red muttered through clenched teeth. "Just shut up and do it."

Lauren was certain Red would have told the man off if he didn't need him.

"Come on, Mr. Durand," Lauren urged. "You drag Red as carefully as you can to the bottom of the service stairs while I go look for bandages in the office. The door's open there. Wait for me. I'll bandage him and help you get him up top so the two of you can slide down together. Okay?"

"Yeah, sure." Still crouched, Durand alternately glared at her and scanned the area. She too was getting jumpy at the mere thought of new fires Evan could be setting. And she thought she smelled fresh smoke.

"But," Durand went on, pointing a bloody index finger nearly in her face, "I so much as catch a glimpse of my demented son again and I'm running for it, Red or not."

"Brad's gone after Evan. I'm sure he'll have him under arrest soon, but his drip torch is as bad as a flamethrower."

"Don't lecture me about drip torches."

She wanted to tell Durand off again, but, as Red had said, time mattered. She got up to go for bandages but couldn't resist one more comment. "I'm sure you're an expert of the same caliber on drip torches as you were on the Coyote Canyon fire in California."

Leaving him sputtering behind her, she headed for the camp office. She could hear the growl of the skidder even more distant. Worse, she could see fresh flames licking at the sky beyond the burning pile of logs Evan had already set aflame.

Brad saw that Evan had run the bulldozer into a barrier of brush and trees at the foot of Mount Nizitopi, but he'd done worse damage with his drip torch. Fire after new fire flared, then burst into flame, spreading through the parched foliage. Brad could even follow the maniac's path by where new blazes were springing up.

He was tempted to get up into the still-running machine and use it to scrape out a firebreak that would cut off the flames from the logging camp and the mountain itself. With the new wind direction, if the fire got a good start up and around Nizitopi, the conflagration could threaten the ski lodge, then Vermillion itself. But he'd followed his heart once before, in going with Lauren to find Nick, rather than pursue Evan, and he had to stop him now, one way or the other, once and for all.

Still holding his gun, exhausted but with adrenaline and rage rampaging through him, he tore toward the spot where the next blaze was breaking out.

Lauren found a large first-aid kit in the back room of the office. She grabbed tape, bandages and antiseptic and started away, then went back for scissors.

A phone sat on the desk. Undecided whether to take the time to make a call—and terrified she might hear that Nicky was still missing—she hesitated, then grabbed the receiver and punched in Dee's number. To Lauren's relief, Dee's familiar voice came on right away.

"Fire Command."

"Dee, it's Lauren."

"Oh, thank God, thank God! Chuck, it's Lauren! Where are you?"

"Brad and I are at the lumber camp. Red's hurt and Evan's starting more fires, so send help up here. Did the rescue planes get Nicky? He was with my plane on the shore of the little lake where the valley meets the canyon."

Silence. Had the phone gone dead? Was Dee crying?

"Dee!"

"A lot of help has just arrived. They'll be heading up there and to you, Lauren. I was in a plane that flew over that area, but the smoke…"

"What about Nicky? Did you see Nicky? I think my plane exploded! He had on his red coat. He'd be easy to spot. Dee…"

"I'm not sure. I'm—"

Lauren's legs gave out; she grabbed the edge of the desk and went to her knees. He had to be all right. Had to.

The phone dangled by its twisted cord. She could hear Dee's voice on the other end, crying her name.

Lauren forced herself to her feet, gathered up the first-aid supplies and staggered out the door. She found Red exactly where she'd asked Durand to deliver him and bent over him quickly, pulling up his blood-soaked shirt. It looked like a single bullet hole but there was very little blood around it. His shirt must have taken most of it. Or was he bleeding internally?

"Wha's matter," Red asked, staring at her strangely. His voice was much more feeble than before and he was slurring his words. "You look bad, Lau'n. He start mo' fires?"

"Yes, but Brad will get him. Red, I'm going to spray your wound with this antiseptic, then pad and wrap it before you have to take that ride down. I talked to Dee. Help is coming but—" she sniffed hard "—just like earlier today, the smoke could hamper rescue efforts. I told them where we are though, so maybe if they get here fast, we won't have to use the flume. Where's Durand?"

"Said go'ng up top—take look…"

"Durand!" she shouted, craning her neck to look up the stairs that led to the top of the flume. "Come down here! I need help with Red!"

In a near whisper almost muted by the crackle of increasing flames, Red asked, "Dee say—'bout Mari?"

"No, but she's as tough as you are. You two deserve each other. Durand should have stayed with you, though I can't blame him for being afraid. Anyone with half a brain would have to be afraid of Ev—"

"You know, dear Lauren," a voice said from behind her. "I think that's the sweetest thing I've ever heard you say."

She jerked her head around to see Evan standing there, the gun still in his hand, his drip torch cradled in the other arm.

"Your father's escaping, Evan," she told him, desperate to keep him from focusing on her and Red. She forced herself not to beg where Brad was, nor to stop wrapping Red's midriff. Keep moving calmly, she told herself. Unless Red was suddenly playing possum, he'd passed out again. But it was just as well, because she must be hurting him terribly.

"Where is he?" Evan demanded.

"He's gone up on the flume to escape to the road below. Maybe you'd better go aft—"

"He left the old man and you? Doesn't that show what a self-centered antihero he is in this drama? Now you see what I've been up against all these years."

His voice was calm but, to her horror, he lifted and pointed the nozzle of the drip torch at them. Then he raised it higher to shoot a spike of flame at the wooden footers of the flume's supporting trestle just a few feet from where Red lay.

Lauren gave a scream that tore at her raw throat. The base of the supporting beams and girders caught fire, and the ladder quickly became a torch.

As she struggled to drag Red back from it, she saw that Evan had managed to nearly encircle the logging camp in flames. Where was Brad? If this was as bad as it looked, Evan had just burned the access to their last way out.

I'm trapped! Brad thought. Evan had enticed him, whether he'd meant to or not, behind a wall of flame outside the camp. He cursed how this whole area was a big tinderbox. And he blamed himself for not shooting Evan the moment he had a bead on his head in the cab of the bulldozer. Lauren was with Durand and Red on the other side of the flames somewhere...

His first instinct was to run up the slope of Nizitopi away from the mushrooming fire. But Lauren had told him that might have been Ross's fatal mistake. She'd said it was better to run through a fire than from it.

At that thought, his legs went weak for one moment. Fear of the orange, gold and red monster devouring everything in sight drove him to his knees. He'd tried to fight fire and catch its creators, but he was now reduced to nothing by its power. Please, dear Lord, he didn't want to die. He wanted to live, to help Lauren and Nick, to save Vermillion and stop the murderer who had made this inferno.

From here, the wall of flames looked twice his height. How wide it was he wasn't sure, but he could not afford to give it more time to grow, to be fed by air funneled between the mountains.

Brad kept his shoes and charred jeans on, but he stripped off his burned jacket and shirt so that the loose cloth wouldn't catch fire. He threw away his gun in case the bullets in it exploded. Scrabbling under a thick pile of dried leaves, he clawed up handfuls of clay soil and smeared it on his forehead, face, chest and arms, praying it might provide some protection.

He knew it was now or never. As he started to run toward the conflagration, pictures paraded through his stunned brain: he was on his horse, Sam, riding with his parents in the forests near Denver; he was flying with Lauren; he was eating dinner with her and Nick...

Now or never!

Hands covering his face, holding his breath, praying he didn't run smack into a burning tree through the thick scrim of smoke, Brad ran downhill and vaulted into the fierce face of the flames.

"I hope that stopped him!" Evan shouted as the top section of the flume collapsed and a column of water splattered the ground farther down the slope. "I'm afraid my sire is like a cat, Lauren—nine lives, or at least three so far, no thanks to all of you."

She saw that he was trembling, but whether from excitement or exhaustion she wasn't sure. The hand pointing the gun at her and Red shook as he cradled the drip torch again. She hoped Evan didn't know that Red had saved his father.

"You know, Evan," she said, fighting to keep her voice calm, praying Brad would soon appear from somewhere like an avenging angel. "I understand now why you hated your father. He's pushy and acts superior, and—"

"That's not the half of it."

"I don't think he's much of an expert witness, either," she went on, carefully touching the pulse at the side of Red's neck. She wasn't sure what would be normal for a man of his age and size who was bleeding internally, but his pulse was slowing. Pretending to be smoothing the bandage on Red, while still maintaining eye contact with Evan, she surreptitiously checked Red's pockets for anything she could use against Evan. Somehow, somewhere, she'd lost the knife that was in her sock.

"I think your father did a terrible job testifying at the Coyote Canyon hearings," she went on.

To her amazement, Evan grinned. From this angle, with his face all blackened, his expression reminded her of a gargoyle's with its strange blend of grotesque humor and horror.

A pocketknife? Her hand closed around it and drew it carefully out of Red's pocket. It was closed, but if she could get it open, then get closer to Evan before he used that gun…

"You're absolutely right," Evan was saying. "He did a dreadful job at those hearings. Now that you mention it, I wish I'd had time to tell him that and why."

Despite blasts of heat from the encroaching flames,

Lauren felt icy chills leap up her spine. "You could tell me now," she said, hoping she didn't do anything to draw him from the near trance he seemed to be in. He was staring at her, but his eyes were not focused on her. He must be seeing other times, other people and places.

"You know," Evan went on, "although that fire didn't begin as an arson fire, I do believe it was further spread that way."

"What do you mean? You said you weren't there, you didn't know my husband," she cried, trying to keep her voice in check.

"Yes, I was there on a hotshot crew and I knew Ross but not well. Like you, he was a meddler, someone I had to simply write out of the script."

"How?" she said, getting off her knees and slowly standing. She held the pocketknife at her side, just behind her right thigh. It had a thick handle, probably with other items besides the blade recessed there. Which one was the blade? How could she open it with just one hand, especially now that what he was implying about Ross made her shake as hard as Evan was.

"I don't have time for this," he said, focusing on her face again. "And neither do you."

"Tell me, Evan! Tell me what really happened that your father got all wrong."

"All wrong—all right!" he said with a crooked grin. "The expert witness, the all-knowing David Durand, did not know that I had, let's say, encouraged the fire after it was started by other causes. The stupid idiots were using fire to sculpt the forests for safety's sake and things just got out of hand. Ha! But Ross Taylor suspected me of spreading those flames—with this very drip torch, actually. He was going to turn me in, I'm sure of it. And I think he told that friend of his, too."

"You set a fire to trap them?"

"I had to knock them out first with this drip torch. Then I took their personal shelters, and just let nature take its course. But I didn't set the original fire to trap them, I didn't assign them to their posts on the fire line and I didn't do any more than knock each of them over the head. That's hardly murder, so don't look at me that way!"

Stunned, she stared wide-eyed at him, then at the drip torch. Ross's killer and the murder weapon. All this time, her gnawing doubts had been fact. This psychopath had dared to come to Vermillion, somehow befriend their son and get into their home. Then he dared to tell her the horrors he had committed.

"Now, Lauren, I'm going to ask you to run back down the hill into the canyon toward Nicky," he said, aiming the gun at her. "If there's any way still out of here, that may be it. The inferno was too great earlier for you to get to him, wasn't it? And if he's still there, be a good mother and don't nag or try to squelch his fine imagination. If you do, you'll pay dearly. Maybe you should pay dearly now."

Suddenly, she couldn't take any more from this man. He'd killed women, he'd killed Ross and Kyle. His meadow fire now screaming into the valley might have taken Nicky from her. She had no idea where Brad was in this new firestorm that might devour entire forests and her town. If this maniac shot her, that was that, but she had to get her hands on him, get this knife in him if she could, or just claw his eyes out…

Though she saw only flames coming closer behind Evan, she cried, "Oh, Brad, thank God you're here!"

Evan spun. She dug out the first two inserted pieces on the knife and ran at him, stabbing, swinging.

He screeched in shock as they went down. His gun flew off somewhere. Cutting his chest and shoulder, she kicked and pulled his hair with her free hand. She was so dizzy, so beside herself with rage, she thought at first that Evan had bested her and was yanking her up off the ground. But it was Brad. Brad, naked to the waist, Brad looking worse than he had before—but Brad!

Evan was screaming and bleeding. Brad set Lauren on the ground near Red, yanked Evan to his feet, then pulled his arms behind him and tied them with the roll of bandages she'd left on the ground. Brad kicked Evan's feet wide apart and started to pat him down.

"I stabbed him," Lauren said. "He told me he killed Ross. He—I had to stop him from killing us…" She held out Red's knife toward Brad. "I stabbed him with—" She gaped at what was in her hand. She had attacked him with only a corkscrew and a bottle opener.

"We've got him now. Any one of the things he's done will put him away for good. But Ross? Lauren, sweetheart, at least you know now. How's Red?"

She felt his pulse again. "I'm shaking so much, I can't tell. Weak, I know that, very weak."

"Hey, FBI agent. Hey, Lauren," Evan said, "I'm really

just a Blackfeet spirit—a ghost, that's what I told Nicky. In like a ghost, out like a ghost."

"You can try to convince a judge or jury about that, Durand," Brad muttered. He came up with a key from Evan's pocket and squinted to read what was on it.

"But how are we going to get out?" Lauren said as reality slapped at her like the waves of heat pulsing from the encroaching flames. "Dee said choppers will arrive soon, but they're going to have the same problem here they must have had looking for Nicky with all this drifting smoke. She said they don't have him back yet, Brad."

It terrified her to see how distraught he looked, how suddenly defeated, despite the fact he'd finally caught BND. Tears burned her eyes again as she looked and pointed upward. "Evan burned the steps to the top of the flume when I said that was how his father got out of here."

"Durand left you and Red here?" Brad exploded. "I wondered where he was. I swear, I'll arrest him, too, but now we'll just have to take a page from BND's arson book of tricks."

She could see how that perked Evan up. Though he was bleeding from his chest wounds, his glazed look departed; he quit sniveling and grimacing.

"Backfires will do you no good here, FBI," Evan said, his voice cocky. "It's too late to use these machines to build a firebreak. You could try to survive by staying in the black in the middle of this camp, but I think the log piles and wooden buildings will just plain burn you out and you'll have nowhere to go. What a great finale and—"

Brad jammed some bandages into Evan's mouth and

shoved him to his knees. Keeping an eye on him, he took a few steps away and retrieved Evan's gun from the ground, checking its clip to see if it was loaded.

"Hold this gun on the prisoner," he told Lauren, putting it in her hand. "Shoot him if he so much as moves—and I know you'll do it. I'll be watching through the window of the crane cab. I've got to rig our way out of here."

She watched as Brad climbed into the cab. Just beyond, water still spewed to the ground where Evan's drip torch had burned part of the long trough of the elevated flume. For the first time she noticed that the water had also put out some of the newer flames below their position, but not enough to stop the growing inferno on the hillside. She wondered how much water was being fed in from the secondary source a bit farther down the rest of the flume, which still stood.

Then, over the noise of the crane engine, she heard another sound. In the sky? A huge roar, coming closer. Not a chopper, but surely some sort of firefighting plane. Maybe Brad didn't hear it since he was obviously concentrating on moving the boom of the crane up and down.

She realized now what he might intend. He could lift them up in the big clawlike tongs of the crane to the unburned section of the flume, but then how would he get up there himself?

She wanted to tell him about the plane she heard coming, but she had to keep the gun on Evan. Hands tied behind his back, gagged, still on his knees with his legs spread for balance, he too was looking upward, waiting. She waved at Brad and pointed up at the sky, hoping he'd see her and realize what she meant as he lowered the top of the crane to just a few feet off the ground.

"Brad, look up!" she shouted, glancing to see if he saw her. At the last minute, she thought, he understood what she meant.

Half hidden by burgeoning smoke, a big-bellied air tanker appeared, flying low. Coming from the direction of the valley and the canyon, it roared over. In a huge wall of spray, the plane dropped a crimson-colored fire retardant. Lauren screamed and bent over Red, trying to protect him, grasping the gun in both hands to keep it pointed at Evan.

The impact of the spewing scarlet foam smacked her hands to the ground. The gun fired once, then slipped away. The foam blinded her, clinging, smothering everything as the air tanker flew onward, dumping the retardant clear across the camp.

Gasping for air, swiping the slick stuff from her face, Lauren turned back to glance at Brad. The windows of the cab looked like they ran red with blood. Would this save them, put out the flames?

She scrambled for the gun but it was so slippery. Would it shoot now? She pointed it back toward Evan, expecting to see him sprawled on the ground.

But like a vanished ghost, he was gone.

24

Lauren gasped and stared. Evan had disappeared.

She knew Brad couldn't see out the crane cab windows, but he jumped out, pressing his hands to his head. At least he wasn't covered with this goo. Leaving Red where he lay, Lauren scrambled to her feet. Brad looked around, stunned, furious. "Evan?" he rasped out.

"He was here when this stuff hit! I shot once, but I don't know if I hit him. He can't be far!" she added, slipping as she ran to cling to a supporting trestle. She looked down the hill. Under the flume itself, the foam was not so thick. "There!" she cried, pointing. "He's running—limping—down under the flume from trestle to trestle, but there's fire spreading below, even creeping up these support bars. He might be stopped or trapped by flames down there. Oh, Brad, I'm so sorry he got away again."

"Air tanker's fault—and mine," he clipped out, but he looked more angry than she'd ever seen him. "Survival time. If we don't get trapped by flames, we'll get slimed to death if that tanker makes another pass. And we can't let that flume burn out from under us, so we've got to move fast. Help me shove that small log over there into these pinchers, then you get on top of it with Red. The crane will lift it to the spot where the flume starts now. Whether we have to slide or swim down, it's our best—maybe our only—bet. As soon as we make it down, we'll get help and go after Nick—and try to find Evan again."

"But how will you get up to us?" she demanded, grabbing his arm.

"I'll climb the boom of the crane."

"It's got this stuff all over it."

"I'll do it, Lauren," he insisted, seizing both her upper arms and nearly lifting her from her feet. He looked frenzied, fierce. "And if I can't, you'll need to get Red down the flume, back to Mari Gates, then get help and find Nick. If Evan makes it down, we'll get him. If not, the world's a better place."

"I won't leave you here. I can't."

"Do what I say. Help me drag this log."

Side by side, they ended up shoving the four-foot log until the pinchers, as Brad called them, gripped it. Lauren straddled it and held Red, balanced against her. To steady herself, she leaned back against the big metal claws.

And then something went right for the first time today as Brad managed to maneuver the boom up so close to the place on the flume where the drip-torch fire had halted that she could roll Red out and clamber onto it herself. But for slippery red foam, it was dry here now, since the secondary flow of water shot in about twelve feet lower.

Hanging on to Red, she thought that, by comparison, it had been nothing to get the injured Chuck down from the mountain on the ski lift. Her thoughts spun out of control. Ross had been murdered, but Evan might never live to tell the truth. And even if he did, would he admit it to anyone but her? Nicky had to be safe or she'd just as soon throw herself off this flume into the forest burning below.

She peered down to the crane where Brad tried to climb the boom. He had it at a steep angle to reach this far and, as she'd feared, it was slippery with red retardant. But he must have found some footholds. As he inched his way up through thickening smoke, she heard the deep roar of what must be the returning air tanker.

The smoke seemed to devour Brad before he emerged from it. Lauren held out her hand to him, praying his added weight on this end of the burned, curved flume would not make it break.

Coughing, he scrambled behind her, turned her to face downward and put both legs around her almost as if she were sitting in his lap. Together they got Red positioned, feetfirst with his head against Lauren's chest, as if they were ready for a three-man bobsled run.

"We've got to get down where the water starts and fight to keep our heads up in it," Brad told her. "I think it will only be about chest deep. I'm going to hold on tight to you! Besides," he added, his voice breaking, "we could all use a bath."

As Brad had feared, the combination of foam and the gush of water below their entry point on the flume got them going faster than he wanted. He wished Red wasn't unconscious because he was dead weight, but he'd probably be in agony if he was awake. Brad had only been with the guy a few hours on their hike back from the ski lift, but they'd taken to each other well. Like with Lauren, it was as if Brad had known the people in Vermillion for longer than just a few frenzied days.

Although Brad sometimes went to see his dad in prison, he'd missed the camaraderie of an older man. Mike and Clay had never filled that void for him.

In the quick, downward rush of current, they fought to keep their heads up, but at least they were going in the same direction as the flow. The water washed the black soot and red foam from their skin and hair. Brad could feel the burns he'd been trying to ignore, but the cool flow of water still felt good.

Beneath the flume, below them, he saw that they raced the latest fires Evan had set. But that was out of his hands now. That air tanker and other help would surely be here soon to fight that battle.

"Brad—below!" Lauren cried.

He looked around her to see that a couple of logs had jammed in a slight turn in the flume. Water was piling up in little rapids ahead of it, and what couldn't get past the jam or what the flume couldn't hold was spewing over the left side. Brad feared Red and Lauren would take the brunt of the collision and they all might be rocked out, down almost twenty feet to the ground.

"Pull your legs up tight!" he shouted. "Lean back into me and try to hold on to Red."

As she did, Brad sat straight up, hoping his bulk might slow their descent. He stuck out both legs beyond Lauren's, down to about Red's knees. The tops of trees on both sides of the flume seemed to rotate past him as time stood still. A chopper with rotors *whap-whapping* suddenly appeared to hover over them.

The buffer of water slowed them a bit more, but they hit into the small logjam with a gush. Brad managed to take the brunt of it. The two logs stuck sideways jerked but did not let loose. Water from above smacked them, shot over them and slammed off both sides of the flume.

He could see no way to get into a chopper rescue basket from here, even if they tried to lower one. Not with these logs and all this water below them ready to pop loose.

"Hold on to the side!" he yelled at Lauren. "If you have to let Red go, do it, but hang on!"

He swallowed and spit out water. How crazy would it be if they drowned in the middle of a wildfire, he thought, then remembered what Lauren said she'd told Nicky. If the fire comes, get in the water.

Brad put his arm around Lauren's waist and clamped her to him. She tried to hold Red between her knees as she gripped the sides of the old wooden flume while Brad kicked at one log then the other.

He pulled Lauren to her knees and, together, they kept Red's face above the deluge. Weeping Wall Falls had failed them earlier, Brad thought, but damned if he was going to be done in by this flume!

Holding Red between them, they knelt against the

two jammed logs in the best airspace they could find. It might have taken only a few moments, but it seemed that water battered them for hours, then sloshed over the side, the way they faced. At least it was a great way to get this lower part of the forest ready to resist the fire, he thought.

That must be what Lauren was screaming about as she looked down over the edge of the flume. Or was she having another dizzy spell like that day they'd climbed down from the old fire tower?

And then Brad saw it, too—saw both of them. About twenty feet below the flume, just above where the water cascaded out to splash the ground and run downhill, lay the charred body of Evan Durand, faceup, next to that of his father.

Brad shook his head to clear it and looked again through the rush of water. Yes, it was Evan, burned and laid out almost formally, as if for his own funeral. The bandages with which Brad had tied his wrists had evidently burned away, for his hands were at his sides, but the gag Brad had stuffed in Evan's mouth partly stuck out, as if Evan were a cartoon character who still had something to say.

And David Durand was definitely also dead. He lay sopping wet, all twisted up as if his neck or back was broken. Evan had run through the flames and gotten this far before he lay down to die. And Durand, trying to get down the flume after deserting Lauren and Red, must have hit this logjam and rocketed out to the ground.

Was it just fate that the Durands had landed side by

side? More likely Evan had stumbled across his father's broken body and decided to die there, too. Still, Brad half expected that if he closed his eyes and looked again, Evan would have disappeared.

Through the wash of air the chopper blades made, driving off the smoke right above them, Brad looked up and pointed down at the bodies. But the moment he freed one hand from holding the side of the flume, his weight shifted. The logs shuddered and let loose. The small dam of water around them gushed downward, taking them with it.

It was a thrill ride he didn't want. He reached for Lauren but snagged only her hair. She grabbed at him, gripping his ankle as they shot downward, out of control, until they landed with a flying, jolting splash amid logs in the holding pond.

Lauren spit water, but that was better than smoke. Brad? When they'd hit bottom, she'd lost Brad. And where was Red? Had they really seen Evan and his father dead up on the mountain?

Brad emerged near her in a whoosh of white water and bare skin. He was holding Red up and she staggered over to help him. The chopper must have landed nearby, because two men in jumpsuits splashed into the pond, fighting their way around logs, pushing them out of the way. She could hear another chopper landing.

"Brad Hale, FBI. This man's been shot!" Brad shouted as they sloshed toward him through hip-deep water. He gasped out his words, and his voice was not his own. "He needs…hospital. The bodies of the arsonist and his father…partway up the mountain under the flume… where I pointed. Tree cover's thick there. You see the fire, working its way down? Someone's got to recover the bodies before they're…burned beyond recognition."

"Burned beyond recognition." The words revolved in Lauren's stunned brain. Ross and Kyle had been murdered and burned beyond recognition, so was this God's justice now?

The men carried Red to the edge of the pond and handed him over to two others, dressed just as they were, who carried him away. Brad hugged her, leaned on her. Exhausted, they staggered after the men. Lauren let their rescuers help her out of the pond while Brad clambered out. Brad pulled on a nylon jacket one of the men handed him.

"Both of you have visible burns," one man said. "We're going to fly you into Vermillion and see that you're transferred to Kalispell."

"Please, my son may be back in the valley, beyond the canyon," she said, gripping the man's hand. His name on his jumpsuit reads Lieutenant Tom Barton.

"We know about the boy."

"You found him?" she cried. "Did you find him?"

"We were going to put down there to search until the air tanker radioed us that there might be people on the ground at the logging camp. We thought the boy might have made it that far."

"No, he didn't make it that far!" she shouted. "Brad, tell them they have to take us there, that—"

Brad scooped her up in his arms and headed for the second chopper as the one with Red took off in a whirl of dust and debris. "That's where we're going, I promise," he said. "That's where we're going if I have to commandeer and fly this thing myself."

The sight of the burned canyon stunned Lauren and Brad into silence. Ahead of them, the once lush valley looked like a bombed-out, blackened war zone. The moment they were over the site where she'd left Nicky, Lauren started to shake so hard that her teeth chattered. All she'd been through and all she'd seen was nothing next to finding her boy.

She saw ragged pieces of the plane on the shore; it had indeed exploded. She was amazed at how little it mattered, yet she began to heave huge sobs. Pulling against his seat belt, Brad leaned over to put a hand on her knee. Then he unsnapped his belt and knelt beside her so that they were both looking out the same window.

She mourned the loss of *Silver*, but that was nothing next to Nicky's life.

The pilot put the chopper down on the shore not far from where Evan had forced her to run the plane into the trees. No one ran out to greet them. Some places were still smoking; a few tree trunks were gently glowing. The area was thoroughly burned, devastated. Even the little lake seemed to glitter black in the morning sun.

The second they opened the chopper door, Lauren rushed out, ducking under the rotors. Weren't they going to shut them down so she could call his name?

"Nicky!" she screamed, running toward where the plane had been. Not only did she see a fierce circle of fire but there was a hole in the shore under stumps of burned trees that had hidden the plane. Brad put his arm around her shoulders, but she pulled away and ran farther into the charred maze of tree trunks. Bushes and brush were obliterated; there was no place to hide.

"Niii-ck-eee!"

The rotors of the chopper finally ceased, leaving only silence.

"Niii-ck—eeeee!"

Her voice seemed to echo across the lake, or maybe it came back to her from the canyon. Could Nicky have fled into the canyon, trying to follow her? If so, he'd been doomed.

Brad and the others fanned out around the lake, calling his name. She knew Brad was keeping an eye on her, and he didn't go far from where she searched. Finally the pilot lifted a sopping, red jacket from the far edge of the lake.

"Dear God, please let him be safe!" she spoke aloud the mantra she'd been reciting silently as she ran over.

She hugged the sodden jacket to her, sobbing into it, then lifted her head. "I've got to stay here to look for him," she told them. "He might have been in the lake for a little while when the fire passed, but he can swim and knows how to hold his breath. I may have to go back into the canyon too. I'm going to—"

"Ma'am, I know this sounds terrible," Lieutenant Barton said, "but we're going to have to use this chopper for other things right now."

"Fine," she said, turning away from them and wading into the water to stare into its depths. "Fine, I understand. Just leave me here."

"Lauren," Brad said and sloshed in to take her arm.

"No. I know you all have jobs to do. Go report in. You, too, Brad. I understand that, so—"

"I don't care if I have a job," Brad told her. "All I've done since I've been here is ignore my so-called duty to the masses so that I could try to help individual people—you, Nick, Chuck, Mari and Red. I keep telling myself that one precious life saved now is more important than FBI statistics down the road."

He picked her up as he had back at the holding pond, then strode toward the chopper. "No!" she cried, hitting at his shoulder with her fist. "I'm staying here!"

"We'll get another chopper or hike right back in through the valley with volunteers from Vermillion— and there will be plenty of those."

"He's just wandered off," she said, collapsing against him. "He can't be in that lake, but if he is…"

"Lauren, I swear to you, wherever he is, I will help you find him. I will make sure, one way or the other, that he comes home to you."

Back on the chopper, she sank into a stupor, staring out the window, not even blinking. She felt empty, sick to her soul. The chopper lifted up and away. Holding Nicky's wet jacket to her, Lauren felt completely defeated.

The Otter River went by under them, black on both

sides. All those lovely flowers burned, she thought, praying she would not need flowers for a funeral. No, he could not be gone…not Nicky. He'd been rescued already and no one had told Dee, that was it.

"Ma'am," the pilot said and put the chopper into a tilted turn, "there's someone walking along the river back there, a small man or a boy."

Lauren and Brad pressed their faces to one window, then to the other side. Yes! Yes, it must be. It had to be!

"Please," she cried, "can you put down here?"

But he was already lowering the big bird to the blackened meadow. Where was the boy? She didn't see him now.

When they landed, she pushed past Brad before he could help her down to the ground. She saw tears streaming down his face. She ran with her arms outstretched, shrieking, "Nicky, Nicky, Nicky!"

Nicky started to run toward her, too, his arms wide. "Mom," he shouted just before she reached him, "don't get mad 'cause I didn't stay where you told me. I got in the water when the fire came and lost my jacket, but I'm really hungry, and I knew the way back home. Sorry, but *Silver* blew up and—"

She hit into him so hard that they both went to their knees. Hugging him, kissing him… Thank God. Thank you, Lord!

Nicky hugged her back hard, his strong, thin arms tight around her neck. A few moments passed, but they didn't budge. Then she heard him say, "Hi, Brad."

"Hi, Nick, my man."

"Did that bad guy get caught?"

"Yes," Brad said. "Yes, he did."

"He shouldn't tell lies. He told lots of them, but I'm not ever telling them anymore."

Her son's high-pitched little voice reverberated through her, as did Brad's lower, raspy tones. He knelt and put his arms around both of them. How she treasured having them both here, both safe.

"You look pretty messed up," Nicky said as he wriggled from their embrace. "Did you guys have to get in a lake to hide from the fire too?"

As their rescue chopper passed over Vermillion on its way to land, Brad thought the place looked like a busy anthill. Darting here and there, some in clusters, people were in the street and on the shore. He was so glad to be back, to see—but for the burned buildings—the place in one piece. It was almost like coming home.

As the chopper put down on a stretch of shore close to town, Brad could see a huge helicopter hovering over the lake, sucking up water to dump on the fire. Tents had been erected close to the dock. At least two hotshot crews wearing hard hats and fire-resistant yellow shirts and green pants lugged axes, chain saws and, yes, drip torches as they boarded a school bus, evidently heading out to contain the fire.

Brad had rejoiced in Lauren and Nick's reunion. Even now, she held the boy on her lap, hugging him tight while Nick expounding on his ordeal and Lauren made light of hers. She had told Brad how, after Ross died, Nick had hardly let her out of his sight; he wondered if the tables would be turned now. But if Lauren would let him, Brad had plans to be in the boy's life as well as in hers.

Dee met their chopper. And when she saw that they had Nick, she jumped up and down, screaming like a kid.

There were plenty of hugs and tears as they piled out. Exhausted and elated, Brad cried too. Then he saw Mike coming his way with Clay and Jen right behind. He swiped at his cheeks with the palms of his hands.

"You sure he's dead?" Mike greeted him above the hubbub. Suze and Larson were in the mix of people now, hysterical with joy, hugging everyone in sight.

Brad nodded.

"You saw him with your own eyes?" Clay demanded as his team surrounded him.

"Both Durands are dead," Brad told them. "I just wish I could have stopped BND before he started this last blaze—or any of them here."

"They say they'll control the mountain fire," Mike told him. "Damn, I wish we could have gotten him alive, but at least you're okay. We're going to have to debrief you now, while everything's fresh in your mind, then be sure we recover the body. Can you go with a team that hikes up there?"

"I told them where he is."

"It's just— He's been so elusive," Jen said, her eyes widening as she looked Brad over. "It would be just like him to have staged his death and then—*poof.*"

Clay said something else, maybe something about Brad getting his burns tended to. But Dee elbowed her way in, thrusting a mug of coffee at him, and Nick had squirmed between Mike and Clay. The kid was breaking a cookie in half that Larson had given him. He thrust part of it at Brad, then hung on to him. Lauren, looking like a flame-haired pagan goddess, was mouthing, "Thank you. Thank you always," again and again to him over Jen's shoulder.

Brad stuffed the cookie in his mouth and took a swig of the coffee. Then, clamping Nick to his side, Brad turned his back away from the team and headed for Lauren. Eating a chocolate-chip cookie with a boy who had come back from the dead, he walked right into the middle of the townspeople milling around him toward Lauren.

Brad supposed he was a failure in the eyes of the arson team. He hadn't captured BND alive or stopped three structural fires and two massive wildfires. But it was over for Evan and over for the hypocrite who had bred and reared him. If they branded Brad a failure, he still felt his coming here had been worth it. Who knows what Evan would have done if Lauren hadn't helped him fight back.

Mike came after him, repeating his order that he needed to be formally debriefed, but he was pushed back by the nurse who had tended Chuck at the clinic. Grabbing Lauren by the other hand, the nurse hustled them both—with Nick tight to Brad—away from Mike.

"Both of you now—and Nicky, too," she said, "come with me. We're going to the firehouse so I can look at those burns, then you all need a good hot meal. Lauren and

Agent Hale, you're both heroes, you know, but even heroes need patching up at times—just ask Sheriff Cobern."

Brad didn't feel like a hero. His long-tended dream of solving arsons and fighting fires might be over, but the fire he felt inside each time he looked at Lauren still burned strong. He guessed the stubborn people of Vermillion thought he was okay because, as the nurse shooed the three of them down the street toward the fire station, people stopped to turn, clap, smile and wave.

Surely they were glad to have Nicky and Lauren back safe. But no, they were looking at him, nodding at him, even calling out his name as if he were a longtime friend.

Mike's voice in his ear muted. For one minute, in his exhaustion, Brad thought the clapping was the crackle of flames, but it went on and on, turning into swelling applause.

He hugged Lauren, then lifted Nick up between them where the boy hooked an arm around each of their necks and pulled them so close to him that their noses and chins bumped.

"I think I just resigned from the FBI," he told her.

"And I don't have a livelihood anymore."

"Finding you and Nick's been worth it."

Lauren nodded and smiled. With Nick screeching, "Way to go!" in his ear, Brad kissed her long and hard.

25

The first snowflakes of the season fell in Vermillion the day Marilyn Gates and Red Russert were married. Mari's sister, in from Omaha, and Chuck Cobern stood up for the couple in the ceremony to which they had extended an open invitation to the community. It seemed the entire town, including Mrs. Gates's first-grade class, had turned out. In a way, two months to the day after the Nizitopi Mountain Wildfire was contained, it was a celebration of Vermillion's survival and recovery as well as a wedding day.

Now, to get the noisy, excited kids out of the reception at Dee's house, Lauren, with the help of the Fencer twins, had twenty hyper, sugar-buzzed first-graders at her house, making Just Married decorations for the inside of the plane that would fly the couple out for their honeymoon. It had been a beautiful day, though the joy of the occasion made Lauren miss Brad even more.

He'd been called to testify again this week in a senate committee in Washington, D.C., about his part in stopping the BND arsonist. It involved FBI funding for a domestic terrorist protection program. Otherwise, he would not have missed Red's wedding. Just as Brad had filled a void in her son's heart, it seemed that Red had become a sort of adopted dad to Brad.

"No," Lauren told Larson, pointing to what he had just printed. She couldn't help herself, but somehow this happy day had made her uptight. "It's not *Just Marred.* That means something else. There's an *i* missing from the word *married.* All of you, listen to me. Copy the sign in the middle of the table. Mrs. Gates is a stickler for spelling, so get the letters right."

"But her name isn't Mrs. Gates anymore, Mom," Nick said. "It's gonna be kinda hard to call her Mrs. Russert."

"I know," Lauren admitted. "Changes are hard but important."

There had been many changes in Lauren's life these last two months. Her insomnia had departed, as had her guilt over not pursuing what had really happened to Ross in the Coyote Canyon fire. It had been in all the newspapers that the arsonist–mass murderer Evan Durand had killed Ross and Kyle and that the ensuing investigation had been a sham.

Posthumously, David Durand's pristine reputation had taken a real hit, so that would have pleased Evan. She wasn't sorry they had found a bullet from the gun she'd been holding in Evan's hip, or the fact that it had probably slowed him down so that he was caught and killed by his own wildfire.

Other changes in her life were more mundane. She tried to help Nick with current events she'd previously ignored. They'd had many discussions about not talking to strangers and telling the truth, but how it was still important to have a good imagination. Lauren could almost hear Evan's voice, telling her not to nag Nick. She and Brad both wondered if the death of Evan's mother in a fiery car crash had been his first death by arson.

And then there was Brad in her life. Brad!

She pulled herself from her reverie as little heads bent over their cutting and coloring, adding stickers and gluing on hearts. Lauren's wedding gift to the Russerts was to fly them into Kalispell, where they would board a jet for Phoenix to soak up the sun and see the sights. It would almost be the inaugural flight for her new Cessna pontoon plane she'd purchased with the reward money for *information which led to the capture and or arrest of Evan Durand, alias the BND serial arsonist,* as the citation, which came with the check Brad had personally delivered, had read.

Both Brad and she had been hailed as heroes and even featured on several nightly newscasts and in an article in *People* magazine. The publicity from all that had worked wonders for ski lodge reservations for this winter. With all the accolades, Brad's boss had not dared to let him go. But Brad had admitted he wasn't happy in his arson-fighting mission anymore. At least he'd made time to visit her and Nick every couple of weeks and called often.

"I know a joke," Susie Parker piped up from down the table where someone had just spilled juice that Ginnie Fencer was mopping up. "Red Russert and Mrs. Gates, sitting in a tree, k-i-s-s-i-n-g! First comes love, then comes marriage, then comes Mrs. Gates with a baby carriage!"

The kids all laughed, but Nick's wide eyes snagged Lauren's gaze. He'd walked in on her and Brad when they were really hot and heavy on the couch in front of the fireplace the last time he was here. They hadn't seen him at first until he'd announced, "I'm not keeping pretend people around or keeping secrets anymore, like you said, Mom. But I can't sleep till I know if you guys are keeping secrets from me."

Startled, they'd scrambled apart, then just sat up to lean shoulder to shoulder, facing him.

"Such as, pal?" Brad had asked, his voice as husky as it had been when they'd inhaled all that smoke.

"I heard where babies come from, and I was wondering if you are trying to get me a brother or sister. I'd rather have a brother, but don't you have to get married first?"

"Nick," Lauren had begun, floundering for words, "you can't just—"

"We're thinking about all that, Nick," Brad had interrupted. "As a matter of fact, we were doing some practice thinking about that just now, so you get on back to bed. Want me to go up with you?"

"No, I'm not afraid of anything anymore, even though I got took out that window by that liar ars'nist. I think he got dead because he was grabbed by a Blackfeet Indian ghost. He lied to me about the Blackfeet, so he got punished. That's what I think. And that's another reason I don't tell lies anymore. It's okay," he'd said, sounding wise and comforting beyond his years as they'd sat there disturbed and disheveled. "You can go back to your thinking now."

After he'd returned to bed, they'd dissolved in laughter, but all that didn't seem funny now. Brad had already won her heart and Nick's, too, but she knew something was holding him back from full commitment. He hadn't asked, but both she and Nick would have given up all they loved here to live in Denver or anywhere else with him—however much leaving would hurt.

"All right, it's almost two o'clock," Lauren announced to the kids, "so you all finish up, and I'll go get changed to fly the newlyweds to Kalispell. I'll decorate the inside of the plane with this beautiful artwork before they get to the dock. I'll tell them what a good job all of you did, but I don't think you should expect any baby carriages. Mrs. Russert has enough on her hands with all of you."

As the plane crested the mountains and descended toward Kalispell, Lauren noted it was snowing halfheartedly here too. Big, lazy flakes spun down from heaven around them.

"We missed Brad today, Lauren," Mari said from where they sat behind her. "But as soon as our new house is finished and you two have a spare evening, you are both to come for dinner."

"We'd love that. I missed him today, too—well, every day."

"Bet he'll be back sooner than you think," Red put in

from the back seat where they'd been holding hands the whole way. Lauren heard Mari smack his knee.

"Have you been talking to him again, Red?" Lauren asked. "Sometimes I think he comes to Vermillion to see you as much as me and Nick."

"If you're not kidding, girl, I think you got blinders on," Red told her. "But then, I've known a woman or two in my day who didn't realize how much they were loved 'til it hit them over the head."

"Talk about getting hit over the head," Mari said. "I still wonder about you sometimes, Red Russert. All we've been through might have been worth it to me just to have those staring, glassy-eyed heads of that mounted game in your living room and bedroom go up in smoke."

"Now, Mari."

"Bring one of those into our new house and your head will be stuffed and mounted right beside it, my love."

Lauren could tell they were kissing again as she brought the Cessna down toward the runway. The landing gear on this plane did not come down with a clunk, and the wheels barely bounced as she taxied toward the main gate instead of the storage sheds this time. She and Nick—with Brad voting, too—had named the new plane *Golden* because of a butterscotch-hued stripe down its side.

"Gold is better than silver, right, Mom?" Nicky had asked. "I'm reading a book about skiing in the Olympics, like I want to do someday when I take some more lessons, and gold is better than silver there."

Yes, Lauren thought now, gold was better than silver. And a new life could be better than the old, she was sure of that, if only it could include Brad. She knew somehow, as soon as Mari and Red got out and hurried off to their honeymoon, it was going to be a long, lonely ride back to Vermillion.

"Cessna Bravo Niner Alpha," came the crisp voice on her new radio, answering her earlier call for permission to land, "you are cleared for gate two. And you have a passenger waiting to go back to Vermillion, Lauren."

"Roger that," she said automatically, then recalled that the last time she'd heard something similar, Evan Durand had been waiting for her.

On the tie-down at gate two, she set the parking brake and shut the engines down. "Well, would you look at that," Red said as she opened the door.

"At what?" she asked, then sensed as well as thought what he might mean.

She spun to face the terminal. Striding out through falling flakes came Brad, grinning and waving, pushing a loaded luggage cart. Her insides cartwheeled. He had flowers.

He hugged Lauren and kissed her hard. Her pulse pounded as it always did when he so much as appeared, even from just the next room. If they were ever really together, would she ever get over this permanent heart condition?

"I was hoping to catch you two before you literally took off together," Brad told the newlyweds and kissed Mari's cheek. He stuck out his hand to Red.

"Oh, hell," Red said and hugged Brad, then set him back and smacked his shoulder.

"More flowers for the bride, for your Phoenix hotel room," Brad said and thrust a bouquet of roses into Mari's arms. So this wasn't a special occasion between Brad and her, Lauren thought. That was fine. Anytime he was here was already special.

Brad helped Red get their luggage out of the plane and put it on his cart, then loaded his gear into *Golden*. The four of them said their goodbyes with more hugs all around. Brad raced ahead to open the terminal door for them, and then they disappeared to start their new life.

"This is way more than you usually bring," Lauren told him as he returned to loading the plane. She tried to sound calm, even businesslike. "Skis? There's not that much snow yet."

"There will be before I leave this time. Dee and Chuck have offered me a room for a while if you don't want me around day and night."

She sucked in a breath. This was starting to sound like a conspiracy—a wonderful one. Because she didn't want to just smother him with kisses or suffocate him with a hug, she blurted, "Nick's going to take ski lessons this winter and—"

"I know. I'm teaching him, with his mother's permission, of course. Besides, I thought you'd have room for skis, but you'd never get six quarter horses into this plane."

"What?"

Still grinning, he piled into the copilot seat and she

climbed in the other side. "If you don't tell me what you're talking about," she said, "I'm going to go see if I can pick up some good-looking, macho guy with impressive creds in the coffee shop across the tarmac."

"I hear you. I've been testifying so long under the glares of grim senators and camera lenses, I think I can handle explaining this to one beautiful woman. Lauren, now that the formal, public fallout from the BND case is over and I won't hurt the team or the terrorist funding, I resigned. The lease on my apartment in Denver's up, so I'm looking for a place in Vermillion to buy or build, where I can have a stable for backcountry packhorses to start my business there. Man, that place needs more than the Fencer twins' two old mares. Besides, Chuck says he wants more time with Dee, so he'll stick with being sheriff and I'll become Vermillion's fire chief.

"Hey," he went on, sounding ebullient when she just gaped at him, "look at all these great heart decorations in here. Perfect."

"Yes, Mari and Red loved them."

"I mean, perfect for this. I was going to wait until we were soaring over the mountains with eagles today—or should I say snowflakes?—but I'm just like Nick. I cannot wait. I have to barge right in with what I want to say."

From his jacket pocket he produced a small box of dark blue leather. It was a good thing she'd just snapped her seat belt on or she might have taken off without the plane.

"I know this part of it is sudden," he explained, "but I didn't want the intensity of our relationship to stampede you into anything. Since we've both been through so much, and getting everything in order took me a while, you can take your time deciding, if you want. Lauren, I had commitments to my cause, but no more. You and Nick and life in Vermillion are now my cause, if you will have me."

The gold ring was stunning, with a round diamond like a little sun nestled in the blue velvet of its own sky.

"Yes," she said as she stared at it, then him, "I will need some time. About as much time as it takes you to put that on my finger."

His big hands shook as he took the ring out and slid it on her trembling hand. They held tight to each other, then kissed endlessly as snowflakes piled up on the cockpit windows, sealing them in together.

"I'm ready to go home," he whispered.

"Yes, home." She swiped at her tears with the handkerchief he handed her. "And we're going to fly over the Vermillion Valley on the way in because, peeking through the snow and charred grass, you're going to see a hint of green already, new growth, new life."

"I'm betting on it!" he said. "Let's go."

AUTHOR'S NOTE

Readers often ask where I get ideas for my novels. The inspiration for *Inferno* came from a trip my husband and I took to the Rocky Mountains in the summer of 2005. We visited several areas where pontoon planes ferried visitors between smaller mountain towns and larger cities. We visited beautiful valleys and saw pristine waterfalls. Most compelling of all, we took a train through a mountain area that was threatened by a wildfire that we could smell even before we saw it. We also observed what I later learned was a hotshot crew, hiking up the mountain to try to build a firebreak.

Because I live in flatland Ohio and the even flatter Everglades area of south Florida, I was thrilled by the magnificence of the mountains and greatly intrigued by the rugged individuals who live there.

As for the arson investigation information, my thanks to arson investigator Marty Robinson of the Columbus, Ohio, fire department and arson investigator Craig Hall of the Worthington, Ohio, fire department. And to my nephew, firefighter Aaron Kurtz, for information about fire engines. Thanks to Laurie Kingery, E.R. nurse and author, for advice about treating burns. And to my author friend Karyn Witmer-Gow for advice on St. Louis neighborhoods and cemeteries. Any mistakes in facts are those of the author.

Also, as ever, very special thanks to my wonderful Rotrosen support team, especially Meg Ruley and Annelise Robey. And thanks to Miranda Stecyk, my excellent Mira Books editor, and the entire Mira family. I greatly appreciate all that you do.

W9-AFV-508

THE
HIDDEN

Also available by Melanie Golding

Little Darlings

THE
HIDDEN

A NOVEL

MELANIE GOLDING

NEW YORK

Published in the United States by Crooked Lane Books, an imprint of The Quick Brown Fox & Company LLC.

Crooked Lane Books and its logo are trademarks of The Quick Brown Fox & Company LLC.

Library of Congress Catalog-in-Publication data available upon request.

ISBN (hardcover): 978-1-64385-297-3
ISBN (ebook): 978-1-64385-318-5

Cover design by Melanie Sun

Printed in the United States.

www.crookedlanebooks.com

Crooked Lane Books
34 West 27th St., 10th Floor
New York, NY 10001

First Edition: November 2021

10 9 8 7 6 5 4 3 2 1

For my mother, Mary

1

She steals to the window, and looks at the sand,
And over the sand at the sea;
And her eyes are set in a stare;
And anon there breaks a sigh,
And anon there drops a tear,
From a sorrow-clouded eye,
And a heart sorrow-laden,
A long, long sigh;
For the cold strange eyes of a little Mermaiden
And the gleam of her golden hair.
　　—Matthew Arnold, "The Forsaken Merman," 1849

NOW
Leonie
Friday, December 21

LEONIE PRESSES HER palm to the outside of the shop window. The glass is cold; the fat little star of her hand leaves an imprint in condensation when she pulls it away. She laughs and slaps her hand back on the window, stamping another and another, a bit like when she does potato printing at the kitchen table, the potatoes soon left aside in favor of dipping her hands straight in the paints. She concentrates on tracing the outlines of the handprints with a fingertip, before they fade away.

"Mamma," she says. "Come look. Me do painting."

Behind her, a handbag stands abandoned on the pavement. She turns around, toddles over, picks up the bag. She looks up and down the street, her whole body turning first one way, then the other. There is no one else there. The chill wind blows in her face, tightening the skin on her cheeks and almost toppling her, almost taking her pink bobble hat from her head. Two bobbles; like a teddy bear's ears.

"Mamma?"

Leonie is still, wearing a small frown. Then, she upends the handbag onto the slabs. Nappies and wipes fall out, nappy bags are whisked up the street by the wind. There is a coin purse, a collection of receipts, a bunch of keys attached to a smooth pebble with a hole in it. Picking up the pebble, she shakes the bunch so that they rattle, then drops the lot back on the ground. A fruit bar, half finished and wound into its torn wrapper is what she reaches for next. She has it in her mouth when she hears the bell on the shop. The heavy door creaks as it opens, spilling yellow light and warmth onto her fingers, now almost blue with cold, that peep out beyond the cuffs of her coat.

Though it isn't late, it's nearly dark; the shortest day of the year. The girl toddles toward the shop's light, toward the Christmas tree just inside, past the stranger at the door who has stepped aside to let her in, who is saying, "Where's your mummy?"

Leonie reaches for a bauble, a shiny thing, sparkling. There's a chocolate bell too, and she drops the fruit bar to take it in her hand.

"Whose child is this?" calls the stranger as the man from behind the counter comes forward, rubbing his hands together, his eyes wide with concern.

"Mamma?" says Leonie to the shopkeeper, recognizing nothing but the worry in his expression. Her bottom lip wobbles in uncertainty. Then, her grip on the foil-covered decoration is lost, and it hits the floor tiles, smashing into pieces that scatter from the wrapping as it splits. There is stillness as she looks at all the bits in turn, her face registering surprise. This, seemingly, is the most upsetting thing. She shuts her eyes to cry, face to the ceiling, fists clenched, mouth open and revealing eight perfect teeth.

The customer crouches, hovering his hand near the toddler, saying, "Shh, it's okay, don't worry. We'll find Mamma."

Both of the adults expect a loud noise and brace themselves for it. But when the cry comes, it is a faint, keening whisper, like distant wind. The child's face is posed in a scream, but there is barely a sound.

The two men exchange a glance, agreeing that something is wrong, but at this moment there are bigger problems than the strangeness of this cry. The customer starts to pat the toddler on the shoulder, the pads of his fingers barely making contact, and all the time he's glancing around, talking to the shopkeeper, saying, "Did you see who she was with?" Leonie opens her eyes and screams silently into his face. The soundlessness of it makes it worse somehow than if the scream were deafening. The man stands, snatches another chocolate decoration from a branch and gently takes one of the child's trembling fists in his hand. He unpeels the small fingers, places the confection on her upturned palm. Her mouth shuts, and she inspects the red Santa figure, turning it over, searching for how to open it. She hiccups once. Snot runs down her chin.

The bell on the door rings as the shopkeeper yanks it open. He steps outside and looks both ways, then up at the darkening sky and finally down, at the handbag spilling its contents. He walks forward, nudges the pile of nappies with a toe, notes the keys, the packet of wipes. He's looking for a phone, or a wallet with something like ID in it, but there's nothing. The coin purse contains only cash. He picks up the empty handbag, weighs it in his hand. He finds a pocket at the front and unzips it. Inside is what he thinks is a rock but on closer inspection is a seashell.

One or two snowflakes swirl in the wind, landing on the concrete and making wet speckles. In the distance, the seals call to each other across the waves, making a sound like human screams, but other than a slight jerk to the head, the man doesn't react. If you live here it's a familiar sound, the seal song, like that of the waves and the gulls.

The sea sighs as the tide licks the shore, sucking the surface of the beach into new shapes: gentle, curving undulations, different from yesterday's, that will be different tomorrow and with every tide that turns.

Just out of sight, a small pile of clothes, buried in haste in the sand, is covered up by the advancing water. Gentle eddies loosen the folds of the fabric, so that a parka slowly unfurls like a flower opening in the darkness. Soon the sea will probe further, uncovering the heel of one boot. Later, the clothes will be completely removed from their rudimentary hiding place by the many strong hands of the currents. Later still they will be scattered on seven different shores. The other boot will remain here, wedging itself between two rocks, unseen by anyone until the litter pickers come in the spring.

CHAPTER

2

NOW
Bathwater
Friday, December 21

THE WATER FILLS the bathtub slowly, over a number of hours. As it does so, the body of the man begins to float, rising with the level of the liquid, the small amount of fat and the air in his body keeping him on the surface for now. Falling from the tap, the water is clear. As the thin stream enters the tub, it mixes with the man's blood so that the color of the bathwater varies from pale rose at his feet, to plumes of bright red near his head, where pulse pressure shoots the blood from the wound in regular bursts. It takes a long time, but when the bath is full, the solution finds its way to the overflow, and from there it trickles through the many meters of pipework to the sewers deep below the block of flats.

In the bathtub, as well as the man and the water and the blood, there is a towel. The towel is drawn toward the overflow until, at last, a combination of the man's legs and the bunching of the thick fabric blocks the hole completely. No one is there to turn off the tap; the bath keeps filling, and keeps filling, so that soon, like a bloody version of the magic porridge pot it goes over, flooding the bathroom, searching out the edges of the vinyl, breaking through, soaking into the floorboards, pooling in the cavity under the floor. There's a layer of sealant there and a layer of soundproofing, but the water finds the lowest point. It accumulates, becomes heavier, weakens the plasterboard. It only needs a tiny gap, a pinprick, to break through.

In the flat below, Mrs. Stefanidis is preparing to eat her lunch, a small cheese sandwich on white bread. She feels rather than hears something drop, disrupting the air close to her face, but when she places her hands on the tabletop and feels around, there appears to be nothing amiss. After a momentary frown, her fingers find the plate and raise the sandwich to her lips, the macular degeneration that has reduced her vision to a sliver of peripheral preventing her from noticing the spreading pink circle that has wetted the middle of the bread, the droplet of blood and bathwater that landed there, that came from the ceiling above. As she opens her mouth, another fat sphere drops and bursts, this time on her hand, and she puts the sandwich down.

Something in the ceiling gives. It starts to come faster, dripping like a broken gutter in the middle of the kitchen table, spattering the walls, flecks of it on the white net curtains, on the clean cups that stand on the draining board. Mrs. Stefanidis feels under the sink for the bucket, locates the leak and places the vessel just so, to catch it. She dries her hands on her apron, then reaches into her apron pocket to phone for the maintenance man. Using the specially enlarged buttons on her handset, she speed-dials Terry's number, listens to it ringing, hopes he won't mind coming to help her; there's no one else to ask. On the table, the bucket is filling, slowly but surely. Soon it will be too heavy for her to lift. The apron she wears is made of crisp cotton. She doesn't see the pinkish prints her fingers have made there.

CHAPTER

3

WHEN RUBY TURNED the corner, she knew she was in deep shit. The plan had been perfect, on paper, but of course they'd realized that the timings were tight, with no room for trains being late. Stupid, then, to think the bloody thing would be on time on this day, of all days. She hurried along the street toward the shop, where blue lights flashed repeatedly from the police car parked outside. If the police were here, it meant that something terrible had happened. What had Constance done—why had they been called? No one was supposed to know about this, a quiet handover of an unknown child on a deserted small-town street, arranged carefully so that the mother could slip away, unnoticed. If the police were involved, then it was all over before they'd even had a chance. Was Constance desperate enough to risk leaving Leonie before Ruby got there? From Constance's state of mind in recent days, Ruby thought she knew the answer to that. Distressing possibilities ran through Ruby's mind: Leonie crushed under the wheels of a car; Leonie drowned trying to follow her mother into the sea. Ten minutes late, that's all it was, and it wasn't her fault—it was the bloody trains.

Ruby's lungs were burning; she'd been running for what seemed like hours. But it was only ten minutes or so. Hardly any time. *Enough time to die,* came the unwanted thought, before she could stop it.

An officer stepped out of the shop, and the sight of the police uniform caused a sickening jolt in Ruby. She thought for a split second that it could be Joanna, before shaking off the notion with logic: Jo lived and worked in Sheffield, fifty miles away. Also, Joanna no longer wore the uniform; as a detective she wasn't on the front line.

"Good evening, madam," said the officer. "Can I help you?"

Through the gaps around the flyers in the shop window, Ruby could see inside, where the shopkeeper was lifting Leonie onto the counter.

"Oh, I'm fine," said Ruby, thinking, *Is she okay? Is she hurt?* And she tried to get past the police officer, reaching a hand to push open the door. The officer moved slightly, to block her.

"I'm afraid you can't go in at the moment. There's been an incident."

Next to the counter, another police officer held the handbag that Constance used as a changing bag, the one she would have handed to Ruby along with the child. He searched through it, placing the items together in a pile as he took them out, one by one. There was no sign, inside or outside the shop, of Constance herself. Ruby became aware of the sound of the waves behind her, and wanted to turn and scan the water for the boat that Constance had said was coming to fetch her, but didn't dare to do so. Even if it were there, in the descending dark Ruby might not have seen it: from the stories Constance had told, her family life was very basic. Ruby imagined them like seafaring Amish, without electricity or modern technology, still living in the way they'd been doing a hundred years ago, or more.

There was a strange, almost musical cry from far offshore, whipped away by the wind as soon as she heard it. Might have been a ship's horn. Might have been the wind itself, whistling through a gap in the rocks where the land met the sea.

She glared at the police officer. "Can you move, please? I need to get inside. That's my baby." *My baby,* she thought, and in that moment, she realized it was true. Perhaps not biologically, but nevertheless true in the only way that mattered. *She's my baby now.* As the thought settled on her, she stood straighter, feeling proud to claim it.

Ruby craned her neck to see, caught the lost look in Leonie's eyes, and tried to take another step toward the door. The child hadn't noticed her yet, and Ruby so wanted to give her a cuddle, tell her everything was going to be okay. She couldn't get past; the police woman was still blocking her way.

"You're the mother?" asked the officer.

"Yes," she said. Ruby's voice was high and quiet, and she worried she'd made her reply sound too much like a question. She cleared her throat. "Can I go in, please? She'll be scared." How long had she been in the care of the police? It was only ten minutes. Maybe twenty. No time at all.

The officer moved forward in a way that made Ruby step back. "If you could come this way please, madam. There'll be someone along shortly to talk to you." With arms held out slightly, the officer ushered Ruby away from the shop, toward the patrol car.

"Can't I see her?" said Ruby, trying to see over her shoulder through the glass. "She's okay, isn't she? Is she safe?" *How to explain it? Even ten minutes is unforgivable.* "I'm so sorry—I let go of her hand for one second, and she ran off. I lost sight of her."

The guilt was crushing. Sharp tears formed in the corners of Ruby's eyes, her throat swelled painfully. She glanced at the expressionless face of the police officer, in which she could read nothing at all. No sympathy, no understanding. Then it hit her: it wasn't just the blonde coloring, and the uniform—this person really reminded her of Joanna, and not in a good way. It was the cool, detached attitude, the way she was observing Ruby the way you would observe another species, an insect, or an alien.

"If you wouldn't mind just waiting in the back of the vehicle," said the officer. *If you wouldn't mind.* There was clearly no choice whatsoever.

"Are you arresting me? I haven't done anything wrong. It was a mistake. An accident."

The officer opened the door of the patrol car and motioned for Ruby to get in. The police radio gave a crackle, and she moved to turn the volume down.

"Do you have children?" said Ruby.

But the officer simply repeated, "If you wouldn't mind."

It was probably best to do as she was told. Ruby climbed carefully into the back seat of the patrol car and sat there stiffly, pressing her knees together, staring at the headrest in front of her.

"Won't be a moment, madam."

When the door was shut, the darkness closed her in. The officer walked away, and Ruby scrabbled at the door, checking for an escape route, just in case. The handle slipped from her fingers as she pulled it; the thing was functionless, child-locked. That must have been a mistake. They weren't supposed to keep her prisoner, were they? When she hadn't done anything wrong?

Inside the shop she could just see the shopkeeper and the male police officer talking to each other. Like the windows, the glass door was plastered with posters and stickers, so only a sliver of the faces could be seen, quick glimpses of hands gesticulating. When the officer who had put her in the car reached the shop door and opened it, there was a clear view of Leonie, sitting on the counter, eating pieces of chocolate from a nest of gold foil that had been placed next to her. A chocolate decoration. Someone must have opened it for her. Leonie was completely absorbed by the process, taking her time choosing a piece and grasping it delicately in her fingers, opening her mouth comically wide to get it in and, even before it was finished, returning her attention to the next selection. Ruby closed her eyes in relief. There were dirty streaks on the little face where she'd been crying, but Leonie was fine. That was really all that mattered. It was going to be okay.

The shop door closed, obscuring most of her view. She could see part of the back of the police woman as she talked to the other officer, then a slice of the male officer's face as he lifted his radio and spoke into it. His eyes slid toward Ruby then, though she didn't think he'd be able to see her: the light was in her favor. She smoothed her skirt and applied some lip balm, tried to control her breathing. This was the big test. She never imagined it would come so soon into the journey. Ruby wasn't sure she was ready.

She took a long, slow breath. *I am all that girl has in the world. I have to do this. I have to try.* Outside there was a distant sound coming from the waves, loud and long and echoing round the bay. This time she knew what it was. The seals calling. She wondered what exactly they were saying. The lullaby came to mind, the one she'd learned from Constance that she often sang to Leonie: *Ionn da, ionn do, ionn da, od-ar da.* Constance had said it was called "The Seal Woman's Joy." The title seemed wrong, now, and in Ruby's head the words sang out in a minor key.

Two cars pulled up: another police car, which parked by the sea wall opposite, and a big black utility vehicle that stopped right behind the car in which she was imprisoned. In the side mirror she saw a woman in a trouser suit exit the black car and go into the shop. After a while this woman came out again, holding Leonie's small hand in hers, leading her away.

Ruby banged on the inside of the window and shouted Leonie's name. The child looked up, perhaps wondering where the banging was coming from. Her mouth formed the word *Mamma,* but she was looking the wrong way, over the wrong shoulder, back toward the shop.

"Here," Ruby shouted, "I'm over here, love. In here. Baby girl? Mamma Bee's here." Her voice faded away as Leonie was pulled out of sight by the suited woman and put into the black car. *She didn't see me. She thinks she's been abandoned, by both of us.* Ruby's eyes started to sting again with withheld tears. Her nails dug into her palms, leaving deep red crescents. She hardly felt it.

When the roadside passenger door of the police car was opened, Ruby jumped. She hadn't seen anyone approaching. She turned to see the woman in the suit, a large woman with glasses and closely cut curls, who got in, shutting the door behind her. Who was with Leonie? One of the cops maybe. One thing was for sure: *they* would never leave the child on her own with no one to look after her.

"Hello. I'm Diane, from Social Services. You're the mother of that little girl, right?"

Ruby nodded.

Diane pulled out a little notepad and pen. "What's your name, please?"

"Constance."

The lie came out before she'd really thought it through. But then, once she'd said it, she relaxed. It made sense to be Constance in this moment. After all, Constance was technically the birth mother. More importantly, unlike Ruby, Constance had no official identity, no police record. She'd never paid tax, had a job, or owned a car. Constance was invisible to authority and society, just like Leonie, her unregistered, invisible child.

NOW
Joanna
Friday, December 21

DETECTIVE SERGEANT JOANNA Harper nodded to Police Constable Steve Atkinson, who'd brought the ram. He swung the front end of the black metal cylinder at the lock with practiced precision, just hard enough to break it.

The door to Apartment 7 swung wide, and Joanna inhaled cautiously, conscious that the smell of a dead body wasn't one she wanted in her nostrils; once it got up there, that very particular stench took a while to shift. Thankfully, all she caught was a strong odor of damp, from the flooded floors. Two paramedics waited outside the flat, along with the caretaker, Terry. She thought of the bucket of bloody water that Terry had shown them and drew a deep breath to steady herself before she stepped inside, her black sneakers squelching on the hall carpet.

Joanna had asked the caretaker what he knew about the owner, a Mr. Gregor Franks.

"He's a single guy, I think. Not too short of cash. I think he's in some kind of sales manager–type job. Or stocks and shares maybe."

"Age?" asked Jo.

"About thirty, I'd say."

"When's the last time you saw him?"

Terry had to think hard. "I don't know. A while now. Two or three years? I only come when I'm called. He never calls."

"I understand you do have a key to Mr. Franks's flat?" said Atkinson. "But you haven't been inside to check on him since the leak?"

Terry looked pointedly down at the bucket that stood between them on the concrete floor. "I didn't know what I might find. I'm not good with stuff like that. Sight of blood. You'd need another ambulance—for me when I hit the floor."

After they'd climbed the stairs to the seventh floor and Jo tried it in the lock, the key didn't work. Franks must have had it changed. Joanna knocked, then knocked again, and shouted for Gregor to open up, but even as she did so, Atkinson dumped the heavy hold-all he carried on to the floor and unzipped it, readying the Enforcer to break it down.

Inside the flat, Joanna led the way. With only the leak to go on, and the occupant not known to police, they were keeping an open mind. With that amount of blood, there could have been anything happening in the apartment: multiple casualties, dangerous suspects still on scene, a terrible accident. Equally, they might find nothing at all. When Jo was sent to the job, the duty Sergeant could only speculate. "Might not even be blood, could be wood stain or paint, or rust. And if it's blood, could be a domestic accident, where the person has taken themselves off to hospital but left the tap on by mistake."

"Or it could be a ritual sacrifice, and the blood belongs to a sheep or something?"

Murray's voice on the radio was without mirth. "Jo, all we have is a bucket of what is apparently bloody water. No other reports of anything unusual, no body, no one reported at risk or missing or injured. Just go with Steve and check it out for me. If you find anything, I'll divert resources immediately."

"I'm assuming you're asking me because you don't have anyone else?"

"You'd be right to assume that. I've got so many immediate response jobs on, they're stacking up as we speak. Firearms are at a stabbing in the city center, and all of my other units are out with higher priority stuff. Ambulance will attend, but they've stated that the police need to clear the scene before they go in."

"Understood."

This close to Christmas, the service always got overloaded. Every year it got worse. A lot of staff took holiday, so that often all they had on duty were a skeleton selection of response officers, half the Control team and a few sergeants, like Murray and Joanna.

"Oh, and Jo? Take a stab vest."

"Yeah, take a stab vest, it's probably nothing," muttered Jo as she shrugged on the heavy garment before walking out of the building and getting in the patrol car with Atkinson. DS Harper enjoyed a good moan, like everyone, but the truth was, she secretly loved it when staff shortages meant that she had to get back on frontline work. Joanna made the move to detective because she thought she'd prefer the investigative side of things. She wasn't going to admit it to Murray, but it turned out she was much happier wearing a stab vest and breaking down doors.

"Mr. Franks?"

Jo edged along the hallway before pushing open the door to the living room. It was cold and dark in there, the power having been shut off along with the water. By torchlight she could see that the place was mostly tidy and relatively clean. A plate of toast crusts was balanced on the arm of the corner couch, along with an undrunk cup of tea. A box of toys had been put away against the wall.

In the kitchen, a packet of bread lay open on the counter. She picked up the nearest slice, felt it, gave it a sniff. Slightly stale. A phone was plugged into an outlet. Jo picked it up and swiped the screen, but it was dead. In the wallet lying next to it, she found a driver's license and pulled it out. A kind face, lightly stubbled, the kind of thick, wavy hair Atkinson had ten years ago.

The next room off the living room contained an unmade double bed and a cot pushed into the corner, the mattress covered in a sheet, an open toddler sleeping bag bunched up on its end, as if the child had just been lifted from it. In the corner, a floral-print summer dress had been tossed, and on top of it lay a single pink baby sock fringed with white lace. Harper quickly scanned the room, then crouched to look under the bed. Nothing there but a collection of seashells in a box.

"Clear," she called.

There was another bedroom, this one spotlessly neat, not a crease in the duvet cover or a single discarded item on the floor. Joanna opened the cupboards and found meticulously ironed shirts and trousers, all arranged in color order.

"Clear," she called again.

Back in the main space the two officers stood in front of the last door. When Atkinson turned the handle, he found that it couldn't be opened.

Joanna banged on the door with a closed fist. "Mr. Franks?" she said. "Gregor? Can you hear me? My name's Jo. I'm with the police. Can you open the door?"

The silence was the buzzing kind, in which you strain your ears, hoping for a sound, any sound. There was nothing.

"We're going to force the door, Mr. Franks," said Jo. "Stand back."

Atkinson picked up the ram. She stepped out of the way as he aimed the front end at the handle and swung.

One great smash and the door was swinging on its hinges. The scene inside was a mess of red and white, blood and tiles, a bath brimful of bloody water surrounding the pale skin of the man's body. Atkinson coughed, to cover a gasp probably. The body itself was unmarked, perfectly still and white, hands and feet bluish and mottled, face peaceful, eyes closed. Harper thought of dumplings in beetroot soup, and her stomach rumbled. She'd skipped lunch, saving herself for dinner tonight. Now it looked like she wouldn't be getting any.

"Anything?" said one of the paramedics.

"There's a body here," called Jo. She checked behind the door to make absolutely sure there was no one else in the room waiting to attack them, but the action was just routine; she'd known already, copper's instinct, that the man was alone. "It's safe. You can come through."

She couldn't see the wrists, only the backs of the man's hands. This was a scene she'd come across a few times in her years as a response officer, and it didn't get any easier to understand. What had made this man do this to himself?

"Is that him, the owner of the flat?" asked Atkinson.

Joanna went back to the kitchen counter for the driver's license. She compared the dead-looking face in the bath with the living one in the image. She showed the picture to Atkinson, who nodded. "That's him."

The two paramedics entered the bathroom gingerly, so as not to slip in the mixture of blood and water on the tiles. One of them knelt by the bath. "Mr. Franks?" he said. "Can you hear me?" He placed a hand on the man's forehead. Then he turned over the arm nearest to them, exposing the inside of his wrist. Joanna fully expected to see a deep cut there, and perhaps later they would find a razor blade that had slipped underneath the body as he fell unconscious. But there was no damage: the skin on the wrist was intact. The paramedic reached for the left arm: also no cuts.

"Where's the blood coming from?" asked Jo.

"I can't tell at the moment. Somewhere on the back of him." He placed his fingers at the man's neck, then listened at his chest; his cheek came away wet.

"He's alive."

This surprised Joanna, who had unwittingly broken the first rule of policing: she had *assumed* Franks was dead because it had been several hours since the leak was spotted, because it was freezing in the flat, because of the blood and the fact that he was lying in a full tub of water. Mostly because it looked so much like a dead body, and she'd seen more than a few in her time.

The paramedic lifted Gregor's head out of the water. "Head trauma. That's where he's bleeding."

Jo spoke into the radio. "Control, update on the situation in Apartment 7 in the North block on the New Park estate. We have a casualty. Repeat: there is one casualty, serious trauma protocol please, head injury, severe blood loss is evident. Unconscious male, positive for signs of life."

Over the radio, Sergeant Murray said, "Copy that, Jo. Any suspects present?"

"No. It's not clear what we're dealing with yet, whether there's anyone else involved. Stand by for update."

"Received, standing by."

The paramedic said, "Gregor, we're going to get you out of the bath now. Can you hear me, Gregor?"

He rolled up a sleeve and pulled the plug in the bath, letting the water out. Then he turned to Atkinson. "Get some blankets or something. The duvet off the bed. And help us lift him out, would you? Both of you—we'll need all of us to do it safely."

As the icy pink bathwater swirled away, the two police officers made a soft bed of blankets on the bathroom floor. Harper placed a hand under the man's head as the four of them lifted him out, and was surprised at the sensation of sponginess, an area of skull that should have been smooth and hard but instead felt like wet cake in her palm.

CHAPTER

5

NOW
Ruby
Friday, December 21

Now that she was Constance to the social worker, Ruby thought maybe Diane would make some comment about the name. When Ruby had first met Constance, she'd done it herself. It was unusual. Old-fashioned.

Diane noted it down, then returned her cool eyes to Ruby's.

"And your daughter's name?"

"Didn't she tell you?" said Ruby. "Only, she's not shy usually. She'll talk to anyone, wander off with anyone. Doesn't see danger. That's how come I lost her. She's quick too."

Stay calm, she told herself. All she had to do was get Leonie and run, slip away so quickly that the police and Social Services had no chance to realize there was anything out of the ordinary happening.

"It didn't take the police long to get here, did it?" said Ruby in what she hoped was an admiring tone rather than one of criticism. "The patrol must have been parked up around the corner. Very . . . reassuring."

Diane blinked. "What's your daughter's name, please?"

"Oh, sorry! Leonie." She spelled it, and Diane wrote it down. "Surname?"

"Hers or mine?"

"Both, please."

There was a hesitation that Ruby wanted to kick herself for. Diane looked up sharply; she'd noticed it too. "Douglas. We're both Douglas." Douglas would have to do; she couldn't use her own name, Harper. It would be just her luck that one of the police officers would recognize it and wonder if there was any link to their colleague in Sheffield.

Diane pursed her lips as the pen moved. Then she glanced up. "What about the father?"

Ruby closed her eyes and saw his face as she sometimes thought of him, that first meeting, the way he smiled shyly and looked away. She shook her head to clear it. Then she glared at Diane.

"Huh," snapped Ruby. "That's a bit personal, isn't it?"

The two women locked eyes. Ruby radiated confident outrage, though below the surface she was unsure the act was working. There was a delicate line to be drawn: don't beg, but don't go too far the other way and make this woman angry or suspicious. After a moment, Ruby lowered her eyes. She dropped the confrontational tone. She said, "I'm sorry. I've been going out of my mind with worry. I didn't mean to be rude, really. May I see my daughter, please?"

Diane appeared to consider the question. Her eyes traveled over Ruby, interpreting, judging the outfit: expensive leather boots, the winter skirt, the trendy parka. Ruby knew she looked nice, but she also hoped she looked plausible—the sort of woman who might make a mistake, but never the sort that would make more than one. Never the sort that needed *intervention*. It was crucial, this first impression, these judgments made in seconds, of a person's trustworthiness, her social standing. Diane from Social Services had the power to take Leonie away just like that if she felt she had justifiable reasons. Ruby prayed that the other woman would decide this wasn't one of those cases.

Diane smiled inscrutably and said, "I'm sure you'll understand, Ms. Douglas, that when a child is found abandoned, alone in a shop, in weather like this, and the police are called, we have to do a certain amount of investigating. It's a child protection issue. One can't be too cautious." Diane tipped her head to the side, her face blandly apologetic as the weighty words found their target.

Ruby swallowed hard. *Think.* "There's no need for all that," she said. "Just let me explain. She wasn't abandoned—I lost her. We were at the seafront, watching the waves. She's got this idea that it's fun to run off—she does it all the time, all the day long, and it's exhausting. So I was buying chips, and I turned round to pay the lady. Then when I looked back, she'd run off again! I panicked—she could have gone two different ways, and I must have run the wrong way. I've been searching for her ever since I lost her, and it's only been—what?—ten, twenty minutes? I asked loads of people. I was about to call the police myself, and they got here so fast. I would *never* abandon her. There's no child protection issue here. You can tell that just by looking at her—she's dressed for the weather, isn't she? She's not undernourished or anything, is she? I just want to see her. I want to say sorry to her. I want to—"

A sob broke off the stream of words. Diane offered a tissue. The social worker's expression seemed to have softened somewhat.

"It could have happened to anyone," said Ruby. She blew her nose. "I'm not a bad mum."

Diane put her notepad back in her bag.

"Where do you live, love?"

"Sheffield."

"So, what are you doing in Cleethorpes? It's a bit chilly for a seaside day trip, isn't it?"

Ruby took a breath before she replied. "You have to get out, don't you? When you have kids. Can't keep them cooped up all day."

Diane raised her eyebrows in weary recognition. *She's got kids of her own,* thought Ruby.

The social worker gave her a long look. Then she knocked on the window, and someone from outside opened the car door.

"I'm just going to have a word with the police officers, Constance. Then we'll let you see your daughter. Okay?"

Ruby tried to say, "Thanks," but emotion choked her voice and she couldn't get the word out in time. She knew she'd done something right if they were going to let her see Leonie. *Careful, though,* she told herself. If anything seemed off when the two of them were reunited, that would be it. She might be imprisoned for attempted child abduction or providing false details. She might never see Leonie again.

A few minutes later and the door on Ruby's side of the car was opened by the police woman. Ruby's legs shook as she stepped onto the pavement, pulling her jacket closed against the wind and sleet. A bit farther along the road, the big black car also had its door open, and she could see Leonie being lifted out. Ruby wanted to rush over and grab her, take up the child and run, but she was aware of the police and the social worker watching them. She took a step closer and saw the toddler look up, recognize her, try to pull her hand away from Diane's.

"Mamma Bee!" shouted Leonie, struggling against the woman holding her.

Ruby couldn't bear it a moment longer. She ran forward and lifted Leonie up, hugged her tight.

"Mamma's here, baby," she said, "I'm so sorry."

"Mamma," said Leonie. "Mamma here. Mamma gone." Ruby hoped that only she could interpret what Leonie was trying to tell her: *"Mamma was here, Mamma's gone."*

"I know, I'm so sorry, my love. I'm back now. I won't let you go again. Not ever."

She covered Leonie in kisses, then pulled back a little to see the child's face. They smiled at each other. "Bee," said Leonie. Or at least, that's what the word *Ruby* sounded like in Leonie's mouth.

Would they pick up on that? "She loves insects. Don't you, baby?"

"Mamma Bee," said Leonie, and giggled. That's what Constance had called Ruby, in front of the baby, almost from day one. *Here's Mamma Ruby, come to give you a cuddle.* As soon as Leonie could speak the words, Ruby was Mamma Bee.

The child still had smears on her face from whatever it was they'd fed her, some sugary crap. The stuff they made those decorations out of didn't even count as chocolate.

"You're all dirty, sweetie. We need to get you a wipe." She licked a thumb and rubbed at the chubby cheeks. She looked around for a baby wipe to clean her, but couldn't see the changing bag.

The shopkeeper stepped forward. "Is this yours?"

"Thank you," said Ruby, taking the bag that Constance had packed that morning with Leonie's things—enough nappies for a day or two, a change of clothes, a couple of toys.

"It was on the pavement outside the shop." He frowned slightly, as if he couldn't work out why that might be a strange place for the bag to be.

"She took it when she ran," said Ruby, a little too quickly. Ruby rummaged inside the bag for the wipes, but Leonie had seen what was coming and was wriggling in her arms to get away. "No wipe!" she shouted, kicking her legs hard so that Ruby had to put her down. In a split second she'd slipped from Ruby's grasp and was running full pelt toward the road. The police woman said, "Whoa," and stepped smoothly into the child's path to catch her.

"I see what you mean about her being a runner," said Diane, and one of the police officers chuckled.

"Looks like you've got yourself an escapee there, love," said the female officer, handing the still-struggling Leonie back to Ruby. She abandoned the wipe.

"She's like this all the time. I'm hoping it's a phase."

"What I'll do, love," said Diane, "is I'll send a report to the social worker that covers your area. There'll be a flag on your file, but that's just to help us keep an eye on things. It won't count against you."

"You're not . . . taking her?"

"No, love. I don't think you need our help at the moment. This is just one of those things. Could have happened to anyone. Your little angel there clearly has a passion for sprinting. Have you thought about one of those child harnesses with reins?"

Ruby nodded. "I've tried. I bought an expensive one in the shape of a ladybird. She just sits and screams the place down until I take it off her, or I let her hold the end of the reins herself, which kind of defeats the purpose."

At the mention of screaming, the shopkeeper made a noise like he was about to say something. Ruby wondered what he'd seen. If Leonie had been crying . . . well. They needed to get going, fast.

"How about a buggy?" said Diane. "You could strap her in?"

Ruby shook her head wearily. "She's very keen on being independent." Leonie was under her arm, still kicking. Ruby crouched down and tried to persuade her to stand on her feet, with little success.

A stern voice spoke then, and Leonie stopped struggling.

"I'm afraid you're going to have to toughen up if you're going to keep that little lady safe, madam." It was the male police officer. "You need to take charge. Listening to her scream is a lot preferable to the alternative in a situation like this."

The child's eyes glazed over. She went limp.

"I know," said Ruby, picking Leonie up and cuddling her, knowing it was the sound of the man's low voice that she couldn't bear. "I'm sorry. I'll put her in the buggy from now on."

"See that you do," he said. "Are you going to be safe on the train journey home to Sheffield? Do you have family members who can meet you from the station?"

Ruby felt Leonie's body stiffen as the man kept speaking, and the toddler began to let out an almost imperceptible whining sound.

"Is she okay?" asked Diane.

Ruby exhaled. "She's just tired, I think." Turning to the male officer, she said, "I'll be safe. I won't let her out of my sight. I promise."

"I could call ahead and have someone escort you home."

"No, thanks. We'll be totally fine. Won't we, kiddo?" She looked at Diane. "I've learned my lesson, okay?"

The officer took the social worker aside. When they returned, the man seemed satisfied. He nodded at his colleagues, indicating that they could leave now.

Diane smiled at Leonie, then at Ruby. "I've got one myself, a bit older," she said. "You'd do anything for them, wouldn't you?"

"Yes," said Ruby, gazing down at the small girl in her arms. "You would."

She turned and started to walk in the direction of the train station. Each step she took away from the police was a step into a new life, a new existence for them both. Her heels tapped out a mantra that echoed in the street: *We did it, we're free, we did it, we're free.* She picked up the pace, turned the corner, started to run. There was no going back now. Her only choice was to take Leonie and disappear completely.

CHAPTER

6

*"Farewell, peerie buddo!" said she to the child, and ran out.
She rushed to the shore, flung on her skin, and plunged into
the sea with a wild cry of joy. A male of the selkie folk there
met and greeted her with every token of delight. And that was
the last he ever saw of his bonnie wife.*
—G. F. Black, "The Goodman of Wastness," 1903

ONE HOUR EARLIER
Constance
Friday, December 21

THE WATER IS a living thing. It heaves, the vast surface of it
shifting beneath the power of the low-hanging moon, of
which only a faint glow can be seen behind thick clouds. At the
ocean's edge, a woman stands, her face toward the horizon. Her
feet are bare, boots and socks at the bottom of the hastily dug hole
in the beach behind her. Where her skin is exposed to it, the offshore wind numbs her. She likes it, the numb feeling. She wants it
to envelop her, for it to chill her body entirely so that she feels
nothing at all. Turning back to the hole, she pulls off her parka
and drops it in. Then she closes her eyes and takes a long, grateful
breath of sea air. The cold salt wind of home.

Although she has stood here—or somewhere very like here—many times before, tonight, the beach feels different. For the first time since she stepped ashore so many months ago, freedom is within touching distance. The sand between her toes, the push and pull of the tide; her heart is beating with excitement, with anticipation. She opens her mouth and sings one of the old songs: *Ionn da, ionn do, ionn da, od-ar da*. Her chest resonates with it, the notes blending with the sounds of the wind and the tide. Seals call back, almost as if they are replying. She hears the response, perhaps only in her head, but oh, the joy of it. A chorus of voices singing: *Hi-o dan dao, hi-o dan dao, hi-o dan dao, od-ar da*.

In the fading light, the woman takes a step toward the water, now a blanket of shining black, the waves ready to take her. She longs to submerge herself, to give herself to it, to swim out as far as she can; to sink down; to forget all that she has been and done, all that has been done to her.

Naked now, the woman hesitates: the child is behind her, the other side of the sea wall, by the shop where she left her. She waited as long as she could for Ruby, but her supposed friend didn't come. A flash of anger within: a sacred trust was broken. Ruby said she loved the child, that she loved them both, but perhaps she lied. Trust is always a gamble. She won't make that mistake again. She won't need to after tonight, as it marks the end of all of that, all of this life and everything attached to it.

She consoles herself that she didn't leave the child entirely alone—there were people inside the shop when she ran. They'll come out and find her; they have to. A small voice says, *But if they don't?* The guilt is heavy on her now, getting heavier with every second. She takes a step away, toward the road. How can she leave, not even knowing if her baby will be safe?

A voice pushes her back in the direction of the water as surely as a hand on her back. *"Constance,"* it says, or seems to say. The second time she hears it, it sounds like the waves on the shingle. Was it real? Or was the voice an illusion, cast by the strength of her longing? She thought she could hear them, singing out to her, calling for her, but now she's convinced she can't. They're not here for her; it's been too long. They haven't come.

A wave wets her feet. She looks down: they gleam.

Salt tears drop, to join the seawater. She ought to go back to Leonie. Soon, the child will notice that her mother has gone. But if she goes back, she might as well be dead. Whatever the water holds, for however short a time, if she goes in now, she'll be free once more.

As she stands there at the cusp of going in, of not going in, she wonders if the knowledge that she has left her will remain with the child forever, a scar running deep, a fear that it was the child's own fault, that the solid fact of her existence was not enough to make her mother stay. She feels the pull of her baby, anchoring her to this place, to this life. But then she hears it again, the song of the seals, and her heart is full. She can't stay. At least under the water, there is a chance she will return to what she was. A chance that she has to take. If it doesn't work, if all she meets is oblivion, even that is better than what she has now. She steps forward, into the water, diving under, letting it take her, deep down, far away.

7

NOW
Joanna
Friday, December 21

AFTER THE TWO officers helped the paramedics haul the man from the tub, together they dried him off as best they could, keeping him warm with the bedding until the stretcher was brought up. They covered Gregor's body in silver space blankets and transported him to the ground floor, where the emergency doctor started administering fluids.

Although still unconscious, the man didn't look quite as dead as he had in the bathroom, which Harper took as a good sign. "Will he live?" she asked.

One of the paramedics paused to look at her. "He's alive now. That's all I can tell you."

The back doors of the ambulance slammed, and a moment later Joanna watched it drive away, slowly at first over the speed bumps, then accelerating, blue lights and sirens blaring the moment they hit the bypass.

Two more patrol cars arrived, with officers on board to help secure the scene. She ordered three of them to guard each of the entrances: one to monitor the lift, one the stairs, and one at the door of Apartment 7. She herself stood at the main door to the block, waiting for her superior, Inspector Thrupp, to arrive.

Momentarily alone, Jo stared up at the West Block and thought of Ruby. Which of those tiny windows was hers? Ruby was top floor, like the victim, but the ones in the social housing block didn't get the label "penthouse." The seventh floor of the West Block was divided into four apartments, each one a quarter of the size of the victim's. She knew this because the last time she'd been here, she'd nearly knocked. She'd gotten as far as the intercom, looked at the row of buttons, but bottled it at the last second, sent a text message instead. That was a month ago, and there'd been no contact since. That message didn't even really count as contact, since Ruby had never replied. It had been early October when they'd last spoken, shortly after Ruby's birthday when she'd phoned Jo from a payphone, claiming to have run out of credit on her mobile. Jo had known it was a lie: their mother still paid the bill for Ruby's phone. Jo had wanted to meet up then, but Ruby avoided making the arrangement, so that Ruby's birthday present, a silver ring set with her namesake stone, inscribed with a line of Latin, was still in Joanna's pocket.

Jo pulled out her phone, scrolled down to Ruby's icon, and pressed to connect. Just like last time, and every time she'd tried for the past six weeks, there was nothing but the recorded message: *The number you have dialed is currently unavailable. Please try again later.* A frustrated sob bubbled up, hard in the base of her throat. She stifled it.

Movement in the corner of her eye made her glance up. Beyond the patrol cars, youths had started to gather, hoods pulled up against the cold, scarves tucked in around faces, eyes glittering. There were around fifteen of them, she reckoned, dotted here and there in groups of two and three.

"I see the rubberneckers have turned up already," said Atkinson, appearing behind her.

She pocketed the phone she was still holding. "They're just interested," said Joanna. "Understandable. There hasn't been a big thing on the New Park for a while, has there?"

"Not since that cannabis farm we found at the top of the East Block. Oh, and there was that pop-up brothel."

"All that was before the refurbishment, though. It's a nice area now, Steve." She arched an eyebrow.

"Well, sure. Shame no one told that lot." He gestured toward the youngsters, who had mostly retreated to the darker places between the buildings, red pinpricks glowing where they sucked on their cigarettes. "What's the status of this job, boss? Suspicious circumstances?"

"I'm waiting for that to be made official. New system. We don't get CSIs, or anything, not until it's been signed off by an inspector."

"Isn't that going to cost the investigation in terms of time lost?"

"Yes, of course it is. But it's a budget issue. Apparently, we need to spread our murders out, or move one or two to the next financial year."

Atkinson paused. "Wrongful death? Did Franks not make it?"

"It's touch-and-go," said Joanna. "Let's see what the next few hours bring. If it's not murder, then it might as well have been: someone's had a good try at killing the guy. We need to act as if it's murder, get all the details nailed. But we can't start properly until the DI's seen it."

Jo kept glancing up at the West Block, at the window she thought might have been Ruby's.

Atkinson cleared his throat. "Are you thinking we need to go door-to-door in that block?"

She snapped her eyes away. "Let's see what we've got, first," she said. "Might not be necessary to knock on everyone's door."

A shadow of something, suspicion or confusion, crossed his features. Their eyes met briefly before they turned as one to go back inside.

It was late when Detective Inspector Thrupp finally rolled into the estate in his large black BMW hatchback. He parked in front of the building and got out of the car, the lock giving an audible click as he made his way toward Harper standing in the entrance to the building.

Tall and striking in his shiny leather shoes and gray suit, Thrupp stared hard at the groups of youths lingering in the darkness between the apartment blocks.

"Nothing to see here, ladies and gentlemen," he boomed. "Off you go, home now." The youths responded by retreating further into the shadows.

"Alright, Joanna, what have you found? And on the night of the Christmas party too. The lads won't thank you for that now, will they?"

"My missus won't thank me either," she said. "I promised I'd be back at a normal time today."

"Normal," said Thrupp. "Ha ha. She knows what you do for a living, right?"

Just then Joanna's mobile started ringing. She pulled it out, looked at it, then swiped to dismiss the call from Amy. They'd planned to go out to eat tonight, before the party. The eight PM reservation had been hours ago. She really hoped Amy hadn't gone on her own, that she'd waited for her.

"You could have taken that," said the DI. "I wouldn't object to a quick call from home."

Jo shook her head. "That wasn't going to be a quick one. She's got plenty of things to say to me, I'm sure. I'll call her back later. This way, boss."

CHAPTER

8

Beneath the depths of the ocean, according to these stories, an atmosphere exists adapted to the respiratory organs of certain beings, resembling in form the human race, possessed of surpassing beauty, of limited supernatural powers, and liable to the incident of death. They dwell in a wide territory of the globe, far below the region of fishes, over which the sea, like the cloudy canopy of our sky, loftily rolls.

—George Brisbane Scott Douglas,
"The Fisherman and the Merman," 1901

THEN
Ruby
August

R UBY WAS WATCHING Yoga Man from the safety of the dark. She was sitting, wrapped in a duvet, on the draining board, her feet in the sink. The routine was familiar; she'd been watching him without fail every day, for so long that the sequences repeated in a pattern she could now predict. Today was headstand day.

Being awake at three thirty AM was standard for Ruby these days, now that a normal person's regime, like having work hours and a social life, was no longer relevant. She dwelled in a permanent half-light; whenever an errant sunbeam edged around the closed curtains and sought her out, it felt as if it burned. The only time the curtains were open fully was at night, when she was watching Yoga Man. A guilty pleasure, perhaps even shameful, but in those silent hours, cocooned in the velvet dark and the warmth of the bedcover, she felt more alive than she had in a long time. His movements both soothed and ignited her. When he walked toward her at the end of the routine, to shut the blinds against the approaching dawn, she imagined he was looking at her, acknowledging her. He seemed to gaze straight into her eyes, though where she sat, behind glass, protected by the dark, he could never have seen her.

When it was over, Ruby would get down from her perch and go to bed, tying a scarf over her eyes to block out the light, sleeping until mid-afternoon. Just like Barbara, her boss, had said, after she'd driven Ruby home from work on the day she'd been signed off sick, yoga practice was meant to be good for your mental health. Barbara meant for her to take a class, but perhaps watching someone else do it was equally effective. It was certainly true that once she'd discovered Yoga Man, Ruby felt she was less depressed and more productive. He was inspirational: when she wasn't watching him, or sleeping, she was working on her music.

Ruby had been spending more and more time playing, perfecting sections from Sibelius's *D Minor Concerto*. The piece was fiendishly difficult, and while she played, she felt she had a sense of purpose, a hope that she might conquer it, do it justice, as only the best players could. Only when the callouses on the tips of her fingers started to bleed onto the ebony of the fingerboard and her shoulders screamed from the tension of the playing position would she wrap the instrument in its ancient duster and place it safely away. Only then would the bad thoughts seep in, along with the loneliness. She tried to keep playing until it was time to watch Yoga Man, but sometimes it wasn't possible. Thank goodness, then, that in the past few weeks she'd felt a new awakening. She'd started to compose something herself; a piece that, when she was immersed in it, chased away the bad thoughts so completely that she was entirely made of music. It was as if when she played, she was losing herself in becoming a conduit for Sibelius or Mozart or

Grieg. But when she sat down to compose, the conduit was something else, not a person. A spirit perhaps, but not a completely nice one. It had personality, this muse of hers.

The melody she was writing had appeared, fully formed, as she watched Yoga Man one night, and she'd scribbled it down, convinced it was something she'd heard before. She hummed it quietly, and its haunting beauty made her think of the ocean at night. The theme began with a tritone—*the Devil's interval*—and in her head the first three notes were played slowly, almost tentatively, on a low flute echoed by a solo viola. Where had she heard it before? It turned out she hadn't. The tune felt so complete, so filmic, and filled with a kind of foreboding. As she went deeper into the composition, it felt less as if someone else had written it, more that it was writing itself. And since then, every time she returned to the manuscript, it seemed like the notes were coming from another place, through her rather than from her. Her fingers held the pen that rested on the paper, and from it the music surged, unexpected, sometimes chilling, and utterly exquisite.

Because of the music, she'd never started the antidepressants that the doctor had given her. More than once she'd picked them up in the packet, taken out the leaflet and read the list of possible side effects, then put them back down again. The doctor had told her the pills would rebalance the chemicals in her brain, but the idea of that was more frightening than the bad thoughts. The pills might dull her creativity, which she already considered to be tenuous and fleeting. They might take away the desire to compose, and with it the first truly beautiful thing she'd created. It was too much to risk.

The tap dripped on her toe, bringing her back to the room. Across the way, Yoga Man was standing at the window, his hand on the pull for the blind. Ruby stared straight into his eyes, as she usually did. He appeared to be looking at her, and she enjoyed the sensation, the fantasy that he knew she was watching and was performing it all for her. Then, he cupped his hand over his eyes to shade them and pressed his face to the window. His body language transformed from relaxed to agitated. He *could* see her. He turned, dashed across to the wall where his light switches were. Suddenly the big window was plunged into darkness.

Ruby scrambled off the drainer, fell heavily on her side, and lay there on the tiles, breathing hard. After a minute she crawled toward the bed-sitting room, avoiding the windows in case the man was still standing there in his darkened room, peering out, wondering who it was that was spying on him.

It was impossible to sleep. Instead, as the sun rose, she worked on her composition, adding a movement that became chaotically discordant, spiky, and unpleasant. Reaching the final few bars, she decided that she hated every bit of it. She crumpled up the new section and tossed it into the bin.

The following day, Ruby practiced the Sibelius past the point at which her fingers hurt. She didn't eat all day, so by the time night fell, she was beyond hunger, enjoying the light feeling of nothing in her stomach, her mind a flighty thing jumping between ideas without fulling exploring any single one, forgetting what she'd been thinking about, not really caring either. At the usual time, in the darkness, she parted the curtains and peeked toward Yoga Man's window, hoping to see him there, in yoga pants and nothing else, just like normal. It was planks day today; she loved to see the straightness of his body, his taut backside the only inter-ruption to the perfect line from head to shoulder, to heel. Disap-pointment stung: the blinds were drawn. Her private show was over, all of her fun spoiled. The yoga would go on, but she wasn't privy to it, not anymore. Ruby felt nothing but shame and loss.

Back in the bed-sitting room, she opened the manuscript she'd been working on and stared at the hundreds of neatly drawn runs of notes. The work had grown, covering both sides of fifty or more pages, but she suddenly couldn't remember why she'd even started it. The melody she'd been so entranced by, that she'd based the whole thing on, seemed trite, derivative. No one would want to hear this, let alone play it. Not even the Devil—especially not him. There was nothing mischievous or dark there, nothing clever or profound. It was all dull, repetitive, predictable. She got up, dropped the entire sheaf of papers into the recycling chute and climbed into bed. There, in a fit of recklessness, she shook four sleeping pills into her palm and crunched them between her teeth before lying down, closing her eyes, and letting the drugs drag her consciousness away.

Waking in the afternoon, Ruby realized she had only half an hour to make her appointment at the GP's. She threw on some clothes and rushed out, hair and teeth unbrushed, bare feet shoved into old trainers. The doctor looked her up and down and briskly signed her off work for another six weeks. He peered at her over the top of his spectacles. "How are you finding taking the antidepressants?"

Ruby said, "Oh, fine. I feel much better, actually."

"No side effects?"

"Nothing significant, no."

She did not mention that she still had no plans to take even a single one.

The doctor gave her another prescription, which Ruby shoved in a pocket on her way out of the surgery. What would happen, she wondered, if she took all of the pills in one go? Would she die quickly, floating away in a blissful cloud of obliviousness? Or would her liver implode, causing untold pain and suffering? It would be interesting to find out, in a way. At least she would feel something other than shame, or loneliness.

On the tram, exhausted and listless, she stared out the window so that at first she didn't notice him: Yoga Man was sitting two rows in front of her. She looked once, then away, wondering, *Is that really him?* She recognized the back of his head, the curve of his neck. Her heart began to pound. She pressed the button for the tram to stop, got up and went past him, holding on to the rail near the door as the vehicle slowed. *Don't make it too obvious,* she told herself, and allowed herself only a short glance in his direction as she got off. He was staring right at her, a slight frown creasing his forehead. She panicked then, hurrying out the doors before they were fully opened, keeping her head down until the tram was out of sight.

Ruby trudged back to the flat in the rain. By the time she got there, she found that a plan had formed, seemingly of its own accord, a bit like the melody had done. There was a quiver of a thrill, that she was being guided by the muse again, but this time not just in music. She made no attempt to resist or to think it through: she walked in the door and got straight into the shower, turned it up as hot as she could bear it and began to scrub. Soon she'd washed away two weeks of grime, shampooed her hair three times. She shaved her armpits and legs, exfoliated her entire body the way she always used to do. She toweled herself dry, applied lotion, used tweezers to shape her eyebrows. She put makeup on and grabbed a dress out of her wardrobe that she hadn't worn in months. *There,* she thought, admiring herself in the mirror. *I'm unrecognizable.*

You're all dressed up with nowhere to go, said a mean voice inside her head.

I don't have anywhere to go yet, she said to the voice. *But maybe I will soon.*

That night, she put on a pair of heels, stood in the dark, and watched the shadows play on the blinds of his living room, imagining the scene within. It was comforting to know that he was still doing the yoga, even if she couldn't see it. That perfectly muscled body had to be maintained somehow.

Ruby went to bed and slept better than she had in weeks, without any sleeping pills, between clean sheets. The next day she dressed carefully, forced herself to eat a breakfast of scrambled eggs and set off to ride the tram.

There was no sign of him, so she rode all the way to the end of the line and back, getting off in the city center to sit and watch the crowds for a while. She was gratified to see that several young men noticed her, though she didn't acknowledge their curious glances. Just yesterday she'd been invisible, a hunched and grubby thing, moving through the press of people without drawing a single eye. Apart from his. He'd looked at her. He'd seen her.

At the market, she bought an apple and ate it while she stood at the tram stop, waiting to get on, heading out of town again, only to come back in.

When he wasn't on the next tram either, Ruby couldn't hold back the disappointment. She stopped hoping but kept riding. There was no reason to go home, really. *See?* said the mean voice in her head. *I told you.*

The apple core was brown and spindly where she held it between thumb and forefinger, and she was about to admit defeat when suddenly, there he was, shuffling on board with his head down. After a moment his eyes swept the passengers with a kind of nervousness and paused, she thought, just for a second, on her. Ruby watched him from the side of her vision, her face turned away. Taller than she'd thought, with longish, wavy hair, dressed in a rather ill-fitting suit, Yoga Man had been waiting at the stop nearest the banks. He didn't strike her as a banker, though: too alternative. A bead on a leather string peeped out from below his cuff, so that the impression was of a surfer who'd been to a job interview. As he passed her in the aisle, she looked straight at him, and their eyes met.

He paused. "Do I know you?"

"I don't think so," said Ruby, and smiled slightly, shrugging with her eyebrows before turning back to the window.

He didn't move. "I'm so sure. You look really familiar. Do you ever go to the gym near the bypass?"

"No, not me."

"Oh, okay." He sounded disappointed in her answer.

"Wait," she said, "are you saying I need to join a gym? That's a bit rude." Ruby straightened her dress and crossed her arms. She knew she wasn't fat—she was far too thin, if anything, though it was true that she rarely exercised. Maybe he thought she needed to tone up.

"Of course not." He started to stutter, and a blush rose in his cheeks. "I only meant that . . . I thought maybe I'd seen you around. My office is near the gym, that's all. I didn't mean . . ."

She watched him for a moment, astounded that anyone would be stumbling over their words because of something she'd said.

He went on, "I don't even go there, myself. I hate gyms. It's just, I just . . ." For an unsettling moment, she thought he was going to cry.

She placed a hand on his forearm. "It's okay. I wasn't offended. I was joking with you."

The movement of the tram yanked his arm away, so that her hand hovered in the air for a beat, and they both stared at it before she took it back. He said, "I'm sorry, I don't usually—I mean, I never . . . I'm just not good at talking to girls. I mean women." He ran a hand through his hair, stared at his shoes, appeared to swallow. "I'm so sorry—I meant *people*." Then he swung his bag onto his shoulder and pressed the bell for the tram to stop. Ruby wanted to grab hold of him, to make him stay exactly where he was.

"Honestly, it was nothing," she said.

"No, it was a dumb thing to say. But you're kind to say that. I'm really sorry."

He was edging farther away from her.

"Wait," she said. "I don't know your name."

Confusion crossed his face, as if he couldn't work out why she would want to know his name. Then he met her gaze, and the blush rose to his cheeks once more. "It's Gregor." He raised his eyebrows in a question.

"Ruby."

"Like the jewel," he said, and then cringed as if he'd said something stupid.

The tram was slowing to a stop, and people were filling the gap between them as they prepared to get off. Although she wanted to say something clever to make him stay, to make him talk to her some more, to reassure him that he hadn't offended her, all she could manage was, "See ya."

The rest of the journey home passed in a blur. She wondered why he'd gotten off the tram early, whether he'd done it just to get away from her because he was embarrassed, or if he had somewhere else to be. He'd seemed to recognize her, which was both worrying and thrilling. It was possible he knew her from the estate or from seeing her around the city in the days before her world shrank to the size of her flat. Perhaps, when she'd still been at work, they'd shared a commute; perhaps she wasn't as invisible as she thought she was.

At her apartment building she had so much nervous energy to burn that she ran up the stairs instead of taking the lift. She'd spoken to Yoga Man! He thought he knew her! He seemed nice! She checked her mailbox and found a letter from Sam, finally. Today was a good day indeed.

At three AM, Ruby was still awake but feeling almost ready to go to sleep. Her practice had gone really well: she'd mastered some of the more virtuosic sections of the concerto and remembered to stop before her arms started hurting. After that she'd written back to Sam, a slightly manic three-page ramble that began:

Sam! I think I've met someone. I mean, maybe not met some-one, but then maybe that is what I've done. I've made a new friend anyway—probably? But I have a good feeling about him. You know how sometimes you just know? And I'm composing again, which is a big thing for me. You'll have to hear it when it's done. I think it might be good, and I've never thought that about anything I've written before . . .

She'd posted the letter, then spent two hours beginning to recreate her composition from the scraps of what she remembered. Despite the difficulty of the task, she eventually concluded that it had been a good thing to throw it out and start again. She had feared that her tricksy muse had gone, that the spirit of *diabolus in musica* had grown bored waiting and left her, but as soon as she started to hum the main theme, it returned, along with her passion. The piece crackled with an urgency that it had lacked in its previous incarnation. In her head she could hear an orchestra playing it; she could even picture herself performing the solo, an image so clear that she could see the exact blue of the dress she would wear, the curve of the stage and the lighting. She could envisage the rapt faces of the audience members, shivers traveling through them and right back to Ruby, on stage. And the applause, washing over her, endless waves of it.

Time was sucked away, and soon the night was almost over. It was just before dawn when she took her makeup off, and Ruby was fizzing with possibility, with positive thoughts of change. She made a pact with herself to start going to bed earlier, to train herself back into normality before she returned to teaching in a few weeks' time. Perhaps she didn't need to stay away so long; she felt so much better. She would ring Barbara and ask to return to work. And she would stop trying to spy on Gregor (she rolled the new name around in her head, relishing the roundness of the vowels, the soft consonants) because that was not normal behavior, was it? Even as she thought this, she went through to the kitchen and found herself looking over at Gregor's apartment building, hoping to see him there, softly lit by a side lamp, tackling a tricky inversion.

The big window was dark, though this time the blinds were open. She turned the lights off and stood, imagining herself on the other side of the drop, standing in his living room, looking over here. The fantasy was so vivid that she could actually see the outline of herself in his window. She pressed a palm to her own window and gazed at the image of her future self, so content to be inside Gregor's apartment, waiting perhaps to start the yoga routine that they would perform together now. He would teach her; she would be a good student, and the lessons would calm her anxious mind.

Then, she froze, fear chilling her, running up her spine. She rubbed her eyes and looked again. The outline she had just imagined had taken shape, become solid, a dark figure forming in front of her eyes as she stared: there really was someone there, standing in the shadowed room, looking out. Not Gregor; it was a woman.

Her panicked brain scrambled for an explanation. She kept darting her eyes away and looking back, hoping not to see it. Was it a hallucination? Just when she'd started to feel on top of things? *Oh,* she thought, *perhaps it could be a reflection, somehow, of me, standing here.* But when she took her own hand down from the glass, the figure's hand remained, white against the surface of the window. And beyond the hand, looming from the darkness, a pale face like the moon, with dark eyes that stared into her own. The face came closer to the glass, almost pressing up against it, a ghostly vision. Ruby ducked down, trying to hide, even though it was too late: she'd been seen.

Whoever it was—whatever it was—turned and walked away, back into the room.

For a while Ruby stood gazing at the blank eye of the big window, heart pounding, wondering if she was dreaming. No, of course she wasn't; she could feel the cold kitchen floor beneath her feet, the rim of the stainless-steel sink under her fingers. She blinked and the woman was back, standing in the same place, but this time there was a bundle in her arms. It looked like a baby. Holding the child with one arm, the woman placed the other hand on the window, palm out, fingers splayed. With the baby she seemed less like a ghost, more like a human, though Ruby was still afraid; the way she stared, as if in accusation. The way her hands clutched the child, and her eyes, unblinking. Who was this woman to Gregor? His wife? Girlfriend?

Oh, Gregor. Ruby felt the disappointment bodily, the sensation of falling from a height, and gripped the edge of the sink to stop herself stumbling. At the same time she chastised herself: Why was she so upset by this? She hadn't lost anything, not really, because she hadn't had anything to start with, only a glimmer of hope. In a sick kind of a way, she was glad to have seen the woman—wife, partner, whatever she was—because it meant that Ruby knew where she stood: back on firm ground, where good things only happened to other people, and all the best men were taken or not interested. Not that Gregor would have been interested in her. How would she have explained the spying, for a start?

The woman in Gregor's darkened apartment continued to stare across the drop and into Ruby's eyes. After what seemed like a very long time, the woman reached across for the blind cord and slowly rolled it down, keeping her eyes on Ruby until the very last second.

CHAPTER

9

NOW
Joanna
Friday, December 21, midnight

"So, all the flats in this block are attached to the video-entry system," said Thrupp.

"Yes," said Joanna, thinking that it was a shame they didn't have such luxuries in Ruby's block. "But this one also has a camera here." She pointed out the CCTV lens embedded in the ceiling near the entrance to Gregor's flat. It was a covert-type camera, flush with the paintwork, but Jo had spotted it immediately. Thrupp paused to consider.

"And have you had a chance to view the footage from either?"

"The entrance system only records when it's activated by the buzzer. The monitor is inside by the door, but there doesn't seem to be anything recorded on this unit since last month. Either there haven't been any visitors, or someone has deleted it."

"And this one?" He pointed at the tiny lens.

"We don't know where the monitor is for that one. It's probably a phone app."

Jo took two pairs of blue crime-scene shoe coverings from the packet she kept in her kit bag. After she'd handed some to Thrupp, she led the way into the apartment, where their feet left damp impressions in the carpeting as they walked through to the large living space. Terry, the caretaker, had recently turned the power back on; Jo used a gloved hand to switch on the lights as they approached the open bathroom door.

The bath had a ring of dried blood near the rim, and streaks of red drew the eye to the plughole. On the bathroom floor there was the crumpled duvet, wet and soaked in blood at one end, a wreath of pink surrounding a reddish-black patch where the man's head had lain.

"The victim was in the tub when we broke the door down," said Jo. "It was full of water. He was floating, his head resting at that end." She pointed to the edge of the bath nearest the wall, where blood had pooled.

"Poor bastard. Unconscious and alone, in a bath full of water. Lucky he didn't drown."

"I don't know how lucky he is, boss. The guy was not in good shape when the paramedics took him away."

Thrupp turned to inspect the doorframe, where splinters stuck out at odd angles from where Atkinson had broken the lock. "Could it be self-inflicted? Attempted suicide?"

"Not unless he smashed his own skull in, sir."

He gave her a sideways scowl. "Did you photograph the scene before you did anything to it?"

"Nope. We walked all over it, I'm afraid. Paramedics did too. Have you had any updates from the hospital?"

"The victim is still unconscious, last I heard. That was about an hour ago."

"Not a murder inquiry then," said Joanna.

"Not yet." He looked her in the eye. "What are you hoping for, resources-wise?"

"We'll need full forensics, a team of investigators—the works."

"With the room locked from the inside? You don't think it was an accident? He could have fallen over, bashed his head. Maybe he stood up to get something from the cupboard."

Her gut screamed that it wasn't an accident, but her training forced her to consider every option. She cast her professional eye over the scene, searching out possibilities that she might have missed. There was a small mirrored unit on the wall next to the bath. Possible to reach from the bath, but it would have been a stretch, and yes, it was likely that if you tried that, you might slip. One of the doors on the cupboard was open slightly. She could see how it might happen. Yet that scenario could easily be ruled out: if the man was reaching for the cupboard, he would have fallen out of the bath onto the floor, not backward into the water.

Joanna considered the velocity of a simple slip-and-fall scenario, if it were the case that he had fallen in the right direction. "I don't see how a person could injure themselves that badly by falling over in the bath. The water would have broken the fall to some extent."

Thrupp stepped forward to inspect the rim of the bath. "I thought the tap was running," he said. "That's why the leak happened, and the neighbor was alerted, correct?"

"Yes."

"So, might have been a dry bath at the time, or only enough water in it to make him lose his footing. Therefore it would have been a harder fall."

"Do you get in the bath before it's full?" she said. "I don't. Something hit the guy hard enough to damage the skull, break the skin, and cause him to go unconscious. I'm not sure a fall would do it." She shuddered at the memory of the place where her hand had supported his head, the cold-porridge feeling of mashed tissue.

On the bathroom tiles, Joanna spotted something that stuck out slightly. Almost the same white as the vinyl, a small triangular piece of something, like a chip from a smashed mug handle.

"What about this?"

Thrupp bent over and squinted at the object. "I can't tell what that is. A bit of tile that's come off somewhere? Doesn't give us much."

"Well, that's the point. We can find out, sir, if we have the forensic team. I'm convinced there was someone else here."

"Based on what? I can't just take your word, Jo. You need something to back it up. Say there *was* someone else here. How did they get out?"

Above the bath there was a high window. Seven floors up, there was no way an assailant could have used it as an escape route. They turned their attention to the door.

Harper crouched down so that the lock on the door was at eye level. "This isn't secure. Could have been turned from the outside with a screwdriver. Easy."

Thrupp said, "It's still not enough. I need a suspect. Or at the very least, a weapon. This case is borderline right now. I could put you and Atkinson on it and be done. Tell me why you need a CSI team."

Jo darted her eyes around the room once more. With her head close to the bath, she spotted a tiny clump of brown hair clinging to the metal rim of the plughole. It was still attached to a fragment of skin. Nothing about the smooth surface of the bath rim indicated that it could have caused skin to detach; no flaws or sharp edges.

"Here, sir," she said.

Thrupp came closer. He took out his phone and photographed the fragment. Then he straightened up, nodded to Harper, and said, "You can have everything you need."

She cleared her throat. "Thank you, sir."

After Thrupp had gone, Joanna radioed for Atkinson to come up. More officers were arriving every minute. Soon the place would be crawling with forensic officers, and she wanted to take one last look around before that happened.

When Atkinson appeared in the doorway, Jo noticed that he'd gone slightly green. He kept glancing at his hands, still stained with Gregor Franks's blood.

"You okay?"

"Me? Yep. Sure. Fine."

Jo knew he wasn't fine. "There's extra psychological supervision available for this kind of situation, Steve. You want me to arrange that for you?"

"It's not that."

She looked him in the eye. "Oh?"

"Well, it is that, sort of. No one likes being covered in someone else's blood, do they?"

"Do you need to take a break?"

He swallowed, stood up straight. "No. I want to get on with it."

She gave him a long look, and decided to take him at his word. There wasn't time to do anything else. "Okay. Gather a team to search for a weapon—heavy object, something with sharp corners, I think, though we can have the details narrowed down by forensics once they've seen the wound."

Atkinson stepped away to convey the instruction to the other officers on scene. As he adjusted the radio, a streak of red on his hand caused Jo to inspect her own hands. Picking at the dried blood under her nails, she felt nothing much except for a trace of sympathy for her buddy, for the fact that Atkinson had been rattled by what they'd found. All police officers were human. Some, like herself, simply found it easier to detach themselves from the grittier parts of the job. Jo saw this aspect of her personality as a strength, though very occasionally she wondered if other people had something she was missing, something overtly emotional.

Back in the living room, Joanna scanned the floor, and although there were no objects that looked like weapons, there by the skirting was a discarded teaspoon she hadn't noticed before. Atkinson came in and she nodded toward it.

"Shall I bag it, boss?"

"No, wait for the CSIs. They'll need a clean run. Also, you'll need to report your movements and your account of my movements from when we both entered the flat, for the record."

"When do you need that report?"

"As soon as possible. Tonight, if you can. What else do you see, Steve?"

He looked around.

"A sofa. A plate. Um. A TV remote?"

"Anything unusual?"

"That box of toys is kind of unusual. The caretaker didn't know there was a kid living here. That doesn't make sense, does it?"

"I don't know. It's a private residence. There's no reason he would know, if he hadn't been told." She stared through the kitchen door at the fridge, where the child's drawings were held in place by lozenge-shaped magnets. "Okay. Here's a different question. What *don't* you see?"

"Do you mean, like, what's missing? Well, not much. The TV is still there. There's a posh wireless sound system. If it was a burglary, then they didn't take anything obvious. I can't imagine what else might be missing unless you mean his personal items, wallet, phone?"

"Nope. They're in the kitchen—look. And his car keys. His phone was plugged into a charger; it only ran out because the electricity had been turned off. That phone is the latest model. They're, like, a thousand pounds."

"Okay," said Atkinson, "we can be sure there was no burglar here then, or all of that would have gone. But I don't know. How can we possibly tell what's missing if we don't know what was here before?"

Joanna narrowed her eyes at her colleague. She gave him another few seconds before she said what was obvious, surely, to anyone. "There are no photos."

Atkinson's eyebrows went up. He swept the walls with his eyes. No photos and no places on the wall where photos might have been. Even in today's digital age, people still had family images on the walls. And here in this smart apartment, where a small child had been living—surely the most photographed species of being in the world—there was nothing. No portraits at all.

"Maybe he'll have photos on his phone?"

Harper thought about it. "Sure, that's possible. But it's still a bit odd, don't you think?"

In her line of work Joanna visited a lot of houses, and where there were babies, there were always baby pictures. Her mother had pictures of her kids everywhere. Grainy baby photos of Joanna and studio shots of Ruby as a small child. Pride of place, above the TV, there was a large portrait of the two of them, Joanna in her police cadet uniform and Ruby in her new school uniform, ages eighteen and four, respectively, both grinning and standing to attention in front of the fireplace. Here, there were pictures, but none of them had any people in them. Moving around the apartment, she realized that every image hung on the wall was a seascape. A photograph of sweeping beach, a print featuring seabirds, a distant horizon. In the bedroom there were more, paintings of stormy seas, calm seas, sunsets over the ocean. But there was nothing displayed of the people who lived here, nothing to show who they were except the scraps of things they'd left behind. She stood in the bedroom where it looked as if a child had been sleeping. No bed toys, no baby blanket; those things would be with the child, wherever it was now. And whoever had the child would be the one who knew what had happened to Gregor. That was who they needed to find, and quickly.

CHAPTER

10

THEN
Ruby
September

THE APARTMENT SEEMED too small and dark to stay inside for yet another day with nothing to do. There were things she *ought* to do: tidying, cleaning, playing her violin, but none of them appealed to her at that moment. The flat was a state, kitchen filthy with grime, but that was usual. What was different was that she hadn't taken her instrument out of its case for many days. It just didn't seem important. Why was she perfecting the Sibelius when she would never perform it? Only a week ago, she'd written to Sam to tell him that things were looking up, that she was composing again, and that she might have met a new friend, finally, though it was early days. She certainly felt stupid for saying that last part. She'd only met someone on a tram and spoken to them for five minutes. Ridiculous to think of Gregor as a "friend," she could see that now. Unfortunately she'd posted the letter a few hours before she'd looked across at the window and seen the woman and baby, which had blown the idea of Gregor away like the fantasy it had been all along.

Sam was an *actual* friend and had been there when she needed him. The only person who had, in fact. If he had a flaw, it would be that he didn't own a mobile phone, but she'd gotten used to writing letters, even though the fact that he moved around the country meant that he sometimes didn't reply for weeks or months. When she'd had to leave her family home the Christmas before, his narrowboat was the first place she'd thought of to go, and he'd welcomed her, let her stay until the council found her the flat. There had been five weeks of blissful boat life, no contact with her family, the longest she'd ever gone without speaking to Jo or Marianne. Then, when the flat was secured, she'd decided to get in touch with Joanna.

Shivering in the February cold in the smoker's shelter outside the folk bar, Ruby had hesitated, then pressed Joanna's icon on her phone.

One ring, two. She'd nearly hung up, but then, there she was. "Ruby?"

For a short while Ruby couldn't speak. Emotion crowded her throat.

"Ruby? Are you there? Is it you? Say something."

Jo didn't sound angry. If she'd sounded angry, then Ruby would have hung up immediately.

"Are you okay? Please, Ruby, just say anything. Tell me you're okay."

"I'm okay," said Ruby, her voice thick.

"Thank God," said Jo. "We were so worried. Have you spoken to Mum?"

"Don't call her that."

"Believe me, there's plenty I could call her. I can't believe she said what she said. I didn't speak to her myself for a week."

"But you're speaking to her now?" Ruby felt betrayed by this. Jo had been there for the fight. She knew how hurtful those words had been.

"I had to. I couldn't let Dad cope with it all on his own. And I would never try to defend what she did but . . ."

"You're about to defend her, aren't you?"

"What do you want me to do, say she's a total bitch? An alcoholic? A failure? We've both had times we've thought those things.

And what she said hurt me too—it was spiteful and stupid. But she didn't mean it. She's ill, Ruby, and what she said was part of that. It wasn't her speaking, not really. We have to make exceptions sometimes. At the end of the day, she's our mum. She brought you up. She loved you, just the same as she loved me. More, if anything."

Ruby snorted in disbelief. Marianne did not love Ruby anywhere near as much as she loved Joanna. If it had been Ruby with an unwanted teenage pregnancy, would Marianne have taken the child in and raised it as her own? Of course not. By the time Ruby was thirteen, the same age Joanna had been when she'd had her, Marianne wouldn't have been able to hide her little problem for long enough to pass the stringent requirements of the adoption process, the way she had the first time. She would have reeked of booze at the assessment interview.

"Drink makes you more truthful, I've heard."

"No, it doesn't do that," said Joanna. "It makes you self-destruct."

Ruby felt a pang of sympathy for Marianne—and squashed it. "I don't want to get into this, not now. I just called to tell you that I've been fine. I've been staying with a friend. But I won't need to now because I've just been given a council flat."

"You're not coming home?"

"Coming home? Where do you mean, Marianne's? It's not as if it's your home, not anymore. You moved out years ago."

She'd told Sam about the fact that Joanna was her biological mother, but in general, Ruby didn't bother to explain to people. She couldn't bear that look in their eyes; the pity, the fascination. Because it was a strange situation, no matter how much their mother tried to normalize it in those early years.

"I always wanted two," Marianne had said to Ruby, more than once. "Yes, it was hard when Joanna got into trouble, but to me you were a gift. You were a gift to all of us. Jo finally got the little sister she always wanted." As she grew up, Ruby thought, *Is that really true, that she wanted a sister?* It started to feel like a story they were using to dress up the fact that Jo conveniently got rid of the child she never wanted. Worse than a story: a lie. Marianne wanted another baby—that she believed—but it wasn't Ruby she'd wanted. Ruby was always going to be a poor replacement for the baby Marianne had tried and failed to conceive herself.

Joanna herself was strangely silent on the subject. Since the older of the two left home to train with the police service, when Ruby was barely five years old, there had always been a distance between them. To outsiders, school friends and so on, they were sisters, but in the house, it was hard to say it out loud. It was only really Marianne who kept on with the "sister" thing. When Jo visited, Marianne would say, "Your sister's home." Ruby would raise an eyebrow, and Jo would look away. It always felt like they were pretending.

As she'd gotten older, in describing Jo to other people, the word *sister* seemed completely wrong, but *mother* wasn't right either, not at all. Most of the time, it was easier not to talk about it. And then there was the fight, when Marianne's true feelings were well and truly aired. And that was that as far as Ruby was concerned. A full stop, but a good one. An end to all of the bullshit.

"So no, Jo. I'm not going *home*. Not after what she said."

There was a short silence. "I think that's . . . fine," said Jo. "It's wonderful news, actually. You're old enough now to get your own place."

"That's right. I'm twenty-six. Hardly a babe in arms."

"Sure. I guess I always think of you as a baby."

"Well, you would, wouldn't you?"

Joanna made a small choking sound.

"So anyway, you don't need to worry about me being homeless or whatever. You can tell Marianne that. And tell her not to keep on calling me. I'll be in touch, but not until I'm ready."

"Just speak to her, for goodness sake—she's in bits."

Ruby held the phone away from her ear, ready to end the call. Her mouth hung open slightly. *She's* in bits, she wanted to yell. What about *me*? Jo ought to have been on Ruby's side. Just this once. But no one was on Ruby's side, were they? They were all too busy looking out for themselves, from the very beginning. From before she was even born.

The tears were coming quickly now. "I was okay until I started talking to you. I've got to go. I'll ring again. But not for a while. Sorry."

She'd ended the call and taken the battery out of the phone.

Since moving into the estate, Ruby had answered calls from Joanna maybe one time out of every three. From Marianne, never. The phone had become a thing for playing music, and not much more.

There was a bench she liked the look of, next to the gardens. The late summer weather was starting to turn, so she pulled on a sweater, took a cup of tea in a travel mug. The buildings rose up in front and behind, but the square itself was a little suntrap. She plugged in her earbuds and let the music take her away, felt the beams of light on her face as if they were healing her, and closed her eyes so that she didn't see Gregor coming out of the North Block and walking toward her, until he was almost at her side.

"Hello again." He held up a hand in greeting.

Ruby smiled, took one earbud out. "Hi." He was better looking than she remembered, but just as awkward, with a blush already rising to his cheeks.

Gregor stopped a meter from the bench, hovering as if he was unsure whether to sit. "What are you listening to? I mean, if you don't mind me asking."

"Rusalka," she said, and waited for his eyes to glaze over the way most people's did.

"The opera?"

"Yes, do you know it?"

"Of course. I love Dvořák. Though I get a bit sick of Number nine."

She sat up straighter. Number nine. Most people would call it the *New World Symphony*. No wonder he was awkward: he was just as nerdy as she was. Gregor sat on the bench at the farthest possible distance away. She shifted to the other edge of the bench, maximizing the gap between them. She took the other earbud out. The music was distracting her.

"'Song to the Moon,'" he said, indicating the tinny stream of music coming from her earbud. "Beautiful. Though it doesn't end well, if I remember rightly. For either of them."

In her pocket, Ruby's phone was digging into her leg. She pulled it out, clicked to stop the music. "These things never do."

"Never trust a fairy-tale prince, I suppose."

"Ha," said Ruby, looking at him sideways, at the way his hair shone gold in the sun. "There's a rule to live by."

There was a silence that got more strained as it stretched on. Gregor cleared his throat.

"When I saw you on the tram . . ." He trailed off.

Ruby took a sip of tea from her mug. "Yes?"

"It's just that . . . I think I know where I recognize you from now."

Ruby felt her own cheeks begin to burn. She stared at the ground, waiting, wondering if she could simply get up and walk away without saying another word.

"You live in the West Block, don't you?" He pointed up to where their windows faced one another. "Seventh floor, right? Your window is opposite mine."

Ruby's grip failed her, and she dropped her travel mug so that it hit the ground and rolled, some of the tea splashing on his shoes. "Oh!"

Gregor leaned down to pick up the bamboo cup. He held it out to her.

"Look, I know what you're going to say. You saw me looking at you, didn't you?" She had to get away. Her voice trembled with the tears she was holding back. What must he think of her? "Well, I'm sorry. I don't know what else to say. It was pathetic. I'm pathetic."

"Hang on," said Gregor, a look of confusion crossing his face. "I don't mind. That's not what I meant. Oh God . . ." His hands flapped, as if he didn't know what to do, how to say what he'd come to say.

"So, what do you mean? You *didn't* see me watching?" The possibility that she'd admitted to something excruciating when she hadn't needed to was somehow worse, in that moment, than the thing itself. Ruby felt a wave of nausea.

"Oh yeah, I did see you. But . . ."

Panic set in. "I have to go."

"Don't."

Ruby looked down. He'd grabbed her hand.

"It's my fault," he said. "I was going to apologize to you. I should draw the blinds. It never occurred to me. I guess I didn't expect anyone to be up at that time in the morning, and your place has the only window that overlooks mine. It's always been empty, so I didn't realize . . ."

She couldn't stop staring at his hand on hers. Anything to avoid looking at his face. He followed her eyes and let go of her then, as if he didn't realize he'd grabbed her in the first place.

"They said, when I moved in, it had been empty. Some kind of council computer mistake. I haven't been there all that long."

"When did you move in?" he asked.

She sat down on the edge of the bench. "A few months ago. But I was working full time up until recently, so you won't have seen me around during the day."

His face had a shadow of stubble, not the designer kind—more of the slightly unkempt kind, as if he probably shaved, as a rule, but hadn't for a day or so. Then there was his scent. Soap and citrus and something almost animal under it all. It reminded her of how her rosin smelled when she applied it to the horsehair of her bow.

"I should be more discreet. I would never have left the blinds up . . . If I knew you were . . ."

Their eyes met and the tension broke. Both of them burst out laughing.

"I shouldn't be awake anyway," Ruby said. "But I've been having trouble sleeping, as it goes."

He studied her face, suddenly serious. "That's a terrible thing, you know. Not sleeping can really screw with your mental health."

Don't I know it, she thought. "Why are *you* awake at that time, then?" she said. "It was always the early hours of the morning when I saw you."

He sighed. "Boring reasons. I go to bed early. I like to do yoga just before the dawn. Not to sound too much like a hippie, but it's . . . magical. The whole world is asleep, even the birds, and there I am, totally at one with body, mind, and nature. Oh. I do sound like a total hippie, don't I?"

She laughed a little, then waited. One of them would have to mention it sooner or later.

"What?" said Gregor.

"Oh, nothing really. I thought you were going to say that the baby woke you up. Your wife must be tired, too . . ."

As she spoke, Gregor's demeanor changed.

"My what?"

"Your wife? Partner? She must have trouble sleeping too. Because of the baby."

"You saw Constance?"

"Is that her name? What a lovely name." What a lovely concept. There were no constants in Ruby's life.

Gregor mumbled what he said next, but Ruby heard every word. "She's not my wife. We're not a couple."

"Look, it's really none of my business."

"No," he said, "it's fine. I can see why you would think that. But she's not—we're not . . . I mean, we were. But."

"What?"

"You know what? It doesn't matter. It's boring anyway." He sat there, slumped over slightly. Then he straightened up and stood, turned toward her with a sad look on his face.

Ruby looked up at him. "Tell me," she said. "I want to know."

"No, you know what? I only just met you. It wouldn't be fair. Seriously, you don't want to know all the tedious ins and outs."

"But how can you decide that? You don't know anything about me either, yet." Yet? What made her say that?

"I know that I like you." He cringed. "I mean, in a friendly way. Not like . . . I mean not that I *wouldn't*—Oh, shit."

His cheeks colored instantly, redder than ever. Ruby looked away, embarrassed for them both.

"I better get back," said Gregor. "It was lovely meeting you, Ruby. I hope we'll bump into each other again one day."

He took a step away. He was going to walk away, and she might not see him again. Having wanted to run away herself, Ruby felt suddenly desperate for him to stay. She said, "Gregor. Just tell me. I can decide myself if it's boring, right?"

He seemed to think about it. Then he sat down.

"Can I trust you?"

"No, of course not. You only just met me."

They both laughed.

Gregor said, "I think I'm a good judge of character. You don't look like a gossip to me."

"You're right. I am confidentiality personified."

She mimed zipping her mouth shut.

He let out a long sigh. "Constance is agoraphobic. We were together, but now we're not. She still lives with me. That's the short version."

Ruby didn't realize she was holding her breath until she started to speak. "And the baby?"

He smiled at the mention of the child.

"The baby—she's nearly two now, so not really a baby—was conceived the night we met. It wasn't supposed to happen. I never planned . . . it isn't like me at all. I don't usually do things like that."

Gregor stole a glance at Ruby. His face was full of regret, embarrassment, hope for understanding.

"These things happen to the best of us," she said. "I know that more than most, actually." He cast a questioning glance at her but didn't pursue it. She was thinking of her own ignoble origins, but then Ruby's mind flitted briefly to her own indiscretions, which amounted to a string of meaningless encounters during one particularly depressing summer. She tried not to feel bad about it, but the shame sat there, deeply rooted and taking up the space where intimacy should have been. "Where did you two meet?"

"A beach party, as it happens."

"Sounds wild."

"It was fun. And I really liked her. But after she got pregnant so quickly . . . we didn't really know each other, you know? I just couldn't stay in a relationship where we were so different."

"So, you ended it?"

"Yeah. But I feel bad every day, that I couldn't make it work. The baby. And everything. I have to take the blame, as it was completely my decision to split, but . . . I just wish I could love her the way she still loves me."

"You can't force these things."

What must it be like for both of them, living together and yet not living together? One of them still holding a candle, and then the baby complicating things. And the agoraphobia must have intensified everything. No wonder he looked so tired. The nocturnal yoga made sense now too—it was probably the only time the apartment was quiet.

Gregor's eyes took on a faraway look. He stood up. "I really should get back now. I only popped out to get milk. Constance gets worried if I take too long."

Ruby stood up too, and the two of them walked a few steps together. "Is it that bad for her?"

"It's variable. Sometimes she's fine, seems to be coping okay. Other days, like today, not so much. Thanks for listening, Ruby. Maybe I'll see you around."

And he was gone, jogging in the direction of the shop before she could say another word.

11

He wooed her so earnestly and lovingly, that she put on some woman's clothing which he brought her from his cottage, followed him home, and became his wife.
—Patrick Kennedy, "The Silkie Wife," 1891

TWO YEARS and SIX MONTHS EARLIER
Constance
The Summer Solstice

SHE SEES THE rocks from offshore and feels a thrill run through her. The solstice is the night of possibilities, the night things can happen. The sand of the beach is a pale strip against the moving water, the darker cliffs beyond. She cuts through the water smoothly, looping under and around her brother, making him laugh because he didn't see her coming. Others are already on the beach, already lighting the fire. Soon the drums will start, and after that her favorite part, the dancing.

It's her special night tonight: she's been given the blessing from the elders. Normally they don't mix with anyone who isn't from the island, but tonight, if she sees an Outsider and she likes the look of him, she can choose him, go with him, give herself to him. Just for one night. It's an ancient rite, practiced for centuries, a way of preserving the ways of their people at the same time as it strengthens the bloodline. It can only happen now, on this night, because tomorrow is her wedding day. Those babies born nine months from the ceremony are all the more special for it, though it can be hard for the menfolk to accept that this is the way it has to be. Her betrothed hasn't looked in her direction all day. He can't wait for tomorrow, for the ceremony that will tie them together until their deaths. They both know that very occasionally, maybe once in a generation, the girls don't come back. They choose to stay with the Outsider. Constance wants to comfort him, tell him she is his, that she would never leave him. Whatever happens tonight will soon be past, never to be spoken of between the two of them. She can tell he is hurt, but he, like her, must wait until tomorrow. It is the way of their people, and there's nothing either of them can do about it.

They emerge from the sea, slick with seawater. She steps onto the sand with feet that feel newly born, with legs that are unsteady at first after swimming so far. But as she gets closer to fire, she hears the rhythm, the drumming; the beat enters her body so that she starts to move, to dance, to lose herself in this one final night of freedom. She mustn't think of tomorrow, of the boy who sits in the shadows, his heart bruised. Tomorrow is the beginning of a long life together; they have time to mend, to journey, and to bear the children who will carry on the traditions.

When the man comes into the circle of light, their eyes meet, and she knows he is the Outsider she's been waiting for. She pushes thoughts of her beloved away so that when he takes her by the hand, she goes willingly.

12

NOW
Joanna
Saturday, December 22, early morning

"CAN I CALL you Sarah?"

The old woman stiffened slightly. "Well. If you have to."

Mrs. Sarah Stefanidis was sitting in her living room in a high-backed floral armchair, her white stick leaning within reach. On her knees was a tray, where Joanna now placed a mug of tea.

"Careful—it's hot."

"I hope so too," said Mrs. Stefanidis. "Nothing worse than a tepid cup of tea." She slid her hands toward the drink, fingertips fluttering on the surface of the tray. "There are a lot of you out there. Up and down the stairs, talking on your radios. Must be serious."

"The man in the flat upstairs, Mr. Franks. We found him unconscious in his bath, taps still running. That's why it leaked through the ceiling. We're treating it as suspicious."

"You think he was attacked?"

"Yes. I'm sorry. It must be a shock to hear that something like this has happened in your building."

"I knew there was something wrong. It was a little worrying, of course, with the water coming down onto the table. But I phoned Terry, and he came straightaway, bless him. I thought it was maybe a burst pipe; it's been so cold lately. But after a while I could smell it, just faintly. The blood." She wrinkled her nose, as if she could still smell it now. Perhaps she could—enough of it had soaked into the kitchen ceiling to cause the plaster to bulge low and stain it rust-red.

"I'm sorry you had to experience that."

"So, his attacker . . . are they still at large?"

"We're currently trying to identify suspects."

Mrs. Stefanidis rubbed her elbows as if she were chilly. "You don't think they'll come back? This building isn't secure, not really. People just buzz anyone in, or come in behind you when you open the door. They say they've business here, but who's to know? I don't have anything worth taking, but they don't know that, do they?"

"We don't think it was a burglary. No valuables were taken, or at least it's not obvious that anything has gone. His wallet was still there, full of cash."

"Really? So, why? I mean, if they didn't want to rob him? Why would anyone, otherwise?"

"That's what we need to establish."

"He used to come around when we first moved in," said Mrs. Stefanidis. "That was when his mother was still alive, of course."

"His mother? She lived with him here?" Jo noted it down.

"Yes, she did. She was a lovely woman, Eva. Only a few weeks after they came, she disappeared. I haven't thought of her for months. Sweet lady."

"Disappeared? Was it reported to police?"

"I don't mean disappeared like that. Only, that's what it seemed like to me. She would pop by every other day or so, have a natter, cup of tea. I thought we'd be friends for life. Last time I saw her she said, *"See you tomorrow,"* but she never came. After a week, I went up and knocked. He answered. *"She's dead,"* he said. Heart attack. I remember the words because he sounded so different to how he normally sounded."

"Different how?"

"I'm not sure. Like he'd been crying, or he had a cold. Also, it turned out I'd missed the funeral. Can't complain too much—I hadn't known her long—but it smarted, you know? I didn't really see him at all after that, which was odd, as if he'd forgotten we were once friendly. Grief can do that to a person."

"So when was the last time you had a conversation with Mr. Franks?"

"Probably nearly three years ago, the time when he told me she was dead. Proper mummy's boy, I suppose—must have hit him hard. Can't blame him really. And now this. Such a lot of blood. Not dead, though—that's good news. Quite a relief that he's still with us. Do you think he'll recover quickly?"

"I'm afraid we won't know that until doctors have finished assessing him. We need to find the assailant as soon as we can. And for that we need your help."

"Well, I don't know how much I'll be able to tell you. Like I say, I don't see him. And I'm almost completely blind, you know. Faces are a particular problem for me." She frowned.

Throughout the conversation Mrs. Stefanidis faced Joanna. The old woman's eyes pointed broadly in the officer's direction, but Jo could tell it was only an affectation, perhaps out of habit or courtesy. When Jo moved, the eyes didn't follow. When she spoke, they swiveled to approximately the right area. "Anything you can tell us about the past few days?" said Jo, "Even if you don't think it's useful. Perhaps you heard something?"

"Just the usual din from her at 6D. When was the attack?"

"This morning, we think. Well, yesterday now, of course. We can't be completely accurate about the time yet. If you don't mind me asking, how is your hearing, on the whole?"

"I'm not deaf, Detective. I wish I were, sometimes. When I open the window, I can hear nothing but children shouting from the playground. Everything on the stairs comes through to me too—stamping and yelling and hollering. Gregor is rather an exception. A very quiet man; I never hear a peep from him, which is more than I can say for the rabble across the hallway, with her screaming back and forth at the kids at all hours. Nothing to complain about with Mr. Franks. I suppose it's because he's on his own."

Joanna thought of the herd of tiny elephants living above her own place.

"Just to be clear. You've never been aware of a child in the penthouse flat, at any point?"

"No. I've not been aware of that."

"No partner, girlfriends? What about visitors, family members, that kind of thing?"

A silence. "Well. Now that you mention it. There was something, but it was probably nothing."

"Please."

"Last week, I heard a child in the hallway on the floor above. I was going down in the lift to get the post from the lobby. I assumed it was one of the kids from this floor, gone up there to play. The mother at number 6D just seems to open the door and push them out every morning, lets them run around unsupervised on the stairs. Little children too. They've fallen in the past, and the ambulance has had to come. Mind you, they fight like rats in a cage—probably pushed each other down."

"But you remember this incident particularly . . ." said Jo, gently nudging her back to the point and leaving the sentence hanging.

"I suppose I do, yes." She pointed in the general direction of the door. "I heard a child's voice talking to someone at the top of the stairs. When I came back up with my post, I couldn't hear it anymore. I suppose I forgot about it until just now."

"Did you hear what they were saying, get a sense of who it might be?"

"No, no. It was baby talk, couldn't catch it. And whoever the child was talking to was mumbling quietly, so maybe that was why I noticed it. Couldn't have been the woman from 6D, you see. She shouts everything, even when she doesn't need to. I know what they're having for dinner, usually, and whether she's out of cider or cigs. Which she always is."

Jo wondered if there would be anything useful to gain from questioning the neighbor any further. She looked around, and something occurred to her. "You have a really nice apartment, Sarah, do you have much help with things?" The room in which they were sitting was extremely tidy and clean.

"You mean, carers?" Mrs. Stefanidis laughed. "No. I don't need them. I can look after myself. I'm not that old."

Jo reckoned Mrs. Stefanidis was at least eighty if she was a day. "I meant cleaners, really. Regular domestic help."

"I do all my own housework. I can't see, but that doesn't mean I'm useless. I can smell things, feel things. The spiders know not to make their webs in here. I go around with a duster every morning."

"What about shopping? Do you do it online?"

"Online? I wouldn't know where to start. Until quite recently I used to walk into town, but now there's a girl from the next block who helps me. She says it's no trouble, that she's going herself anyway once a week, so we get the tram together. She's great. Plays the violin for me sometimes. Beautiful."

At the mention of the violin, Joanna became quite still. A memory rose and bloomed, Ruby playing Christmas carols on the fiddle, with Marianne accompanying on the piano. This year, on Christmas Day, the piano would probably remain under the embroidered cloth, the way it had all year. They might use it rest their drinks on, but without Ruby, her mother wouldn't bother. It would stand there in silence, like a piece of furniture or a coffin.

"Beautiful?"

"Yes. Beautiful playing. I don't know what she looks like, of course. She has a beautiful soul too. That's all that matters, isn't it?"

"What's the name of this person?" But it was as if she knew already, before the old woman pursed her lips to make the sound of it.

"Ruby. Ruby Harper."

Joanna suddenly noticed the headache she'd been ignoring. It felt like she was being stabbed in the temple.

"What it is, detective? Are you alright?"

The possibility that Ruby knew something about what had happened to Gregor entered her detective's mind and stuck there, flashing in neon. "Yes, of course. I'm sorry. I feel a little unwell. I think I might have a cold coming on."

"I hope not," said Mrs. Stefanidis. "That's the last thing I need."

"Do you have anyone who can come and keep you company tonight?"

The old lady shook her head. "My husband died, oh, ten years ago now. No children."

"What about friends, other members of your family?"

"Friends apart from Ruby? I'm afraid not. And no family apart from two nieces who never bother."

"And this Ruby," said Joanna, breathing mindfully, "when did you last see her?"

"The day before yesterday. She dropped off some bread and milk."

"I'll need an address for her, please, and a phone number if you have one."

Mrs. Stefanidis reached into her pocket for her phone handset. "I have it all stored on here. Feel free to look."

"Thank you," said Jo, standing up to take the phone. Scrolling through the contacts, she found Ruby's name and there, under the address she knew by heart, was an entirely different number from the one she had for Ruby. Quickly, she added this new number to her contacts and handed Mrs. Stefanidis the handset. She sat down, fiddled with the clipboard she carried, aware that she was supposed to fill in a potential witness contact form with Ruby's details, reasoning that she could easily do that later, but also knowing she was deceiving herself; that she was making up excuses not to do it.

"I haven't known her very long, six weeks or so. She saw me struggling with my shopping bag out there, and carried it up for me." When she said the words *out there*, Mrs. Stefanidis waggled a hand toward the window.

Just like Ruby to help an old lady. Just like her to keep on helping, every week, to see someone in need and step in selflessly.

"Is there anything else I can help you with?" asked Mrs. Stefanidis.

"Oh," said Joanna, realizing she'd been staring into space, not speaking. "Not for now, thank you. I might need to talk to you again. I can have the police liaison officer come and sit with you for a while if you're feeling shaken."

"No, thank you. Don't feel sorry for me. I like my own company. I'll be completely fine."

Harper was almost out the door when Mrs. Stefanidis called her back.

"Leonie," said Mrs. Stefanidis. "I just remembered. That's what the person said, the mumbling person, to the child upstairs. I couldn't make out anything else but I heard them say the name Leonie. "Leonie, come back here"."

"Does that name mean anything to you?"

"No. None of the children on this floor are called that, from what I hear them yelling. This wasn't a yell, more of a loud whisper. Strange."

Harper wrote the name *Leonie* on her notes.

"I'll be in touch," she said, and closed the door.

CHAPTER

13

THEN
Ruby
September

HER PHONE WASN'T in any of the usual places. Ruby went through her pockets, then her bag, even looked in her workbag, which she hadn't opened since being signed off. It wasn't under the bed or on it or in the kitchen. She tried to retrace her steps—she'd definitely had it on the bench, because she remembered Gregor asking her what she was listening to.

There was no sign of it on or around the bench. The model she had really wasn't worth stealing, and for a moment she considered checking inside the bin to see if someone had thrown it away. Maybe, on his way back from the shop, Gregor had seen it. She walked up to the North Block and pressed the button for Apartment 7. There was a click, followed by the sound of static, a channel opening. She looked straight into the camera.

"Hello?" She thought she could hear breathing. "Gregor? Are you there?"

Another click, then silence.

She pressed the button again. No response to the buzzer, not even the click this time.

He probably didn't have it. It was annoying to lose the phone, but not the end of the world. Sam had lectured her for so long about information safety that she never even accepted cookies. If the phone was gone, it was gone. No one would be able to empty her bank account or anything.

"Would you give me a hand, dear?"

An older woman was approaching the door to the building, struggling with two shopping bags. Ruby took them from her. They cut into her fingers painfully.

"Wow, these are really heavy. Are you going far?"

"Only in there. Sixth floor." As she took out her key card and opened the door, Ruby noticed the white cane, folded and hanging from a belt loop.

Ruby was amazed that the woman, whose name was Sarah, had been managing alone all this time, what with being elderly and visually impaired. There were no friends or family to help, Sarah explained; she had no choice but to manage.

"I'll help you next time. We can go together."

"Oh, I couldn't."

"It's no trouble," said Ruby. "I'll be going anyway. It'll be nice to have some company."

"Well, if you're sure. Give me your phone number, so I can call, and you can call me."

"Ah. My phone. I can't find it."

"Oh no! When did you see it last?"

"I was talking to the guy who lives upstairs."

'Mr. Franks? Have you met him, then?" Sarah sounded surprised at that.

"I bumped into him on a tram. Then today he was outside the block, on his way to the corner shop."

"Nice man, but he's so shy and quiet. Very much a lone wolf, these days. Good catch for the right lady. If she can bring him out a bit, you know?"

Yes, thought Ruby, picturing the way Gregor had stumbled over the awkward parts of the conversation. He is shy and quiet. Not really a lone wolf, though—not yet. She was about to say something, when she remembered his words: *"Can I trust you?"*

"Anyway," said Sarah, "what's he got to do with your phone?"

"He might have seen it or seen who picked it up. I can't find it in the flat, so I thought I might have left it on a bench out there, when I was chatting with him."

"Oh well, it could have been anyone who took it, then. People will take whatever they like, in my experience. They'll see a thing they want and just take it, as if it belongs to them already. Especially round here."

Ruby said goodbye to Sarah and climbed the stairs to the seventh floor. On the landing there was a single doorway, the door painted shiny black, with a silver number seven at the center.

Before she could knock, the door opened.

Music swelled, seeming to fill the hallway. Tears sprang to Ruby's eyes. Elgar's Cello Concerto always had that effect on her.

Gregor stood there in an old gray T-shirt with sweat at the armpits, moisture beading on his forehead. At the sight of her, he frowned and smiled at the same time.

"How did you get into the building?"

"How did you know I was here?" Ruby said.

"Slightly embarrassingly, I have motion sensors. On the stairs. They alert me when people are coming up."

She could barely hear his voice. "Why are you whispering?"

He beckoned for her to step inside, and shut the door behind them.

"It's going to sound paranoid."

"I can tell that."

"I had a thing with one of the downstairs people. A bit of a falling out."

She couldn't imagine what this unassuming person could have done to annoy anyone in the building. From what Sarah had said, she was hardly even aware of his presence. "What happened?"

"It was my music. A man came and banged on the door, said it was too loud. He threatened to 'fill me in' if I didn't turn it down."

"Really? But you can't even hear it in the corridor."

"No, that's right—not anymore. I had the entire place sound-proofed after that, to make sure it never happened again. It was really scary. Oh, wow. I'm not making myself sound very manly, am I?"

They both laughed. "Not really, no. Have you seen the man since then?"

"No, I've been avoiding being seen too much. I don't want to bump into him. Or anyone else I might have unwittingly annoyed, of course."

"You're so brave." She laughed again, teasing.

"Well, too late—it's public knowledge now. I'm a nerd and a chicken, and I'm proud."

"Me too," she said. "Someone in my block complained too, but I was practicing in the middle of the night, so I can't really blame them."

'Practicing?'

"Yes, I play the violin."

"Professionally?"

"That was the dream. But no, unfortunately not. I'm a teacher."

"Huh." He looked thoughtful.

"I'm not very good."

He frowned. "I bet you're amazing."

"I meant I'm not a very good teacher, actually. I wasn't too bad as a performer. But a lot of it is down to luck, you know. Whether you get to do it for a living."

"I'd love to hear you play."

Ruby went red. "Um . . ."

"Not in the middle of the night, of course. Though I get why you might do that. Some music sounds better when the world is asleep, doesn't it? And some things, like yoga. They're better too."

For a moment, they just looked at each other. Ruby felt like her cheeks were on fire. "So," he continued, "you never said. How did you get in? Not that I'm not happy to see you, but unless somebody . . ."

"The woman downstairs let me in. Sarah?"

'Mrs. Stefanidis? She's a sweet old thing. Sometimes I wonder how she manages, all alone. I'd help her out, but—"

"You have enough on your plate, sneaking around and trying not to be beaten up?"

"Well, yeah, that and the other thing. The . . . family thing."

She followed his eyes to the door across the hallway. Ruby assumed that was where Constance and the child were right now.

"I actually did try your doorbell first, but no joy."

"You buzzed?" Gregor went to the wall by the door, where there was a panel with a video screen. He pressed "Play" on the last recorded footage, and sure enough, there was Ruby, waiting by the entranceway. "It must have been Constance who answered. Sorry about that. I was working out. In my room."

Ruby noted the use of the term *my room*. Not *our* room, then. He lived with her, but he wasn't *with* her. She was gathering evidence, still unsure whether to fully believe it.

"Ah yes. You hate gyms. But not exercise, clearly."

He gave a half smile. "Come through—you can meet them."

The short hallway led to a large, immaculate living room. There, seated on one of the couches was a small woman in a green, skin-tight jumper dress, with bare feet, her dark hair plaited in a long rope that coiled over a shoulder and reached almost to her lap. Standing, holding the edge of the couch, was a small child in a red sleepsuit, with a cockscomb of black hair, rosy cheeks, and pale skin.

"This is Leonie," said Gregor. "Say hi to Ruby, baby girl." He waved a hand at the toddler, who stood completely still and stared at Ruby with huge gray eyes just like her mother's. "And this is Constance." To Constance he said, "Ruby lives in the West Block. Remember, I told you we met on the tram the other day. Ruby plays the violin."

The woman raised her eyes to Ruby's. The only person smiling was Gregor. When Ruby glanced at him, he made a kind of reassuring yet apologetic face and a half shrug, as if to say, *"Sorry about them."* Looking back at the mother and daughter, the way they regarded her seemed guarded, almost startled. Wild animals caught in a beam of light, alert to whatever might come next.

"Hiya," said Ruby, grinning and waving, not knowing whether to try any other kind of greeting. Constance and Leonie continued to stare at her. There was no vibe whatsoever for a hug or a double-cheek kiss.

The living space was bigger than Ruby's entire apartment. There were two identical couches arranged around a stylish coffee table, facing a very large flatscreen TV affixed to the wall. Floor-to-ceiling blinds concealed the impressive picture window onto the city, and if they had been open, she would have seen that it was overlooked by only one window, her own. Four doors led off the main space. The door to the kitchen stood open; the others were shut.

Ruby settled herself on the couch opposite Constance. Gregor took the remote and turned the music down a little. She was grateful for that. It was impossible to concentrate on anything else when music was playing.

"Nice place," said Ruby. "How long have you lived here?"

"Two years, three months," said Constance, her voice dreamy, almost wistful. "And six days."

Very precise, thought Ruby. "We were just talking about the neighbors," she said. "Have you met any of them?" Was she babbling, talking too fast? Ruby thought perhaps the woman hadn't heard, and was about to repeat herself when Constance shook her head.

"No." There was a trace of an accent. "I don't really go out."

She looked at the child, at how pale she was except for those cheeks. Leonie moved toward her mother without taking her eyes from Ruby, who smiled in a friendly way to try to put everyone at ease.

"I just met the woman who lives underneath you," said Ruby. "She seems nice."

"I don't know her." Constance narrowed her eyes at Ruby, then glanced at Gregor. "How do you two know each other, again?" Scottish, that was the accent. But softer, somehow worn at the edges, musical.

"We, er, don't—not really. I bumped into Gregor out there this afternoon, but when I got back to my flat, I couldn't find my phone. I'm always leaving it places." She turned to him. "I meant to ask: Did you happen to see it?"

His eyebrows went up. "No, sorry. I would have brought it back to you if I had. Was it not there when you went back?"

She shook her head no.

"You could try the police station Lost Property? Someone might have handed it in."

The idea of the police station Lost Property made her feel tired. She wondered if she even needed a phone. She only used it to play music and to ignore calls from her family. "I've probably lost it in the flat somewhere. Wouldn't be the first time." Maybe Sam was right, and life would be simpler and healthier without technology. She could get a record player. The more she thought about it, the less likely it seemed that the phone had been stolen. She should really have checked inside the bin.

Ruby sat down cross-legged on the carpet, in front of Leonie. "Hi," she said.

The baby dropped to her bottom and shuffled across the room in a sort of traveling lotus position, using her feet to propel her forward in little bum-hops.

"That's an interesting way of getting around," said Ruby to Constance.

It seemed as if Constance wasn't going to talk anymore, but then she gave a slow blink and said, "Yep. She doesn't like to crawl. It's not quick enough, apparently. She's a speedy one."

They heard the kettle being switched on and the water beginning to boil. Gregor whistled tunelessly as he opened and closed the cupboards and the fridge.

Leonie was heading toward Ruby with a toy lion in her hands. "Is that for me?" she said when the baby was close to her.

Leonie thrust the toy at her. "Line" was what it sounded like.

"Lion! Amazing job, well done! What else have you got in there?"

Leonie shuffled off, back toward the box.

When Ruby turned to Constance, she was gazing intently into Ruby's eyes. The kettle was loud. "You're the girl from over there," said Constance, pointing at the drapes. "I saw you."

Ruby went cold. "Yes, you're right. I wasn't spying or anything. I've got insomnia, so I'm up at funny hours. Sorry if I—"

"And is what he said right? You're a musician?"

"Yes. Do you like music?"

On the stereo, the Elgar reached a crescendo at the same time as the kettle, and Constance leaned in.

"What's he told you about me and Leonie?" She spoke with an edge of, what, panic? Desperation? Ruby felt accused, as if she'd been gossiping.

"Nothing, really," said Ruby.

"Nothing?" Constance made a face indicating that she clearly didn't believe her. "He didn't say anything about where I came from? About the sea?"

She couldn't tell Constance what he'd said to her about the beach party and the one-night stand that resulted in the pregnancy—it suddenly seemed so personal.

"We didn't talk for long. He just said that you were together, and now you're not, but you live together for the baby's sake."

Constance closed her eyes momentarily, as if the revelation pained her somehow. When she opened them, they were clear and full of determination. She reached out a hand and placed it on Ruby's wrist, gripping her, holding her there when Ruby recoiled, tried to pull away. The concerto ended just as the kettle clicked off, so that the only sounds were Leonie dropping wooden bricks from the box onto the floor, and in the other room, the pouring of water from kettle to mug. "Did you believe him?" Almost a whisper now.

From the kitchen: "Do you take milk, Ruby?"

Ruby kept her eyes on Constance. *"Do you take milk?" "Did you believe him?"*

"Yes," she said, to both of them, though when Constance's face fell, she wasn't sure anymore that it was the right answer.

CHAPTER

14

NOW
Joanna
Saturday, December 22, early morning

THE MOMENT SHE was out of Mrs. Stefanidis's flat, Jo tried
Ruby's new number. In the seconds before it connected, hope
soared in her breast, only to be crushed by the recorded message:
This person's phone is turned off.

Back in the lobby, she briefed the CSI team, then excused
herself and made her way to the West Block doors. Part of her
knew there wouldn't be a response to Ruby's buzzer, so when there
was not, she was only half devastated. But of course, it was party
season. There had been a new group of friends recently, but Jo
didn't know the first thing about them, just a passing comment
back in October, the last time she and Ruby had spoken. "Any
boyfriend potential?" she'd asked. Ruby had made a strange noise
and said, "One of them's a guy, but it's complicated." Joanna had
so many questions about that, but at the time it hadn't been right
somehow to interrogate her. *Complicated* usually meant bad news.
Maybe Ruby was with the new friends now.

Joanna wondered how everything had gone so very wrong.
Right up until the day of the fight, she'd thought the family,

unconventional though it may have been, was functioning okay. Throughout Ruby's childhood everything had been fine. She'd seemed well-adjusted—happy even. It was easier for Jo not to be there, to listen to Ruby call her mother Mum, and not her, but she thought she was making things better for everyone by staying away. She'd missed so much and hidden how much it hurt; she'd assumed her own issues were the only fallout from the decision taken—while she was still a child herself—with the best intentions for everyone involved. How wrong she'd been about so many things.

Everything had come to a head on Christmas Day. Jo walked into the living room and found her mother sitting with a glass in her hand.

"Where's Ruby?" Jo asked. Dad was in the kitchen, banging tins and running the tap.

Marianne took a long sip. The glass was full of ice and clear liquid, but Joanna did not assume it was water. She glanced at the clock and saw that it was 11:52. Close enough to lunchtime for a first drink, she supposed.

"She's sulking," said Marianne, and from her voice Jo knew instantly that the half-finished drink in her mother's hand was far from the first of the day. She walked out of the room to find Ruby sitting on the stairs, her lips set in a thin line.

"She's been drinking since breakfast," hissed Ruby.

"Did you have a fight?" asked Joanna.

Ruby shook her head. "I just . . . can't deal with it today." She went back up to her room, making it clear she didn't want Joanna to follow.

Later, Dad served lunch, fussing and flitting about, asking everyone three times if they would like more of this or that, if they were sure they didn't, trying to jolly everyone along, the way he'd done for years. Ruby had joined them but declined to pull crackers. She'd barely spoken a word, in fact, until she suddenly interrupted Dad's flow as he tried to push more sprouts on to her plate. Glaring at Marianne, she said, "You need help."

Marianne was pouring red wine into her glass, a third refill that saw the bottle emptied. "What have I done?"

"Ruby," said Jo, "It's not the best time—"

"Why, because it's Christmas?

"No, because . . . well, we've all had a drink, haven't we?"

"You haven't. I haven't." She pointed to their drinks. The wine in their glasses had barely been touched. "It's never a good time, is it?" She jabbed a finger at Marianne. "She's drunk all the time. Why does no one ever talk about it?"

In the silence, the question presented a natural response. A trap to fall into.

Dad was the one caught by it. "Talk about what?" He froze, half standing, with oven mitts raised. He glanced from Marianne to Joanna, to Ruby. In that moment, they were all thinking the same thing. Not the alcoholism, which they also never talked about. The other thing.

"Your father was a mouthy little shit too," said Marianne to Ruby, and Jo stood up, as if to get between them. She wanted to slap a hand over her mother's mouth.

"Ru—"

Dad said, "What? I was a what?"

"Not you," said Marianne, reaching for the corkscrew. "That boy. The one that got Joanna pregnant. Apple doesn't fall far from the tree." She popped the cork on a new bottle of red and filled her glass to the brim. "I think he's in prison now, right, Joanna?"

"Mother, stop." Jo took a step toward Ruby, but she flew out of her chair and over to the doorway, where she hesitated, staring at Joanna. *"Do something,"* she seemed to say. In a rage, Jo snatched her mother's wineglass as she tried to take a swig, and the deep red liquid splashed across the table, the carpet, the walls. Marianne cried out, as if in pain. Then she placed her palms on the table, head down like a hyena about to strike.

"You're so ungrateful. Both of you. I don't know why we did what we did, Phillip. It wasn't worth it."

"Marianne, what are you saying?" said Dad. "Don't listen, girls—she's not herself. We love you, both of you. Why don't you go and have a lie-down, darling?" The oven mitts fell to the floor as he tried to wrestle his wife to a standing position.

"Get off me," shouted Marianne, falling back into her chair.

"I'm leaving," said Ruby.

"Good," said Marianne. Then she looked at Jo. "You should never have had her, Joanna. Would have saved us all a lot of trouble."

Damage control was impossible this time. As Jo and Dad scrabbled for what to do, how to limit the damage, Ruby turned, walked straight out the front door and didn't look back. She left all of her things, turned off her phone, and disappeared, only days later sending a text to Jo saying to tell Marianne never to call and that she'd be in touch again when she felt ready. Which wasn't for almost two months, when she rang to tell Jo the news about her council flat on the New Park. However, Jo wasn't to visit or tell the parents (in Ruby's mind no longer her parents) where she lived. "I trust you," she'd said. "I'll be ready one day. Just not yet."

"So why give me the address now?"

"Just so you know where I am. If, say, someone dies or something. Otherwise, I'll call you. You're not like her. At least I can rely on you to respect my wishes."

Since then, she'd spoken to Ruby maybe once a month, and never for very long. Jo felt she was being punished for something, and furthermore that she deserved it. Most recently, contact had completely dried up. In her day-to-day life, Joanna tried not to dwell on it, especially on her part in the way the family was falling to pieces. Their mother did need help, but Jo wasn't the one to give it. It was up to Dad to get something sorted. As for Ruby, the mantra Jo repeated became *If you love someone, set them free.* Jo was holding tight to the hope that Ruby would come back eventually, if she was patient; if she didn't push it.

She tried the new number once more, listened to the recorded message almost to the end before hanging up. The words *this person's phone is turned off* at least offered the possibility that it might one day be turned on again. She imagined what Ruby might say to her if she ever answered. She hoped it would be *"I've missed you,"* but she knew it would more likely be *"I told you not to try to get in touch until I'm ready."* Trying to get in touch was a reflex action, though, and she had little control over it; she almost called the number again as she spun on her heel and jogged back toward the North Block, just to see if it had been turned on in the last few seconds, but the other cops were watching her approach so she slipped the phone into her pocket instead. She was furious with herself for letting the silence go on for this long, but Ruby could wait a day or two longer; this case couldn't. There was a suspected attempted murder and zero leads.

Atkinson had just finished briefing another officer in the lobby when Jo walked in.

"Did you get much from the interview with the neighbor?" he asked.

Jo explained that Mrs. Stefanidis was visually impaired, but her hearing was perfect. She told him the name that Sarah had heard being said. "It might be the child that's been living there, though she seemed convinced, like Terry was, that Franks lived alone. Might be worth checking against the names of any children known to be living in the block—can you put someone on that? I'm heading over to the hospital to have a look at the victim, see if anything's changed."

"Do you want me to come with you?"

"No, you get home, Steve."

"Really?"

"Sure." She indicated the constable on door duty. "Box can cover you for this shift. He probably needs the overtime to pay for my Christmas present."

The young officer laughed, a little nervously.

Atkinson patted his pockets for his phone, probably eager to call his partner. "Thanks, boss."

"You make sure you get some sleep. I'll need you nice and fresh in the morning."

His face fell. "Tomorrow morning? I've, um, booked it off, ma'am."

"Sorry, Steve, you might need to unbook it. You're needed on this one, what with being first on scene. I'll warn you now, this case might be a long one. It won't stop until it stops."

She gave him a steely look, challenging him to start complaining about the sanctity of Christmas, only a few days away. She didn't think he would: people knew what they were signing up for when they entered the service. Goodbye, private life. It shouldn't have come as a surprise that crime continued to occur even on high days and holidays. Imagine if all police officers decided not to bother working at those times.

He seemed about to speak, but then he dropped his eyes. "Yes, of course. Sorry, it's not me. It's Felicia; she's all set for a day at home."

"You don't have to work, Steve. I can have another officer replace you on the case. But if you were hoping to make detective, a case like this could really give you the edge. It's up to you."

As she walked toward her car, she felt confident that Atkinson would make the right decision. The truth was that Steve was like Jo when it came down to it: married to the job. Of course he loved his girlfriend; that was clear from the way he was around her. But Felicia was going to need to accept that she was always going to come second in Steve's life to what he cared most about: making the world a better place.

As she drove through the deserted streets, Joanna felt fortunate that Amy wasn't anything like Felicia. Broken dinner dates didn't matter between them, not in the long run, because Jo sometimes needed to prioritize work. Amy understood that. It was confusing to Jo, then, that as she approached the house she shared with her girlfriend she could see Amy coming out the door, holding a large suitcase and wearing a decidedly pissed-off expression on her face.

Jo parked up and got out just as Amy slammed her own car boot shut. It was so full of stuff that the lock wouldn't quite catch. She stood and watched as Amy tried to force it closed.

"What's going on?" asked Jo.

Amy gave one last push, and the boot clicked shut. "What does it look like?" she said, turning and leaning on the car, arms folded.

"Hey, I'm sorry I missed dinner. There was a big case and I had to—"

"I don't care."

"What?"

"I don't care what it was. For once, I thought you'd be able to keep a promise to me."

"But Amy, I didn't have a choice—"

"That's bullshit, Jo, and you know it."

Amy was shivering in the wintry air.

"You're cold. Why don't we go inside, and we can talk about it."

"There's no point. You don't listen to me."

Jo felt surprised at that. "I do listen to you."

"The fact is, Joanna, there's always something. Some little shit has always done something that desperately needs your attention on a Saturday night, or someone's dropped dead, or they've found a haul of drugs. And sure, I understand that the police service needs to respond. But it doesn't always need to be you, does it?"

There was a pause, during which the only sound was the chattering of Amy's teeth. Joanna was listening, hard. *I do listen to you,* she thought. *See?* She stepped forward to put an arm around Amy, who flinched away, pointed at Jo's trousers.

"Is that blood?"

She looked down at herself. Her coat and the thighs of her jeans were soaked. She looked like a butcher. "Oh. Yes."

"What's going on? Is it a murder?"

"Honey, you know I can't tell you anything until the details are made public."

Amy threw her hands up. "Oh, for fu—"

"Where are you planning on going, anyway?"

"A friend's. What's it to you?"

"I don't want you to go, obviously."

"I don't want to either. But I think it's time. I'm too young to be someone's dreary home-sitter. I'm not good at waiting. Or being stood up. I think I'm worth a bit more than that."

"If I could tell you what I'm working on, you'd understand. It's big."

"If you could tell me what you were working on," said Amy, "maybe we wouldn't be in this mess."

"What do you mean?"

"When you and I weren't involved, you didn't have to keep everything from me. We were working together. Talking to you was part of my job, a part I liked. Remember when I was a plucky journalist, and you were my best cop pal?"

"Yeah, but what we've got now, Amy—it's special, right?"

"Being a police officer's partner isn't what I thought it would be. I thought I'd get more information, not less."

"So, that's what it's about? You can't grill me for the details in newsworthy cases anymore, so you want to leave?"

"Don't you think it was more exciting before we were a couple? When the confidentiality standards didn't apply?"

"They did apply, Amy, but it was different. We had a professional relationship. I can't share details of a live case with my wife."

"I'm not your wife."

"You could be."

She hadn't known she was going to say that, and for a moment she wanted to take it back. Was she proposing?

Amy almost laughed, but then she stopped. "Are you proposing?"

Perhaps she was. The idea filled Joanna simultaneously with excitement and dread. The last thing she wanted was to lose Amy. The next to last thing she wanted was a wedding. But she'd said it now. And perhaps, if she proposed, it would make her stay. "Yes? Yes. I am. Will you?"

"Will I what?"

"Marry me?" Even to Joanna it sounded unconvincing. And terrifying.

Amy sighed and pushed her away, not unkindly. She gazed into Jo's eyes and smiled with half of her mouth, the way she did when she was sad. "You'll be relieved to hear that the answer's no, Joanna. I don't want this life for me. And you don't either."

Jo could feel her slipping away. "I can change things at work if it matters that much. I can move departments—"

"No. You won't be happy doing that."

"You breaking up with me isn't exactly going to make me happy either."

Amy searched Jo's eyes. A tear slipped from her cheek and fell into the darkness. "I wouldn't be so sure about that."

Jo watched as Amy walked to the car without looking back. She made no move to stop Amy from getting into her car and driving away. The hard truth was, Amy was right. It had been better before they moved in together, before Amy had started trying to change the way Jo lived. They'd been playing house, but it wasn't a game either of them liked. Jo knew it wasn't just the work too: the training was another source of friction. There was a timetable on the wall in the kitchen that clearly set out the hours of cycling, swimming, and running Joanna needed to do to keep competition-fit, yet Amy had always seemed surprised and annoyed by Jo's dedication to it. Triathlon was a passion for Joanna, but also a lifeline. It allowed her to process the more stressful parts of the job. It got the anger out, and the frustration. Without it, she would have come undone, and she wouldn't have given it up for anything.

Jo climbed the stairs to the building, her mind a jumble of feelings. She loved Amy, but she also loved being alone. She was sad that her first attempt in years at a proper relationship had failed after less than six months, and then angry that Amy seemed to be more worried about her own job than anything else. Then she thought about their history together, that heady, wonderful few weeks when the friendship had developed into something more; the way Amy looked in the morning, sleep-ruffled and makeup free, and she was back to feeling sad again. Finally, as Jo entered the flat and saw that all of Amy's flowery mugs had gone, her stacks of shoes were missing from the hallway, and that terrible painting she'd insisted on hanging pride of place above the fireplace had been removed, she felt something she wasn't proud of but couldn't deny: a wave of quiet relief.

Jo quickly got changed out of her bloody clothes and into a fresh set of smart jeans, a long sleeved shirt, and a warm jacket. She trotted down the stairs and jumped into her car. It was as if a weight she didn't know she'd been carrying had been lifted from her shoulders. When she returned later to grab some sleep before what would inevitably be an early start, an empty bed would be waiting. Jo smiled at the thought of it, then felt guilty for smiling, and wondered where Amy was now and whether she would be okay.

Work mode kicked in, sweeping aside the feelings, keeping them on ice for later. She started the car and set off for the Royal Infirmary Hospital, where a severely injured man needed her help to find his attacker and bring whomever it was to justice.

CHAPTER

15

THEN
Ruby
September

G REGOR OPENED THE door before she got there, dressed in a
clean T-shirt and jeans. "You came," he said. "And you
brought the violin."

Ruby felt a rush of joy that he was so pleased to see her.

"How did you get in the building, though? Mrs. Stefanidis again?"

Ruby nodded. "I've told her I'll help her with her shopping.
You know she's almost blind?"

"You didn't mention Constance to her, did you?"

The door to the living space opened a crack, and a tiny girl
shouted "Hi!" as she yanked it completely open, then bum-shuffled
toward them before using the doorframe to stand up.

Today, Leonie wore a yellow sundress, with white sandals on
her feet, which she used as levers to get her across the carpet super-
fast. "You look ready to go to the beach, honey," said Ruby.

"Beach!" shouted Leonie. When Ruby glanced up at Grégor,
he winced and made a shivering motion.

"Yeah, your Dad's right. It's a bit cold for that today. Hey, why
don't you show me the rest of your toys?"

Leonie had spotted the violin case. She dropped to the floor, shuffled across and reached up for it as Ruby drew it away instinctively.

Gregor said, "Oh, don't touch, baby girl. Precious."

The child's eyes flitted between Ruby and Gregor. Then the little hands reached for the violin again. Gregor squatted and picked her up. "Ruby's going to play something for you, Leonie. Shall we go in the living room?"

Constance was sitting in the exact same place as before, wearing a blue woolen skirt and a long-sleeved top. She acknowledged Ruby with a small movement of her head before resuming staring at the big picture on the wall, a large photograph of the ocean during a storm. Her hair was coiled into its rope, gleaming black against her shoulder. The way she stared at the seascape, as if she longed to dive in, suddenly brought to mind a ballet Ruby had played for, back when she was a student at the conservatoire: *Ondine*. Constance's long limbs, so graceful as she sat there, pointed feet crossed; Ruby could imagine her dancing the character of the water nymph. It was as if her pose was simply a pause in the choreography, and at any moment she might rise, wraith-like, from the couch and perform a slow pirouette.

"See?" Gregor said to Constance. "She's come back. I told you she'd come back. And she's going to play for us."

"Oh," said Ruby, "only if you don't mind."

Constance looked back at them and nodded, almost imperceptibly. Her expression was hard to read, her eyes glassy. It was past lunchtime, but despite her physical poise she looked vacant, as if she'd just woken up.

"What songs do we know?" said Gregor to Leonie. "'Twinkle, Twinkle'?"

"Yay!" said Leonie.

"Can you play that, Ruby?"

Ruby was unfolding her music stand. 'Twinkle, Twinkle'? Maybe she wouldn't need the stand. She took out her instrument and played the tune from memory. While the sound of the nursery rhyme filled the room, only Constance looked away, still focused on the print. The sun streamed through the window, surrounding her in a kind of ethereal glow. It was as if she held herself apart, was only half there in the room. Ruby wondered where the rest of her was, which world her attention had wandered to. Certainly one with a wild sea and a dark, brooding sky.

At the end of the song, Leonie applauded wildly. Gregor stared. "That was so beautiful," he said.

"What?" Ruby laughed. "It was just a nursery rhyme."

"Yes, but the violin. The sound it makes, that you make, it was . . ."

She noticed that Constance had turned her head, was staring at him, her lips pressed together. Ruby suddenly felt acutely aware of the attention Gregor was showing her.

She lowered the instrument.

"Don't stop," he said. Leonie wriggled in his arms, and he put her on the floor, where she bum-shuffled toward the toy box.

Ruby put the violin under her chin and played "Twinkle, Twinkle" again. There was a sound coming from the baby, who was turned away from them as she piled up bricks in a stack. This kid was singing. A perfectly clear tone, in tune with the violin.

"Is she . . ."

"Yes," said Gregor. "She sings all the time. It's amazing."

Leonie fell silent, as if she could sense them listening. She turned around. "Twinkle, twinkle?" she said, though it came out *Tingle, tingle?* Ruby began to play again.

This time she played Mozart's variations on the same tune, *Ah, vous dirai-je, Maman.* Leonie picked up bricks and arranged them into piles, all the while humming along in tune. Constance looked like she'd zoned out again, her eyes having returned to the sea scene, but Gregor stood transfixed, watching Ruby. When she'd finished, he was full of questions: How long had she been playing? How much training had she had? What was her conservatoire like? Had she ever wanted to give up as a child?

"I used to play the piano but I gave it up when I was eleven," said Gregor. "I thought I knew better, but I regret it now—exactly the way my parents told me I would. I wish I'd listened to them and kept on practicing."

"Well," said Ruby, "I wasn't given the option, thankfully, or I might have given up too. I hated her for it at the time, but now I can see why she was so strict."

"Your mother?"

"My . . . yes." Gregor frowned at her, wanting her to explain the hesitation. She just smiled; it was too soon to go into all of that.

He said, "I'd love for Leonie to play. You say you started when you were three?"

She nodded. "My folks were pretty keen. They were a bit like you, gave up playing when they were young, always regretted the decision. You know, you could take it up again now, if you wanted to. I know a few good piano teachers."

Gregor laughed, as if the notion were ridiculous.

"I'm serious."

He shook his head, still laughing. "I was never very good anyway."

"Your parents must have thought you were if they willing to pay for lessons."

His face darkened, she thought, for a split second. "I suppose."

"I was sorry to hear about your mother, by the way. It must have been a shock for you."

"My mother?" he said, and for an instant she thought he looked angry. Then his face smoothed out into wide-eyed bafflement. "But how did you . . . oh yes, of course. Mrs. Stefanidis." He rolled his eyes.

Ruby felt awkward, that she'd admitted she'd been discussing his business behind his back. She knew how he felt about gossip.

"I'm sorry . . ."

"Don't be. It was a long time ago," he said in a way that made it clear he didn't want to talk about it. Ruby didn't think three years was very long, but what did she know about grief? In some ways, she felt, she was very lucky indeed.

Gregor said, "But Leonie, she's got potential. You could teach her, couldn't you? I'd pay you, of course."

"I could, but she's a bit too little now. When they're little you just need to sing to them. How old is she exactly?"

Ruby had directed the question to Constance, but the other woman hadn't noticed. She was concentrating on coiling a strand of hair around a finger, watching as it slipped around and back, around and back.

Gregor cleared his throat and said, "She's not quite two."

They both looked over at the child, who might have been able to sing in tune but wasn't even walking yet. Something worried Ruby slightly about that. She vaguely remembered a video of herself, on her first birthday, running across a lawn into her father's arms. She doubted there were any videos of her singing, though— not until much later.

"Next year, then," he said. "And it will be worth it, right? What a skill to have, Ruby. I know she'll pick it up quickly; she's got an amazing ear. Like you." He smiled at her, his eyes full of admiration.

Ruby caught a movement in the corner of her eye, Constance's head turning once more to look at them. All of a sudden, Gregor seemed flustered. "I haven't even offered you a drink."

"Don't worry, it's fine. I just had one . . ."

"I'll make coffee." He rushed out.

The energy in the room, without Gregor, was completely different. Ruby put the violin away, and when she looked up, she realized that Constance hadn't said anything for a long time. The quiet settled, both of them listening to the sound of Leonie shuffling here and there over the carpet.

"Thank you, little lady." Ruby took the wooden brick that was offered. "So, Constance." Leonie shuffled across the length of the room. "Where are you from originally? You have an accent."

Constance looked in the direction of the seascape print and pointed. "I'm from there."

Ruby stood up to get a closer look at the image. There was no land in it, only water and sky, in different shades of gunmetal gray and green, with white on the tips of the waves. The ocean during a storm.

"Where was this taken?" asked Ruby. Thinking of the accent, she said, "Somewhere in Scotland?"

Gregor came in holding a tray with three mugs and a cafetière.

"It's nice, isn't it? I bought it in an online auction last year. Somewhere off Orkney, apparently. They get a lot of weather up there. Sideways rain."

"It's a beautiful image. Are you from the island, Constance?" Ruby thought the picture was kind of bleak. She hadn't decided if she liked it or not.

There was a long pause before Constance said, "Yes and no."

Confused, Ruby looked at Gregor.

"It's a story," he said, with a small dismissive gesture, "but she tells it as if it's true."

"It is true," said Constance, offended. "All of my stories are true."

She sat back on the couch, suddenly bristling with anxiety, twisting the end of her plait faster and faster. At the edge of the room, Leonie stopped what she was doing, one hand frozen in the act of turning the page of a fabric book. She looked at her mother, but she didn't move or make a sound. In that moment the child reminded Ruby of a startled bird, hoping that if it stays completely still, it won't be noticed.

Gregor's face was suddenly full of regret. "I'm sorry, Constance. You go on. Of course, it's true. I was just being insensitive." He gave Ruby a look, then, apologetic perhaps.

"All stories are true in a sense," said Ruby. Leonie relaxed as the tension in the room eased. She went on with her page-turning. Ruby turned to Constance. "Tell me. I'd love to hear about where you're from."

Constance looked away. "I don't want to now. Not with him here. He doesn't believe any of it, clearly."

"Maybe I should leave," said Gregor.

"No," said Ruby. "You don't have to."

But Constance glared at him, triumphant. "Maybe you should."

Gregor picked up his cup of coffee, got up, and headed for one of the bedrooms. "I'm sorry, Connie. I didn't mean to upset you. Really."

"But you don't really have to go, do you?" asked Ruby. She wasn't sure she wanted to be alone with Constance. Something about the woman's mood was making her uneasy.

Gregor glanced at the wall clock. "Actually, I do have to make a call for work. It shouldn't take long. Sorry. I'll be a few minutes. Then I'll be back."

After he'd gone, Ruby wondered about the office in the city and why he wasn't there now. Maybe he worked from home sometimes. What did he even do for a living? The opportunity hadn't arisen yet to ask him. She felt suddenly unsafe, and stupid, not knowing why she'd come up here, to Gregor's flat, to these people about whom she knew so little, and this strange, glassy-eyed woman.

Leonie, having come to life, bum-shuffled toward her and handed her the book.

"Raf," she said, pointing to the giraffe on the front page.

"Amazing! You're so clever!" Ruby clapped her hands in applause, and Leonie laughed.

For a while, Ruby played with the baby, who would bring things to her, hand them over, and name each one as she did so. Leonie knew the name of everything, even correctly identifying a tarantula in a nature book.

"She knows so many words," said Ruby.

"Yes."

"And she sings. I've never seen that before. Not that I see a lot of children this age. Usually they sing, but they don't really sing, you know? They just sort of yell."

Constance turned her head and smiled at Leonie. "She's done it since she was tiny. I could sing a note, she could sing it back. She was just a baby in the cradle."

"Tuss!" said Leonie.

"Tuss?"

"She means tortoise."

"Tortoise! Of course." Leonie went over to the toy box, and Ruby turned to Constance. "So," said Ruby, "you're from Orkney?"

"Not Orkney. The island is West of there, in the Hebrides. He bought me that picture because it reminded me so much of the sea near where I was born. I look at it, and I can see my family."

"You have family out there still?"

She nodded. "I have everything there. When I came here, I lost it all." As she said this, they both looked over at Leonie, and Ruby was puzzled. How could she say she'd lost everything if she'd gained this astonishing child? The relationship with Gregor might not have worked out, but Leonie was something, wasn't she?

"Your family must visit, though? And you visit them?"

"No. They can't; they won't. Not after I left the way I did."

Ruby felt suddenly very sorry for Constance, for the predicament she found herself in. How on earth could she go back if the agoraphobia was keeping her prisoner? Quite apart from the traveling required to get there, Ruby wondered how a person afraid of the outside would fare, living on an exposed island in the middle of nowhere. No wonder she was homesick. "Tell me about them?"

Constance stared at Ruby, holding her gaze for the first time, for so long that Ruby felt sweat prickling on her forehead. It was the intensity of it that unsettled her. The woman radiated an unstable energy, nervous and full of something else, suppressed rage perhaps. She spoke, eventually, through a clenched jaw. "I'm not sure you'd believe me either."

Ruby said, "Try me," and for a while Constance just continued to stare, distrust etched on her face.

Then she tipped her head, deciding. "We're a community. Like a clan. We have our own island."

Ruby thought it sounded wonderful. She imagined the women in long, rough-hewn dresses, waiting on the shore for the fishermen to return. "Sort of like a hippie commune?"

"What? No . . ."

"I don't mean that offensively . . ."

"We are *Roane*," said Constance.

Ruby didn't understand. "Is that your surname?"

"How are you two getting on?" said Gregor, from the doorway. He looked from one to the other, then at Leonie and down at the scattering of objects on the carpet around Ruby's legs. "Making a mess, baby?" he said, tutting as he scooped up all of the offerings before taking them over to the toy box. "Shall we tidy up?"

"Di-dee up!"

Ruby stood. She needed to get away. "Well, thanks for the coffee." She picked up her violin. "I should be going."

"Of course, we mustn't keep you. You must have to practice for hours to be as good as you are," said Gregor. "I don't suppose . . ."

"What?"

"Well, I don't suppose you'd come back and play for us again?"

Ruby wasn't sure if she wanted to or not. "Um . . ."

"Only if you have time," he said.

Ruby found herself looking into Constance's eyes. Then Leonie came toward her and pulled on her trouser leg, using it to stand up. Ruby reached down and offered her a finger to hang on to instead. That black shock of hair and the rosy cheeks.

"I could make time," she said.

"Ba-ba," said Leonie, waggling her hand like a balloon on a stick.

"Bye-bye," replied Ruby, mirroring the action. Leonie laughed.

Gregor walked her down the stairs, out and across to her building, then without Ruby really knowing how it was happening, he was riding in the lift to her door. She fumbled with the keys, turned to say goodbye, but somehow after that he was in her flat, pretending not to notice the state of the place, tactfully stepping through into the tiny kitchen while she bundled up her dirty washing into a corner, straightened the duvet, kicked a couple of used plates further under the bed. There wasn't much else she could do to improve things after that; the bare bulb in the bed-sitting room made everything seem cheap and ugly. Cheaper and uglier than it was already, anyway—nothing she had was expensive or beautiful except for the violin. She tried turning the light off. It was completely dark. She turned it on again. Ruby wished she had a couple of lamps to soften the atmosphere.

"You really can see right into my place from here, can't you?" Gregor said from the kitchen.

She went through and stood behind him, inhaled his smell. "Yep. Sort of asking to be watched, aren't you?"

"I thought I was safe, actually. Until I saw your little head peeping out, and by then it was too late. My cover was blown."

She wished he would stop mentioning it. So embarrassing. "I'm sorry about that. I really didn't mean—"

"I'm not sorry," said Gregor, turning quickly so that they were standing far too close together. "It meant that we met, didn't it? I don't meet many people."

"You don't?"

"No. Well, I sort of do, for work and so on. I don't usually like them." He smiled, shy and unsure.

Ruby took a step backward. It was dangerous being this close to him. He might be technically single, but he was tangled up in something nevertheless, with Constance and the child. She didn't want to get involved. Despite this, her body responded to him. It had been so long since she'd been touched.

"Why don't you like them?" she asked, leading the way out of the darkened kitchen and into the harsh, unforgiving light of the bed-sitting room.

He shrugged. "Most people are paste, that's why."

"Paste?"

"Oh, you know. Sort of gray and uninteresting. Or pretending to be something they're not."

"Huh."

"But you're not, Ruby. You shine."

She blushed, and not knowing what to say, she said nothing. She didn't feel shiny. She felt, if she were honest, like paste. Ruby stood there awkwardly, leaning against the wall nearest the door. Gregor walked the few steps to the window and looked out.

"I've got a weird thing to ask. You can say 'no.'"

"Oh, okay. What is it?"

"I wanted to ask you, if you wouldn't mind . . . not talking about us to anyone?"

"Why would I talk to anyone about you?" she said, thinking, *I don't really talk to anyone, about anything, right now.*

He grew serious then. "I meant about Constance, really. And Leonie. No one can know they're there with me."

"Why not?"

"It's hard to explain, but because of her background . . . there are a few legal issues. To do with Leonie."

"What?"

"Nothing bad. Only that, since Leonie came along, I've been helping Constance manage her mental health. The agoraphobia, and the . . . other stuff."

She thought of her own GP, the antidepressants she was supposed to be taking. That look in Constance's eye, the volatility she sensed, a firework about to blow. "So, I'm assuming she hasn't seen anyone about it?"

He shook his head, no. "If it got much worse, I'd have to think about it. But right now we're doing okay, I think. I don't want anyone getting involved. Doctors, Social Services, or whatever. You understand."

"But if she's unwell, wouldn't it be better if she got treated?"

He sat down slowly on the edge of the bed and stared at his hands. "Would it, though?"

"What do you mean?"

"I hear what you're saying. But once you start down that road . . . I just look at Leonie and I think, how terrible it is for a child to grow up without a mother."

Gregor's back was hunched, his eyes in shadow. He drew in a breath and let it out slowly, but she could hear the slight tremor, the emotion in it.

Ruby went to him. She sat down next to him, not quite touching. His breathing was ragged. "What is it, Gregor? What happened to you?" She reached for his hand, but he drew it away.

"I know how these things end. Once someone is in the grip of mental illness, if you let them out of your sight, abandon them to strangers, to medics. They try to . . . leave."

She barely dared ask, "Did you lose someone?"

"I . . . just can't. Not yet. One day I'll tell you, I promise."

He must have had some terrible experiences to have become so cautious and mistrustful. That he would confide in her, this man who hardly let anyone in.

"I worry that I wouldn't be enough for Leonie. If we ended up alone."

Ruby reached again for his hand. "You're not alone."

He looked at her then, searched her face for meaning. "But, Ruby, you barely know me."

She thought of Leonie, that joyous child, that gleaming ball of potential. She thought of Constance, her strange, ethereal mother, who already seemed so faded and distant, as if she had one foot in another world. The two of them with many complex needs; such a heavy burden for one person to carry. She held his gaze. "I know enough."

He shook his head, perhaps in disbelief, but when he looked at her, she saw deep gratitude in his eyes.

"Can I ask you a question now?" said Ruby.

"Go on."

"What's *Roane*?"

His brow furrowed. "What did she tell you?"

"Nothing, just the name. She phrased it strangely, that's all. Made me wonder."

"It's her family name. Her clan, if you like. But, Ruby, it's more to her than that. *Roane* is an old word meaning 'seal,' or 'selkie.'"

"Selkie? Isn't that like a mermaid?"

"Kind of. They're shape-shifters: seals in the water, humans on land. But because of it, she believes that she comes from the sea, that she's part of that myth."

So, the significance of the name had gotten distorted in her mind somehow. Poor Constance. A disordered thought, looming larger than it should have done in her confusion about what was real and what wasn't.

Gregor said, "So you won't say anything about them living there with me?"

"I can tell you one thing: your downstairs neighbor doesn't know about them."

"You haven't told her?"

"No. She thinks she knows all about you, of course, from when your mother died. But Constance and Leonie didn't come up in conversation, really. I'm not sure she even knows that I've been coming over after I see her. To be honest, she spends most of the time talking rather than listening."

He took her hand. "Thank you, Ruby. I knew I could trust you. And thanks for tonight. I know that Constance is quite . . . unusual, I suppose. It's partly that she doesn't see many people. Because of the illness."

"She's not paste?"

He shook his head. "No, she's not paste. She's special in her own way. One of a kind. And you, well. You've got skills and passion. What you did to 'Twinkle, Twinkle' back there . . ."

"Not me. Mozart."

"But you played it. You interpreted it. And you could probably have written it."

Ruby laughed, slightly hysterically. "No, I couldn't."

"But you do compose, don't you?"

Suddenly shy, she said, "I don't, not really. I mean, I have, but nothing any good. Nothing I would show to anyone. And nothing that could even touch Mozart with a hundred-foot pole."

She thought he would laugh then, but he remained serious.

"I want to hear it."

"What?"

"Your music. The stuff that comes from you. That you wrote."

"But it's not very—"

"Please, Ruby."

"But I—"

He was at the door, opening it. "Just think about it, yes?"

Before she could answer, he was gone.

16

NOW
Joanna
Saturday, December 22

G REGOR FRANKS WAS very good-looking, even unconscious. Not pretty-boy good-looking but old-school handsome, so that his three-day stubble only added to the effect of rugged, symmetrical masculinity. He had a substantial upper body with defined pectorals, slim waist, strong thighs—clearly a gym bunny. She hadn't noticed when they hauled him from the bath, but he was tall: his bare feet were right at the end of the bed, almost hanging off. The fit body made his presence here even more tragic. For all of his physical grace, the man lay motionless on the bed, his arms draped at his sides, his head encased in a protective foam helmet.

"There's really nothing you can do for him?"

When Joanna had arrived at the ICU, Doctor Locke had shown her into the patient's room, a private space separated from the rest of the unit.

"The team worked on him for almost four hours after he came in. We tried everything to get his blood pressure up, but nothing improved it."

"What does that mean exactly?"

"It means unfortunately his blood pressure is so low as to be incompatible with a life expectancy of any more than a few hours. Days, perhaps."

The oxygen mask on Gregor's face misted gently at the nostrils.

"What are the machines for? Is that a ventilator?"

"No, just oxygen. And the other one is monitoring his heart rate."

"He's breathing on his own?"

"For now."

"But you don't think he'll recover?"

"I'd say it's highly unlikely."

A large, bearded nurse entered the room, picked up the chart at the end of the bed, and made a note.

"Are you the next of kin?" he asked Joanna.

"No, I'm a police officer."

The nurse flipped the pages up on the chart and frowned. "Is there anything you can tell us about him?" he asked. "All we've got is a name, and that hasn't actually been confirmed."

Joanna reached into her satchel for a plastic bag containing Gregor's wallet. "The ID we have for him is all in here." The wallet and its contents had already been swabbed and dusted for prints by the CSI team. There wasn't much in it that could help them trace family; only cash, a single VISA bank card and the driver's license. The nurse took the wallet out of the plastic bag and retrieved the license. Jo looked from the photo to the man in the bed, to his slack, unconscious face, as smooth and unmoving as a marble statue, all the life that was present in the photograph gone.

"So there was considerable brain damage, from being hit on the head?" said Jo.

"The head injury wasn't as bad as we thought. It was the drugs he ingested that have caused his system to shut down."

"Drugs?"

"Everything points to opiates. There are no track marks, so not injected. Probably some kind of prescription drug. I couldn't say what at this point, only that it's too late to reverse the effect. None of the usual antidotes revived him."

"What about the head injury? It felt pretty serious to me." *Like his brain was coming out,* she thought, with a degree of revulsion.

"I agree it did look dramatic, but the CT scan showed only a large extracranial hematoma and some skin abrasions. If he hadn't ingested the drugs, I think the outlook would have been much more positive."

Jo said, "Any sense of how he might have been injured? There was an initial theory that he slipped and fell in the bath, hitting his head on the edge."

The doctor was shaking her head before Joanna even finished the sentence. "I don't think so. The bath wouldn't have broken the skin like that."

"You won't mind if we have someone come in to examine him?" said Jo. "One of our medical forensic people will need to see the injury, have access to the medical records, and so on."

"You're welcome to examine him. But I'm afraid, while he's alive, you would need his consent to get access to the medical records."

Joanna looked at the still and silent patient, then at the doctor. "How do you suggest I go about obtaining that?"

"That's your department. You might need to get a court order. I can't release the notes without one."

Someone would come forward with information about this man soon. Young, good-looking chap like that had to have friends and family. *The phone will be the key,* she thought. Scroll through to the most-called number, and bingo. It was locked with a password, but the tech boys could open anything, given enough time.

"So, what's the next step?" asked Jo.

"We're monitoring him. That's all we can do for now, apart from keeping him as comfortable as possible."

The doctor approached the bed, where Gregor's head was supported by the padded helmet device and a small rubber ring–shaped pillow. "This is to keep pressure off the wound. Tissue damage and so on."

Jo said, "Can I get a look at the scan?"

The nurse turned to a computer monitor that was mounted on the wall and made a few clicks, and the scan appeared. Harper and the doctor stepped closer.

"You see this area, this sort of circular impression? That's the site of the injury."

Jo could just make out the place she indicated, which was about the size of a tennis ball.

"But as you can see, there's no bleeding to the brain," said the doctor. "I'd say he was hit with something roundish. And heavy. Maybe a large hammer or a mallet. Something with a sharp edge or corner. Big swing from behind—*pow*. Or, could have been more than one blow, and that's why the skin was broken. But I'm not an expert in weapons."

Pow, she'd said, and done the action to go with it, like an underhand shot in tennis. Jo had seen many people become desensitized to the horrific nature of their work. In the police it was more than commonplace. She felt it was important to remember that in both professions they dealt with extremes. In such a position you had to choose: try your best to keep a sense of perspective, or let the job turn you into the kind of person that looked at a man in a coma and found it interesting rather than shocking. She considered herself to have achieved a good balance, so far. She could look at Gregor Franks and feel terrible for him. Then she could put those feelings away and get on with the job.

Just then, an alarm sounded somewhere in the main ward.

"Excuse me," said Doctor Locke, and he was gone. The nurse followed, absenting himself with such swiftness that Jo stood there with her mouth open for a few seconds, her hand on the edge of the open door. There were sounds of feet running, trolleys being wheeled across, a cry of *"Clear!,"* and the unmistakable loud bleep and clang of the defibrillation machine. Jo turned back to Gregor, letting the door fall shut behind her, closing the noise out. She watched his chest barely moving as he breathed. Her mobile rang into the silence.

She prayed it wasn't Amy, her cheeks flushing in shame with the memory of the not-proposal. Then, for a moment she thought—hoped—it could be Ruby, who might have turned her phone on when she awoke this morning and saw the missed calls. But no, neither. It was Atkinson.

"I thought I told you to go home."

"We think we've found her. The woman and the kid who were staying in Gregor's flat. We've got a woman on CCTV leaving the building and heading straight across the forecourt, holding a child of about the right age. This was yesterday, in the morning. She's got her hood up, and she's hurrying. I can't say exactly what drew me to her, but she just stood out from the crowd, you know?"

Jo did know. Copper's nose was real, and Atkinson had a good one.

He went on. "So, we traced her movements. We've got images of her going to the train station and buying a ticket. The whole time, she's facing away from the cameras, as if she's avoiding them getting an image of her face."

"Where did she travel to? Can you get a hold of the train station ticket office people?"

"Not right now, boss. The ticket office is shut. Opens in an hour."

"Well, shake them up, Constable. We need a good image of her."

"Are you at the hospital?" asked Atkinson. "How's Franks?"

"Not good. He's got a load of drugs in his system. They don't think he can survive."

"Drugs? I didn't see anything at the flat, no packets or bottles or anything."

"Me neither. Let's see if the CSI search turns up anything."

"Maybe the person who attacked him also spiked him, just to make sure?"

"That's why I like you, Steve. Always striving to see the best in people."

"I learned from the best, boss."

She smiled grimly.

Atkinson said, "It makes it even more urgent that we find this woman, though, if his condition is so critical. I think we need to do a media shout-out. Local radio, TV. Someone will have seen her face, even if the cameras didn't."

Jo thought of Amy, and the time before they'd been a couple, when she would have been the first person to call in this situation. Perhaps one day, that would be the case again.

"Good idea. I'll leave it with you, if you don't mind."

"No problem."

"After that, go home, will you? You haven't slept." She hung up before he could point out that she hadn't either.

Jo examined the X-rays for a while longer, then moved across, behind the head of the bed to stand near the emergency button, just in case Gregor should start flatlining while the medics were otherwise engaged. She watched the machines closely for any sign of alarm, but nothing happened. Heart kept beating. Lungs kept inflating. The patient just lay there, eyes closed, splayed feet pointing to the corners of the ceiling. She moved to the other side of the bed and glanced at the man's fingernails, at the white skin like wax, bloated and wrinkled from being so long in the water.

He was alive. But for how long? Despite what the doctor had said, she didn't want to believe there was no hope of recovery. Someone, somewhere, cared about this man and would be willing him to live if they knew what was happening. Until those people were found, all he had was Joanna.

"Hold on, Gregor," she said to him. "If you can hear me, we're going to find the person who did this to you. So just hold on, okay?"

17

THEN
Ruby
September

"CLOSE YOUR EYES and open your hands."

Ruby did as he asked. Gregor placed something flat on her palm.

She opened her eyes. "That's not my phone."

"It is now."

The model in her hand was top of the range. It probably cost several hundred pounds, maybe more.

"Do you like it?"

"I can't accept this."

His face fell. "Whyever not?"

"I mean, thank you so much for thinking of me, but honestly, you really shouldn't have."

"But it's your birthday, isn't it?"

Ruby was shocked; how could he have possibly known it was her birthday? "Well, actually it was yesterday."

Gregor burst out laughing at her surprised expression. "I didn't know! That's so funny—I was just going to say that as a joke. Was it really your birthday yesterday? How perfect! Oh, brilliant. What a coincidence. Well, you'll have to accept it now, won't you?"

It had been a little over a week since the phone had been lost, and for those few days Ruby's life seemed stripped back, simple in a clean, uncomplicated way. She'd been to the library to find some Scottish folk tunes for Constance, and what time she hadn't spent practicing, she'd been using to develop her own piece. On her birthday, apart from playing her violin and working on her composition, she'd had a bath that lasted for two hours while she listened to *Tosca* on the secondhand record player she'd treated herself to. Perfection, added to by the fact that she didn't even need to actively ignore any annoying calls from Joanna and Marianne.

She turned the device over in her hand. It was sleek and sophisticated. The kind of phone she would never have bought for herself, whether or not she could have afforded to, which she could not.

"I don't know what to say." She certainly couldn't say she was enjoying life without the hassle of a smartphone. It would have sounded so ungrateful.

"You don't have to say anything."

"I was going to get myself a phone soon." If only to prevent her family panicking or, God forbid, trying to visit in person. "But it wouldn't have been as fancy as this one. This must have cost a bomb."

"It's a gift, Ruby. I bought it for you."

"But—"

"No buts."

She hesitated. "This is a bit embarrassing, but the thing is, I'm not sure I can afford the monthly fee. I wasn't paying the bills for my other phone. My parents were paying for it. Without my income from teaching at the moment, there's no way I could—"

"Don't worry. I've set you up on a really cheap deal. And I've paid up for the first six months."

"The first six months? It's too much." She tried to give the phone back, but he put his hands behind him.

"The first three months were free if you bought the next three, that kind of thing. So, it barely cost me anything. I'm seeing it as a way to support the arts. My first deed as your patron."

Ruby pressed a finger to the screen so it lit up. The wallpaper was a picture of him, pulling a silly grin.

"You can change that," said Gregor. Then he looked at her and frowned. "Did I do something wrong?"

Don't be so proud, she told herself. *He can afford it. He's just trying to be nice.*

"No," she said. "Of course not. It's very generous of you, Gregor. Thank you. I'll pay you back as soon as I can."

He looked hurt. "Don't be silly, Ruby. It's a gift."

"Sorry, I didn't mean to . . ."

"And look," he said, unlocking the phone and scrolling to the contacts page, where just one person was listed. "You have my number already."

She couldn't remember any of the other numbers she'd once had, apart from the home landline number and Joanna's mobile. All the others—mostly friends from school, a few bad dates, and a handful of ex-pupils—had been lost along with her phone. Gregor's gift made her feel pressure to get in touch with some of those people and ask for their numbers again. Then she had another thought. *Does it really matter that much?* The only people apart from Jo to ring regularly were Barbara at work and Marianne, neither of whom she particularly wanted to talk to. She supposed she could put Mrs. Stefanidis in there. And then there was Sam, who didn't even have a phone—his address had been stored in the other phone, but she still had it written down on a sheet of paper back at the flat. So, with Gregor, Sarah Stefanidis and Joanna, that made a grand total of three contacts, four if you counted Sam. Was that beyond pathetic? *When did my world get so small,* she wondered.

Maybe it was fine. Maybe she didn't need anyone else anyway.

"Come through," said Gregor, leading the way further into the apartment. "Leonie's asleep, I'm afraid. But Constance is here."

He opened the door to the sitting room. "We haven't had the best day today, unfortunately."

Constance was reclining, catlike, on the same couch as always. There were dark circles under her eyes; her gaze was dull, her hair loose and tangled.

"Is she okay?" asked Ruby.

"She will be. She's had a sedative. Sometimes things get a bit . . . too much." He raised his voice. "How are you feeling, Connie? Any better?"

There was no response apart from a flicker of the dull eyes in Ruby's direction.

"Should I go?" asked Ruby.

"No, no. It'll help her to see you." He lowered his voice to a whisper. "She might not show it, but I think it was really therapeutic for her to hear you play last week."

Ruby was unsure, but Gregor smiled encouragingly.

"Hey, Constance. I found you some songs," she said, taking out her instrument, and the book she'd borrowed. *"Hebridean Ballads, Jigs and Reels.* Yes?" She started to play. It was a folk song, beautiful, ancient, and solid, sounding very Scottish to Ruby, reminding her of the folk bar she and Sam went to whenever he was in town. When she got to the end of the first chorus, she fell silent. Constance hadn't moved or made a sound.

"Maybe I should come back another time," said Ruby.

"No, stay," said Constance at last. There was a creak to her voice, as if she hadn't spoken for a long time. "I know that one. It has words, doesn't it?"

"I don't know them. It's just the tune in the book."

"Play, please."

With effort, Constance moved to a sitting position, her thin arms straining against the cushions to push her upright. After a few bars, she started to sing, in Gaelic.

> *Chuir iad mise dh'eilean leam fhìn,*
> *Chuir iad mise dh'eilean leam fhìn,*
> *Chuir iad mise dh'eilean leam fhìn,*
> *Dh' eilean mara fada bho thìr.*

There was something terribly sad in the sounds, in the way she sang them. Gregor stood and stared at Constance, as if seeing her for the first time. It was the way he'd looked at Ruby when she'd played for them the week before. Ruby watched him, watching the mother of his child, and wondered what had passed between these two that they should have become so distant from one another.

Something powerful remained, clearly, though the nature of it was far from obvious.

When the song was over, there was a silence in which nobody breathed. Ruby lowered her bow.

Gregor said, "What's it about?"

Constance raised her eyes to him, slowly. They never quite reached his face. "It's about being sent to an island, far away and all alone."

Gregor looked from Constance to Ruby and back again. "You make such beautiful music together. I can't quite take it in."

"Gregor," said Constance. "I'm thirsty. Can you . . ."

"Of course. I'll get water."

"Something hot?" she said. "Tea?"

When he left the room, Constance seemed to come to focus. She fixed Ruby with her eyes and hissed urgently across the gap between the couches. Ruby moved closer.

"He locked me in the bedroom today."

The words were so surprising that Ruby could only stare. "He *what?*"

"He locks me in so he can hide my coat. My sealskin. I need it so I can go home. He's a bad man, Ruby. You should stay away from him."

"Your sealskin?" Ruby didn't know what to say. It was possibly the most peculiar thing she'd ever heard. Perhaps she meant *oilskin*, like a rain slicker. But then Ruby remembered the conversation with Gregor, about the name *Roane* linking to the shapeshifters, the seal people: *she thinks she's part of the myth.* Constance's face was a tight grimace, with veins standing out on her forehead, which was shiny with sweat.

"I can't go outside without it. That's why I'm stuck here. It has to be with me. It has to . . ."

Gregor came back into the room. "It's a yes for milk and no for sugar, right, Ruby?" he looked over at Constance, and his face changed to one of concern. "Oh, hon, you don't look well. Much worse than earlier on—sure you want tea? I can make lemon and honey? Or cocoa?"

She waved a dismissive hand and leaned back into the cushions. "I feel fine. A bit sleepy, maybe."

"You should probably go to bed. Do you need any help getting up?"

Constance glared at him. "I do not need anything from you," she said. "And neither does Ruby." Her eyes drooped and closed; her hand went to her head.

"Let's get you to bed," he said, taking Constance's hand.

She yanked it away. "Don't touch me."

"Okay, I'm sorry." Gregor held his hands above his head in a gesture of surrender. "I won't if you don't want me to. But I'm right here, if you change your mind." His voice had a tremor; he was upset, trying not to let it show.

Constance struggled to her feet, pushing herself up with effort. Whatever she'd taken was affecting her balance. "Remember," she said to Ruby, "everything he says to you is a lie. I tell the truth. I tell . . ." She trailed off, her eyes drifting almost closed. With the gait of a person fifty years older, the dark-haired woman walked slowly across to her room and went in, shutting the door behind her.

The room was mostly in darkness, lit only by the table lamp, the pool of light not quite reaching the walls. Gregor handed Ruby her tea, then sat where Constance had been on the other couch. In the dimness, she couldn't see his eyes, but as he turned his head, there was a glint where tears were gathering.

"I'm so sorry about that," he said.

Ruby wasn't sure how to respond. She said, "It's not your fault. She seems so . . ."

"Paranoid?"

"I was going to say different, from last week."

Gregor nodded slowly. "When it's good, I think it will be good forever, that she's better. That maybe she'll be able to live independently. But then, out of the blue, she'll wake up in the morning, and there will be a look in her eye. And I'll know."

"Know what?"

Gregor seemed to struggle with what he was about to say. He winced, as if in pain. "I think of it like a demon now. When it's bad, it's like there's a demon inside her, controlling her. Not letting the real Constance speak."

"Sounds like it's really hard for you."

"Yes. For both of us. Though when she's better, she often forgets what she's said."

Ruby thought of Marianne then, and how it was hard to understand how very different she was when she was bad, how far from her sober self. She had blackouts too, though Ruby wasn't sure whether Marianne really forgot what had happened or blocked it out deliberately because of the shame. That wasn't the same, though. To an extent, Marianne could have helped herself. Constance couldn't do that.

"You're so good to take this on, Gregor."

"Not really. It was my carelessness that got us both into this mess in the first place. I'm simply seeing to my responsibilities. Leonie, I mean, though she's more than just a responsibility."

"Yes, but with Constance. I don't know anyone who would do what you've done."

"That's just it. You don't know the half of it. There are things I've done that I knew were wrong at the time. I thought I was helping her, I really did, that it was worth the sacrifice. And now it's too late to go back."

"What things?"

"I'm not sure I should tell you. I don't want you to think I'm a bad person."

She moved closer. "I'd never think that."

After a long pause, he began. "I helped her hide the pregnancy. And the birth. When it came to the labor, we did it on our own."

"Do you mean, you delivered Leonie? Without help? No midwife or anything?"

He nodded, his forehead crumpling.

"But anything could have happened."

"I know that. Don't you think I know that? She was in so much pain, I begged her to let me call an ambulance. But then, it all happened so fast, and afterward they both seemed to be fine. So I just went along with it."

"My god, Gregor." She couldn't get her head around it. "What did you do with the umbilical cord? With the afterbirth?"

He shuddered, looked like he might throw up.

"I don't want to talk about it. Can we not?"

Gregor's head dropped into his hands. Ruby heard a soft sob. She went to him, put her arm around him as he cried.

"I loved her once, you know. I still do, as the mother of my child. But when someone's ill, and you become a carer, it can kill it dead, even if you don't want it to. That sounds awful, doesn't it?"

"No, it doesn't," said Ruby. "It's understandable. And nobody's fault." She thought she understood now why he wanted Ruby to keep Constance and Leonie a secret: the birth was the first lie, and to cover it up he'd had to keep lying. It was illegal not to register a birth. Every day they went without declaring it would compli-cate things further, make explaining their actions ever more diffi-cult. Could he go to prison? Could Constance? Perhaps that was what he was really scared of, not the mental illness.

"It is my fault, though. I failed them both when I ended it between us. It doesn't matter that we didn't intend on having a baby. Leonie deserves two parents."

"Of course. Two good parents, and she's got that. It doesn't mean they have to be a couple." She thought of her own parents then, who were really her biological grandparents. They'd stayed together and provided a stable enough environment for her early years, but the cracks were there even for them, growing wider with the secret amounts of vodka that Marianne poured in. As for her biological father, Ruby had no idea where he was now. He was just a name without even a face attached. A teenage boy at the time of her conception, he'd probably forgotten Ruby even existed.

"And now all I want is for her to be happy, to be well again. Because despite everything, she's a brilliant mother. Or she would be, given the chance."

"Yes," said Ruby. "And you're more than a brilliant father. You're having to take care of Constance too."

He turned toward her, looked into her eyes. "Ruby. Can I ask you something?"

Her heart started racing. "Of course."

"When I was out of the room, what did she say to you?"

Ruby hesitated. "Why?"

"I feel like I don't know what's going on in her head anymore. I hate to have to ask you, but she barely speaks to me these days."

"She said something about a coat. I didn't understand it. I think it was part of her delusion." She remembered the horrible accusation then and instinctively moved away from him. "She also said you locked her in the bedroom. Did you actually do that, Gregor? Because if so . . ."

"Oh, Jesus," said Gregor. "Oh no. This is how it started last time. It's worse than I thought."

"What?"

"Look, I'll show you."

He took out his smartphone and pressed "Play" on a video. It took Ruby a second to realize what she was looking at. There on the screen was the room they were sitting in, from above. She looked up, searching for a camera, but could see nothing. In the video the room was disheveled, and there was a figure moving around it, frantically searching.

"A burglar?"

"Look closer."

It was Constance. She was pulling the room apart, removing cushions from the sofas and throwing them, tipping chairs, pushing over the coffee table. She disappeared from the shot, and the camera switched to the kitchen.

"Do you have cameras everywhere?"

He grimaced, nodded his head yes. "I have to. It's for everyone's safety."

On the screen, in the kitchen, Constance opened the cupboards and threw everything on the floor, packets of food, jars—the lot. The kettle went flying, water splashing against the wall. Shards of smashed plates scattered. She climbed on top of the surface and searched above the cupboards, dislodging rolls of kitchen towel, bottles of bleach. The next moment her face filled the screen. There was no light in her eyes, only anguish, her lips pulled back, teeth bared. Then, she jumped off the kitchen counter and opened the fridge, scooping out the contents and throwing food, cartons of drink, everything onto the floor, liquids spilling in pools. After she'd rummaged inside it, she started to drag the fridge toward her, out of its alcove, her small form demonstrating surprising strength.

"What's she doing?" said Ruby. "She looks like she's totally out of it."

"She's looking for the coat."

"What coat is it, Gregor?"

"The one she told you about that I'm supposedly hiding from her. The one that doesn't exist."

Constance returned to the main room. She tried one of the doors, but it wouldn't open. Though there was no sound on the film, Ruby could feel the scream of rage and frustration that escaped from her then, her back arching, mouth twisted, fingers like claws, ripping out handfuls of her own hair.

"That's my room. I have to keep it locked, or she'd tear it apart."

On the screen, the woman dragged an armchair toward the locked door. She struggled with it for a few seconds. Then she picked it up above her head and threw it straight at the door. As she did so, the outline of the baby bump was clearly visible.

"She's pregnant in this video?"

"Yes."

"But Gregor, isn't this dangerous? For the baby? I mean, the stress and everything." She thought about how small Leonie was, how she wasn't yet walking. The way she was alert to everything her mother did.

"This is why I started working from home. I realized I couldn't leave her for any amount of time. When she was pregnant, she couldn't take anything to help, no meds, not even herbal things. She was talking about the coat all the time, and when I wasn't there, this would happen."

"Why a coat? Is it significant in some way? Seems pretty random."

"It's to do with her family, the place she grew up. Did she tell you much about it?"

"She said they were from the Hebrides. That the community has their own island."

"You could call it a community. But I say it's a cult."

"A cult?"

"When we met, at the party on the beach, at first I thought it was wild. The drumming, the dancing. We had a great time. The best. But once I got her away from the crowd, she was babbling such nonsense to me. I thought was she on drugs then, but it was just that she was so indoctrinated. She was malnourished and brainwashed, and when I took her back in the morning, they'd all gone without her. Good riddance, I said, but she was heartbroken, couldn't accept that they'd done that, that they didn't care about her and wouldn't wait for her. She had nothing but what she stood up in, and I swear nothing she was wearing would constitute a coat. Anyway, I brought her home, got her some proper clothes, fed her up. She seemed to get better. We were so happy, for a short while. When she was about three months pregnant, that's when the delusions took hold. She said I'd taken her coat, meaning her skin. It's gotten tangled up in her mind. She thinks she puts on her coat and *turns into an actual seal*, Ruby."

There was so much to take in. "So, her family . . . abandoned her there?"

He nodded. "So cruel. It sent her mad, I think. She needs therapy, a kind of decompression, anti-brainwashing. She never had the chance for that."

Ruby felt it like a gut punch. It explained why she was losing her mind. Constance's problems suddenly made Ruby's seem trivial.

"What about all the seal stuff, though? It can't just be about the name."

He sighed. "Within the community, cult, whatever—there are stories. They're all to do with seal worship. Their version of Bible stories I suppose. And they have rituals. When they come of age, there's a ceremony. On the solstice or the equinox or whatever, they wrap a sealskin coat around themselves, throw themselves into the sea and swim until dawn. They're convinced, when they come ashore, that they've been seals all night long, catching fish in their teeth, sleeping on rocks, all of that. Hallucinations brought on by the exhaustion, probably."

"Must be freezing, the sea up there." Ruby wrapped her arms around herself, shivering at the thought of it.

"It is. And the thing is, they don't all come back."

"You mean they drown?"

"Well, yes. But that's not how they see it. If they don't come back, to them it's because they've decided to live as seals for the rest of their lives. The tribe are actually happy when that happens. The parents do a special ceremony, with dancing and feasting, and so on."

"Wow," said Ruby. "So, you lose your kid forever, and you're happy?"

"I know. The things some people believe." Gregor stared into the middle distance. "Do you know there are hundreds of unidentified bodies that wash up on beaches, in morgues up and down the country?"

"Hundreds?"

"I'm not saying they're all from the *Roane* clan. But those that don't return have to wash up somewhere. Healthy, young people. Throwing themselves into the sea, thinking they'll turn into seals. The police probably assume it's suicide, but really, in my view, it's murder."

Ruby rubbed her temples.

"I can't believe you've been dealing with all of this on your own."

"The tranquilizers I got for her help a little bit, but I don't like to give them to her. I only do it when I need to go out, for work or to the shops."

"You leave Leonie alone with her when she's in that state?"

His face was suddenly angry, defensive. But then his shoulders slumped and he nodded. "It's never for long, and she would never harm the baby. Never. I don't know what else to do. I couldn't work if I had Leonie with me. I can't get anyone to help me; there's no one I trust enough to keep our secrets."

"No one at all?" He seemed to miss the implication: *What about me?*

"I told you, Ruby, there are things I've done, that if anyone found out, I'd be arrested. We both would. The birth . . ." He shuddered. "If I could go back, I'd do it all differently. But I can't. I have to deal with it."

Ruby looked down at the video, still running, of Constance hurling herself at the bedroom door repeatedly. The baby bump was barely visible under a loose shirt.

"I'll do it."

"What do you mean?"

"I said I'd help. I can keep them company. Then you won't need to give her any tranquilizers. I can make sure she's okay. I'm not talking about care—I couldn't do that. Just company. And if she gets really paranoid, I can call you. From my new phone."

"You would do that for me?"

"Yes. For you and for Leonie." She nearly said, *For Constance too,* but stopped herself, not quite understanding why she wanted to hide from him her quiet sympathy.

Ruby had an urge to get away then. To be alone to process everything. She stood up. "I should go. It's late."

"Already?"

She patted her pocket. "I'm just on the end of a phone."

Ruby bent to pick up her violin. When she turned back, he was right there, standing close to her. She could hear his breath.

"It's good to be able to talk to someone finally. I think I've been lonely. I just didn't want to admit it."

She raised her face. His hand caught hers, thumb gently stroking. *I should step away,* she thought. Her feet did not move.

"I didn't mean to spend all night talking about Constance again."

"Then stop," she said, her fingertip tracing his knuckle.

"I don't want to take advantage of you," he said, leaning closer, letting his lips brush hers.

Ruby's eyelids fluttered closed. Her lips parted. Gregor's hand encircled the back of her neck with gentle fingers.

Suddenly, she went cold, realizing what she was about to do.

"No," she said, grabbing his wrist. "Stop."

Gregor stepped away, looking shocked. "What's wrong?"

"This is," she said.

"I thought you . . . wanted to."

She did. So badly. The hurt on his face cut her deeply, and she wished with everything she had that things could be different.

"I'm sorry" was all she could say.

Ruby let the door to the flat slam shut as she ran down the stairs, wondering if she'd done the right thing, if she should have just gone ahead and let it happen. He was so perfect. And yet.

There was too much to lose here. She couldn't betray another woman in that way. If there was even a chance that when Constance was better, she and Gregor might get back together, for Leonie's sake she didn't want to be in the middle of that. And even if there was no chance, he'd said himself that she wasn't the one who wanted to split. If Constance still held a candle for the father of her child, then Ruby wasn't going to be the one who destroyed that dream for her. She was better than that. She had to be.

CHAPTER

18

NOW
The Injured Man

H E HEARS MUFFLED sounds. Voices. Two or three people are speaking, but he can't make out what they're saying. They're not talking to him, only to each other. There is darkness and the beeping of machines. He appears to be floating, weightless, unsure which way is up; the voices are all around, above, and beneath him, as if he's suspended among them. Then, a sharp certainty about what this is: he's in hospital. He can smell it now; cleaning fluid and the faint stench of human waste. Someone leans over him; their voice is booming near his face and he tastes perfume, thick and chemical in the back of his throat. He doesn't understand the words, though they are being pronounced clearly enough; nonsense syllables. No, that's not right. They're just speaking in a language he doesn't understand. He can't think in a straight line; the links between ideas are broken, thoughts floating as freely as he is. Nearby, someone is unfolding a blanket or a sheet and shaking it out. It swishes, plasticky, and then it's laid on top of him. He fades out.

19

NOW
Joanna
Saturday, December 22

THE OFFICERS GATHERED in the incident room, seats pulled out into rows facing front, where Joanna stood before a whiteboard. Atkinson sat nearby, to the side, his arms crossed, feet planted.

"Okay folks, we have a critically injured male, age thirty-eight, who was found at his home on Friday night, unconscious, with a suspicious head wound. We are treating this as attempted murder, and so far we have no suspects in custody."

She turned around and pinned a large photograph of the injury on the back of Gregor's head to the board. There were one or two indrawn breaths, but mostly no reaction. Every person in the room often saw much worse.

"Unfortunately, Gregor is not expected to recover. Apart from this injury, he is also suspected to have ingested a quantity of prescription drugs, which we are also treating as suspicious. The charge therefore is likely to become murder, so watch for updates. Our priority is finding the perpetrator or perpetrators, but also any family. We know next to nothing about this guy. Clive, any movement on next of kin?"

An officer seated by the window shook his head. "Not yet, boss. I'm working on it."

"Keep looking. There must be someone. No one in his phone that you can ID?"

"The numbers don't seem to connect."

"What do you mean, they don't connect?"

"I mean, where there is a number for Dave or whatever, it literally won't connect. Some of the numbers aren't even long enough to be phone numbers. It's weird, as if his phone is full of fake contacts."

There was a ripple of interest in the room. Harper had never come across this before. Once they'd opened up a phone and retrieved the contacts, finding a next of kin was usually fairly straightforward.

"What about call history?"

"There's an app on the phone called *Whypr*. It deletes all information, cookies, searches, etcetera, at least once an hour. There's no way of recovering any call history at our end, we could try to contact the makers of the app, but I doubt they are storing any data, what with the data protection laws."

"Also, why would they store it if they're in the business of getting rid of it?" said Jo. "Did you find any photos on the phone? What about social media? Email?"

"No photos, and emails were connected to the *Whypr* app too. And as for social media contacts, the few that we have for him aren't current. There are one or two old school friends, but he hasn't interacted with them for over three years. He doesn't seem to use his Facebook or Instagram accounts at all, or very rarely. From everything I've seen, I think he's a bit obsessed with online privacy."

"It would seem so."

"We can try to get the phone cleared for tracing, to see where he's been in the last few weeks at least. We might even be able to get more from phone company data."

Joanna addressed the assembled officers. "Okay. Until then it's the old-fashioned way. We need to look at his post, knock on doors, question all the neighbors, and try to find some family or associates using local knowledge. Someone will be missing this person, and they will want to know what's happened to him."

She pinned another photograph to the board. In this one, Gregor Franks was shown face up, eyes shut, tubes bisecting his face, with attachments entering his nose. Harper put her fists on her hips and frowned at it. "Don't we have a better image than this? Steve?"

"Sorry, boss, yes, we do. We have his driver's license. I'll get the headshot blown up."

"What about profile pictures? He must have something up on Facebook even if he doesn't use it much."

"The profile picture he uses for everything isn't actually of his face. It's there on the desk. I printed it."

Harper found the printout and pinned it to the board. It was a picture of crossed feet on a poolside lounger, a bottle of beer gently condensing on a side table.

"Did you mine the data on this photo?"

Clive said, "Yes, it was taken five years ago in the south of France, but I don't think those are our victim's feet: I also did an image search. It pops up everywhere, almost like a stock photo. Been used for various things—holiday websites, blogs."

"What does he do for a living? Something to do with finance?"

"Property development and investments. He works alone on a laptop. Doesn't even have an office."

"If he's buying property, he must know people. He's a landlord, so what about tenants?"

"He uses an agency. Never met any of his tenants, as far as I can tell."

"He has to have a solicitor. And an accountant, probably. Find out who it is, would you? And we've got his bank details, so can someone get the data from the bank, please? At the scene we have Forensics working on DNA and fingerprint evidence, with a report expected today on the print profiles and later this week for DNA. We are currently looking with priority urgency for a female who was seen leaving the area with a child on the day the neighbor reported a leak through the ceiling that turned out to be from the bathroom above. That was Friday."

One of the officers put a hand up.

"Yes?"

"Do we know when the victim was last seen alive?"

"He's not dead, Louise. Keep up."

Nervous laughter burst from several people in the room. Louise Reynolds, a young community support team officer, was shame-faced. "Sorry, boss. When was he last seen before the incident?"

"A good point. I don't have that information, but perhaps you could find out. We did a door-to-door of the immediate neighbors last night, but we need to expand that now. Get that sorted, would you, this morning?"

"Yes ma'am. Also . . ."

"Yes?"

"I did notice something. Might not be relevant."

"Go on."

"The window, on Gregor's flat. It's overlooked by the window of one of the West Block flats. Is it worth asking the tenants if they've seen anything?"

"Good idea," said Harper, concentrating on not glancing at Atkinson, whose eyes she could feel on the side of her face. "You might need to knock on all of the seventh-floor flats . . ."

"I looked at a floor plan. I know which one it is. Apartment 7B."

Ruby's place. Of course it was. Harper could barely control the nervous tic in her cheek. It wouldn't be anything to do with Ruby, though. There was no need to mention the connection. Was there? She said, "Great. I'll follow that up, then."

"You will?" said Atkinson. She looked straight at him. He was frowning, probably because, as senior investigating officer, she should have assigned a junior officer to take a statement.

Joanna wasn't going to be questioned. "Anything to add, Steve?"

It took him a couple of seconds to gather his thoughts. "Um, yep. We've managed to get a good likeness of the woman we sus-pect was living in Franks's apartment with the child. This is a still from the train station CCTV."

The woman in the picture had her hood up, as she had in the footage from the estate, but her pale face had been captured finally. The dark eyes seemed haunted.

"What's she looking at?" asked Jo. In the wide shot the woman stood away from the other passengers, holding the child tightly against her chest. She stared intensely into the middle distance, as if frightened of whatever it was that she could see. But there was nothing there.

"We've circulated the picture to news outlets, and this morning there will be an appeal for witnesses. At this point we're thinking child protection, mainly. We don't know the name or circumstances, but we need to find this woman and child, to check there's nothing amiss."

Another young officer said, "She's not a suspect?"

"We need to rule her out."

Harper said, "In terms of evidence. Did anyone manage to find any images of this woman inside the actual building?"

"Not yet," said Atkinson. "But we got this a few minutes ago."

He pressed a button, and the video projector came to life. It showed footage from the ticket office, a high angle showing the woman buying a ticket. Audio had been recorded from the microphone intercom system.

"Single to Cleethorpes, please." The woman's voice was muffled, but it was clear she didn't have a Sheffield accent.

The officer issued the receipt, but the woman didn't take it immediately. She turned and shouted for the child, who'd run away into the crowds. *Leonie, stop.*

Atkinson paused the tape and looked at Jo. "It's the same name," they said together.

"That's confirmation of a link to Gregor Franks. So let's comb the system. Any child with that first name of the right age, involved in any incident, child protection or not."

"Worth a shot," said Atkinson, opening up his laptop.

20

THEN
Ruby
October

THE NEXT DAY, Gregor didn't contact her at all. Ruby stared at the blank screen of the new phone and tried not to fret. Yes, she'd pushed him away, cut him off when he was at his most vulnerable. It might have even looked, to him, like an out-and-out rejection. But couldn't he tell that she would have kissed him if things had been different? Didn't he understand that it wasn't him that had set her running, but the fact that to have let it happen would have complicated things too much for both of them? She was sure that he'd gotten the wrong idea, and his silence confirmed it.

Sleeping was a challenge, as the new phone glowed brightly every few seconds so that she kept thinking there was a message. Eventually, to end the madness, she forced herself to turn it off.

The day after that, hope returned. Switching the phone on, she remembered how pleased he'd been when he gave it to her. She was ashamed that she'd felt so ungrateful.

After it had started up, silence. There were no notifications, no messages that had been sent while the phone was off. Clicking on

Gregor's name, the chat box was empty. *Last seen at 3:42 AM*, read the header. Yoga time.

Before she could think it through too much, she'd typed out a message:

Hi Gregor, how's things?

The answer came forty-two anxious minutes later, though the app told her that he'd seen the message the second she sent it.

Yes, fine thanks. Busy! Leonie wants to see you, maybe you could come tomorrow? Bring the fiddle?

So it had been three full days when, as requested, she stood at the entrance to his building, thinking, *Maybe I'll just leave it. Maybe I'd be better off without him in my life; without any of them.* She thought she might not press the buzzer, that she ought to turn and walk away. Last week, in that brief window of having no phone, her life had been so peaceful. There was no one but herself to worry about. Maybe that was what she needed now, to focus on herself rather than get involved with these people. Even if they were, in turn, gorgeous, mysterious, and cute as hell. It was more than she could handle right now. The sensible thing—the healthy thing—would be to leave.

She could post the phone he'd given her into his mailbox. Imagine how freeing that would be. But despite the thoughts, her decision to go home, her feet didn't move. Then, just when she was willing herself to turn away, the door buzzed and clicked open. *The cameras,* she realized, as she went through and toward the lifts. *He must have been watching.*

Gregor beamed from the doorway, welcoming her, delighted to see that she'd brought the violin. It was as if nothing had happened or—maybe better—that he'd forgiven her entirely and put aside his hurt feelings. He took her jacket, made her a drink, smiled warmly. While Constance rested in the bedroom, the two of them spent a delightful hour playing with Leonie, and when Constance appeared, she seemed cheerful, asked if Ruby would like to help with bath time. Later, as Leonie settled down, Ruby played lullabies. When the child was asleep, she played a soothing nocturne, mainly for Constance, who seemed tired by then but much calmer than before. As the bow moved across the strings, Gregor watched Ruby, his eyes full of admiration.

Finally, after Constance headed to bed, Ruby and Gregor were alone. Without the presence of either Constance or Leonie, Gregor's demeanor changed. The temperature in the room seemed to drop. She glanced at him and caught a shadow of the awkwardness she'd seen the last time they were alone, right before she ran.

She sat next to him on the couch, cleared her throat. "Are you okay?"

He moved infinitesimally further away. "Why wouldn't I be?"

"I wanted to apologize for what happened the other night."

"Nothing happened, though, did it? So you've nothing to apologize for. Everything's fine."

She swallowed. His body language had shifted, his hands clutched together in his lap.

"It's clearly not fine," she said.

"I get it, okay? I've been friend-zoned."

"No . . ."

"Look," he turned to her, softening, the warm smile returning. "I understand, I really do. It's happened before. I know I'm not much of a catch. Too much baggage. Why would anyone want this?" He gestured to himself, to his handsome face, his strong, supple body, toned by hours of nocturnal yoga sessions and daily cardio. She frowned.

"Are you going to force me to compliment you?" He must have been aware of how he looked, of the effect he had on women. He was solvent, handsome, well-spoken, tall. Up until this point she would have said he was modest, but this outlandish display of self-deprecation simply didn't ring true.

He folded his arms. "I wouldn't try that. I'd be waiting a long time."

Ruby had had enough. "Well, you can wait a bit longer then." She took a deep breath, stood up, and gathered her bag and jacket.

"Please don't go," he said. "I'm sorry. I was being a dick."

She walked toward the door.

"You're coming back though, right?" he said. "Tomorrow?"

She stopped but didn't turn. "I don't know."

"Leonie loves you," he said. "And Constance does too."

"Constance loves me? Really? I doubt it."

He paused. "Well, she likes you. I can tell."

"But what about us? I can't keep coming over if it's going to be awkward."

"It won't be. I guess my pride was hurt a little. But I'll get over it."

"It might be better if I stay away for a while."

"No, please, Ruby. Even if it's only for the music. I think I'd die if I couldn't hear you play."

Will that always be enough for you, though? she wondered. And for how long will it be enough for me?

As she walked out the door, he called after her. "You said you'd help me. Didn't you?"

Ruby turned to face him. "Of course I'll help you. I just need some time. A day or so. Then I'll be back."

Their eyes met and she hesitated, as if she might go to him, embrace him, let it happen the way she both wanted it to and didn't want it to. She took a breath, to strengthen her resolve. She left without another word.

CHAPTER

21

NOW
The Social Worker
Sunday, December 23

D IANE IS DRIVING home from a job when she turns on the radio. It's the news.

A man has been found in a critical condition at his home in Sheffield. Police are appealing for witnesses. A woman, wanted for questioning by police, is missing, along with a child between eighteen months and two years old. The pair were last seen boarding a train from Sheffield to Cleethorpes on Friday afternoon. If anyone has any information about their whereabouts, they are asked to contact Greater Yorkshire Police on . . .

Diane's first thought is *I don't have time for this.* She keeps driving, grimly determined to go home, thinking that she deserves a bit of rest now despite whatever this is. Probably nothing anyway. It's Sunday, and she's just removed three children from their mother, having been called in on her day off. The mother is a drug user, but it's mostly her partner the children are being protected from: there's a legal order of no contact between the man and the children, but the mother seems as addicted to him as she is to the heroin. Diane took them early this morning, with the help of specially trained enforcement officers. She unpeeled the middle one's fingers from the mother's scarred and unresisting wrist, carried her to the car. She delivered them to foster carers, all three children stunned and dirty and the little one screaming his head off. Diane is brewing a cold. She just wants a sit down, and have a cup of tea and some more painkillers.

She turns off the radio, but she can still hear the announcer in her head, like an echo. *"A missing woman, and a child between eighteen months and two years old."* On Friday. In Cleethorpes. From Sheffield. *Could be a coincidence,* she thinks. It can't be the two she had in the police car, outside the shop, the nice woman, the big fuss over nothing. Constance and Leonie, the mother she'd spoken to, that she let go without so much as a background check. The little girl they found on the seafront, who turned out to be not abandoned, but simply lost. Surely not. And yet she is suddenly filled with the cold possibility that she's made a giant, career-derailing mistake.

She feels sick and giddy, and fears that she'll lose control of the car. She manages to pull up in a side street and turn off the engine. Closing her eyes, Diane takes one slow breath, then another.

She literally jumps in her seat when her phone starts ringing. It is Belinda, the senior social worker for the area. Her voice is as harsh as dogs barking in Diane's ear.

"I've just had a call from Detective Sergeant Joanna Harper at Greater Yorkshire Police. She says police officers attended a missing child incident of yours on Friday, and the mother is a person of interest in an inquiry into a serious assault. I can't find anything on the database."

Diane doesn't say anything. She hears the blood rushing in her ears.

"Diane? Are you still there? What's the reference? Name of the mother? Maybe you made a mistake inputting the date."

"No, it's not that. I didn't write it up yet."

This time Belinda doesn't say anything. She clears her throat with such powerful passive aggression that Diane shivers.

Diane goes on, "I've got the notes. Handwritten. I just . . ."

"Where are you?"

"It might not be the same people. I mean, this was just a lost child, not anything that needed our attention. The woman I saw was genuine. It was a genuine mistake. I was sure."

"It is the same woman. The local police officers who were attending have already given a name and the description matches the person they're looking for. They said they left it to you to deal with the details."

"I did deal with it as far as I thought was appropriate. I was sure it didn't require intervention. At the time. She seemed really normal. I didn't think . . . it can't be her. They must have made a mistake. Maybe there were two missing child incidents?"

"Oh, and two Diane Rathbones, I suppose? They've got your name in their report. They want to see yours. To cross-reference the details."

"What's it got to do with the man they found in Sheffield? I don't see how it can be connected."

Diane's head feels like it is being compressed in a vise. The cold she's had coming for days has laid itself down on her like a wet blanket over her face. She blows her nose, and a palmful of green snot collects in the tissue, some of it escaping and running down the heel of her hand. She wipes it up best she can. She feels like crying, but she knows she won't; it's just that she always feels like crying when she's talking to Belinda.

Belinda says, "I don't need to tell you how badly you have screwed this up, Diane. You need to go into the office now and write up what you can, and explain to the police why your report is dated two days late."

The phone goes dead.

When she arrives at the office, Belinda is waiting, arms folded, bum perched on Diane's desk. She is wearing a holly-green velvet dress with a silver tinsel trim around the bottom, but her face is far from festive.

"That DS is coming over to see you. She'll be here in about an hour."

Diane nods. "I'll be ready."

"What were you thinking, Diane?"

"I was trying to see the good in people, alright? I'm always judging people, playing God with their lives. I just wanted to let everyone forget about it and get on with their day. How was I supposed to know she'd . . . done whatever it is she's supposed to have done? I can't know everything, can I?"

Belinda narrows her eyes.

"How long have you been in this job?"

"Sixteen years. Give or take. Why?"

"What made you think you didn't need to follow procedure in this case?"

I just couldn't face it, thinks Diane. *The forms, the grief, the mother's inevitable protest. I wanted to be the good guy, for a change.* That child was happy—she was sure of it. Absolutely certain.

"I decided there was no need for intervention. So the procedure was irrelevant. That's all."

Belinda's voice is low and dark. It cuts like tiny knives. "The procedure was irrelevant? Not even an incident form, a statement from the mother?"

Hearing Belinda say it, she realizes how very unprofessional it sounds. She sinks into her chair and rests her arms on the desk, allows her head to droop momentarily.

"I'm not very well, Belinda." It comes out whiny, like a child declaring that she has a tummy-ache.

The other woman snorts, implying that Diane is pathetic. *Fair enough,* thinks Diane; *what kind of an excuse is that, for a grown-up?*

"Well, I hope you have the contact details at the very least."

Diane presses a tissue to her streaming nose. "Of course. I was going to pass them on to the service in Sheffield when I had time."

"I suppose that's something. Let me see."

Belinda holds out her hand for the note, then takes it over to her desk. She types for a few seconds.

"Huh. Fake address. Haven't you checked it?"

"No, I told you. I've been snowed under."

"Fake name too, I'll bet."

Diane's head throbs. She wonders again if it is too soon for another painkiller.

22

NOW
Joanna
Sunday, December 23

O N THE MOTORWAY, Joanna mused on the particular tragedy of this year's Christmas, trying to look at the positives. Yes, Ruby had gone AWOL from their lives, and at this time of year it hurt more than usual. She'd been dreading Christmas Day without Ruby, the empty spot at the table sure to bring back memories of the fight the previous year. Marianne would be drunk as usual, Dad would be struggling to keep up the pretense as usual. Jo had hoped that the day after the fight, when Marianne sobered up and learned what her words and actions had brought about, she might seek help in earnest. Instead, she'd sunk further, had progressed from being drunk almost every day to being drunk every day without fail, allowing herself to pour the first measure a fraction earlier each time. Joanna found it hard not to let her anger toward her mother show; Whenever they were together, Jo fantasized about grabbing Marianne's frail shoulders and shaking her back to sobriety. So, on the upside, it was a relief to have an excuse to duck out.

Atkinson, in the passenger seat, sighed dramatically, breaking Harper's train of thought.

"Honestly, if people could just choose to try to top each other any other week, it would really help my personal life."

"Ah, she at home is not happy, I take it?"

"She's not. And, I was going to . . . never mind."

"You were going to what?"

"Oh, it's just— I bought a ring."

Without taking her eyes off the road, Jo let out a little whoop of joy, leaned over and slapped Atkinson on the knee. "Congratulations!"

"I haven't actually asked her yet—don't jinx it."

"Mate, she will say yes. I'm really happy for you."

"Well, we'll see, won't we?"

"How could she not?"

"If you get me home before Christmas is over completely, then there might be a chance. A slim chance."

Harper laughed, assuming he was joking. Atkinson grimaced and looked out the window at the traffic.

Whatever Felicia ended up saying to Steve in response to his proposal, it was unlikely to go as badly as it had for Joanna the previous morning. He'd planned it, for a start, bought a ring. He actually wanted to get married too, wasn't just throwing it out as a pathetic attempt to hold onto something he wasn't even sure was the right thing. Jo still didn't know where Amy had gone, though she planned to try to find out later, to make sure things were okay between them. This morning, after a starfish sleep and a quick series of hill sprints, she had returned her road bike to its familiar place in the hallway, where the stacks of high-heeled shoes had been until very recently. The feeling was bittersweet.

Grimsby was suitably named. Although it was on the coast, the industrial town wasn't a typical tourist destination, dominated as it was by the fisheries and the seafood processing factories. It didn't look good, it didn't smell good. Cleethorpes, a couple of miles south, with its famous beaches, was the place people were drawn to, but the bigger town of Grimsby was where the police and Social Services were based. Much of the older housing stock appeared neglected, and as they got closer to the center, the sky turned from gray to muddy brown with approaching rain.

So much for a white Christmas, thought Harper, turning up the radio for a bit of festive cheer in the face of Atkinson's persistent scrooge-like countenance.

They parked on the street outside the concrete-and-glass municipal building where Social Services was housed, and were soon shown into an interview room by a woman in an ill-fitting suit who said her name was Belinda Sumpter.

"I spoke to you on the phone, didn't I?" said Jo.

"That's right. Diane's the one who dealt with the case in question. She won't be long. She's just locating her notes. I'll let her know you're here."

They followed Belinda past the main office, a large room with about fifteen desk booths. Only one of the booths was occupied, by a sweaty-looking woman, typing furiously. A few minutes later, very apologetic, she appeared at the door, clutching a sheaf of printouts.

The social worker looked absolutely fucking terrible. Red nose, streaming eyes, skin almost gray.

"Thanks for making the time to see us. Have a seat. You know why we're here?"

Diane nodded.

"Just before we start, are you feeling okay?"

Diane tried to smile. Her eyes were small and red-rimmed. She withdrew a lump of damp tissue from her handbag, started trying to straighten it out. "I've got a bit of a cold, that's all."

Joanna took out some hand sanitizer and squeezed a blob into her palm, rubbed her hands together, feeling the alcohol evaporate, relaxing slightly as she imagined all those germs dying. The last thing she needed was to get ill herself. Beside her, Atkinson drew out a package of tissues and handed Diane a fresh one.

"Thanks, love." There followed a great wet nose-blowing.

Jo said, "Yesterday, my officers entered the apartment of a man called Gregor Franks, who lives in the New Park estate over in Sheffield. He's been quite badly injured and taken to hospital, and has yet to regain consciousness. We're trying to trace a woman who we suspect may be connected to the victim. She's traveling with a child. I believe, on Friday, you attended an incident along with some local officers, in which a woman and child of the right age were detained."

"Initially, they were detained," said Diane. "It seemed to me that there wasn't a problem, so they were allowed to be on their way."

Jo nodded. "Just to confirm the details, what were their names?"

"The mother was called Constance Douglas. The girl was called Leonie Douglas."

Atkinson made a note. "Tell us what happened. From the beginning."

"We had an emergency call from the police about a lone child, a toddler, who'd been found on the seafront. A shopkeeper had opened his door, and she'd just wandered in. No adult to be seen anywhere nearby, and it was freezing. I went there expecting to do an emergency referral, but by the time I got there, the mother had turned up."

"What did she say?"

"She explained that she'd lost sight of the child, who was a bolter, always running off. She said she'd been looking for her everywhere. It seemed fine. Genuine mistake. Tragedy averted." Diane did a small, unconvincing "ha ha." Both police officers regarded her with stony faces.

Atkinson said, "Did she say why she hadn't called the police? The nine-nine-nine was from the shopkeeper."

"She said she'd been frantically searching. And it hadn't been that long either. The police must have gotten there very quickly."

Harper checked her notes. "Less than three minutes from the call to when the first officer arrived on scene. Impressive. I guess sometimes you're in the right place at the right time."

Diane threw her hands in the air. "Well, there you go. If the mother hadn't found her when she did, she most probably would have called nine-nine-nine. But she did find her, and she would have done so whether the police had been involved or not. If the shopkeeper had waited a minute or so more, the situation would have resolved itself. But there was no harm done."

Jo thought that Diane Rathbone's body language seemed overly defensive. She glanced at Atkinson, who gave a bland smile. To Joanna, his eyes conveyed his skepticism.

"What did you put in the report?" he said. "Will there be any follow-up?"

"I was going to hand the details to Sheffield Social Service so that they could do a routine check in six weeks' time."

"You were going to? You didn't do it already? How long does it usually take?"

There was a tight pause. "I've got a lot on. As you can imagine. I was going to do it, and then it was the weekend, so it was going to have to wait until tomorrow. And like I said, it wasn't a priority."

"Was there anything on your database about them, the mother or the child? Any previous contact with Social Services?" asked Joanna.

Diane pursed her lips. "I didn't check."

"Oh?"

The social worker gave Jo a hard glare. "I had to remove three children from their mother this morning. Two days before Christmas. Do you know what that feels like, Detective Sergeant?"

Joanna's voice was calm and pleasant when she said, "Have you checked now?"

Diane mumbled something incoherent.

"What's that?"

"I said, Belinda did. Turns out the address the woman gave me was a false address."

Harper left a pointed pause. She was starting to get very slightly annoyed by Diane Rathbone. "What I don't understand, from what you're telling me, is why you decided it was nothing to worry about. What was it about Constance Douglas that made you think she wasn't a risk to the child? She'd lost her, for a good amount of time, and not thought to call for help."

"I had to make a judgment call. I assumed she just wasn't thinking."

Jo had to assume that Diane wasn't thinking either. She should have known better. As for suggesting the shopkeeper ought to have waited to call 999, no social worker worth their salt would recommend a delay in alerting the authorities if a child was found alone on the street in wintery conditions. The cold Diane was suffering from must have been brewing for days; perhaps it had skewed her judgment.

"Okay, Diane. Let's see if we can start again. Our victim is named Gregor Franks, and there's a possibility that he is the father of the child. Let's assume that Leonie is the child's real first name. Can we try searching for the name Leonie Franks on the Social Services database? And maybe Constance Franks? Also, this address?" She gave Diane a piece of paper with Gregor's address on it. Then she turned to Atkinson. "Can you . . ."

He was already opening his laptop. "I'll search for the names Leonie and Constance Douglas on the police database, boss, right away."

A few minutes later, they had each drawn a blank.

"So. Constance Douglas doesn't appear on the Social Services database. Nor Constance Franks, nor Leonie Douglas or Leonie Franks."

Jo had to assume from now on that all the names were false. They were looking for an invisible mother and an invisible child.

"But she seemed so normal," said Diane. "She seemed so—and I know this sounds terrible—but she was middle class. I don't see many like that. Very nice, you know?"

Jo squinted at Diane. The woman had lost all sense of perspective. She wouldn't be surprised if this case led to an internal investigation by the service, and even this person's suspension. That might not be such a bad thing for the vulnerable children of Grimsby. Diane could do with a rest, at the very least. She had the word *burnout* written all over her.

"There's one more thing we need you to help us with. I have a CCTV image of Constance in Sheffield train station on her way to Cleethorpes. Then the cameras catch her again leaving the Cleethorpes station, but we can't find her returning or getting on a train. She certainly never came back to Sheffield. We need to know where she went."

"That doesn't make any sense. I know there's a camera opposite the entrance."

"We didn't pick her up after she got off the train at Cleethorpes."

"So, she never got on the train? She's still in Cleethorpes?"

"Possibly. Or she was covering her face when she went past the cameras. I've got an officer scouring the footage at the moment, but it's a slow process. Here's the image we have of her."

She showed Diane the image on the police tablet. There was the woman, her hood pulled up, dark hair showing. Those haunted eyes. Diane's face creased in confusion.

"That's not her. That's not the woman I spoke to. I knew it. I knew there had to be a mix-up."

"That's not Constance?"

"No. The woman I talked to wasn't as thin. She had different hair. Let me see it again."

Harper watched as, if it were possible, even more color drained from Diane's face.

"Oh no. How can that . . ."

"What is it?"

"That, without a doubt, is not the same woman I spoke to on Tuesday. But it's the same child. That's Leonie."

"What?"

They all stared at the screen.

"What does this mean?" said Atkinson.

"It means," said Jo, "that whoever's got Leonie, it isn't the same woman who left the New Park Estate on Tuesday, carrying her."

"So, the woman I spoke to . . . wasn't her mother? Or was her mother? If . . . then . . . so who is this?" Diane grabbed her own head as if she was in sudden pain. Harper thought, *Yup, investigation, suspension.*

"Could have been anyone," said Joanna. "And who knows where the real Constance has gone. If this woman is even really called Constance. Meanwhile, there's a seriously injured man lying comatose in a hospital bed, whose child may have been abducted."

Joanna looked again at the image on the tablet. An invisible child, no records, no way of knowing that she even exists, except for this bit of footage. *Well,* thought Jo, *she's not invisible to me.*

She turned to Atkinson. "We can do facial recognition with Leonie. We'll be able to track her that way and find out where she's gone, and who with. Come on."

They stood up and started to leave the room.

"Wait," said Diane. "Let me see it one more time."

Harper handed over the tablet.

"So strange," said Diane.

"What is?" asked Harper.

"This woman, she's wearing exactly the same clothes as the woman I spoke to."

"Really?"

"Yes, and she had the same bag, that changing bag."

Very odd indeed, thought Jo.

"There is one difference, though."

"What's that?"

"That leather hold-all thing she's got. I never saw that."

When they zoomed in, the item was clear to see. Strange that they hadn't noticed it before, wrapped across the woman's body exactly like a papoose. In the footage, while she held tightly on to the child with both arms, at all times one hand possessively gripped the edge of this papoose as if it contained something equally as precious.

23

THEN
Ruby
November

"MAMMA BEE!"

Ruby lived for the sound of the little feet padding down the hallway in her direction. The baby had progressed this week, from bum-shuffling to running in a matter of days. Ruby wasn't worried about her development anymore; she'd looked it up. Sometimes kids didn't walk until they were two, sometimes they talked nonstop from before the age of one. Leonie was a child of extremes, but she certainly progressing within the wide range of "normal." It was like a miracle; you could almost watch this person growing in real time.

"Look, Mamma Bee, got socks!" Leonie pulled her socks off, one by one. "Here go!"

"Thank you, honey." As Ruby bent to take the socks, she caught an unmistakable odor coming from Leonie. "Hey, you need a change, baby?" Ruby picked her up and took her through to the changing table in the bathroom. She was getting to be quite the expert at nappies and feeding and all the other things she'd been helping with recently. She pulled up the little girl's tights and set her back on her feet, let her lead the way through the door to where her mother was.

"All clean!" Leonie declared, thundering into the space, heading straight for the toy box.

In the living room, Constance was curled on the couch in her usual spot. Ruby tried to discreetly gauge how unfocused she was today, how vague she seemed, how distant. Sometimes it was as if the other woman couldn't keep her eyes open. Other times she didn't seem to be aware that Ruby was even there until she started playing her violin. Then, there were good days.

"Hi, Constance."

It was a good day. Constance smiled. "Hi, Bee." Her eyes drifted across to the seascape, but they came right back to Ruby.

Gregor leaned in the kitchen doorway, arms crossed, still in his yoga pants. The two of them had fallen into an almost easy friendship, punctuated with occasionally awkward moments when they accidentally touched, or she caught him gazing at her for a little too long. What had passed between them hadn't gone away, but she thought they'd found a balance and that it was worth making the effort to keep it steady.

"Moosic, Mamma Bee. Pleeeease." Leonie was tugging Ruby's violin case toward her so that she'd play all the tunes Leonie loved to dance to. And Ruby loved to see it, the little hips swaying from side to side, arms pumping. Pure joy. She played "Molly Malone," and Leonie's favorite, "A Fox Went Out on a Chilly Night," bending the notes just like on the old American bluegrass version she knew so well.

"I know a song," said Constance.

She started to sing, a haunting melody, sad and moving.

Ionn da, ionn do ion da, od-ar, da.

It made Ruby think of the ocean and of the night sky, deep and mysterious. After a few times round, she joined in with her violin. Leonie swayed to the slow beat. Gregor didn't say anything. His face was strangely blank.

"Beautiful," said Ruby. "What's it called?"

"It's hard to translate," said Constance. "It's a cry of joy. 'The Seal Woman's Joy'? We sing it to each other. I mean, back home they do. They did."

Just then, Leonie tripped over her feet and fell, her head catching the corner of one of the wooden bricks. Constance sprang from the couch in an instant and scooped up the little girl, whose face was contorted with pain. Leonie inhaled for a few long seconds, then started to cry. Or she looked as if she was crying, but she wasn't making any sound.

"Did you hurt yourself, baby? Don't cry," said Constance. A lump was forming on Leonie's head. She continued to cry, but the only noise coming out between the girl's jerky inhalations was a high wheeze, like air escaping from a puncture.

"I'll get an ice pack." Gregor went to the kitchen.

"What's wrong with her?" Ruby whispered to Constance. "Why is she silent? Is she choking?"

"This is how she cries. Always. Barely a sound."

"But that's not normal. You know that, right?"

A frown creased Constance's forehead as she stroked Leonie's hair. She tipped her head toward the kitchen. "He doesn't like noise."

"Dammit," said Gregor, from the other room. "No ice."

Ruby thought she saw Leonie's small body tense up at the sound of his voice. She curled closer to her mother, became very still.

"Hey, baby," said Ruby, touching Leonie's arm. She flinched, and Ruby drew away. "Daddy's not angry with you—don't worry."

Constance's face was solemn, her eyes intense as she gazed at Ruby over her daughter's head.

By the time Gregor returned with a pack of frozen peas wrapped in a towel, Leonie had stopped the silent crying. She wriggled to be let down, had apparently forgotten that she'd even hurt herself, despite the half egg protruding from her forehead. Constance tried to put the cold pack on her forehead, but the child batted it away and toddled off, bump and all, to carry on playing as if nothing had happened.

"So brave," said Gregor. "That's my girl."

Later he walked Ruby to the door. "Thanks for tonight. You're a good friend to us."

"It's no trouble. I love coming over. And that song—wow. It's like a gift every time she teaches me something new."

Their eyes met, and Ruby was suddenly aware that they were alone together. Gregor shuffled his feet awkwardly. "Well, I'll see you next time, then."

Ruby said, "I wanted to ask you . . ."

"She's been better recently, Constance. Don't you think so?"

Ruby wasn't sure she agreed, in general. "She's better today, sure. But Gregor, when Leonie was crying . . ."

"Oh, that. I've gotten used to it now. She's not like other kids, right? You don't need earplugs." He laughed a little, then stopped when he realized she was serious.

"But why is she like that? Is there something wrong with her? Did you teach her not to cry?"

Gregor's eyes darkened. "And how do you imagine I would teach a baby not to cry, precisely?"

"Well, I don't know, but Constance said—"

He hissed at her, angry now. "Constance said? Didn't I explain what's going on with her? You can't trust anything she says. The woman's delusional."

"Gregor, let go—you're hurting me."

He looked down at where he'd grabbed her upper arm and immediately released her. Mouth open, he stared at his hand like he didn't recognize it.

"Ruby, I'm so sorry, I didn't mean . . ."

She backed away from him, rubbing her arm, a bruise forming. Then she looked at his face and saw that he was about to cry.

"It's fine," she said, though despite the pity she felt for him, it was not. "No harm done."

"Are you sure? Oh god, I don't know why I did that. Seriously, I'm really sorry. Did I hurt you?"

He searched her face, but she couldn't quite meet his eye. "Not really."

"I'm such an idiot. Let me see . . ."

She drew farther away, toward the door, as he reached out to try to touch her. "No, honestly, I'm okay. But I should go, anyway."

"Don't—I mean, you can leave, of course you can. And I would understand if you didn't want to come back after what I just did."

A tear slid from his eye. He hung his head, shoulders slumped.

"I'm sorry too," said Ruby. Though for what, she wasn't entirely sure.

CHAPTER

24

JOANNA GATHERED THE team together in the incident room. She brought up a grainy image, an enlarged section from the train station CCTV, of the little girl wearing her pink bobble hat.

"Priority number one is safeguarding this child. Leonie, assuming that's her real name, is not registered with any midwife or health visitor team, nor with Social Services or the National Health Services. Also, although we strongly believe that Leonie and her mother live or have lived recently in Gregor Franks's apartment, neither the electoral roll or the council tax listing show anyone apart from Gregor at the address. As for the mother, all we have so far is this image." She pointed to the photo from the station CCTV in Sheffield of the woman with dark hair buying a ticket.

"And this is where it gets interesting. Whoever this person is, it's not the same person who was allowed to leave with the child on Friday night. This is the reason facial recognition software didn't track where she went after she returned to the station, because she never did."

One of the constables said, "I don't understand."

"I can't explain it either, Jade, but these are the facts we're working with."

Harper stuck a silhouette of a woman's face next to the picture of the woman at the train station. It was a drawing, meant to represent the woman they didn't have an image of yet. It had a white question mark in the center.

"Two different women, one name: Constance. I want to know, firstly, what happened to this one, the one who had the child first of all. And secondly"—she pointed to the silhouette—"who is this one, what does she look like, and where is she now? She was the one last seen with the child, and therefore she's the one we need to track as a priority. Any update on the media shout-out? Any leads?"

Clive said, "We haven't had any useful calls from the public yet after the news bulletin. Maybe we should do another one."

A young man knocked and was waved into the room. Dressed in civvies, tall and lanky, he looked like a member of the tech department, which was exactly what he was. "Jo?"

"Yes, Eddie?"

"We found her. The second one."

"Good work," said Harper. "From the Cleethorpes station cameras?"

"Yes. We loaded Leonie's face into the software, and it pinged straight away. She might have told the Social that she was going back to Sheffield, but from the time code on the ticket office camera, you can see that she actually bought a ticket to Edinburgh."

She's running, thought Joanna, and held out her hand for the A4 printout. When she looked at the photo, she immediately wanted to throw up. She tried not to react outwardly in any way, not in front of all these officers.

"I have a bigger image with more detail," said Eddie. "This one is a close-up of the face, but in the wider image she's waiting on the station platform, holding the child."

"I think I need to see that one, if you don't mind." Even Joanna could tell that her voice was uncharacteristically soft.

Eddie said, "Sure, not a problem. Give me a few minutes." He left the room.

How can it be her? thought Jo as she turned slowly toward the whiteboard, still holding the image in both hands. It didn't make any sense.

Someone cleared their throat, and she realized she hadn't said anything for a weirdly long time.

"Um," she said, "this is our second person of interest. So." She pinned the image up and took down the question-mark silhouette. As she faced the room, thirty inquisitive pairs of eyes studied her, every one trained to spot a liar. Joanna rubbed her palms together uncertainly. What did she just do? Why didn't she say anything? It wasn't if she could keep the truth from them forever. She needed to tell them. Now.

"That's it for now, folks. Get to work."

Chairs scraped as they were pushed back and everyone got up to leave. Atkinson was staring at her. He waited until the room was clear before he spoke.

"You okay, boss?" he asked. "You look like you've seen a ghost."

For a second she considered telling him. In the corner of her eye, she could see Ruby staring down at them from the board, so much older than she'd seemed the last time Joanna had seen her. Apart from evident anxiety, Ruby's face was closed, expression indecipherable; holding on to her secrets, as always.

"Oh, nothing," said Jo. "I mean yes, fine. Sorry. I've just got a bit of . . . indigestion. I think I need a drink of water." She pushed past him and out of the room before he could respond.

In the bathroom, she splashed water on her face and stared at herself in the mirror. She was pale as paper; her hands shook as she retied her blonde hair into its topknot. When she reached into her pocket for a tissue, her fingers touched the box containing the silver ring she'd been carrying around since Ruby's birthday, that she hadn't sent, that she'd hoped she would be able to give to Ruby in person. She took it out, slipped the tip of her finger inside it to feel the engraved inscription. Not simply a birthday present, the ring was an apology, a promise, and an olive branch, supposed to be the first step in healing the rift between them. She turned the ring in the light and the letters glinted. *Filia mea et soror mea et cor meum:* my sister, my daughter, my heart.

25

NOW
The Injured Man
Dreams

H E HEARS THE faint slap-slap of a spinning rope, a pair of feet taking off and landing, over and over. The dark place has transformed into a hospital room, but it's not the muted white and gray tones of a normal hospital. The walls have no windows or doors, are twice as high as they should be, and they glow with lurid menace. The whole scene is wonky, oversaturated with color. There is a girl in the corner, skipping.

> *Cinderella, dressed in yella,*
> *Went upstairs to kiss a fella*
> *By mistake, she kissed a snake*
> *How many doctors will it take?*
> *One, two, three, four.*

She's holding up her fingers with the numbers. When she gets to number four, the wooden handle falls from her hand. She comes closer, her bare and toughened feet shuffling along the vinyl, the rope trailing behind her. The man tries to move, to sit up, and finds that he cannot. The girl seems to know that he is trapped, a fly in her web. It's a dream, he tells himself, and she's been conjured by his imagination. Perhaps if he shuts his eyes, when he opens them, she'll be gone. He shuts his eyes tight and waits.

When he opens his eyes, she's right up in his face. He jumps, hard, and lets out a scream. All he sees is her wide, white-and-blue eyes, her grinning mouth, the black holes of her nostrils, her fringe hanging down. He smells her breath, sweet and foul with rot, but he can't turn his face away. She is sitting astride his chest, crouching there like an evil little imp. He tries to scream again, to make her move. But either she can't hear him, or she doesn't care.

Get off me get off help me someone please help.

The grin grows slowly on her face as she sits up and regards him with a cold kind of interest, as if he is a specimen that she has collected. The fact that he's sure this is happening inside his head is no comfort. There's no escape. He is trapped there with this malevolent girl, who he thinks he knows and is sure hates him, and he can't move or speak or get away, and it's not fair—why is this happening to him?

Then, the girl lifts her arm and fans out her fingers over his face. The pinkie is missing, cleaved off at the base. He remembers then who she is and how he knows her, and the knowledge of it makes him freeze with dread. He looks again, to make sure, but there's no mistake. It's his sister, Dora. She died in 1997, aged eight. He remembers, as a teenager, feeling angry with her because after she died, he was the only one there to help on the farm. Their parents barely spoke to him again unless it was to talk about the search for his sister. They never found the body, and yet here she is.

A drop of blood from the stump of the girl's little finger falls in his open eye, turning half of the world a grisly red. He screams. He fades out.

CHAPTER

26

NOW
Joanna
Sunday, December 23

Eddie looked at her over the top of his thin-framed spectacles. "I got the image you wanted."

This time, when he handed it over, she was ready. Atkinson was watching her carefully. She shot him a look, a kind of what-are-you-looking-at-exactly?, and he shifted his eyes away, pretended he hadn't been watching.

Briskly, she pinned up the print. There was her baby girl, without question. The picture captured the way she held herself, her limbs and body shape, the way she inclined her head. Ruby's form was as individual to her as a fingerprint and as familiar to Joanna as her own face in the mirror.

"This is great, Eddie—thanks."

In the full-length image, Ruby was wearing the exact same clothes as the other woman had been: a long, hooded parka and knee-high boots. The jacket had a thin fur trim on the hood, the boots had a low heel. What was Ruby doing? Who was the other woman? And the most important question of all: Where the hell were they now?

"I don't get it," said Atkinson. "Why did they wear the same outfit?"

"They want to look the same," said Joanna.

"Well, obviously, but—"

"Maybe it's so that if they get seen, witnesses only think there's one of them," said Eddie.

"Hmm," said Atkinson, "Not going to work in the age of CCTV, though, is it?"

"Not for long, no. But maybe they didn't think they would be scrutinized this closely," said Eddie.

"Maybe," said Joanna, almost to herself, "when they planned this, they weren't thinking of trying to avoid the police. Maybe it was a game."

"Not much fun, though, really," said Steve.

She thought of Ruby's voice on the phone when she said she'd met some new friends. The way she sounded when she said the word *complicated*. The case was certainly that: she couldn't get a sense of what they were doing, what or who they were running from or to.

No one spoke for a minute, their eyes on the photographs.

Atkinson pointed at the most recent image. "What are we calling this one?"

Ruby appeared in her mouth like a prayer. "B," said Jo, swallowing the first part of the name. "Constance B, because she was the second one we found. The other one is Constance A. Until we know better."

"Better than Jane Doe. Suppose neither are called Constance?"

One of them definitely isn't, thought Harper, but she said, "That's a possibility. But it's such an unusual choice for a pseudonym, don't you think? It must have some significance. Good to keep the name at the front of our minds."

"We've been scouring the available CCTV, like you asked," said Eddie. "We tracked B to where she started her journey to Cleethorpes. She came from Sheffield, was caught on the same camera as Constance A, but a couple of hours earlier."

He showed her another image of Ruby, head down into the wind, hands thrust in pockets, waiting at the tram stop near the

New Park for the next one to take her to the interchange. She could just be identified in profile. She seemed cold, vulnerable. Joanna thought she looked lonely. What had she gotten herself into?

Atkinson looked at the data on the sheet of paper Eddie had given him. "So, Constance B gets a train to Lincoln, where she waits for a connection to Grimsby that is due to get in at 15:34."

"Right."

"You know, she could easily be the one who attacked Gregor Franks."

"No, I don't think so," said Harper.

"Why not? There's no evidence to say otherwise. It would make more sense, actually, for it to be her, because Constance A had a kid to look after, which could be considered a deterrent. Maybe Constance B did him in, then a couple of hours later Constance A went round to his place and found him like that."

"We don't even know if B was in Gregor's flat. She could have come from a different neighborhood. We have her on camera at the tram stop, but not in the actual estate, correct?"

"Yes," said Eddie, "but . . ."

"Whereas," she said, turning to face him, her face a picture of calm, "we do have a positive ID for Constance A, from the neighbor. A was in the building. Not B."

Atkinson said, "The neighbor didn't ID Constance A, boss. She heard someone say the word *Leonie*, and that was days before the attack. Hardly hard evidence. She never *saw* either of them. She couldn't have."

"Well, no, but A is the one who carried the child from the block. The neighbor might not have seen her with Leonie, but the camera on the estate did. And A is the one we have on camera getting the train at the later time. All we have on B, the lighter-haired one, is footage of her at the tram stop, showing that she's wearing similar clothes and heading for the same place, albeit by a completely different route."

"They're working together," said Atkinson. "The outfits prove it. The lighter-haired one is a person of interest and should be a potential suspect. For the assault and for child abduction. She was in the right place for the assault, and she definitely took that child. But we don't know why."

"The outfits prove nothing. And, yes, she took the child. Maybe it's her child," said Harper, trying to appear reasonable but sounding snippier than she would have liked, and surprising even herself at what she was suggesting. There was no way it was Ruby's child.

"Hang on, she can't belong to both of them. You were the one who prioritized the kid as high risk, boss, based on the assumption that it wasn't B's child. I thought that was still the working theory? Unless there's something you're not telling me?"

"Of course not," she said, reminding herself to stay calm, wondering again if it was time to come clean. No, not now, not with Eddie in the room. "I'm just tired—sorry. Not much sleep last night. You're absolutely right, it could have been either or both of them. Or neither. We'll stick to the working theory. Until more evidence presents itself."

She couldn't conceive of Ruby hurting anyone. Certainly not doing something like what had happened to Franks. But then, did she really know Ruby at all? She hadn't seen her for so long. What the hell *was* she doing with that child?

"So," said Harper, "we know the movements of Constance B, after she left Sheffield and up to the point where she gets on the Edinburgh train with the kid. What about Constance A?"

"After she left the New Park in the afternoon, she got a direct train, with the girl, from Sheffield to Cleethorpes. It stopped at Grimsby at 15:37," said Eddie. "I'm wondering if they were supposed to meet up at that point and travel to Cleethorpes together. Or if A was going to hand the kid over to B and travel to Cleethorpes alone."

"B only had a ticket to Grimsby, which backs up that theory," said Atkinson. "She had to buy another ticket to get to Cleethorpes. I suggest the plan didn't take into account the trains being delayed. Looks to me like the rendezvous should have happened at Grimsby station, and would have if B's train had been on time."

"I still don't get why A would abandon the kid, though," said Eddie. "Why couldn't she have just waited a few more minutes if she was planning to hand her over to B all along?"

"I found footage of what happened at the seafront," said Eddie. "Watch this." He set a laptop on the table in front of them.

The woman in the image was waiting with the child. The camera picture was hazy, all in shades of green, darkening as the light drained from the day. Shot from above, both figures were foreshortened, but it was definitely the same pair that had traveled from Sheffield.

"They're there for quite a while. I'll forward it a bit."

The sped-up Constance kept glancing at her wristwatch and staring off-camera in the direction of the sea. "She must be waiting for B," said Jo. "But what's she planning to do?"

"You'll see," said Eddie.

On the screen, Constance held the little girl close, pressing her face into Leonie's hair. Then she put the child down, took a step away. Looked back at the little girl. Her hand went to her mouth.

Eddie said, "She's hesitating. She doesn't want to do it."

"Do what?" said Atkinson.

Then the child toddled toward a shop window, and at the same time the woman disappeared from the shot.

"Where's she gone?"

"I can slow it down slightly. Hang on."

The split second in which the woman disappeared was like watching a sprinter shooting out of the blocks. One last look at the kid and she crouched, then ran in the direction of the sea.

"Is there no camera that covers the beach?"

Eddie shook his head no.

Atkinson said, "So she's running toward the water, right? For what? To drown herself?"

"What else could it be?" asked Eddie.

"Are we thinking that A wanted to kill herself, and B was trying to help her do it?"

Joanna said, "B would never do that." She blurted it, too fast and too loud. Both of the men looked at her, baffled. "I mean, the evidence doesn't point to that. It makes no sense for that to be the reason. And let's say she did go into the water to drown herself. There would be a body washed up by now."

"Not necessarily," said Atkinson. "It can take days, months, years. If she caught a riptide, then the body might never wash up." He gave her a look that said, *"Are you feeling okay?"*

"What we do know for sure," said Eddie, "is that after this, A isn't seen again on any cameras we can find. She ran in the direction of the sea. And she never came back."

They paused for a second to take this in.

"What about B?" said Jo. "You say she got on a train to Edinburgh. Can we track her from there?"

Eddie said, "We're still looking. I'll let you know the moment I find something."

After Eddie left the room, Atkinson and Harper studied the laptop screen, where the child on camera, now completely alone, was fiddling with something on the ground. "What is that?" said Jo.

"Her handbag. That's what the kid was found with."

"Where is it now?"

"B has it. The police gave it to her, assumed it belonged to her. But Constance A is the one who carried it to the seafront."

Harper shook her head. "I can't understand how they missed that. I've read the report. B told the social worker that the kid must have run off carrying it. That child can barely pick it up."

"If she'd stopped B then, or simply asked a few more questions, none of this would be happening."

"That's a bit harsh, boss. Gregor Franks would still have been floating unconscious in his bath, whether or not they'd been apprehended at that point by Social Services."

Harper could feel her professionalism slipping. She realized she hadn't been considering the terrible attack on Franks; she was only thinking about Ruby, about the trouble she was in and how she might be helped to get out of it. She told herself to focus on the task at hand. It shouldn't have mattered that she had connections to any person in this case; she should be able to do her job without prejudice, for the sake of equal justice for all. But at the same time, she already knew what she was going to do, and it wasn't the most sensible plan.

She turned to Atkinson. "We need to go and search the beach at Cleethorpes. See if there's anything we've missed."

"Okay, let's go."

"You go. Take Jade if you like. I've got a few things to do. Let me know what you find."

Atkinson stood up, but he didn't immediately leave the room.

"Boss, I just wanted to make sure . . ."

"What?"

"There's definitely nothing you're not telling me?"

"Don't be silly, Steve. On you go now." She smiled tightly as she gathered up her stuff before pushing past him, out of the room.

27

THEN
Ruby
December

Now that she had a spare key, Ruby had developed a technique of opening the door to the flat stealthily, like a burglar, making almost no sound. Then, when Leonie caught sight of her, she was even more delighted. Gregor usually knew she was there, of course, because of the motion sensors on the stairs. Today, it seemed he'd missed his phone alerting him to her approach. He and Constance were arguing.

Silently, she closed the front door behind her and stood in the hallway, listening. She reached inside her bag for the fruit snack she'd brought with her, the organic kind that Leonie loved, but her hand stopped when she heard his voice.

Gregor sounded agitated.

"She has everything she needs, right here. Why would you want to put her in danger like that?"

"It's not dangerous out there," said Constance. "It's a playpark. She should be allowed to play, like the other children."

"If people around here see her, they'll start to ask questions. And that can only end one way, with Leonie being taken away."

"But she's our daughter. Why would anyone take her away from us?"

"We've been through this. They won't care about that. They'll say we've been neglectful. They'll ask for birth certificates, for proof of residency. Then, when you can't show them, you'll be thrown into a detention center and she'll be put with a foster family."

"That's not going to happen. Ruby knows how to be careful. Please, for Leonie if not for me. You don't want to take her yourself, fine. Let Ruby take her out. I'll stay here. It's not as if I can go very far, is it? Not without my coat."

"You realize how insane that makes you sound, don't you?"

Constance mumbled something that Ruby couldn't hear.

"I haven't got your fucking coat, for fuck's sake! If you want to leave, go ahead!"

"Gregor, please, you're hurting me. Leonie's upset—look at her."

"If she's upset, it's because of you, not me. You're ranting again. You're so indoctrinated, you know that? I wish you'd just let it go."

"I'm not going to let it go. I won't let anything go until you agree to let her go outside. I won't ever—"

There was the hard crack of a slap, skin on skin, then another. *He's hitting her.* Ruby froze.

A thudding sound, a person collapsing to the floor. Then silence. At once Ruby wanted to storm into the room and shout at him to stop, but at the same time she was fixed to the spot, praying the door to the living space would remain almost shut, that Gregor wouldn't come out now and find her, listening; that he wouldn't do to her what he was doing to Constance.

"She should be in fucking bed. Why is she still up? It's your fault she saw that. If you'd put her to bed, then she wouldn't have had to be here. You're a terrible mother. You made me do that, and you made her watch. You're sick. Maybe I should let the police know you're here—then I'd be rid of you. I'm sure they'd love to hear all about your weirdo relatives as well. How about it? They'd break that oddball cult up quick as you like, and prosecute half of them for all kinds of crimes. The child protection people would be over there like a shot. One phone call, that's all it would take."

A mumble that she couldn't hear.

"Oh, you want to stay, do you? Well, I'll think about it."

Ruby heard Leonie hiccup. She could imagine the anguish on her small face, the silent cry. So, this was the truth of the man. Why hadn't she seen it? Ruby's body trembled with the shock of it, and her cheeks burned with humiliation at how she'd been fooled.

"Shh." Constance's voice.

Ruby's hands formed fists.

Gregor sighed with irritation. "She'll never sleep now. I'll give her some tonic."

"No, Gregor, it's not for children."

"Oh, it's fine, I'll give her a little bit less than what you have."

"Really, I don't think you should—"

"Would you *shut up* with your *fucking whingeing?*"

Another slap.

"See what you made me do? When are you going to learn to go along with things? You always have to argue." Ruby heard him go through to the bathroom, the cabinet opening and shutting. When he returned, his voice had changed, softened slightly. "Here, baby, open wide, medicine for you."

"Please . . ."

"Well, hold her fucking head, would you? Hold her mouth open. Come *on.*"

There was a gurgling sound, and Leonie started to cough and splutter. Ruby needed to go in there, right now. But the fear gripped her, rooted her, even as the shame of doing nothing crept into her stomach.

"That was too much, Gregor. You said—"

"It's fine. She's spat most of it out on the carpet anyway, hasn't she? I'll have to clean that up now, won't I?"

Ruby hardly dared to breathe. Perhaps she ought to go outside and come in again, pretend she hadn't heard any of it. But that other part of her, the brave part, wanted to burst through the door and punch Gregor in the throat.

There was the sound of paper towels scrubbing on the rug.

"I'm sorry I shouted, baby." It was if a switch had been flipped. This was the voice of the Gregor she knew—gentle, considered.

"I'm sorry. I just get so angry when you ask me things that we can't do. It's for your safety, don't you see? This isn't easy for me either, having you both cooped up here the whole time. I'm trying as hard as I can to find a way she can go outside safely."

"But we could let her go out now, if it was with Ruby."

There was a pause then, in which Ruby silently begged Constance not to bring that up again, because of how angry he'd gotten the last time. But he didn't shout, only sighed. It seemed that the danger had passed, for now.

His voice was kind. "It's too risky. Some nosy old neighbor would make the connection between Ruby and this flat, and then the social worker would come sniffing around. We'd no longer be safe here. And as for the coat, I wish you'd let it go. There was never a coat. You were all but naked when I found you, drugged up on something, don't you remember? I told you before, love. You must have dreamed it. The coat doesn't keep you in here. Your mind does that."

His voice grew louder as he approached the door where Ruby was standing but it was too late to make any kind of move. He opened it and stopped dead.

"Oh," she said, "Hello." She tried to push the fear away, to look normal, not so panicked that her smile would seem fake. She could almost hear her heart pounding; perhaps he could too.

"Hello." He narrowed his eyes at her, patted his pockets for his phone but didn't find it. "How long have you been standing there?"

"Sorry, I just came in. Is everything alright?"

He pulled the door shut behind him, took her to one side, whispered in her ear, his breath moist against her skin. "She's ranting about that coat again. Will you be okay, do you think? I need to go out for a few hours. Can you keep Constance company, and make sure nothing happens? Not that it would. But just in case."

Her skin bristled in revulsion at the closeness. She wanted to push him away; only a primitive kind of self-preservation prevented her. "Sure."

"You can ring me if there's any need to."

"Do you think there will be?"

"I don't know. Maybe." He placed a gentle hand on each of her upper arms. She tried not to flinch away, not wanting him anywhere near her, not wanting him to know that was how she felt.

"I've been thinking, actually, that maybe you were right about treatment for Constance. Maybe it's too much for us to handle."

"You think she ought to see someone?" Ruby felt a small rush of hope then. If Constance could get to a doctor, maybe she could get away from Gregor.

"I found a residential treatment program that might be right for her. It's a commitment, though. She'd have to go away for a few weeks and wouldn't be allowed contact with us."

"Oh, I see. No contact at all? Not even with Leonie?" The hairs on her neck stood up.

He shook his head, the regret apparently genuine. His act was so convincing. "The therapy is quite intense, but what with her being as bad as she is now, I think it might be worth it." It was as if he were a different creature entirely from the cruel and violent man from moments ago.

"Where is it, this therapy place?"

"It's going to be hard for all of us, not to contact her. So, I think it's best I don't tell you."

She knew then, with a cold certainty, that if Constance went away, she wouldn't be coming back—he'd make sure of it. She felt as if her heart would pound out of her chest. "H-how long would she be gone?"

"Until she's better, I guess."

Ruby stared at him, trying to work out what he wanted her to say, how she ought to respond. If he could fake it, so could she. Outwardly, she managed to look relieved and hopeful. Inwardly, her guts churned with fear. "Okay," she said.

"But would you—I mean, if it came to it, if I can get her on the program—would you help me with the baby when she's away? You'd come to stay?"

So, that was the plan. With Constance gone, he'd need a replacement there, to do the bulk of the childcare. She pretended to consider it. "Just while she's away? I can do that, sure."

He grinned with relief. "Thank you. Seriously, you don't know how much that means to me. You're so good with Leonie. She loves you more than she loves me, I think."

Ruby forced herself to laugh, to show that she thought that was ridiculous. But it wasn't. It was the only true thing he'd said so far.

There had always been caution in the way Leonie interacted with her father. She should have known there was something very wrong.

"I don't need an answer now. But think about it—would you promise to do that? It's a lot to take on. Too much to ask, really."

"I don't mind, honestly."

"If it wasn't for you, I never would have considered sending her away, you know. But I think it's the right thing now."

"You do?"

He nodded. "Don't you?"

Though she felt sick with dread, she forced her face into a smile and nodded that she agreed it would be best to send Constance away for treatment.

"I don't know how to thank you, Ruby. For everything."

Ruby rolled her eyes. *It's nothing.*

He checked his phone screen. "Is that the time? I've got to run. She might need her sleep tonic tonight. It's in the bathroom. Can you make sure she gets it? It's awful when she doesn't sleep."

"Sleep tonic?"

"Yeah, it's just a herbal thing. Brown bottle. One spoonful is usually enough to do the trick, but tonight I think two would be better. She's a little antsy."

Gregor kissed her on the cheek, grabbed his jacket and left. When the door clicked shut, she wiped the kiss away with the back of her hand.

In the living room, Leonie was asleep in Constance's lap, her arms and legs limp and splayed. As Ruby entered, Constance swiped at her eyes with her sleeve. Ruby expected bruises on the other woman's face, but there was no redness on the pale skin, no marks from the beating she'd endured. He must have hit her in places that didn't show. Always the long sleeves, the high-necked shirts. It made sense now. *Where does it hurt?* she wanted to ask. There was a carefulness in the way Constance held her head, and now that Ruby looked, one ear was bright red and swollen at the lobe.

"Hey, Mamma Ruby. You're too late; she's all ready for bed." Constance held the small girl close, studied her face, and stroked it gently with a fingertip as she sang.

Ionn da, ionn do, ionn da, od-ar da.

Ruby sang the answer.

Hi-o dan dao, hi-o dan dao, hi-o dan dao, od-ar da.

"You almost sound like one when you sing it like that," said Constance. Her voice was low and resonant so that Ruby struggled to catch the words.

"One what?" The air seemed electric, and Ruby felt light-headed. She didn't know if the feeling came from the long shadow of what had just happened or from her worried anticipation of what Constance might be about to say.

Constance lowered her voice further and glanced from left to right, imparting a secret. "One of the seals. From the old skerry."

"They sing?"

"Of course. All the time."

Ruby felt anxiety take hold at the strange look on Constance's face as she spoke, her gray eyes too large, too bright, the way she was when she was beginning to detach from reality. But there wasn't time to worry about Constance's delusions now. It was more important to get her away from there—they could deal with her mental health when they were in a safe place. A place that wasn't rigged with cameras and listening devices.

As Constance went to put the baby down for the night, Ruby switched the TV on and turned it up loud.

She laughed—then worried it sounded false—at Constance's confused expression when she came back into the room. They never usually watched TV. "I love this one," said Ruby—too loud? "Let's watch it together." It was one of those talent shows, all glitter and ballgowns. Constance looked sideways at her, questioning. Ruby turned it up even louder, and flicked her eyes at the ceiling. After that, Constance seemed to understand. Almost without moving her lips, keeping her eyes trained on the screen, Ruby said,

"I heard what he did to you just now."

Ruby could almost feel Gregor watching them from the overhead cameras. Her head itched, though she didn't scratch. The bad feeling crept down her neck, spreading over her skin. Her whole body ached with the effort of not moving, not reacting, not trembling, though her heart was drumming so loudly she was sure it could be picked up by the hidden microphones.

Constance said nothing for a while. From the corner of her eye, Ruby saw a fat tear sliding down the other woman's cheek, changing color in the light from the TV.

"Does he ever hit Leonie?"

She turned to look at Constance, who nodded, almost imperceptibly. Rage made Ruby's cheeks burn. Her fingers twitched, as if they would have grabbed something to hit him with, had he been there. She tried to breathe slowly.

"I can help you get away. You can't let her stay here any longer. You could go anywhere you like, another city—there are hostels for people like you, with small children."

"No," said Constance. "I need to go home. Back to the island. The *skerry*. They'll come and get me, if I can get to the coast at the right time, on the solstice."

"Are you sure that's where you want to go?" Of course it was home, to Constance, but everything she'd heard about the place was awful. The rituals, the strange beliefs that resulted in drownings. Although, Ruby realized, all of that had come from him. The man whom, until recently, she'd trusted without question. Ruby hadn't listened properly to Constance because Gregor had made her believe Constance was mad. But Gregor had lied about so much, from the very start. She had no idea who he even was.

Constance's eyes shone with tears. She muttered, "I was happy before I met him."

Then Ruby's phone beeped. Gregor. *Has she taken the tonic yet?*
Just doing it now, she replied.

"He says you need to take your medicine."

"Good," said Constance. "At least I'll be unconscious for a while." She went to the bathroom, and Ruby heard the cupboard opening and shutting, the clinking of a glass bottle. When she returned, Ruby spoke out of the side of her mouth, still aware of the camera overhead, hoping the sound of the TV was masking them completely.

"We need to think about the next steps," she said. "The plan for getting you both out of here."

"Not now," said Constance. "It's too much. Today I sleep."

"But he said he might send you away soon. I don't know how long we've got."

"Send me away? Where?"

"For treatment. But you can't trust him."

"I can't leave. Not without my coat."

"Your coat?" Was it real, then, after all? Ruby decided that even if it wasn't, she had to pretend she believed in it if Constance was to trust her. "Can't you get a new one?"

She shook her head no. "It's part of me. I was born in it."

Ruby imagined the scene, a wind-blown stone cottage on an island, the mother in labor with nothing but an old coat to cushion the baby from the packed earth floor.

"But what if he's gotten rid of it?"

"I don't think he has. The man keeps things, forever if he can. I think he's planning to keep you too, Ruby, one way or another." The tonic was starting to take effect, as Constance's speech slowed and she slumped deeper into the cushions.

Ruby felt her heart rate increase. They could go right now, if they were quick. But Constance curled on the sofa, her eyelids starting to droop.

"Is it really worth staying here for the sake of a coat?"

"I stay here *only* because of the coat. Otherwise, don't you think I would have gone already?"

When she looked into Constance's eyes, she thought she understood, finally. The coat was a link to her past, to her real self, to everything Gregor had been keeping from her. It was more than a symbol, more than a possession. Ruby wanted so much to help Constance regain something of what she'd lost, something of her fragile sanity, her sense of self. But more than that, she needed to get them away.

When Gregor came back an hour later, Constance was fully asleep and snoring. She didn't even stir when he hauled her up into his arms, carried her to bed.

Ruby hid her fear, or she hoped she had. She yawned and stretched, started to get up to leave.

"You off?" he said.

"Yup. I'm not sleeping brilliantly at the moment. Bloody insomnia. I'm trying not to stay up too late. Get a bit of a routine back. Maybe I need some of your sleep tonic."

He laughed. "Maybe you do."

"What's in it? Constance was out like a light after she had some."

"Secret recipe," said Gregor, tapping his nose. "Well, I guess it's not that secret. Chamomile, essence of lavender. Valerian. And a tiny bit of alcohol, of course."

Ruby had to stop herself from blurting, *Alcohol? And you gave that to the baby?* She covered her reaction with a cough and an interested smile.

"Help yourself. No more than half a spoonful, though, if you're not used to it. It's pretty good stuff."

In the bathroom, Ruby opened the cupboard above the sink. There was a brown bottle with a spoon beside it. She took out the bottle, unscrewed the cap and sniffed. It smelled sweet and chemical, not like alcohol at all. She poured a full spoon and swallowed. Bitter.

Before she even arrived at home, her legs were as heavy as concrete. She woke up fourteen hours later, face down on the carpet in her apartment, the front door ajar, unable to remember how she got there. Thankfully no one had robbed her. As she dragged herself to her knees, felt the roughness inside her mouth and the pain in her head, one thought surfaced, white-hot and shining with fury. He gave that fucking stuff to *Leonie*?

28

NOW
Joanna
Sunday, December 23

ON THE WAY to the New Park Estate, Joanna thought only of Ruby. There was so much she'd never said to her that she thought perhaps she should have. It had never been the right moment, and now it might be too late. Rain started falling as she crossed the city, the sky blackening with her thoughts.

Jo had been so careful to avoid getting between her mother and Ruby in the early years, that for most of Ruby's childhood she'd absented herself, keeping herself busy at first with school and college, after hours with her sports, and in later years with her police training. She'd learned to live with the nagging, aching feeling that she worked hard to suppress, knowing deep down that this was the urge to be a real mother that she had not only been denied but had actively denied herself. For all those years the family went from day to day, doing their thing, ignoring the reality of the adoption, ignoring their mother's alcoholism, ignoring Ruby's feelings of rejection and Joanna's of replacement. Right up until they couldn't ignore it anymore. And Ruby had left them, taking half of Joanna's heart.

Immediately after the fight, Jo had been so angry that she'd decided she never wanted to see her mother again either. But as the days went on, she realized the blame had to be shared. There was a kernel of truth in what had been said, as there always was in the most hurtful things: none of it would have happened if Joanna hadn't given birth to Ruby in the first place. It took a week for the worst of Joanna's anger to subside and be replaced once more with pity. She'd persuaded Marianne to give Ruby the space and time she needed. Joanna was convinced that if they did that, she would come home, she would forgive Marianne the way Jo had done. But it hadn't happened in the twelve months they'd waited patiently. Ruby had just gotten further away.

As the looming apartment blocks appeared in her eyeline, she wondered if it was too late to make any of it right. Ruby had always needed her, not just as a sister. Jo should have admitted that sooner, when her baby was still a child, when it mattered most of all. Now she felt like she was being given a chance to do something to show how much she cared. Whatever Ruby had done, whatever crime, Jo could forgive her. More than that, she knew how she could help her stay out of prison. It was her duty as a police officer to apprehend and arrest suspects, but her duty as a mother came first.

Joanna parked and approached the West Block, glancing at the entrance to the North Block only briefly. She knew that Gregor's flat had been sealed by the CSI team, who would be back the next day to complete the work. They'd taken samples, finger-prints, and photographs. Tomorrow, the search would get a bit more structural: one of the officers had noticed an area of plaster that was newly replaced, and had sought permission to open up the wall. For now, though, the entrance to the block looked as it always had. There was no police tape, no officers guarding the building, no sign that anything untoward had happened there. Apart from one small thing. Someone walking by wouldn't notice, but Harper knew that if you looked carefully, there were still drops of Gregor's blood on the paving. She refused to imagine Ruby wielding the weapon that caused those injuries; the figure she pictured carrying out the crime was faceless, with a rope of jet-black hair. Whatever she imagined, she knew it was probable that Ruby had been in Gregor's flat very recently, and it was only a matter of waiting for CSI to analyze the DNA and fingerprints. If—or more likely *when*—they connected those samples to Ruby, it was a short step from Ruby to Jo. Joanna would find herself answering one or two awkward questions about withheld information and bias. She had to make the most of what little time she had.

At the entrance to the flats, she pressed buzzers randomly until she got a response.

"Yes?"

"It's the police. I need access to this block."

Whoever it was simply hung up on her, so she tried again, and the second person who answered was more amenable. She heard the buzz as the electric lock disengaged. She pushed open the door to the stairwell.

On the seventh floor she found Ruby's door and knocked loudly, announcing her name and rank, mostly for the benefit of the neighbors. She wasn't expecting an answer, and so there was barely a hesitation before she swung the bag containing the Enforcer off her shoulder onto the floor and unzipped it. She took out the heavy metal cylinder, positioned it, took aim at the lock.

"Step away from the door. I'm going to force the lock, in five, four, three, two—"

"What are you doing?"

She froze, looked to her left. It was Atkinson. Surprise turned quickly to anger.

"What am I doing? What are you doing? You're supposed to be searching the beach at Cleethorpes."

"I ended up behind you in traffic. Then I saw you were coming in here and I thought maybe you'd need help."

"You followed me."

"I called out when you got out of the car. You didn't hear me. I didn't want to use the radio, in case . . . well, I didn't know what you were doing. Whether it was related to the case, or . . . personal."

Harper lowered the Enforcer. She took a step toward Atkinson. "Whatever you think you're seeing here, just forget it, okay? That's a direct order. Turn around and go."

Atkinson took a step backward. He seemed uncertain.

"Who lives in there, boss?"

For a few seconds she just stared at him.

He went on, "It's 7b, isn't it? The flat that overlooks our victim's. You said you'd take the statement, but I guess they didn't answer?" He glanced at the Enforcer that she still held in one hand. When their eyes met, she got the feeling he was nervous. He thought she'd gone rogue, that she wasn't in her right mind. She too looked down at the Enforcer and then at the door. Maybe she had, and maybe she wasn't.

"Do you trust me, Steve?"

A very slight hesitation, then. "Yes, boss."

"I feel like I could explain," she said.

"Yeah?"

"But first I'm going to do this."

Joanna turned, and in one fluid movement lifted the Enforcer and rammed it into the lock. The frame splintered, the lock gave, and the door swung inward, banging hard against the wall. Harper turned and glared at Atkinson.

"Now. As you can see, what I'm doing here isn't strictly by the book, so I'm going to give you two options. You can either keep your mouth shut and stay aboveboard. Turn around right now. Go and do the task you've been assigned to do." She paused.

"Or? What's the alternative?" said Atkinson.

She met his eyes. "The alternative is that you take that look off your face and help me find out where she's gone."

29

The Injured Man
Remembers

H E IS FOLLOWING a man through the churchyard. The target
is unaware of his presence, as he has been for the past month.
As he follows, keeping a safe distance away, he copies exactly the
target's gait, his way of running his fingers through his hair every
few seconds. When the target stops walking to check something
on his phone, he stops too, checks his own phone, mirroring the
same stance. The target glances up at him, but he's not really looking, not really noticing. If he were, he might have thought it odd
that the person he is looking at has the same haircut as his, and the
same shoes.

The target has no significant friends, though he is very rich.
Only those who use the BDSM website the target frequents know
him at all, and none of them know his real name. They wouldn't
recognize his face, as the target is careful never to post selfies
online. He keeps himself to himself, happy in his own company,
though he shares his large apartment with his elderly mother,
whom he is devoted to. The target probably enjoys the fact that
the tenants in the block of flats that he owns don't even realize that
he's the landlord and that he lives above them. They don't know

that he had the penthouse flat soundproofed thoroughly when it was being refurbished, and that he hardly ever has to leave the building. The target orders his entertainment in, easy as pizza, every Friday. His mother never hears a single thing. The person following him knows this, because he has been taking careful note. The person following has been watching from the opposite flat, the empty one in the social housing block that just happens to overlook it, that he has managed to keep empty for his own purposes by means of a little light hacking of the council housing portal. The person following has been waiting for the right time to strike, enjoying the wait, the game of it. And now, finally, he's decided the persona has been perfected. There's nothing more he can gain from allowing the target to continue. Tonight's the night. It couldn't be better.

He lets the target enter his building, and walks on for a few minutes before he uses his phone to log on to the BDSM website where he has set up a profile he is certain will appeal. In moments, they have a date.

He waits another thirty minutes before he presses the buzzer and is let in to the block. He walks up the stairs, knocks on the door, watches it open. The two men exchange a matching slow smile. The target moves aside to let him in, and he takes in the large living space, the tasteful decor, the high ceilings. *Nice place*, he thinks. *I think I'll be very happy here.*

The scene cuts to a few hours later, and the target is kneeling on the bed, naked except for a blue shirt. He's helpless, his eyes big and pleading, mouth swollen slightly, blood dripping from one corner. The handcuffs the target owns fit the wrists perfectly; they were made to measure. The soundproofing the target has had built into the fabric of the flat is excellent. No matter how much the target screams, no one outside the room or downstairs will hear it at all. The man turns and picks up an old green embroidered tie that he has found in a wardrobe. The target sees what the man has in mind, and as anticipated, begins to fight. As the tourniquet is tightened around the throat, the end of the tie becomes frayed where the target is scrabbling at it. Together they struggle, and together they fall, twisting slightly so that the target's head catches the corner of the bedframe badly on the way down, the sound of it a wet crack, and by the time they hit the floor, those sparkling eyes have glazed over. He stands up and brushes himself down, watching with fascination as the pool of blood spreads blackly outward like a pupil dilating in the darkness. It occurs to him that the rug on which the target lies will need to be replaced. Also, he's not sure about the wallpaper.

Now for the old lady, he thinks, wrapping the tie around his hands, noticing with irritation that he has pulled a muscle in his shoulder during the fight with the target. It's unlikely to affect his finishing the old lady, but there's a great deal of salt to be brought up, eight sacks of it, ready to deal with the bodies. He supposes it can wait a day or two, until he's at full strength again—there's all the boxing in and plastering to be done, too, after all, once they're finished. No particular hurry. He knows from experience that bodies don't ripen for at least a week if you keep the heating off.

He cracks open the bedroom door and peers into the living space. The old woman, seated facing away from him, jerks as if she's just woken up. She tries to look round but doesn't quite have the flexibility in her neck.

"Gregor?" she says. "Is that you?"

CHAPTER

30

NOW
Joanna
Sunday, December 23

JO TOOK A few steps inside Ruby's flat and held up a hand for
Atkinson to stop. They waited, listened. All was still; the place
was empty. She flipped the lights on. The bare bulb dangling from
the ceiling illuminated the bed-sitting room in a stark yellow light.

It was clear from the state of the apartment that the occupant
was not a natural homemaker. It was a tip, by anyone's standards.
Jo felt a pang of protectiveness, but also one of recognition. Her
own place might have been bigger, but it had looked similar before
Amy moved in, with pictures still leaning on the wall where she'd
not had time or inclination to hang them, washing drying on the
radiators, and piles of unopened post. It didn't seem right, somehow, that Ruby's place was so untidy, so uncared for. The Ruby
that lived in Harper's head was the sort of person who liked order
and neatness; her bedroom at home had always been pristine. Jo
had pegged her as a neat freak. Another thing she'd been wrong
about, by the looks of it.

What furniture there was in Ruby's place was well-worn, secondhand stuff: a small TV on a low table, a carton of tatty books.

The bed, which had been made up with cotton sheets that showed their age, stood out as the only tidy corner of the room. By the door there was a tangle of dirty washing spilling from a plastic laundry sack. She picked up the familiar washed-out gray T-shirt featuring "Last Splash" by The Breeders, that Ruby used to sleep in. She'd "borrowed" it from Joanna probably fifteen years previously, when it was already a relic. Jo pressed the fabric briefly to her face. Her throat swelled up and she choked back tears. Ruby had kept this old thing for all this time; it must have meant something. But now it was screwed up in a dirty ball in this unloved apartment, and Ruby was missing.

"What's that?" asked Atkinson.

"Nothing," said Jo. "Just stuff. Doesn't matter."

She tossed the shirt back with the rest of the washing. Atkinson was giving her that look again. It occurred to her that it wasn't usual to sniff things during a search. She ignored him.

Joanna wondered about practicalities: Who had helped Ruby get the bed up here? Gregor? Someone else entirely? Why hadn't she bought nicer stuff, or more of it—she earned good enough money at the Music Service, or she had been when Jo last saw her. Ruby loved that job. Jo remembered her saying she'd been lucky to snag it without a teaching degree, that they'd taken her on audition and recommendation. It was only part-time, though, and when she lived with Marianne, Ruby would also teach from home to make up the shortfall. How was Ruby supplementing her income now? No student would want to come up here, to this.

Shame flooded Joanna at the fact that she didn't know this much about her own . . . what was she? *Sister* had always felt wrong. Why hadn't she admitted that before now? *Hi, Sis,* she used to say when they met, but it wasn't sincere, hadn't been for years. *Sister* had become a kind of dark joke shared between them and in front of Marianne. The word stood in place of what they wanted to say to each other, a poor substitute, a thing they'd both been forced to accept.

Jo knelt down to search under the bed.

"Oh no," she said.

"What have you found?" said Atkinson, dropping to his knees to see.

She pulled it out and unzipped the case. Under a yellow duster that had never seen dust, had only ever been used to lovingly polish the instrument's curves, was the burnished form of Ruby's violin. Jo stared at it, letting the significance of it being here sink in.

Atkinson said, "Are you okay?"

"She never leaves this thing anywhere," she said. "It's like a child to her." *Or it used to be,* thought Joanna. Things must have gone really badly wrong for Ruby to abandon her violin.

"Are you going to tell me, then?"

"Tell you what?"

"Whose place this is? Or do I have to guess?"

"It's Ruby's place."

"Your sister, Ruby?"

She looked at the carpet. Then she nodded.

In the kitchen, she and Atkinson stared across at the big window onto Gregor's flat. It was dark in there, the open curtains offering nothing more than a vague impression of the plush living space they'd searched the day before.

"Can I ask you something, boss?"

"Sure," said Joanna.

"Why haven't you told the DI that your sister lives here?"

"It's not relevant."

"But the address is already part of the investigation. I can see now why you wanted to take the statement yourself, but there's nothing stopping one of the team looking up who lives here. Louise seemed keen to start digging."

"Louise isn't going to make that link. Harper's a common enough name."

"I think you're underestimating Louise. And me, actually."

She looked at him. "Fine, maybe it might be relevant to the case, but I want to find her first, talk to her. Give her a chance to explain."

"Explain what?"

"Where she's gone. Why she left. She won't answer her phone, Steve—she won't talk to me. Hasn't for months. I think she's changed her number."

"Hang on, this has been going on for months? How long has she been missing?"

"I didn't realize she was missing until today. I thought she was still avoiding me. There was a big family bust-up. I haven't spoken to her since October."

"But she might be a witness in this case, Jo. You need to tell someone. If she's involved somehow—"

"She's not involved," Jo snapped.

Atkinson raised an eyebrow. "You can't know that. You're too close to this. Maybe you should think about handing it to another SIO."

"No. I need to be the one in charge, Steve."

"Why?"

She stared at the floor, hating that she was having to discuss her private life with a colleague. She never mentioned anything to anyone at work that didn't involve sport or jokes or police work. She took a deep breath. "Ruby. She's not my sister, not really, that's a . . . force of habit. She's my kid. But I didn't bring her up—my mother did. Does that explain it well enough?"

Atkinson paused before he said, "It explains some things pretty well."

They locked eyes.

"Are you here to help or just to make snarky comments?

"Sorry. That must be hard for you. I didn't mean to be flip. Wow, I mean, I can see why you're so worried about her."

"Yes, well. Now you know. Can we get on with searching the place? Or is this a therapy session?"

They moved back into the main space.

"What are we looking for, boss?"

"Anything that tells us where she might have gone. How about you start with the post. I'll look for devices."

"Some of these aren't opened," said Atkinson, holding up the letters.

She took them from him, tore each one open and handed them over. "They look open to me."

He stared at them, then at her, in disbelief. "If we reported her missing, we could have done that legally."

"Done what?" She raised her eyebrows in a challenge. Atkinson shook his head, and started going through the contents of the envelopes.

Joanna pulled out a plastic box from under the bed. It contained mostly stationery. She rummaged and found a notepad and pen, a sheaf of envelopes with several missing. Ruby had been writing to someone. Harper held the pad up to the light, turning it this way and that, trying to read the jumble of illegible impressions left by the pen before the sheet above had been torn away. All she could make out were two words at the top of the page: *Dear Sam.* Sam Douglas, the fiddle-playing crusty from the folk music bar. Who lived on a boat and made no secret of the fact that he hated technology, that he owned no phone or computer and never would. Sam made his living as a joiner getting jobs by word of mouth. He moved around all the time for work. If you wanted to hide, Sam Douglas would be the man to help you do it.

Dear Sam, she read, *Don't* . . . what? It was impossible to see. She would need to have it properly analyzed. They'd decode it in seconds at the lab.

Frustrated, she tucked the pad and pen into an evidence bag and continued the search.

"There's no phone here. Not even a charger," she said. "No laptop, nothing."

She went through to the kitchen again, to see if she'd missed something in there. There was nothing plugged in and nothing in the cupboards but a box of out-of-date cereal. When she opened up the fridge, a puff of rotten air escaped, and she shut it hastily.

"This place. It's not like there's anyone living here, not really. She's been sleeping here maybe, but not much else."

"Certainly looks that way," said Atkinson. "I think she must have come back regularly to check the post, though. There's nothing here older than a week."

"Did you find anything interesting?"

"Only one thing, but I'm afraid it won't give us much to go on."

Us, she thought, experiencing a begrudging little glow at the fact that Atkinson had thrown his lot in with her despite the risk to himself if he went along with her off-the-record antics. He handed her a yellow envelope handwritten in blue ink. On the back, when she closed the flap, a capital *S* had been drawn where an old-fashioned seal might have been.

"What was in it?"

"Nothing. Just the envelope. But if you look closely, there are some words on the inside where the ink has transferred."

The postmark was smudged, impossible to read. "I can get this to the lab. They'll be able to tell us more. And they'll be able to lift prints, hopefully." She slipped it into an evidence bag and folded the flap closed.

"The lab?"

"Yes, the lab. You remember. Where we send things to have them analyzed."

"I know that. I just meant how are you going to square that with Thrupp? What code are you going to use?"

All official evidence was coded with a catalog number that indicated where it was found, at what time, and what case it related to. There were no exceptions: if the lab couldn't categorize it, they wouldn't process it. Joanna was well aware of the procedure. She'd planned to deal with that when she had to. Solutions would present themselves, she was sure of it.

"Just leave that side of things to me, will you?"

"Look, I get why you'd want to protect your kid, but we should think about stopping before we go too far. Why don't you put it on the record? Then you can run as much evidence through the lab as you like. It's not too late to get the search authorized if I vouch for you. Ruby's a potential witness. If a witness is reported missing, then we can throw everything at it. And there'd be no need to sneak around."

"But if they find out I'm related to a witness, they'll take me off the case."

"Maybe that wouldn't be such a bad thing."

She stopped, turned. "What?"

"I saw the way you reacted when Eddie gave you that picture of Constance B. It was a picture of Ruby, wasn't it?"

Jo couldn't react quickly enough; she fumbled for an answer. "I . . ."

"You know she could be the one who attacked Gregor?"

"Nobody asked you to be here, did they? In fact, I recall asking you more than once to be somewhere else entirely."

"I want to help you, Jo. I won't tell the DI. Just be straight with me, now and in the future."

Joanna studied her friend's face. After a while, she decided to trust him. "If Ruby was involved in the attack on Franks, then she would have had a good reason. She's a good person, Steve. She helps people—she doesn't hurt them. She was helping the old woman, wasn't she?"

He nodded. "I'm sure you're right. But if she's committed a crime, that changes things."

"She hasn't. I know her. And if anyone asks you what happened here, you'll tell them. I broke the door down, I ordered the search. That is a direct order. Though you don't seem to be putting much store by those today."

Just then there was a sound in the hallway, and both of them froze. Harper crept to the spyhole and peeked out, caught a glimpse of a neighbor walking toward the lifts. The noise must have been their door closing. Had this neighbor noticed the broken lock? Jo knew they had to get out of there. Someone from work would see her car parked in the lot, and then, if they went to Gregor's flat and she wasn't in it, they'd start to wonder. Even if they didn't notice her unmarked vehicle, Atkinson had come in a patrol car.

"Listen," she said, her voice a controlled whisper, "I only need a couple of days. If I can speak to Ruby, find out what's going on, then I'll put it all on record after that. Two days. Tops. Then if I haven't reported it, you can do it."

"I can't blow the whistle on you. And you know it."

Their eyes met. Then she nodded, pulled open the door onto the brightly lit corridor, and they went through.

31

THEN
Ruby
December

"Hurry up," said Constance. "He might come back."

"Just a few more seconds," said Ruby, "I've nearly got it. There."

The lock on the bedroom door finally turned. She left the hairpin where it was—sticking out of the keyhole—knowing she would have to perform the tricky operation of picking it the opposite way if she was going to avoid Gregor finding out what she'd been up to. She straightened up, took a deep breath. Then, she turned the handle and pushed.

Inside the bedroom it was dark. Ruby started to reach for the light switch, but Constance grabbed her arm. "He'll probably have a tripwire or something. There'll be a booby trap."

Ruby didn't think so. Gregor can't have known about her lock-picking skills, which she'd learned one long summer from YouTube videos, quietly practicing until she was able to open an old cupboard at her music school, to which the key had been lost. There was a rumor that inside was a treasure trove of baroque instruments, but when she finally got inside, it was empty apart from a dusty Hoover from the 1950s. It had been a fun challenge, though, and a useful skill to have.

In the days since Ruby had witnessed Gregor's violent, bullying nature, she and Constance had been biding their time. When he was there—and even when he wasn't—they made a show of maintaining their expected roles. Ruby was still the "babysitter," looking after Leonie and helping Constance cope, making sure she took her medicine whenever Gregor hinted or texted that she needed it. In actual fact, Ruby was making sure she didn't take that stuff, tipping it one spoonful at a time down the sink. Constance pretended to be sleepy and vacant, when in truth, she was getting stronger and more focused every day. She still longed for home, though, and Ruby would catch her gazing wistfully at the seascape pictures, lost in thought.

Ruby played her violin for them often, and they sang shanties, sea songs, and lullabies from the old skerry, as Constance called her home. Gregor listened, his eyes gleaming. He loved the sound of the two of them as much as they loved it themselves, but when the songs were over, the women were careful to hide their affection. They made up complaints about each other to tell Gregor when the other wasn't in the room so he didn't think they were too close. Constance said Ruby was a bossy, nosy little busybody. Ruby complained that Constance was bad-tempered and uncommunicative. So far, the plan was working. Maybe a little too well.

On his way out that evening, he'd pulled Ruby aside.

"You're an angel for staying," he said. "I've told her she needs to stop being such a bitch to you, when you do so much to help us out."

"I don't mind," Ruby said. "I know she doesn't really mean it. Some of the stuff she says to me when you're not here can be hurtful, sure, but it's nothing I can't handle. But I'm not here for her—not really. I'm here for Leonie."

"I've seen the kind of things she says to you, on the cameras. You shouldn't have to put up with that. Not with everything you do for her and for us."

It was good to know that the occasional spats they staged for him were being noted and having the desired effect.

"We don't fight the whole time, you know."

"No, I know. Sometimes you watch TV."

"You watch us doing that?"

He laughed. "No, I don't have time for that. I just . . . check in sometimes. That's all. You don't mind, do you? Too 'stalkery'?" He laughed but didn't wait for her to answer. "She's out of order, picking on you. I could have another word with her. Make her stop."

She stroked his arm, attempting a distraction. "Honestly, it's not needed. I think you're being overzealous."

He caught her hand, pulled her toward him. "Have you thought about us recently?"

"It's all I've thought about."

He kissed her, then, before she could pull away. He held her arms as she struggled to free herself, keeping her there a little too long. The strength of him. If he'd wanted to do anything to her, she wouldn't have been able to stop him. She stilled herself with every ounce of strength, fighting the urge to fight him, to push him away. He smelled of cloves; his tongue darted past her teeth, sweet and poisonous.

"Gregor," she hissed, fear coursing through her, making her tremble. She hoped he assumed it was because she wanted him so badly. "We can't—I told you before. It wouldn't be right."

"I'm sorry," he said. He studied her face, his lips parted. She tried to gaze at him with the longing she had once felt, which had now turned to ash. "I find it so difficult to be near you at the moment." He pulled her into a too-tight hug, the hard muscles of his arms bruising her cheekbone. "Can I come and see you later? At your place, I mean."

No, never, she thought. *I don't want to be alone with you even for a moment.*

"At my place?"

"I want to hear your piece. I haven't heard it for so long. The opening section has been in my head all day." He hummed the theme, the tritone that spanned the first bars, setting the mood for the rest.

"You don't need to come over, Gregor. I can bring my violin, play it for all of you. I'll bring it tomorrow, yes?"

He gave her a long look. "I suppose."

She stopped then, blinking to cover the widening of her eyes, pulling him in for a second hug as she tried not to show her reaction, her skin prickling all over, events slowing with her breath as every single hair on her body stood up. Despite the heat in the apartment, she felt suddenly ice-cold, and her jaw clenched.

I have never played him that piece. How does he know it? There was only one possibility. He was spying on her. There were listening devices, and maybe even cameras, over in Ruby's flat too.

It was important that Gregor thought she was still in love with him, only denying herself because of Constance and Leonie. So it was useful now that the fear looked so much like desire. Standing there with her pupils dilating, her tongue wetting her lips, trembling, she must have looked to him like a fruit ripe for the picking.

They had to get out, and soon. Tonight they would act. As she'd watched him disappear into the stairwell, she'd known they would need to search fast. If she and Constance were going to access his private space without him knowing, it had to be after he'd set off in the car and before he arrived at wherever he was headed, because he couldn't be watching them and driving at the same time. They didn't know how far he was going or, therefore, how long they had. The moment his car started to move, she'd given the thumbs-up to Constance, who stuck a piece of masking tape over the tiny camera lens in the light fitting so that Ruby could pick the lock without it being recorded.

They checked all around the door for traps and wires, but could find nothing, not even the telltale borehole of a hidden camera.

"I think it's safe."

Ruby walked into Gregor's scrupulously neat and clean bedroom, flipping the light switch as she went. The bed was covered in a white cotton top sheet, folded back to reveal a white cotton duvet. Crisp white pillows were perfectly symmetrical. There was a white chest of drawers and a matching wardrobe. The painted walls were bare. Ruby got a feeling of blank nothingness. Like a hotel room, but with even less character.

Having been reluctant to enter the room, Constance suddenly pushed past her and flung open the wardrobe doors. She shoved aside the shirts, dragged the bottom drawer open.

"It's not in here," she said. "It has to be somewhere. Where's he hidden it?"

Ruby opened the top drawer of the bedside cabinet and found nothing, not even dust. In the second drawer, also nothing, but when she shut it she heard a soft metallic sound and opened it up again. There, at the back of the empty drawer, was a small silver key. She picked it up, looked at it. A serial number was marked on it, but nothing else. She replaced the key where she'd found it and closed the drawer.

Constance moved fretfully around the room, looking for more places to search. She looked under the bed and made a grunt of frustration.

"Nothing here."

Inside the open wardrobe, Ruby could see Gregor's shirts arranged in color order, a row of shoes neatly placed. She moved toward it and started straightening them out where Constance had rummaged.

"What are you doing?" said Constance, still on the carpet, feeling the underside of the bed for hidden pockets. "Help me look, will you? There's nothing in there—I checked."

"We need to tidy, though. We've got to leave it all the way we find it. Otherwise, he'll know we've been in here snooping."

Constance rose and wrenched open every drawer in the chest, her search becoming more frantic. "Maybe I don't care if he knows. Maybe he needs to know." By the end of the sentence, she'd lost her conviction. She stared down at the mess she'd made, the bundle of underwear she'd thrown to the floor. She dropped to her knees and gathered it all up, folded the items carefully, replaced them with shaking hands. She started straightening out the rest of the drawers. "This was a mistake. We should get out of here, Ruby. It's not in here."

"Yes," said Ruby, "just let me sort these shirts." She placed each hanger equidistant from the next, then ran a hand down each front and back to smooth them. Soon the wardrobe looked the way it had when Constance first opened it. She was about to close it up when she noticed a wrinkle in one of the middle shirts. This time when she ran her hands down the fabric, her fingers grazed something at the back of the wardrobe. Parting the shirts carefully, she bent to look.

"What is it?" said Constance. "What have you found?"

"I don't know."

She pulled gently and the box came toward her. It was about the size of a shoe box, made of metal painted black, and fastened with a small, gold-colored padlock.

"The coat won't be in that," said Constance. "It's not big enough."

Ruby tried to pry the lid off. As she did so, there was a noise from the front door.

"Is that him?" They listened.

There was the sound of a key sliding into place. Gregor's key.

"Quick," said Constance, "Put it away. I'll get the tape off the camera."

Ruby shoved the box back where she'd found it and slammed the wardrobe doors. Scanning the room for things out of place, she blanked, couldn't tell. She hoped there was nothing; she'd no time for anything more than hope. Constance was outside the bedroom; Ruby could hear her panicked breathing. She stepped out, flicked the light off, closed the door. Just the lock to turn now. From behind her, an urgent whisper. "Come on, Ruby. He's coming in."

She turned the pin too hard at first; she thought it was going to snap. But then, as the front door opened, she wiggled the lock, the cylinder turned, and she wrenched the hairpin free and took a step away from the bedroom door.

"What's going on here?" said Gregor.

"Oh," said Ruby, realizing how suspicious they must look. "We weren't expecting you."

He stared hard at each of them in turn. "What are you doing, though?"

"We were exercising," said Constance.

"We . . . were?" said Ruby. "That's right. You weren't watching, were you? That would be embarrassing." Both of them were red-faced, breathing hard and sweating. It was the perfect lie.

"No, of course not."

Gregor walked through to the kitchen with the shopping bag he was holding. "Glad to hear it, though, about the exercise," he said. "You need to shift a bit of that baby weight, right, Connie?"

He stuck his head out the door. "Oh, hang on—if you're planning to get in shape, should I not have bought these cakes, then?"

Ruby had pulled herself together, though her cheeks still burned. "Don't be silly. She can eat whatever she likes. She's barely there."

"I'm not sure that's true," he said. "You can overcompensate. She's not fat now, but everyone's only a few calories a day away from weight gain. Even me."

"I don't even like cake," muttered Constance. "You can eat them, Ruby."

"Are you staying for dinner?" said Ruby to Gregor. "I thought you were working tonight?"

"I'm not staying. I still need to go to Liverpool tonight. Business. I just popped in to drop off some shopping. In fact, do you think you could stop over again, Ruby?"

"You don't need to," said Constance to Ruby. "We'll be fine."

"I'd be really happy to," she said.

"That's settled, then."

When he'd gone, they waited, the way they should have waited the first time. Constance checked on Leonie and found her awake in the cot, needing to be soothed. She brought the sleepy tot through into the living room, where they all watched half an hour of mindless kid's TV, Ruby taking none of it in. Then they waited a bit more. Ruby got up and made sure that Gregor's car wasn't in its space before she dared to relax even slightly. They had to pray that he really was going to Liverpool; if it was true, they had about two hours to search before he stopped the car and checked the cameras from his phone. If it wasn't true, and he suspected them, then Ruby reasoned that they were already fucked, so it didn't matter what they did.

Ruby stuck the tape over the camera in the ceiling light.

"Maybe we should leave it off," said Constance. "If he checks the camera and can't see a picture, he'll know we're up to something."

"Better that he sees nothing than what we're actually doing," said Ruby, fishing the hairpin from the pocket where she'd shoved it.

Picking the lock was easier the second time. She knew what to feel for, where the pressure needed to be applied, and when to be gentle. Soon the lock gave and she was inside, where she went straight to the wardrobe and pulled out the black metal box. After a moment's thought, she went to the bedside unit and fetched the small silver key. Back in the living room, the key slid easily into the padlock, which opened with a satisfying click. More proof that Gregor trusted they wouldn't go in his room, if all there was to find in there was a padlock and the key that opened it. Something tugged at her mind, though, a quiet warning. It seemed a bit too easy. She pulled at the tightly fitted lid until it came free, swinging open on its hinge.

Constance was on the sofa, feeding Leonie a cup of warm milk. "What's in there?"

"Bills," said Ruby, leafing through the file folders as she pulled them from the box and placed them one by one on the coffee table. "Papers, certificates, boring stuff. The deeds for this place. You'd think he would have a proper filing system." She pulled out his birth certificate, looked at the dates, the name of the Royal Infirmary Hospital. "Funny," she said. "According to this, he's thirty-eight."

"And?"

"Don't you think he looks younger than that?" She thought about his voice. Born in Sheffield. Gregor's accent was carefully neutral, which he'd explained by the fact that he went to a fee-paying school. But sometimes his long vowels shortened unexpectedly, and he sounded almost Bristolian to Ruby.

Underneath the last file was something she recognized.

"Oh my god," she said, picking up the phone that she'd lost, that she thought had been stolen, or thrown away. Her old phone, containing all of her numbers, her text message conversations, her passwords. Gregor had had it all along. Her whole life was on there, or her life before she met him, anyway. She turned it on, not expecting, after all this time, that the thing would have any power, but it chimed into life, the battery at seventy-five percent. Ruby was halted by the chilling knowledge that not only had he been keeping the phone, he'd been regularly charging it up. She saw that there were no unread notifications. Gregor had been reading them all. But why? In the calls menu, there were hundreds of missed calls, mostly from Marianne, but some from Joanna too.

Her breath caught, and she felt sick with guilt and regret for ignoring them, for not contacting and telling them she'd changed numbers. Scrolling through, she saw that every Sunday, Marianne would start calling in the morning, then continue every hour or so until the early hours of Monday morning. Drink and dial—her specialty. She immediately stopped feeling guilty. If Ruby had answered any of those desperate calls, she would have spoken to a person still ruled by drink.

She switched the phone off again, pushing thoughts of Marianne and Joanna away. No time for that now. Also in the box was a black device almost the size and shape of a mobile phone, but unlike any make or model she'd seen before. She turned it over, found the "On" button, pressed it. The word TRAX flashed up in blue and disappeared before the screen filled with a map. It took a few seconds for her to realize what it was she was looking at.

"It's a tracking device," said Ruby.

Constance leaned over to look. She pointed at the flag icon in the center. "Is that the apartment?"

Sure enough, the map was recognizably of the local area, centered on the New Park estate, shown from above. The flag was in the North Block.

"Must be," said Ruby. "I don't get it, though. What's it tracking? Itself? Is that like a 'Home' flag?"

"No," said Constance. "Look, there're two flags, but they're really close together. There'll be a locator device, a small thing. He told me once he had one for his car, in case it ever was stolen."

Ruby ran to the window, panicking that he'd come back again. The space was still empty. "His car isn't here, though."

"Is the locator in the box?"

Ruby turned the box upside down. Nothing. She felt in the corners. "Not in here."

"Maybe it's faulty."

Ruby scrolled through the menu. She clicked on "Locate at close range," and the screen changed to a set of concentric circles pulsating from a blue central dot. The word in the dot was *Receiver*.

"This must be the receiver, then," she said. Next to the receiver dot was a smaller red dot, labeled with the word *Locator*. At the bottom of the screen, the words *Less than 0.5 m.*

"That means it's here somewhere. In the room. You're sure it's not in the box? Have a good look, might be stuck on. They're magnetic, probably."

Constance ran her hands over the box, inside and out. Nothing. They both looked around them.

Ruby lifted the cushions on the sofa. "How big is the locator, do you think? Did you ever see the one on his car?" She got up and walked across to the bathroom, went inside, and began to feel along the top of the cabinet.

"Ruby," said Constance. "It moved."

"What?" She went back into the main room and walked across to where Constance was sitting.

"Stop," she said, and Ruby stopped. Constance's eyes flicked between her and the screen of the tracking device. "Okay, go again."

She'd only taken three steps when Constance said, "It's you."

"It's me? What do you mean?"

"When you went to the bathroom. The dot moved with you. It's on you somewhere. What have you got in your pockets?"

"Only my phone." She reached into her pocket and pulled out the phone. "But it's turned off."

"Here," said Constance, taking the phone and handing her the tracker. "Watch the dots."

Constance walked toward the bathroom. The locator dot moved. The distance marker went up as she got farther away: *Less than 1.5 m, Less than 2.5 m, Less than 3.5 m.*

Ruby threw the tracker down and grabbed the phone from Constance. She unclipped the back and took the battery out. There was a flat, black circle underneath it that she'd never seen before.

Gregor was tracking her. He'd given her a phone that meant he could follow her every move. She'd been carrying it around, not knowing that at any given moment, Gregor knew exactly where she was. The few times he'd phoned her when she'd been in town, she'd always been at the bus stop by the police station. Not a coincidence, then, as she'd thought; he didn't fully trust her, suspected she might have been about to betray him to the authorities.

Quickly she bundled everything into the box, hoping she'd put it all in the right order. She wedged the lid on, fastened the padlock, replaced the box exactly where she'd found it hidden in the wardrobe. Finally, she wiped the padlock and the wardrobe door where her prints might be found. Paranoid, perhaps, but she'd seen just how far Gregor would go to keep tabs on her. The idea of him routinely dusting for prints seemed perfectly plausible now.

32

The Injured Man
Remembers

THE GIRL IS running ahead of him through a field of maize, her small form disappearing into the high stalks, reappearing again in flashes of white cotton and yellow hair. It's a game: he's laughing as he chases her. She ducks to the left and disappears. He stops to search the rows. He can't find where she's gone, but then he steps forward and sees a foot quickly drawn away under the low leaves. He creeps along. He can feel himself grinning, the sun on his back, stalking his prey, the thrill of a good chase. She's hiding, perfectly still. She thinks he can't see her. Then, the crops shudder as she realizes he's there and takes off, running chaotically, here and there like a startled rabbit, and he's after her. She's an arm's length away, and he reaches for her, grabbing her wrist and turning her to face him. She stares at him, her mouth wide in a scream. Up close, the white dress she wears is covered with uneven red spots. She struggles to get away, so he goes to take hold of her with his other hand but can't because he's holding something already. He opens up his palm to reveal a severed finger, and in that moment she twists and slips out of his grasp.

Next, he is standing at the edge of a deep hole, looking down. There on the distant bottom, the girl's limbs make a star, still and pale, with a fan of yellow hair in an angel's aurora around her head. She stares in his direction, but the eyes no longer see.

He is pushing the front door open, heading to the kitchen for a glass of water.

His mother is saying, "Where's your sister?"

He turns, looks her in the eye. "I haven't seen Dora all day." As he leaves the room, he slips his hands in his pockets. His left hand grips his penknife that he knows he must wash. His right hand caresses the nestled finger, a gruesome treasure, his first and his best.

33

NOW
Joanna
Sunday, December 23

S TREETLIGHTS SPREAD WEAK orange light on the paving
between the apartment buildings. Jo followed Atkinson to
where the cars were parked, her breath billowing in puffs of vapor,
though she didn't feel cold. When she reached the car, she paused
in the act of unlocking it.

Across the top of the car, Atkinson followed her eyes to the
seventh floor of the North Block.

"You're not thinking what I think you're thinking, are you?"

"I just want a quick look."

"You can't go in there now. They've sealed it up to preserve the
evidence."

"I had no idea Ruby was involved when we went in before.
There might be something I missed." Jo pocketed her keys and
started toward the brightly lit lobby of Gregor's building. "Go
home, Steve," she said, but when she reached the door and he was
right behind her, she was secretly pleased.

At the apartment door, she ripped the yellow police tape from
the frame and pushed the key into the lock. As she did so, she

noticed that the utilities cupboard in the corridor to the right of the door was ajar. There was a padlock lying open on the floor, its key still inserted. Inside the cupboard there was nothing but the water stopcock, the energy meters, and a space underneath with a gap in the dust, as if something that had been there for a long time had been recently removed.

Not knowing what or if this meant anything, she tucked the information away, cataloging it along with the other scraps she had, none of which seemed to her to be connected yet, though she knew they had to be. Cases came together for Harper all at once like illusions, puzzle pieces falling randomly until she took a step in a different direction and suddenly it would come to her, the links, the gaps, shining a light on it all so she could see the way through. She turned each fact over, searching for the kinks, the points at which each one joined the rest: first, a child abandoned on the seafront; a mysterious woman disappearing; Ruby convincing the Social Services to let her take the woman's child, then disappearing herself. The state of Ruby's flat. The last phone call they'd had, Ruby's tone of voice when talking about the people she'd met. The neighbor, who thought Gregor lived alone. The invisible child, with no records, slipping through the cracks. The invisible mother, Constance. Where did Ruby fit into the picture? Something in Franks's flat might tell her. But she had to be quick. Atkinson was on her side, but the fingerprint evidence would point the investigation at the name Ruby Harper soon enough, no matter how hard she tried to obstruct it.

Jo stepped into the flat, with Atkinson close behind. She went into the first bedroom, the one with the crib in it. She started opening drawers, slamming them when she found nothing but women's clothes, kids' clothes, toiletries. In the box under the bed there were shells of varying sizes and colors, the larger ones with intricate, earlike curves on the inside, shining pinkly, almost glowing. Jo weighed one in her hand. It was heavy, like a rock, its edges sharp and brittle.

In the other bedroom, it seemed at first that there was even less to find, until she opened the wardrobe and pushed aside the shirts. There was a metal box, padlocked shut. For a split second she paused, considering the consequences of what she was about to do:

tampering with evidence, ignoring direct orders, interfering with an investigation. Together it spelled court order, disciplinary, maybe even gross misconduct. Then she thought of Ruby's expression in the photograph from the train station. So far away, so lost and alone. Up until recently Jo had assumed Ruby was fine, but she had to admit that it was a convenient assumption—if Ruby was fine, then Jo didn't have to do anything. She realized now that it wasn't just the past few months: assuming that Ruby was fine had been her default position ever since the baby was born and handed over to Marianne. Well, she couldn't use that excuse now, or ever again. Ruby was in trouble, and the only person in a position to help was Joanna. She loved her job; she'd dedicated her life to it. But if it came to a choice, there was only one way to go. In that moment it didn't even feel like a difficult decision.

She took a pair of bolt cutters from her satchel and set them at an angle on the flimsy padlock bar, squeezing only slightly before the lock came apart with a metallic pinging sound, and she opened the box.

Underneath a sheaf of legal paperwork, at the bottom of the box, her hand closed around a black device, which on closer inspection turned out to be the receiver part of a high-end tracking device of the kind used by undercover operations.

Placing the device on the bed, she returned her attention to the box. There was a phone in there, the same make and model that Ruby had owned before the number changed. Was it Ruby's? Too risky to leave it here, just in case. She pocketed the phone at the same time as she noticed: the metal box was much deeper, by two or more inches, from the outside than from the inside. There was a secret compartment.

"Jo? Have you found anything?" Atkinson's voice floated through from the living space.

She felt in the bottom of the metal box, found a small ring attached to a chain and pulled. The false bottom came away.

"Maybe. I'm not sure."

"I heard on the radio, they're sending a patrol to check the apartment. We need to scarper."

She stared at the items revealed in the secret compartment, picked one of them up, flipped it open.

Atkinson came into the room where Harper was sitting on the bed, still with the metal box open on her lap, the bolt cutters and the broken padlock lying beside her.

"Did you cut that?" said Atkinson, pointing at the lock.

She ignored him. "Did we check Gregor Franks on the police computer?"

"Of course we did. I ran his details myself. He has a clean record, but I don't see how—"

"Did we check his prints, I meant?"

"The prints from this place matched the ones we took from Franks at the hospital, yes."

"But did anyone check the prints against the records on the police computer? To see if they matched any unsolved crimes?"

"No, of course not. I just told you, we checked his name and he had a clean record. We're not investigating Franks, we're trying to find out who attempted to kill him. Franks is our victim, Jo."

"He's a victim, sure," said Harper, "but whether or not he's actually who we think he is, that's another matter."

She handed over the passport that she'd found in the bottom of the box. The name was right: Gregor Christopher Franks. But the photo was of a different man entirely.

"I don't understand," said Atkinson.

"Whoever that man in hospital is," said Harper, "he's not Gregor Franks. And look," she said, indicating the other item lying in the bottom of the box. It looked like a rolled-up handkerchief, edged in blue stitching, a posy of embroidered flowers at one corner. The white cotton was stained with something dark.

"Is that—"

"Yes," said Harper, "I think it's blood."

With a gloved hand, she picked up the handkerchief and unwrapped it. Lying in her palm was a curl of something that looked like tree bark, but on closer inspection had a fingernail. A child's pinkie finger, brown from age, dried up, mummified, and stored in the bottom of a box as if it were a keepsake.

34

On a fine summer's evening, an inhabitant of Unst happened to be walking along the sandy margin of a voe. The moon was risen, and by her light he discerned at some distance before him a number of the sea-people, who were dancing with great vigour on the smooth sand. Near them he saw lying on the ground several seal-skins.
—Thomas Keightley, "The Mermaid Wife," 1870

The Injured Man
Remembers

THE MAN HAS traveled to the coast to inspect some property he is thinking of buying with the money he has now that he is Gregor. It's the second night of the trip. After he's gone to bed, he hears drumming coming from the beach, and is curious enough to get dressed and head out there. Might be a party, someone to play with. It's been so long since he's had the urge for a girl. He grabs a bottle of wine and leaves the rented cottage, barefoot.

The half-moon swims and flickers on the waves in multiple versions of itself. There is a soft lapping at the shore, but otherwise the sea moves silently, gleaming and swelling under a matte sky pierced with stars. It's too dark to see properly, but he feels his feet

"Long way
Cleethorpes?"

"We always t

He takes the

She moves up

skin on his thigh

"You know w

He looks dov

easy. He shakes h

"We girls get

A grin spread

When the wir

got a place we car

"I don't have

"Swim?" he l

miles.

Her face twit

tides."

"I don't see a

She's already

one shoulder. "D

At the rented

after that, she is o

trunk of his car. F

proofed apartmen

to be fun.

sinking into the wet beach as he walks, the water occasionally sucking at the sand beneath his soles. He likes the idea that as he makes his way toward the gathering of people at the bonfire, whatever impressions his bare feet leave behind will be erased by the sea as quickly as they are made.

From far out in the darkness, a scream. He stops and listens, straining his eyes in the direction of the horizon for the source of it. He glances farther up the beach at the dancers around the fire, but the drumming doesn't falter, and the silhouettes of the moving bodies keep the steady rhythm; they haven't heard it. Their laughter drifts toward him on a soft breeze. Gregor knows that he ought to run, to call out for their help with whoever is screaming. He wouldn't go into the water himself; he isn't a particularly strong swimmer. But maybe someone at the party has lifeguard training or knows of someone who does. He's not at all concerned for the person who may be in trouble in the water. His worry is that people will expect him to do something about it and that he will be obliged to make the effort to appear as if he is concerned. He stands on tiptoe, listening, watching the dancers.

The scream, when it comes again, pushes him down onto his heels. The breath he is holding comes out in a sigh. Not a human cry; it's a seal. Moonlight falls on the animal's pointed face as it nods in the inky darkness, whiskers dripping with saltwater, before disappearing under the surface.

Of course it was a seal—how ridiculous. He wishes he has someone to laugh at him then, that he'd brought a friend along after all. But then, he doesn't have any friends, not really. He hardly ever thinks of this, and even now, as he examines the fact, he doesn't feel anything about it. Not even a numbness, merely an absence.

He's close enough now that they will see him the moment they turn to look. He hovers in the shadows, waiting to see what will happen, whether he'll be welcomed, if it is that sort of a party. There are twelve or thirteen of them around the fire. None of them immediately turn in his direction, and he thinks about clearing his throat to draw their attention, but he does not. He's content, for the moment, to watch without being observed himself. A young woman is playing a hand drum that hangs from a strap over her shoulder, and next to her a young man sits the big woman, something passing between hits with a stick on the offbeats. Three girls danc[e] woman glances over at him, and her face has der, young men and women both, are around a[...] n't smile, but the accusation is gone. She returns leaning on each other, making patterns in the oung woman, and he thinks—no, he's sure, and pebbles. imperceptible—that she nods. Then, she sits

And that is when he sees her. Her hair is [...] mming starts up again. The scene resumes as her skin patched with sand. The curve of her a[...] s beginning to move to the beat. Gregor sits the muscles move, and the collarbone, dipped in e sand and opens his screw-top bottle. up to an exquisite jawline. n the seal calls once more, and the sound is

Beautiful creature, he thinks. And a second [...] *from me. She won't want me. Not at first, anyway* makes her way over to him, as he knows that she *They always do eventually.* njoying the rhythms, letting the drumming and

From where she crouches, drawing with a d[...] him as he waits for her. When she sits down at his the packed sand at her feet, she raises her eyes bottle from his hand, he notices a young man on something between them, as quick as that. He e fire get up and walk away. This young man of it, and he sees it in her eyes too, like a chim ce at them before he disappears into the shadows. same note within them both. etects bitterness in the other man's expression.

You're mine, he thinks, but her eyes dart y?" says Gregor. woman he hasn't noticed, seated on a crate behi the young man for a moment, then draws her The young woman's eyes dart back to meet his nglish?" Slowly the older one stands, a big woman, wid struck by her facial features, her wide-set eyes the drums falter, then stop. The old one's face is kbones. She has a strong nose and full lips. He warning. Gregor sees this, but he can't take l ght, the exact color of her eyes nor the shade of younger one for long. She's twitchy, like a w n that both are dark, and the hair hasn't been caught in a beam of electric light. *What's sh* time. He expected, when she was this close, wonders. l the tang of unwashed body that you often get

Gregor walks forward into the circle of fir ypes, but he can detect only a faint hint of sea- and smiles, friendly, unthreatening. "Hi," he say sh fish. The smell of her makes his stomach

"Can I help you?" says the big woman, he outh water, though he is not hungry. Still, he resonant. Even as she says it, she seems to rela smile he is wearing. It melts people. es. I'm from the north."

"I was just passing," says Gregor. "Looks lik ead sideways to look at him. "How north?" He shines the smile around the circle and b wine out to show them. There are murmurings. "that is not north. We're from the north. From women appraise him openly, their eyes roamin down his body, their hands rising to cover their u win then, I guess. What are you doing here?" tell they are whispering to each other. His attent On the summer solstice we party on the beach. her, to the young woman he has connected with nt place each time."

CHAPTER

35

THEN
Ruby
Thursday, December 20

R UBY NO LONGER felt safe anywhere. She carried the phone
he'd given her, even though it felt wrong to do so now that
she knew it was tracking her. The night she'd realized he was listening to her in her flat, she'd stopped spending time there alone.
It was better when she slept over at Gregor's on the sofa. Something about the fact that they all knew the cameras were there
made it less sinister. Occasionally she would wake, sweating, in
the small hours, stare up at the light fitting and think about phon-
ing Joanna, telling her everything, asking her to come rescue
them. But then she'd remember, she couldn't do that without him
knowing, and if he found out he'd been betrayed, then what? He
was clearly capable of violence. He had her old phone with all her
contacts—did he therefore realize who Joanna was, that she was a
police officer? No, she was just listed as Joanna, so there was no
reason he would know that. The idea that she still had secrets
from Gregor was a comfort. Something she could use against him,
if it came to it.

She thought of the Yoga Man days, when she would spy on him in the dark, convinced she was being so secretive, watching him when he didn't know. But he did know; he'd always known. At the time she'd enjoyed the fantasy that he was performing for her, but now the thought of it made her shudder. She'd started to take sleeping pills again, and several times found herself dosing up on beta blockers during the day for the anxiety.

It had been a week since they went looking for the coat and found the box. Ruby had repeatedly tried and failed to make Constance leave without it. Time was running out—Gregor's words still rang in her head, the idea that he might be getting ready to send her to a "residential treatment program." She didn't believe that was his plan—not for a moment. It was too awful to try to imagine what his actual plan might be.

Perhaps she couldn't save them both. She'd decided she would try once more, and then, if Constance wouldn't come, she would simply take Leonie. It was monstrous to allow Gregor—and Constance—to continue to keep the child here. Ruby was prepared for a fight, a physical one, if it came to it. Leonie had to come first. None of the needs of the adults were as important as that kid's safety. She was even prepared to phone Joanna, to let the police deal with it if her hand were forced. Anything was better than this. And if, as a result, the child was taken into care, then so be it. At least if Leonie were in care, she'd get to go outside.

Ruby opened the door to the flat with her key. Leonie was seated in the living room, cross-legged on the rug, facing the big screen, with headphones concealing her ears. *Peppa Pig* was on. Ruby kissed her on the head, but she was too engrossed to respond. Gregor wasn't there; she could tell from the atmosphere. When he was in the flat, it thrummed with a certain kind of palpable tension, even if he was in the bedroom with the door shut. When it was just mother and daughter, there was a much more pleasant vibe. But there was nevertheless a background hum of vigilance, of awareness that they were being watched at every moment. That feeling never fully went away. Every word she spoke out loud was for the benefit of Gregor, to reinforce the things they wanted him to hear and to hide the things they didn't.

Ruby could hear the shower shutting off in the bathroom, the sound of the glass door opening and shutting. "I did your shopping," she called, going through and unpacking the bag in the kitchen. "They didn't have the rice you like."

After a short while, Constance appeared in the doorframe, her long hair wetting the shoulders of her top. She came into the kitchen and flicked the switch on the extractor fan, another trick allowing them to speak more freely.

"I found it."

Ruby's eyes reacted before she could think. She wanted to jump up and down but stopped herself. If she'd found the coat, they could leave right now. "Where? How? You've looked everywhere."

"Everywhere inside, yes, many times. But he went out yesterday, and he didn't lock the door. Come."

They were silent as they stepped outside onto the landing. Ruby listened hard for movement from below. Constance reached up to stick a piece of tape over the tiny lens of the camera that covered the doorway.

To the side of the door, there was a utilities cabinet set into the wall. Constance held up a small key. "This was in the kitchen. I never knew what it was for, until now." She unlocked the padlock and opened the door, then quickly drew out something that looked like a swathe of gray fabric and bundled it into her arms. She hurried inside. Ruby bent to close the cabinet, and as she did Leonie came running out the door, laughing, heading for the stairwell.

"Leonie, come back here!" Ruby grabbed the small girl and carried her inside the flat, just as a door closed softly on the floor below. Sarah. She had to try to check in on Mrs. Stefanidis before they went, make sure she had everything she needed for a few weeks. It was possible Ruby wouldn't be coming back for a long time.

Once in the living room, Ruby stuck another piece of tape over the pinhead camera in the light fitting.

Leonie started to fuss, trying to get to the front door again, restrained by Constance.

"Here you go, honey," said Ruby, handing her half a peeled banana. It seemed to do the trick for the moment. The child went back to watch her TV program.

Constance sat with the old leather coat draped on her knees. It was dark gray in color and looked dry and cracked, like it hadn't been cared for.

"That's it?"

"Yes." She stroked it tenderly, as if it were a second child of hers.

"It's kind of . . . tatty, isn't it?"

"Yes," she said, letting her tears fall on the rough surface of the leather.

Where the salt tears fell, circles of the cloth became lumines-cent. Constance rubbed at it with her thumbs in sweeping motions, spreading the moisture across the garment. As she did, more tears fell, and as the circles of gleaming anthracite gray grew on the surface, they met and joined together, spreading across the coat until it shone. Soon it was completely transformed.

"It's so beautiful." Ruby watched as Constance ran her hands over the skin, a strange light seeming to come from within it, illu-minating Constance's face. But no, now that she looked closely; the glow was coming from Constance too.

Ruby couldn't believe what she was seeing. How were the tears having such an effect on the fabric? It was as if each one, as it splashed and spread across the coat, was capable of rehydrating much more surface area than one tiny droplet ought to have been. *It's like magic,* she thought, swiftly followed by *Don't be ridiculous.*

Then she caught sight of something else that made her pause. "Your hands," said Ruby, and Constance quickly hid them under the coat. "Let me see them. I never noticed before but . . ." Was she imagining it?

Constance stayed very still for a long time, looking down at her lap. Then she brought out one fist and uncurled it slowly. The skin in between her fingers was webbed.

"Have you always had that?"

Constance nodded.

"Why didn't I see it?"

She shrugged. "People only notice the things they expect to be there."

"Can I . . ." Ruby reached for the shining pelt, but Constance yanked the thing away from her.

"No, don't touch it."

Ruby withdrew, slightly hurt. "I wasn't going to do anything."

"If you touch it, something is lost. And I've already lost so much. Do you understand?"

Constance's wide eyes were bright with hope, shiny with tears.

"I'm so sorry," said Ruby. "I didn't believe it was real. Or if it was real, I didn't think he would have kept it. I thought you were crazy to stay here just for that."

"He had no choice but to keep it if he wanted me alive. It would be like asking me to live without a head."

Ruby thought she knew what Constance meant; she felt that way about her violin. More recently, she'd started to feel the same way about Leonie.

From beneath the coat, Constance brought out a white comb, carved from a shell. Ruby couldn't understand where the comb had been hidden; the coat didn't appear to have any pockets, or even any arms. It was more like a cloak or a long, unfilled pillow-case. Constance turned the comb over in her hand, held it out for Ruby to take.

"It's exquisite," said Ruby, and tried to hand it back, aware of the strange impulse she'd had to touch the coat, to possess it. Constance indicated that it was okay this time, that she should keep it.

"There's only one like that. After I go home, that's how you'll find me."

Ruby looked at the teeth of the comb, so finely crafted she was afraid they might snap if she touched them; at the shape of it, how it fitted into her palm. On the edge of it, the maker had created an intricate, intertwining mermaid pattern. It must have taken weeks of work.

"I don't understand what you mean."

"Don't worry. You'll understand when you need to."

Ruby felt light-headed. The way the coat had transformed before her eyes from a cracked old thing to a soft, rippling fabric somewhere between leather and suede. She'd never seen anything like it. What kind of fabric did that? She held the comb in one hand, but she couldn't take her eyes from the coat. Once again she could feel the draw of the garment. She wanted more than anything to take it in her hands, to stroke it, to hold it to her face. Constance caught her looking, must have seen the covetous gleam in Ruby's eyes, because she held it closer to her, crossed her arms over it, and leaned away. Ruby held out her hand; she couldn't help it.

"Just let me touch it. Please." Her fingertips reached out, trembling. Constance was saying something, but the words weren't quite clear. She reached a little further. If she could only hold it, feel it for a second . . .

A sharp pain seared Ruby's knuckles, and she jumped back, shouting out with surprise. Constance had slapped her hand, hard.

"What did you do that for? It really hurt."

"You weren't listening to me. You were under its spell."

The coat had gone; she'd put it away somewhere out of sight, and without the presence of it, Ruby felt shame at what she'd tried to do. This is what Gregor must have felt, though he wouldn't for a moment have thought to fight it. He saw it, liked it, and took it for himself. The way he'd been planning to do with Ruby. He'd hidden her phone, put a tracker on her. Would he have gone as far as to keep her violin? No, he hadn't needed to. Leonie was the reason she couldn't stay away. She saw then how—and why—he'd offered Leonie up to her in pieces, like bait. All the small things he'd encouraged her to do for the baby over the past few weeks—the nappies, the feeding when Constance wasn't able, the babysitting of both mother and child. It was real, the trust they shared, the bond. But it did exactly that: she was bonded, now, and it felt unbreakable, love and confinement in one, like sweet shackles.

Ruby was so glad the coat existed, that it was as wonderful as Constance had hinted at. For all this time she'd thought Constance was delusional. Turned out she was telling the truth about it all along, though what she'd seen only a few moments ago, as the coat transformed, already seemed like a strange kind of dream. It ought to make sense, and yet it did not. There wasn't time for reflection; for now, the fact that it was real was enough. She thought back to what else Gregor must have lied about, and concluded that it was in fact everything. He breathed lies with every word he spoke. There was no cult, only a community with very particular ways. He'd taken Constance and kept her here; it was as simple as that. All the seal talk was unusual, sure, but Constance was under extreme pressure, and to her, the stories were true. The stories were part of their way of life. And poor Leonie, living her small life within these walls, never imagining the size of the world outside. It wasn't too late for the child, Ruby realized. Not by a long shot.

"You've been looking for the coat all this time. And you've finally found it."

"Yes," said Constance. She didn't look happy. Not at all. Her eyes followed Leonie as she made her way around the room, chatting to herself, picking things up, exploring.

"So, you can finally leave. If that's what you want to do?"

"More than anything."

"Constance. Why are you crying?"

"I want to go home."

"Then go. Gregor's not here—he might not be back for days. There's enough time. You can contact your family, and they can come and get you. Right?"

She nodded slowly. "They will come and get me. Now I have my skin."

My skin. What a strange way of putting it. "That's right. So, you should get ready. All of Leonie's stuff will need packing. I can help you." Ruby started to walk to where the shopping bags were kept. There were no suitcases that she knew of; shopping bags would have to do.

"Wait, you don't understand. They will come and get *me*. But they won't take Leonie."

Ruby paused. She turned slowly. "Why can't they take Leonie?"

"Because she wasn't born in the skin, like I was. She doesn't have a coat."

"Can't they give her one when she gets there?"

Constance shook her head. "It doesn't work like that."

Ruby said, "Can't they make an exception? She's your baby. Your parents' grandchild. They'll be thrilled. Won't they?"

Constance was shaking her head. "No. They won't be thrilled. They'll be disappointed. They might even reject me, too, when they find out about her."

"But . . . how? Why?"

"When he took me, I was supposed to be married to someone else the next day. On the island, babies outside marriage simply don't happen. I went with him because it was part of my rite, the way that we—how can I put it—strengthen the bloodline? But children, whether conceived on the wedding night or during the *wandering* night before, must be born into wedlock. Otherwise, they don't exist, not in the eyes of the elders."

"That's bloody ridiculous. It's the twenty-first century."

"It doesn't matter. Tradition and the old ways are what we live by. They are like your laws."

"Well, why would you want to go back, then? If you can't take her with you?"

There was a pause, and Ruby thought perhaps Constance would change her mind, see how unreasonable she was being. But she shook her head. "It's my home. They're my family. I have to go."

Ruby stared at her. She didn't think she would have to say it. The silence stretched out, and it became apparent that she would. "But, Constance, Leonie's your family too."

Constance blinked. She gazed at Leonie while she spoke. "I must persuade them. But it would mean going back without her, first of all." She turned to Ruby. "I need your help. I can't do it without you. I can't leave her with him and I—"

"I'll do it," said Ruby, although she had no idea what it was she was being asked to do. All she knew was that she would do it, whatever it was. Because she loved Constance, but mostly because she loved Leonie. And the little mite had no one else.

They worked out what they had to do, what false trails they could set to throw Gregor off. Ruby would get a train to Lincoln, where she would take the tracking device out of her phone and put it on a train heading south. They would dress the same as each other so that when Gregor tried to follow, if he asked anyone whether they had seen either of them, the stories would be confusing. Constance would take Leonie and meet Ruby at Grimsby, where Ruby would take the baby so that Constance could meet her family at the beach.

"So they'll come for you in a boat, to the beach at Cleethorpes? Why there? Why not the docks at Grimsby?"

Constance's face twitched slightly before she answered. "That is where they last saw me. They come and look for the lost, every solstice, in the place they were lost. It's a tradition."

"They won't have forgotten you? Or assumed that you'd run away?"

Constance looked stricken. "I hope not. If so, then I'm lost forever."

They straightened out the rest of the plan. After the handover, Ruby and Leonie would get on a train with a ticket to Scotland but get off somewhere else and hide out for a few days, just in case Gregor had somehow managed to track them that far. After that, Ruby would make her way to a secluded beach on a tiny island in the Hebrides, by any means possible and without being detected. Constance would meet them there, having persuaded the elders to take Leonie in. Then, Constance and Leonie would start their new life together on the old skerry, where they belonged.

"What will you do, though?" asked Constance. "Once we're gone?"

Ruby thought of her broken family, the increasingly desperate missed calls and messages from Marianne every Sunday night; the last, brief phone call she'd allowed herself with Joanna. Once she was done with this, perhaps she'd be strong enough to deal with all of that.

"I'll be free of him. We both will. I can start my life again."

"How will you? He won't stop searching for me and Leonie. My family will protect me from him. But you? You won't be free of him until he's dead."

Ruby hoped it wouldn't come to that. Gregor was away, not expected back until the evening of the next day. By then they'd be long gone and impossible to track.

36

NOW
Joanna
Monday, December 24

"THERE'S BEEN NO change in his condition," said Dr. Locke. "To be honest, I'm surprised there hasn't been a deterioration."

"But you said on the phone that you needed me to attend. If there's been no change, did I really have to come all the way down here?"

Joanna had been expecting to find Gregor awake. She'd wanted to ask him so many questions.

"I need your help to proceed. You may be interested to learn that a colleague of mine has selected Mr. Franks for a medical trial involving a functional MRI scan."

"I don't know what that is."

"Essentially, it's a scan where you can view the brain in real-time and see different parts lighting up in response to different stimuli."

"Like, you poke him with a needle and see if he feels pain?"

"That's among the things they may do, yes. Another is to ask him questions."

"But if he's a vegetable . . ."

"Well, that's kind of the point of the trial. To find out if he has any brain function, any consciousness remaining."

"I can ask him questions?"

The doctor's eyebrows shot up. "You?"

"I can sit in on the scan, right? Isn't that why you asked me to attend?"

"I suppose you could. But the reason I needed to see you was because we would need to obtain permissions to go ahead. There's an ethical procedure we have to follow."

"I can okay it. Where do I sign?"

"I was hoping you'd obtained that court order, in the absence of next of kin?"

"I don't need one," said Jo. "Not if it's part of a police inquiry and in the public interest. As the SIO I can authorize it for the purposes of assisting the current investigation."

"But the study isn't part of the investigation, Detective."

"It will be if you let me sit in the control room."

"I honestly don't see how . . ."

Joanna pointed at the still form of the man who, until recently, she'd thought was called Gregor Franks, lying on his back in the hospital bed. "He *knows* things. If I can gauge his reaction to some questions I have, it might make the difference between finding the little girl we're looking for and not finding her."

The doctor paused, considering.

"I need to make some calls first. And it'll take a while to get the patient ready for the scan and have him brought up from the ward. I hope you're not in a hurry."

After the doctor left, Joanna walked up to the bedside and stood next to the man who had been living as Gregor Franks. She watched his motionless face. "Soon I'll be able to speak to you and see how you react," she said. There was no response. She bent closer. "You won't be able to hide for much longer, whoever you are. I'm going to see right inside your brain."

While she waited in the control room of the MRI, Joanna dialed Ruby's number and listened again to the bot reciting the phone-switched-off message. She pulled out the phone she'd taken from Gregor's flat and looked at it. It couldn't tell her anything more than it had when she'd gone through it the night before—it was Ruby's old phone, and it hadn't been used since September. The missed calls page made her sad, but not as sad as the gallery, where she found only one photo of herself, grimacing, trying to avoid being captured. She remembered Ruby taking it, laughing at Joanna's camera-phobia, how Jo had held up a hand to try to block the lens. She wished now that she'd simply smiled, like a normal person.

The door opened and Atkinson entered.

"Jo. What the hell are you doing?"

"How come you're here, Steve?"

"I came to find you. Someone from the hospital contacted me to confirm we were okay to go ahead with some kind of fancy scan on Franks. Apparently, you've said it's part of the investigation."

"Well, it is. They can look inside his brain. I'm going to see how he reacts to certain things."

"But he can't answer."

"I have a plan—don't worry. His reaction will be enough. Unless Dr. Locke's right, and the bugger's brain-dead."

"They said that because it was part of the police investigation, some of the cost should come from the police budget. Do you know what fifty percent of an fMRI scan costs?"

"Oh. Does Thrupp know?"

"He will soon. And then he'll wonder why I didn't tell him."

"Ah."

Atkinson sank heavily down into a chair.

"Jo. What we did last night was stupid. And dangerous. We've got information the investigation needs, but we can't tell anyone because of how we got it. That passport—and the finger, for fucks sake. The fact that Gregor isn't who we think he is."

"Relax, Steve. We were one step in front, that's all. CSI will be opening up that box as we speak. They'll find the passport and then they'll know everything we know, and they'll start running checks on Mr. Mysterious immediately. And then there's this scan. If I ask him a question and his brain lights up in response, we'll be able to work out where Ruby has gone."

"Oh, so you're planning to stake your reputation on a highly expensive version of the yes or no game, with no guarantee that it will even work?"

"It will work. You'll see."

"Even if it does work, we'll still be in trouble. You think Thrupp's going to overlook the fact that we broke into a suspect's property and then carried out an unrecorded search of the victim's place?"

"We won't be in trouble if we get the results. Plus, he's not going to find out about either of those things."

"You broke the lock on Ruby's apartment."

"After you left, I went back and fixed it. Good as new."

"You cut that padlock on the box in Gregor's wardrobe."

"I replaced the padlock too. It was only a cheap model. Anyway, they already cataloged the key, so they'll have to cut it themselves if they want to get inside quickly."

Atkinson rubbed his temples and made a low, frustrated groan.

There was a tense silence, in which they both stared through the glass into the MRI scan room at the huge, space-age machine.

"This is too risky, boss. I think you should—"

"I'm only going to ask a few routine questions."

"Of a man who can't consent to being asked. The ethics of this are all over the shop."

The door to the control room opened, and a technician entered, along with Dr. Locke and a short, bald man who introduced himself as Mr. Cunningham, the consultant radiologist in charge of the trial.

On the other side of the large glass screen, the patient was wheeled into the white-walled scan room by a porter. A moment later a team of staff entered and transferred the man's limp body to the platform that would feed him into the cylinder at the center of the MRI. One nurse remained in the room and began to place straps on the patient. Through the speakers they could hear her talking to him as she worked.

"I'm just getting you ready for the scanner, Greg, okay? It'll be almost the same routine as last time with the CT. Don't try to move while you're in there; it can distort the results."

Joanna found it touching that the nurse talked to the patient as if he could hear. She wasn't writing him off as brain-dead, then.

The technician in the control room started adjusting the equipment, switching on every screen on the bank of monitors in front of them. She pointed out the microphone Jo would need to speak into so that Gregor would hear her questions.

"What should I be looking out for on the scan?"

The radiologist brought up a recorded scan of another patient.

"This area here"—he pointed with a pen—"is the hippocampus, associated with emotions and memory. That's the bit you need to keep an eye on. I'd expect it to light up at anything personally meaningful."

The scan video showed splashes of red and yellow appearing and dissipating on the screen.

"We're obviously presenting the patient with stimuli here. The darker colors represent increased activity."

"And was this patient as outwardly unresponsive as Mr. Franks is now?"

He nodded. "Every patient in this trial has been selected because they have been diagnosed with persistent vegetative state due to infection or drug overdose. The head injury Mr. Franks has sustained complicates things slightly, but he's still eligible. A bonus of the scan is that if the head injury turns out to be more significant than the CT showed, we'll be able to consider further treatment."

Jo was only half listening, thinking about the things she was going to ask. *Do you know where Ruby is?* was the first question. She could already picture the bloom of orange and purple caused by the reaction that question would get. *Who does that finger we found belong to?* The screen would light up like a firework display. She'd need to think carefully about how to frame the questions if this was actually going to help in any specific way beyond confirming her suspicions. All she would see would be emotional response. Perhaps she would need to take a very methodical approach, listing every major UK city Ruby might have gone to until she got a response. It could take a very long time.

"How long do I have to question him?"

"We generally scan for about ten minutes."

"Can I have longer if I need it?"

"No," said Mr. Cunningham.

"Ready," said the nurse, her voice metallic through the speakers. She left the patient alone in the room. The technician pressed a button, and the platform started to draw the man's body into the machine.

From the angle Joanna was looking from, the patient's face was obscured by the foam helmet as he was slowly inserted into the aperture. She hadn't noticed when she stood next to his bed earlier on, but his body seemed different. Thinner than when she'd inspected him on Saturday. Perhaps a couple of days on a liquid-only diet will do that to you.

Once the man was fully inside the scanner, the doctor leaned forward and pressed the button on the intercom microphone.

'Mr. Franks, in a moment we're going to ask you a few questions. If you're able to, just think of the answer for me. We'll be able to pick up any brain activity on the scan. If you can hear me, this is your chance to communicate with us, okay?"

The patient started to cough and splutter. He was coming round. Joanna stood up. She could see his feet kicking in the restraints.

"Oh, shit," said the doctor, scanning the readouts on the heart monitor. "That's not right."

"What's happening? Is he waking up?"

"We need to get him out. Right now."

The technician pushed the button to slide the platform from the machine. The doctor left the control room and appeared a moment later in the scan room, followed by two nurses.

"He's fitting," shouted the doctor. "Let's get him back on the trolley."

As more staff entered the room to transfer the patient, Harper and Atkinson stared through the glass at the carefully managed emergency happening on the other side of it. Someone pressed the resuscitation alarm. Blood dripped from the patient's head as he was lifted across. And Joanna saw a strand of hair peeping from the foam helmet, the wrong color, the wrong length. The man was too skinny. His legs didn't reach the end of the hospital bed. She wrenched open the control room door and ran around to the scan room, but she didn't need to get a good look at the much younger man lying there. She knew already.

"That's not him."

"What?" said Atkinson. "But how?"

Jo started running in the direction of the exit, but there were too many options. The hospital was huge. It had about forty exits. She raised her radio and pressed to connect, summoning assistance to help with the search, still running down corridors and flights of stairs, with no sense of where she should run, knowing that it was useless because she was looking for a man in a porter's uniform, a man well-practiced at disappearing, who could move through the hospital—and through the world—without being seen by anyone.

37

NOW
Joanna
Monday, December 24

THE HOSPITAL LIFT security tape made grim viewing. Thrupp joined Harper and Atkinson in the CCTV monitoring station, the DI having made his way across town on blue lights the moment he heard what had happened.

The first part of the footage showed an apparently unconscious patient being wheeled into the lift by the porter. The porter then stood facing away from his charge, so that he didn't see the patient's fist uncurl, revealing what he had stolen from the trolley, unaware of the length of tubing being unraveled, until it was looped around his neck and pulled tight. During the struggle, "Gregor" managed to use an elbow to press the emergency stop button to halt the lift between floors. The porter collapsed, lifeless, and the next moment, the patient grabbed the smaller man under the arms, dragged his limp body up on to the hospital bed and started removing his clothes.

"I've never seen anything like it," said Thrupp.

"How long do you think he's been lying there, pretending to be in a coma?" said Joanna. She knew then that when she'd spoken to him that morning, he would have heard every word. *"I'm going to see right inside your brain,"* she'd said. Her face had been inches from his.

On the screen, now wearing the porter's uniform, "Gregor" had removed the protective helmet he'd been wearing and was fitting it on the porter. He took the other man's glasses and used them to inspect his reflection, tidying his hair under the uniform cap before putting the glasses on as a final touch, then releasing the emergency stop mechanism. A moment later the lift doors opened, and he maneuvered the bed out confidently, as if that had been his job all along.

Thrupp turned to Jo. "He can't have gone very far. I've mobilized all the patrol vehicles and officers we can spare. Let's hope he collapses from blood loss—after all, the man does have a head wound."

Joanna said, "I think he's stronger than we imagine, sir. You saw what he did with that porter. He's cunning too."

"More than you know," said Thrupp. "I've got a confession to make, in fact."

"Oh? What's that, sir?" Jo and Atkinson exchanged a micro-glance.

"First thing this morning, one of the CSI's found evidence in Franks's flat that the victim might not be called Franks at all. There was a passport with a different photograph. We showed it to the agent who deals with Franks's rental property, and he identified the man in the passport picture as Franks. The photo of our patient on the driver's license, however, turns out to be a fake. The agent didn't recognize our man at all. Apparently, they've been doing business entirely over email for the past three years. Haven't even spoken on the phone."

Atkinson said, "What? He's stolen another man's identity? Oh my god." Harper wanted to kick him for his terrible acting.

Thrupp carried on, oblivious. "We checked his fingerprints against unsolved cases in the system. Should have done that to start with, but there was no reason to suspect the man."

"What did you find?" asked Jo.

"A few years ago there was a spate of burglaries, all with the same fingerprint evidence, but we never found the perpetrator. Our man's fingerprints were a match."

"I don't understand, sir. You said you had a confession to make," said Harper. "I don't see what you could have done wrong."

"I made a judgment call. First thing this morning, I knew this man had committed a crime in stealing Gregor Franks's identity, but I decided not to organize a guard for him because he was in a coma at the time of discovery. Why would a man in a coma need security? And now this has happened. So I have to take some of the responsibility for the injury to that poor porter."

Atkinson was apparently studying his own shoes, in detail.

"The burglary offenses connected to this man weren't of a violent nature," said Jo.

"No."

"Therefore you had no reason to believe he was a danger."

"I suppose."

"And, like you say, we'll find him soon enough. He's not going to get far, the state he's in. Steve and I can join the search."

"No. You need to concentrate on finding the girl—and the two women. We've still no leads on that. I'll see you back at the station."

"Yes, sir."

"Oh, and I'd appreciate it if you used your discretion with what I've told you. No obligation, of course; you're both upstanding officers. I don't want a cover-up, just for you to keep it under your hats for the time being. Gossip, you know. I'll be making a full report, detailing my decision-making process. Hopefully, the chief constable will see fit to accept my reasoning."

"Of course, sir, no problem," said Atkinson.

"Don't beat yourself up about it, sir," said Joanna. "Any one of us would have done the same."

"One last thing," said the DI, fixing Joanna with a steely eyeball. "Don't try to charge my investigation with any more MRI scans. Unless you want to pay for them yourself."

"Yes, sir. Sorry, sir."

* * *

She drove back to the police station, the police radio turned up so she could monitor the search. By the time she'd parked and made her way to the incident room, she was feeling despondent about

their chances of catching him. There'd been no sightings whatsoever since he'd escaped from the ward. It was as if he were the
Invisible Man.

In the incident room, Eddie was waiting with news of the
search for Constance B and Leonie. Like the doctor, he'd been up
most of the night, and it showed.

"Hi, Eddie. Did you find them?" Joanna struggled to control
the slight tremor in her voice. If they'd found Ruby and Leonie, at
least she'd have a chance at getting to them first, at keeping them
safe from the fugitive.

"We checked CCTV at the Edinburgh train station, where
their journey was supposed to end. There's nothing. She didn't get
off there. So, we've had to search cameras at every stop on the line,
but I'm afraid to say, it's not a straightforward process. Some of the
systems are still analog. We've been uploading all the tapes and
programming the face-recognition software to search. It all takes
time. As a result, we don't have anything yet, I'm afraid."

"How long until you do?" said Harper.

"Maybe another couple of days."

"Can't you make it happen quicker?"

"I'm afraid not. Today we're having the tapes couriered over,
but getting them into our system is a bit of a laborious task, as you
can imagine. We have to convert them to digital in real-time, and
then—"

"Well, get some more people on it, can't you?"

"There isn't anyone. And I'm going home."

"Can't you stay? Do a bit of overtime?"

"No," said Eddie. "In case you haven't noticed, I've done ten
hours overtime already. And tomorrow's Christmas. My annual
leave started yesterday; I should be at home relaxing by now."

She thought about ramping up the pressure, letting him know
just how urgent it was. Maybe she could try yelling at him. But
there was no point burning bridges that might be useful in the
future, if she could help it.

"Fine," she said. "You go home and have a break—you deserve
it. But if you could do one small, tiny favour for me before you
do."

"What is it?"

"I need you to set up email alerts for any mobile phone or data usage that happens on this number." She wrote down Ruby's new phone number and handed it to him. "Now, I realize we're not supposed to have alerts going to personal emails, but this phone belongs to a suspect, and I'm sure you understand the need for urgency on this case. I wouldn't ask you, but it's Christmas Day tomorrow; there won't be anyone manning the surveillance system, and if the person turns the phone on, to contact family, for instance, then there'll be an opportunity there that we don't want to miss."

"You'll need the DI to authorize that."

"I will, of course, but he's not in right now, and if you want to get home quickly . . . It's on my head, shall we say."

"Right, fine. I'll do it. But then I'm out of here." He hurried away, clutching the paper with Ruby's number on it.

"Thank you, Eddie," she said. "I love you, Eddie."

She thought she heard him mutter, "Yeah, right," before he disappeared from view.

CHAPTER

38

It happened that one of the children, in the course of his play, found concealed beneath a stack of corn a seal's skin. Her eyes glistened with rapture—she gazed upon it as her own—as the means by which she could pass through the ocean that led to her native home. She burst into an ecstasy of joy, which was only moderated when she beheld her children, whom she was now about to leave; and after hastily embracing them, she fled with all speed toward the seaside.
—Charles John Tibbets, "The Mermaid Wife," 1889

Constance
Friday, December 21, early morning

THERE ARE ONLY a few hours until she will be gone from this place forever. Ruby has left—she went last night so that she could start her journey in a different place from Constance's, to make the tracks they leave behind them as confusing as possible. Soon Ruby will set off to catch the first train south, and later they will meet up to make the switch. Constance couldn't have chosen a better guardian for Leonie; Ruby is a true friend. A savior. Without her, none of this would be possible. She stares at the hands of the clock, willing them to go faster.

When she hears it, she instantly remembers the tape. The small pieces of masking tape she put on the cameras, that she forgot to remove. He's looked on the camera feed, he's seen that some of the cameras are obscured. He's come back, and he's angry enough to make a noise loud enough to alert her. She gathers Leonie into her arms, runs and hides as quickly as she can. He'll kill her if he finds her trying to leave. She knows this in her bones.

The conch shell rests on the side of the bath. Heavy and curved, with delicate white edges and a polished interior, it sits just as it has since Gregor bought it from the gift shop in the seaside town where he first met Constance. Until this moment, the shell has always been an ornament, something to look at.

This should not be happening. They had expected him to be gone the entire night, and the next day too. She eyes the conch shell as she crouches behind the door, an idea forming in the split second before his footsteps slow to a stop outside the room.

"Are you in there?"

She doesn't answer. Silently, she slips her hand inside the shell. It is cool and smooth, hard and heavy as a rock. The weight of it, hugged to her belly, comforts her.

There is a soft whimper from the bundle of towels under the sink, and she reaches to stroke the child, to quiet her. It won't be long. Only a few seconds more. Then it will all be over.

He speaks through the door. "Leonie? It's Daddy. Don't worry, sweetie. I'm coming in. Don't be scared, okay? There's going to be a big bang."

But before he can charge at the door, she unlocks it. The sound of the bolt being drawn makes him pause. He waits, perhaps to see if she'll come out. For a while nothing happens. Then, he opens the door and steps inside.

The shell flies through the air, her hand inside it, a deadly knuckle-duster, connecting with the man's skull with such force that the shell is cracked. The man is felled; he drops quickly, though to her it seems in slow motion, a building demolished by dynamite. In the silence that follows, she turns to check that Leonie didn't see anything. The bundle of towels is shaking, but it's still intact. She lets go of the shell and picks up the girl, holding her head so she can't see, taking her away from the slowly growing pool of blood and into the bedroom.

"Wait here, baby girl."

She lays Leonie in the cradle. Her silent cry contorts her face, but Constance can't comfort her—not now. The job isn't finished.

Constance takes the brown bottle from the bathroom cabinet, and goes through to the other bathroom where Gregor is starting to stir. He is trying to sit up. He eyes her with confusion.

"Gregor," she cries, "what's happened? Don't try to get up too fast. Here, let me help you."

She grabs an arm as the man tries to stand up. He slips on the blood, and Constance only needs to push him a little to help him fall backward into the tub, where he hits his head again and lies still.

She kneels, using towels so that she doesn't get covered in his blood, and drips the brown liquid from the bottle into his mouth. She squeezes his nostrils shut to make him swallow. When he's had the whole lot, she stops.

Constance wonders if it's going to be enough. She wonders if he's going to die. She hopes he does, and then she hopes he doesn't, because Ruby will be the one left behind. She'll be the one they try to blame.

Either way it's too late now. His breathing slows, becomes steady, until she almost can't tell whether he's breathing or not. It's better for Ruby if he's dead. It's better for all of them.

Constance chews her thumb and stares at the man, bent and broken-looking in the empty tub, a towel bunched at his feet.

Later, when she's dressed and ready, Constance returns to the bathroom and turns on the bath taps. She takes a pair of scissors and cuts off his clothes, to make it look like an accident, as if he was alone, that he has slipped and fallen badly. He groans when she shifts his body to get the clothes out from under and she jumps back, afraid he will rise up and attack her, the way he has so many times before. His eyes don't open. He settles, grows still, but the fear doesn't leave her. She pulls his head forward, hits him again with the conch shell, in the same place as before. This time, the blow lands with a squelch. Constance doesn't notice the small piece of the shell's lip that breaks off and lands on the tiles. She bundles up the cut clothes; she'll drop them in a litter bin somewhere in the city.

She locks the bathroom from the outside, using a teaspoon wedged in the groove of the bolt to turn it. She wraps her coat across her body, picks up Leonie in one arm and swings the changing bag over a shoulder. Time to go. Tonight she'll return to her old life, but even as she feels the joy and anticipation of that, she is brokenhearted. Because it means letting go of everything she has in this life, including her baby girl.

39

NOW
Ruby
Monday, December 24

THE COLD CLAMPED itself around Ruby's head and made the inside of her ears hurt. She zipped up Leonie's jacket and pulled the hood over the child's head. Then she tried to fasten her own coat, letting go of Leonie for a second. Almost in the same moment, her arm shot out to grab the child again as she got ready to run off. Ruby hauled her up to eye level.

"Baby girl? Please don't do that. You scared me so much."

Leonie stared blankly at Ruby, as if she didn't understand. Then she laughed and started wriggling to be let down. Ruby had to hold the little hand tightly to stop Leonie wrenching it away. With her free hand, Ruby struggled to jam a beanie hat on her own head, tried to hold her jacket closed with frozen fingers as they made their way down the platform and out onto the streets of York.

They'd spent the past two nights holed up in bed and breakfasts, one in Leicester, the other on the outskirts of Leeds. The landlady this morning had served fizzy orange in a wineglass in lieu of bucks fizz to mark the season, but she'd also folded her arms and looked at her watch, anxious for her unwanted guests to leave. The woman had made no secret of the fact that Ruby and Leonie were inconveniencing her when they'd turned up late the previous night. ("I never open on the twenty-third; I'm afraid you'll have to go elsewhere.") Ruby's distraught face had softened her slightly, but it was Leonie's silent weeping when she saw Ruby was upset that had swung it in the end. ("Fine, stay the night. But you'll have to change the sheets yourself.") On their way out, the woman had half-heartedly asked Ruby where she was going for Christmas, though as she spoke, she was opening the front door and ushering them through it as if to make sure they definitely were going somewhere, and she didn't really care where exactly that was.

"Don't worry about us," Ruby had said, thinking, *As if you would.* "We're going to see an old friend."

"Oh, good," said the landlady, seemingly relieved to be let off the hook after being such a Scrooge. "You have a lovely Christmas now, won't you?"

Ruby worried now that she'd said too much. If Gregor some-how found out that they'd been at that B&B and questioned the owner, would "an old friend" give him anything to go on? She couldn't recall ever mentioning Sam to him. Not that Ruby would have talked about Sam in any great detail to anyone. The pair had a patchy history, had shared a fair few dark moments. They'd helped each other when they'd been at their lowest points; those stories were no one else's business. She also knew, deep down, that Sam was in love with her. But she couldn't recall every single thing she'd spoken about to Gregor, especially in the time before she knew what he was.

The taxi driver was wearing a Santa hat, but his face was thin and pinched. "It's double time today, love."

"Merry bloody Christmas," she muttered as they pulled away.

When the cab arrived at the wharf car park, the night was closing in around them. Only a few windows were lit in the barges that wintered there. Leonie was almost asleep again and had to be carried. The moment they'd paid and left, the taxi reversed away at high speed, leaving them alone, standing under the single streetlamp that burned at the edge of the water.

In the silence she watched the gentle bobbing of the tethered boats, wondering where Sam might have moored.

"Hey, matey. How was your trip?"

"Jeez, Sam. You made me jump."

She hadn't seen him sitting there on the old lock in the gathering dark. They both laughed, and Sam stood up and came close. He'd grown his beard longer, but the eyes were the same, wide and kind. When he put his arms around her and around Leonie, Ruby tried not to cry.

He gave them a long squeeze. Then he stepped back a little. "So. This must be Leonie."

"You're sure it's okay for the baby to stay too? We don't have anywhere else to go. We stayed in this B&B last night and the woman was really mean."

"Hey, hey. You're here now. It's okay. I love kids." He rubbed Ruby on the back. She leaned into him, into the familiar feel of his wiry frame, his strong arms. Finally, she was safe. Arriving at Sam's, she thought it might have been the closest thing she'd ever felt to coming home.

The boat was just the way she remembered it. She carried Leonie down the steps into the cozy warmth, the smell of liquorish tea and woodsmoke. After the bed and breakfasts, which she had chosen on the basis that they were clearly run-down, ask-no-questions-type establishments, she felt she could finally relax.

"Nice boots," said Sam, with a smile in his voice. On her feet were a pair of ex-army boots she'd found in a charity shop. "Not really you, though, are they? And what's with the hair?"

Still holding Leonie, Ruby twirled a strand of her newly orange hair in her fingers. Yesterday she'd bleached it, tinted it, and cut it herself into a rough bob. (She knew she ought to feel bad about the mess she'd made of that landlady's sink. But she didn't. Not even a bit.) This morning she'd teamed the hairstyle with heavy eyeliner and a tweed jacket that was a size too small. The steampunk getup was her third disguise this week, and not her favorite if she was honest. She looked at her friend for a moment without speaking.

"It's so good to see you, Sammy. I can't tell you how much I've missed you." And she cried then, letting her head fall into the padding on the shoulder of Leonie's thick coat.

Sam sat next to Ruby on the narrow bench. Leonie's eyes were open, and she sat up and started patting Ruby on the head. "Mamma Bee sad," she said. "No sad, Mamma Bee." Her little hand stroked the orange hair, a bit too roughly. "Ahhhh," she said. "Ahhhh."

Ruby laughed through the tears. She pulled the little girl into a hug. "Thank you, baby. I'm happy now."

"She's lovely, isn't she?" said Sam. "Very caring."

"Yes, she is," said Ruby, "I'm really lucky."

"Milk," said Leonie. "I want milk, Mamma Bee."

She looked at Sam. "Can I heat some milk for her? She'll sleep then."

Sam heated milk in a pan, and Leonie drank it from the sippy cup that Ruby had brought. Then Ruby said, "Can I borrow your fiddle?"

She sat Leonie on Sam's knee and played "The Seal Woman's Joy," singing the words at the same time.

Ionn da, ionn do . . .

"What is that?" he said. "I don't think I've heard it before. Is it Orcadian?"

It was rare for Sam to hear a tune he didn't know at all. The music filled the boat with calm. Rich and sonorous, the fiddle and the lullaby worked their magic on the baby, who gave a huge yawn.

"Do you like it on the boat, tiddler?" said Sam, stroking Leonie on the cheek with a knuckle. "She's beautiful. Aren't you, honey?"

Leonie gave a tired smile from around the sides of her thumb.

"She's sleepy," said Ruby. "I might put her down."

Sam arranged a purple corduroy beanbag on the floor of the boat, and Ruby laid Leonie in it. She curled up on her side, her thumb wedged firmly in her mouth, and her breath came and went, long and slow.

"Now," said Sam, after a moment's silence. "There is a fuck of a lot to tell me, I think you'll agree."

Ruby held her head in her hands for a while. Then she said, "I'm not sure where to start."

"Let's start with whose child this is, and go from there."

She shut her eyes. "She's mine. Like I said in the letter."

"Is it an adoption?"

"Yes, exactly."

"An official one? I thought it took ages. That you had to own your own house, have a steady job, all of that."

"Mmm," she said. Her eyes ached.

He waited until she looked up at him. Then he tipped his head to the side, gave her a knowing look. "Come on, Roo. Tell me the truth."

Ruby shifted her eyes away, to where the stove glowed red and gold, a blackened log at its center, turning to ash. He could always see the truth; it was stupid trying to pretend. Other people could never tell when she lied to them, but Sam saw through it every time. Though, it may have been that she didn't want to hide things from him. With most people, Ruby wanted them to leave her alone. With Sam, she wanted him to see her properly. But in that moment, it was too much for her to think about trying to explain it all to him.

"Not now," she said. "I just need to sleep now."

"Fine," he said. "But if it turns out you've stolen someone's kid, then I'm not sure I can help you with that."

"I haven't. I promise you. The mother knows about it. She asked me. And I'm like a mother to her anyway. You saw how she is with me."

Sam nodded slowly. He didn't say anything for a minute or two. He passed her a cold bottle of beer. A short while later he inhaled as if he was about to speak, then made an indecisive *mmm* sound that could have been a yawn. She felt him observing her, which made her feel awkward in the unfamiliar clothes she was still wearing, and when she glanced up in the dim light, she could tell he was frowning.

"I'll tell you in the morning, I promise."

"Is that going to be my Christmas present, you answering all my questions?"

"Oh, mate. Christmas present? Yeah, I guess it'll have to be."

"Don't feel bad. I didn't get you anything either."

They both looked at the sleeping form of Leonie.

"I should have done something for her, though," said Sam.

"No, don't worry. She's too young to be aware. Christmas is overrated anyway. In my house it's been a sham for the past few years, my mother drunk all day, everyone pretending things are normal, that we're the perfect family. I know they tried their best, but even as a kid I never felt like I belonged. Not properly."

She caught Sam's eye. He hadn't stopped watching her. "You belong here, though. So, you can forget all that, can't you."

"I can try. Christmas is like fucking Groundhog Day. The same songs, the same shit in the shops. The same food." She looked up. "Oh, I just thought; you didn't get a turkey, did you?"

"Of course not, you tit. I'm a vegetarian. I was going to do curry."

"Well, thank goodness for that. I can't stand the stuff. And gravy granules make me hurl."

"No danger of turkey. Or Christmas telly, of course, because I haven't got one. And looks like no presents either."

She smiled. "Sounds completely perfect."

"We can all pretend it's not even Christmas Day." He inclined his head at Leonie. "Then we can have curry and secrets for lunch."

She stopped smiling and stared at her knees for a while. "I'm not keeping secrets from you, Sam. I won't, not anymore. It's a long story, that's all. Let's get some sleep first." Her exhausted eyes were starting to close on their own. She forced them open. "Just so you know, she wakes up early."

"That's fine—so do I. Up with the dawn."

They shared a few more minutes of companionable silence. After a while he disappeared into the back of the boat, returning with two military-style blankets that he handed to her. He closed up the fire and made his way to the cabin, where he shut the partition door with a small click.

Ruby took a swig of her beer, which had gone warm in the heat from the fire. She let her body relax for the first time in days, so that when the tears came, they were a raging wave that closed her throat and made her clap a hand over her mouth to stop the sobs from waking the baby.

CHAPTER

40

NOW
Joanna
Monday, December 24

THE MOMENT THRUPP entered the department, he made a bee-line for Joanna. He was holding a sheaf of paper and had a strange look on his face.

"Jo. How are you?"

Harper looked sideways at her superior. She couldn't remember a single other occasion on which he had asked her how she was.

"I'm fine, sir."

"This morning was quite shocking, wasn't it?"

"Well, yes. Just another workday, right? How are you?" She couldn't remember ever having asked him that question either. Neither of them were small-talk people.

"Oh, good, thanks," said Thrupp. There was an awkward pause. "Shall we go somewhere a bit more private?"

"Sure." Every fiber of Joanna's body screamed that something was very wrong. They went through into her office and shut the door.

"Forensics just sent me this," said Thrupp. "It's the fingerprint report for Franks's flat."

The alarm bells that had already started ringing in her head got suddenly more urgent.

"Thanks, sir." She held out her hand for the report, but he didn't hand it over. She swallowed. "What's it say?" She thought she could guess what it said.

"Well, it's very . . . revealing. It details four separate profiles. One is the fugitive. One is the child, from the size of them. The other two are, presumably, the two women we are searching for. So one of those will be, or might be, called Constance. And the other is this person."

He opened up the report and placed it on the desk in front of her. He pointed at a name: Ruby Harper.

Harper stared at the report. She cleared her throat a couple of times.

Thrupp took his finger away and crossed his arms. "Relation of yours, by any chance?"

"Harper's a pretty common name, sir."

"How long have we known each other, Jo?"

The memory hit her like a slap for being so stupid. Of course. Ruby had met the DI at the Police Local Heroes awards ceremony four years ago. Only for a few seconds, but still. They'd shaken hands. How could she have forgotten? Thrupp clearly hadn't.

Quietly, she asked, "When did you realize?"

"Oh, I didn't. Terrible memory for faces, unfortunately. That young community support officer, Louise, made the connection. She saw the name on the lease on the flat opposite Mr. Franks, then had a quick look at social media when she couldn't get access for a statement. Ruby doesn't have a profile on Twitter or Facebook, but there are ways of finding people, as you well know."

Anger colored Joanna's cheeks. *I told Louise I was going to follow that up myself. The snitching little—*

Thrupp went on. "In fact it was very easy indeed to identify Ruby Harper as your relation. There's a photo of you together. On your social media. Several, actually."

Jo wanted to cry. She forced the feeling downward, into the pit of her stomach where it sat, hard and heavy, waiting to come back up.

"You knew it was her from the start," said Thrupp. "The photograph on the station platform. You'd have known immediately. Why didn't you tell me?"

"I can explain."

Thrupp held up his hand. "Actually, there's no need. I know you can get a bit . . . emotional sometimes. When family's involved. Hell, we all do. So, I'm not going to bollock you. But I'm transferring you, for now. With a note of caution."

Jo was so surprised that she couldn't speak at first. Where was the almighty tirade, the lecture about holding up an investigation? Why wasn't he angrier? What she'd done—and this was only the parts he knew about—could have been a sacking offense. "You're not punishing me?"

"Not this time. I've spoken to Constable Atkinson. He explained that Ruby is your, um, well, he said the situation was complicated. That you're going through the wringer right now with family stuff. You're not getting away with it completely— there will be a level of monitoring for the next few months."

"Please don't take me off the case." She needed to be on the case. Nobody cared as much about the safety of these people as she did, and that could only be a good thing, surely.

"It's unethical for you to continue. You know that."

"Why is it?"

"I shouldn't need to spell this out for you: it's unethical because one of the suspects in the case is related to the investigating officer. It makes you biased."

"She's not a suspect yet. There's no evidence to suggest she did anything to that man. Ruby would never do anything to hurt anyone. She's a loving, gentle person. And anyway, he deserved it."

He threw up his hands. "My point exactly. You can't be objective."

"But sir, I—"

"Fred West was someone's little boy, you know. Ted Bundy's mother said he was the perfect son."

"This is nothing like that. Why are you—"

"No arguments. You know what's right, Jo. Don't force me to suspend you, because if it comes to it, I won't need much persuading."

"Couldn't I be kept on as an advisor? Even unofficially? I've got more of a chance of talking her round. For instance, she'd hand the kid to me, if it came to it."

He hardened his expression, ignoring what she'd said. "I'll send you your new case in a day or two. Why don't you take a couple of days off? Have a nice rest, a Christmas break. Gather your thoughts."

"But—"

He held up his hand, his palm facing her. "Stop talking. Get your stuff. Go home."

She crossed her arms. "Did you tell the chief constable yet about what happened this morning when your delay in communication meant that man could assault that porter?"

The DI stepped toward her and waggled a finger in her face. "Don't threaten me, Joanna. I can guarantee it will not end well for you."

They locked eyes for a tense few seconds.

"Fine. I'll go." She grabbed her jacket and picked up her satchel. "Who are you putting in charge?"

"Steve Atkinson can hold the fort for now. I'll keep a close eye on proceedings. Don't worry. We'll find the fugitive."

"Before he finds Ruby and Leonie? How can you be so sure? You saw what he did."

"It's not your concern anymore. You need to leave it to us now. Go home."

"Not my concern?"

"Would you like to speak to a family liaison officer?

Harper didn't trust herself to speak. She stalked from the room without another word.

CHAPTER

41

NOW
Ruby
Tuesday, December 25

A T FIRST LIGHT, Ruby was woken by a scream. She opened her
eyes to find Leonie standing by the wood burner, her hand in
front of her face, mouth wide, eyes wide, shock and pain and outrage all at once. The child inhaled quickly and began crying her
silent cry, in which the only noise came from snatched breaths in
between each soundless sob. Ruby jumped from the narrow bed
and picked her up, held the small hand and turned it over, looking
for what was wrong.

"Did you touch the stove, honey? Did you burn yourself?"

Sam thundered from the other end of the boat, topless and
sleep drunk. "What's going on? Is she hurt?"

"She burned her hand, I think." There was a red rectangle on
the toddler's palm. "Is it hot? Does it burn, sweetie?"

Leonie bawled and the tears came down, those not wiped away
by Ruby disappearing into her collar. If there had been sound, it
would have been deafening. Mouth wide open, teeth bared, she
nodded her head in slow motion, yes, it's hot, it hurts.

Ruby said, "I'm so stupid—I should have known. She's never seen a stove; she won't have known it could hurt her. I'm sorry, lovely, it's okay."

Between sobs, Leonie whispered, "Mamma? Where Mamma? Want Mamma." She took a deep breath and screwed up her face, shaking with the force of the soundless cry.

"I know," said Ruby, stroking her back. "I know." And her heart was breaking then, for although she loved Leonie like she was her own child, to Leonie, Constance was irreplaceable. And she wasn't here.

"What's she doing? Why isn't she making any noise?" Sam frowned in confusion.

"Can you get some cold water?"

He filled the washing-up bowl from the tap and brought it over, but Leonie's hand stayed rigid, arm outstretched, and she couldn't be persuaded to bend it at the elbow. Ruby picked her up bodily and dunked the hand in, held it there. When she instinctively took it out again, Ruby grabbed it and forced it in.

"I'm sorry, sweetie, but this will help to cool it down."

The girl just cried and cried, her face a mask of pain and terror, and all without any noise at all but a high squeak, air being let out from a balloon.

Sam was wringing his hands and shifting from foot to foot, causing the boat to rock slightly "What's wrong with her voice, Ruby? Should we take her to the hospital?"

She looked at him. He saw her hesitate, and frowned. If Leonie was badly burned, then they wouldn't have a choice, of course, but the hospital would need names, addresses, background checks. And then, when they didn't find Leonie on the system . . . it was too risky. Ruby brought the child's hand out of the bowl. It was a little pink now, but there was no blistering. Tentatively, she touched the top of the stove with her own finger. Hot, but not burning. Perhaps they wouldn't need to go.

"That's just how she cries. I don't know why. She's always been like that."

"But she talks fine. She screams *silently*."

Ruby felt shame for what she was about to say, even though she had nothing to do with it. When she'd first met Leonie, she never cried. It was many weeks before she realized what happened when she did.

"I don't think there's anything physically wrong. I think it's learned behavior."

"Learned how?"

"I—oh, she's fine now, look at her."

Leonie had stopped crying, though there were tears still wetting her cheeks. She was splashing in the bowl of water with her other hand. Soon, she dragged the injured hand away from Ruby and started to play in the water with both hands. Sam found a beaker to fill up and pour, and Leonie went toward him to get it. As she toddled over, apparently perfectly happy now, the hood of her top brushed the wood burner, and Ruby drew in a sharp breath. "I think we might need a fireguard, though."

He nodded. "I'll make one. We won't light the stove again until it's done."

Later he crouched in the tiny space next to the table, picked up a spoon and handed it to Leonie, who tried to add it to a pile of three other spoons. The pile fell over.

"Ups-a-daisy," said Leonie.

"How old are you, honey?" said Sam.

"Spoon," said Leonie.

Sam turned his head toward Ruby. "How old is she? Two?"

"Nearly."

"And I dropped you off at the New Park when, February? How long have you known her?"

"Okay, I'm sorry. I should've told you the whole story. I planned to."

Sam heaved himself up from the floor to sit on the bench.

"Hit me."

So, Ruby told him everything. How she'd met them when she was struggling with her own personal stuff, the way she'd felt about Gregor and the lies he'd told to reel her in. He listened to her account of everything Gregor said about Constance being mentally ill, and how she'd fallen in love with little Leonie and eventually become friends with Constance.

As she spoke, the child was roaming the boat, looking for things to explore. Ruby pulled out a notepad and pen from her bag and handed it to Leonie, who held the biro in her fist and concentrated on drawing spirals of scribble on all of the available space.

Ruby told of the moment she'd learned the truth about Gregor, and how she'd promised to help Constance escape by looking after Leonie until she could persuade her folks to let them live together

"We waited until Gregor was out. And we just ran."

Leonie toddled over and handed the pen to Sam. "Thank you, sweetie." A second later, she took it back with a "Taaank-yoo!" and resumed drawing, scribbling over what she'd done already.

"She said she lived on an island in the Hebrides. A skerry. So that's where we're heading." The song came to her then, the folk tune she'd found in the book and learned for Constance. "Can I play your fiddle again?"

Ruby played, and Sam listened. Afterward he said, "I know that one, I think."

"I can't pronounce the Gaelic name. In English it's called 'They sent me to an island by myself.'"

"I learned it as 'The Song of the Seals.' Here." He took the violin and played the tune, slower this time.

"It's different. The chorus is different."

Sam said, "Yes, the man who taught it to me said it's the actual tune the seals sing to each other."

"Do you think that's true?"

He laughed. "It's only a story. Seals don't sing."

"Play that bit again. It's beautiful."

As he played, Leonie became still, and started to hum along. Ruby watched her, swaying slightly, for a moment transported.

"It's a lament, I think," said Sam, putting the violin away. "Kind of sad."

"Not to me," said Ruby. "I think it's full of hope."

Sam looked at Leonie, who had stopped singing and gone back to scribbling. "Musical bones, that one."

"Yes."

He sighed. "How could her mother just go off and leave her?"

"It was terrible, Sammy. But she must have been so desperate. I was late for the handover, and she went anyway. When I got there, the police had the kid."

"The police? You were lucky to both get away then."

"I know. It was close. But I wasn't going to let the social worker take her. Her mother might have abandoned her, but I would never."

"What did you do? How come they let you have her, when her mother had left her?"

"I told them I was Constance."

Sam sat up straight then. There was the sound of Leonie dropping the pen on the floor. "Ups-a-daisy," she said.

"The woman's name is Constance? Not Constance Douglas?"

"How do you know? I mean, that's the name I gave them, but how—"

"Have you heard the news the past two days?"

"No. Why?"

Sam was scrabbling for the radio, turning it on, looking for a news station. There was nothing but static and Christmas pop songs.

"Stupid bloody thing. Do you have your phone?"

"Yes, but I turned it off so I can't be traced. You taught me that."

"Turn it on."

"Really? Here?" She looked at him, still unsure. He'd said so many times that he didn't want the boat contaminated with mobile signals.

"Yes. Do it now. There's something you have to see." He said it with a grim determination, so she grabbed her bag and found the phone, pressed the button to start it up. Sam took a step backward, away from it, as if it might explode.

"What am I searching for?" she said.

"The name should do it. Constance Douglas."

She typed it in. The first result was a national newspaper website headline, dated the twenty-second:

Woman and Child Missing After Murder Attempt

A man was found badly injured and unconscious at his home in Sheffield yesterday. He is currently in a critical condition, being treated at Sheffield Royal infirmary. It is not known whether he will recover. A woman, going by the name of Constance Douglas, is missing, wanted by police for questioning in relation to their inquiries. She is traveling with a child, a female around 2 years old. If you have any information, please contact . . .

"You used my name," said Sam.

Ruby couldn't speak. She stared at the phone, reread the article. There was no photograph, and the details were vague. But the name they had was the same made-up name she'd given to the social worker in Cleethorpes on Friday. What else did they know now?

She wanted to look for more information, but Sam took the phone from her, took the battery and dropped the separate bits into her bag.

"Did you try to kill that man, Ruby?"

"I had no idea he was injured. He must have come home early. I left before Constance did, so she must have . . ."

She could imagine how frightened Constance would have been when Gregor appeared. The desperation that would have caused her to defend herself so violently. She left him for dead. Part of her was horrified. Another part was deeply impressed. Constance surely meant to tell Ruby when they met up. But then, they never did.

"So he's in hospital? In a coma?"

She'd been terrified. The idea that the man was in a critical condition gave her a sick kind of hope.

"He might not be looking for you, but the police are. But they have eyes everywhere. It's only a matter of time. They'll have you on camera, on the streets, in the estate. Especially if you've been to a train station."

And if Joanna's seen the footage, thought Ruby, *then the game's up.*

"What should I do, Sammy?"

"Go outside," he said, "Get the rope in. We're moving. Now. We'll think about what to do when we're on our way."

"Everything I did, I did to help Leonie."

"They don't know that, do they? It doesn't matter to them either, if it fits the story they're telling themselves. Quickly—we need to get going. This friend of yours, she knows how to drop you in it, doesn't she?"

Within five minutes Ruby had released the ropes, Sam had fired up the engine, and they were traveling. Although they weren't going very quickly, she felt safer on the move, in the boat with her old friend. As they chugged serenely along the waterways, her heart slowed, and she smiled a little to herself. She realized she was in the strange position of being relieved that the police were after her. Compared to the fear she'd had over the past few days, the terrible knowledge that Gregor would surely track her down, being wanted by the police was frankly a much lesser threat. She'd witnessed what that man was capable of, how strong he was, how relentless. And worse: how charming, how plausible. Her relief was cautious, however. Now that she'd tricked him and wronged him, and helped to take away both Constance and his precious daughter, she was in no doubt: whether discovered unconscious or not, if Gregor was still alive, one day he'd find a way to get to her.

CHAPTER

42

NOW
Joanna
Tuesday, December 25

S HE'D MESSAGED AHEAD of time, but Marianne still pretended
not to understand the situation when Jo arrived.

"What, you're not staying?"

"No, Mum. I told you. I've got to work."

It was just after nine AM. Her mother had opened the front
door, holding a champagne glass that she sipped at anxiously.
Today was supposed to be the one day of the year on which morning drinking was acceptable, yet Joanna couldn't help but glance
judgmentally at the beverage. Her mother noticed her looking and
smiled. "Would you like a drink? Little festive drinkie-poo?"

"No, thanks, Mum. I can't turn up smelling of booze. Even
today."

"Champagne is not booze, sweetie. It's virtually pop."

Jo tried not to make any comment, but she was aware that her
lips were pressed together in irritation. Marianne took a sip of the
pale liquid and looked around as if she'd forgotten something.
"Where's lovely Amy?"

"We're on a break."

"Oh, darling," said her mother, "I'm so sorry."

Her mother didn't look sorry, not in the slightest. She'd never fully approved of Amy. Joanna remembered the time her mother had complained that Amy laughed too loudly.

"What's wrong with that?" Jo had asked.

"Well, if you like that sort of thing, it's fine," her mother had replied. "Seems a little, I don't know. Brash."

Jo hadn't forgotten that comment—probably never would—but Marianne had, almost instantly. The conversation had taken place rather too late at night, and although her mother was adept at hiding how drunk she was, especially on the phone, Joanna had had years of training in spotting the signs. That had been a two-pints-of-vodka sort of an evening. Sober Marianne would absolutely never have made such a remark, but knowing that didn't make it any easier to forgive her.

Marianne turned toward the kitchen. "Did you hear this, Phillip? Joanna isn't coming for lunch. So it's just you and me. No children this year. No children! On Christmas Day." She turned off the hallway, stumbling slightly as she disappeared from sight into the lounge. Jo would have bet her life that the champagne glass her mother was sipping from had been given a good fortification from the vodka bottle.

In the kitchen, her father was intent on a huge half-cooked bird, peering through steamed-up glasses, doing something with juices. "What a shame you can't join us. We'll have so much left over. Plenty for four, and now only the two of us. Oh well. Did something come up?"

The turkey was wedged into the biggest oven tray her parents owned. Plenty for a hundred and four, more like.

"Sorry Dad. I know you've made a real effort. What time did you have to wake up to get this beast in the oven?"

"Oh, not too early. Sixish. I'd have been up anyway," he said, waving away her apologies. "What's happened with Amy? You haven't broken up, have you? I liked her."

Dad actually had liked Amy, and Amy adored Phillip. They'd bonded over a game of sevens and a mutual love of true crime podcasts. Joanna felt sad all over again that the two of them wouldn't get to hang out again. Then she felt relieved all over again that she wouldn't have to force Amy to endure any more visits with her mother.

"It's fine, Dad. We're spending some time apart. You know what I'm like. Hard to take, sometimes. I don't blame her."

"You're lovely, Joanna. Just a little bit . . . independent, perhaps. For a girl like Amy. She's a bit of a homebody, maybe."

"You don't have to say that, Daddy. I screwed it up, that's the truth. She deserves better."

"No, no, I don't believe that. She was a darling, but not right for you. You need someone a bit more outdoorsy."

Joanna filled the kettle and set it to boil.

"Maybe."

"It must be a big case for you to go in today, right? Tell me about it?"

"Oof, it's a bit messy. Do you really want to know?"

"Of course."

She spooned coffee into mugs, added milk and boiling water. There was no need to ask what her dad was drinking because it was always the same. Instant coffee, black, a mug of it on the go constantly until twelve noon. Then, tea with milk until bedtime. Never alcohol. That was Marianne's department.

"We found a man in a bit of a bad way. He'd been attacked. We weren't altogether sure he was going to make it, actually, but then he woke up."

"Oh, that's good, right?"

"Yes and no. When he woke up, he attacked a porter, and now he's on the run."

"Ah."

"Then there's this missing woman and child, who may or may not be involved." Jo tried to deliver this information without emotion. She couldn't let on that Ruby was involved—not yet. Her dad wouldn't be able to sleep for worrying.

"Oh, I think I heard about it on the news. Terrible business."

"We put something out today too, on the radio channels and the TV. Did you see it?"

"No one listens to the news on Christmas Day. Too busy cooking."

As if to demonstrate, he got up and tipped a sack of potatoes into the sink, turned on the tap.

"Still," said Jo, "someone has to be at the office just in case. It's the baby we're most concerned about. Can't really stop until we know she's safe."

Her father opened the oven and, with a great deal of clanging and swearing, jammed the turkey inside. Then he turned and looked at her. "Sometimes I don't know how you carry on, the things you have to deal with. How are you so strong?" He pulled her into a hug, still wearing the oven mitts. "I'm so proud of you, Jo-Jo. Always."

You wouldn't be so proud if you knew the truth, she thought. If she dared to go into the office today, she'd probably be given a formal warning for disobeying orders. Her actual plan was to drive straight to her flat and spend the day listening in to the response team on her radio, in case they found "Gregor." And she might go for a run in the woods down by the hospital—no harm in that, was there? If she happened to find the fugitive herself, well, so be it.

Marianne called through from the living room. "Are you coming in here, darling?"

"In a minute, Mum."

"Bring a fresh bottle of pop, would you? Get yourself a glass."

Of course, Marianne had forgotten what Jo had said about not wanting any. Standard. "I'll be right through."

She met her father's eyes.

"Don't be angry, sweetie. She can't help it."

"How can you say that? There's help available. Why doesn't she—"

"She knows she's got a problem. She's promised to deal with it after today. I thought I'd let her, you know, do whatever she needs to do to get through Christmas. Especially since what happened last year. Bad memories, you know."

She looked at him properly then. He'd lost a little weight. The strain was showing in the deep lines around his eyes, in the slight tremor in his voice. But he was strong; he always had been. Reliable. A rock for Marianne, for all of them. None of this was fair to him.

"You haven't heard from Ruby?" she asked.

"No. Nothing at all." After a moment he said, "What about you? Usually she'll speak to you."

"Not this time. I've tried ringing. I went to her flat. She doesn't answer the door if she knows it's me knocking."

"What about that boyfriend you said she told you about? She hasn't said anything more about that?"

Jo deeply regretted mentioning that conversation to her parents. The information had slipped out, and Dad had clung to it, probably because there'd been nothing else.

"I still don't know anything more. She hasn't rung me, I told you."

"You're not just saying that because she's asked you to pretend?"

"No, Dad. I wish I were."

"It's good that she's found someone though, isn't it?"

"I keep telling you, dad, it's not a boyfriend. She just said she'd met some new friends and that one of them was a man."

The driver's license in the name of Gregor Franks came to mind, the face of the fugitive staring out. It occurred to her that they needed to add Gregor, the real Gregor, to the list of people they had to find. The list of people this invisible man had caused to disappear.

"Don't be like that, Joanna. It's a comfort, to know that she's not on her own. Since last year we haven't known who she's with, whether she's eating properly, nothing at all. Only the updates we get from you. I like to imagine he's a lovely man, that she's happy and settled."

She took a deep breath before she said, "Her phone is switched off. Has been for a couple of weeks."

"Oh no. Don't tell your mother that, will you?"

"I'm not sure she'd remember if I did."

"Marianne wants to give her something, a Christmas gift. She missed her terribly on her birthday. We never sent anything because we were hoping she'd come home. I hope it didn't make things worse."

Jo thought things couldn't be much worse.

"If you see her, could you pass it on? Even if it's just the card."

"You're not listening to me, Dad. She won't see me either."

He was facing away from her, his hands rummaging in the sink for potatoes. When he turned, his face had crumpled in a way she'd never seen before and made her heart lurch with pity. She caught him in a tight hug because it seemed as if he might collapse right there on the kitchen floor. Joanna held her father up as he cried, and thought about how we never really leave our childhood selves behind. The little boy that grew up to be her father still lived inside him, just as the little girl she'd once been lived in her. It was the little girl part of Ruby, too, that was hurting now.

"Why does she hate us, Joanna? We tried to do the right thing. I loved her like a daughter. I still do. Exactly the way I love you. Maybe even more because of who she is."

Me too, thought Jo. "I don't know what she's thinking, Daddy," she said.

He turned back to the potatoes. "Your mother and I tried to catch her at work last week."

"Oh, Dad. What happened?"

"Well, I was starting to think maybe she doesn't work there anymore. Once or twice, I've sat outside that music service building when the schools finish. Just on the off chance, you know, because she told me once that she runs the after-school orchestra on Wednesdays. I've never seen her. And then last week, she wasn't there either. One of the other tutors told us—and I had to really lay it on thick because they gave me all this data protection bullshit—that she's off sick. Your mother was so upset."

Harper felt a surge of anger at Ruby. If she was in some kind of trouble, why didn't she ask for help? If she was sick, she needed her family around her. "I didn't think it would go on for this long. If I had, I would have tried to do something much sooner. After everything you've done for her—for both of us. I don't know how she could just cut you off. Mum, I can understand, but you?"

Dad looked at his slippers. He dried his hands on a tea towel and placed it on the side. "Well, that's the problem, isn't it? She thinks what we did—what we all did—was the wrong thing to do."

"If she can't see that—"

"Shh, Joanna. Don't get upset. Your mother doesn't need it today."

There was a sound then from her mobile phone, still in the pocket of her coat in the hallway. The distinctive *boing* of an email notification.

"I better go, Dad. Work's calling."

"Proud of you, sweetheart. Making the world a better place. Come round later for some leftovers, won't you? Please?"

In the living room, her mother was sitting very straight in her chair, facing the telly.

"Bye, Mum. I'll try to drop by later." Joanna knew that she probably wouldn't.

Marianne smiled thinly and tipped her head at the Christmas tree in the corner, decorated with paper angels. The familiar sight of them tugged at Jo. She remembered making them with a six-year-old Ruby, gluing the silver foil, cutting sprigs of tinsel to make the crowns. Under the tree were two piles of beautifully decorated presents, ten or more in each pile, with a card on top.

"Don't forget your gifts, darling," said her mother. "And Phillip said you wouldn't mind passing on little Ruby's presents when you see her?"

One card said *Joanna*. The other said *Ruby*. Tears pricked at the corners of Jo's eyes. She bent and picked up Ruby's card. It was thick, probably with cash. Marianne rose and stood behind her daughter, both of them facing the decorated tree. The anger she felt toward her mother was still there, but it had faded into the background, replaced by pity.

"Mum, I don't think I'll see her today."

"Tomorrow, perhaps?"

"I . . . maybe."

The next thing her mother said was almost a whisper. "I know she's gone, Joanna. I know we've lost her. I lost her." The words were flat, emotionless. But repeated in the reflection on every bauble, Harper could see the tears rolling down her mother's face.

"She hasn't gone, don't say that. I can't take the presents but I'll give her the card, Mum. I'll find her. I'll make sure she gets it. Then she'll come over and you can give her the presents yourself."

She gave her mother a quick hug, then walked out the front door and climbed into her car, pushing the envelope into the zipped pocket of her satchel. She took out her phone and checked her email, hoping to see a message from the automated mobile phone signal detection service that Eddie had set up for her, which would ping whenever Ruby's phone number was used. It was a spam email from a sports drink company. She set off for home.

CHAPTER

43

NOW
Ruby
Tuesday, December 25

T HEY TRAVELED ALL day, not even stopping for their lunch of
the promised curry: Ruby heated it up and took the tiller
while Sam ate and watched Leonie. It was a bizarre situation;
here they were, on the run from the police and Social Services,
with a child that didn't belong to them. Yet there was a sense of
peace as they cruised along the canals and rivers. It was a different world from the one Ruby usually inhabited, that of cities
and buildings, roads and vehicles. There was only the water,
which meandered through farmland, and the boat, gently
churning up the surface as they escaped almost comically slowly,
at a leisurely walking pace. It was too serene to get stressed,
though when she thought of the news article, her stomach tightened. She wanted to turn her phone on and search for more
information about the case, specifically, which DS was working
it. Did Joanna know already that it wasn't Constance, but Ruby
at the seafront?

The fact that it was Christmas Day made her think about
what happened last year, and the many missed calls she'd seen on

her old phone. She realized she wasn't angry anymore, only home-sick. Joanna hadn't done anything wrong, not really. As for Marianne, she probably couldn't even remember what she'd said. In the end it didn't make much difference whether Ruby forgave her or not; the woman barely remembered anything from one day to the next. Forgiveness wasn't about the other person, though. It was about drawing a line under something, and moving on. What Ruby had realized since knowing Leonie, was that once there was child in your life, you no longer had the luxury of deciding whether or not to forgive. What you did, you did for them. Her mother—both of her mothers—had sacrificed a lot for her, per-haps more than she would ever know. And they did it, not from a sense of duty, but because they chose to. Joanna chose to carry her to term; Marianne chose to bring her up. Neither was forced into anything. Constance, in contrast, hadn't been given a choice at all.

That night, they moored on a deserted stretch of canal bank between two derelict working boats. Sam let Ruby steer as he jumped onto the towpath with the rope, guiding them in, using the light from his powerful head torch. Leonie was already asleep on the bean bag underneath the table, her thumb in her mouth.

In the frozen dark, Ruby helped him to tie the boat up, then they both went aboard, down into the saloon, and shut the doors behind them. The heat enveloped her like an embrace. After a while they sat together to eat another delightfully unfestive meal of canned spaghetti on toast, washed down with fizzy orange.

"We should go on the run every year," she said. "It's kind of nice."

He grew serious then. "Don't make the mistake of letting yourself feel safe." He stood up to pull closed an infinitesimal gap in one of the blinds. "That's when they'll get you."

Sam started to list all the ways in which she had to modify her behavior if she wanted to stay free. Avoid cities, train stations, buses. Don't call anyone. Don't turn on your mobile phone.

"You can't take any money out either. Not from cashpoints."

"What? How are we supposed to eat? And I need some toilet-ries, moisturizer, lip balm, you know."

"You can't be thinking about beauty stuff now, Ruby."

"It's not for me. It's for her. She's got sore lips. The cold weather isn't good for sensitive skin." She looked at the baby, nestled on the beanbag like a little pup in the warm glow from the fire. There was a patch of skin on her chin that she couldn't seem to stop licking, that by the end of the day was sometimes bleeding. Ruby's own skin was sore too. Her cheeks were tight from the extreme changes in temperature from outside to inside. Her cracked lips cried out for relief. But it was the baby she wanted the balm for, first and foremost. Her priorities had shifted without her really noticing.

"We'll be able to get some money," said Sam. "There are ways to do it without them finding us. We'll be okay, but you might need to give me your bank card, for security. You'll get it back."

"Why can't we just go and get some money out ourselves?"

"Because they will have set up an alert on your account."

"They don't know it's me, Sam. They're looking for someone called Constance."

"If you're on camera with Leonie, then someone is going to recognize you eventually, and people love to snitch."

He was right. It was likely they would have made the connection by now. It was safest to behave as if they had.

Ruby checked her wallet. There was a ten-pound note and a few coins. "There'll be a corner shop in one of the villages. I'll go there tomorrow."

"But you can't go, Ruby. I'll go."

"Surely it's safe to go to some random village shop?"

He shook his head no. "That's how they get you. You can't go in any shops. Not if you really want to avoid the hunters."

"The hunters?"

"That's what they are, the police. Professional hunters. They think they've got the upper hand, too, with all their equipment and tracking technology. But it's not foolproof. We can beat it, if we're careful."

It seemed so far from them, this danger. Thinking about it hurt her brain. She looked at the sleeping child, felt the heat of the fire, the sensation of floating on the river, the occasional pull of the ropes in the mooring when the wind took them.

"You're not listening. Ruby? What did I just say?"

She jolted back to the conversation.

"Sorry, Sam. I guess I'm too tired."

"We both need to get some rest if we're going to stay one step ahead of them."

Sam went into the tiny bathroom. She heard him brushing his teeth. When he came out, she said, "Why are you helping me?"

"What's that supposed to mean? Why wouldn't I help you? I'm your friend. Why do you even need to ask?"

"Only because it must look really bad. I'm here with someone else's kid, being chased by the police after a man has been attacked. And you, without even really asking many questions, you just accept it."

"Yes. Because I trust you."

"You could get into trouble."

"I don't care. Anyway, where else are you going to go?"

"I just don't know if I'd be able to do the same. If the tables were turned."

He narrowed his eyes in the dim light. Then he sighed. "I suppose it's a good job that you won't have to, then, because I'm never going to get into the kind of trouble you can create. Not anymore. And when I needed you, you were there. This is payback."

"Payback?"

"For saving my life."

They held each other's gaze. "It was nothing."

"No," said Sam. "I know we joke about it, but in all seriousness, if you hadn't picked me up off the street that night, I would have died."

"Someone else would have come along."

"No, they wouldn't," said Sam. "I don't know if I would have done that myself either."

Ruby considered for a minute. Then she nodded. "Okay. But then we're square. We don't owe each other anything."

Sam's expression changed, as if he had more to say. But then he tilted his head, smiled slightly, and went through into the cabin.

*   *   *

Wednesday, December 26

The tip of the narrowboat nosed through the thin ice on the surface of the river, driving a dark path up the middle and leaving
floating white islands drifting in its wake. She and Leonie were
dressed in their gloves, hats, and coats, huddled low in the bow
against the cold wind, their heads sticking up over the side. Sam
was at the stern, holding the tiller with one hand, only his eyes
visible between his woolly hat and the scarf he'd wrapped over his
face. Leonie was pointing at birds in the winter trees as they
passed, calling, "Wobin!" whenever she spotted anything remotely
winged. The proximity of the water, combined with the toddler's
complete obliviousness to any danger, made Ruby nervous. She
kept one hand wound tightly in the fabric of the little girl's coat.

Since the incident with the stove, Leonie hadn't mentioned her
mother. She'd been fully engaged with discovering everything
new about the world she found herself in. Having been confined
for the entirety of her life so far, Ruby was impressed with the way
she took everything in her stride, delighted in everything, laughed
and charged about all day with an energy she hadn't seemed to
have when in the apartment. But minding a tiny human with no
sense of danger was a full-time occupation. By six PM both of
them were exhausted. Leonie slept for twelve hours every night,
her little brain soaking up all of the newness and assimilating it,
ready for her to leap up in the wee hours and begin all over again.
Ruby had to be ready for anything, and although she found it difficult to be on duty so unrelentingly, the rewards were huge. She
was seeing everything through Leonie's eyes, as if it were new to
her too. And it was wonderful.

Ruby was about to suggest to Leonie that they go inside, get
warm by the fire, when the sun came out in glorious ribbons of
gold, and the way it caught the ice crystals that had formed on the
branches of the trees gave the scene an achingly festive, greetings-
card beauty. "Look, baby, there's a sparrow."

"Wobin!" shouted Leonie, pointing at the small brown bird.

Sam cut the engine. The boat edged toward the towpath,
where he jumped ashore and banged in a mooring pin with a mallet, securing the stern. "Throw us the rope," he called, and he did

the same with the bow end. They'd stopped by a small gate in the hedge, which led to a farmer's field.

"Let's go for a leg-stretch," he said. "There's a village just down there."

They set off at toddler's pace, the path cutting straight through the fields to a weighted kissing gate at the far perimeter of the second one. It would have been a few minutes' walk but for the fact that every couple of meters, Leonie found something to stop and look at. She would examine it, hold it up for approval. "Look, Mamma Bee, stick!" "Look, Mamma Bee, stone!"

After about twenty minutes of this they'd barely made it past the first field and were only halfway to the gate. Sam said, "I'm going to go ahead. I've got a few things to do, okay? I'll meet you at the boat in an hour."

"What are you doing? I thought we were keeping out of sight?"

"Should be fine as long as you don't draw attention to yourself. Try not to talk to anyone, don't go into any establishments. You'll just look like a tourist. I need to make a phone call. I think there's still a call box here—there was last year."

"Who are you calling?"

"We need some money. I'm going to get us some."

"But Sam—"

"Don't worry about it. I'll see you soon."

As Sam paced ahead and disappeared, Ruby took hold of Leonie's hand and steered her toward the gate. On the other side of it, there was a street of old stone cottages leading toward a village green, at the center of which, a picture-perfect duck pond. "Ducks!" shouted Leonie, and set off running.

"Wait," said Ruby.

In slow motion, Ruby saw it play out, but she was slightly too far away to stop it happening: Leonie's welly boot made contact with the curbstone, she toppled like a domino, the hat came off her head, her head connected with a sharp piece of gravel on the ground, all in one short second that seemed to last forever. As she went down, Ruby's fingers barely brushed the edge of the girl's coat, her hand grabbed at nothing. The blood came before the screaming, running down her face and into her eyes and mouth, turning her baby teeth pink. A dark bruise formed quickly at the site of the injury, a lump started to swell there. Ruby picked her up and held her, searched for a clean tissue to press to the cut. All the while, she was trying to contain her emotion. Because for the first time, Leonie was crying out loud.

And she wanted to say, *Please don't cry,* but she also wanted to tell that sweet baby she could cry whenever she liked, as loud as she liked, for as long as she liked.

Don't draw attention to yourself. So much for that. As the baby screamed at full volume into her ear—such a joyous moment, the fact that she finally felt safe enough to, but why did it have to be now?—Ruby rubbed Leonie's back in soothing circles. She stood up and looked around to see if she could tell where Sam had gone. There was no phone box nearby that she could see. A curtain twitched in one of the houses, and she turned to retrace her steps, but as she passed the entrance to the pub at the edge of the green, a large woman dressed in chef's whites and a stripy apron appeared at the open door. "Are you okay, love?"

"Yes, fine, don't worry. It's only a scratch. She's just making a fuss. It's nothing."

The woman came close. She lifted up Leonie's fringe. "Doesn't look like nothing to me. Might need stitches. I'd go to hospital with that. Are you local?"

"No. Yes." What was the best thing to say? Ruby just wanted to get away.

The woman frowned, and examined them both a bit more closely. This was a village, where everyone was bound to know everyone else. Ruby laughed, a simulation of amusement that felt flat even to her. "Sorry, that doesn't make sense does it? I'm not local, but I'm hoping to be. We're looking at a house this afternoon, just getting a feel for the place."

"Oh, you're looking at the Simonsen's place?"

"Yes," said Ruby, then, "I think so. It's a lovely building. Lovely area. Lovely." *Stop, Ruby, you sound manic.*

"I see," said the woman, narrowing her eyes. "Well, hope this hasn't put you off. The hospital is a few miles down the main road. I can give you the postcode to put in your phone?"

Leonie had stopped crying. Ruby was always impressed with how quickly she got over things. The girl leaned into Ruby's chest, sucking her thumb and gazing at the chef with her big eyes. The woman covered her face with her hands for a second. "Boo," she said, opening her hands wide and grinning in a silly way. Leonie laughed.

"Thanks," said Ruby, "but I think she just needs a plaster."

"What?" said the chef, frowning slightly. "You're not going to take her? Looks pretty deep to me."

"I'm a nurse," said Ruby, rather too defensively. "I think it's superficial. Don't suppose you have a first-aid kit in your kitchen?"

The first-aid kit contained steri-strips, which Ruby used to close the cut after she'd cleaned it. The chef was right, the cut was deep and probably needed stitches, but of course there was no question of going to the hospital.

"How old is she?"

Leonie had been handed a bottle of apple juice with a straw sticking out of it, and she sat, dangling her legs on the stainless-steel kitchen counter, slurping the sweet liquid and humming.

"Nearly two," said Ruby, thinking, *Why did I come in here?* She needed to get away, get back to the boat. Every second she spent here, every bit of information she gave to this woman, would put them in danger of being caught.

Just then there were footsteps on the stairs above them. It was too early for the pub to have any customers yet. They both looked up. "That's the landlord," said the chef. "What's your name, lovely?"

"Lonie!" shouted Leonie.

"Ha ha," said Ruby, picking her up and making for the door. "I don't know why she says that. Her name's Anna, actually. Funny, the things they come out with, isn't it? Better be off—thanks for the first-aid kit."

Ruby hurried through the bar. As she did so, she caught sight of the TV, where a news channel was silently rolling along. She read the words on the banner. *Police are still searching for a man who escaped from hospital after seriously assaulting a member of staff. The man, who was using the name Gregor Franks, until recently was in a coma after being found unconscious on Friday. The public are being asked to help search for a woman in relation to the inquiry, who was last seen traveling with a young child who may answer to the name Leonie. . . .*

The chef followed Ruby's eyes to the TV and then looked at the child. Ruby saw her frown, look again at the TV, again at Ruby.

"Which house did you say you were looking at, love? The Simonsen's? Maybe I could put in a word for you." But her face had changed. She wasn't friendly anymore, she was suspicious.

Without saying another word, Ruby backed into the swing door and went through. It was bad enough that the police were after her, that she might have given away their location by talking to this person. But the thing making her heart pound was the other part. Gregor was no longer in hospital. He was on the run, and he'd be coming for her. She needed to get moving as quickly as possible.

"Hey," shouted the chef, as Ruby held Leonie close and started to run across the green and back to the gate.

44

NOW
The Injured Man
Wednesday, December 26

FROM THE BENCH at the edge of the green, the man watches the gate bang shut, the woman and child disappear into the furrowed field beyond. Standing in the doorway of the pub, the chef looks over at him and raises a hand, but she frowns slightly, as if she can't quite place him. He flashes a reassuring smile, and the chef smiles back. The trace of suspicion is gone, just like that. Villages like this, they always clock an outsider, but the injured man has taken steps to appear as if he ought to belong, and that's the most important thing. Dressed in a tweed jacket and walking boots, he knows that he looks the epitome of a middle-class, higher-income-bracket, older man, taking a rest after a morning stroll. The chef steps inside and shuts the pub door, no doubt forgetting she even saw him, her mind moving on to the next thing. She can't have guessed that the man has taken the jacket and boots he is wearing from the unlocked boot room of a large house ten miles south, that he's been walking the canal path, searching for the boat he knows was, until recently, moored at a wharf near York. She can't have guessed that the flat cap covers up an almost circular injury on the back of the man's head, or that his hands bear small wounds where he ripped out his drip.

The man leaves the bench and makes a slow circuit of the village green, standing for a while to admire the ducks on the pond. No one is watching him as far as he can tell, but it's worth a little stroll around to make sure, if there are curtain-twitchers in the vicinity, that he isn't considered suspicious. After a minute or so, he climbs into his stolen car and sets off at a leisurely pace in the direction of the Ripon terminal, knowing he'll have more than enough time to change both his vehicle and his appearance before *Nessie* has traveled even halfway there.

45

NOW
Joanna
Thursday, December 27

J OANNA WAS AWOKEN by the soft *boing* of her email alert.

Ruby had turned her phone on, and the system had sent her the location. She knew there was a time lag, but when she saw exactly when the phone had been turned on, she swore. It was forty-eight hours ago; time she'd spent listening in to the police radios and conducting her own ground searches of local wooded areas, using the hospital as a midpoint. There had been no sign of the fugitive. She'd been crossing her fingers that he'd be found dead in a ditch, but after what she'd seen, she knew better than to underestimate him. Jo scrambled out of bed and into the car.

It took the better part of three hours to drive through the heavy back-to-work traffic to where Ruby's new mobile phone had pinged, a small canal wharf in the middle of nowhere, north of York. The data contained in the email stated that the phone had activated the nearby mast on Christmas Day. Therefore it was unlikely she was still going to be there, but at least it was a starting point.

At the wharf she parked and started walking toward the first narrowboat in the row, where she knocked on a window, three sharp raps. The afternoon was crisp and cold, frost laced on the edges of leaves, floating islands of ice on the river. The craft's curtains were drawn, but she knocked once more anyway. There was no answer.

Jo glanced at the chimney of the next boat, from which she could see a curl of smoke escaping. When she knocked this time, a curtain twitched, and a few minutes later, a woman's head appeared out of the hatch. Her white hair was messed up, and she had a face brown and wrinkled like a walnut. Clouds of steamy breath filled the space between them.

The woman squinted into the bright slanting sun. "Yes?"

"I'm from the police," said Harper. "I'm looking for a young woman called Ruby. She's traveling with a little girl called Leonie, about eighteen months to two years old."

The woman climbed from the hatch onto the small deck where the tiller was, dragging a blanket that she wrapped around herself tightly in the cold. "No one here by that name, not that I know of."

"What about a man called Sam Douglas?"

"*Nessie*? Yes, he was here."

"Nessie?"

"That's the boat," said the woman.

"When was he here?"

"Day before yesterday. I saw her leave, oh, late morning, I'd say."

"Her? I thought you said there wasn't a woman?"

"I was talking about the boat."

Joanna was holding it together, but the boat woman was starting to annoy her very much. At times like these, she did well to remember the tips she'd picked up at the two politeness training sessions she been obliged to attend as part of her CPD.

"Just to be clear," said Joanna, "Sam Douglas, the man, not the boat. He plays the violin. Do you know him?"

"Yes. He built my kitchen. It's very good. Are you looking for a handyman? Or a violinist?"

"No. I'm looking for a woman called Ruby and a little girl. I know they've been here, because we had a mobile phone alert from the area. You're sure you haven't seen them?"

"You know, there was something strange that happened. Sam's a real loner. I've never seen him with anyone before, so I suppose I wasn't expecting it. But the other morning, we heard a scream, coming from over there, where he was moored. I thought it must have been someone passing by, a gongoozler. We get families walking on the towpath all the time. Especially on Christmas Day. Morning walk with the family, you know. It's like Paddington bloody station round here."

"You heard a scream?"

"Yes. Very high-pitched scream. I never imagined it could be from Sam's boat. I didn't get a chance to ask him whether or not he'd heard it too, because later he'd gone, which in itself isn't unusual. Anyway I didn't connect the two things. But now that you're here, maybe it does make sense. What's he done, run off with someone's wife?" The woman seemed strangely delighted by the prospect. Bent over, wrapped in her blanket, Harper couldn't help thinking she was just like the witch in so many of the fairy tales she'd read as a child.

"Who do you think was screaming?"

"I don't know. I got the impression it was a child, from the pitch of it."

"Not an adult?"

"Well, could have been a woman, I suppose. Do you think he was strangling her? Is that why you're looking for them? Is it a murder inquiry?"

Jo kept her face completely still.

"You say that Sam's boat left on Christmas Day. Do you know which way he went?"

"That way," said the woman, pointing to one of only two routes out of the wharf. "North. Very itchy feet, that one. Always on the go. I never thought he might be a criminal, though."

Joanna noticed the boarding ramp from the woman's boat, which rested on the towpath. There was grass growing all around it. "You don't move, though?"

"Not me. I pay for this mooring, so I don't have to. Some boat people like to be able to move. That's part of why they choose to live onboard. Very small world though, especially in the winter. I've seen Sam here a few times. He's not one for farewells. Or hellos, actually. And he's not a terribly festive chap; no decorations or anything."

She fingered the wrinkled berries on the holly wreath adorning her cabin door. "It's always the quiet ones, isn't it? I never took him for a violent man."

"Can you show me exactly where he was moored?"

"Just across there," said the woman, indicating the other side of the wharf, which had space enough for about fifteen boats. "And I wouldn't bother knocking on any of those other boats. No one's in. Mostly holiday craft."

Joanna gave a tight smile. "Thank you for your time, madam. We might be in touch again."

As she started to move away, the woman shouted after her, "Hey, this isn't about that missing woman with the girl, is it? I heard it on the news."

Well, I did mention that it was about a woman and a child, thought Joanna. "Oh?"

"Only, if it is, I did find something on the towpath. Thought it was an interesting coincidence that someone would drop one so similar. Maybe it wasn't a coincidence at all. Look, I hung it on the fence, just down there. It looks like the hat they were talking about on the news, doesn't it?"

Jo walked toward where the woman was pointing, and there on the fence was a scrap of pink something. Harper picked it up and brushed the ice off. It was a woolen hat with two bobbles like a bear's ears. Identical to the one Leonie had been wearing in the images from the train station. She tucked it into a plastic evidence bag.

Just then, Jo's phone rang. It was Atkinson.

"Hello, boss," he said.

"Hello, Steve. Have you found the fugitive yet? Any leads?"

"Where are you?"

"I'm . . . at home."

"No you're not. I'm standing outside your place right now. Your car's gone."

"What, are you checking up on me now?"

"I came over to tell you that the surveillance system recorded a location flag from a number that I didn't recognize, that I hadn't keyed in. I couldn't get in touch with Eddie, but I assumed it was something to do with you. Something to do with the case that you are not supposed to be investigating anymore."

"You'd be right about that, *Detective*. It's Ruby's number. I got an email notification about it this morning."

"Is that where you are now? I could have come with you, if you'd said."

"Probably best you stay away from me, Steve. You're in charge of the operation, and you don't want to chuck that opportunity away. Could be great for you, career-wise. It's different for me. It's personal."

"There's more to this case than your daughter disappearing, Jo. I had that preserved finger we found fast-tracked by forensics. It was a child's, like you thought it might be. Around eight to ten years old."

"Can they tell if it's from a male or a female? When was it severed?"

"They couldn't say much more than the fact it wasn't recent. They're running DNA, but Thrupp is also talking about opening several linked inquiries."

"Several?"

"One for each victim. They opened up the wall yesterday. There were two bodies inside. A female and a male."

Harper felt her blood run cold. She thought of Gregor's mother, how she'd disappeared so suddenly just after they moved in. And how, when the neighbor had knocked to ask about it, "Gregor" seemed to have forgotten who the neighbor was.

"I've been inside the apartment. We both have. There was no smell, no sign."

"No. There wouldn't have been. The bodies had been preserved, much like the finger was. They're trying to work out what the process was. It might help us identify the killer."

Preservation. A deliberate act. The murderer had really thought things through.

"Can you identify them?"

"Forensics are working on it. They say they should be able to reconstruct the face of the male, make a computer simulation and compare it with the passport image we found, but I have a strong suspicion—"

"It's Gregor Franks. The real one."

Joanna walked a little way down the path in the direction the boat she suspected Ruby was aboard had gone. The silence out here was unnerving, especially for a city girl.

Atkinson said, "One more thing. They found a bottle with traces of . . . hang on, I'll read out the description. "A cocktail of liquid paracetamol, diamorphine, Valium, and GHB." This was in an unmarked bottle in the bathroom. Take a spoon of that, you'd be out for a week. Take two or three, you might not wake up."

"Do you think that's what he'd taken?"

"I'd say it's likely. Though I don't know if he took it on purpose."

Joanna could see that she'd been right all along. If Ruby had given the man a head injury—and if she'd dosed him up with that stuff—then it was for a very good reason indeed.

"You're not safe up there, boss, not with him on the loose. This man is a killer. There are two bodies already, and the finger, the drugs—all indicating further crimes. And there's Constance, throwing herself into the sea—I know we haven't found her body, but it looks most likely that she drowned herself just to get away from him. That kind of man wouldn't think twice about attacking a police officer."

"He wouldn't think twice about attacking a woman and a little girl, Steve. I have to keep looking for Ruby and Leonie."

"You can't do it on your own. It's too dangerous."

She ended the call.

Joanna stood on the towpath in the fading daylight and found a map of the waterways on her smartphone. There were only thirty miles of canal left in that direction, until it ended in the terminus at Ripon. She eyed the sign sticking out of the reeds that stated the speed limit was four miles per hour. She could probably catch them up if she'd had her bike with her. Or she could borrow a boat. *Nessie* couldn't have gone anywhere especially difficult to find, confined as she was to the waterway. On the other hand, thirty miles was a huge search area, and checking every boat, in the dark, would take hours.

"There's a quicker way to find them, you know," said a voice from behind her. It was the woman she'd spoken to earlier. "If you were interested."

"Go on."

"All of the boats are registered, and the men from the Canal and River Trust monitor where you are. It all goes on a database."

"They monitor where you are? How?"

"Man on a bike. They go up and down, note down the registration numbers, make sure you've moved far enough if you're a continuous cruiser. They're a bit like traffic wardens."

"How often do they do that?"

"Not sure, actually. They're quite secretive. I suppose they don't want people to cheat the system. But I saw him go by yesterday, as a matter of fact. Might be worth checking with them?"

Jo searched for the number and pressed to connect, held the phone to her ear.

"No answer," she said to the boatwoman.

"Office hours, dummy," said the old woman, rolling her eyes. "Try in the morning."

Jo called Atkinson back.

"You hung up on me," he said.

"I'm really sorry about that, Steve. It turns out I do need your help."

CHAPTER

46

NOW
The Injured Man
Wednesday–Thursday, December 26–27

THE BOAT RESTS in the dark, its engine ticking as it cools. The water is completely still, disturbed only by occasional movements from inside the boat, rocking the vessel slightly, causing small ripples.

The man is crouching, his body hidden by the brambles and the darkness. He is cold, but he doesn't move at all.

In one of the nearby houses, there is a shrill voice complaining.

"You need to move that boat," it screeches. "You can't moor here, you know. I'll call the authorities. They'll be along to move you."

It's true there are no other boats moored here, only the ancient hull of a pleasure boat, and a speedboat, covered with canvas and pulled up on to the bank for the winter.

A man with graying hair and a scruffy beard sticks his head out the top of the boat. The injured man can see him, lit from below by the light coming from the boat's cabin. He knows that the man is called Sam. He first became aware of Sam almost a year ago, when the cameras he'd installed in the empty flat opposite his window were triggered by the girl moving in. He'd had a plan in place for this eventuality—that was why he'd set up the cameras in the first place. The idea was that when someone moved in, he would contain the problem by first observing and then eliminating the tenant—he'd even stockpiled several sacks of salt to deal with the body, as it had worked so well the other time. But through the listening devices he'd heard her playing, and it was like a siren song, urging him to change his plan, attempt something new for once, despite the risks. He realizes now that this was the decision that changed everything, the point where things had started to get complicated for the injured man. He should have gone ahead and done what he'd always intended. The injured man doesn't like things to be untidy. And things, as they stand, are very untidy indeed.

To befriend Ruby had seemed like the perfect solution at first, and for a while he'd thought that the two women could remain under control indefinitely. Ruby kept Constance and Leonie entertained. She was lonely—he knew from her phone history that she had no friends nearby or family to interfere. And she had seemed so trusting, so pliable. Even when she rejected his advances, he saw it as a victory, understood it was because of the story he'd told her about Constance still being in love with him.

He should have anticipated that it couldn't stay that way forever, though. The child had started walking, and Constance had begun whining about letting it go outside. Ruby appeared to feel strongly for the child in a way she didn't feel for him. Those kinds of feelings made people unreliable. There was a point when he realized the whole setup could easily spiral out of his control, and for that reason it had to be scrapped. He had it all planned out, would pick them off one by one, Constance first, telling Ruby she was going for treatment. He'd just finished getting everything ready when they betrayed him. Thinking of the things he has prepared, the man is annoyed that he has wasted his time, that his efforts will amount to nothing. A few miles away from the apartment in an abandoned warehouse, behind a secure door, there are three bathtubs standing ready, the salt sacks leaning against the wall, next to the shovel.

"I'm sorry, we're not staying long," says Sam to the screechy person, and he shuts the cover and zips it.

"We're not staying long"—that's what Sam said. So, Ruby is still aboard. The man doesn't want to be seen by her, but the fact that he hasn't laid eyes on Ruby or Leonie since the village green is worrying him slightly. Recently she's shown a talent for deception of which he was previously unaware. Right up until the day they attacked him and stole themselves away, he'd thought Ruby was at least partly on his side. No matter. He can get the upper hand again. He already considers himself to be one step ahead of her. The tracker being taken from the phone and placed on the train as a decoy would have been a cunning move if he hadn't been able to visit the warehouse after leaving the hospital, where he picked up the cloned phone he uses to track her online life, such as it is. It's inconvenient that he can no longer track her physically, but he can watch, in real-time, whenever she uses the internet to try to evade him. The first escape may have taken him by surprise, but he knows what she's been planning this time. He was watching as she booked the tickets yesterday. His first thought was that he ought to go there and wait for her, but all of Ruby's lies have undermined his confidence in predicting what she's going to do next. If she's somehow guessed he has access to her search history, there's a risk that the tickets themselves are a decoy, intended to send him hundreds of miles in the wrong direction.

Part of him wonders if he ought to draw a line under it all. Finish the three of them on the boat now and move on permanently, let Constance go. "Gregor" has become rather tedious, and although he has enjoyed spending all of that rental money, one can get too comfortable. It will be fun to take on another challenge, another persona. He's done his research, he just needs to take the leap, start again in the new life he knows is waiting for him—once he's dealt with the man currently living it. A surge of anger turns his thoughts around. The rage he feels now is caused by his humiliation, the injustice of it. He's been made a fool of, and he no longer wants to finish Constance, but to punish her. Killing Ruby and Leonie is part of that, but if he does it here and now, she'll never know.

The screechy person cuts through his thoughts. Apparently, they have lots to say, but it seems to be all along the same lines. The injured man stops listening.

Many hours pass, but the man does not fall asleep. He waits, to see what will occur. Ruby should come out at any moment, he thinks. He imagines her passing by in front of him, unaware that he's hiding there, waiting to follow her wherever she goes.

And then, when the winter night is at its darkest, the injured man can't bear the suspense any longer. He creeps from the shadows and places silent fingers on the zip of the boat's rain cover.

CHAPTER

47

NOW
Joanna
Thursday, December 27

JO BROKE THE speed limit twice on the way to Ripon, which
Atkinson had found out was the last recorded location for
Sam's boat. She followed satnav directions to the canal terminus,
parked hastily next to the water, and got out. The sky was completely dark, but the canal was illuminated by a handful of streetlights scattered around the almost deserted basin. A single
narrowboat floated in darkness, moored a short distance from
where the waterway came to a dead end.

As she approached the black-and-red-painted craft, Harper
read the name on a plank propped in the window, hand-drawn
letters picked out in white on a blue background.

Nessie.

From above her, a harsh, disembodied voice yelled, "Is that
boat anything to do with you?" and Joanna looked up to see a
person leaning from the window of one of the houses backing
onto the canal side where *Nessie* was moored. "There's no overnight mooring here. So you better move it, or I'll get it moved for
you."

"I'm a police officer," said Harper.

"Oh, good. Are you going to tow it? I'm sick of looking at the scruffy old thing."

"How long has it been here?"

"More than twenty-four hours now. The Canal Trust man came by, left them a fixed penalty notice, serves them right. Since then I've been keeping an eye out."

"You haven't seen anyone on board?"

"A man, yesterday. He didn't say much, refused to move. I'm glad the police are interested, finally. When I rang up, they didn't seem to care. They said it was a civil matter."

"Just a man? No one else? What did he look like?"

"White guy. Straggly beard. Looked like they all do. Boat dwellers."

"Thank you, madam, go inside now. I'll deal with it."

Once the person had shut the window and drawn the curtain across, Jo turned back to the boat.

No light burned in any of the windows, but when she put her hand on the chimney, she found that it was very slightly warm. The fire had been lit, perhaps this morning, and allowed to burn out. She knocked on the side. No sounds.

There was a waterproof shelter attached to the deck, a kind of awning that had been left unzipped. She pushed it aside and stepped on board, seeing that the hatch was ajar. Quickly she descended the steps into the saloon, and there, by the light of the torch on her phone, she saw the form of a man, slumped and bloody on the floor of the small galley.

"Sam Douglas?" He was facedown, his body twisted, one arm at an unnatural angle. She crouched and put her fingers at the side of neck. A pulse, but very weak.

Joanna looked around the inside of the boat. There were books thrown everywhere, cushions on the floor, everything turned out of the drawers and cupboards. There wasn't anything Harper could see that belonged to Ruby. Except . . . she reached out and pulled on a small furry thing sticking out from under a heap of papers. She held up the child's teddy bear in the shaft of light from her phone. They'd been here, she was sure. But so had Gregor.

Harper's mind was racing. Had he taken them? Were they injured, dead?

From the floor of the boat, the man let out a soft groan.

"Sam? Can you hear me?" She knelt over him, willed him to look at her. His eyelids flickered open.

"Jo?" The voice was breathy, almost inaudible. The fact that he recognized her was a good sign, though; they hadn't seen each other in years.

"Who did this to you, Sam?"

Sam started to cough, and she thought he might choke. He spat out a mouthful of blood.

"Listen. Don't try to talk. Just blink once for yes, twice for no. Was Ruby here when this happened?"

Sam blinked twice.

Joanna felt a wave of relief. She hadn't been caught. But how long ago had she left? And where was she headed to?

Blood had dried on the floorboards and cupboards where it had splashed. The attack on Sam must have been many hours ago.

"Do you know where she is now?"

One blink.

"And did you tell him where she was going?"

Two blinks. A tear ran down his cheek. He tried to say something, but it was so quiet that she couldn't hear what it was. She leaned closer and could barely make out the words.

"He already knew."

48

NOW
The Injured Man
Thursday, December 27

THE MAN STANDS at the window, feeling the great rumble of the boat's engine beneath his feet, watching as the lights of Castlebay, gleaming like flecks of white gold in the distance, draw slowly closer. The winter night fell hours ago, and now it is as if they sail through space; the thick dark of the sea can be distinguished from that of the sky only by the occasional streak of white foam at the top of a wave, and the way the heaving swell catches the reflection from the ferry's lights at a certain angle.

He is light-headed, delirious from the pain that has been getting steadily worse since he boarded. The fight with Sam in the early hours was more difficult than it ought to have been. When he'd seen that Ruby and Leonie had already gone, he'd been too angry to react efficiently. He must have made a noise that woke Sam, who'd managed to get a few good punches in before things were properly under control. All that time wasted waiting to follow them, when he hadn't even needed to. Imagine if he'd left it any longer—he might have missed the ferry altogether.

The drive up in the car he'd stolen at Ripon had been calm-
ing, the landscape through the Scottish lochs and valleys sooth-
ingly dramatic, but something about being at sea seemed to
disagree with him. The moment he was on the ferry, he'd slipped
into the first bathroom he'd come across, knowing that Ruby and
Leonie were somewhere nearby. The choice of hiding place was
rather appropriate, it turned out, because only minutes after the
boat set sail, he'd been overcome with the worst seasickness he'd
ever experienced. The force of the first great expulsion of vomit
was too much for his injured head: he'd blacked out.

In the darkness, the dreams returned. Constance was standing in front of him, her gaze steady. She had big, sad eyes and a
baby in her arms. She opened her mouth to speak, but all that
came out was a terrible scream, a high-pitched, barely human
shriek. It had the ocean in it somehow; it sounded exactly like the
seals on the night he took her. As he watched, her eyes became
entirely black, the whites disappearing. Her mouth grew bigger,
her nose became elongated, her skin darkening to gray. She was
half seal, now, a horrific chimera, with a human's legs and torso
but a thick neck and the head of a seal, and she was screaming
that awful scream. He wanted to cover his ears, but he couldn't
seem to move his arms. She put the baby down on top of him and
turned away, and he wanted to shout, *Don't leave it here. I can't
have it, it's not mine. What have you done? Where are you going?
She's your baby—come back for her.* But no sound came from his
lips, and she kept moving away. Now the baby, another half seal,
Leonie but not-Leonie, was looking at him with its big dark eyes,
but even if he could have picked it up, he wouldn't have done so.
He was repelled by it. He shouted, *Come back Constance and do
your duty,* and he knew that if she didn't, then the thing was
going to die. He experienced the thought in a matter-of-fact sort
of way, because he couldn't, wouldn't—and what is more, didn't
want to—look after it, not in a million years. And even though
there was no sign that she would come back, somewhere in the
depths of his brain he knew that she wouldn't just walk away
from Leonie. He had started to feel angry. She was messing with
him. She'd turn around in a minute. And yet she kept getting
smaller and smaller as she receded into the distance, and she

didn't look around, not once. Her legs were gone then, replaced by a seal's tail. The last he saw of her, she was diving in a perfect arc, disappearing into the black. The baby opened its mouth and started to scream, and the sound was just like the mother's: distant, soulful, and so terribly loud.

Someone was shouting, then, and there was a loud knocking sound. The man had opened his eyes and remembered where he was.

"Are you alright in there? Do I need to get the doctor?"

"No," he'd managed to say, trying to sound convincing. His voice cracked, and he said it again, more forcefully. "No, thank you. I just feel a bit sick. I'm not used to boats."

"Well," said the voice, "if you're sure."

"I'm sure. Thank you. I'll be fine."

"You've been in here for half an hour."

"I'm—" he cut himself off with another wave of nausea, head down into the bowl, his whole body clenched. Matter rose up from his stomach and splattered into the toilet.

"I'll check again in a bit," said the person, and went away.

With every heave, the pain in his head intensified, and with each bright burst of it, he pictured Constance coming toward him with the rock or whatever it was that she'd used to bash his head in. This picture was not a memory; he'd been hit from behind, he hadn't even known she was there. After Ruby led him to Constance, the first thing he was going to do was make her pay for that.

The man had ventured from the bathroom a couple of hours into the journey, but he hadn't been able to go far. He kept needing to dash back and hold himself over the toilet, though after a while mostly he'd been dry-heaving. When he first saw the lights of the island, he'd been convinced it was a mirage, but as they came closer, he saw that there were streetlights, and a few lit windows punched out of the dark, seemingly set into the dense blackness of rock. When the moon broke through the clouds for a moment, the island loomed from the sea, both bigger and smaller than he had expected, like the hump of an impossibly large whale; an ancient, treeless mound with the edges of cottage roofs silhouetted against the sky like giant limpets.

The boat tips very slightly and he loses balance, his stomach turning with the movement, but there is nothing left to come up. Leaning with one hand on the cool glass, the man hears the sound of the child's—unmistakably Leonie's—chatter behind him, and discreetly moves away to the other side of the ferry. The child's noise is like an early-warning system; he can hear them coming and get out of the way before they spot him. There had been only one moment, about an hour ago, when he'd realized that Ruby was coming toward him, heading for the toilets without Leonie, and he'd had to duck sideways into the bar area to get away. There, he saw that Leonie was asleep under a coat on one of the benches at the edge of the room. He watched her for a minute, until he realized he too was being watched, by the bartender. When their eyes met, the man smiled, but the bartender did not. He just stared back steadily, continuing to polish a glass with a cloth.

"You feeling alright, mate?"

The man was on the verge of replying that he was fine, when he realized he was about to be sick again and ran for the gents with a hand clamped over his mouth. As the door swung shut, he could hear the bartender's soft chuckle and his comment to a colleague. "First-timer, that guy. You can spot them a mile off."

As the ferry docks, most of the people on board begin to gather near the stairs to the car deck. The man hangs back—as a foot passenger he will be exiting the same way as Ruby and Leonie, but he doesn't want to risk being seen at this crucial point. He keeps his eye on them. In Ruby's arms, the child is almost asleep, her head on the woman's shoulder. He lets them go in front, with another six or seven people between them. Leonie's eyes are just closing when she spots him. He looks straight at her for a split second, then bends quickly pretending to tie a shoelace. Shit. He was so close. It couldn't be spoiled, not when he'd come so far.

"Mamma Bee?" he hears Leonie say, talking around her thumb so that the words aren't quite clear.

"Yeah, baby?" says Ruby.

"Daddy there."

He holds his breath. It isn't a question, but Ruby answers it as if it is. "No, honey, Daddy's not here."

When he peeks above the heads of the other people, he sees that Ruby has whirled around and is searching the crowd, standing on tiptoes, scrutinizing every face. He ducks in the nick of time.

"I seen him," says Leonie. "Daddy there."

Perhaps aware of listening ears, or wary of frightening the girl, Ruby merely says shhh, and Leonie stops talking. Hemmed in by the crowd, Ruby faces the front and rocks the child gently, though he can tell from the way she holds her shoulders that she's tense. The man moves so that he isn't directly in Leonie's eyeline before he glances again and sees that she is asleep.

The door clanks open, and he stands aside to allow everyone to get off before him so that he can put as much distance between him and Ruby as possible. Gingerly he pulls down the baseball cap that covers his wound, and wraps the fisherman's jacket tightly around himself as he disembarks. By the time he walks slowly up the freezing dock, the two of them have gone into the nearby hotel; he can just see them through the window as Ruby speaks with the receptionist. It's too late, too dark to try to find Constance now. They'll be planning a daytime rendezvous, and he needs to be ready in the morning, the moment they set off.

He waits until all the locals have dispersed before he starts trying the doors of the cars parked in the street that leads from the bay. He has his pick. No one here locks their car, it would seem. The first in the row is a Mini, too small for him really, so he tries the next, a large BMW. The door opens. He slips into the back seat, curls up and falls quickly into an untroubled sleep, lulled by the sound of the waves against the nearby shore.

CHAPTER

49

H EAVY FOOTSTEPS ON the towpath outside alerted her. Sam lay on the floor of the boat, so Joanna crouched in a position from which she could defend them both. Silently she grabbed a broken bottle and gripped it, ready to strike.

"Boss?"

She relaxed. "Steve. You scared me."

Atkinson thumped down the stairs into the saloon, shining a heavy-duty torch around the trashed inside of the boat.

"I guess the fugitive beat us to it," he said. "Did you find Ruby and the girl?"

"No, but I know where they are. On a ferry in the middle of the sea."

Sam groaned softly.

"Is he alright?"

"Not really."

Once Sam had been attended to and taken away by the paramedics, Harper and Atkinson climbed into the patrol car and started driving north, heading for the port at Oban. As they joined the motorway, Steve wordlessly handed her his phone, on the screen of which was an email from the mobile phone surveillance system, informing them that Ruby had turned her phone on again and that it was located off the coast, en route to the Western Isles. Such a remote place—why did it have to be there? The alert was from only an hour ago. Jo took out her own phone and tried Ruby's number, and this time it connected. She listened to it ring three times, four, imagining her daughter holding the phone in her hand, thinking about whether or not she should answer. Then, she did.

"Joanna?"

"Ruby."

There was a pause as they both choked into tears. Harper searched in her bag for a tissue, ended up wiping her nose on the back of a hand. The distance between Jo and Ruby was huge: six hours driving, six hours on the ferry. It was as if they were on separate planets. Yet just hearing that voice, Joanna felt closer than she had in years.

"Are you okay?"

"Yes," said Ruby. "I'm in trouble though. I need to tell you—"

"It doesn't matter."

"Joanna, don't. I'm trying to explain."

"You don't have to explain. I know already."

"What do you think you know?"

"That you took that child, that you pretended to be someone else."

"You make it sound like I committed a crime."

"Technically, you did. But that's not what I meant, Ruby, honey. Can we start over?" How come they always ended up here, no matter how much Jo tried not to? Atkinson side-eyed her. This was no time for an argument. Don't make her hang up and turn off the phone again. Jo took a slow breath and tried again. "I'm not blaming you. I know why you did it, Ruby. And we're not going to arrest you."

"We? You mean, the police? But, Jo, I thought I was talking to you. As a person, not as a copper." She sounded hurt, then angry. "Nothing ever changes, does it?"

"Please, Ruby. I'm sorry. Is Leonie okay?"

"Yes, she's fine. She's the best thing in the world, actually. She's asleep right now."

"And you're on the boat?"

"Yes. We should dock soon."

"I need to ask, have you seen Gregor anywhere?"

Suddenly Ruby's voice was panicked. "Why would I have seen him? Is he in Scotland? I know he escaped from the hospital, but I hoped, because of the injury, maybe he wouldn't have gotten very far."

"He went to see your friend Sam."

"Sam? Is Sam okay? What did he do?"

"He'll be fine. But Gregor, he knows where you're going. He's trying to find you, and maybe hurt you. He's angry. Perhaps he wants to take his daughter back. And he's ahead of us, though we're coming as fast as we can."

"But I'm on a ferry." Ruby sounded shaken. "I've been on it for nearly five hours, and he's definitely not here. I haven't seen him. Although . . ."

"What?"

"It's nothing. Only, Leonie said something about seeing him. But she was half asleep at the time."

Joanna stiffened in fear. "You're sure? You checked he wasn't there?"

"Yes. I'm sure."

There was a tremor in her voice, though, that neither of them acknowledged. She must be terrified. And the little girl; surely she was traumatized too. No wonder she was seeing that man around every corner.

"That's great," said Jo. "He must have missed it, like we thought. He might try to get on it tomorrow, but we'll be there in time to stop him. We won't let him get to you."

"If he catches me, I don't know what he'll do."

"I know, honey. I know what he's capable of. I know why you had to defend yourself. Just a shame you didn't hit him harder."

"Me? You think that was me? I didn't even know about it until I saw it on the news."

Jo exhaled. "I knew it couldn't be you."

"But if you think I'm a criminal . . ."

"What are you even doing up there, Ruby? What's on the island you so desperately need to get to?"

"Leonie's mother. Constance. She asked me to bring her. So I'm keeping my promise."

"Constance? But we don't know if she's still alive. She ran into the sea, Ruby. She didn't even have a wetsuit."

When Ruby spoke again, her voice was full of doubt. "But she said she'd be here. For Leonie."

Ruby was so far away. If only she'd told Joanna what she was planning, she could have talked sense into her before it was too late. Constance had clearly been a woman with a severely troubled mind. Jo gave a frustrated groan.

"Even if she is there, after what she did, abandoning her child on the seafront, do you really think she's a fit mother?"

Ruby went quiet. Then, "That is fucking rich, coming from you."

Click.

"Ruby. Ruby? Oh, shit."

"Did she hang up?" said Atkinson.

"Yeah."

"Huh."

"I always say the wrong thing. I don't know why I can't just keep my stupid mouth shut."

A few seconds later, Atkinson's phone rang through the speakers of the car. It was DI Thrupp.

Steve put his finger to his lips as he pressed to allow the call.

"What do you mean, you're going to the Outer Hebrides?" Thrupp wasn't quite yelling.

"Like I said," Atkinson replied, "that's where Ruby's gone with Leonie. I just spoke to her; she's about to disembark from the ferry at Barra."

"What state of mind is she in? Is there any risk to the child?"

"No, of course not," said Joanna, interrupting. "None whatsoever."

Atkinson grimaced. He mouthed, *Shut up.*

"Who is that? Steve? Who just spoke? DS Harper, is that you?"

"Yes, sir."

Thrupp's voice rose a half octave. "What do you think you're doing? Can someone explain what is going on?"

"Well, sir—"

"Not you, Jo. I don't want to hear from you after what you've done. In the morning I'm meeting with Hetherington to discuss what's happening, but I wouldn't be surprised if he recommends a suspension —"

"But, sir—"

"But nothing. Stop talking. Learn to follow an instruction, would you? Steve, I want you back here as soon as possible."

"But what about the little girl? Don't we need to bring her home?"

"She's not our priority right now—neither of them are. Yes, it's important that we locate the child and bring her back, of course it is. I'm going to liaise with Highlands and Islands police and get them to help by directing some manpower. They can pick up Ruby and Leonie. But our team only has so many resources, and at the moment all of our focus needs to be on finding this man."

"But that's who we're chasing, sir. He's attacked Sam Douglas, and he's gone after Ruby. We're right behind him."

There was a short silence. "He's on the island now too?"

"No, we don't think so," said Atkinson. "It would have been tight for him to catch the ferry, and Ruby wasn't aware of him on the boat during the crossing."

"We need to get an officer to the island as quickly as possible. Can you fly from Glasgow?"

"Me?" asked Joanna

"One of you. The other one needs to go to the port in case he's waiting for the next crossing."

"So I'm back on the case?" said Jo.

"For the moment. You said you'd spoken to Ruby?"

"Yes, but she hung up on me. I put my foot in it, slightly."

Harper could almost hear the sound of Thrupp hitting his forehead with a palm in frustration. "Jo. If you weren't the only copper available for this I would . . ."

During the pause, Harper and Atkinson exchanged a glance.

"Fine," said Thrupp. "I mean, it's not fine, but I don't have much choice in the matter, do I? Jo, get the plane. Steve, go to the ferry port, intercept him if you can, arrest him. I'll send backup, but it might take a while. Keep me updated."

The call ended. They drove in silence for a few minutes.

"What do you think that man's planning to do to them? To Ruby and Leonie, I mean."

"The guy's a psychopath," said Jo. "Who knows what he's thinking? One thing in our favor, though: he's got quite a severe head injury to contend with, and Sam said he managed to land a few blows before he was overpowered. Hopefully that will slow him down enough for us to catch him."

"Yeah," said Atkinson, though to Jo he sounded far from certain.

50

NOW
The Injured Man
Friday, December 28

DORA IS KNEELING on his chest, holding his eyelids shut. *Get off me, you little shit,* he tries to say, but his mouth seems full of cotton wool, his tongue too thick to move properly.

I won't let you do it, says Dora. *You've done enough now. Just leave them alone, won't you?*

It's a dream. He knows it's a dream, yet he can't shake it off. He can't shake her off; he bucks his body, but she clings to him like a goblin. *You're dead,* he tries to say. *You can't stop me doing anything.*

Dora lets go of one of the man's eyelids and reaches behind her. When she brings her hand around, she's holding a penknife that he recognizes. It's the one he used, to take off her finger, just before he . . . just before she fell, so tragically.

You pushed me, she says, as though she can read his thoughts. Then, she plunges the blade of the penknife into the soft part at the back of his head, and the pain explodes like a grenade.

With the pain, clarity returns. He stops struggling and lies still. *This is not real,* he thinks. *You're not real. It's all in my head.*

Dora stops what she's doing. For a moment she seems unsure. Then she glances to her right, and Constance is there, floating beside them, her bottom half a fish, top half human. The man tries to say, *This isn't fair,* because now there are two of them, and he still can't move. *You're just a dream, both of you,* he thinks. Then he sees that behind Constance is an old woman, and next to the old woman, though it takes him a while to place him, is the man whose name he took. *Now this is getting ridiculous,* he thinks. Both Gregor and the old woman are laughing at him. *I don't see why you're laughing,* he thinks. *I killed you.*

It's because we know what's coming next, says the old woman. *And I don't think you're going to like it very much.*

Constance comes near.

What are you? she asks. *You're not a man. You took my skin. You kept it.*

You're not real, he tries to scream. *None of you are real.*

Dora's still crouching above him, her hand on the knife sticking out of his wound. Her lip curls, like a shrug. *Real is relative,* she says, twisting the knife, and the pain he feels is real, excruciating. The last thing he sees before he blacks out is Constance, swimming away into the distance, to the sound of Dora, Gregor, and Gregor's mother laughing.

He awakes into darkness, remembering where he is, that he's in a car and he needs to get out before anyone sees him there. His head throbs violently, and when he reaches up to feel it, he realizes he has been resting his head on the seat-belt connector. He must have jerked his head in his sleep, and that is what has stabbed him. *Dora, you crazy little hallucination, he thinks,* smiling bitterly. But still, his pulse races with the memory of the vicious apparitions, and he can't shake off the uneasy feeling for some time.

The woman at the hotel crosses her arms. "I'm sorry," she says, "We have no one of that description staying here, I'm afraid."

"Look," says the man, "I know she might have told you not to let me know where she is, but I'm her husband. It was just a little fight, honestly. I only want to talk to her."

"I don't know who you're talking about."

"But I saw her come in here last night. You were serving her. You must remember."

The woman shrugs.

"I'm worried about her, that's all. And my daughter. She's such a daddy's girl. She'll be missing me."

The shy smile, that beautiful smile, and the bashful eyes. It never fails. He smiles it right at her, and the woman cannot look away. She takes a deep breath, visibly softening. "She only came in to ask for a taxi. She didn't stay."

Well, why didn't you say that first off, thinks the man. He smiles again, not completely hiding the irritation that he feels. "Do you know where she went in the taxi?"

"Nope." How can that be true? The second smile hasn't been as effective, clearly. She stares at him, daring him to ask again.

"Ah," says the man. "Well, thanks for your time, I suppose." He turns to leave.

"Not many places she could have gone, though."

"Oh?"

"Only three other hotels on the island, and one of them is shut for the winter."

"Thanks," says the man, pulling open the door.

"This is a small place," says the woman, with a warning tone. "There are eyes everywhere, you know. No police, but eyes everywhere."

This is interesting. "No police?"

"There was one, once. But he tried to arrest one of ours, so we locked him in his own cells. We police ourselves, these days. Have done for twenty years. And we are very, very, good at it." She folds her arms and lowers her chin to look at him from under her brow.

The man sits on his rage. He takes a slow, deep breath. Then he holds up a hand in farewell, leaves the hotel, and goes down the steps to the road.

CHAPTER

51

NOW
Ruby
Friday, December 28

I T WAS PITCH dark outside. In winter, this far north, the hours of
daylight were limited to the middle part of the day; in summer,
the opposite was true, with only a few hours of darkness. When
Ruby drew the curtains open, she could barely make out the
expanse of the beach that she knew stretched out in front of them,
and to the right of that, the ocean. The hotel boasted the best view
of any of the three hotels on the island. She'd chosen it because of
the location, close enough to where she needed to be, but not so
close that anyone would see what she was doing or try to interfere
with the plan.

Leonie was sleeping, her chest gently rising and falling in the
light from the bathroom door. Ruby had an idea that she might
just slip out, leave the comb where Constance had said to, and be
back before the toddler awoke, but almost as soon as the thought
had surfaced, she dismissed it. Leonie was coming with her, of
course she was. It was unthinkable that the child would wake up
alone and think she'd been abandoned again. By the time Ruby

had dressed herself, the little girl was rubbing her eyes and sitting up.

They made their way to the front door of the hotel, avoiding the restaurant, where the smell of breakfast wafted tantalizingly toward them.

"I mungry, Mamma Bee," said Leonie as the door swung closed, and Ruby began walking fast along the coast road, heading north, with the child strapped to her back.

"We'll eat soon, baby," she said over her shoulder. "Just got to do one thing. Then it's brekky, okay?"

"Yay! Brekky."

As she hiked around a corner, the landscape rolled out in front of them, and she almost had to stop to get her breath. Even in the weak, predawn light, with the freezing wind whipping her face, the harsh beauty of it floored her. The road was cut into the rock, which stretched craggily down to meet the sea, that heaving, blue-black, infinite thing. The island curved to one side, with coves and crevasses breaking up the flat edges of the machair, falling away to beaches with sand that shone white, as if they held the light inside them for times such as these.

Ruby pressed on, shushing Leonie as she complained of being cold, heading for the outcrop that Constance had described, the barren, exposed peninsula with a single, half-derelict cottage on it. It was further away than it looked at first. Leonie started to moan softly and wriggled against the scarves that Ruby had used to wrap and secure her on her back.

"Just a few more minutes, baby. Don't worry. Nearly there."

Up close, the cottage was even more of a wreck than she'd thought. The windows were boarded, the door rotten in the corners, with only a few flakes of paint left on its surface. It was clear to Ruby that it was abandoned, had been for years. She screwed her eyes shut against the wind that was causing tears to sting her face, and leaned close to the wall, hoping for a little shelter, finding none; the wind whipped the house on all four sides. It was a mystery as to why it had been built. No one could live here. No one would want to. She went to the door and knocked, not expecting a response. Sure enough, all she could hear was the crashing of the sea, the whistling of the wind. Then she kicked the door, feeling the planks give way a little against the toe of her boot. Finally, she tried the doorknob, and it turned.

They stumbled into the cottage, grateful to get out of the weather. The only furniture in the single room was a rickety table pushed up against a wall. On the table, a large and beautiful conch shell, much bigger than any she'd seen before; twice the size of the one that had been in the bathroom at Gregor's. The table on which it stood was thick with dust, but the shell itself was spotless. Something shifted in Ruby and she let out a sob, steadied herself against the damp stone wall. She realized that until she saw the conch, part of her hadn't believed it was real.

"It dark, don't like it," said Leonie.

"Don't worry, only a minute more," said Ruby. She took the carved white comb from her zipped pocket and placed it inside the conch shell. It made a small, musical clanging sound as it slipped out of view, into the pinkish interior. She stood there, breathing, wondering if this was really going to work; if someone from Constance's family really came and checked the conch every day, the way Constance had described when they were planning how to meet up again. The family had no phones, no other way of communicating.

"We've people on the big island," Constance had said. "Some of our children, cousins who weren't born in the skin, who can't live where we do. Like you, my lovely." She'd kissed Leonie on the head as she slept in her mother's arms. "When the comb's in the shell, we come across to the beach at Seal Bay. It's a message. This one, they'll recognize. I carved it myself."

"Wanna get down, Mamma Bee," said Leonie, wriggling and kicking. Instinctively, Ruby started to bounce on her heels and sing. *Ionn da, ionn do* . . .

So far away from anyone, in this remote spot at the edge of the world was the last place she expected thoughts of Joanna to find her. Nevertheless, as she backed out of the dark room, into the wind on the headland, pulling the door shut behind them, Joanna was who she yearned for. Leonie had taught her what it was to put someone else's needs before your own. She realized then, that perhaps Joanna had been trying to do that, all those years ago. Jo hadn't abandoned Ruby. She'd sacrificed the chance to be a mother, the gift of experiencing the joy and the fear that came with being the provider of unconditional love. Alone on the rock with Leonie, Ruby wanted to find her mother, Joanna, and say she was sorry, that she was forgiven—and that there was nothing to forgive, really, because she understood everything now. Most of all, she wanted to hold her, be held by her, and to say that she loved her.

Seagulls circled above them as she hiked over the rocks, then over the machair to the road. Soon they would be back in the warm hotel, eating breakfast and waiting until it was time.

52

NOW
Joanna
Friday, December 28

THE FLIGHT FROM Glasgow to Barra, which lasted a little more than an hour, wasn't the kind of flight you could sit back and enjoy. Joanna watched her knuckles turning white as she gripped the seat in front and prayed for it to be over.

She supposed she had been warned, up to a point. "It's a wee bit windy today," the man she'd bought the ticket from had said. "Keep your eye on the board for a delay, or a cancellation."

"Is it likely to be canceled?" There was only one scheduled flight a day. A cancellation would be unthinkable.

The man tipped his head in thought. "They fly in a force eight. But they won't fly in a force nine."

"What's the gale force now?" she'd asked. Outside, trees were bent sideways. People leaned at unlikely angles, clutching their coats to them, hair battened to scalps by the driving might of the wind and rain.

"Eight point three." The man laughed at her. "Don't look so worried."

She shut her mouth.

The plane circled back on itself, and if Harper hadn't been gripped by the certainty that she was going to die, she might have appreciated the moment when they broke through the cloud cover and the island came into view. There was no airport, no runway that she could see. She tapped on the newspaper of the man next to her, who lowered it and raised an inquiring eyebrow.

"Where do we land?" she asked, trying to keep her voice steady. When the man answered, she was sure she'd heard him wrong, that the accent had somehow made her mistake his meaning. The second time he said it, she understood, with a kind of sinking feeling, that she'd heard it correctly the first time.

"On the beach," he said, nodding out the window as the aircraft tipped to make a turn. She could see a long stretch of sand between two needles of rock. "Only at low tide, mind. In a couple of hours, all that'll be underwater." He grinned at her before returning to his paper. A second later he lowered it again. "First time, I assume?"

She nodded. "Last time, too, I think."

He laughed, low and phlegmy.

To distract herself, she looked out the window and almost forgot she was scared. The sun had come out, turning the sea a translucent blue-green, the ripples on the water sparkling silver. The sand was pure white at the edges of the island. It reminded her of the colors of the Caribbean. The island itself was unspoiled, almost devoid of civilization, apart from the airport building, itself a stark reminder that humans had conquered this place, even if the tide was still in control of the flight times. From what she could see of the coastline, apart from the huge white beach that served as a runway, there were no accessible beaches on this side of the island. With probably sixty or more miles of coastline on the eight-mile-wide island, she wondered how she was going to find Ruby. There was no way of ringing. Straight after the badly judged conversation yesterday, Ruby had switched off her phone.

As the plane made its descent, she turned again to the newspaper-reading man. "Do you know where I can hire a vehicle?"

He folded his paper, finally. The plane was low now, the engines loud as it prepared to land.

"Sure," he said, "I'll show you if you like."

"Maybe you have a number?" She pulled her phone out of her pocket and saw that there was no signal.

The man chuckled gently. "Who's your service provider?"

She told him, and he shook his head. "Nay chance wi' them, lassie."

Joanna's hope wilted a little more. Even if Ruby did turn her phone on, there would still be no way of connecting.

The plane touched down on the sand, and Harper had to hold on tight to stop herself bouncing around as the brakes roared, came to a mighty crescendo, and died away. Finally, the aircraft was still.

"I wonder, can you also tell me where the local police station is?"

The man chuckled again.

"No police on Barra," he said, standing to retrieve his bag from the overhead locker. He turned and looked her in the eye. "No need. No crime to speak of."

"That can't be true," said Harper.

"Well, not entirely. But nobody really likes police, do they?"

When he grinned knowingly at her then, she raised her eyebrows. "How did you know I was police?"

"Apologies," he said, "Didn't mean to hurt your feelings. Just saying. What are you here for, anyway? Can't be anything big; I'd have heard about it."

"I'm here to find my daughter."

And she realized, then, that she'd stopped thinking and speaking of Ruby as her sister altogether. She was a mother, and her child needed her. Perhaps for the first time, she knew she would be there, no matter what; she was the only person who could do it. And it felt completely right.

53

I am a man upon the land
And I am a silkie in the sea
And when I'm far and far frae land,
My dwelling is in Sule Skerrie
—"The Great Silkie of Sule Skerrie." Scottish: Traditional

NOW
Ruby
Friday, December 28

THE SUN WAS bright as she hiked across the machair to the beach, with Leonie tied to her back once again in the makeshift sling, and Sam's violin strapped across her front. Ruby heard the sea before she saw it, the hiss and tumble of the waves against the sand, and the screeching of the seabirds above them. As the horizon came in sight, she spied the old cottage they had visited that morning, hunched and lonely on the headland.

Constance had entered the sea in a very different spot, so many miles away at Cleethorpes, on a freezing winter's night. Did she ever meet her family? If only Ruby could have caught a glimpse of them as they left. The way Constance expressed herself in fanciful tales of ancient lore, stolen skins and an island where seals danced on the beach as humans—the metaphors were so tantalizing, and being here made Ruby see how you could grow up believing the stories were true. In the moment of helping Constance escape, Ruby had been convinced she was sending her into the arms of her family. But in recent days she'd become less and less certain that she hadn't simply helped a madwoman to her death. Coming to Barra had been a decision taken in desperation; she'd seriously doubted that Constance would be here, but it seemed as good a place as any to hide from Gregor. But the conch, that beautiful shining shell. That had been the proof that she'd needed to carry on. There *was* a colony, a secret island clan. They existed, and Constance was among them. Ruby was so close now, to what she'd come to do, to return the baby to her mother and her people so that they could live freely in the traditional way, away from prying eyes.

The deserted bay was pristine. White sand led to the ocean, clear blue-green in the bright wintry sunlight. Shaped like a perfect crescent, the beach was surrounded by rocky outcrops. Ruby turned toward the water, the wind coming straight off the sea and flattening her hair to her head, whistling past her ears. Right in front of them, about a hundred meters out, was a large rock, its edges washed by hundreds of tiny waves.

With Leonie still secured in the sling, Ruby took out the violin and began to play. First she played the folk song, *Chuir iad mise dh'eilean leam fhìn*. When she got to the chorus, she played the part Sam had taught her, that he learned as "The Song of the Seals." In that moment, she could see how the song could be sung both ways. She felt as if she'd been sent to an island, but it wasn't in exile. She'd come here for a reason. And as she played, a seal lifted its head, appearing as if out of nowhere on the rock in the bay. Of course, it had been there all along, just camouflaged and sitting very still. She smiled, imagined it thinking, *Who's that playing our song?*

Leonie started to sing along. The song transported Ruby to the folk bar where she'd first heard it, and from there to the dark interior of the flat on the New Park that she hoped never to see again. Playing it here washed all of that away. She knew from now on that the song would forever make her think of this beach, this perfect morning.

The wind should have whisked the notes from them, but the music seemed to echo in the bay. When she finished, the wind dropped and she felt the sun on her face. She put the instrument under her chin again and played "The Seal Woman's Joy." All of the tension she'd been holding in her body drained away. Leonie relaxed against her, singing softly the words, *Ionn da, ionn do* . . .

The final note quietly faded away. For a while she could hear only the wind, the sea, and the birds. Something screamed, then, and she jumped.

"What that, Bee?" said Leonie, wriggling in the wrappings that bound her to Ruby's back.

"It's a seal, honey. Can you see it?"

Once she'd seen one, her eyes adjusted, and she perceived three large gray seals, all of them watching Ruby and Leonie on the beach. One opened its mouth and made the noise again, but this time it didn't sound like a scream; more like a yelp, or a cry of recognition; perhaps even of joy. The seal heaved itself off the rock into the water, where only its head could be seen above the waves for a moment before it disappeared.

Ruby unwrapped Leonie and let her down, so that she ran with arms open wide toward the ocean, stopping just short of the lapping waves. She bent and tried to touch the edge of a wave, laughed when it disappeared, started to chase another as it withdrew and was only saved from a soaking by Ruby, who scooped her up and ran back to the dry sand. More games of "touch the waves" followed. The child was looking down, so she didn't see the seal's head pop up, much closer now, before disappearing again.

Soon the two of them were sitting on a rock, Ruby drying the child's hands on one of the scarves, doing the counting rhyme, one-little-piggy, both of them laughing when the little one went wee-wee-wee all the way home. As she tickled her under the chin, Ruby suddenly realized that when the *Roane* arrived, when she handed her back, Ruby wouldn't be doing any of this anymore. Constance would take her daughter with her to wherever she lived now, and Ruby might never see them again. Of course it was the right thing for Leonie to be with her mother, and her other relatives. Ruby was never intending to keep her; that wasn't the plan. Only, now she wished it was. She squinted into the sunlight, scanning the beach for signs of Constance. *Maybe she won't come,* she thought.

Leonie, now with her gloves on, trotted down toward the water to look for shells. Ruby followed. The wind dropped to a light breeze; the sea was flat and calm. A chill crept up her spine and she whirled around, sure that she was being watched.

"Constance?"

But there was no one there, only the empty sand dunes, the seagulls, and out there in the ocean, the seals. Would she be in a boat or a vehicle? If the colony lived on an island, then it would be a boat, but she didn't see any craft in the bay. Perhaps there was a causeway just out of sight somewhere. She shaded her eyes and searched the horizon. Two of the three seals she'd seen were still on the rock. The other one was nowhere.

"Mummy!" cried Leonie, and started running along the sand. There was Constance, at the edge of the sea, barefoot, glowing, and smiling, and running toward her daughter with her arms out, ready to catch her. The sight of it filled Ruby up with joy, and yet pierced her heart at the same time. Mother and daughter, reunited. Just the way it should be.

The girl reached her mother and fell into her arms. Constance lifted her up in the air, both of them whooping. The woman's hair was loose down her back, threaded through with small shells, and she was wearing a sleeveless dress made of a patchwork of fabrics roughly sewn. Just behind her, on the rocks, Ruby saw that she'd placed her sealskin coat, which seemed good as new, shining like polished pewter in the sun. Constance balanced Leonie on a hip, walked toward Ruby. As she did so, Ruby could see the difference that a few days with her people had made. Constance seemed truly alive, for the first time, in a way Ruby had never seen; her eyes sparkled, her skin was illuminated. Whatever had been missing back at the New Park estate had been returned. Leonie lay her head on her mother's bare shoulder; apart from the dress, she wasn't wearing anything. Ruby shivered, wondering how Constance could stand the cold.

"You came," said Constance.

"Of course. I promised."

"Thank you for coming, for bringing her."

When Constance moved forward to embrace her, Ruby jerked away.

"What is it?" said Constance, finally seeing Ruby properly, how her expression had darkened.

"Where were you?" said Ruby, her voice sharpened by anger. How could she look so happy, after everything she'd done? "At Cleethorpes. You left her on her own. How could you do that?"

"I didn't want to." Constance set Leonie on the sand, straightened up and looked at Ruby. "I had no choice."

The wind had picked up. Ruby's words were being whipped away as it took her breath and stung her eyes. But she didn't feel it. "Of course you had a choice. You could have chosen to keep her safe. You could have chosen not to leave her all alone."

"I would have died if I'd stayed there. You know that."

"You? *She* might have died because of what you did. How could you leave her—how could you choose yourself over your daughter, what kind of mother does that?"

"If it's a choice between my daughter or death, then it's not a choice. What use am I to her, without my own life?"

"Some people might say that it's your duty to sacrifice yourself for your child."

Constance grimaced. "I thought you understood. Clearly I was wrong. I don't have to explain myself again."

"Right. And I don't have to do anything to help you, or your kid. You treat me like I'm an idiot. Just like everyone does."

"You can choose whatever path you feel is right, Ruby. That's always been the case."

"You asked me to help you."

"You didn't have to say yes."

Leonie looked from one to the other. Her bottom lip had started to stick out. "No shouting," she said, and a tear escaped from her eye. Both of them rushed toward her. Ruby got there first.

For a second she thought the child would reject her, reach for her mother. But she snuggled there, sucking a thumb, watching Constance with big eyes.

"I'm sorry, baby," said Ruby. "We won't shout anymore."

Constance reached out a hand to rub her daughter's back. Her arm was shiny with seawater. Sand clung to her elbow and her bare shoulder.

"Aren't you cold?"

"I'm used to it. I like it."

Ruby noticed that Constance's hair was wet. "Surely you didn't swim from the island?"

She nodded. "It's the quickest way. It's not too far."

"But I didn't see you coming."

"I know how to stay hidden." Constance shifted her eyes toward the sea. "You can't really see the island from here—look, see that rock just beyond there?"

Ruby looked where she was pointing. There was a rock, quite far out, disappearing behind the edge of the island they stood on. Waves were crashing against it.

"Not that one there? That's miles out."

"It's only part of where we live. I'll show you, one day."

"Will I have to swim there?"

Constance smiled.

"Mummy Mummy Mummy," said Leonie, and Constance took her from Ruby. "Down," she demanded immediately, so Constance squeezed her, kissed her, set her on her feet, where she squatted down to inspect a small stone.

"You can't swim back, though, can you?" said Ruby. "Not with Leonie."

Constance looked at her steadily. "No," she said. "I can't."

"Look, Mummy, look," said Leonie, holding up a shell for Constance to see.

"Yes, baby, I see. It's beautiful."

Constance looked back at Ruby. "I can't keep her," she said. And although Ruby expected to see tears glistening on Constance's cheeks, there were none. "She can't come home with me. She wasn't born in the skin. She has to live on the land. With you."

Born in the skin—that phrase again. Ruby didn't think it was literal, despite her notion that the sealskin coats might once have been used to catch the newborns. She'd assumed it was an expression meaning "born to the harsh island life." She glanced again at the sleek sealskin behind Constance, and then over at the rock in the middle of the bay from where the gray seals watched them.

So many questions crowded her mind. "But . . ."

Both seals called, loud and sharp, a warning bark.

Ruby heard a sound behind her, and she turned. Constance gasped. Ruby's throat closed.

The man they knew as Gregor was only a few meters away from them, where the beach became the machair. The sight of him chilled Ruby so that for an instant she couldn't move or speak. He was dirty, unshaven, dressed in unfamiliar clothes. His lips were cracked, there was dried blood on his neck, but that wasn't the most terrifying thing. It was that finally, he wasn't trying to hide who he really was; she looked into his eyes and saw that the Gregor she had known was gone, if he'd ever been there at all. The creature standing in front of them was made only of spite, and hate. He looked as if he wanted to kill her, and not only that, but he was quite looking forward to it.

"Daddy," said Leonie, and she was too far away to catch before she started running toward him.

Constance set off sprinting. Her fingers grazed Leonie's coat as the man picked up the child and took several steps backward.

"Give her to me," said Constance, and Ruby could tell she was making a huge effort to keep her voice steady.

The man laughed, a harsh, percussive sound. "What, so you can leave her alone on the seafront again? Not likely. You're not fit to be a mother."

"Fine, give her to Ruby then."

"Ruby? She'll run off with her, and I'll never see her again. My own kid! What were you planning to do, anyway, Constance? Take her away to your backward little sect? To live like a bloody scavenger? I don't think so."

"You don't care about her, Gregor. You never have. Just let her go."

"You thought you were so clever, didn't you? Sneaking up on me, spiking me when I couldn't defend myself. But you can't win at this. I'm in charge here. She belongs to me. And so do you."

The man was holding Leonie too tightly. "Daddy, ow! Let go!" But he wouldn't.

"Don't, you're hurting her," said Ruby.

He looked at Ruby as if he'd only just realized she was there. "I'll do whatever the hell I like with her. And I'll have you know, for the record, that I could have done whatever the hell I liked with you, too, at any time. You were nothing to me. A game that got boring."

"I won't say anything," said Ruby. "I'll take her far away. We'll start a new life, new names, everything. You won't need to worry about us. I've got as much to lose as you, Gregor, if the police catch up with me."

He narrowed his eyes at her in disbelief. "Firstly, I can't believe a word you say, honey, not after what you did to me. And secondly, I won't need to worry about you saying anything to the police because pretty soon you won't be saying anything to anyone ever again. But kudos for trying, I suppose." He turned to Constance. "You ready to come home?"

"Never."

"Hmm." He shrugged. "I really wanted to make you sorry for what you did. But actually, this might be better. Makes things simple for me. No loose ends, shall we say."

Still clutching the small girl, he turned and walked away from them, started hiking over the rocks, up the steep part at the edge of the bay. Ruby felt her arms twitch with the urge to fight him for the baby. Both women followed, gasping when he stumbled and nearly dropped the child, afraid to go too close for fear of what he might do to Leonie if they did. At the top of the cliff, he turned to face them. Leonie had gone limp, was whimpering silently, her eyes red with tears. *You've silenced her again, you bastard.*

Ruby stepped towards them, but Constance held out a hand to stop her. The man took another step backward, edging closer to where the ground fell away to a deep crevasse.

"Okay, so, kid first, I guess?" He grabbed a fistful of Leonie's coat and held her out toward the edge.

"No," shouted Constance and Ruby together.

They were fifty feet above the sea, perhaps more. A few steps away from a long drop into deep water, with needles of rock sticking up like teeth.

He took another step, held the child out at arm's length.

Ruby shrieked, tried to run toward him, but again Constance stopped her.

"He'll kill you," she said.

"I don't care!" Ruby struggled with Constance to get away, "I'd rather die than let him hurt Leonie."

"There are two of us and one of him," said Constance, shouting so that Gregor could hear. "If he throws her, we'll both go for him." She turned toward him, his laughing face, mocking them and their panic.

"You're weak," he said. "I'm not afraid of you."

"If you hurt her . . ." said Ruby.

Constance said, "Gregor, if you do anything to Leonie, we're both going to take you down."

His smile faltered as he glanced over the cliff at the rocks. He looked at each of them in turn, seeming to weigh things up. Then he drew back his arm as if to throw the child.

"Maybe I'll risk it anyway."

"Leonie!" Ruby shouted. But she was too far away to stop him.

"I'll come with you," said Constance, and he hesitated, the arm holding Leonie dropping to his side so that she dangled there like luggage.

"Come with me?" He glanced again behind him at the crashing waves.

"Not like that. I'll come back with you." She was holding out the sealskin coat. "If you let her live." Her face was set like stone.

His eyes narrowed as if he might believe her. Then he laughed. "Nice try. It's a trick."

Leonie squealed and wriggled. Ruby felt like her heart would burst out of her chest. They were so close to the edge now. "Stay still, Leonie. Please. Just for a minute. For me." She held eye contact with Leonie, who stopped struggling, seeming to understand. "Good girl."

Constance stepped forward, holding out the coat. "Take the coat. I can't go anywhere without it—you know that. Here." She dropped it on the ground between them and it lay there, gleaming and still, seeming almost alive.

He grinned, his perfect white teeth glinting in the sun.

"Told you I'd win."

Constance said, "I'll count to three. We'll switch. Let her go, Gregor."

He rolled his eyes, as if completely bored with the whole situation. "Well, if you want her that much." Ruby couldn't allow herself to believe that he was going to let her and Leonie go. He was toying with them the way he'd been doing all along, since the yoga, since before that even, when he'd bugged the flat. She and Leonie were dispensable now, and there was no predicting what he might be about to do. He might have been waiting for her to pick up the child so he could shove them both together over the cliff. Gregor eyed Ruby as she stood there, his tongue darting out like a snake's every few seconds. If she could get a bit closer, she would be able to touch Leonie, maybe even save her. *I dare you,* he seemed to be saying.

Slowly he set Leonie on the ground but kept tight hold of one of her arms. With the other hand, he reached for the coat that Constance had left on the ground. His fingers brushed it as Ruby rushed forward for Leonie. She grabbed her, then nearly overbalanced as she changed direction, sensed the man's hands almost touch her neck where he tried to get hold of her, and twisted away, feeling the sting of pain as he tore out a fistful of her hair.

"Stop! Police!"

Ruby dropped to the ground and rolled away from the edge of the cliff, Leonie held tightly in her arms. As she did so, she turned her head to see who had shouted. There was Joanna, running across the machair toward the rocks, cupping her hands to shout, "Stop!" once more. What was she doing here?

"No!" she shouted, though the wind took her words away. "Stay back."

Gregor had picked up the sealskin. "Oh, look, Ruby. It's your mummy. Come to save you." He started to laugh, as if it was the funniest thing he'd ever heard. Ruby tried to signal to Joanna again to stop, that she was making things worse, that she might be putting herself in danger too. She could feel Leonie's slack body against her, shaking softly with the silent cry.

"Come on then," said the man, and Ruby felt him take hold of her upper arm, drag her to her feet. "Looks like the three of you will have to go together, after all. Don't worry, Mummy will be with you soon, Ruby."

What happened next can't have taken more than a split second. She saw a flash of dark hair as Constance swooped her head down, her mouth open, teeth bared. She bit the man on the wrist where he held Ruby's arm, and he let go with a yelp, blood from the wound arcing out, specks of it landing on her face. Ruby stumbled away with Leonie, protecting her, comforting her as she cried and cried, the noise no more than a breath of air, but the shuddering of her body shaking them both. Joanna was there. She put her arms around Ruby, blocking out the wind, blocking out the world with her words: *Don't worry, you're safe, I've got you.*

Over Ruby's shoulder, Jo saw something that made her gasp, and Ruby turned just in time to see them fall. Constance went headfirst as if in a dive, her hand tightly gripping the arm of the man they had known as Gregor, as his other arm windmilled, his eyes huge with shock. Time slowed: for a moment his body seemed suspended, feet cartoonishly scrabbling, first at grass, then rock, then nothing. His mouth opened in a scream.

As quickly as it started, the scream was cut off. Far below, the waves crashed against the rocks.

Leonie was wide-eyed.

"Mummy Daddy gone."

A seal called from somewhere far offshore. Another, much closer, answered. The sound was loud and terrible.

54

Joanna

WITHIN AN HOUR of the pair falling from the clifftop, a team of specialist officers from the mainland arrived on the island by helicopter. With direction from the coastguard, Joanna offered to help organize the search parties. Rescue boats worked alongside local fishermen to comb the surrounding areas for the bodies overnight, but found nothing. At around five AM, the pair of them freezing, huddled together in the old police station waiting for news, the sergeant turned to Jo. "You get to the hotel, get some rest. If we find anything, I'll call you."

The call came with the morning, yanking her from a flimsy slumber. It was fortunate that she'd been too exhausted to get undressed; she levered herself upright and into her boots in minutes.

A body had been found floating not far off the coast, and towed in to shore by a fishing boat. Jo hiked over to where it lay, spread-eagled facedown on the sand, surrounded by the fishermen who had found it, the scene lit red and orange by the dawn.

Two of them turned the body on its back, one arm flopping wetly and splashing her shoes. "This him?" asked one of the fishermen.

"Yes," said Joanna. Jo felt nothing that he was dead, except frustration. In the hospital she'd spent too long staring at this same slack face and wondering. So many unanswered questions. Now, not only would she never have the chance to question him, he would never face justice for what he'd done. Not in this life at least.

The fishermen shuffled their feet. "Right then, lads," said a big bearded one, who appeared to be the skipper. "We'll be off." Waders squeaking, all four men started for the rowboat they'd pulled into the shallows. The fishing vessel was anchored a little way offshore.

"Hang on," said Joanna, "You're still going to help search, right?"

"Search for what?" said the skipper, continuing to walk away. "We found your man."

"There's another body to find. The woman, Constance."

They stopped walking. One exchanged a glance with another. "Ah, but she's *Roane*, isn't she?" said the youngest of the group. The bearded one punched him on the upper arm; the others shushed him.

"Whoever she is, she's still missing. We can't call off the search yet."

The skipper stared at her, his face unreadable. "You won't find that one, Detective. Be a waste of our time and yours." He turned and waded into the surf, the other three men following.

She turned to the local sergeant. "You just going to let them all go home?"

He shrugged, embarrassed. "They're volunteers. And fishermen, you know. A law unto themselves."

"But what about the rest of the search? What about Constance?"

They both looked out to sea, where the coastguard's boat was no more than a speck on the horizon. "She's dead, Harper. We can't spend any more money looking for a body, not when there are live cases to deal with."

She stared at him. "I can't believe—"

"I've seen a lot of these," said the sergeant. "When the sea's done with her, she'll give her back. It's just a case of waiting."

Joanna thought of the little girl, not even two years old, now an orphan. Her parents had plunged to their deaths together in this bleakly beautiful place, right in front of her. That kind of thing left a mark, even if Leonie might not remember it consciously. Echoes of trauma would cascade down the generations, seeping into corners that love should have filled. Unless of course she was lucky, and the love got there first.

At the hotel, Joanna watched Leonie carefully for signs of distress, but all she saw was a sunny, happy girl, playing with Ruby, whom she adored. Mamma Bee. They seemed so happy together, so natural. The bond was obvious.

"What's wrong, Joanna?" asked Ruby. "You seem troubled. Not like you."

"Oh, nothing. Just tired."

How could she tell Ruby that in a matter of hours, Leonie would be taken away, perhaps forever? That safeguarding systems and Social Services would be even now deciding what was best for the child, and while they did that, they would almost definitely take her into local authority care? Unless someone could find living family members to take her.

"I need to see if I can find the family, this *Roane* lot," she said, and headed out once more.

Jo went door to door. At every house, the same response: folded arms, closed faces. As the short time she had started running out, she became more desperate.

"There's a community on an island nearby. You haven't heard of it? What about the name *Roane*? Mean anything to you?" Each person feigned an unconvincing denial. One man said, "Oh, you mean the selkies?" but his wife dragged him away before he could say any more. At the Castlebay Hotel, a strange expression crossed the face of the woman who ran it. Her words declared that she'd never heard of the secretive clan; her face and body language said the opposite.

Jo returned to the beach just as the helicopter landed, come to pick up Ruby, Leonie, and her. As the island drifted out of sight, Jo looked at the little girl—excited to be so high up, her head too small for her ear defenders—and felt sad that if it was true her mother was from here, this might be her only visit. Whatever her family setup looked like after this, Leonie would be changed by it, like the roots of a sapling encountering a rock, and growing differently forever after. But maybe that was just life; maybe that's how we all grow.

EPILOGUE

Three Months Later
Joanna

THE TWO BODIES in the wall of the penthouse apartment were eventually proved to be that of Gregor Christopher Franks, a local property developer, and his elderly mother, Eva. Forensic examination of the bodies suggested they had been killed at around the same time as each other and sealed in the wall for at least three years. The murderer had gone to great lengths to make sure they didn't rot, using salting processes that the pathologist described as "more usually applied to the making of serrano ham."

The pathologist was oddly chirpy, as Joanna found that pathologists often were when they came across something out of the ordinary. "He would have needed to salt them for a few months. I imagine he needed sacks of the stuff—the bodies would have been covered completely. In the bath, probably. To get all the moisture out, you see. The ancient Egyptians did something similar with mummification."

"So he mummified them? Why?"

"I imagine it was so that the bodies didn't start to smell and give themselves away. Ingenious, really."

"I'm not sure I'd go that far. Sick, certainly."

Both bodies were devoid of innards, hanging upside down from butcher's hooks in the well-ventilated cavity, so that they had slowly dried out completely, finishing the job the salting had begun.

As for the man who'd killed them and stolen Franks's identity, while it took a lot of detective work to determine exactly who he was, assigning him to crimes he'd committed was initially a much simpler affair. As well as the many unsolved crimes which could be matched to him from the national police database, his DNA and fingerprints were found all over a disused industrial building on the edge of town, owned by Gregor Franks. From the equipment he'd been stockpiling, it looked as if he'd been planning to use the building to dispose of a number of bodies, three in total. Or three to start with. Joanna hadn't been part of the team who searched the building, and no one would tell her what exactly they'd found, but her imagination filled in the blanks. It made Jo angry all over again that he was dead because that meant she couldn't kill him herself.

"What do you think he was doing, when he left us alone all those nights?" said Ruby.

Jo knew exactly what he'd been doing, from the information that had been found on his various phones and devices. When he hadn't been building his body-disposal unit, he'd been stalking single gay men in neighboring cities, using online dating apps. He'd met several of them, but others he'd simply been watching, researching, finding out everything he could. He was hunting for his next persona, Planning to jump from "Gregor" into another lonely life via a little light murdering.

"I don't know," said Joanna. "Bad things, probably."

"The worst thing is," said Ruby, "that he knew I was there from the moment I moved in."

Joanna was cooking for the two of them in her flat. She thought it was hard to choose what the worst thing was but that this was certainly among the top five.

"But he didn't speak to me until August. I'd been there since February."

Jo nodded. "He was watching you. Two years before you were given the flat, around the same time he took over Franks' life, he hacked into the council system to prevent anyone from renting it. He must have known that the housing people would notice the glitch eventually. So at some point in those two years, he fitted the spyware. I suppose, if a random stranger was going to be in a position to be observing him, he wanted to be watching them first." Or maybe, and Joanna thought this more likely, he did it initially to amuse himself. One thing she knew from the many psychopaths she'd encountered over the years was that they tended to get bored easily. The crimes they committed had to get steadily more disturbing each time, ramping up the level of violence or deviance in order to achieve the same thrill.

"All those hours of practice, when I thought no one was listening. I never realized until he mentioned a piece I'd written that I'd played in the flat but never played him. After that I spotted three tiny cameras. There was even one in the bathroom."

"Don't think about it too much. You'll drive yourself mad."

Ruby's hand flew to her mouth. "Oh, Jo, no one from the police had to look at that, did they? You didn't—"

Joanna shook her head. "You don't have to worry. We've destroyed the footage."

"What really puzzles me, though, was that he knew so much about classical music. We talked for hours about the vagaries of Brahms or which was our favorite Schubert lieder."

"I guess he was genuinely a fan," said Joanna.

"I don't know if he was genuinely anything. He'd certainly done his homework, but there was this Mozart thing that he thought I'd written . . . doesn't mean much. I guess I'm just going over everything he said to me in the early days, and wondering how I fell for it."

Jo opened a bottle of red to let it breathe. "I shouldn't tell you this, but we've found his fingerprints at crime scenes in almost every county. Mostly house burglaries, dating back ten years. One or two very odd ones, though . . ."

The frightened look on Ruby's face made her stop, then, before she got into the story behind the preserved finger from the metal box and how it led them to discover the dead man's identity. As she poured the wine, Jo kicked herself for oversharing; she ought to keep in mind that gory details are not for everyone. In a similar way to the psychopaths, she'd become immune to horror: over the years it took ever more violence and deviance to shock her. This, however, was nothing ordinary, a case she would remember for a long time and one she thought she would never cease to be sickened by.

What she didn't say to Ruby was that familial DNA testing had proved that the finger belonged to a sibling of the man who had stolen Gregor's identity, and from there it was a short step to scouring records, first of murdered children with missing fingers and then of missing children whose bodies were never recovered, of whom no one could know the state of their fingers. Thankfully both categories of crime were few and far between. They found whom they thought was the right person almost immediately. Joanna had studied all the newspaper clippings before heading to the village with Atkinson to confirm it.

Eight-year-old Dora Jones had lived on a remote farm in rural Wales with her family. She had disappeared in 1997 on a sunny day, after going out to play in the fields. Hope of finding her alive started to wane after a week. Police scaled back the search after two months, but the family and the community continued to search for Dora every day for half a year before they were forced to call it off because of the harsh winter that had set in. Dora's parents never stopped looking for her, though it would turn out they didn't have much time left to search.

The deaths of both parents two years later were recorded as accidental carbon monoxide poisoning, though many in the area assumed, when they heard the news, that it was a double suicide, brought on by the guilt and grief of losing Dora. The couple were dead before they ate their sausages, having sat down to eat in a very enclosed kitchen space with a new, but faulty, gas heater. Only the older brother, Daffyd, survived, what with being away that night, sent by his father to tend the furrowing sows, and therefore missing dinner. He came home late to find them with their faces in the mashed potatoes. When questioned by Joanna, it seemed that no one in the small rural community had seen or heard of Daffyd since the funeral. "A cold fish," was the most she could get out of anyone who'd met him. Everyone remembered Dora, but some had forgotten she even had a brother. Not everyone: one retired schoolteacher shuddered in alarmed recognition at the sound of his name. She looked at a photograph of the dead man and confirmed it, providing old school portraits that proved it without a doubt. At the time of Dora's death, Daffyd would have been fifteen years old. His sister's body had never been found, but the finger was buried with her parents at the family plot in a ceremony attended by those who had known her.

One day, Ruby might want to know the extent of the man's crimes. But for now, it could wait.

Joanna looked at her daughter. Her cheeks were pinkly flushed. "You look good, Ruby. Healthy. Sam must be feeding you well." Since what had happened, Ruby had moved back onto the boat with Sam to help him recover. The relationship had developed too: they were officially a couple, had been for almost three months.

"Yeah, right. He's a terrible cook." She looked away, hesitated.

"What is it?"

"I know what you're going to say, okay? But just let me speak."

"Go ahead."

"Me and Sam, we're thinking about adoption."

"Whoa, Ruby. That's a bit fast, isn't it? You've only just moved in together."

"See? I knew that's what you'd say. We've known each other for years, you realize. Nine years, Jo. I think that's long enough to know if it's going to work."

Jo moved to the hob, started throwing chopped vegetables into the wok. Ruby sat on a stool at the breakfast bar.

"But . . . children?" said Jo. "Do you really want to tie yourself down, at this stage in your career? Now that you've landed that soloist role?"

"It's a local operatic society. Hardly the Royal Philharmonic Orchestra."

"No but it's a step in the right direction. And the boat—it's not exactly brilliant for kids, is it?"

Ruby waved a hand in the air, as if the words were a bad smell. "That's just details. We can get a bigger boat. But we've got to do it soon because she's two now. Time goes so quickly when they're little, don't you think?"

Joanna turned the hob off. She came around the counter and took Ruby's hand, led her to the couch, made her sit.

"You're talking about Leonie, aren't you?"

"Of course I am. Who else would I be talking about?"

"Honey, I'm so sorry. I was going to tell you, but I never got the chance; it was never the right time."

"What is it? What's happened to her—is she alright?"

"She's fine, sweetie. But she was placed for adoption a month ago. With the foster family she's been with from the start. Turns out there might be a family connection: the mother said her great-aunt was from the *Roane* clan . . ." she trailed off when saw Ruby's reaction. Ruby seemed so angry that Jo thought she might be about to hit her, and braced herself for the blow by closing her eyes. When she opened them again, Ruby was sobbing.

"Why didn't you tell me?"

Jo felt that her heart might burst. The guilt, the powerlessness. In that moment she would have done anything to swap places with her daughter, to take some of that pain from her. "I'm sorry. I'm so sorry."

"I loved her so much."

Jo held Ruby as she cried. She'd been expecting something like this for a while. Ruby had starting talking about trying to apply for permission to see Leonie and wouldn't understand that there was little chance, as an unrelated person, that the child protection order would allow it. Adoption by Ruby and Sam would have been entirely out of the question. Things simply didn't work that way.

"When you're ready," said Jo, "I have some photographs. I've been keeping them for you. If it's too much, then I can—"

"Let me see them. Please."

In each photo, Leonie was happy. They had mostly been taken in a large and wild back garden full of play equipment, where she laughed as she went down a slide, smiled as she marveled at some frogspawn, giggled as she was pushed on a swing by an older girl.

"That's her new sister there, with the red hair," said Jo. "She's one of four, now."

"So many children to play with," said Ruby. "She really looks happy, doesn't she?"

"She really does."

"So why do I feel so sad?" Fresh tears spilled on to Ruby's knees. "How did you do it, Joanna?"

"Do what?"

"How did you let me go the way you did? I only knew Leonie for a few months. I didn't give birth to her. How do people do these things? And Constance. I'll never understand the choice she made at Cleethorpes."

"I understand why Constance did what she did. And although it's hard, I understand why you're going to let Leonie go too. Because the choice you have is almost the same one Constance faced. To keep her and sacrifice everything that you have, or to let her go so that she can be happy elsewhere—so that you can live. That's not a choice, is it? Constance would have been kept by that man her whole life if she'd stayed. At least she had a few days with her family before . . . she fell."

"But I could have taken care of her. I promised Constance that I would."

"You would have been battling the system for years, unable to get on with your life. Leonie wouldn't have been free either. Look at her."

In the photograph, Leonie was about to blow out the candles on a huge cake in the shape of a number two. Just behind her, a cheeky boy had been caught in the act of trying to blow them out for her, and the big sister was policing the situation by grabbing him, a fierce look on her face.

"I see that it's the right thing for her," said Ruby. "I see it and yet. I want her with me. I miss her. It hurts."

"And this is why I'm so grateful for what Marianne did for us."

"Marianne?"

"I never had to let you go, Ruby. You were right there all the time. She stepped in and allowed us both to live."

For a minute Ruby was silent. "How is she?"

"She's good. She's been off the booze for a few months. She misses you, though."

"I miss her too. I think I'm going to go and see her. Do you think she'd like that?"

"I think she'd be the happiest mother in the whole world. And I think I would too."

*   *   *

ONE YEAR LATER
Ruby

It felt like a pilgrimage, to come back. Seal Bay was exactly as she remembered it. The gleaming white sand, the sharp wind, the machair. Across the unspoiled landscape she hiked to the cottage and pushed open the door, was amazed to see that the conch was still there, spotless in the center of the dusty table. The comb she placed inside was a cheap plastic one from Boots, but it was all she had. She'd been here before, with the same thoughts in her head; Constance had gone, but there was no body, no way of proving she was dead. Every day since she'd last visited the cliff top, she'd thought about her friend and wondered about what had happened, until finally she had to come back. Had Constance drowned? She'd been such a strong swimmer, but if she'd landed on rocks, she wouldn't have had a chance. Ruby hesitated before reaching into her pocket for the photographs she'd brought with her. The print she chose was dog-eared, one of the three precious images that she owned. There was Leonie, happy in the big garden, blowing out the candles on the cake. *What if she doesn't come?* The photo would mean nothing to other members of the *Roane*, but to Constance, it would mean the world. She kissed the photograph, then placed it carefully into the conch shell. As she returned the remaining photos to her pocket, her fingers brushed the edges of the small brown envelope she'd been given at the hospital the week before. Her face broke out in a smile, but she didn't need to look again at what was inside; the black-and-white scan, that coiled spring of new life, sucking its thumb. The shape of it, like a miraculous bean with new shoots of limbs, was imprinted on her brain.

Back on the beach, Ruby sat down and took out her violin. As she started to play the tune she'd learned from her strange friend, the rock in the middle of the bay came alive. She saw five, six, seven gray seals raise their heads and start to call. One of them dropped into the water and disappeared. A flip, then, inside her, and she cried out with surprise, with joy. A tiny fish turning over, the first time she'd felt it, her little acrobat.

With one hand resting low on her belly, Ruby waited where the ocean met the land, to see what might happen. She caught sight of the head of the gray seal as it appeared once more and wondered what was happening in that other world, just beneath the surface.

ACKNOWLEDGMENTS

Thanks go to the following people, without whom the book would not exist.

Madeleine Milburn, for her unwavering support, brilliant advice and so much more. Many thanks also to the wonderful, talented team at the MM agency.

For their excellent guidance and supremely wise editorial input, and for steering the book toward the market with such passion and professionalism: Manpreet Grewal and the team at HQ; Jennifer Lambert and all at HarperCollins Canada; Chelsey Emmelhainz for her early input; Matt, Melissa, and the entire team at Crooked Lane Books.

To my first readers: Jennifer Usher, Mel Sellors, Chloë Kempton, Kitty Fordham, Alison Dunne, Mary Reddaway. Big kisses to all of you wonderful people. To Jenny Parsons, for medical advice and guidance. All omissions, mistakes, and examples of willful misrepresentation are my own.

To my supervisors at Bath Spa: Fay Weldon, CJ Skuse, and most especially Tracy Brain. Your input was invaluable: wise, crucial, and transformative.

To my children, who are the absolute best.

To Jonathan Golding, who is always there, ready to listen to all of my nonsense.

AUTHOR'S NOTE

FOLKTALES LIVE ALL around us. If you look hard enough, you can find one in the bones of every story, every bit of gossip, every film you watch, every book you read. The seed of this book sprouted when I read a folktale about a selkie, but the story may well have been waiting there in my mind all along, ready for me to water it so that it could grow into the novel you have just read.

The folktale in question is called "The Mermaid Wife," which is said to be from the isle of Unst, the most northerly island in Shetland, and therefore the British Isles. Unst is at the edge of one of the few places in the world where, in autumn, the sky is fleetingly lit with the mysterious and astonishing Northern Lights. Strange happenings and odd things coming from the sea there are not unusual, and the story goes that one evening, a very long time ago, a local man came across a group of selkie women dancing on the sand. He found their sealskins lying nearby and took one so that when the selkies saw him and fled, slipping into their skins as they ran for the surf, one of them was stranded. In the way of many fairytales, the selkie woman's beauty worked against her: although the man saw that she was heartbroken, he could not bring himself to free her by giving her back her skin, dressing her instead in human clothes and taking the weeping woman home with him. Having no other choice, the woman lived with him for many years and had several children.

According to the story, she eventually seemed content, though it is noted that she often spent hours gazing out to sea. One day, while the man was out at work, the children came across an old sealskin hidden in the barn. They brought it to their mother, who fell upon it with joy, hugged her children one last time, and ran down to the water, where she dressed in her skin and swam away.

This story chimed in a particular way with me. I felt the reason could be found in childhood, in the stories many of us share, in a kind of subconscious, half-remembered collective knowledge that draws people toward such things. Folktales are retold in different versions the world over. As children, the music of story is sung to us so often that sometimes, we don't even realize that the story we are telling has been told before, time and time again.

Selkies exist in the folklore of Ireland, England, Scotland, and Iceland, as well as the Scandinavian countries whose shores border that particular area of the globe. They are related to Finfolk, and perhaps to swan maidens, as well as other creatures of myth and legend the world over who transform from animal to human form, and back again. Like "The Mermaid Wife," many versions of the selkie stories tell of a magical creature trapped by a human man, forced to marry him and bear his children. She sometimes appears happy with her lot until she finds her stolen skin, the means to return home. At this point she escapes, often gleefully, into the sea, with only a passing, regretful glance back at her earthborn children. I was excited by this aspect of the legend because it seemed so taboo: a woman who leaves her children? Shocking. But is it? Should it be? If that woman has been captured and kept for years against her will? And would it be shocking if a man did the same? Constance didn't choose to get pregnant or give birth, but she does love her daughter. She has this in common with generations of women the world over: her story is their story. It is my story and the story of my ancestors.

There's no way of knowing, but I like to imagine that the selkie legend has roots in real events. Imagine a fishing and farming community on a remote island centuries ago. One day a woman emerges from the waves, wearing sealskins, speaking a language no one can understand. Those big gray seals with their intelligent eyes, always watching from a nearby skerry. The onlooker glances from the seals to the woman and makes the connection, sees the evidence: she is a seal. Modern, logical minds might suggest that there is a more earthly explanation; perhaps the onlooker has missed the fact that the woman has come from a shipwreck, that she was always human. Nevertheless, the rest of the story is the same: she cries when her sealskin is taken away. She reluctantly becomes a wife. He hides her skin, naturally assuming that she would try to return to the ocean if he let her have it, despite her love for her children that anchors her to him and to the land. Perhaps she would. The question is, would you blame her?

EPIGRAPHS AND SOURCES FOR FURTHER RESEARCH

Chapter 1

Excerpt from "The Forsaken Merman," in Matthew Arnold, *The Poetical Works of Matthew Arnold* (New York: Thomas Y. Crowel, 1897), available at https://en.wikisource.org/wiki/The_poetical_works _of_Matthew_Arnold/The_Forsaken_Merman.

Chapter 6

Quotation from "The Goodman of Wastness," in Black, G. F. and Thomas, N. W., *Examples of Printed Folk-lore Concerning the Orkney & Shetland Islands* (London: The Folklore Society, 1903), available at: https://www.alternatewars.com/Mythology/Example _FL_Orkneys_Excerpt.htm.

Chapter 8

Excerpt from "The Fisherman and the Merman," in George Douglas, *Scottish Fairy and Folk Tales* (New York: Dover, 1901), available at https://www.sacred-texts.com/neu/celt/sfft/sfft57.htm.

Chapter 11

Excerpt from "The Silkie Wife" in Patrick Kennedy, *Legendary Fictions of the Irish Celts* (New York: Macmillan, 1891), available at https://www.sacred-texts.com/neu/celt/lfic/lfic028.htm.

Chapter 34

Excerpt from "The Mermaid Wife," in Thomas Keightley, *The Fairy Mythology Illustrative of the Romance and Superstition of Various Countries* (London: Whittaker, Treacher, 1870), available at https://www.sacred-texts.com/neu/celt/tfm/tfm063.htm.

Chapter 38

Excerpt from "The Mermaid Wife," in Charles John Tibbits, *Folk-lore and Legends: Scotland* (London: W. W. Gibbings, 1889), available at https://www.worldoftales.com/European_folktales /Scottish_folktale_16.html#gsc.tab=0.

Chapter 53

Quotation from "The Great Silkie of Sule Skerrie," by Capt. F. W. L. Thomas, in *Proceedings of the Society of Antiquaries of Scotland* (1855): 86–9, available at https://archaeologydataservice .ac.uk/archiveDS/archiveDownload?t=arch-352-1/dissemination /pdf/vol_001/1_086_089.pdf.

Song Lyrics

"Chuir Iad Mise Dh'eilean Leam Fhìn" (They sent me to an island by myself): Traditional Gaelic song, perhaps connected with Uist. Additional source notes can be found at *The Session*, https:// thesession.org/tunes/4468.

"The Sealwoman's Sea-Joy" (Ionn-da, ionn-do): This song is popular among choirs and has been variously attributed to Icelandic, Scandinavian, and Scottish cultures. The version I know is transcribed in David Thomson's *The People of the Sea*, first published in 1954, in which he ponders whether the seals themselves wrote the song and taught it to the islanders on Uist.